D0455165

AT THE SIGN OF TRIUMPH

TOR BOOKS BY DAVID WEBER

AT THE SIGN
OF TRIUMPH

DAVID
WEBER

TOR

A TOM DOHERTY ASSOCIATES BOOK
NEW YORK

AT THE SIGN OF TRIUMPH

Copyright © 2016 by David Weber

Map by Ellisa Mitchell

A Tor Book
Published by Tom Doherty Associates
175 Fifth Avenue
New York, NY 10010

www.tor-forge.com

Tor® is a registered trademark of Macmillan Publishing Group, LLC.

The Library of Congress Cataloging-in-Publication Data is available upon request.

ISBN 978-0-7653-2558-7 (hardcover)
ISBN 978-1-4299-5211-8 (e-book)

Our books may be purchased in bulk for promotional, educational, or business use. Please contact your local bookseller or the Macmillan Corporate and Premium Sales Department at 1-800-221-7945, extension 5442, or by e-mail at MacmillanSpecialMarkets@macmillan.com.

First Edition: November 2016

Printed in the United States of America

0 9 8 7 6 5 4 3 2 1

For Father George Anson Clarke.
I really did listen that half-century ago,
and you were right.

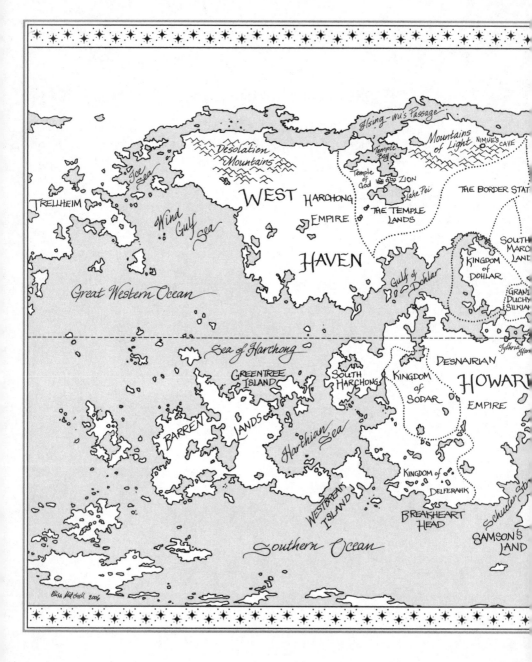

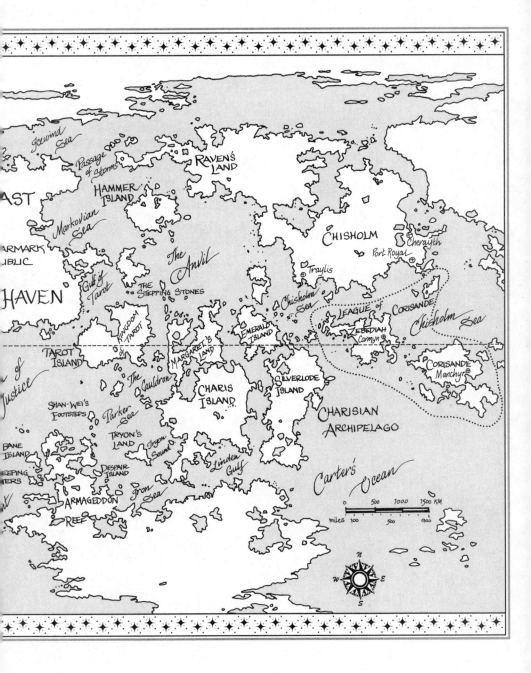

For further relevant maps, please go to
http://www.davidweber.net/downloads/index/recent/series:6/key:maps.

OCTOBER

YEAR OF GOD 897

The Earl of Thirsk's Townhouse, City of Gorath, Kingdom of Dohlar.

Forgive me for intruding, My Lord, but you and I need to talk."

The Earl of Thirsk stared at the black-haired, blue-eyed guardsman in his townhouse study. Sheer, disbelieving shock froze him in his chair—a shock deep enough to reach even through the agony of his dead family—because he knew that sapphire-eyed man, and that man couldn't possibly be here. Not in the middle of the city of Gorath. That man was with his emperor in Siddar City, thirty-four hundred miles from this spot. Everyone knew that. And even if he hadn't been, there was no conceivable way a man in the livery of the House of Ahrmahk could have traveled into the very heart of the Kingdom of Dohlar's capital city without being spotted and accosted.

Yet there he stood, and Thirsk felt his good hand fumble at his belt, seeking the dagger that wasn't there.

"I assure you I intend no harm to anyone under this roof," Merlin Athrawes continued. "I'd appreciate it if you didn't raise a hue and cry, though." He stroked one fierce mustachio with a quick smile. "That would get messy, and I'm afraid quite a lot of people would be harmed under those circumstances."

Rain pelted against the study windows, gurgled in waterfalls from eaves and gutters, swirled down paved streets or cascaded into storm drains, and distant thunder rumbled somewhere beyond the thick clouds of midnight. Streetlights in Gorath were both dim and few and far between, even on nights when pounding rain didn't reduce visibility still further. Perhaps that might explain how he could have passed through those same streets unnoted. Yet even as the earl thought that, it only created its own preposterous questions, for Athrawes' blackened chain mail and the black tunic beneath it were dry, and so was his raven-dark hair.

Of course they are, a voice said in the back of Thirsk's brain. *After all, what's a minor impossibility like that if he can be here at all?*

That inner voice sounded preposterously clear, given how much whiskey he'd consumed that evening.

Athrawes closed the door behind him and crossed the study floor, and his gleaming *dry* boots were silent on the thick carpet. He stopped fifteen feet away, and Thirsk drew a deep breath as lamplight gleamed on the "revolvers" holstered at both hips and the curved blade sheathed across the *seijin's* back. God alone knew how many men those weapons had killed, and a chill ran through him as he thought of how the Inquisition would explain how this man might have come to stand before him.

"Does that 'no harm to anyone under this roof' apply to me, too?" he heard himself ask, and his voice sounded almost as unnaturally calm as his . . . visitor's. "I don't imagine there'd be many more legitimate targets."

"Oh, trust me, My Lord." Athrawes' smile was thinner this time. "I can think of dozens of targets more 'legitimate' than you. Which isn't to say—" the smile disappeared "—that Charis doesn't have a few bones to pick with you, too."

"I imagine." Thirsk settled back in his chair and his good hand rose to the fresh pain that stabbed through his healing shoulder as he moved. "I won't blame Cayleb if he's sent you to deliver the same sentence he's passed on inquisitors taken in the field. And to be honest, I won't really mind, either. Not anymore." His lips twitched in a parody of a smile. "At least I could trust you to be quick, Master *Seijin*, 'demon' or no. That's more than I could say for some 'godly' men I might mention. And it's not as if you wouldn't be doing me a favor."

The other pain, infinitely worse than any physical hurt, roused to ravenous life as the anesthesia of shock began to fade, and the anguish of his family's death ripped at him with claws of fire and ice.

"I can understand why you might feel that way."

There was no anger in Athrawes' tone. Indeed, there was . . . compassion, and that only made Thirsk's pain worse. He didn't *deserve* any Charisian's sympathy, not after what he'd allowed to happen to the men who'd surrendered to his navy. He damned well knew that, and he remembered a passage from the *Book of Bédard*: "Do good to those who despise you and return kindness to those who smite you, and so you will heap coals of fire upon their heads." He'd heard that scripture countless times in his life, yet until this very moment, he'd never truly understood what the Archangel had meant. But now—as he heard the simple compassion in Merlin Athrawes' voice, received the gift of sympathy from someone he'd given so many reasons to hate him—his own sense of guilt, the knowledge of how much Athrawes *ought* to hate and despise him, crashed down upon his soul like Shan-wei's hammer.

"I can understand it," Merlin repeated, "but that might be premature. You still have things to do, My Lord."

"I have *nothing* to do, *Seijin*!" Thirsk snapped with a sudden flare of fury spawned by grief . . . and guilt. "That bastard in Zion's seen to that!"

"Maybe he hasn't . . . quite," Athrawes replied.

Thirsk stared at him. Athrawes *had* to know what had happened to his family—the entire *world* knew that! He opened his mouth to spit back a reply, his face dark with anger, but Merlin raised one hand.

"I'm not here tonight only for Cayleb and Sharleyan, My Lord. I have a message for you from someone else, as well."

"And who might *that* be?" Thirsk's demand was harsh.

"Your daughters, My Lord," Athrawes said very quietly.

"How *dare* you come into this house with that kind of—?!"

Thirsk got that far before words failed him entirely. He thrust himself up out of his chair, heedless of the pain in his mending shoulder, confronting the armed and armored *seijin*—a foot and more taller than he—with no other weapon than his rage.

"My Lord, your daughters are alive," Athrawes told him unflinchingly. "So are your grandchildren and your sons-in-law. *All* of them."

Lywys Gardynyr raised a clenched fist, prepared to assault the towering *seijin* physically as the Charisian mocked his pain. But Athrawes made no move to deflect the blow. He simply stood there, arms folded unthreateningly across his breastplate, and his unflinching eyes froze the earl's fist in mid-strike.

They were very dark, those blue eyes, Thirsk thought, a sapphire so deep it was almost black in the lamplight, but they met his fiery gaze without flinching. That was what stopped him, for there was no lie in those eyes, no mockery . . . and no cruelty.

And yet Athrawes' words were the cruelest trap of all, for they held the whisper of possibility, an invitation to breach the armor of acceptance, to open his heart once more, delude himself into hoping. . . .

"So are you going to tell me now that Charis can bring people back from the dead?" he demanded bitterly, grinding that deadly temptation under his heel. "Not even Langhorne could do that! But they do call Shan-wei Mother of Lies, don't they?"

"Yes, they do. And I don't blame you for a certain . . . skepticism, My Lord. But your family wasn't aboard *Saint Frydhelm* when she blew up. They were aboard a schooner, with two of my . . . colleagues."

Thirsk blinked. Then he stood there for a heartbeat or two before he shook his head like a weary, bewildered bear.

"What?"

The one-word question came out almost calmly—too calmly. It was the calm of shock and confusion too deep to express. And the calm of a man who dared not—*would* not—allow himself to believe what he'd just been told.

Merlin reached into his belt pouch. His hand came back out of it, and the earl sucked in a deep, shocked breath as gold glittered across a calloused swordsman's palm. Disbelief and fear froze the earl and he stood as if struck to stone, listening to the pound of rain, the crackle of the hearth fire, eyes locked to the miniature he'd known he'd never see again. He couldn't—for at least ten seconds, he literally *couldn't*—make himself touch it. Yet then, finally, he held out a trembling hand and Athrawes turned his wrist, spilling the miniature and its fine golden chain into his cupped fingers.

He held its familiar, beloved weight, looking down at the face of a gray-eyed, golden-haired woman—a very young woman. Then his stunned gaze rose again to Merlin Athrawes' face, and the compassion which had edged the *seijin*'s tone filled his sapphire eyes, as well.

"I'm sure there are all sorts of ways that might've come into my possession, My Lord. And many of them would be little better than what you thought actually happened to Lady Mahkzwail. But I could hardly have obtained it if it had gone to the bottom of the Gulf of Dohlar, could I?"

Thirsk turned the miniature in his hand, seeing the intertwined initials engraved into its back. It was hard, with only one working hand, but he managed to wedge a thumbnail into the thin crack, and the back of the glass-fronted locket sprang open. He turned it to catch the light, and his own face—as young as his beloved Kahrmyncetah's—looked back at him from the reverse of her portrait.

He stared at that image of a long-ago Lywys Gardynyr, then closed the locket and gripped it tightly enough to bruise his fingers. It was possible someone in Charis might have known his daughter Stefyny wore that miniature around her neck day and night. They might even have known about the initials on its back. But no mortal hand could have so perfectly forged its duplicate. So unless Cayleb and Sharleyan of Charis truly served demons. . . .

"How?" His legs collapsed abruptly, refusing to support him, and he thudded back down in his chair, scarcely noticing the white-hot stab from his shoulder. "*How?!*"

"My Lord, Cayleb and Sharleyan have known for years how the Group of Four's held your family's lives over your head. It's hardly surprising Clyntahn would do something so contemptible, and you're scarcely the only one to whom he's done it. If he understood how to *inspire* the Church's children a tenth as well as he understands how to terrify them, perhaps the Temple wouldn't be losing this jihad! But there's a problem with terror; if the threat's removed, it becomes useless. Is it really so hard to believe Cayleb and Sharleyan would strike that sort of weapon from Clyntahn's hand if they could?"

"But. . . ."

"You may have noticed that our spies are *very* good." For a moment, Athrawes' smile turned almost impish. "We knew about Clyntahn's plans to move your family to Zion even before you did, My Lord. It took longer to discover how he meant to transport them, but once we did, my companions intercepted *Saint Frydhelm*. The weather was on their side, and they managed to board undetected."

Thirsk had suffered too many shocks in far too short a time, but he'd been a seaman for well over half a century. He knew exactly how preposterous *that* statement was, and Athrawes snorted as he saw the incredulity in his expression.

"My Lord, the world insists on calling me a *seijin*. That being the case, my fellows and I might as well act the part from time to time, don't you think? And there is that little matter of Irys and Daivyn, you know. With all due modesty, this was no harder for Gwyliwr and Cleddyf than that was. It was certainly *over* sooner! And it seems to be becoming something of a specialty of ours. I'm thinking that after the jihad we *seijins* might go into the people-retrieving business. Just to keep our hands in, you understand."

Thirsk blinked in incipient outrage that the *seijin* could find anything *amusing* at a moment like this! But then he drew another deep breath, instead.

"A point, *Seijin* Merlin. Definitely a point," he conceded. "However, there was still the matter of a war galleon's entire crew to deal with."

"Which they did." The amusement of an instant before vanished, and Athrawes' face tightened. "*Seijin* Gwyliwr saw to your family's transfer to their fishing boat—where, I might add, she says your sons-in-law and young Ahlyxzandyr and Gyffry made themselves very useful—while *Seijin* Cleddyf . . . prevented the crew from intervening."

Thirsk looked at that grim expression for a long, silent moment, then nodded slowly. He'd heard the stories about the bloody path Merlin Athrawes had carved through the crews of no less than three Corisandian galleys. How he'd cut his way single-handed through a wall of swords and pikes, leaving no man alive behind him, as he'd raced to save Haarahld of Charis' life. How he'd held *Royal Charis*' quarterdeck alone against twice a hundred enemies while his mortally wounded king died behind him in a midshipman's arms. They were incredible tales, whispered to close friends over tankards of beer or glasses of whiskey when there were no Inquisition ears to hear, and Thirsk had seen far too much of battle and death to believe the half of their wild exaggerations . . . until tonight.

"They deserved better, those men," Athrawes said now, harshly. "But the moment Clyntahn put your family aboard that ship, he signed their death warrants."

"*You* blew her up, didn't you?" Thirsk said softly, and it wasn't truly a question.

"We did." Merlin's nostrils flared, but he refused to look away. "We had no choice. If Clyntahn had suspected for a moment that your family was alive—far less that they might be in Charisian hands—you and I would never have had a chance for this conversation. You know that as well as I do."

"Yes." Thirsk's voice was barely audible, but he nodded slowly. "Yes, I do."

Silence fell, perfected by the backdrop pound of winter rain. It lingered for several seconds before Thirsk straightened in his chair, still clutching the miniature of his long-dead wife.

"And now *you* intend to hold them over my head," he said. "I don't suppose I can blame you. God knows your Emperor has reason enough to hate me! In his place, I'd be remembering the mercy he showed off Armageddon Reef and comparing it to what happened to his men when they fell into Dohlaran hands."

"I think you can take it as a given that neither he nor Sharleyan—nor I, for that matter—are likely to forget that, My Lord," Merlin said bleakly. "But you've met Cayleb. Do you really see him using your daughters and their children as *weapons*? He'd die before he became Zhaspahr Clyntahn!"

The blue eyes were fierce this time, and shame twisted in Lywys Gardynyr's soul, because he *had* met Cayleb, knew the man who lived behind the Charisian Emperor's larger-than-life legend. Yet he knew too much of the necessities and imperatives of war, as well.

"*Seijin* Merlin, if I lived to twice my age, I could never express the gratitude I feel at this moment. You—and Cayleb—have given my family back their lives, and I genuinely believe you did it because it was the right thing to do." He shook his head, faintly surprised to realize he truly meant that. "But Cayleb's an emperor, and he's at war with Mother Church. He can't possibly fail to see the opportunity—the *necessity*—of compelling me to do his will. No ruler worthy of his crown could simply ignore that! And he wouldn't have to threaten to harm *them* to accomplish that, either."

"Of course not." Athrawes nodded. "All he'd have to do is inform the world they're alive and in Charisian hands. Clyntahn would no doubt deny that, given how it cuts against the narrative he's constructed. But that wouldn't keep him from recognizing that you'd just become a potentially deadly weapon in Charis' hands, one he could no longer hope to control. At which point, his reaction would become a foregone conclusion. Unfortunately for that scenario, Cayleb and Sharleyan would really rather keep you alive and un-martyred."

"Out of the goodness of their hearts, I'm sure," Thirsk said dryly.

"Actually, there *is* quite a bit of goodness in those hearts. But, no, you're right. They do have responsibilities of their own, and they're as well aware of them as you are of yours. But they aren't going to threaten your children, and they aren't going to reveal the fact of their survival. I'm afraid they aren't going to do what Lady Stefyny asked us to do, either, though."

"What Stefyny—" Thirsk began, then stopped and shook his head. "Of course. She would ask you to 'retrieve' me, as well, wouldn't she?"

"She loves you very much," Athrawes replied, and the earl smiled at the seeming non sequitur.

"Unfortunately, though, that's not why I'm here," the *seijin* continued, and there was an edge of genuine regret in his deep voice. "I do have *this* for you." He reached into his pouch once more and extracted a thick envelope, sealed with wax. "It's briefer than I'm sure she would have liked it to be, because she knew the person who delivered it might not be able to spend a great deal of time in Gorath and she wanted time for you to write at least a brief reply. I'm afraid I do need to be gone before much longer, but I think I can give you a quarter hour or so in which to reply. And—" he held out the envelope "—I'll also ask you to be sure you burn it afterward. Letting it fall into the Inquisition's hands would probably be a bad idea."

Thirsk glanced at the envelope, then almost snatched it from Athrawes' hand as he recognized his daughter's handwriting.

"I'm sure she'll give you her own version of what happened that night, My Lord. *Seijin* Cleddyf promised her I'd deliver it unread, which I have, so I can't be certain, but I doubt her account will differ much from the one he shared with me. Not that I expect it to be *identical* to his. She'll have a rather different perspective, after all." The *seijin* smiled again, briefly. But then the smile disappeared. "I'm afraid Cayleb's asked me to deliver a rather different message to you, however."

"What sort of message?"

"It's a fairly simple one, actually. Just as you once sat across a table from Cayleb, he sat across that same table from you, and he's almost frighteningly good at taking the measure of other men, He took *yours*, and he knows how little you've relished some of the actions the Church has demanded of you. Notice that I said the *Church*, not God. There's a difference, and I think you know what it is."

"I won't pretend I don't know what you mean. But the fact that Clyntahn's vile and corrupt doesn't automatically grant Cayleb and Maikel Staynair license to destroy Mother Church and defy God's will."

"And you don't believe for a moment they *are* defying God's will," Athrawes countered. "I doubt you ever did. And even if you did once, you *stopped* believing it long ago."

The *seijin's* riposte lay between them, a steely challenge Thirsk declined to pick up. He only looked back at the other man steadily, refusing to admit the charge . . . or to deny it.

"My Lord, as I say, time is pressing, you have a letter to read and another to write, and I still have a long way to go tonight, so I'll be brief. Cayleb and Sharleyan make no demands in return for your family's safety. And they fully understand that not only were you raised a son of Mother Church but that you take your oaths to the Crown of Dohlar and your responsibilities to the navy you command seriously. A man of honor has no choice about that . . . unless an even greater duty, an even deeper responsibility, is used against him. That deeper responsibility's been lifted from you now, yet neither Cayleb nor Sharleyan would expect you to act against what *you* believe are the best interests of your kingdom and your own soul. If they tried to force you to, they'd be no better than the Group of Four, and because they refuse to be that, they've sent me to give you the deadliest gift of all, instead."

His level gaze held Thirsk's in the lamplight.

"Freedom, My Lord. That's Charis' gift to you. The freedom to do what *you* think is right . . . whatever the consequences."

NOVEMBER

YEAR OF GOD 897

S hit," Lieutenant Klymynt Hahrlys said with great precision and feeling as he got his hands under himself and pushed up out of the knee-deep mud which had just pulled the boot off his right foot.

"Getting a bit thick, Sir," Gyffry Tyllytsyn, his platoon sergeant said sympathetically, and waded through the soupy, treacherous mess to extend a helping hand.

Hahrlys spat out a nasty-tasting glob of muck and scrambled up as Tyllytsyn half heaved him to his feet. The toes on his bootless foot cringed as the cold, wet mud enveloped them, and he wiped more of the slimy stuff from his face as the sergeant bent to thrust a hand into the churned swamp where the boot had vanished. Tyllytsyn felt around for a moment or two, then grunted in satisfaction as he found it. It took both hands and the full power of his arms to wrestle it out of the deep pothole the sea of mud had hidden, but he managed at last. Then he upended it, pouring out its porridge-like contents in a splattering, splashing stream. The flood dwindled to a trickle, and he shook the boot firmly before he handed it to its owner.

"Happen you'd best lean on m' shoulder till we get you out o' this patch, Sir," he offered. "Might not be a bad idea t' see if you can convince the quarter-master t' scare up another pair, too." He grimaced. "'Bout time you had a new pair—one with laces an' everything, this time—and gettin' this one cleaned out an' dry again'll be no easy task."

"And what makes you think the quartermaster *has* a pair my size?" Hahrlys asked sourly, accepting the boot and tucking it under his left arm as he draped his right arm around the sergeant's shoulders and started hopping one-footed through the shallower mud that bordered the pothole.

"Well, as t' that, there's that bottle o' whiskey Edwyrds an' I have squir-reled away. Happen that might jog his memory."

"Bribery is against regulations." Hahrlys gave Tyllytsyn a stern look, then shrugged. "Besides, it probably wouldn't work. Boots seem to be in short supply at the moment."

"Never know till you try, Sir," the sergeant said philosophically, and Hahrlys snorted in amused agreement.

They reached solider ground, and the lieutenant took his arm from the noncom's shoulder with a smile of gratitude. That smile faded quickly as he looked distastefully down at the boot. The thought of shoving his foot back into it was hardly palatable, but there wasn't time to clean and dry it. Captain Maizak had scheduled an officers' conference in less than two hours, and the company CP was over a mile away. The thought of covering that distance barefooted—or even half barefooted—was even less palatable. Besides, the foot in question was as liberally coated with mud as the boot's interior, and it would probably warm—gradually—to something almost bearable.

He sighed, wishing the QM *did* have a pair of field boots—the sort that stayed put under the most arduous circumstances—in his size. Unfortunately, he had big feet, well outside the normal size range, and he'd already worn out two complete sets of proper, laced field boots. Which was why he was now stuck with a pair of the jackboots the Imperial Charisian Army's mounted infantry wore. Of course, he was scarcely the only member of his platoon who needed new boots. Hopefully, they'd be available soon enough to do some good—like before half the platoon was down with pneumonia!

He grimaced and jammed his foot back into its squelchy nest.

"Best be back to it, Gyffry." He couldn't quite keep the sort of resignation a commissioned officer wasn't supposed to display to his enlisted personnel out of his voice, but Tyllytsyn had been with him a long time now and the platoon sergeant only chuckled.

"Happen you're right, Sir," he agreed, and went wading off through the mud—rather more cautiously than Hahrlys, avoiding the more treacherous patches—towards the engineers working to repair what was left of the high road that paralleled the Sheryl-Seridahn High Canal.

Yet another in the endless chain of dragon-drawn freight wagons—laden with barely a third of the load decent road conditions would have allowed—churned by, and Tyllytsyn paused to let it pass. The wagon's wheels were damned near man-high, yet it was hub-deep in places as the straining dragon hauled it forward. There were a lot of those wagons, and a lot of hard-working dragons, yet in these conditions, they could move only about two-thirds of the supplies the Army of Thesmar's forward elements truly needed. The ruined high road offered even poorer going, however, which forced them *off* the road . . . which *created* the mud which made the going so hard *there* and slowed the hard-working engineers' efforts to repair the high road to get them back onto it again.

And the retreating Dohlarans had made sure his men wouldn't have much to work with, Hahrlys thought glumly as he followed the sergeant through the gently sifting rain. At least it wasn't another downpour . . . at the moment. Winters in the South March were less brutally frigid than those farther north, but that was about the best that could be said for them. They might not freeze as hard or as often, but they were cold, wet, miserable, and—within the next five-day or two—the weather *would* get cold enough to start freezing the mud overnight. By the end of the month, it might get sufficiently cold to freeze it solid enough to provide decent footing instead of a crusty, treacherous skim that only looked firm until someone was stupid enough to try walking across it. It might not, too, though. Frankly, Hahrlys doubted the temperature would be considerate enough to do anything of the sort.

Mother always said any of a pessimist's surprises were going to be pleasant ones, he told himself. *And given the weather's track record so far, anyone who isn't a pessimist'd have to be a frigging* lunatic, *instead!*

He stopped and turned, looking westward in the freight wagon's wake as distant thunder rumbled. Despite the current rain, that thunder had nothing to do with the weather, and his jaw tightened as the artillery growl swelled louder. It was a reminder of why his men were working knee-deep—even waist-deep—in mud and water to restore the high road to something remotely serviceable. The front line was less than five miles from his present position, and the Army of Thesmar's advance had slowed to an agonizing, mucky, sodden crawl.

He wiped rain out of his eyes, removing another swath of mud in the process, and peered along the canal as if he thought he might actually see the muzzle flashes. He couldn't, of course, but he didn't have to see them to know what was happening. The difference between exploding mortar rounds and the bellow of heavier guns was quite distinct to an ear which had heard so many of both, and the artillery duel was no longer purely one-sided.

Sir Fahstyr Rychtyr's Army of the Seridahn hadn't been heavily reinforced—the Royal Dohlaran Army seemed to be finding it difficult to come up with trained manpower—but the men in its regiments had received a steadily mounting trickle of Dohlaran-designed breech-loading rifles. That was bad news; the fact that a growing number of banded, rifled artillery pieces—including the first Dohlaran-built angle-guns—had come forward was even worse. Fortunately, there were still very few of the latter and neither the Dohlarans nor the Army of God was able—yet—to match the indirect fire of Charis' mortars and angle-guns. That meant their artillery remained far more exposed to Charisian counter-battery fire, since their guns had to have direct lines of fire, which meant their opponents had direct lines of fire to *them*. The Dohlarans had become steadily better at building protected—and much harder to destroy—emplacements for them, however, and they no longer had to deploy within range of their enemies' rifles, which meant their gunners were no longer being picked off by snipers in large numbers. And those angle-guns of theirs *were* trickling forward. It was unlikely Dohlaran artillerists would be anywhere nearly as proficient in their use initially, but that didn't mean they wouldn't be painfully effective, and the Charisian Empire had discovered the hard way that Dohlarans learned quickly when someone was shooting at them.

And Earl Hanth doesn't have as many mortars and angle-guns of his own as he'd like to shoot at them with, either, he thought unhappily. *In fact, the bastards outrange his thirty-pounders now, and that's still two-thirds of his total field artillery.*

But they were still driving towards the Siddarmark-Dohlar border, he reminded himself. Even at its present snail-like rate of advance, the Army of Thesmar would cross into the Duchy of Thorast before the end of the month.

Unless something new was added, of course.

In the meantime, the men cursing, bleeding, and dying at the sharp end of the stick still needed to be supplied, and Klymynt Hahrlys turned back from the distant thunder to the men laboring to get those supplies to them.

▼ ▼ ▼

"Sorry, Sir."

Sir Hauwerd Breygart, otherwise known as the Earl of Hanth, grimaced and waved his hand, actually grateful for once for the wet air's damp cold as it eased the sting in his fingers.

"Firing squad at dawn, Dyntyn," he said, giving his personal aide a stern look. "Make a note of that!"

"Yes, Sir. Of course, after you have me shot, you'll have to find someone else who can find your maps for you." Major Dyntyn Karmaikel smiled crookedly. "That's my secret weapon, you know. I figure if no one else can find anything for you, you'll have to keep me around."

"Sneaky bastard, aren't you?" Hanth stopped waving his hand and examined it carefully. There was no sign of blisters, although the back of his ring finger was undeniably red-looking.

"Let's try that again, more carefully," he said, and took the enormous mug of hot cherrybean tea from Karmaikel's hand without further misadventure.

It wasn't really the major's fault the hot brew had slopped over the brim, and at least he'd kept it off the map spread out under the dripping tarp's protection. Besides, as long as no fingers were burned entirely off, a little scorching around the edges was a small price to pay.

The earl sipped deeply, treasuring the warmth and the caffeine. His addiction to cherrybean was relatively new, acquired only after he'd come ashore in Thesmar. It wasn't a common beverage in the Old Kingdom of Charis, although it was popular in Emerald. It was even more—one might almost have said *ferociously* more—popular in the Republic, however. That wasn't hard to understand, given Siddarmarkian winters, and restocking the militia companies who'd held Thesmar in the teeth of everything the South March Temple Loyalists could throw at them had been a high priority once Charisian galleons were able to reach the port city. It was a staple at any senior officers' meeting—especially early ones; Siddarmarkians in general seemed incapable of rational thought before their first cup of the morning. Under the circumstances, Hanth's addiction had probably been inevitable, although he remained a little bemused by the fact that he'd actually succumbed to drinking it *black*. For a man who'd been brought up on milder teas and hot chocolate, that was going a bit far.

What happens when a man falls into bad company, I suppose, he reflected, wrapping both hands around the heavy earthenware mug to warm his palms. *And there are worse habits to get into.*

"Anything more from Brigadier Snaips?" he asked out loud.

"Not a full report, My Lord, but he sent an update right after breakfast." Dyntyn grimaced and gestured at the the charcoal-gray sky's low, drifting cloud belly and misty curtains of blowing drizzle. "Not too many heliograph or semaphore reports making it through this muck, so he had to send it by runner. His forward units are still counting noses, but he says the casualty totals aren't going to be quite as bad as he thought. According to Colonel Brystahl, the platoon he thought had been completely overrun held its positions, instead. It sounds like it took more wounded than KIA, too, and its CO actually had twenty or thirty prisoners to hand over when he was relieved."

"Good!" Hanth nodded vigorously.

Brigadier Ahrsynio Snaips' 4th Brigade was his leading formation, and Colonel Fhranklyn Brystahl's 7th Regiment had been 4th Brigade's point for the last two five-days. It was a thankless task, especially in weather like this, and Hanth worked hard to rotate the duty. That was why 8th Regiment would be moving up past Brystahl's men to take over the offensive next five-day. The miserable terrain was cramped enough—and logistics were poor enough—that a regimental frontage was about the widest advance the Army of Thesmar could support at the moment. Clyftyn Sumyrs' Alyksberg Division, its Siddarmarkian pike companies made back up to strength and rearmed entirely with rifles, was deployed to cover both of his flanks, but they were rather far back from his spearhead—if such a slow, slogging advance could be called that—because they could move no farther forward than the repaired high road unless he wanted to starve his entire army.

Those same considerations had put a stop to the repeated turning movements he'd used early in the year, working around the Army of the Seridahn's flanks to force Rychtyr to pull back instead of grinding straight into the Dohlaran's prepared positions. He'd tried to continue them after the rains set in in earnest . . . for a while. His men referred to that unhappy experience as "Grimaldi's Mud Bath," which he had to admit was thoroughly reasonable of them. He could still have moved infantry and cavalry cross-country—slowly—and he knew the men would have done it for him, but moving the supplies to *feed* them was another problem entirely. For that matter, he was finding it damned hard to keep his advance grinding forward even along the direct line of the canal!

Off-road conditions were even worse than he'd expected, and he began most mornings by kicking himself for not having paid more attention to the local Siddarmarkians who'd tried to warn him about that. It wasn't that he hadn't believed conditions would be bad; he'd simply been unable—or, he acknowledged, un*willing*—to think they could be *this* bad. In his defense, no one else had ever tried to move entire armies through the area, even during the wars between Desnair and the Republic, which meant they hadn't experienced just how shallow the water table east of Fyrayth and the line of the Fyrayth Hills truly was. As a result, not even his Republic of Siddarmark Army allies had been able to warn him about the swamp the nice, flat ground would turn into as soon as he sent a few thousand infantry, cavalry, and supply wagons churning across it.

The Army of the Seridahn's logistics, unfortunately, were rather better than his. All his intelligence reports indicated that the Royal Dohlaran Army remained short of trained men, and even shorter of new weapons for them to use, but they seemed to have ample stocks of food and ammunition, and the high road behind General Rychtyr remained intact. Worse, the terrain west of the Fyrayths was far better drained—and was a lot less swampy—and the canal was still operable to within thirty miles of his front line. Rychtyr's troops might be wet and miserable, but they were well fed and full of fight and he was becoming more confident . . . or at least less timid about risking casualties of his own.

He'd also assigned command of the units in contact with the Army of Thesmar to General Clyftyn Rahdgyrz, arguably his most competent division commander . . . and certainly his most aggressive one. Last night's counterattack launched under the cover of last night's darkness, was typical of Rahgyrz, unfortunately. His men didn't call him "The Slash Lizard" for nothing, and he'd chosen the conditions for it well. The low cloud base and rain had reduced the effectiveness of the Charisians' illuminating rockets and the even newer "star shells" with which Admiral Sympsyn's gunners been supplied. That had let Rahdgyrz' men cross what both sides had taken to calling "no man's land" with far fewer casualties than they ought to have taken, and the fighting had been close, nasty, and costly. Brystahl had retaken the lost ground, but the Dohlaran attack had cost him time, as well as men, which had undoubtedly been Rahdgyrz' primary purpose. There'd be no further advance before tomorrow; given its casualties, 7th Regiment would need at least all of today just to reorganize.

Hanth considered that unhappy fact as he held his cherrybean mug one-handed and ran his left index finger across the crayon-marked lines indicating 4th Brigade's positions on his oilcloth map.

"I think we need to see about asking General Sumyrs if Brigadier Snaips can borrow the Third Alyksberg to shore up his right for a few days, Dyntyn," he said thoughtfully. "We might ask for the Seventh South March, too. The high road's in good enough shape to get them forward, and I want to pull Major Klymynt's battalion completely off the line while it refits."

"Yes, Sir," Karmaikel said, jotting a brief memo in his notebook.

"And after you've gotten that message sent off, send another one asking Admiral Sympsyn to plan on joining us for lunch. I'd like to discuss how to get the best use out of our new angles, once they arrive."

The earl tried—mostly successfully—to keep the bitterness out of his last three words, and he knew it wasn't really anyone's fault. But that made him no happier that so far he had one—count them, one—battery of the new 6-inch angle-guns. Despite how hellishly difficult they were to move under current conditions, that single battery had already proved worth its weight in gold, however, and if Ehdwyrd Howsmyn's word was as good as usual, he'd see at least four or five more batteries within the next few five-days.

"I could wish they were sending us a few of the new four-inchers, as well," he continued. "Langhorne knows I don't want to sound like a whiner, but angle-guns and mortars can only do so much, and I'd love to be able to pull the thirty-pounders completely off the line right along with Klymynt's battalion. Still, let's be grateful for what we're getting."

This time Karmaikel only nodded as he went on writing, and Hanth stood a moment longer, looking down at the map.

You're only trying to delay the inevitable, Hauwerd, he thought. *It's still going to be raining whenever you finally get your arse into the saddle.*

He entertained an ignoble temptation to send young Karmaikel on the scheduled trip to inspect the progress of Ahrthyr Parkyr's engineers' without him. Surely the major could bring back all the first-hand impressions he needed!

They need to know you appreciate the way they're busting arse, he reminded himself. *And having the general lean over their shoulders can't hurt their . . . sense of urgency, either. Especially if the general's feeling wet, cold, and grumpy while he does the leaning! Just remember they need* positive *encouragement, too. And that it's not their fault you're going to be wet and cold.*

He snorted again, this time in amusement, and took another long swallow of cherrybean.

"All right, Dyntyn," he sighed then, lowering the mug. "I suppose you'd better go collect the horses." A harder burst of rain pattered on the shielding tarp, and he shuddered. "I'll just stay here and finish my cherrybean—and hope the morning gets this—" he waved his mug to indicate the rain splattering across the tarp "—out of its system while you see to that."

"Is this another of those 'rank has its privileges' moments, Sir?" Karmaikel asked with a small smile.

"Why, I believe it is, Major." Hanth's smile was considerably broader than his aide's. "I believe it is."

.II.

HMS *Serpent*, 22,
and
HMS *Fleet Wing*, 18,
Trosan Channel,
Gulf of Dohlar.

B ugger'll be up to us in another two, two and a half hours, Sir," Lieutenant Karmaikel Achlee said quietly in his CO's ear. "She's faster'n we are, damn her."

Lieutenant Commander Truskyt Mahkluskee nodded, trying his best to keep his unhappiness out of his expression. It wasn't that he doubted the capability or courage of his crew, but the Royal Dohlaran Navy had learned the hard way that crossing swords with the Imperial *Charisian* Navy on its own terms was almost always a bad business, and the fellow chasing him wouldn't have been if he wasn't confident he *could* engage on his terms.

Mahkluskee clasped his hands behind him, spyglass tucked under his right armpit, and gazed back across the taffrail at the schooner-rigged sails sweeping steadily closer. The wind was almost directly out of the northwest at about twenty miles an hour, with six-foot waves—what sailors called a topsail breeze—but it was steadily strengthening, and cloud banks rolled down upon it. There was rain in those clouds. Mahkluskee could almost smell it, and he would have vastly preferred for that rain to have already appeared, preferably in driving squalls that cut visibility to nothing. That wasn't going to happen, however. Or not until long after the vengefully pursuing schooner overhauled *Serpent*, at least.

Oh, stop being an old woman! he scolded himself. *Yes, they're Charisians and they're chasing you. Is there some reason that should surprise you? Any Charisian warship's going to be out for blood after Hahskyn Bay—hard to blame them for that!—so this fellow may be pissed enough to run risks he wouldn't otherwise. And Charisians or not, they aren't ten feet tall and they don't pick their teeth with board-*

ing pikes. Best you remember that . . . and don't let any of the lads think for a minute you ever doubted it!

"Actually, I think it'll be closer to two, Karmaikel," he said judiciously. "Pity nobody's had time to get us coppered."

Achlee grunted in agreement. The RDN had learned how to copper ships to protect them against borers and weed only after they'd captured a few Charisian ships and taken them apart to find the bronze fittings below the waterline. No one knew why that worked, but they did know every attempt to attach copper with *iron* nails had been a dismal, disintegrating failure. Yet even after they'd discovered the secret, coppering a ship which had been put together originally with those same iron nails was a significant challenge. New construction was one thing, but simply pulling all the iron from an existing ship and replacing it with bronze was a time-consuming—and expensive—proposition. Eventually, however, the shipwrights had figured out how to sheath a ship's hull first in an additional layer of planking, well coated with pitch and fastened to the original hull with bronze, before screwing the sheet copper to it. It was still expensive as Shan-wei herself, but it worked, and any trifling speed which might have been lost to the additional beam was more than compensated for by the copper's immunity to the long, dragging tendrils of weed which started cutting an un-coppered hull's speed within five-days after it was scraped clean.

Serpent, unfortunately, was a lowly brig. The Navy realized ships her size needed speed even more than larger ships, but they were also more expendable, and the galleon fleet had been given a much higher priority. Then the screw-galleys had been added to the mix, and *they* took priority even over the galleons.

Which had left *Serpent* sucking hind teat.

Again.

"How do you think they'll go about it?" Achlee asked after a moment.

"They're bringing the wind down with them," Mahkluskee said, and shrugged. "They're faster, they're schooner-rigged, and they'll have the weather gauge. Unless they screw up—and when's the last time you heard about a Charisian screwing up in a sea fight?—they'll be able to choose the range. The question, I suppose, is whether this fellow's a dance-and-shoot type or a drive-straight-in type. To be honest, I'd prefer the latter."

"Me, too," Achlee agreed.

There wasn't much to choose between *Serpent*'s armament and that of a typical ICN schooner. The brig mounted twenty 25-pounder carronades, with a pair of 18-pounder long guns in her forward ports to serve as chasers. Depending upon its class, the schooner pursuing them might mount anywhere from sixteen to twenty guns, most probably 30-pounder carronades, although some of the larger schooners had reduced the number of their guns by as much as half in order to replace them with 57-pounders. A 57-pounder's 7-inch explosive shell was devastating—well, so was its *round shot*, to be fair—but he could always hope this one had retained her 30-pounders. Both sides had now equipped their broadside weapons with shells, although the RDN had decided there was little point developing shells for anything lighter than a 25-pounder, given how small the explosive charge would be, and it didn't make a lot of difference to something the size of a schooner or a brig if the shell that hit it was technically a 30-pounder or a 25-pounder. The effect on its frail timbers was pretty much the same.

In a fight like this one, however, it would probably come down to who hit whom first, and while Mahkluskee had enormous faith in the quality of his crew, the Charisian Navy had *invented* naval gunnery. They were still the best in the world at it, too, and no shame to admit it. But that meant a "dance-and-shoot type" was likely to stand off until he'd gotten that first hit or two, then close in only if he had to and settle it with cold steel.

"He'll have to be at least a little careful," Mahkluskee mused. "We're a hell of a lot closer to home than he is. If he gets banged up, he's likely to be easy meat for anybody else he runs into."

"Here's hoping *he* bears that in mind, Sir!" Achlee grinned.

"Couldn't hurt," Mahkluskee agreed, then drew a deep breath. "We're coming up on lunch in about two hours. Tell the cook to bring that forward. Let's get a good meal into the lads before it gets lively. And tell Fytsymyns I want a word. After they're fed, I think we need to do a little rearranging."

▼　　▼　　▼

"I think it's about time to clear for action, Zosh," Lieutenant Hektor Aplyn-Ahrmahk, known on social occasions as His Grace, the Duke of Darcos, said thoughtfully.

At eighteen, the duke was technically old enough—barely—to command an imperial Charisian warship. He was also the adopted son of Emperor Cayleb and Empress Sharleyan, and there were at least some who suspected that that lofty connection explained how he happened to be the commanding officer of HMS *Fleet Wing* at such a tender age. None of the people who thought that, however, had ever served with "the Duke," as he was almost universally known in the fleet, as if there'd never been another Charisian duke. He'd been at sea since he was ten years old, his king had died in his arms when he was only eleven, and he'd earned a reputation for fearlessness second to none over the past half decade. Despite his youth and the crippled arm left by a near-fatal wedding day assassination attempt, any man in his crew would have followed him in an assault on the gates of hell themselves, and he'd learned his seamanship from Sir Dunkyn Yairley,

Baron Sarmouth. There might—possibly—have been two ship handlers in the Imperial Charisian Navy who were better than Sarmouth; there damned well weren't three. And unlike too many skilled seamen, the baron was one of the best teachers to ever walk a quarterdeck . . . which went quite some way towards explaining why Aplyn-Ahrmahk handled his fast, sleek command with the confident skill and judgment of a man twice his age.

He'd also served for over a year as Sarmouth's flag lieutenant. That gave him an insight into the Navy's strategic needs which was vanishingly rare in an officer of his youthfulness, which was how he'd ended up picked for the task of examining Chelmport on Trove Island.

Chelmport had served Admiral Gwylym Manthyr as a base during his ill-fated foray into the Gulf of Dohlar, and Trove—on the southwestern corner of the Dohlar Bank—was about equidistant between the ICN's current forward base on Talisman Island and Gorath Bay, the maritime heart of the Kingdom of Dohlar. Five months had passed since the Battle of the Kaudzhu Narrows, and although Dohlar had unquestionably "won" the engagement, both navies had suffered heavily. At the moment, the RDN was as busy repairing, rebuilding, and commissioning new construction as Charis, and they'd had an advantage in the number of new galleons almost ready for launch at the time of the battle. Charis, on the other hand, had a much, much greater existing fleet, including some new construction of its own, from which to draw reinforcements. In Baron Sarmouth's opinion, that meant quite a few of those reinforcements were undoubtedly en route to join Admiral Sharpfield at Claw Island. As soon as they did, Sharpfield would just as undoubtedly look for ways to use them as aggressively—and as far forward—as possible, and a base at Chelmport would be well placed to allow those galleons to dominate the Mahthyw Passage, the Hilda and Trosan Channels, and the Fern Narrows. That would effectively blockade the eastern end of the gulf, sealing the RDN—and all the kingdom's carrying trade south of the Dohlar Bank—into Hankey Sound and Salthar Bay and threatening any coaster rash enough to dare the Gulf of Tanshar, as well.

It seemed . . . unlikely that as canny a fox as the Earl of Thirsk would be less aware of those possibilities than any Charisian, especially since Manthyr had used Chelmport to do exactly that during his incursion. The question in Admiral Sarmouth's mind was what Thirsk had done to preclude a repeat of the Manthyr treatment, and that was what Hektor had been sent to discover.

The answer, he'd found, was quite a lot, actually. It was clearly impossible for Thirsk to fortify every potential port along the sixteen thousand miles of the Gulf of Dohlar's coastline, not to mention the scores of islands where a raiding squadron might temporarily drop anchor. He could eliminate quite a few of those potential ports on the basis of depth of harbor, availability of fresh water, exposure to prevailing winds, and all the other factors which would weigh in the mind of a professional mariner, but that still left far too many possibilities for him to have any hope of protecting all of them.

Chelmport, however, had received special attention. The harbor entrance was now covered by a powerful battery of 40-pounders. There were no more than twenty guns or so, but they were well sited and protected by heavy earthen ramparts, and new positions were being prepared. From their locations, it seemed likely they were intended for some of the new Fultyn Rifles, the banded, rifled cannon the Church's foundries were rushing into production. Defenses on that scale were more than capable of dealing with any unarmored galleon. And that, since the Royal Dohlaran Navy currently possessed the only ironclad in the Gulf of Dohlar—HMS *Dreadnought*, which had retained her Charisian name after her capture—meant Chelmsport was useless as a forward base.

That was always subject to change, however, and Hektor Aplyn-Ahrmahk and Sir Dunkyn Yairley had certain advantages when it came to predicting the future.

"Do try to remember you have to get home to make your official report," a voice said dryly in his ear, as if to remind him of those very advantages, and his lips twitched as he suppressed a smile he couldn't very well have explained to Lieutenant Hahlbyrstaht. Suggesting to his executive officer that he "heard voices" probably wouldn't be a good idea, even if the voice in question belonged to Admiral Sarmouth. And it would be an especially un-good idea since it happened to be true.

And it's also entirely unfair that the Admiral can natter away at me when he knows damned well I can't say a word back.

Not that Sarmouth didn't have a point. The truth was that he and Hektor had known exactly what Hektor would see at Chelmsport long before his lookouts started calling reports down from aloft. The orbital SNARCs provided far more detailed information than he'd ever be able to include in his official report, but there was no way—or, at least, no non-*demonic* way—to explain how he might have come by that information. And if he was so careless as to get himself killed or his ship sunk so his written report never got back to Talisman Island, there'd still be no way Sarmouth could act on their knowledge when the reinforcements they both knew were already en route actually arrived.

On the other hand, I have no intention of getting myself killed, he thought dryly. *Quite apart from not getting the Admiral's report back to him, Irys would be really, really pissed.*

"I think it behooves us to tread a bit cautiously, Zosh," he told Hahlbyrstaht for the benefit of the SNARC he knew Sarmouth had focused upon *Fleet Wing*. "I'm not too concerned about our ability to take this fellow, but we're a long way from home, and I imagine the Admiral would really prefer for us to report back."

"Probably a safe bet, Sir," Hahlbyrstaht acknowledged wryly. "Matter of fact, I'm sort of in favor of the idea myself, now that you mention it."

"In that case, let's pass the word for Master Zhowaltyr."

"Aye, aye, Sir."

Hahlbyrstaht put two fingers in his mouth and whistled shrilly. It wasn't exactly the official Navy technique, but a midshipman popped up out of the after hatch almost instantly, like a rabbit from its hole, with his index finger holding his place in the navigation text he'd been studying with the sailing master.

"Yes, Sir?"

Ahlbyrt Stefyns was the junior of *Fleet Wing*'s midshipmen. Two years younger than Lawrync Dekatyr, the only other midshipman the schooner boasted, he was actually two inches taller and quick-moving. But whereas Dekatyr was an athletic sort, Stefyns was never happier than when he was curled up with a good book. He was also a Tarotisian, which remained a rarity in the ICN, and, as authorized by regulations, he wore the traditional kercheef headgear of his homeland instead of the Navy's standard three-cornered hat.

"I believe the Skipper would like a word with the Gunner," Hahlbyrstaht told him, and waggled his fingers in the general direction of the foredeck.

"Aye, aye, Sir!" Stefyns acknowledged with a grin and went thundering off.

"You really could have used your speaking trumpet to get Bynyt's attention, you know," Hektor observed quietly.

"True, Sir," Hahlbyrstaht acknowledged, forbearing to mention that Hektor could have done the same thing. "But it does a midshipman good to know he's needed. Besides, it'll keep the lad occupied instead of worrying."

"*Worrying?* Ahlbyrt?" Hektor shook his head. "You're sure we're talking about the same young man?"

It struck neither him nor Hahlbyrstaht as odd that he should use the term "young man" for someone less than four years younger than himself. For that matter, Hahlbyrstaht, who was actually on the young side for his own rank, was three years older than his captain.

"Probably 'worrying' was a mite strong." Hahlbyrstaht shrugged. "How about 'thoughtful'?"

"That might be fair," Hektor agreed, then looked up as Stefyns returned with Bynyt Zhowaltyr, *Fleet Wing*'s gunner, in tow.

At thirty-five, Zhowaltyr was one of the oldest members of the schooner's company, and he'd learned his trade as a gun captain in then-Commodore Staynair's first experimental galleon squadron. *Fleet Wing* was damned lucky to have him, and Hektor had wondered occasionally if that was more than simply a happy coincidence. Zhowaltyr *had* been transferred into the schooner about the same time Hektor assumed command, and it was entirely possible Admiral Sarmouth had had just a little something to do with that. He'd certainly insisted that Stywyrt Mahlyk, his personal coxswain, go along to "keep an eye on" Hektor!

"You wanted me, Sir?" the gunner said now, touching his chest in salute.

"Indeed I did, Master Zhowaltyr. You see that fellow over there?" Hektor pointed with his good hand at the Dohlaran brig *Fleet Wing* had pursued for the last five and a half hours. She was still doing her best to avoid *Fleet Wing,* but little more than three thousand yards now separated them, and the range was falling swiftly.

"Yes, Sir," Zhowaltyr acknowledged.

"I'd like to make his closer acquaintance . . . on our terms, not his. And it occurs to me that you're the man to make that happen."

"Do my best, Sir." Zhowaltyr grinned broadly. "The fourteen-pounder, I'm thinking?"

"That certainly seems like the best place to start," Hektor agreed. "And I'm sure that the fact that you've been looking forward to playing with your new toy has nothing at all to do with your choice."

"No, Sir! O' course not!" Zhowaltyr's grin got even broader.

"I thought not. So, now that we've cleared that up, what range would you like?"

The gunner glanced up at the sails, then cocked a thoughtful eye at the sea. The breeze had continued to freshen—enough that Hektor had been forced to take in a reef in the big foresail which was actually *Fleet Wing*'s primary working sail—and the waves were approaching eight feet in height. Bursting clouds of spray glittered around the schooner's bow in the early afternoon sunlight as she drove through exuberantly through the sea, and the wind sang in the rigging.

"Bit lively underfoot, Sir," Zhowaltyr said thoughtfully. "I'm thinking a thousand yards, maybe eight hundred."

"He'll probably have a pair of long eighteens forward," Hektor pointed out. In fact, he knew exactly what *Serpent* carried, although he couldn't exactly share that with Zhowaltyr.

"Aye, Sir, he will. An' they'll be smoothbores an' he's a Dohlaran." Zhowaltyr didn't spit, but that was only because the Navy frowned on people who spat on its spotless decks. "Won't say they couldn't hit a barn if one happened to float by, Sir. Not going to hit *us* at much over six hundred yards, though."

"Fair enough," Hektor said. He had a bit less contempt for Dohlaran gunnery than Zhowaltyr did, but the gunner still had a valid point . . . probably.

Under ideal conditions, both the Dohlarans' 18-pounders and *Fleet Wing*'s long 14-pounder had a range of over two thousand yards. The carronades which constituted the primary broadside weapons for both ships were shorter ranged, although *Fleet Wing*'s had been rifled. It didn't increase their *maximum* range, which was still about twenty perecent less than that of a long gun of equivalent bore, but the improved accuracy definitely increased their maximum *effective* range. So, *in theory*, both ships should have been easily capable of hitting the other at half that range.

Theory, however, had a sad way of failing in the face of reality, especially when one was trying to fire accurately from one vessel underway in a seaway at *another* vessel underway in a seaway. Moving targets were challenging enough even when the gun trying to hit them wasn't moving simultaneously in at least three different directions itself—forward, up and down, and from side to side—at the moment it fired. Under present conditions, any gunner would be doing well to mark his target at anything much in excess of five hundred yards.

Charisian gunners were still the best trained and most experienced in the world, however. Other navies, even the Dohlarans who'd demonstrated they were the ICA's only true peers, concentrated on maximum rate of fire at the sort of minimal ranges where hits could be expected.

Desnarian doctrine had relied on engaging at longer range and shooting *high*, trying to cripple the other side's rigging, but that was because Desnarian captains (and quite a few Navy of God captains, if the truth be told) had always concentrated on *getting away* from any Charisian warship they met. Dohlarans, on the other hand, were perfectly ready to fight whenever the odds were close to even, and like the ICN, they wanted *decisive* combat. That was why *their* doctrine relied on getting in as close as possible—to within as little as a hundred yards, or even less, if they could manage it—where missing would be extremely difficult, and then pouring as much fire as they could—as quickly as they could—into their enemies' *hulls*. It was a technique they'd learned from the Charisians themselves, but the ICN's gun crews exercised with their weapons for a minimum of one full hour per day. And unlike navies who drilled solely for speed, going through the motions of loading and running out again and again without ever firing, the *Charisian* Navy also "wasted" quite a lot of powder and shot shooting at targets it intended to actually *hit*. Its rate of fire at least equalled that of any other navy in the world, when speed was needed, but its gunners were also trained to *aim* their pieces and to allow for their ships' own motion.

Hektor intended to use that advantage as ruthlessly as possible. The last thing he wanted was to enter *Serpent*'s effective range for a broadside duel, and for a longer-ranged engagement, what really mattered were the opponents' long guns. Although *Serpent*'s 18-pounders were heavier and she had two of them, *Fleet Wing*'s single 14-pounder was pivot-mounted, able to fire in a broad arc on either broadside. And unlike *Serpent*'s guns, it was rifled. The "long fourteen" had been famed in Charisian service for its accuracy from the moment it was introduced. Rifling only made it even more lethally accurate . . . and increased the weight of its projectiles. The schooner had received the new weapon only three months ago, and Hektor knew Zhowaltyr was eager to try its paces in action.

"I believe we can have you in range in the next, oh, thirty minutes," he said. "I trust that will be satisfactory?"

"I think I can make that work, Sir," the gunner assured him solemnly.

"Then I suppose you should go do your noisy, smoky best to make me a happy man."

"We'll do that thing, Sir."

Zhowaltyr touched his chest in salute once more, then turned and cupped both hands around his mouth.

"Ruhsyl! Front and center!" he bellowed.

The tallish petty officer who answered his gentle summons had a sharply receding hairline. In fact, he was well along in the process of going bald, although none of his subordinates would be rash enough to describe it in precisely those terms. The hair fringing that gleaming expanse of bald scalp was worn very long and pulled back in a braided (if somewhat moth-eaten) pigtail that hung well down his spine. As if for compensation, he also sported a full, bushy beard and a magnificent specimen of what would have been called a "walrus mustache" on a planet called Earth. Both arms were liberally adorned with tattoos, a golden hoop dangled from his right earlobe, and there were strands of white in both that beard and pigtail. Not surprisingly, perhaps. At forty-seven, Wyllym Ruhsyl was close to three times Hektor's age and the oldest man in *Fleet Wing*'s company.

He was also the schooner's senior gun captain and effectively Zhowaltyr's assistant gunner, with an uncanny kinesthetic sense.

"Aye, Master Zhowaltyr?" he rumbled in a subterranean voice.

"You're on the fourteen," Zhowaltyr told him. "Don't miss."

▼　　▼　　▼

"'Vast heaving, there!" Oskahr Fytsymyns bellowed.

HMS *Serpent*'s solid, muscular boatswain stood with his hands on his hips, scowling at the sweating party of seamen. Shifting heavy weights about on the deck of a ship underway was often a tricky proposition, and just the tube of a long 18-pounder weighed well over two tons. With the carriage added, it topped three and a half, and that much weight could inflict serious damage—less to the hull of the ship, though that could be quite bad enough, than to the fragile human beings of her crew—if it got out of control on a moving deck.

Fytsymyns had no intention of allowing that to happen, and he'd watched with a king wyvern's eye while the second carronade in *Serpent*'s starboard broadside was transferred to her larboard broadside and replaced by the larboard 18-pounder chase gun. Now he stalked forward to inspect the fruit of the sweating seamen's labors, and they watched him with rather greater anxiety than they did the oncoming Charisian schooner. The Bosun's formidable temper was a known danger, after all.

"Aye, that'll do," he growled, then turned to Tohmys Prytchyrt, *Serpent*'s third lieutenant, who'd hovered in the background while the true professionals got on with it. "I think you can tell the Cap'n she's 'bout ready, Sir," he said.

"Very good, Bosun," Prytchyrt acknowledged and gestured to one of the waiting gun captains. "Best get your people stood to, Klynmywlyr."

"Aye, aye, Sir." Jyrdyn Klynmywlyr touched his chest in salute and jerked his head at the two waiting gun crews. "Y' heard the Lieutenant, you idle buggers! Let's get these bastards loaded!"

▼　　▼　　▼

"Guns're ready, Sir!"

"Good!" Truskyt Mahkluskee nodded in satisfaction.

He remained far from in favor of engaging the Charisian, especially after he'd gotten a good look at her through his spyglass. Although she showed only ten ports per side, she was very nearly as big as *Serpent*, she was eating up the range between them with greyhound grace . . . and she'd cleared away her midships pivot gun.

Mahkluskee would have dearly loved a pivot of his own. Unfortunately, that was another thing he didn't have, so he'd done the best he could to compensate by shifting both 18s to the same broadside. Unless he missed his guess, the Charisian captain intended to stand off and peck away with that 14-pounder from well up to windward, and as long as he retained the weather gauge, he could prevent *Serpent* from closing to bring her carronades into effective range. On the other hand, that told Mahkluskee exactly where to find him when the shooting started; hence the rearrangement of his own battery.

Now all I have to do is keep them pointed in the right damned direction, he told himself. *Shouldn't be all that hard, especially if the bastard doesn't want to get in close. Of course, the* Writ *does say the road to hell is paved with 'shouldn't be's.*

▼　　▼　　▼

"Another quarter point, I think," Hektor Aplyn-Ahrmahk said calmly.

"'Nother quarter-point larboard helm, aye, Sir," Senior Petty Officer Frahnk Seegairs acknowledged, easing the wheel, and *Fleet Wing* swung three degrees farther to starboard, taking the wind almost directly on her starboard beam. The Dohlaran brig lay to the southwest, starboard-side to, and the range continued to slide downward, albeit far more slowly than it had.

"Whenever you feel best, Master Zhowaltyr!" Hektor called out, and the gunner waved his hat in acknowledgment.

He stood close enough to the pivot gun to supervise, but he had no intention of joggling PO Ruhsyl's elbow. At the moment, the balding, pig-tailed petty officer was totally focused on the 14-pounder. He'd waved the rest of the crew back out of the recoil path, and his eyes were almost dreamy as he crouched behind the mount, peering along the barrel.

"You heard the Skipper," the gunner said, just to be sure, and Ruhsyl nodded.

"Aye, so I did," he murmured back, and waited a moment longer, feeling the rhythm of the schooner's motion in his brain and bone. And then thirty years at sea, coupled with five long years of intensive gunnery training and an inherent sense of movement no mere training could have imparted, came together behind those dreamy eyes, and he stepped smartly to the side and jerked the lanyard.

The friction primer worked perfectly, and the 14-pounder bellowed, spewing out a smoke cloud that shredded instantly on the wind.

▼　▼　▼

Truskyt Mahkluskee pursed his lips as dark brown gun smoke spouted from the Charisian's pivot gun. She'd opened fire at a greater range than he'd hoped for, but at least he'd been right to anticipate that she'd come to a south-westerly heading to hold the wind and the weather gauge. Barring some catastrophic damage aloft, *Serpent* should be able to keep her opponent in the play of her starboard guns—and both of her 18-pounders. Of course, at this range and in these seas, the chance of actually *hitting* the bastards wasn't especially good. Still. . . .

"As you bear, Klynmywlyr!" he called to the sandy-haired gun captain crouched over the aftermost 18-pounder's breech, firing lanyard in hand, and—

Something punched through the brig's jib. It plunged into the water forty yards off her larboard bow.

And exploded.

Both 18-pounders fired as one, like an echo of that explosion, but Mahkluskee felt the blood draining out of his face as the water spout rose on the far side of his ship.

▼   ▼   ▼

"Not so bad, Sir," Stywyrt Mahlyk remarked thoughtfully. Admiral Sarmouth's coxswain—who'd somehow become *Lieutenant Aplyn-Ahrmahk's* coxswain—stood in his customary position, festooned with pistols and cutlasses, arms crossed, watching Hektor's back. "Mind, I'd not be telling Wyllym that. Man's head's already too big for his hat!"

Hektor snorted, but Mahlyk had a point. In fact, that first shot had landed remarkably close to its target, and he smiled thinly as the SNARC's remotes projected Mahkluskee's reaction to it onto his contact lenses.

Instead of the 14-pound round shot or 8-pound shell the smoothbore 14-pounder had fired, the new, rifled weapon fired a cylindrical solid shot that weighed almost forty-five pounds . . . or a 30-pound explosive shell packed with just over five pounds of black powder and an improved version of Ehdwyrd Howsmyn's original percussion fuses. It was longer ranged, heavier, and far, far more destructive than the old "long fourteen" had ever hoped to be.

Serpent's forward gunports flashed fire, belching their own smoke clouds, and he watched the round shot slash across the wave crests in explosions of white. Like the 14-pounder, they had more than enough range to reach their target. What they didn't have was Petty Officer Ruhsyl, and the Dohlaran gun captains hadn't fired at exactly the same moment. One shot actually plowed into the water fifty or sixty yards short of *Fleet Wing's* side. The second, fired at a different point in the brig's roll, went high, whimpering across the ship without hitting a thing and plunging into the sea at least two hundred yards *beyond* the schooner.

Not good enough, Commander Mahkluskee, Hektor thought coldly.

▼   ▼   ▼

"Shit!"

Unlike Mahkluskee, Lieutenant Achlee couldn't hide his reaction as the Charisian shell threw up that telltale column of water. He wheeled around to his commanding officer, eyes wide, and opened his mouth, but Mahkluskee's sharp headshake shut it again before anything else came out.

"See if you can edge a little closer to the wind," the lieutenant commander told the grizzled seaman on the wheel, and showed his teeth in a thin smile. "I think we'd best get as close to her as we can."

"Aye, aye, Sir," the helmsman acknowledged, but he was an experienced man. His eyes met his captain's with the knowledge that *Serpent* was getting no closer to *Fleet Wing* than *Fleet Wing* chose to allow. No square-rigged vessel could match a schooner's weatherliness at the best of times, and *Serpent* was slower, to boot.

"Get forward, Karmaikel," Mahkluskee continued, turning back to his first lieutenant. "I want you as far away from me as possible in case something . . . untowards happens. Besides—" his smile was even thinner than the one he'd shown the helmsman "—it can't hurt to have your presence encouraging Klynmywlyr's efforts. Just don't joggle his elbow."

▼ ▼ ▼

"That's right, lads," Wyllym Ruhsyl encouraged as the fresh charge went down the barrel and the loader indexed the shell's studs into the barrel's rifling grooves. It took a fraction of a second longer than simply inserting a round shot or a smoothbore shell, but this gun crew had fired well over a hundred rounds since they'd acquired their new weapon. The loading number could have seated the rifling studs in the dark in the middle of a driving rain—in fact, they'd practiced blindfolded to simulate doing exactly that—and the shell slid smoothly down onto the bagged charge. A gentle stroke with a rammer settled it against the charge, a fresh primer went into the vent, and Ruhsyl reached for the lanyard.

"Clear!" he snapped, and waited long enough to be sure every member of the crew was safely out of the way.

Then he bent over the breech again, lining up the dispart sights which only the Charisian Navy used, watching the muzzle of his gun rise to point only at sky, then slowly dip until it pointed only at sea. The trick was to catch it at precisely the right point in the cycle—the point at which the inevitable delay in the charge's ignition would coincide with the moment the muzzle aligned perfectly on the Dohlaran brig. It helped immeasurably that Ehdwyrd Howsmyn's quality control assured such uniform burn times on the primers supplied to the fleet, but the best quality control in the world couldn't guarantee *truly* uniform times. There was always some variation, and the only "fire control" available was an experienced human eye and sense of timing.

As it happened, Wyllym Ruhsyl had both of those.

▼ ▼ ▼

Fresh smoke blossomed from the Charisian's waist, and a second shell screamed through the air. This time, the gunners had fired a little high, however. The projectile made a sharp, flat slapping sound as it punched through *Serpent*'s main course and exploded at least a hundred yards clear.

Maybe that first shot was a fluke, Mahkluskee told himself. *It could've been.*

He told himself that very firmly . . . and never believed it for a moment.

▼ ▼ ▼

"*Shan-wei!*" Ruhsyl snarled as his second shot went high.

"Told you *not* to miss." Zhowaltyr had to raise his voice, but his dry tone came through Ruhsyl's protective earplugs quite well. "Not like those shells grow on trees out here, y'know!"

The gun captain glared at him, but wisely didn't reply.

"Load!" he barked instead, and his crew sprang into motion once more.

▼ ▼ ▼

"Fire!" Jyrdyn Klynmywlyr snapped, and the 18-pounders bellowed afresh.

The stinking cloud of gun smoke streamed back across the deck, and he squinted through it, straining to see the fall of the shot. At this range, there wasn't much time for the smoke to clear, but he saw the flash of white as at least one of the round shot went bouncing and bounding across the waves well astern of the Charisian schooner.

"Damn and blast!" He shook his head angrily. Problems in elevation were one thing; being that far off in deflection was something else entirely.

"I want that frigging *ship* hit, not the Shan-wei-damned *water*!" he snarled. "Anybody not understand that?!"

He glared at his own gun crew for a moment, then swiveled the same fiery eyes to the other crew and held them for a pair of heartbeats. Then he inhaled sharply.

"Load!"

▼ ▼ ▼

"Fire!"

The 14-pounder lurched back on its slides, coming up against the breeching tackle, and the smoke cloud—not the dirty gray-white of conventional gunpowder but the dark brown of the much more powerful Charisian chocolate powder—blasted up and out. The shell shrieked across the water between the two ships and landed perhaps thirty feet short of its target.

▼ ▼ ▼

The deck jerked under Mahkluskee's feet, and he threw out a hand to the compass binnacle for balance.

The Charisian shell had hit the water and continued forward. Its down-angle had been too sharp to actually hit *Serpent*'s hull below the waterline, but the fuse had activated just as it passed under the brig's keel. Fortunately, it was too far away and the charge was too light to break the ship's back or stave in her planking, but the caulked seams *between* those planks were another matter. Half a dozen of them started, and water began spurting into the hull. It wasn't a dangerous flow—not yet—but there was time for that to change.

"Fire!"

▼ ▼ ▼

The 18-pounders thundered again . . . and this time, Jyrdyn Klynmywlyr found his mark. A single 4.6-inch round shot slammed into *Fleet Wing*'s hull right at the waterline and continued onward through one of the schooner's iron water tanks before it lodged in her timbers on the far side of the hull.

"Hands below!" the ship's carpenter snapped, sending his assistants below to check for leaks. Hektor absorbed that information, but his attention remained fully focused on *Serpent*.

The only man aboard his ship more focused on the brig than *he* was, was Wyllym Ruhsyl.

"Fire!"

▼   ▼   ▼

Serpent bucked as a 4.5-inch shell slammed squarely into her hull, punched through her planking, and exploded in her cable tier. The tightly coiled hemp absorbed much of the explosion . . . but it was also flammable, and smoke began wafting upwards.

"Away fire parties!" Oskahr Fytsymyns bellowed, and half a dozen men vanished down the forward hatch.

The Royal Dohlaran Navy's firefighting techniques had improved radically over the last couple of years, especially once Earl Thirsk started contemplating the ramifications of explosive shells hitting wooden hulls. *Serpent*'s firefighters dragged a canvas hose behind them, and four more men tailed onto the forward pump, ready to send water surging through the hose when—if—they reached the source of that smoke.

The smoke rose through the hatch behind the firefighting party, rolling along the deck like ground fog, wreathing around the gunners' knees before it topped the bulwark and the wind snatched it away, but they ignored it.

"Fire!"

▼   ▼   ▼

The two ships forged through the water as the minutes dragged past and the artillery duel raged.

The carronade gunners on both sides stood watching, rammers and handspikes in hand, waiting until the moment might come for them to join the exchange. But Hektor Aplyn-Ahrmahk had no intention of giving *Serpent*'s shorter-ranged weapons the opportunity to fire upon his ship. Mahkluskee's gunners were better than he'd anticipated, and they'd managed to hit *Fleet Wing* three more times over the past twenty-five minutes. In absolute terms, that was a dismal percentage of the shots they'd fired; in terms of gunners aboard a small ship in eight- or nine-foot waves, it was a very respectable accomplishment, and the last thing he wanted was to let the *rest* of *Serpent*'s gunners join the fray.

Wyllym Ruhsyl's gun crew, however, was even better. They'd fired barely more than half as many shots and hit their target *five* times. *Fleet Wing* had suffered six casualties, none of them fatal; *Serpent* had seven dead and eight wounded, and she'd been hit twice below the waterline. Her pumps had kept pace with the inflow handily . . . until six minutes ago, when one of Ruhsyl's shells had landed with freakish perversity right on top of her forward pump.

With only the after pump still in action, the water was gaining, slowly but inexorably. The brig had also lost half the pumping capacity dedicated to her firefighting teams, and although the fire in the cable tier had been contained, it hadn't been *extinguished*. It continued to smolder, and another shell had exploded in Mahkluskee's cabin, starting a second fire. That one had been smothered quickly, but the Dohlaran skipper could feel his people's growing desperation. They'd hit the Charisian several times—he *knew* they had—yet there was no external evidence of it, and that accursed pivot gun continued to flash and thunder with metronome precision.

"Hit 'em, lads!" he heard himself shouting. "*Hit the bastards!*"

A rigging hit, he thought bitterly. *That's what we need*—one *hit on the bastard's rigging!*

That was the schooner rig's one weakness as a man-of-war; it was more vulnerable than a square-rigger to damage aloft. If they could only bring down a mast, or even shoot away the foresail's gaff! Anything to slow the Charisian, give *Serpent* a chance to break off. It would have to be a truly devastating hit to give the brig any hope of clawing upwind into carronade range, but at this point, he'd be more than willing to simply run.

I don't care how accurate those bastards are, we could take them if they weren't firing shells while we fired round shot! Who ever thought of fitting a gun that small with shells? And how did they get so damned much powder inside them? Why the Shan-wei can they do things like that, and we can't? Which side are the Archangels really on?!

Something quailed inside him at the blasphemy of his own question, but that didn't rob it of its point. *Dohlar* was the one fighting for God and Langhorne, so why was it that—

▼   ▼   ▼

"Fire!"

Wyllym Ruhsyl yanked the firing lanyard for what seemed like the thousandth time. The 14-pounder bellowed, smoke blossomed . . . and HMS *Serpent* disintegrated in a massive ball of fire, smoke, and hurtling splinters as a 4.5-inch shell drilled straight into her powder magazine and exploded.

.III.
Lake City
and
Camp Mahrtyn Taisyn,
Traytown,
Tarikah Province,
Republic of Siddarmark.

It would appear all is in readiness," Captain of Horse Medyng Hwojahn, Baron of Wind Song, remarked. His breath rose in a cloud of steam as he gazed through the tripod-mounted spyglass at the formidable lines of snow-shrouded fortifications. They stretched as far as he could see, even with the spyglass, and he straightened and turned to the tall—very tall, for a Harchongian—officer at his right shoulder. "Whenever seems best to you, Lord of Foot Zhyngbau."

"Yes, My Lord!" the lord of foot at his shoulder bowed and touched his chest in salute, then snapped his fingers sharply. An aide bowed in turn and lifted the signal flag which had lain ready at his feet. He raised it and swept it in a vigorous circle high overhead, sharply enough that the swallow-tailed banner popped loudly in the wind of its passage.

For a few moments, nothing happened. And then, from well behind Wind Song's vantage point, thunder rumbled like Chihiro's kettle drums. Forty heavy angle-guns, the product of the Church of God Awaiting's steadily growing steel foundries, hurled their shells overhead. They came wailing down the heavens, shrieking their anger, and impacted on the fortifications in a hurricane eruption of fire, smoke, flying snow, and pulverized dirt. For five minutes that torrent of devastation crashed down, stunning the ear. Then ten. Fifteen. *Twenty.*

The awesome, terrifying display of sheer destruction lasted for a full thirty minutes. Then it ended, if not with quite knife-like sharpness, sharply enough, and Wind Song reached up and plucked the cotton-silk earplugs out of his ears.

"Impressive, Shygau," he said to the lord of foot, and Shygau Zhyngbau permitted himself a somewhat broader smile, bordering perilously closely upon a grin, than Harchongese etiquette would have approved in a properly behaved noble.

Of course, Zhyngbau's connection to the aristocracy was . . . tenuous, at best. Technically, he was some sort of distant relation of Lord Admiral of Navies Mountain Shadow, although he and the duke had never met. The relationship was sufficient, barely, to make him at least marginally tolerable as the senior artillerist of the Mighty Host of God and the Archangels. Personally, Wind Song wouldn't have cared if the man had been a serf, given his sheer capability. Then again, Wind Song's own horizons had been some-what . . . broadened since his uncle had assumed command of the Mighty Host and he'd come face-to-face with the realities of the Jihad.

"From here, it looks pretty bad," Wind Song continued, turning to the considerably shorter officer standing to his left.

Unlike Shygau, Captain of Horse Syang Rungwyn had no aristocratic connection whatsoever, and he was—sad to say—totally deficient in the graces, deportment, and exquisite rhetoric of the Harchong Empire's great houses. He wasn't even connected to the bureaucrats who ran that empire. In fact, his sole qualification for his position as the Mighty Host of God and the Archangels' senior engineer was that he was even better at *his* job than Zhyngbau was at his.

"It does," Rungwyn acknowledged. "May I, My Lord?"

He indicated the spyglass, and Wind Song moved aside to allow him to peer through it. There was still enough drifting smoke—and flailed snow—to make detailed observation difficult, but it was beginning to settle. Rungwyn's gloved fingers adjusted the glass carefully, then swung it in mi-nute increments as he studied the churned, cratered wilderness the artillery storm had created. His expression was impassive, and when he straightened, his eyes were merely thoughtful.

"Actually, My Lord, I believe first impressions may have been mislead-ing." He twitched his right hand in a brushing-away gesture. "The trenches have caved in in many instances, and the obstacle belt's been severely dam-aged, but I think we'll find the majority of the deep bunkers fared much better than that."

"Truly?" Wind Song arched one eyebrow, then bent over the spyglass to examine the battered fortifications. It was possible, he conceded, that Rungwyn had a point.

And perhaps you should have looked first yourself before you began spouting opinions, Medyng. How often has Uncle Taychau suggested that to you? It doesn't always follow that something which looks *irresistible truly is.*

"I believe you may have a point, Captain of Horse," he said as he straight-ened his back. "I propose we go and take a closer look."

"But not too precipitously, My Lord," Zhyngbau put in. Wind Song looked at him, and the lord of foot shrugged. "I regret to point out that our fuses are still less reliable than the heretics', and I would truly prefer not to be blown up by—or, even more, not to blow *you* up with—an unexploded shell's delayed detonation. I suspect Earl Rainbow Waters would be mildly perturbed with me for allowing anything like that. May I suggest you wait another twenty minutes, perhaps . . . and that my gunners and I precede you?"

"Since I have no greater desire to be blown up than you have to see that sad fate overtake me, suppose we make it a full hour, instead? Or, for that matter, two. I see it's almost time for luncheon, anyway. I invite both of you to share the meal with me." The baron smiled with an edge of genuine warmth. "It will give your gunners an opportunity to check for those unexploded shells . . . without *you*, since I fear my uncle would be only marginally less delighted to lose you than to lose me. It will also give us an opportunity to share our pre-inspection impressions and perhaps hit upon some additional thoughts for the test of the new bombardment rockets when they arrive."

▼   ▼   ▼

Well, that's . . . irritating, Kynt Clareyk, Baron Green Valley and the commanding officer of the Army of Midhold, thought as he crossed to his office stove. *In fact, that's* intensely *irritating*.

At the moment, his army—which was due to be rechristened the Army of Tarikah next month—lay encamped along the Lakeside-Gray Hill High Road. "Encamped" was probably the wrong word, given its implication of impermanence, when applied to the solidly built barracks the always-efficient Imperial Charisian Army Corps of Engineers, was busily constructing. Those engineers had been encouraged to even greater efficiency in this case by the current weather, and by the time they were done, Camp Mahrtyn Taisyn would sprawl over several square miles of New Northland Province and provide snug, weather-tight housing for upwards of eighty thousand men. That was still very much a work in progress at the moment, but some buildings—like the one housing the commanding general—had been assigned a greater priority than others, and Green Valley listened to the icy midnight wind whining around the eaves as he used a pair of tongs to settle two new lumps of Glacierheart coal into the stove. He pushed the door shut with the tongs, then returned to his desk and tipped back in his chair to consider the implications of the latest SNARC report.

It shouldn't really be that much of a surprise, he told himself. *You already knew Rainbow Waters had a brain he wasn't afraid to use, and then you went and gave him plenty of time to do the using. What did you* think *would happen?*

That wasn't entirely fair, and he knew it, but he wasn't in the mood for "fair."

There was no doubt in his mind that the delay imposed by liberation of the Inquisition's concentration camps had been both a moral and a strategic imperative. Charis and her allies had to save as many of the Inquisition's victims as possible. Their own souls, their own ability to look into the mirror, demanded it. And even if that hadn't been the case, they had to demonstrate to friend and foe alike that they *cared* what happened to Zhaspahr Clyntahn's victims. So, yes, the Army of Midhold had had no alternative but to stop short of the Hildermoss River while its logistic capability was diverted to rescuing and then caring for, feeding, and transporting thousands upon thousands of sick, half-starved, brutalized prisoners to safety. In the end, they'd rescued considerably more than the three hundred thousand he'd estimated they might get out . . . despite losing every single inmate from three of those camps.

The inmates of Camp Raichel had been successfully marched deeper into captivity by the Inquisition and their AOG guards. Twenty percent of them had died along the way, but the death toll would have been far higher if Dialydd Mab hadn't . . . arranged a change of command for the guard force. The inmates of Camp Urtha and Camp Zhakleen, unfortunately, had *not* been marched to the rear. They'd simply been massacred . . . all hundred and twenty thousand of them. In Camp Zhakleen's case, they'd been joined by over a third of the camp's AOG guard force, who'd mutineed against Zhaspahr Clyntahn's orders and attempted to protect the prisoners, and Kynt Clareyk prayed regularly for the souls of the men who'd made that choice. Just as he'd seen to it that the guards of Camp Hainree, who'd mutineed *successfully* and marched eighty-seven thousand Siddarmarkian civilians to safety, had been treated as honorably and humanely as humanly possible when they reached the Allies' lines barely five hours ahead of the pursing AOG cavalry.

That kind of humanity—and courage—was far too precious to waste.

But whereas he'd estimated they might recover as many as three hundred thousand, they'd actually saved well over half a million, and that had held them up even longer than he'd feared. In fact, it had cost the entire remaining campaign season in North Haven.

Actually, I suppose we could *have resumed the advance after we cleared our supply lines . . . if we'd wanted to end up like Hitler's army in 1941. There are a lot better Old Earth generals to emulate, though. Carl Gustav Mannerheim comes to mind, for example.*

He grimaced at the thought, which was especially apropos, in a less than amusing fashion, given what Owl had just projected across his contact lenses. Green Valley's troops would *probably* have fared better than the Wehrmacht had fared in Russia, given the ICA's specialized winter equipment and training. But they might not have, too, in which case the end result would have been to leave the Charis-Siddarmark alliance at the end of tattered, overextended supply lines, fighting to haul desperately needed food and fuel forward through the wasteland the retreating Army of God had left in its wake.

The consequences of that could have been . . . unfortunate, and the

Alliance had experienced entirely too many of those sorts of consequences when the Sword of Schueler spread blood and destruction across more than a third of the Republic. In the opinion of its leaders—and of Kynt Clareyk— it was time to visit some of that blood and destruction on someone else for a change, and even with the early halt the camps' liberation had imposed, they'd made a decent down payment over the preceding northern summer's short campaign season. Far better to get their troops into winter quarters before the full savagery of the *long* (and bitterly harsh) northern winter caught up with them.

The eight-plus inches of snow currently burying the ground outside his office lent that logic a certain point, especially to the tender sensibilities of a native Old Charisian, and more of it was swirling down on the teeth of that cold, wailing wind. According to Owl's meteorological projections, the eight inches which would have accumulated by sunset would be closer to ten by morning. Until his first winter in Chisholm, Green Valley had never even seen snow, except for an occasional, innocuous white mountaintop admired from far, far away. Chisholm had been a sobering experience . . . and not a patch on a northern East Haven winter! It amused him that a Charisian boy had become the most successful practitioner of winter warfare in Safeholdian history, but he was never going to be fond of winter sports.

Stop distracting yourself, he thought sternly. *You know this is going to make things a lot tougher when it's finally time to start advancing again. So what kind of brilliant brainstorm are you going to come up with* this *time?*

Unfortunately, nothing suggested itself to him.

Lord of Horse Taychau Daiyang, the Earl of Rainbow Waters, commanded well over a million men. Last summer, before the halt imposed by the camps' liberation, only about eight hundred thousand of them had been at the front, and a third or more of those had been deployed as far south as the Tymkyn Gap in the Snake Mountains, over seventeen hundred air-miles south of Rainbow Waters HQ at Lake City on West Wing Lake. But by spring, the Mighty Host of God and the Archangels would have been reinforced to close to two million men. The Army of God would have several hundred thousand new troops in the field, as well, and Allayn Maigwair was already reinforcing the Army of Tanshar, which had moved up to take over the extreme southern end of Rainbow Waters' enormous front. That relieved Earl Silken Hills, the Southern Mighty Host's commander of his responsibilities in that area, and *that* allowed Rainbow Waters to pull his right flank in closer, building an even deeper and better defended defensive zone between the Allies and the Holy Langhorne Canal, the lynchpin of the Church's northern logistics. By the time the weather permitted the Allies to resume offensive operations, they might well be facing as many as three million welldug-in troops along a front that extended all the way from Hsing-wu's Passage to Hankey Sound. Worse, many of those troops would be equipped with far better weapons than the armies the Allies had shattered over the previous summer. And there'd be even more—far more—of those weapons than the Allies had previously estimated, as well.

I'd really love to be able to blame Ehdwyrd for that, but the real culprits are Duchairn and Brother Lynkyn. Well, I suppose we shouldn't forget Master Bryairs or Brother Sylvestrai, either. And Duchairn and Maigwair's willingness to pull skilled artisans out of the AOG's manpower pool came as a bit of a surprise, too. But still. . . .

He grimaced and shook his head. In retrospect, he should have seen it coming, he thought, reflecting on certain research he'd done in Owl's databanks once the discrepancy between estimates and actuality became evident. Oh, perhaps he might be excused for doubting Duchairn could find a way to *pay* for all those rifles and artillery pieces, but given the frenetic rate at which the Church had expanded the number of its foundries and manufactories ever since the Battle of Darcos Sound, the output he was achieving actually made sense.

During the American Civil War back on Old Terra, the Union's population had been roughly 18,500,000. In the course of the four terrestrial years—almost four and a half Safeholdian years—that war had lasted, the Union had put almost 2,700,000 men into its army and another 85,000 into its navy. It had also equipped all of those men with uniforms, saddles, food, rifles, cavalry sabers, cutlasses, pistols, knapsacks, canteens, and ammunition out of its industrial base. That industry had, admittedly, had the advantage of railroads and steam power—for some of its manufactories and ironworks, at least—but Safehold's dragons and canals actually gave it better freight-hauling capacity than the Union had boasted, and water had remained the primary source of power for the United States until the 1870s. The need to expand the Union's industrial capacity during the Civil War had given a significant impetus to the changeover to steam, but the widespread availability of fast-moving streams and the abundance of waterfalls in the Northeast had made water far cheaper. In many other respects, however, that industrial base had been inferior to pre-Merlin Safeholdian manufactories . . . and the Union had still produced over eighteen hundred bronze and cast-iron field guns—and another thousand 3-inch Ordnance Rifles out of far more expensive, far more manpower-intensive wrought iron—while simultaneously producing the artillery, machinery, and—ultimately—armor to expand its fleet more than fifteen fold.

The Church had just a few more hands—and a few more foundries—to put to work than the Union had ever boasted. In fact, in just the Border States, the Temple Lands, and the Harchong Empire, the Temple still controlled over 384,000,000 human beings, almost *twenty-one times* the Union's wartime population. Worse, Safeholdian agriculture—outside North

Harchong, at least—was more efficient than mid-nineteenth-century North America's had been. That meant more of that manpower could be taken from the farm and put into uniform—or reallocated to those newly built foundries—by a "central government" with the sort of ruthless reach and compulsory authority Abraham Lincoln and Edwin Stanton could have imagined only in an opium dream. And the massive increase in the Church's steel output over the last year or so hadn't done anything to reduce its productivity.

At the moment, those foundries were producing almost seven hundred pieces of artillery—split between field guns, all of them rifled now, and angle-guns—every single month. And while they were doing that, they and the manufactories they served were also simultaneously producing Brother Lynkyn's infernal rocket launchers in indecent numbers. Not to mention around eighty of the new, heavy coast defense guns each month.

The Army of Glacierheart and the Army of the Seridahn had lost their entire artillery parks in the previous year's fighting, but the Mighty Host of God and the Archangels' artillery hadn't even been touched yet, and the majority of its existing smoothbore field guns had been sent back to foundries in the Border States to be banded with wrought iron and rifled. Those were almost all back at the front already, and the last of them would have returned to Lord of Foot Zhyngbau long before spring. They were inferior to the cast steel guns emerging from the new and upgraded Church foundries. For that matter, they were inferior to the Fultyn Rifles already in service, but there were a lot of them, and Zhyngbau and Rainbow Waters had given careful thought to how they could be best used when they were withdrawn from frontline service in favor of the newer weapons.

The one bright spot on that front was that Allayn Maigwair seemed to have dropped a stitch—unusually, for him—in the relatively low priority he'd assigned to putting the new Church-designed mortars into production. That was a mixed blessing, since most of the capacity which might have gone into them had been diverted into the rocket program, instead, but at least it meant the Mighty Host and the newly raised Army of God divisions would have far fewer of them, proportionately, than Charis or Siddarmark. That would hurt them badly once the fighting turned mobile again, since even the best field gun was less portable than a mortar. On the other hand, perhaps it hadn't been as much of an oversight as Green Valley might like to think, since Rainbow Waters had also spent so much of the time he'd been given rethinking his entire strategy. He'd gone right on stockpiling supplies at Lake City—and, even more so in some ways, in strategically dispersed depots at other points behind his front line—but he'd clearly decided not to take the offensive during the coming summer after all. He'd been careful to avoid explaining his new thinking to Zhaspahr Clyntahn, but even a cursory look at his

fortifications and deployment indicated that he intended to fight from fortified positions and allow the Allies to pay the attacker's price whenever possible. In that sort of fighting, rocket launchers—especially massed rocket
launchers—would probably be much more valuable to the defenders than
mortars might have been.

Whatever Rainbow Waters might not have spelled out in his dispatches
to Zion, Maigwair, at least, seemed to have realized his intentions quite
clearly . . . which probably explained the captain general's production and
procurement choices.

But whether Maigwair's decision had been a mistake or not, the unhappy
truth was that despite Charis' vastly superior productivity *per man-hour*, the
Church's artillery would substantially outnumber that of the Allied field
armies in the spring. Their guns wouldn't be as good, they wouldn't be as
mobile, a far higher percentage of them would be converted smoothbores,
and the cast iron Fultyn Rifles, especially, would be much more prone to
bursting when fired than the Allies' steel and wire wound guns, but there'd
be hell's own number of them.

There was some good news on that front, though. In the short term,
matters in the Gulf of Dohlar were about to take a distinctly downward trend
for Mother Church. But far more dangerous for the the Group of Four's long-
term hopes, the Church of God Awaiting was straining every sinew to the
breaking point to achieve its current production miracle.

The Temple had already lost all of the Kingdom of Dohlar's not inconsiderable production capacity, given Dohlar's desperate need to reequip the
troops facing the Army of Thesmar. The need to confront the Charisian naval
offensive everyone in Gorath knew had to be coming was a major factor, as
well. But the diversion of Dohlaran attention—and weapons production—
was scarcely the only consequence of that impending naval offensive.

Even after the Battle of the Kaudzhu Narrows, Earl Sharpfield's cruisers
had managed to effectively shut down all Church shipping across the western third of the Gulf, and less than half the Church's foundries and manufactories were located north of the Gulf, in the Temple Lands and North
Harchong. All the rest of them were in *South* Harchong, and every gun,
every rocket, every rifle or grenade produced in those foundries had to make
it to the front.

And *that* meant they had to travel by water.

For the moment, galleons from Shwei Bay could still make the crossing
to the Malansath Bight's Fairstock Bay or Tahlryn Bay, where cargoes could
be barged upriver to the Hayzor-Westborne Canal. The light cruisers operating out of Talisman Island took a toll of that shipping, but until Baron
Sarmouth was further reinforced, he could use *only* his light units for that purpose. The galleons had to stay closer to home, protecting against a possible

sudden pounce by the Dohlarans' heavily reinforced Western Squadron from its base on Saram Bay.

Unfortunately, the RDN had learned a lot about convoy protection from the Charisian Navy, and Caitahno Raisahndo, the Western Squadron's new CO, had put those lessons to good effect east of Jack's Land Island. At the moment, he was operating what amounted to a shuttle service of escorting galleons over the five hundred miles between the Shweimouth and the northern end of Whale Passage, which meant as much seventy or eighty percent of the cargo which had used that route before Sharpfield retook Claw Island was making it through. And if those galleons sailed another nine hundred miles or so, to Mahrglys on the Gulf of Tanshar, their cargoes could be barged up the Tanshar River to the Bédard Canal and from there straight to the southern Border States, which was by far the fastest way to deliver it to the Church's field armies.

For now, those three routes were carrying an enormous flow of munitions, but given what Green Valley knew would be happening shortly, that shipping would soon require another route. It damned well wasn't going to be sailing through the middle of the Gulf of Dohlar anymore, at any rate!

The inland canals from south Shwei Bay to Hankey Sound would compensate for some of that lost capacity, at least as long as the Dohlaran Navy could keep the eastern end of the Gulf open. But not even Safeholdian canals really compared to the cargo capacity of blue water transport, and if Hankey Sound should somehow happen to be cut off from the northern portions of East and West Haven in the same fashion as Shwei Bay . . .

A lot of those new guns and rockets will never make it to Rainbow Waters or the Army of God, Green Valley reflected. *Unfortunately, given the sheer numbers we're talking about—and the fact that Sharpfield and Dunkyn aren't going to be able to shut the Gulf down tomorrow morning—a lot of them* are *going to make it. It'll be a hell of a lot better than it might've been, though!*

That would help—help a *lot*—in the upcoming campaign, and the truth was that the Allies didn't actually need to repeat their battlefield successes on the same scale as the previous two years. Victories were needed, yes, but the Church simply couldn't sustain its current level of production indefinitely. Even Rhobair Duchairn's coffers would inevitably run dry and the permanent isolation of South Harchong from the north would cut off any future weapons production from that source for the Mighty Host.

All of which meant there was no way the Temple would be able to replace losses on anything remotely like last year's scale a second time. The bad news was that it was up to the Imperial Charisian Army and the Republic of Siddarmark Army to *inflict* those losses, and Rainbow Waters wasn't cooperating.

That's why they call the other side "the enemy," Kynt, Green Valley thought sardonically. *Why, oh why can't all of their field commanders be as stupid as Kaitswyrth or Duke Harless? Or even only as smart as Nybar or Wyrshym? But no!*

Rainbow Waters was as determined to avoid experiencing blood and destruction as the Allies were to visit them upon him. He had entirely too cool and calculating a brain with which to do that avoiding, too, and Carl Mannerheim would have strongly approved of his latest brainstorm. What Green Valley had just finished viewing was only the latest in several full-scale field experiments the Harchongian had authorized. He knew he couldn't match the full capability of the Allies' new-model artillery, but he was beginning to receive enough heavy guns of his own to let him at least approximate a Charisian-style bombardment, and he'd held many of them near his headquarters in Lake City to keep them concentrated while he experimented not simply with the best way to *use* them but the best way to defend *against* them.

Captain of Horse Rungwyn had built a fortified "line" a mile wide and three miles deep, and then Lord of Foot Zhyngbau had done his dead level best to blow it up again. Constructing something like that in the early stages of a northern winter had been no picnic, even for Harchongese serfs accustomed to a still harsher climate, but Rungwyn had persevered.

In a lot of ways, Rungwyn reminded Green Valley of Admiral Sir Ahlfryd Hyndryk, the Baron of Seamount, except that Rungwyn had possessed no military experience before the Harchong Empire raised the Mighty Host of God and the Archangels. He was a civilian engineer, and a very good one. That was one reason Rainbow Waters had selected him for his current position. Another was the fact that he was almost as smart as, if thankfully less innovative than, Seamount, and his commoner background left him blissfully unhampered by aristocratic prejudices. But the fact that he had absolutely no training as a *military* engineer was perhaps his most important qualification, since it meant he'd had so much less to unlearn.

The IHA's engineers, like every other Harchongian, were the best, most effective practitioners of their art (whatever that art might happen to be) in the entire world. *They* knew that, whether anyone else did or not. The fact that they had exactly zero experience with the new-model tactics and weapons Charis had introduced was a mere bagatelle. Certainly those new-fangled toys were no reason to panic or allow themselves to be stampeded into abandoning the tried-and-true techniques they knew worked!

It was possible that existing senior officers could have been taught better, but it was unlikely it could have been accomplished in time to save the Mighty Host from disaster. So Rainbow Waters, with a directness Alexander the Great could only have envied, had cut his own Gordian Knot with a blade named Rungwyn. It hadn't made the captain of horse any friends. In fact, he was as well aware as Rainbow Waters of the innumerable enemies he'd made. Unfortunately for the Allies, he was just as focused on winning the jihad as the Mighty Host's CO, and he'd already moved his family to Shwei Province in the South Harchong Empire. He liked the climate better there . . . in more ways than one, and many of the merchant and banking families of Southern Harchong were already floating tentative post-jihad employment offers in his direction.

In the meantime, however, he'd approached the question of new-model fortifications with a completely open mind, and the results promised to be extremely painful. Good as current Charisian artillery was, it had yet to approach the effectiveness of the TNT-filled shells of Earth's twentieth-century wars. Sahndrah Lywys' version of TNT might change that, but not in the next few months. Pilot lots had already been completed at the Delthak Works' new satellite facility, and the new explosive—designated "Composition D" after the site of its development—had been tested *very* enthusiastically by Sir Ahlfryd Hyndryk at his Helen Island proving grounds, but the new explosive wouldn't achieve true volume production until late spring or early summer. That meant all of the artillery shells available when the upcoming campaigns began would still be charged with black powder, and black powder—even the current Charisian "prismatic" powder—was an anemic explosive compared to something like dynamite or TNT. And, unfortunately, some of Rungwyn's efforts would have been a serious challenge even for the massive artillery bombardments of 1916 and 1917.

He'd demonstrated that in experiments like the one Green Valley had just watched. Worse, he, Wind Song, and Rainbow Waters between them were in the process of formulating an entirely new doctrine to use those fortifications. It was one the Imperial German Army of 1916 would have recognized: a deep zone of successive belts of trenches and fortified strong points designed to absorb and channel an attack, diverting it into preplanned defensive fire zones. And just as Rainbow Waters had been prepared to modify the Mighty Host's hand grenade design to produce a weapon his slingers could launch to extraordinary range, he'd signed off on the local production of the equivalent of Charis' landmines. He didn't have barbed wire—yet, at least—and the Mighty Host's mines were less powerful and less reliable than the current-generation Charisian product, but within those limits, he was well on the way to producing something Erich von Falkenhayen would have recognized only too well. Neither Rainbow Waters nor Rungwyn had quite gotten to the point of deliberately allowing the attacker to advance until he'd outrun the effective support of his own artillery before throwing in a crushing counterattack. Given the way their current discussions were trending, the competent bastards were almost certainly going to arrive there eventually, though . . . and quite probably before the Allies were prepared to resume the offensive.

Perhaps just as bad, Rungwyn had been devising ways to *attack* his own fortifications. Some of his notions about combat engineers and demolition charges were unhappily similar to those the Imperial Charisian Army had worked out. Whatever Rainbow Waters might be telling his superiors in Zion, he clearly expected the Mighty Host and the AOG to be defending their positions this summer, rather than attacking. He wasn't about to pass up any offensive opportunities that came his way, however, and Rungwyn's mindset—and the mindset he was instilling into the engineers he was cycling through his training programs as rapidly as possible—was likely to provide Allied commanders with some very unpleasant experiences if that happened.

And Zhyngbau's no prize, either, Green Valley thought grumpily. *The man's spent entirely too much time corresponding with Maigwair and Brother Lynkyn, than actually thinking about the best way to use his new guns. And he's done too damned good a job of analyzing what* we've *done with them. His tools won't be as good, and he won't have the advantage of Ahlfryd and Ehdwyrd's new toy, so we're still going to have a huge advantage in reach, range, and flexibility. But he's damned well going to evolve the best technique he can for what he* does *have, and he's got a hell of a lot more than they ever had before.*

If the new Balloon Corps worked as well as promised—or even only *half* that well—the Allies' qualitative artillery advantage might well over-balance the Church's numerical advantage. No balloon had ever been used in combat yet, though, and it was possible their carefully worked out doctrine wouldn't work as well in practice as in theory. Even if it did, even the heaviest currently available guns would be hard-pressed to deal with the sorts of fortifications Rungwyn was designing. Charis simply didn't have the high-explosive shell fillers needed to blast a way through deeply bunkered positions. Yet, at least. That might change if Sahn-drah Lywys was able to expedite her progress, but the Allies couldn't count on that. They had to fight a campaign this year, and even if Lywys achieved miracles, they'd still have to *begin* that campaign before the new shells could possibly become available, and that was likely to prove expensive.

The ideal solution would be to go somewhere his men wouldn't have to face Rungwyn's fortifications or Zhyngbau's dug-in and prepared artillery, and under normal circumstances, the ICA's emphasis on mobility would have let him, Duke Eastshare, and the other Allied army commanders do just that. But the Church's retreating armies had demolished the canal and road net behind them too efficiently, and weather was already shutting down Chari-sian and Siddarmarkian repair efforts.

And, unfortunately, even the Imperial Charisian Army needs a supply line. The fact that we've managed to hang onto Spinefish Bay and Salyk this winter will help, and when the ice melts onthe Hildermoss—not to mention in Hsing-wu's Passage—our logistics will get a lot better. But even then, we're going to have to advance along depressingly predictable lines, and Rainbow Waters is obviously prepared to evade even Zhaspahr Clyntahn's demands if he has to. We can't count on sucking him into indefensible positions like Wyrshym's or Kaitswyrth's. And if it looks like we're about to do that, he'll damned well retreat, whatever *Clyntahn wants, unless we can figure out a way to fix him in position.*

Green Valley had become an intense student of Earth's military history since he'd been recruited for the inner circle, and the situation, he thought, had some resonances with the last year or so of World War Two. In Zhaspahr Clyntahn's eyes, Harchong held much the same position the *Waffen SS* had held in Adolf Hitler's. He trusted Harchongese devotion to the jihad—or, at least, to preventing the success of the Church of Charis—in a way he trusted none of the other secular armies who'd answered Mother Church's call. In fact, he trusted the Harchongians more than he did the Church's own army, given his current relationship with Allayn Maigwair. That meant a Harchongese commander enjoyed far greater latitude when it came to Clyntahn's demands, and Rainbow Waters had amply demonstrated that however intelligent and willing to think "outside the box" he might be, he was also a consummate practitioner of the Harchongese aristocracy's ability to game the system.

Not even he would be able to simply ignore Zhaspahr Clyntahn, and if the military situation began to crumble, his ability to *manipulate* Clyntahn would probably crumble right along with it. But he'd begin the campaign, at least, with a far greater degree of flexibility than any of the Allies' previous opposing field commanders.

And that's going to be painful, Green Valley thought glumly. *Even with the Balloon Corps, and even assuming it works perfectly, it's going to be painful. Especially since he's also going to begin the campaign with forward-deployed supply stockpiles big enough to support his operations all frigging summer long.*

Well, the Empire of Charis had confronted apparently insoluble problems before, he reminded himself. They'd just have to do it again.

As soon as he or someone else came up with a clue as to *how* they did it.

.IV.
The Delthak Works,
Barony of Lochair,
Kingdom of Old Charis,
Empire of Charis;
Nimue's Cave,
The Mountains of Light,
The Temple Lands;
and
Siddar City,
Republic of Siddarmark.

So you're happy about Ahlfryd's latest brainstorm?" Cayleb Ahrmahk asked.

"They seem to be working just fine," Ehdwyrd Howsmyn, the recently elevated Duke of Delthak, replied over the com as he leaned back in his chair and gazed out his office windows at the bustling, never ceasing activity of the largest industrial complex in the world.

"In some ways, I'd have preferred Ahldahs Rahzwail's suggestion," he continued, his expression a bit more somber as his eyes rested on the still incomplete roof and walls of the newly named Kahrltyn Haigyl Barrel Finishing Shop. "Compressed air for the burner isn't really that much of a challenge and fire vine oil's a lot less explosive than hydrogen, not to mention easier to transport than hydrochloric acid. Doesn't have the same corrosive effect on the gas cell linings, either. But it's also got about seven times the lift of hot air, and the varnish Rhaiyan's people came up with to the steel thistle gastight also cuts down on the corrosive effect. Can't completely *stop* it, but each cell should be good for at least a month or so of use before it needs routine replacement." He shrugged. "Generating the gas will be easier for the Navy, and hauling around multi-ton lots of hydrochloric acid and zinc will present the Army with some significant safety hazards. On the other hand, they'll be able to haul a lot more of both than a ship at sea can cram into its available volume."

"True, and I don't think anyone's going to complain about the transport problems once they realize what it means to them," Kynt Clareyk put in from Camp Mahrtyn Taisyn. "That look down from above will be huge for our forward observers, especially given what Runwyng's done with their fortifications. And if we manage to turn it back into an open field battle, it may be even more important. For one thing, it'll be a relief not to have to rely on 'hunches' and 'guesses' I can't explain to anyone about what's happening on the other side of the next hill! For that matter, we'll be able to give Ruhsyl and the others some of the same edge without needing *seijins* to turn up fortuitously with critical information just when they need it. And God knows we're going to need every edge we can get against Rainbow Waters."

"Amen to that," Cayleb agreed fervently.

"At any rate, all the first-wave aeronaut detachments should reach Transhar within another three or four five-days," Delthak continued, still gazing at the barrel shop. "I'd really prefer for them to be able to go on training—hydrogen doesn't respond well to sparks, and I worry about safety precautions that get rusty—but I suppose that's out of the question?"

"I'm afraid so," Merlin replied. "Oh, they can train in the basic procedures, but they can't deploy for real field training until it's actually time to use them. This isn't something we could hide from the casual observer—like anyone within, oh, twenty or thirty miles—and somebody like Rainbow Waters would recognize the implications of it just as quickly as anyone on our side. I don't know how much good that would do him, but if it would do *anyone* any good, he'd be the one. So the detachments will just have to stay undercover until it's time to move up to the front. I know you're worried about accidents during the inflation phase, but we'll be generating the hydrogen on demand, not hauling around huge pressurized tanks of it, and it's a lot more likely to just burn—violently as hell, I'll grant you—if it catches fire when it's not pressurized. And given the way it rises, it won't hang around at ground level even if they have a major leak. Those sparks you're worried about are a lot less likely to ignite it than you might think just because they can't catch it before it gets out of range!"

"Which I'm sure will be a great comfort to the survivors if one of them *does* catch it!" Delthak said a bit tartly. But then he inhaled and shook his head.

"I don't like it, but that may be because I've been extra skittish about potential accidents—and especially ones that involve things like flammable gasses—since our fire. It's only been about four months, and a thing like that . . . tends to stick in a man's mind." He grimaced and swiveled his chair back around, looking away from the nearly completed replacement barrel finishing shop. "And I may have done just a little too much reading about Lakehurst, I suppose. Either way, I can't argue with the 'military logic,' Merlin. And I have to admit I'm looking forward to the Temple Boys' reaction when *they* see it for the first time!"

"I think you can safely assume all of us are," Cayleb observed dryly. "When you come down to it, it's probably our biggest hole card for this summer's entire campaign. Timing or no, though, I'm not really looking forward to explaining to Hauwerd Breygart why *he* didn't get any of them."

"I'm sure he'll forgive you . . . eventually," Merlin said soothingly. "He understands the value of surprise better than most. Besides, Ehdwyrd's gotten him all that splendid new artillery, and he's doing just fine the way things are."

"Can't argue with that," Cayleb said approvingly. "In fact, he's doing well enough I think it's time to start the process of elevating Hanth to a duchy."

"Seems to be a lot of that going around lately," Merlin observed with something suspiciously like a chuckle, and Delthak's image made a rude gesture in his direction.

"That's because as nasty as this campaign's looking, we're not worried about whether or not we're going to *survive* it." Cayleb's tone was considerably more sober. "When you're confident you'll still be here at the end of the year, you've got a lot more leisure to think about handing out tokens of appreciation to the people who've made sure you will. People like *you*, Ehdwyrd."

"It's been a joint effort, Cayleb," Duke Delthak replied with a hint of embarrassment. "I won't pretend I haven't worked my arse off, but so have a lot of other people. And at least no one's been shooting at *me*."

"True, but there's not a single man in uniform who doesn't realize this war will be won just as much on the manufactory floor as any battlefield," Merlin said. "And the truth is that beating the Group of Four's the easy part. You and your people are what may let us win the war against the *Proscriptions* in the end."

"But winning the war against the Group of Four has to come first," Nahrmahn put in from his computer in Nimue's Cave. "And I think our little psychological warfare campaign is starting to wear on friend Zhaspahr's nerves. His agents inquisitor are spending an awful lot of time tearing all those broadsheets off of walls all over the Temple Lands, and they seem to be getting just a bit frustrated by it." The portly little prince smiled seraphically. "The word's getting out, too. None of his city and borough bishops inquisitor can pretend they're only a local phenomenon anymore."

"No, they can't," Nynian Rychtyr agreed in tones of profound satisfaction, and Merlin smiled across the breakfast table at her.

It must be driving Clyntahn and Rayno to frothing madness, he thought. For the better part of two years, they'd managed to prevent the majority of the Temple's supporters from realizing how broadly Owl's remotes had been distributing their broadsheets. To be fair, Nahrmahn and Nynian had been careful about ramping up that distribution. Clyntahn was going to blame it on demons in the end, whatever they did, but they'd wanted awareness of the bulletins posted on walls and doors to seep into people's awareness slowly. To become an accepted part of their world gradually, giving them time to get over the "demonic" novelty of them as familiarity wore away the taint. To help that along, they'd strictly limited the number of "bombshell" revelations in each issue, filling out at least half—and more often two-thirds—of the space with homey local news items. News items people could check. Whose accuracy they could verify for themselves and which tended to validate the items they *couldn't* check by a process of association.

Once they'd pushed them into their readers' awareness as an alternate source of information, they'd started broadening their attacks on Clyntahn's version of events. In the last year or so they'd even started carrying statements from the Fist of God, including devastating lists of the crimes for which the Fist had struck down literally dozens of vicars and archbishops, almost all of whom had been Clyntahn allies or toadies. The damage *that* had done to the Grand Inquisitor's credibility would be almost impossible to overestimate, and in the last five or six months, Owl's remotes had begun distributing them even more widely. They were *everywhere* now, and little though anyone in the Inquisition's reach would admit it, many of their readers had decided they were telling the truth . . . and that Clyntahn wasn't.

Another consequence of that greater saturation, however, was that people had become aware the same sorts of broadsheets were appearing *everywhere*. Despite the communication limitations of a pre-electronic civilization, the Inquisition could no longer pretend even to the average man in the street, much less to their own agents inquisitor, that they were restricted only to a single locale, or perhaps to one or two of the Temple Lands' greater cities. Nor could they hide the fact that they were appearing despite everything Clyntahn's minions could do to prevent it, which ground relentlessly away at the Inquisition's aura of invincibility. Zhaspahr Clyntahn's cloak of authority and power was growing progressively more tattered, and when it came completely apart. . . .

" 'The moral is to the physical as three to one,' " he quoted. "Napoleon didn't get *everything* right, but he nailed that one. The more we've got Clyntahn's bastards—and everyone in the Army of God and the Mighty Host, for that matter—looking over their shoulders, the shakier they'll be when the hammer comes down."

"Yes, but I've been thinking we might want to look at a few ways to further improve our own people's morale, as well as grinding away at the Temple Loyalists' confidence," Nahrmahn said.

"I know that tone," Cayleb said warily. "What have you been up to this time?"

"Oh, I haven't been up to *anything* . . . yet, Your Majesty. I do have a . . . call it a prototype morale booster for Ehdwyrd's manufactories, though."

"My manufactories are just a bit busy with other things at the moment, Nahrmahn," Delthak observed. "Like, oh, balloons, bayonets, hand grenades, angle-guns, armor plate, shell production, rifle ammunition, steam engines—you know, little things like that."

"Oh, I know that! And it won't cut into your military production at all. In fact, you may want to farm it out to one of the plumbing manufactories. Or possibly to one of the ceramics works."

"What in the world are you talking about, Nahrmahn?" Nynian demanded with a smile. She'd had more experience than most of how the devious little Emeraldian's mind worked.

"Well, I don't know about the rest of you, but back when I had to waste all that time breathing, I did some of my most profound thinking when I was enthroned in the privacy of my water closet," Nahrmahn said with his most serious and profound expression. "The isolation, the quiet—the ability to focus upon my reflections secure from any interruptions or distractions—were always rather soothing."

"Should I assume this is *going* somewhere? Besides into the crapper—you should pardon the expression—anyway?" Cayleb seemed torn between laughter and exasperation, and Nahrmahn grinned at him. But then the prince's expression sobered once more—a bit, anyway.

"It is, actually," he said, "and it goes back to what Merlin just said about morale. Our people have plenty of determination, Cayleb, but sometimes they need a little laughter, too, and there are times mockery can be more deadly than any amount of reasoned argument. So I got to thinking about how we might provide that laughter, especially in a way that gave another kick to Clyntahn's image, and it occurred to me that indoor plumbing isn't really all that widespread, especially in rural Siddarmark or places like Delferahk and Zebediah. For that matter, it damned well doesn't *exist* in North Harchong or anywhere in Desnair outside a palace! And that suggested *this* to me."

He held out an empty left hand and waved his right hand above it like a stage conjurer. Unlike the conjurer, however, Nahrmahn Baytz truly could work "magic"—within the confines of his virtual reality, at least—and an object appeared on his palm. It was a largish white, bowl-shaped ceramic vessel with a handle and a cover, and Merlin frowned as he recognized the chamber pot.

"*That's* your magic morale weapon?" he asked skeptically, and Nahrmahn glanced down at it.

"Oh, excuse me! I didn't quite finish it."

He snapped his fingers, and the plain white chamber pot's sides were abruptly decorated with a tasteful pattern of intertwined leaves and vines. Then he held it up at an angle and removed the lid with a flourish, allowing the others to see down into its interior.

"Oh, Nahrmahn! That's *perfect!*" Nynian exclaimed before a chorus of laughter swamped the com net, and Nahrmahn's smile became an enormous grin.

The bottom of the chamber pot was decorated with the jowly, readily recognizable face of a man in the orange-cockaded white priest cap of a vicar. His mouth was open and his eyes were wide in an expression of pure outrage, and a six-word label ran around its rim.

"A salute to the Grand Fornicator," it said.

.V.
Earl Thirsk's Townhouse,
City of Gorath,
Kingdom of Dohlar.

Thank you for coming, My Lord," Earl Thirsk said as Bishop Staiphan Maik followed Paiair Sahbrahan into his library. He climbed out of his chair—a bit of a struggle with his left arm still immobilized—despite Maik's quick, abortive wave for him to stay seated. The earl smiled faintly at the bishop's distressed expression and bent to kiss Maik's ruby-set ring.

"There's no need for this sort of nonsense when no one else is looking, Lywys," Maik scolded. "Sit back down—immediately!"

"Aye, aye, My Lord." Thirsk's smile broadened, but he obeyed the prelate's command, settling back into his chair with a slight sigh of relief he couldn't quite suppress. Maik heard it, and shook his head.

"All silliness about formal greetings aside, you shouldn't push yourself this hard," he said seriously, brown eyes dark with a very personal concern. "Langhorne knows you've been through enough—*lost* enough—for three men!"

"Others have lost their families," Thirsk replied, his smile vanishing. "And others have been 'through' quite a lot since the Jihad began."

"Of course they have." Maik's hair gleamed like true silver in the lamplight as he shook his head, and his expression tightened. "But I've seen and shared more of what *you've* been through. And try though I might, I can't avoid the thought that God's asked too much of you."

"I don't think so, My Lord."

There was a curious tranquility in Thirsk's tone, and he leaned back in his chair, his good hand waving for Sahbrahan to leave. The valet withdrew, closing the door behind him, and it was the earl's turn to shake his head.

"Men can ask too much of someone," he said. "And sometimes Mother Church—or the men who serve her, at least—can do the same. But God and the Archangels?" It was his turn to shake his head. "We owe them all we are or can ever hope to be. How can *they* possibly ask 'too much' of us?"

The bishop sat back in his own chair, his eyes narrowing, and frowned.

"I've known you and worked with you for several years now, Lywys," he said slowly. "I think I've come to know you fairly well during that time."

"I'd agree with that," Thirsk conceded.

"On the basis of how well I've come to know you, I think you just chose your words very carefully."

"Because I did." Thirsk's good hand pointed at the whiskey decanter and glasses on the small table at the bishop's elbow. "Would you pour for us, My Lord?" He smiled thinly. "It's Glynfych . . . from Chisholm."

"Is it?" Maik smiled slightly as he unstoppered the decanter and poured the amber liquid into the glasses. "I'm sure the bottle was imported long before the Grand Inquisitor prohibited any trade with Chisholm."

"Oh, of course!"

Thirsk accepted his glass and the bishop re-seated himself and sipped appreciatively. Yet his eyes never left the earl's face, and a subtle tension hummed in the modest-sized, book-lined room. The coal fire crackling on the hearth seemed unnaturally loud in the stillness, and Thirsk allowed that stillness to linger as he took a slow, deliberate swallow of his own whiskey and wondered if he was right about the man sitting across from him. He hoped he was. He *believed* he was. But he also knew Staiphan Maik had been handpicked by Wyllym Rayno and Zhaspahr Clyntahn for his present assignment because of how implicitly they'd trusted his judgment and his devotion to Mother Church.

Of course, there's just a tiny difference between devotion to Mother Church and devotion to Zhaspahr Clyntahn, now isn't there? Thirsk thought. *And time and experience have a habit of changing a man's opinions, if his heart's good and his brain works.*

The library was smaller than his formal study, and it was also an interior room with no windows, although it was well illuminated in daylight by an extensive, domed skylight. Its size and internal location meant it tended to stay warmer this time of year, despite the skylight's expanse of glass, but warmth wasn't the primary reason he'd invited the Royal Dohlaran Navy's intendant to join him here. The lack of windows, and the fact that no one could enter it—or eavesdrop upon any conversation within it—without first getting past Sahbrahan and Sir Ahbail Bahrdailahn, Thirsk's flag lieutenant, were far more pertinent at the moment.

"I'm pleased to see you looking so well. Relatively speaking of course," Maik said into the stillness. "I was . . . concerned about what I was hearing."

"You mean you'd heard I was doing my best to drink myself to death." Thirsk shook his head and waved the glass in his hand as Maik started to protest. "I'm sure that's what you heard, My Lord, since it's exactly what I was trying to do."

The bishop closed his mouth, and the earl chuckled softly. There was very little humor in the sound.

"I'm afraid I'd come to the same conclusion you had, My Lord—that too much had been asked of me. I just didn't think it was God or the Archangels who'd done the asking."

The humming tension intensified suddenly, and Maik settled slowly back into his chair.

"That's . . . a very interesting statement," he said at last.

"I doubt somehow that it comes as a total surprise to you, My Lord. I remember the day you mentioned the sixth chapter of the *Book of Bédard* to me. I'd come to the conclusion that I'd waited too long to comply with the Holy Bédard's commands in that chapter."

"That was scarcely your fault, Lywys," the bishop said quietly.

"Perhaps not." Thirsk sipped more whiskey and gazed down into his glass. "No, definitely not—you're right about that. But the fact that it wasn't my *fault* doesn't change the fact that seeing my family into a place of safety was my *responsibility*. And now that that's . . . no longer a factor, I've been forced to reconsider all of my *other* responsibilities, both as the senior officer of His Majesty's Navy and—" his eyes lifted suddenly, stabbing into his intendant's "—as a son of Mother Church."

"Have you, my son?" Staiphan Maik asked very softly.

"Yes, I have." Thirsk's eyes held the bishop's gaze very, very levelly. "And the true reason I invited you here today, My Lord, is that one of those 'other responsibilities' includes explaining to you as my intendant, my spiritual councilor, and—I believe—my friend how that reconsideration has . . . shaped my thinking."

"You used the term 'spiritual councilor,'" Maik said. "Should I assume you're telling me this in my priestly office and treat anything you say as covered by the confidentiality of the confession?"

"No." Thirsk's voice was very soft, but there was no hesitation in it. "I want you to feel free to treat what I'm about to say in the way that seems best to you. I trust your judgment—and your heart—as much as I've ever trusted any man's. And, to be honest, you and your office are . . . rather central to my present thinking. Your response to it will probably determine exactly what I do—or can do—to better meet those responsibilities of mine."

"I see." Maik sipped more whiskey, rolling the golden glory over his tongue before he swallowed. "Are you very sure about this, Lywys?" he asked then, his voice even softer than the earl's had been.

"Staiphan," he said, using the bishop's given name without title or honorific for the first time in all the months they'd known one another, "I've never been more sure of anything in my life."

"Very well, then." Maik set his glass back on the side table and settled himself squarely in his armchair, his elbows on the armrests and his fingers interlaced across his chest, thumbs resting lightly on his pectoral scepter.

"In that case, I suppose you'd best begin."

.VI.
HMS *Lightning*, 30,
Claw Island,
Sea of Harchong.

Wyverns and seagulls rose black against the sunset in winged, raucous protest as the saluting guns thudded from the defensive batteries. The spurts of smoke were the gray white of conventional gunpowder, not the dark brown of the ICN's current propellant, and they merged into a ragged line that rolled southeast on the fitful breeze out of the northwest, There were fewer guns in those batteries than there had been, since two-thirds of the smoothbores which had defended Hardship Bay under Dohlaran ownership had been replaced by less than half as many rifled Charisian guns with twice the effective range and far greater destructive power. There were still a lot of them, though, and the crews of every single one of them— aside from the saluting guns—stood atop the earthen ramparts, cheering as the weather-stained line of galleons made their way into the bay through North Channel, close-hauled on the starboard tack.

A return salute rippled down HMS *Lightning's* side as she led that line, flying the streamer of Admiral Tymythy Darys. They were three months out of Tellesberg, those galleons, and more than one man aboard them had wondered if Claw Island would still be in Charisian hands when they arrived.

Silly of us, Darys thought, standing on *Lightning's* quarterdeck and studying the bay through a raised angle-glass. *Baron Rock Point was right. The bastards may've taken* Dreadnought *from Kahrltyn, but there's no way in Shan-wei's darkest hell they could have her back in commission yet. Not with any ammunition for her guns, anyway!*

The admiral's mouth tightened as he thought about Kahrltyn Haigyl, HMS *Dreadnought's* captain. He would miss that giant of a man, but the

Imperial Charisian Navy would never forget *Dreadnought*'s last fight. It did seem that perhaps *Dreadnought* wasn't the most fortunate name in the world for Charisian warships, he acknowledged, but neither this *Dreadnought* nor her predecessor had gone without one hell of a fight . . . or failed to achieve the goal for which she'd fought.

Could have a lot worse tradition for the next one *to live up to,* he reflected. *A lot worse. And her* skipper'*ll have some damned big boots to fill, too. Even if he was a lousy navigator!*

His tight mouth relaxed into a smile at that thought, and he straightened from the angle-glass.

"Well, we appear to still be here," he said dryly to his flag captain.

"Never doubted we would be for a moment, Sir," Captain Sympsyn, who happened to share Darys' first name, said stoutly.

"Oh?" Darys cocked an eyebrow. "I seem to recall a moment or two there, about the time those headwinds in the Sea of Harchong were so . . . uncooperative. Wasn't there *someone* in *Lightning*'s company who was fretting that we might not get there in time? Let me see . . . I can't quite seem to recall the name, but I think it was a captain somebody."

"I'm sure you're mistaken, Sir. Couldn't've been anybody aboard *my* ship!"

"Of course I am." Darys chuckled, then clapped Sympsyn on the shoulder. "Probably just somebody who was pissed off by the weather and had to vent. But for now, I'd best get below and change." He indicated his comfortable, well-worn seagoing uniform, with its brand-new, golden collar kraken and single gold cuff band. "Wouldn't want to turn up in front of the Earl poorly dressed, would I?"

"Frankly, Sir, I think you could turn up naked and he'd still be glad to see you. And all the rest of us, of course."

The flag captain waved one hand to take in the twenty-five warships and sixteen supply galleons following *Lightning*.

"You may have a point," Darys agreed. "Not that I intend to find out the hard way!"

▼　　▼　　▼

"Somehow I doubt this will surprise you, Tymythy," Sir Lewk Cohlmyn, the Earl of Sharpfield, said dryly as his flag lieutenant showed Admiral Darys into his office in the ICN's steadily expanding Hardship Bay base, "but I'm extraordinarily happy to see you."

He clasped forearms with his visitor, his thinning silver hair gleaming in the lamplight. Sailing ships were not the fleetest things upon the face of the world, and the wind—capricious more often than not, as any professional mariner could explain at length, usually taking at least several of the

Archangels' names in vain in the process—had decided to drop while Darys' squadron worked its way towards the anchorage. As a result, he hadn't gotten ashore until well after supper had been served, and the tropical night outside Sharpfield's office was blacker than the inside of Kau-yung's boot.

"Admiral Rock Point thought you might be, Sir," Darys replied. "He tried to send enough friends along with me to make you that way, anyway."

"I'm especially glad to see *Lightning, Floodtide,* and *Seamount,*" Sharpfield said frankly, "and *Zhenyfyr Ahrmahk* and *Iceberg* are nothing to sneer at, either. I didn't really expect to see them, but they certainly can't hurt! To be honest, I'm a little surprised Thirsk hasn't already sent *Dreadnought*—and the rest of his Western Squadron—to call on us." His expression darkened and he shook his head. "Not like him to let grass grow under his feet, and he has to've understood that the High Admiral would be sending replacement ironclads."

"I've brought along the Baron's personal dispatches to you, of course, My Lord." Darys extended the thick, heavy canvas envelope with its ornate wax seals. "Before we sailed, though, he and I discussed *Dreadnought* and getting her back into service with Master Howsmyn and Sir Dustyn. Based on Sir Bruhstair's report and what the prisoners Sir Dunkyn rescued were able to tell us, it seemed likely to them that *Dreadnought* had been battered badly enough to need at least some repairs. More to the point, the High Admiral and Master Howsmyn both estimated it would take months, at least, to provide ammunition for her guns, unless they wanted to completely rearm her with their own artillery. Then, too, Thirsk is no idiot. He'd have his shipwrights crawling all over her for five-days just to figure out how she was put together. In the long term, he probably thinks that's more important than getting her back into service as quickly as possible. And—" he smiled unpleasantly "—given what he thinks he knows, he'd be right. Unfortunately for him, he *doesn't* know what's coming along behind us, though, so it would be perfectly logical for him to think that learning to duplicate her—assuming they could produce the armor for it—would give the Dohlarans something like a fighting chance."

"Hard to blame him if he does," Sharpfield agreed, waving his guest towards a chair and laying the envelope on the blotter of his desk. "Especially after the fight Kahrltyn put up!" He shook his head, his expression one of mingled pride and bitter grief. "One thing that did occur to me after I'd thought about it a while was that Kahrltyn must've put the fear of God into the entire Dohlaran Navy. They took his ship in the end, but he pounded half their fleet into scrap single-handed before they did, by Chihiro!"

"Like Baron Green Valley says, 'putting the fear' into the other side's always worthwhile." Darys nodded, then sighed. "I could wish the price hadn't been that steep, though."

"We all do." Sharpfield settled into his own chair while Lieutenant Tympyltyn poured brandy for him and his guest. "And I'll certainly read all of these as soon as I can," he continued, laying one palm briefly on the envelope Darys had handed him. "In the meantime, though, I'd appreciate it if you could bring me up to speed on the High Admiral's thinking in general."

"Of course, My Lord."

Darys accepted a glass from Tympyltyn and sat back. He wasn't surprised Sharpfield would want his take on the High Admiral's thinking. Until the relief for Claw Island had been organized, he'd been Sir Domynyk Staynair's flag captain, a post he'd held for well over two years, and no one in the entire ICN could have a better read on Rock Point's analysis of the Empire's current strategic imperatives. In fact, that was one reason he'd been both promoted and chosen to command the relief squadron in the first place.

"First," he continued, "Sir Domynyk specifically told me to assure you he fully approves of your response to what happened to Captain Ahbaht's squadron. In fact, there's a letter of commendation—and a promotion to commodore—for the Captain in that envelope somewhere. As the Emperor himself put it by semaphore, 'It's not given to mortal men to simply command a victory. Wind and weather have a part to play, and all man or God can ask of anyone is that he give the very best he has, which is exactly what Sir Bruhstair and all his men did.'"

"I have to admit I'm relieved to hear that." Sharpfield sipped brandy, then set the glass down. "I couldn't fault a single decision he made, and I'd far rather worry about our people's aggressiveness than that they might *avoid* a fight! And Langhorne knows the last thing we need is to hammer a good officer who damned well wouldn't deserve it. If nothing else, the effect on the next flag officer who has to make a hard call probably wouldn't be very good."

"That's almost exactly what Sir Domynyk said, My Lord." Darys nodded. "And, obviously, everyone in Old Charis was elated when we got word Sir Dunkyn had rescued our people. Archbishop Maikel proclaimed masses of thanksgiving throughout the Empire.

"Now, I'm sure the High Admiral's dispatches to you will cover exactly what he had in mind when he sent us out, but he asked me to give you a brief overview of his thinking before you get to them.

"It's his thought that deploying as much of our strength forward as possible would have to have an . . . efficacious effect on Admiral Thirsk's thinking. Towards that end, it occurred to him that—"

.VII.
Rydymak Keep,
Cheshyr Bay,
Earldom of Cheshyr,
and
King Tayrens Chancellery,
City of Cherayth,
Kingdom of Chisholm,
Empire of Charis.

Rydymak Keep was spectacularly beautiful, in an old-fashioned, drafty-icehouse, freeze-one's-arse-off sort of way.

Karyl Rydmakyr, the Dowager Countess of Cheshyr, still remembered the way the keep had struck her to the heart the first time she saw its steep-pitched, red-tiled tower roofs and sheer, storybook walls from the deck of the ship bearing her home to Cheshyr with her newlywed husband. She hadn't known Styvyn well—indeed, when she came down to it, she hadn't known him at *all*—before the wedding, but he'd been handsome, athletic, considerate of his young and very nervous bride, and unswervingly loyal to the House of Tayt. As a daughter of a cadet branch of that house, she'd understood how important that was. She'd also known how unusual it was among the Chisholmian aristocracy of her youth, for she'd been raised to be sensitive to the treacherous currents which swirled among the kingdom's nobility. And because of that, she'd realized very clearly that Styvyn was a far greater matrimonial prize than the lord of an impoverished holding like Cheshyr might normally have been . . . especially then.

King Irwain had been a good man, and she'd respected him as her king, but he'd lacked the steel spine to stand up to the kingdom's great nobles. His son, though . . . Prince Sailys had been a different sort. Young she might have been, but there'd never been anything wrong with Karyl Tayt's brain, and despite the distance of their relationship—fifth cousins normally weren't extraordinarily close—she'd strongly suspected her crown prince had plans he wasn't discussing with his future adversaries.

More to the point, perhaps, her *father* had cherished the same suspicions, and when Prince Sailys had casually expressed himself as favoring the proposed match, Sir Ahdam Tayt had found it in his heart to accept the young earl's offer for his second eldest daughter's hand. It hadn't been the sort of dashing, wealthy marriage young Karyl had dreamed of, but given the penurious fortunes of her branch of the Tayt dynasty, it hadn't been anything to turn her nose up at, either. And he *had* been good-looking, her Styvyn. Better still, he'd had a sense of humor and a brain *almost* as good as hers. And even more than that, he'd had a heart that dearly wanted his new wife to be happy and to love him . . . in that order.

With all of that going for him, she thought now, smiling as she drew the shawl more tightly around her shoulders while she sat very close to the hearth, how could she not have done both?

The memory of his presence wrapped itself about her more warmly than any shawl, and her hazel eyes softened, gazing into the flames at something only she could see. They'd had thirty good years, she and Styvyn, years in which he'd risen to general's rank in the Royal Army and stood foursquare by first Prince Sailys' and then King Sailys' side.

And he'd died by his king's side, as well.

Her smile faded, and she huddled deeper into the shawl, turning away from the pain of that memory, choosing instead to remember again that first glimpse of Rydymak Keep against a spectacular summer sky of crimson coals and smoke-blue cloud banners. The Sunset Hills upon which it stood weren't much, as hills went, compared to the lofty Iron Spine Mountains in whose shadows she'd grown to young womanhood. But in low-lying Cheshyr, they'd amply deserved the title, and she'd fallen in love with the stone cottages of her new husband's capital city even before she'd finished falling in love with him. Even today, she made it a point, weather permitting, to walk Rydymak's streets, personally visit the school built close up against the church, and chaffer with the vendors in the farmer's market at least once every five-day. She often thought she knew every inhabitant by name, and if she didn't, it certainly wasn't for want of trying!

Yet for all its scenic beauty, Rydymak Keep was a monumentally uncomfortable place to live. Styvyn had built her a beautiful little solar as a fifth-anniversary wedding gift. Given the state of Cheshyr's exchequer, it had been ruinously extravagant of him, but he hadn't cared. And the bedroom of their suite had been carefully draft-proofed. He'd even installed an enormous Harchong-style tiled stove, despite her protests, and she'd scolded him mercilessly for *that* indulgence. After all, she'd grown up in Tayt! A Cheshyr winter was a mere trifle to an Iron Spine girl. Besides—she smiled again—she'd never needed a *stove* to keep her warm whenever Styvyn was home.

The rest of the keep, however, was just as drafty, cold, and thoroughly miserable in winter as it looked, and she wondered why she was sitting here in the library in the middle of the night. The high-backed, thickly cushioned chair was comfortable enough, but that could scarcely be said of the shadowy, high-ceilinged, frigid chamber in which it sat.

You're sitting here because you're lonely, you're worried, and you're frightened, she told herself tartly, looking up to watch the fire-flicker dance on the exposed beams overhead. *And because this is the chair where you used to sit in Styvyn's lap while the two of you read the same book. Because sitting here, with a little piece of him, you don't care if you're cold . . . and you're just a little less frightened than you are lying awake in that big, warm, lonely bed.*

She snorted and jabbed irritably at the single tear that leaked its treacherous way down her cheek. Feeling maudlin never solved a problem, she reminded herself sternly. Unfortunately, she didn't know what *was* going to solve the one she found herself facing this time.

If only that miserable, unmitigated son-of-a-bitch hadn't gotten his hooks into Young Styvyn, she thought bitterly. *Or if only Young Styvyn had half the brain his grandfather and his father had! Bédard knows I love the boy, but—*

She chopped that thought off. It wasn't her grandson's fault he wasn't the most brilliant young man ever born, and maybe it was at least partly *her* fault that he'd fallen so readily into Zhasyn Seafarer's hand. She did love him—she truly did—but she'd always been . . . disappointed by her inability to interest him in the books, the poetry, the history she and his grandfather—and, for that matter, his own father—had loved so much. Perhaps he'd sensed that disappointment, decided it meant she didn't love him, or—even worse—that she thought poorly of him. Could that be why his glamorous second cousin had found it so easy to worm his poisonous way into the boy's affections?

Doesn't hurt that the slick bastard's a duke and as rich as Cheshyr is poor, either, does it? she reflected. *And he is family, whether I like it or not. Somehow that whole marriage didn't work out the way Styvyn and Sailys hoped it would, and, oh, how I wish I hadn't found myself in a position to say "I told you so" to the pair of them! I truly did love Pahtrysha, though. Of course, she couldn't stand Zhasyn either.* A brief, fond smile flitted across her lips. *Always did have good taste, Pahtrysha did, especially for a Seafarmer. Look who she married!*

The smile vanished as completely as the hope she'd once cherished that Pahtrysha Seafarmer's marriage to her son Kahlvyn might open at least a small crack in the Dukes of Rock Coast's adamantine opposition to the Crown's dominance of Chisholm. The only Seafarmer they'd won to their cause in the end had been Pahtrysha herself . . . and she'd died in the same carriage accident which had paralyzed Kahlvyn and left him incapable of speech.

Sometimes I wonder what we did to draw Shan-wei's hatred so strongly, she thought bitterly. *Why has the world gone so far out of its way to demolish my family? Not even Father Kahrltyn can explain that one to me! It's not like we haven't always—*

"Excuse me, My Lady."

Karyl Rydmakyr bounced out of the chair with an agility at odds with her seventy-six winters. She landed at least a yard from it and whipped around, heart pounding, to stare at the blue-eyed young woman who couldn't possibly be there. She opened her mouth, but before she could speak—or shout for help—the intruder raised a swift hand.

"Please, My Lady!" she said quickly in an accent that never came from Chisholm. "I'm a friend. In fact, Her Majesty sent me."

Lady Karyl closed her mouth with a snap as she took in her impossible visitor's blackened chain mail and the black-and-gold kraken and blue-and-white checkerboard blazoned across her breastplate. The mere fact that the intruder wore the accoutrements of the Imperial Charisian Guard didn't guarantee one damned thing, but it certainly bore thinking upon.

"*Friends* don't creep uninvited into locked rooms in someone else's house, young woman!" she said acidly, instead of shouting for help.

Which might be just as well for the any servants in the house in question, she reflected as her pulse slowed and she took in the curved sword and what had to be a pair of the newfangled revolvers holstered at the intruder's waist.

"They do if Her Majesty's impressed them with the importance of making contact with you without anyone else knowing about it," the young woman said respectfully, and Lady Karyl's eyes narrowed.

"That's an interesting assertion." She settled her shawl around her shoulders. "I trust you'll understand that I'd like some verification that it's also a *truthful* assertion." She smiled with very little humor. "I'm afraid I've become somewhat less trusting of late."

"According to Her Majesty, My Lady, you've never been exceptionally trusting where enemies of your house are concerned." The younger woman's smile was much warmer than Lady Karyl's had been. "She tells me that her father spoke to her often about your husband's loyalty to the Crown . . . and yours. In fact," those blue eyes, so dark they were almost black in the lamplight, met Lady Karyl's levelly, "she told me to tell you she hopes the doomwhale is still hidden in the cliff lizard's mouth."

Lady Karyl never actually moved a muscle, yet her spine—as steely straight as the Iron Spines she'd grown up among—seemed to relax ever so slightly. She stood for several more seconds, gazing at the interloper through narrow hazel eyes. Then she stepped back to her chair and pointed imperiously at a corner of the library's enormous hearth.

"Move where I can see you," she said, settling back into the chair she'd shared so often with Styvyn. "Besides," she added with a small, crooked smile as the other woman obeyed her, "you'll be at least marginally warmer!"

"Yes, My Lady."

Lady Karyl studied her more carefully. Cheshyr couldn't afford to waste first-quality kraken oil on its lamps, even in the library, and her eyes were no younger than the rest of her. The brain behind them was still capable of careful observation, however.

The other woman was perhaps half a hand shorter than her own five feet and seven inches, with extraordinarily dark brown hair touched with auburn highlights. She was slim and graceful, almost delicate looking, yet there was nothing fragile about her. She stood very straight, despite the obviously heavy saddlebags over her shoulder, waiting patiently, sapphire eyes level, enduring Lady Karyl's meticulous inspection with complete composure. Indeed, she was almost too composed for comfort, Lady Karyl thought. That sort of calm wasn't normally the property of someone as young as she was.

"Very well, young woman," she said finally. "Suppose you tell me what that nonsense about doomwhales and cliff lizards was all about."

"I'd be happy to, My Lady . . . if I knew." Her visitor, Lady Karyl discovered, had dimples. "From the way Her Majesty made sure I had it straight, I assume it's some sort of recognition phrase. And if I had to guess, I'd guess it goes back to your husband's relationship—or perhaps yours—with King Sailys. Unfortunately, a guess is all it would be."

"I see."

Lady Karyl gazed at her for another moment, then pushed back up out of her chair. Her father-in-law had disdained anything as effete as books, and in his day the room which had become Styvyn Rydmakyr's library had been the keep's trophy room. Since neither Styvyn nor Lady Karyl had wanted to shelve their precious books against an exterior stone wall, the trophies which had looked back into the room from between the windows during Truskyt Rydmakyr's day looked back still, and she paused beside one of them.

The cliff lizard had been a giant among its kind, probably over three hundred pounds, and its mouth was open, displaying teeth equally apt for chewing meat or grazing. She laid a hand affectionately on it for a moment, then reached into that gaping mouth and extracted something that gleamed faintly in the lamplight. She carried it back over to the hearth and held it up, and it was the other woman's eyes' turn to narrow.

It was an exquisitely rendered doomwhale, about five inches long and cast in solid silver . . . except for the golden crown no true doomwhale had ever worn. That crown gleamed more brightly than the tarnished silver, and Lady Karyl turned it deliberately to catch the firelight on its thorny points.

"King Sailys gave this to Styvyn," she said softly. "I believe there were less than twenty of them, and anyone who received one was charged to keep it hidden and keep it safe. Unless it was needed."

She met those shadow-darkened blue eyes, and the other woman nodded.

"Tokens of his authority," she said slowly, her voice soft. "From what

Her Majesty told me, I knew your husband had been high in King Sailys' confidence, but I hadn't realized how high."

"Few people ever did." Lady Karyl's long, still-strong fingers tightened around the small statue. "He and the King were careful to keep it that way, for a lot of reasons. And that fool thinks I'm going to forget everything Sailys—and Styvyn—fought and died for?!"

Her lips worked as if she wanted to spit, and the young woman laughed. There was very little humor in the sound. Indeed, if doomwhales had laughed, one of them might have owned a laugh very like it.

"That question I already knew the answer to, My Lady." She bowed deeply, then straightened. "With your permission, I'd like to finish introducing myself."

"Of course." Lady Karyl seated herself once more, holding the doomwhale in her lap, clasped between both hands. "And when you've done that, perhaps you could explain how you got into this locked library without any of my admittedly understrength staff seeing you on your way here? Or, for that matter, without alerting *me* when the hinges shrieked like a soul in hell?"

"The introduction is easy, Lady Karyl." The younger woman touched her breastplate in formal salute. "Men call me Merch O Obaith."

"Ah." Lady Karyl nodded. "I hope you'll pardon my saying so, but your name seems rather . . . outlandish. In fact, it reminds me of a few other names I've heard. Would it happen you're familiar with a gentleman named Athrawes?"

"As a matter of fact, I am."

"Fascinating." Lady Karyl leaned farther back and crossed her legs. "It would appear his reputation for coming and going as he wants despite any silly little things like locked doors is well deserved. And it would also appear *seijins* are coming out of the woodwork, as Styvyn would have said."

"I wouldn't go quite that far, myself, My Lady," Obaith corrected politely. "Although, if pressed, I would admit they've become rather more visible. I believe *The Testimonies* say that *seijins* will appear when they're most needed, though."

"And at this moment, I need one very *badly*," Lady Karyl said somberly.

"Perhaps the *services* of one, at least," Obaith acknowledged. "I'm afraid that tonight I'm only a messenger, however."

"And what sort of message do you bear?" Lady Karyl's eyes were intent in the flickering firelight.

"My Lady, Her Majesty wants you to know her agents are aware of what's happening here in Cheshyr, not to mention in Rock Coast and Black Horse. Those agents are keeping a very close eye on the situation, and I regret that it's taken so long for her authorization to share that information with you to reach Chisholm. We know about Duke Rock Coast's efforts to ensnare your grandson, and we also know they're in communication with Lady Swayle. Unfortunately, there's very little we can do about the Duke's machinations where your grandson is concerned. It would be . . . awkward for Her Majesty to rely on the sort of evidence we could provide in a court of law, particularly given the way Zhaspahr Clyntahn and the Inquisition have branded all of the 'false, so-called *seijins*' demons and servants of Shan-wei. The fact that everyone with a working brain knows that's a lie wouldn't prevent the Duke's supporters from fastening on it as a means of discrediting evidence procured by such . . . irregular techniques."

"I can see that."

Lady Karyl succeeded—mostly—in keeping the disappointment out of her tone. It wasn't easy, but the decades she and Styvyn had spent working circumspectly on King Sailys' behalf stood her in good stead.

"The fact that we can't act openly against him and his fellow conspirators—yet—doesn't mean we aren't aware of their plans in far greater detail than they could possibly suspect." Obaith shrugged. There may be some small details of their strategy we *don't* know about, but if so, there are very few of them. And we've been sharing our information—fully—with Earl White Crag, Baron Stoneheart, and Sir Ahlber Zhustyn."

"Thank God." Despite herself, Lady Karyl sagged in her chair. She inhaled deeply, then ran both hands over her still thick and luxuriant silver hair. "I've shared what little I've been able to glean with them, as well, although finding ways to get that information to them without anyone's suspecting I've done it hasn't been the easiest thing in the world. But I've always realized I'm seeing only bits and pieces of whatever it is they ultimately intend."

"Her Majesty realizes that. And although your grandson—Young Styvyn—doesn't dream for a moment that his glamorous cousin might do anything that could endanger you personally, I'm afraid Her Majesty—and *His* Majesty, for that matter—are less confident of that. Especially given how much time the Duke spends with Father Sedryk."

"That mangy son-of-a-bitch." The cold, searing anger in Lady Karyl's voice made the icy wind outside Rydymak Keep seem almost balmy for a moment. "If I could find a way to tie a rope to that bastard's ankles and drop him into Cheshyr Bay with a hundred-pound rock for ballast, I'd die a happy old woman."

Obaith chuckled.

"Nothing would give me greater pleasure than to accomplish that minor chore for you, My Lady. Unfortunately, Father Sedryk's rather more central to the conspirators' plans than it might appear. I know you must especially hate the way he's made himself Young Styvyn's newest best friend, but, trust me, that's only a small part of his role. Among other things, he's most definitely not the Chihirite he pretends to be. The truth is—although it's one of those things we can't prove without resorting to those 'irregular methods' of ours—he's actually a Schuelerite . . . and an Inquisitor. In fact, he was dispatched to Chisholm from Zion by Wyllym Rayno in person."

Lady Karyl's jaw tightened. She'd known Sedryk Mahrtynsyn was far more than the "simple priest" he tried to pass himself off as, but not even she had suspected he was a direct agent of the Office of Inquisition!

"My Lady," Obaith's expression was very serious, "we need Mahrtynsyn to implicate and incriminate Rock Coast and as many of the others as possible. So far, they've all been very cautious about anything that might be set down in writing, and we don't anticipate their suddenly getting careless now. But as their plans move into the end game, they'll have steadily more opportunities to create the chain of documentary evidence—or eyewitness testimony—we need. He's only one of the people we're hoping will do that for us, but he's one of the bigger fish in that particular pond, and Her Majesty believes he'll play a pivotal role in the actual exchange of any written messages."

"And the longer you wait to net him, the more likely he is to draw my grandson into that pond with him to drown," Lady Karyl said grimly. "He's charming, he's suave, and he flatters the hell out of a fifteen-year-old."

"We know," Obaith acknowledged unflinchingly, "and we don't like it. Her Majesty intends to bear in mind every mitigating circumstance she possibly can where Young Styvyn is concerned, however. And from what we've seen, it's highly likely that in the end, Rock Coast and Mahrtynsyn will make a serious mistake in his case. He's young enough, and—forgive me—foolish enough to see something romantic and exciting about pitting himself against the Crown in the service of Mother Church. But he also loves you very much, My Lady. The time's going to come when he realizes that whatever Rock Coast and Mahrtynsyn may tell him, they must know that when they demand you join them, you'll tell them to go to hell. And when he realizes that, he'll also realize they must have planned for that eventuality. Which means they've lied to him from the start when they promised no harm would come to you." The *seijin* smiled. "He was very adamant about that from the very beginning, My Lady," she said gently. "*Far* more adamant than Rock Coast ever expected he might be."

Lady Karyl's eyes softened and her mouth trembled for just a moment. Then she nodded sharply.

"Thank you for telling me that." Her voice was husky, and she paused to clear her throat. "Thank you for telling me that," she repeated. "I told myself that had to be the case, but—"

"But there's been so much treachery," Obaith finished for her. "And when someone like Rock Creek or Mahrtynsyn plays the 'will of the Archangels' card with a fifteen-year-old, the consequences can get very ugly very quickly."

"Exactly."

They gazed at each other for a moment, and then the *seijin* shrugged.

"While I'm speaking with you here, My Lady, another of *Seijin* Merlin's friends is in Cherayth, where he's delivering Her Majesty's messages to Earl White Crag. As a consequence of those messages, you're going to be in a position to augment your personal armsmen in the very near future. I realize you aren't as plump in the purse as you'd like to be, and that you've been worrying that anyone willing to accept service with a small, out of the way earldom like Cheshyr—especially for the wages you'd be able to pay—might very well have been sent to you by someone who . . . wishes you ill.

"As far as the first of those points is concerned, Her Majesty sent along this," the *seijin* said, and the saddlebags she'd held draped over one slim forearm clunked heavily as she set them on the floor.

She opened one of them, and Lady Karyl inhaled sharply as she saw the neatly rolled golden marks gleam in the dim lamplight. If both bags were equally full, she was looking at well over two years of Cheshyr's revenues. How in Langhorne's name had even a *seijin* carried that much weight as if it were a mere nothing?!

"There'll be more funding if you need it, My Lady," Obaith continued. "Obviously, you'll need to be careful about revealing the fact that you've got it, but *His* Majesty observed that there are very few problems in 'human relations' that can't be smoothed with a little gold, and it's always nice to be able to outbid the opposition when you need to. Especially when the opposition doesn't think you *can*."

The *seijin* dimpled again, then sobered.

"You won't need it to pay the armsmen who'll begin trickling in to find work over the winter in the next few months, however. And you won't have to worry about where they come from. I assure you they've been thoroughly vetted. Or they will've been, by the time they're sent, at any rate."

"They will?" Lady Karyl sat straighter again, and her hazel eyes began to glow in the firelight. "And just how many of these wandering armsmen are likely to come Cheshyr's way, *Seijin* Merch?"

"How interesting that you should ask, My Lady." The *seijin*'s smile would have turned a kraken green with envy. "As a matter of fact—"

▼   ▼   ▼

"—so it's essential, in Their Majesties' view, that Lady Karyl's security be bolstered at the earliest possible moment," the tall, blond-haired man emphasized, leaning slightly forward over the conference table towards Braisyn Byrns, the Earl of White Crag and First Councilor of the Kingdom of

Chisholm. Sylvyst Mhardyr, Baron Stoneheart, who served as Chisholm's Lord Justice, sat beside White Crag, and Sir Ahlber Zhustyn, Sharleyan's domestic spymaster, stood at the First Councilor's shoulder.

"I'd rather just move in, round them up, and detach a few heads," Stoneheart said flatly. "I'd think that would 'bolster' Lady Karyl's security quite nicely!"

"Now, Sylvyst!" White Crag shook his head, his cataract-cloudy eyes gleaming with grim amusement in the lamplight. "Aren't you the person in this room who should be most concerned with little things like due process?"

"I'll be perfectly prepared to get back to due process the instant the blood stops spurting," Stoneheart replied, and it was obvious he wasn't even half jesting.

"I understand exactly why you feel that way, My Lord," the man who'd introduced himself as Cennady Frenhines said.

Although his accent was that of Chisholm—indeed, he sounded as if he was from Serpent Hill, in the Earldom of Shayne—that was a name no Chisholmian had ever borne. Which was hardly surprising. As nearly as White Crag, Stoneheart, or Zhustyn could tell, every single one of the *seijins* who'd offered their services to the Empire of Charis had equally outlandish names.

"Her Majesty is adamant about this, however," Frenhines continued very seriously. "It may not be my place to say this, but I think *His* Majesty would prefer to do it your way, because he's worried about how many people may get hurt before this is over. But the Empress is determined to cut out this cancer once and for all. For that, she needs any nobleman as senior as Duke Rock Coast to implicate himself too thoroughly for *anyone* to question his guilt. I believe the phrase she used to the Emperor was 'I need my own Zebediahs.'"

"And she's right, with all due respect, My Lord," Zhustyn told Stoneheart grimly. "This problem's crept out of the shadows every few years from the moment King Sailys began the Restoration. And it's going to keep on creeping until the people who want to turn back the clock finally get it through their heads—those of them who still *have* heads—that it isn't going to happen. Her Majesty's never been hesitant about doing what needs doing, but she's in a far stronger position today than she ever was before. I understand exactly why Her Majesty wants these people to make their move. And I *also* understand why she wants *enough* object lessons to be sure the lesson finally goes home."

Stoneheart looked back at the spymaster for several seconds while the midnight wind prowled restlessly around the eaves of the King Tayrens Chancellery. That wind was just as cold as the one whining outside a drafty library in Rydymak Keep, two thousand and more miles west of Cherayth, but this one was heavy with snow flurries turning rapidly into something much more like a blizzard.

"Sir Ahlber's put his finger on exactly what Her Majesty hopes to accomplish," the hawk-faced Frenhines agreed somberly, his wrist-thick braid gleaming under the lamps which were considerably brighter than those in Lady Karyl's library. "But that doesn't mean she doesn't want precautions taken."

"What sort of precautions, *Seijin* Cennady?" White Crag asked.

"She's sent along written instructions for General Kahlyns."

Frenhines reached into the imperial courier's shoulder satchel he'd carried into the chancellery and extracted a heavy canvas envelope. He passed it across to the First Councilor, who handed it on to Stoneheart without comment. The Lord Justice glanced at the label—unlike White Crag, his vision was still clear and sharp—and nodded to his colleague as he recognized Sharleyan Tayt Ahrmhak's personal handwriting and seal.

"And did she summarize those instructions for you?" White Crag inquired, and smiled thinly when Frenhines nodded. "It's unfortunate the General can't hear your impression of them directly."

"My Lord, it's over two hundred miles from Cherayth to Maikelberg." The *seijin* shook his head with a smile, sapphire eyes glinting. "Not even *Seijin* Merlin could be in both places at once when he was here with Their Majesties! And if there happened to be some way I might actually accomplish that, you *know* what Clyntahn would say the instant he heard about it!"

The other three chuckled, albeit a bit sourly. And Frenhines didn't really blame them for that sourness. There wasn't a more reliable, more honest man than Sir Fraizher Kahlyns in the entire Kingdom of Chisholm, but he wasn't the Imperial Charisian Army's most brilliant officer. It was unfortunately true that he was more comfortable with written orders when they were accompanied by the opportunity to clarify any ambiguities by personally discussing those orders with whoever delivered them.

"Sir Fraizher won't have any qualms about these instructions, My Lord," Frenhines assured White Crag, although he was actually speaking to all three of them. "The important thing is to keep Rock Coast, Black Horse, Countess Swayle, and Dragon Hill from realizing how many of the reinforcements he's sending forward will have rather different actual destinations. And Their Majesties would really prefer for none of them to realize how many Marines will 'just happen' to be in Chisholmian waters come spring, either."

"Oh, I *like* that," Zhustyn murmured, and Stoneheart gave a sharp nod.

"In the meantime, however, we need to increase Lady Karyl's personal security," Frenhines continued. "One of my colleagues has been sent to discuss this with her, and Her Majesty suggests it might be possible for Sir Fraizher to release a few highly skilled, highly experienced, career Army noncoms from active service after . . . training accidents or some other mishap leaves them unsuited to arduous duty in the field. Obviously, men such as that will have limited skills for civilian life. So it should hardly be surprising if a few score of them were to trickle slowly into a place like Cheshyr—hitching rides on some of the coasting trade vessels, perhaps. And if men who've loyally and ably served the Kingdom find themselves out of work due to no fault of their own, I doubt anyone would be surprised if someone like Lady Karyl, given her own husband's long Army career, found a way to put roofs over their heads. For that matter, she'd probably even find the invalids token positions in her own household—just to satisfy their self-respect, you understand."

"That's *devious*," Stoneheart said approvingly.

"Her Majesty can be that way," Frenhines agreed with a thin smile. "And *His* Majesty's contribution was to observe that the frantic efforts to increase weapons output at Maikelberg almost have to have resulted in some clerical errors. Why, it's entirely possible enough modern rifles, shotguns, and pistols to equip forty or fifty armsmen—perhaps even a mortar or two—could simply have been lost. And if *that*'s happened," Frenhines' smile turned even thinner and far, far colder, "there's no telling where all those . . . mislaid weapons—and possibly even the ammunition for them—might eventually turn up, is there, My Lords?"

.VIII.
Merlin Athrawes' Chamber,
The Charisian Embassy,
Siddarmark City

G ot a minute, Merlin?"

Merlin Athrawes looked up from the revolver he'd been carefully cleaning and oiling.

Sandrah Lywys had finally gotten her new "smokeless" powder—they'd actually gone ahead and called it cordite, since it was extruded in narrow rods that looked exactly like the Old Earth propellant of the same name—into production. The field armies had several million rounds of old-fashioned black powder ammunition to use up, but the Imperial Guard had already switched completely to the new propellant. In addition to virtually no smoke, it produced far less fouling than gunpowder had, but the ICA's fulminating primers still left a corrosive residue which could damage a weapon if it wasn't promptly cleaned after firing, and Merlin had spent over an hour at the range this afternoon, putting several hundred rounds downrange. Not because a

PICA's programmable muscle memory needed the practice, but because he'd discovered how much he enjoyed it. And because he'd figured he was due the downtime. He'd been back from Cherayth for barely a five-day, and this was the first opportunity to do something remotely like relaxing that had come his way.

"I'm not especially busy right this minute, if you don't mind my going ahead and finishing this—" he told the image projected across his vision as he waved the oil-soaked swab in his hand "—while we talk. Nynian and I are having dinner tonight, and I want to grab a shower first. I'd really rather not smell like I've been bathing in gun oil when we sit down to eat."

"Dinner with Nynian, is it?" Nahrmahn Baytz murmured with a smile. Merlin gave him a moderate glare, and the dead, rotund little Emeraldian's expression straightened quickly. "Well, I don't see any reason you shouldn't go on playing with your toys," he said more briskly. "I've just had a thought about Rainbow Waters and Maigwair's troop deployments, though."

"Oh?" Merlin cocked his head. "What sort of thought would that be?"

"Well, as I understand Kynt and Eastshare's plans for this summer, they'd really like to be able to hook around an open flank, right?"

"Except for the minor fact that there's not going to *be* an open flank, yes, they certainly would," Merlin agreed a bit sourly.

By all rights, there *should* have been open flanks, he reflected. The Church's defensive front stretched from Hsing-wu's Passage in the north all the way south to the Bay of Bess and the northern border of Dohlar. That was considerably better than two thousand miles—more than eight hundred miles farther than the Russian Front in 1942, when it had stretched all the way from Murmansk to the Caucasus Mountains. No one could hold a contiguous front line that long. Even if the Church met its full three-million-man target, Rainbow Waters and Maigwair would have less than fifteen hundred men per mile of front, and that was assuming the front was a straight line, unaffected by any terrain features, which it most definitely was not.

Some of those terrain features—like the Snake Mountains and the Black Wyvern Mountains on the western borders of Cliff Peak and Westmarch—would actually help economize on manpower, of course. Others would consume it voraciously, however, so that was pretty much a wash. Still, there was plenty of relatively firm, flat (or at least firm*er* and flat*ter*) ground out there.

What there wasn't was an intact road net and internal combustion engines. Dragons bestowed a degree of mobility and flexibility on Safeholdian armies for which any preindustrial Old Terran general would cheerfully have sold his firstborn child, but they weren't magic. And the dirt roads which served local communities once one got off the magnificent high roads didn't make things a lot better. The farther one got from canals or navigable rivers, the harder it became to keep an army supplied, and there was damn-all in the way of forage for an army trying to live off the land in western Siddarmark. The Sword of Schueler had been a huge head start towards making sure of that, and Rainbow Waters had spent the last several months moving every remaining civilian farmer within two hundred miles of his front line still farther west. There would be no crops, no livestock, to support an attacking army anywhere in that zone.

And because that was true, the Allies had very little choice about their axes of advance. They could ring up local tactical variations, but the waterways, the high roads, the mountain passes, the forest paths they'd have to follow were easy to predict, and Rainbow Waters intended to make them pay to break his frontier

He clearly recognized that the Allies' primary strategic objective in the upcoming campaign. Destroying or crippling the Mighty Host, the Church's single truly formidable field force, would give them the keys to the Temple Lands, and he knew it.

That was the true reason he'd rethought his dispositions so carefully, just as it was the reason he'd pulled Silken Hills so far back north. He was far more prepared to risk the loss of Western Cliff Peak and the Duchy of Farlas—even the Princedom of Jhurlahnk—than to expose his own right flank in western Westmarch or open the door to Sardahn . . . and a direct line of advance to the Holy Langhorne Canal in Usher. He'd also made careful plans to demolish roads, bridges, and canal locks in his wake whenever and wherever he was forced to give ground. The ICA's mounted infantry would provide commanders like Eastshare and Green Valley with exploitable opportunities despite anything he could do, but there was no point pretending their flexibility wasn't going to be straitjacketed by the Harchongian's carefully thought out deployments.

"I know Rainbow Waters isn't going to leave any *open* flanks," Nahrmahn said, "but what if we could convince him and Maigwair to *weaken* the Northern Host's right flank?"

"How *far* to his right?" Merlin asked, frowning thoughtfully as he consulted his mental map of the front, and Nahrmahn's computer-generated image shrugged.

"I'm not the military man Kynt or Cayleb are, so I can't say exactly how Maigwair and Rainbow Waters would react to what I have in mind. But what I think we might be able to do, if we manage it properly, is to convince them to move Silken Hills' entire force several hundred miles back to the south and fill the gap with brand-new Army of God formations."

"You think you've come up with a way to convince them to hand some or all of Silken Hills' area of responsibility over to Teagmahn and the Army of Tanshar?" Merlin couldn't quite keep the skepticism out of his voice, but Nahrmahn only smiled like a cat-lizard with a brand-new bowl of cream.

"I think I *may* have come up with a way to prompt them to at least consider it," he said. "A lot depends on how well Earl Hanth continues to do, of course, and even more of it depends on the proper . . . misdirection. Which, I have to admit, makes it especially attractive to me, since the Group of Four's managed to misdirect *us* a time or two. I'd rather enjoy turning the tables on them that way."

"I sort of thought that was what Zhapyth Slaytyr and I did to the Army of Shiloh," Merlin pointed out mildly.

"Yes, but that was so . . . so *crude.*" Nahrmahn lifted his nose with an audible sniff. "That was simply a case of taking an opportunity chance presented, not one that you'd generated on your own! Effective and neatly done, I'll grant, but so *reactionary*, without the flair of your *truly* despicable and underhanded intriguer. Besides, you took unfair advantage of your ability to play chameleon. *My* idea is far more elegant and doesn't depend on any high-tech chicanery."

" 'High-tech chicanery,' is it? And I suppose the fact that you're even here to present your 'elegant plan' has nothing at all to do with high-tech *or* chicanery?"

"Well, perhaps, in the *broadest* sense," Nahrmahn's virtual personality conceded.

"All right." Merlin shook his head with a chuckle. "Go ahead and dazzle me with this elegance of yours."

"Well," Nahrmahn said rather more seriously, "the first thing we'll need to make this work is to bring Breyt Bahskym in on it. We'll need to send him some bogus orders, and he's going to have to arrange some artistic leaks of information. I expect you or Nimue can provide a *seijin* or two to help with the necessary leakage?"

"As long as we can keep straight who's leaking what to whom," Merlin said dryly. "We've got quite a lot of irons in the fire in that regard already, you know." He shrugged. "On the other hand, I don't suppose one or two more will make it any *worse!*"

"In that case, we also need to get Nynian involved in this, because—"

FEBRUARY
YEAR OF GOD 898

✦

"—So I don't think there's any need for long-term worry, My Lady," the nun in the caduceus-badged green habit of a Pasqualte said. "Zhosifyn is a . . . sturdy little girl." The nun smiled wryly. "In fact, I think I can safely say she's going to be a right handful in nine or ten years! She reminds me quite a bit of me, in that respect. But as far as the dreams are concerned, I think they'll pass. I'm no Bédardist and, unfortunately, we don't have any Bédardists here on Green Tree, but Pasquale only knows how many children I've taught over the years!" She shook her head, brown eyes twinkling, but then her expression softened. "I know what she saw and heard aboard ship was ugly and terrifying, but this is a little girl who knows she's deeply loved, who has her family around her, and knows she and that family are safe. It may take some time, but it's been less than three months, and the dreams are already less frequent. In time, I'm confident they'll fade completely."

"Thank you, Sister Mahryssa," Lady Stefyny Mahkswail said sincerely.

She rose from her rattan chair and walked to the edge of the shaded veranda. It was technically only spring, but Green Tree Island lay less than a thousand miles south of the equator—little further below it than the city of Gorath lay *above* it—and she was deeply grateful for the shade as she looked out across the peaceful garden at the small cluster of children busily spading what would eventually be a tomato patch. She smiled at all of them, although her eyes lingered longest on the fair-haired toddler gleefully flinging trowel loads of dirt in every direction as she "helped." Then she looked back over her shoulder at the nun.

"I appreciate your taking the time to put my fears to rest," she said, "and the truth is that I pretty much knew what you were going to say." Her smile turned into something suspiciously like a grin. "God knows you're absolutely right that she's a 'sturdy' little girl, and I won't have to wait any nine or ten years for her to turn into a handful, either!"

The nun chuckled, and Stefyny turned to face her squarely. She leaned a hip against the veranda's waist-high stone wall, and her expression turned serious once more.

"We tried to protect her from . . . unpleasant realities back home," she said, her tone somber. "It wasn't the easiest thing to do—all of them are really smart kids, and Bédard knows they're sensitive to emotions at that age. They couldn't help knowing that all of us were worried as Shan-wei about their grandfather. And about what might happen to *them*, to be honest. And you're right about what it was like aboard that ship." She shuddered, chilled to the bone for a moment despite the sunlight and heat. "That was absolutely terrifying to *me*; God only knows how badly it frightened *her*! But I'm not surprised she feels safe here."

"Because she *is*, My Lady," Sister Mahryssa said firmly. "And so are you."

"I certainly feel a lot closer to 'safe' than I did back in Gorath!" Stefyny snorted harshly. "It'd be hard not to. But I'm afraid I've learned just a little more than Lyzet has about how even the 'safest' place can turn out to be less safe than you thought. And in some ways, feeling safe myself only makes me worry more about . . . other people."

"I'd be astonished if you felt any other way," Sister Mahryssa said simply. "And what I just said about Lyzet's true for you, too, My Lady. It hasn't been three months yet. I'm sure you're still processing what's happened."

"Oh, I think you could definitely put it that way!" Stefyny agreed. "On the other hand, I—"

"Excuse me, My Lady."

Stefyny turned as another nun stepped onto the veranda.

"Yes, Sister Lytychya?"

"Mother Superior asked me to find you and tell you a messenger's arrived with a letter for you."

▼   ▼   ▼

Sister Lytychya paused outside the study door and rapped gently.

"Enter," a clear soprano called, and the nun smiled at Stefyny, opened the door, and waved for her to precede her.

A tall, red-haired man with a spade-shaped beard and dark blue eyes turned from his conversation with Mother Superior Ahlyssa as they entered the book-lined room. He bowed gracefully to Stefyny as she paused on the threshold, obviously surprised to see him. She stood for a moment, gazing at him, her eyes suddenly touched with a sharper anxiety. Then she gave herself an almost invisible shake and crossed the room to him, holding out one hand with an air of composure.

"Thank you for fetching Lady Stefyny so promptly, Sister," Mother Ahlyssa said. "Now if you'd be so good as to go help Ahbnair rescue the kitchen garden from the children's ministrations, the entire Abbey will be eternally in your debt!"

"Of course, Mother," Lytychya agreed with a smile. "My Lady, *Seijin* Cleddyf."

She inclined her head to each of the mother superior's guests in turn, then withdrew and closed the door behind her, and Ahlyssa turned to Stefyny.

"As you can see," she said with a smile, "there's someone to see you, my dear."

▼　　▼　　▼

Cleddyf Cyfiawnder, who actually rather favored Merlin Athrawes around the nose and eyes, watched Stefyny Mahkswail's face as the silver-haired mother superior smiled at her. Stefyny looked better than the last time he'd seen her with his own eyes, just before the boatswain's chair lifted her to HMS *Fleet Wing* from the deck of the fishing boat he'd never gotten around to naming. This elegantly groomed, assured-looking young matron—at thirty-seven, she wasn't quite thirty-three terrestrial years old—was a far cry from the frightened nightgown-clad mother trying desperately to reassure her terrified children that they were safe when she was far from certain of that herself.

"Lady Stefyny." He took the hand she'd offered and bent from the waist to kiss its back. "It's good to see you looking so well."

"Mother Ahlyssa and the sisters couldn't have been kinder or more attentive, *Seijin* Cleddyf," she replied. "In fact," she met his eyes levelly, "they've been everything you and *Seijin* Gwyliwr said they'd be. I'm glad to have this opportunity to thank you for our rescue in more . . . seemly fashion, but I must confess I'm also surprised to see you. Especially so soon."

"My Lady," Cyfiawnder said in his mellow tenor, "I promised you we'd get your message to your father as quickly as possible."

"So you did, but I hardly expected a *seijin* to personally spend his time delivering my mail. I'm sure Emperor Cayleb and Empress Sharleyan have all sorts of other things they rather desperately need you to be doing at the moment. Besides, Green Tree Island's almost six thousand miles by sea from Gorath, and I'm an admiral's daughter." Her smile was quite a bit tighter than it had been. "I also know the prevailing winds between here and Gorath. You've made what I could only describe as . . . miraculous time if you traveled all the way to Gorath with my letter before coming here."

"First, My Lady," he said calmly, "I didn't have to personally deliver your message to your father; *Seijin* Merlin did that." He smiled considerably more broadly than she had. "It seemed to us that the Earl might find it easier—or at least marginally less difficult—to accept the word of a *seijin* he'd personally met than of someone who simply walked in and announced you'd sent him."

"*Merlin?*" Her gray eyes widened. "But he's—"

She cut herself off, and he nodded.

"You were about to say that he's in Siddar City with Emperor Cayleb."

"Since you brought it up, yes, I was, which brings me back to that adjective—the 'miraculous' one—I used a moment ago." She regarded him narrowly. "I'm sure you'll forgive me if I wonder how he could possibly have reached Gorath from there? Particularly with my letter to Father in hand?"

"Well, Siddar City *is* better than a thousand miles closer to Gorath than Green Tree Island is," he pointed out with a lurking smile. Then his expression sobered. "My Lady, I understand exactly why you used the word 'miraculous,' just as I know the other sorts of adjectives you might have used instead. And in some ways, I wouldn't have blamed you, given how many lies—even more of them than usual—Clyntahn's spun about Merlin and the rest of us. But while that man wouldn't recognize the truth, much less the true will of God, if it walked up and bit him, the truth is that we *do* have certain advantages over other messengers. We seldom display them openly—or any more openly than we can avoid, at any rate—*because* of those lies of his. In this instance, however, Merlin and the Emperor decided to make an exception to the rules. I won't pretend their motives were completely altruistic, but I will say that reaching your father with the news that you were still alive as quickly as we could, to spare him as much pain as we could, was a factor in their thinking. As for how your letter reached Merlin before he set out for Gorath himself, there are such things as messenger wyverns, you know."

"I suppose there are."

Stefyny glanced quickly at Mother Superior Ahlyssa, but if the nun was perturbed by the suggestion that the *seijins* serving Charis truly were capable of superhuman feats, there was no sign of it in her calm expression.

"I suppose there are," Stefyny repeated, turning back to Cyfiawnder. "And while a dutiful daughter of Mother Church probably shouldn't admit it, I wouldn't be terribly astonished to discover that that lying bastard in Zion truly has lavished a few of his lies on you and *Seijin* Merlin."

"My father always told me you could tell even more about someone by the enemies he made than by the friends he kept," the *seijin* said.

"*My* father told me much the same thing, upon occasion." She smiled again, briefly. "And speaking of fathers, how did mine react to the news?"

"I think it would be best to let him tell you that in his own words," Cyfiawnder said gently, reaching into his tunic. "He didn't have a great deal of time in which to write, under the circumstances, but Merlin promised we'd deliver his reply to your letter, as well." He extended an envelope to her. "I wish there *had* been time for him to write a longer response," he said seriously. "Still, I hope this will ease your heart at least a little. There are several things you and I need to talk about while I'm here, but I think they can wait until after he's spoken to you."

Despite her formidable self-control, Stefyny's fingers trembled as she took the envelope from him. She held it in both hands, staring at him, and then her eyes flicked to the mother superior as Ahlyssa cleared her throat.

"My dear," she said, indicating the door behind her desk, "why don't you retire to my private chapel while you read that? And don't rush yourself, child! *Seijin* Cleddyf and I will keep one another entertained until you've had time to fully digest it."

"Thank you, Mother," Stefyny said gratefully, and glanced back at Cyfiawnder. "And thank you, *Seijin*, as well."

"Go, read your letter." The *seijin* smiled at her. "As Mother Ahlyssa says, we'll be here when you've finished."

She nodded, still clutching the envelope in both hands, and vanished through the chapel door.

Cyfiawnder watched her go, then crossed to gaze out one of the study's windows across the manicured lawn of St. Kahrmyncetah's Abbey while he thought about the woman who was even then opening that envelope. He could have watched her through one of the SNARCs' remotes, but he spent too much time spying on people already. There was no need to play the voyeur this time, and Stefyny Mahkswail—yes, and her father—deserved for her to read his letter in privacy.

"How would you say they're adjusting?" he asked over his shoulder, and Mother Ahlyssa stood and walked around her desk to join him.

"As well as anyone might have expected." She shrugged. "Certainly better than anyone could have *counted* on! After all, it's been a bit difficult for *me* to accept there are true *seijins* once more walking the living world in my lifetime, and I had Mother Nynian's letters to help."

She snorted, and Cyfiawnder chuckled softly as he nodded in acknowledgment of her point.

It's a good thing she did *accept it, too,* he thought. *Of course, most of the Sisters of Saint Kohdy seem to be rather more . . . flexible-minded than other people. I suppose that's a requirement for the Sisterhood, when you come down to it.*

St. Kahrmyncetah's Abbey—and the true ironic appropriateness of that name hadn't struck him until he'd accepted the miniature of Stefyny's mother from her as her token to her father—was far from the largest religious institution on the face of Safehold. It was bigger than many abbeys, or even a few full-scale convents, perhaps, but certainly not huge, although many of those larger, grander convents would have envied the sheer beauty of the spectacular view laid out before the mother superior's window. The abbey looked down from its perch in the Talon Branch Mountains on Green Tree's northern coast across the deep blue of Markys Bay, stretching to the sun-drenched horizon, and the steep slopes of even taller mountains rose behind it like huge, sleeping dragons furred in lush, green trees. It was officially affiliated with the Order of Pasquale, and all of its sisters truly were Pasqualates. The majority of them, however, were also Sisters of Saint Kohdy, which made it a bit easier for them to accept the extraordinary comings and goings of "*seijins*" in general. Unfortunately, not *all* of them were adherents of the out- lawed saint, and the number who weren't had risen over the last year or two as the abbey's mother order reinforced it in light of Green Tree's recent upsurge in immigration.

Green Tree Island had long been a place of refuge, and many a would- be refugee had paid a steep price to reach it. The Straits of Queiroz, which separated it from the Harchongese province of the same name, were almost two hundred miles wide. That was enough to pose a formidable challenge, and over the centuries, hundreds—probably thousands—of Harchongese serfs and their children had drowned trying to cross it. But other thousands had succeeded, fleeing the Empire's repressive regime, and they and their descendants had emerged with the kind of stubborn independence that sort of test engendered. They were, he thought, quite possibly the only people he'd ever met who were even stubborner—in their own very Harchongese way—than Zhasyn Cahnyr's Glacierhearters. The flow had eased consider- ably over the last century or so, as the institution of serfdom had lost much of its rigor in South Harchong. But there'd still been a steady trickle, in- cluding hundreds of serfs who'd somehow made their way south from *North Harchong*, where the institution remained at least as harsh as it ever had been. No one knew exactly how the story of Green Tree had made its way into the folklore of those brutalized serfs, but somehow it had, and as the jihad's intensity grew and worsened, the refugee volume had begun growing again.

The authorities in Queiroz Province were just as happy to funnel every refugee they could straight through to Green Tree, even though they were fully aware that many of them had fled the land to which they were legally bound in perpetuity. For that matter, they were equally well aware that a very high percentage of the *male* refugees were fleeing—with their families in many cases; by themselves in most—involuntary service with the Mighty Host of God and the Archangels.

In Cyfiawnder's opinion, that said some really interesting things about the provincial governor and his staff. South Harchong had never been espe- cially sympathetic to its northern compatriots' savage abuse of its serfs. Indeed, quite a few of its more powerful merchant and banking families were quietly agitating to have the institution completely abolished, at least in the south- ern half of the Empire. But serfdom remained the official law of the land and powerful North Harchongese nobles were vociferous in their demands that any escaped serfs be seized and "repatriated" . . . where they were inevitably turned into object lessons for the benefit of their fellow serfs, and Cyfi-awnder made another mental note to have Nahrmahn and Owl take a closer look at Queiroz's internal dynamics. If its administrators were prepared to turn that blind an eye to that sort of traffic, who knew what *else* they might be prepared to ignore?

More to the immediate point, however, the Sisters of Saint Kohdy had infiltrated—or, more accurately, co-opted—St. Kahrmyncetah's Abbey over two hundred years ago. Not because they'd seen any tactical or strategic advantage in it, but because one of their number who was also a Pasqualate had been assigned as the abbey's mother superior and been allowed to select a half-dozen assistants to accompany her to her new posting. She'd seen no reason not to take advantage of the opportunity, and the Sisterhood had effectively controlled the abbey ever since. When the plan to rescue Earl Thirsk's family had first been discussed, Aivah Pahrsahn had been quick to suggest that St. Kahrmyncetah's would be a perfect place to hide them away. After all, they'd hardly be the first refugees she'd hidden there. And not only was the abbey isolated, the sparsely settled island's inhabitants provided a defense in depth against any outsider.

Like all Pasqualate abbeys and monasteries, St. Kahrmyncetah's was as much hospital as house of worship, and the sisters had cared for the islanders for centuries. They midwifed their births, nursed them and their children through illnesses, and buried them in Mother Church, and the islanders repaid their care with a fierce devotion. The fact that St. Kahrmyncetah's sisters' version of the Church of God Awaiting was more "humanist"—and far, far gentler—than the one in which the islanders or their parents and grandparents had been reared didn't hurt one bit, either. Nor did the fact that they remembered the oppression they'd fled, which meant any outsider would meet an automatic conspiracy of silence if he started asking questions about *anyone* on Green Tree, much less about the sisters.

Given how vital it was to prevent Zhaspahr Clyntahn from ever suspecting that Thirsk's daughters and grandchildren were alive, concealment was the order of the day. And hiding them someplace they could live almost normal lives, confident no one would recognize them or report them to the Inquisition, had been almost equally important in the inner circle's eyes. Cayleb and Sharleyan truly had no intention of holding their safety over Earl Thirsk's head, and sending them to St. Kahrmyncetah's—where their only "guards" were nuns sworn to a healing order—had struck them as the best way to make that point to Stefyny and her sisters and, especially, to their *children*, as well.

And it's not as if they're completely *unprotected, either,* he reminded himself.

Concealment was their best defense, and the only one that would keep the earl himself alive, but Ahbnair Truskyt, St. Kahrmyncetah's chief gardener and handyman, was more than he seemed. As a member of Helm Cleaver who'd attracted the Inquisition's attention just a bit too closely, he'd found it expedient to emigrate from the Temple Lands when he was much younger, and Nynian Rychtyr had sent him here almost twenty years ago. He'd overseen the abbey's physical security ever since, and Zhustyn Kyndyrmyn, his "assistant gardener" had once been a sergeant in the Temple Guard.

Unfortunately for the Temple Guard, Kyndyrmyn had become thoroughly disgusted by some of the things the Guard had been called upon to do in the Inquisition's service. The true turning point for him had come when he'd been required to falsify the report of his investigation into the death of young Dahnyld Mahkbyth on the direct orders of Wyllym Rayno. He and Sergeant *Ahrloh* Mahkbyth had been friends for over seven years at the time, and he'd longed to tell Ahrloh the truth about how his little boy had died. He'd known Ahrloh too well, though, and Zhulyet Mahkbyth had needed her husband alive. So Kyndyrmyn had kept his mouth shut, but his rage had slowly, slowly eaten him up inside, and hard though he'd tried to hide it, that festering anger had been evident to his platoon commander. Indeed, that anger—though the lieutenant hadn't known its source—had led him to ask his battalion CO to have a word with the sergeant, see if he could get Kyndyrmyn to open up before whatever demon was riding him destroyed him. And that battalion CO had been a young auxiliary bishop, not yet a vicar, named Hauwerd Wylsynn.

Hauwerd had always been the sort of officer who attracted the trust and loyalty of men under his command, and he'd been a Wylsynn. That combination had been enough to convince Kyndyrmyn to open up, and that was how Hauwerd and Samyl's circle of reformers first learned the truth about the carriage accident and Zhaspahr Clyntahn's intervention to suppress the investigation into it. Kyndyrmyn had been astonished by Hauwerd's reaction to his bitter charges of corruption at the Inquisition's highest levels, and even more when Hauwerd asked him to write up an *accurate* version of his report for the files the reformers were assembling in hopes of someday bringing Clyntahn down.

That had never happened, unfortunately, but the same reports had drawn Nynian Rychtyr's attention to the sergeant, and he'd been quietly recruited for Helm Cleaver . . . which was probably the only reason he was still alive. When Clyntahn purged the Wylsynns, Nynian had whisked Kyndyrmyn and half a dozen other members of the Guard who'd been too close to Hauwerd out of Zion and sent them to places of safety. Three of them—four, counting Kyndyrmyn—had ended up at St. Kahrmyncetah's, where they were safely out of sight and simultaneously provided Truskyt with a few trained soldiers.

It's not like they could stand off any sort of organized assault, Cyfiawnder acknowledged. *They're certainly able to look after Thirsk's family, and especially to keep an eye on the kids, though.* He shook his head, lips twitching on the brink of a smile. *Their parents know to keep their heads down, but that's a little harder to explain to kids, so I'm in favor of giving them all the babysitters—especially tough,* competent *babysitters—we can find! And if it comes to anything more serious than that, I can trust Ahbnair and Zhustyn to at least get them all out from under long enough for one of the "mysterious seijins" to swoop in and get them the hell out of Dodge.*

Of course, the temptation to smile faded, *if that ever happens, it's probably going to mean Thirsk is dead. I never thought that would be a good idea, and judging from his conversation with Maik, it would be an even worse idea now! Besides, I like that man . . . and his family. And it's about goddamned time I got to keep someone alive instead of killing them for a change!*

.II.
City of Zion,
The Temple Lands.

"I don't think you should go, Krys." Alahnah Bahrns shook her head without ever looking up from her sketchpad, but her expression was worried. "Things are getting so . . . crazy. There's no telling what might happen!"

"Someone *has* to go," Krystahl Bahrns said stubbornly. "You're right—things *are* getting crazy, and somebody has to do something about it!"

Alahnah looked up from the hat design she'd been sketching, and her brown eyes were somber. She looked across the table at her cousin and tapped the tabletop with the point of her pencil.

"Maybe *somebody* has to do something," the words came out in time with the tapping, "but it doesn't have to be *you,* and Uncle Gahstahn's already worried about you. Don't you dare go and make it worse!"

"I know Daddy's worried, and I don't like it. But he knows as well as I do that Mother Church needs all her sons and daughters to stand up for what's right. He *taught* us that, Alahnah!"

Her eyes held Alahnah's until the other woman was forced to nod. Gahstahn Bahrns had become Alahnah's second father after his younger brother, her own fisherman father, drowned in a Lake Pei gale. And he had, indeed, taught both his niece and his own daughter the devotion Mother Church and the Archangels deserved from all of their children. But that had been before the world went mad, and now was not the time to be drawing that madness' attention to oneself.

"Yes, he did, but you're talking about criticizing the *Inquisition*, Krystahl. That's never a good idea, and it's a lot worse one right now."

"We're not talking about *criticizing* the Inquisition," her cousin replied. "We're talking about asking for a little . . . moderation. And we're going to be just as respectful as we possibly can in our petition. And Langhorne himself said in the *Holy Writ* that any of God's children *always* have the right to petition Mother Church so long as they do so respectfully and reverently."

Alahnah bit her lip and looked back down at her sketch, smoothing one of the lines with the ball of her thumb to buy time while she considered what to say next. It felt odd to be the voice of caution, since Krystahl was five years older than she was and had always been the sober, sensible one when they were girls. But she also cared about things—she cared a lot—and once she had the bit between her teeth where that passion for justice was concerned she was hard to stop.

But someone needed to talk some sense into her. Bédard knew Alahnah agreed that "moderation" was in short supply in Zion these days. But that was the entire point. The Inquisition had grown progressively sterner as the Jihad wore on, and over the past few months some of its agents inquisitor had started making sure their arrests were widely publicized. In fact, she thought grimly, they were deliberately making examples in an effort to quell any public discontent with the course of the Jihad, and Langhorne help anyone who sounded as if he blamed the Grand Inquisitor—or any other member of the vicarate—for how badly things were going.

And then there were those whispered rumors about the arrests that *weren't* made public. About people who just . . . disappeared.

And that dreadful Fist of God isn't making things one bit better, she thought fretfully. *What do those people think they're doing?! I don't approve of everything that's happening any more than Krys does, but that doesn't give anyone the right to go around murdering consecrated priests and even* vicars! *No wonder the Inquisition's getting so strict. I would too if I were the one who's supposed to catch those terrorists!*

"Krys," she said finally, "you're right about what Langhorne said. But he never said a Jihad wouldn't change things! With everything that's going on, with how bad things are in Siddarmark if even half the reports are true," her lip quivered briefly in remembered pain, but she made her gaze hold her cousin's steadily, "don't you think the Inquisition *needs* to be stricter? Needs to stay on top of the sorts of rumors and accusations that support the heretics?"

"Last five-day, they arrested Sharyn Lywkys," Krystahl said quietly, and Alahnah inhaled sharply.

Sharyn Lywkys? That was . . . that was *ridiculous!* She and Krystahl had gone to school with Sharyn, they'd been friends since childhood. And if there was a single person in Zion who was more devout, more dedicated to

God and the Archangels, than Sharyn, Alahnah didn't know who it could possibly be.

"It has to be a mistake. I mean, it just *has* to be!"

"That's my entire point. *Lots* of 'mistakes' seem to be getting made, and people are getting hurt. *Innocent* people."

"Well, what did they tell Madam Lywkys after Sharyn was arrested?"

"Nothing." Krystahl's expression was grim, her hazel eyes dark.

"Nothing?!"

"She went to the parish office and asked about Sharyn, but the local agents inquisitor said they didn't know anything about it. They promised they'd find out where she was, why she'd been arrested. But they haven't yet, and her mother's been back to the office twice since then. The last time she was there one of the lay brother agents inquisitor told her very quietly— she says he looked like he was afraid someone might overhear him—that she should go home and wait without making trouble that could have . . . consequences."

Alahnah swallowed hard. She'd heard the rumors that people were simply disappearing, but she knew now she hadn't truly believed them. Not until this very moment. But as she looked into her cousin's eyes, she knew it was true . . . and that was *wrong*. The *Writ* required the Inquisition to at least tell the family of anyone it took into custody where he or she was and *why* they'd been arrested, no matter what that person might have been accused of doing.

"I don't know what to say," she admitted after a long, tense moment. "But if they could arrest someone like Sharyn—if they could make *that* kind of mistake—then they could arrest *you*, too, Krys!"

"I haven't done anything against the *Writ*, and I'm not going to," Krystahl fired back, her head tilted at a stubborn angle Alahnah knew only too well. "Sebahstean and I checked Scripture very carefully before we decided to organize the petition drive. We've fulfilled every requirement, and it's not like we're going to be issuing any *demands* or anything! Besides, everyone says Vicar Rhobair's a good man. Down at the shelters, they're starting to call him '*Saint* Rhobair,' for goodness sake! He won't let anything bad happen to us if we only ask him reverently and respectfully to . . . to look into what's been happening."

Alahnah bit her lip, her eyes more worried than ever. It was true that Rhobair Duchairn was undoubtedly the most beloved and respected member of the entire vicarate here in Zion, and she never doubted that he was the good man Krystahl had just called him. For that matter, his position as Mother Church's Treasurer was the third most powerful in the entire Church hierarchy. But there were those rumors . . .

Alahnah was always very careful never to use the term "Group of Four" to anyone under any circumstances, but she knew what it referred to. And if it really existed—and she thought it did—then Vicar Rhobair was only one member of it . . . and not the one in charge of the Inquisition.

"I think it's a mistake, Krys," she said. "And with all due respect, Sebahstean's not exactly the most . . . cautious person we know. For that matter, you know how he tends to obsess over things like rules. Remember when he and I used to play chess all the time! Uncle Gahstahn didn't call him the 'local law master' because he was *reasonable* about things, you know!"

"I read the same passages he did, and 'local law master' or not, he's right this time."

"You're going to do this, whatever I say, aren't you?"

"Somebody has to," Krystahl repeated. "Mother Church 'is a great beacon, God's own lamp, set upon a mighty hill in Zion to be the reflector of His majesty and power, that she might give her Light to all the world and drive back the shadows of the Dark. Be sure that you keep the chimney of that lamp pure and holy, clean and unblemished, free of spot or stain.'" Alahnah's heart sank as her cousin quoted the Archangel Bédard. "That's what we're doing, and that's *all* we're doing." Krystahl's spine straightened and she squared her shoulders with an odd mixture of devotion and defiance. "It's all we're doing . . . and it's also the least we *can* do."

▼   ▼   ▼

"Do you have a minute, My Lord?"

Zakryah Ohygyns looked up from the latest report and the ruby ring of his episcopal rank glittered as he beckoned with his right hand.

"At the moment, I'd welcome a distraction," he said wryly, pointing at a chair on the other side of his desk. "I know I officially have to sign off on all these reports, but do you think the Grand Inquisitor *really* needs to know how many copies of the *Book of Sondheim* we have in the borough library?"

"Probably not," Father Erek Blantyn said, but his smile was less amused than it might have been, and Ohygyns felt his stomach tighten in reflex reaction.

There were a lot of reasons Father Erek might be un-amused by any number of things . . . and very few of those reasons were anything the Bishop Inquisitor of Sondheimsborough really wanted to hear about. Unfortunately, it was Father Erek's job to bring exactly those sorts of things to Ohygyns' attention.

The bishop inquisitor tried—really *tried*—not to hold that against him.

"Why do I suspect you're here to tell me something I'd really rather you didn't?" he asked now.

"Because I haven't found anything to tell you about that you *wanted* to hear for the last year or so, My Lord? Or perhaps because you noticed this?"

He waved the folder he'd been carrying under his left arm.

"Probably." Ohygyns sighed and pointed at the chair again. "I don't suppose there's any reason you have to be uncomfortable while you tell me. Sit."

"Thank you, My Lord."

Blantyn settled into the chair and laid the folder in his lap, then folded his hands on top of it. Ohygyns wasn't surprised when he didn't open it. Blantyn always brought the documents to support one of his briefings with him, just in case Ohygyns wanted to see them for himself, but he couldn't remember the last time the priest had needed to refresh his own memory before presenting an absolutely accurate account of what those documents contained.

"What is it, Erek?" the bishop inquisitor asked now, his tone and his expression both much more serious than they had been.

"We have a new report on one of the seditionists we've been watching," Blantyn said. "I think he's moving into a more active phase. One active enough to bring him under Archbishop Wyllym's Ascher Decree."

Ohygyns' jaw tightened. Wyllym Rayno, the Inquisition's Adjutant, had recently issued a heavily revised *Decrees of Schueler*, the codified regulations and procedures of the Office of Inquisition, over the Grand Inquisitor's signature. Ohygyns found himself in agreement with the vast majority of the revisions, although he regretted the stringency—the *temporary* stringency, he devoutly hoped—forced upon Mother Church by the heretics. If the schismatic Church of Charis wasn't crushed, utterly and completely—if it survived in any form—the ultimate unity of Mother Church was doomed, and that could not be permitted.

But that didn't mean Zakryah Ohygyns *liked* what the new *Decrees* required of him, and he especially disliked the Ascher Decree, named for the fallen Archangel Ascher, who held sway over the lies crafted to lure loyal children of God away from the truth. Obviously anyone who truly did lend himself to that sort of despicable deception and temptation had to be cut out of the body of the Faithful, but he didn't like the way Archbishop Wyllym's most recent decree lowered the threshold for exactly what constituted deliberate deceit.

"Who is it?" he asked levelly. "And have I already been briefed on whoever it is?"

"No, you haven't been, My Lord," Blantyn replied, answering his second question first. "As to who it is, it's a young fellow named Sebahstean Graingyr. He's a journeyman printer with a shop over on Ramsgate Square."

"And what brought him to your attention in the first place?"

"We suspect he's been producing broadsides critical of the Grand Inquisitor." Blantyn's face had become utterly expressionless, and Ohygyns felt his own expression smoothing into a similar mask. "There's evidence—pretty strong evidence, actually—that he not only printed them but personally posted them in half a dozen places here in Sondheim."

"Wonderful." Ohygyns leaned back and pinched the bridge of his nose. "I assume you didn't find anything linking him directly to the Fist of Kau-Yung?"

Blantyn winced very slightly as Ohygyns used the proscribed label for the terrorists stalking Mother Church's prelates. It wasn't a term the bishop inquisitor would have used with just anyone, but they had to call the organization *something*, and Ohygyns flatly refused to use its self-bestowed title and call it the Fist of *God*. Other Schuelerites constructed all sorts of awkward circumlocutions to avoid using either phrase, but Ohygyns was too direct for that. Plainspoken to a fault himself, he preferred subordinates who were the same.

"No, My Lord. There's no evidence linking him directly to the terrorists. To be honest, the quality of the printing amply demonstrates there's no direct link. The ones we're certain came from his presses simply aren't anywhere near as finely produced as the ones attributed to the Fist of God." Blantyn used the term without flinching. "And to be fair to Master Graingyr, he's never posted a single word in support of the heresy. In *direct* support, I mean, of course."

Ohygyns grimaced at Blantyn's qualification, but he understood it. So Graingyr was another of those who found Vicar Zhaspahr's stringency difficult to stomach and he'd decided to do something about it. Well, in many ways, the bishop inquisitor couldn't blame the people who felt that way. And, under normal circumstances, he would simply have had someone who did quietly brought in and counseled, probably with a fairly hefty penance attached, for criticizing the mortal custodian of God's *Holy Writ*. Unfortunately, under those same normal circumstances, it would have been far easier to separate that mortal custodian—who, like any mortal, could be fallible—from the *Holy Writ* he preserved, which could *never* be fallible. When the entire basis of Mother Church's authority was in question, when she was fighting a desperate war for her very survival, *nothing* could be allowed to undermine the integrity of the *Writ* . . . and her custody of it.

That was the entire point of Archbishop Wyllym's Ascher Decree.

"What, precisely, has he done?"

"Up until the last five-day or so, he's restricted himself to quoting scripture—especially from Bédard—that emphasizes the godly responsibility to show mercy wherever possible. It's been pretty plain from context that he's speaking directly about the new *Decrees* and the degree to which the Inquisition's been required to become more . . . proactive. But yesterday one of our agents inquisitor brought in a broadside that's almost certainly from Graingyr's press, and it directly criticizes the Grand Inquisitor."

"How are you sure it's from his press? And what sort of criticism?"

"One of the 'e's in his type case appears to have a very distinctive flaw, My Lord. There are three other letters with less easily identifiable flaws, and two of them turned up in the same broadside." Blantyn shook his head. "My people can positively say this broadside and the earlier ones we believe he posted were printed on the same press. Without actually seizing his type case, we can't *prove* he's the one who set them, but if we're correct that he printed the originals here in the borough office files, then he printed this one, too."

Blantyn paused until the bishop inquisitor nodded, then continued.

"As for the criticism, it's not really what I'd consider blatant. He begins by suggesting the Inquisition may have been 'betrayed into excessive sever-ity' by the 'undeniable severity of the crisis Mother Church confronts.' Then he quotes from the *Book of Bédard*—Bédard 8:20, to be exact—and suggests that the Inquisition has forgotten that 'there is no quality more beloved to God than that of mercy.'" The priest shrugged. "To that point, he hasn't strayed any farther into dangerous waters than he's already been. But then he suggests that the Grand Inquisitor has 'allowed his personal ire and anger' to lead him into 'intemperate actions' and into forgetting *Langhorne* 3:27."

Ohygyns' nostrils flared as the words of the twenty-seventh verse of the third chapter of the *Book of Langhorne* ran through his mind. *See that you fail not in this charge, for an accounting shall be demanded of you, and every sheep that is lost will weigh in the balance of your stewardship.*

Under the circumstances, there couldn't be much doubt what this Grain-gyr was implying.

"What else do we know about him?" he asked after a moment.

"We have a lay inquisitor inside his circle of acquaintance, My Lord. I wouldn't call him the most reliable source we have," Blantyn held out his right hand and waggled it in a so-so gesture, "but he's usually fairly dependable. And according to him, Graingyr will be meeting with several like-minded friends the day after tomorrow to finalize a petition of some sort. Appar-ently, once the wording's been agreed to, Graingyr will produce a couple of hundred copies to circulate for signatures."

"And does this lay inquisitor know what that wording is likely to in-clude?"

"He *thinks* he does, My Lord," Blantyn said in a tone that sounded very like a sigh. "If he's right, then the petition in question will be directed not to Vicar Zhaspahr but to Vicar Rhobair and it will request Vicar Rhobair to 'bring some solace' to the families and loved ones of those '*apparently* arrested' by the Inquisition. And it will request him to 'lead the Inquisition into an exercise of that quality of mercy beloved of the Archangel Bédard.'"

Ohygyns' face settled into stone. A mere bishop inquisitor wasn't supposed to know about the complex, competing currents swirling at the very heart of the vicarate. He wasn't supposed to know that there actually was a 'Group of Four,' for example, or that the Grand Inquisitor had ample reason to distrust the iron at Rhobair Duchairn's core. For himself, Ohygyns understood exactly why the poor of Zion, in particular, had taken to calling Duchairn "the Good Shepherd." For that matter, he couldn't fault the vicar's obvious determination to discharge his shepherd's office among God's sheep. But there was a time and place for everything, and at this moment, with the Jihad going so poorly and the Fist of Kau-Yung becoming ever more brazen, anything that suggested Duchairn and the Grand Inquisitor might be at odds could be deadly dangerous. And, he acknowledged unwillingly, if they truly *were* at odds, anything that strengthened Duchairn's standing in the eyes of Zion's citizens at Vicar Zhaspahr's expense might be even more dangerous.

"Our lay inquisitor knows when this meeting is to take place?"

"Yes, My Lord. There are only ten or twelve of them, and they plan to meet at Graingyr's Ramsgate Square shop."

"In that case," Ohygyns said unhappily, "I suppose we should do something about them."

▼　▼　▼

"—so I think we need to be as forceful as we can," Gahlvyn Pahrkyns said, tapping his finger emphatically on the frame of the printing press.

"I don't think 'forceful' is what we want to be where the Grand Inquisitor's concerned," Krystahl Bahrns objected. "He's the one specifically charged to protect the *Holy Writ* and Mother Church. Even if we think the Inquisition's being . . . too rigorous, he deserves to be addressed with the respect God and Langhorne would want us to show him."

"I see your point, Krys," Sebahstean Graingyr said. "On the other hand, I see Gahlvyn's, too." He frowned, his thin, scholar's face intent. Then he held up his right hand, ink-smudged index finger extended. "I guess what we really need to be is as forceful as we can without showing any disrespect."

"That's likely to be a hard line to walk," Krystahl argued. "I think we'd be far better served leaving the Grand Inquisitor—specifically—out of the petition entirely. We can ask Vicar Rhobair to investigate and intervene, assuming intervention's in order, without ever directly attacking the Grand Inquisitor."

"I'm not talking about *attacking* Vicar Zhaspahr, for Langhorne's sake!" Pahrkyns said. "But people are *disappearing*, Krystahl. We don't even know what's *happening* to them! It's being done in the name of the Inquisition, and Vicar Zhaspahr is the Grand Inquisitor. I don't see how we can criticize the Inquisition without criticizing him, and if that's the case, we ought to be forthright about it. Respectful, yes, but we can't just pretend he doesn't have anything to do with what his agents inquisitor are doing!"

"That's my point," Krystahl replied. "I don't think we should be *criticizing* anybody. Not yet. Maybe, if Vicar Rhobair accepts our petition and nothing happens—maybe *then* actual criticism would be in order. But right now, what we ought to do is ask for *explanations*, ask to be told what's happening and why, and humbly petition the Inquisition to temper necessary stringency with mercy."

Graingyr and Pahrkyns looked at each other. It was evident the situation was already past that sort of request, as far as they were concerned. On the other hand, judging by expressions, at least half of the other eleven people crowded into the back of Graingyr's shop agreed with Krystahl.

"If you're afraid to be involved with anything that looks like it's criticizing the Inquisition, you don't have to help circulate the petition, Krys," Pahrkyns pointed out.

"I'm not *afraid* to be involved." Krystahl's hazel eyes flashed. "Anyone who isn't nervous about having his or her words misconstrued at a time like this obviously isn't the sharpest pencil in the box, though. We're here because we think the Inquisition's turning too harsh, too repressive, in response to the threat of the heretics. It's also possible we're not in the best position to judge how much harshness is really necessary at this point, though. I think it would be more appropriate for us to ask Vicar Rhobair to explore that very question for us before we start openly condemning the Inquisition's actions. And—" she added in a rather unwilling tone "—if the Inquisition *is* acting . . . capriciously, or without respect for the due process established in the *Writ*, the last thing we need to do is to turn that capriciousness in our direction until we have to."

"There's something to that, Gahlvyn," Graingyr said. "In fact—"

The sudden crash of shattering glass cut the youthful printer off in mid-word. He started to whirl towards the workshop windows as the broken panes cascaded across the floor, but in the same instant both the back door leading to the service alley behind his shop and the door to the public area where he took orders crashed open. More than open: they flew off the hinges, smashed and broken by heavy iron-headed rams in the hands of a dozen Temple Guardsmen.

"Stand where you are!" a voice shouted, and Krystahl Bahrns paled as she recognized Father Charlz Saygohvya, the agent inquisitor who headed the Inquisition's office in her own parish of Sondheimsborough. "You're all under arrest in the name of Mother Church!"

"*Shit!*"

The single word burst from Gahlvyn Pahrkyns. He whipped around, then bolted towards the broken-in windows.

It was pointless, of course—a panic reaction, nothing more. The guardsmen who'd smashed those windows were waiting right outside them when he came scrambling through the opening, slicing both hands on the broken glass still in the frame. A heavily weighted truncheon smashed down across the back of his neck, and he crashed to the cobblestones face-first.

Krystahl's hands rose to cover her mouth as icy wind sliced into the printing shop's warmth, then she turned in place and found herself face-to-face with a thick-shouldered, dark-haired Schuelerite monk with the flame and sword emblem of the Inquisition on his cassock.

"*Please*," she whispered. "We weren't . . . we *didn't*—"

"Be still, woman!" the monk snapped. "We *know* what you were doing!"

"But—"

"Be *still*, I said!" he barked, and the truncheon in his right hand slashed up in a flat, vicious arc. Krystahl Bahrns never saw it coming before it impacted savagely on her face, shattering her cheekbone and jaw and clubbing her to the floor, less than half-conscious.

"You're all coming with us," she heard Father Charlz' voice saying, and then she faded into the darkness.

.III.
HMS *Floodtide*, 30,
Rahzhyr Bay,
Talisman Island,
Gulf of Dohlar.

Bosun's pipes twittered, the side party snapped to attention, and a commodore's streamer broke from HMS *Floodtide*'s mizzen peak as Sir Bruhstair Ahbaht climbed through the entry port to the ironclad's deck. The entire ship's company was drawn up in divisions on the broad deck, or manned the yards overhead, in clean, tidy uniforms, and the captain waiting for him at the side party's head saluted sharply. Ahbaht returned the courtesy with equal precision and, despite the solemnity of the occasion, felt his lips trying to smile. The towering, broad-shouldered captain was almost a full foot taller than his own 5'4"—indeed, he was every bit as tall as Merlin Athrawes himself—and Ahbaht hoped he didn't look too much like a teenager reporting to his father after staying out too late.

"Welcome aboard *Floodtide*, Sir Bruhstair," the captain said, taking his right hand from his chest and extending it to clasp forearms.

"Thank you, Captain Tohmys," Ahbaht responded gravely. "She looks like a beautiful ship."

"I'm proud of her, Sir," Kynt Tohmys agreed.

"I'm sure you are—and with good reason. For the moment, though, allow me to present Lieutenant Commander Kylmahn." He gestured to the auburn-haired, green-eyed officer who'd followed him through the entry port. "My chief of staff," the commodore added as Kylmahn and Tohmys exchanged salutes and then arm clasps.

"And this," he indicated a considerably younger officer, "is Lieutenant Bairaht Hahlcahm, my flag lieutenant."

"Lieutenant," Tohmys acknowledged as the slender, dapper young lieutenant—who was only an inch or two taller than his commodore—came to attention and saluted.

"Captain Tohmys," the lieutenant acknowledged in a pronounced working-class accent.

That accent might have seemed . . . out of place to some people's ears, given his immaculately groomed appearance. Not to Tohmys', though. The captain might be a Chisholmian, but he recognized the sound of Tellesberg's docks when he heard it, and there were at least a score of "working-class" Tellesberg families who qualified for the newfangled term "millionaire." And unlike most Mainland realms, where the newly rich worked hard to extirpate any vestige of their origins from speech and mannerism, Charisians saw things rather differently. They were just as adamant about their children's educations, about acquiring the better things in life for spouse and family and learning how not to embarrass themselves in business discussions, but they were just as adamant about not forgetting where they'd come from. It was one of the things Mainlanders who persisted in regarding all Out Islanders as ignorant bumpkins most despised about Old Charis . . . and one of the things Tohmys most liked.

"If you'll accompany me, Sir," he said, turning back to Ahbaht, "I'll escort you to your quarters. Unless you'd care to address the ship's company?"

Ahbaht looked at him, head slightly cocked, but Tohmys looked back steadily. The line between the authority of a flag officer and the captain of his flagship was drawn very clearly for a great many reasons. A commodore or an admiral could order his captain to do anything he wished *with* his flagship; he had no authority over *how* the captain did it. There could be only one commander aboard any ship, especially any *warship*, and it was essential that there never be any question in anyone's mind who that one commander was.

Because of that, the ICN tradition was that flag officers addressed their flagship's companies only at their flag captains' invitation. It would take a hardy captain to refuse a commodore or admiral permission to address his crew, but there was a distinct difference between granting permission and extending an invitation.

"I would, indeed—with your permission, Captain," Ahbaht said after a moment. "And I thank you for the indulgence."

"Sir Bruhstair," Tohmys said, still meeting his eyes levelly, "it will be my honor—and my men's."

Ahbaht might have colored ever so slightly, but he nodded and stepped up onto the raised coaming of the midships hatch. The elevation raised his head above shoulder level on Captain Tohmys, but not by much, and the flag captain stepped back. Ahbaht wondered whether he was tactfully . . . deemphasizing the altitude differential.

"Ship's company, tennnnn-*huttt!*" the officer of the deck barked.

The Imperial Charisian Navy placed rather less emphasis on immaculate military drill and formality than most armies did. It was a . . . practical sort of service, the Navy—one which prided itself on getting the job done and on thumbing its collective nose at the aristocratic Mainlander realms' punctilio. But it was also completely capable of executing that drill whenever the mood took it, and *Floodtide*'s company snapped to attention with a precision not even the Temple Guard could have bettered.

"Stand easy," Ahbaht said, raising his voice to be heard through the wind humming in the shrouds and the seabirds circling the anchorage, and feet moved, again with that same precision, coming down on the deck in a single, crisp movement as they folded their arms behind themselves. It wasn't the position of "stand easy"; it was the far more respectful position of "parade rest," and Ahbaht felt a suspicious prickle at the corners of his eyes. He wondered if Tohmys had drilled them especially for this moment, yet somehow he doubted it.

"I thank you and Captain Tohmys for your welcome," he told them, clasping his own hands behind them and letting his eyes sweep slowly across those hundreds of attentive faces, "and I won't keep you long. All of us have a great deal to do, and I know all of you know just as well as I do why we're here."

He took one hand from behind himself to wave it in a circle that indicated the crowded waters of Rahzhyr Bay. Half of Admiral Sarmouth's squadron was at sea; the other half was right here at anchor, and Admiral Darys' arrival had filled the hundred and sixty square miles of Rahzhyr Bay to capacity. The truth was, he reflected, that the ICN was going to need a larger, more commodious forward base. Or even, if things went well, several of them. Personally, he was in favor of Stella Cove on Jack's Land, at least as an interim measure. Of course, they'd have to take it away from the Royal Dohlaran Navy first, but that only made it more attractive to Sir Bruhstair

Ahbaht . . . and *Floodtide* and her consorts might just give Baron Sarmouth the wherewithal to do that taking.

Unless, of course, he has something even more . . . adventurous in mind.

"All of you know what happened in the Kaudzhu Narrows last July," he continued, his voice harder and harsher, and a quietly ugly sound hovered above the listening seaman and officers. "Well, that's what we're out here to do something about, and I'm deeply honored that Earl Sharpfield and Baron Sarmouth have seen fit to give me this division. There was never any question in my mind which of its units I wanted as my flagship, either . . . and that was before I saw the handsome way you brought her into Rahzhyr Bay. Seamanship alone doesn't make an effective warship, but good *seamen* do."

He let that sink in for a moment, then continued.

"We have a great deal to do, and I'm going to demand a great deal *of* you. I'm going to drive this division, and I won't settle for less than the very best you can give me. And don't forget—we're the Imperial *Charisian* Navy. I *know* what you can give me, so don't expect to fob me off with anything less than the finest navy God ever put on the surface of Safehold's seas. That's what you are," the words came slowly, measured, "and that's what you're going to be for me, because the Charisian Navy has a debt to collect and the Dohlaran Navy's account is about to come due. When that time comes— when that bill's presented and that account is rendered; not just for Dohlar but for *everyone* in the Group of Four's service—this division—and HMS *Floodtide*—will be in the van, and there's not a man or an officer in Dohlaran service who will *ever* forget that day."

He paused once more, letting his eyes sweep those silent faces once more, seeing the grim determination, the fire in the eyes, and he nodded slowly.

"*That's* what I'm going to demand of you," he told them, his voice like hammered iron. "And when you give it to me, we'll teach the Dohlaran Navy not to fuck around with the ICN . . . and show that fat, fornicating pig in Zion what God *really* has in mind for him!"

The roar that went up from *Floodtide*'s deck should have stunned every bird and wyvern in Rahzhyr Bay unconscious.

.IV.
**Protector's Arms Hotel
and
Aivah Pahrsahn's Townhouse,
Siddar City,
Republic of Siddarmark.**

Y ou're late!"
The very attractive young woman smiled and pointed accusingly at the clock outside the restaurant's entrance as the dark-haired colonel came through the street door into the hotel lobby vestibule.

"Nineteen-thirty, that's what you said!" she continued. "I've been waiting here an entire *twelve minutes*, I'll have you know."

She elevated her nose with a distinctly audible sniff, and the colonel grinned at her.

"Considering the weather, you're lucky it wasn't at least a couple of hours," he told her, stamping snow off his boots. He took off his heavy great-coat, handed it to one of the bellmen, and crossed the lobby to wrap his arms around her. She snuggled against his chest and he pressed a kiss to the part in her hair.

"Miss me?" he asked in a much softer voice, and she snorted.

"If I had, the last thing I'd do would be to admit it! Can't have you taking me for granted, you know."

"Never!"

He laughed and tucked one arm around her and they started for the restaurant. The maître d' was waiting for them with a broad smile.

"Should I assume our regular table's available. Gyairmoh?" the colonel asked.

"Of course, Colonel Fhetukhav. It *is* Friday," the maître d' pointed out.

"Are we really that predictable?"

"Only to some of us, Sir."

"Well, please make sure this gets into the hotel strongroom till I leave," Fhetukhav said much more seriously, handing across his briefcase.

"Of course, Sir. I'll take it myself. And in the meantime," the maître d' accepted the briefcase and snapped his fingers, and a waiter materialized out of thin air at his elbow, smiling just as broadly in greeting as he had, "Ahndrai will see you to your table and take your drink orders."

"Your efficiency never ceases to amaze me, Gyairmoh."

"The Protector's Arms has a reputation to maintain, Sir," the maître d' said, and bowed gracefully as the waiter escorted them to their table.

▼   ▼   ▼

Airah Sahbahtyno sat at his own table, watching through the diamond-paned glass wall which separated the restaurant from the lobby, as Gyairmoh Hahdgkyn crossed to the elevated, pulpit-like front desk. The good-looking young woman behind it looked up at his approach and shook her head with a smile as she saw the briefcase.

"I take it the Colonel's arrived?"

"It's Friday," Hahdgkyn said with an answering twinkle.

"You know they're discussing marriage?" the desk clerk asked.

"I think that would be wonderful." Hahdgkyn's expression was more sober than it had been. "They're good people, Sairaih. And it would certainly be a happier ending than a lot of things have been in the last few years."

"It certainly would," she agreed, and reached out to accept the briefcase from him.

She stepped back through the open wicket gate to the massive, iron-strapped door of the hotel strongroom and used the key hanging from the chain around her neck to open the door. She stepped inside and slid the briefcase into one of the numbered heavy cabinets against the back wall, then closed and locked the cabinet door—also reinforced with iron—behind it. Then she closed the strongroom door, relocked it, as well, and returned to the desk, where she pulled a slip of paper from a pigeonhole, dipped her pen in the inkwell, and wrote in a quick, neat hand. She blew on the ink to dry it, then handed it to Hahdgkyn.

"Here's his receipt," she said, then spurted a little laugh as the maître d' accepted it. "Not that he really needs one anymore. Charlz knows that brief-case as well as I do by now!"

"The light's usually a little better when the Colonel collects it in the morning, though, I imagine."

"Oh, I'm sure it is," she agreed, and Hahdgkyn headed back to the restaurant to deliver the receipt.

Sahbahtyno watched him go, waited thirteen minutes by the clock—last time he'd waited only five, but the time before that he'd waited for thirty-three—then stood, folded his newspaper, signed the check lying beside his dessert plate, and ambled out of the restaurant. He crossed to the desk, and the clerk greeted him with a smile.

"Good evening, Master Sahbahtyno. How was dinner?"

"Excellent, as always," Sahbahtyno replied with a matching smile. "Would you happen to have any mail for me, Sairaih?"

"I don't believe we do tonight, actually," she said. "Let me check."

She ran her fingertip along the long row of wall mounted pigeonholes until it came to the one for Room 312, then turned back to him.

"I'm afraid not. Were you expecting something? I can have one of the bellboys run it up to your room when it arrives, if you are."

"No, no." He shook his head. "Just checking. There's some routine paperwork en route from one of my suppliers, but nothing urgent. If anything does come this late, it'll keep until tomorrow. No point sending one of the boys upstairs. Besides, I'm going to be turning in early tonight, I think." He glanced out through the double-paned lobby windows as the snow driving along Lord Protector Ludovyc Avenue at a sharp angle and shivered theatrically. "I always sleep better on nights like this. I think listening to the wind howl on the other side of the wall makes the bed feel warmer."

"It seems that way to me, sometimes, too," she agreed. "Sleep well."

"Thank you."

He nodded pleasantly, turned from the desk, and headed across the lobby.

As one of the Republic's capital's premier hotels, the eight-floor Protector's Arms boasted no less than three elevators, and he took the center one to the third floor, then strolled to his room, unlocked the door, and turned up the wick on the lit lamp housekeeping had left on the small table just inside it. A small, banked fire burned on the small grate—housekeeping always laid one for him promptly at sixteen o'clock, at the same time they lit the doorside lamp for him—and he closed the door behind himself and locked it. He crossed to the fireplace, setting the small lamp on the mantel while he poked up the fire and settled three or four lumps of fresh Glacierheart coal into the suddenly crackling flames. Then he lit a taper from the jar on the mantel and used it to light the larger lamp on the pleasant little sitting room's table and the still larger one suspended from the coffered ceiling on a chain. The Protector's Arms used only the finest first-quality kraken oil, and the lamps burned brightly and steadily as he settled into the armchair parked in front of the cheerfully dancing fire.

Despite his conversation with the desk clerk, he had no intention of sleeping. Not anytime soon, anyway. It would be—he pulled out his pocket watch and consulted it—another three hours or so before Sairaih Kwynlyn handed the desk over to Charlz Ohbyrlyn, her relief. And it would probably be at least another hour after that before Ohbyrlyn knocked ever so quietly at Sahbahtyno's door.

He sat back in the chair, opened his personal copy of the *Holy Writ*, and resumed his study of the *Book of Chihiro* while he waited.

▼   ▼   ▼

It was actually closer to five hours than four, but the knock came eventually.

Sahbahtyno marked his place, set the *Writ* on the table, and crossed quickly to open the door.

The man in the hall was at least ten years older than Sairaih, with brown hair and eyes, and his expression was nervous. It was also determined, however, and he held out a very large briefcase—almost large enough for a small suitcase, actually, and monogramed with the initials "ARS"—without a word. Sahbahtyno took it, the brown-haired man turned and walked quickly away, and the door closed and locked behind him.

Sahbahtyno moved with the smoothness of long practice as he opened the briefcase with his initials on it—the one which had been parked in the strongroom since the day before—and removed the considerably smaller briefcase which had been concealed within it He picked the locks securing the straps on the second briefcase, opened it, and gazed down into it, touching absolutely nothing for well over a minute while he carefully memorized how its contents were arranged. It would never do to put them back in a different order.

Finally he nodded to himself and extracted the neatly banded folders. He stacked them on the table, careful to maintain their order, and arranged a pad of paper and a pen at his elbow. Then he drew a deep breath, opened the first folder, and began to read.

Halfway down the first page, he paused, eyes widening. His gaze darted back up to the heading, rereading it carefully, and his nostrils flared as he reached for the pen and began jotting shorthand notes at a furious pace.

▼　▼　▼

"Well, so far so good," Merlin Athrawes murmured.

He and Nynian Rychtyr sat side-by-side on a comfortable, deeply upholstered couch in "Aivah Pahrsahn's" luxurious townhouse. A carafe of hot chocolate sat on the small side table at Nynian's end of the couch, but Merlin nursed an outsized mug of cherrybean tea. He hadn't actually realized how much he'd missed Nimue Alban's favorite hot beverage until he'd rediscovered it here in the Republic, and he wondered sometimes why it had taken him so long to reacquire Nimue's addiction.

Probably because I'd spent so much time going cold turkey in Charis, he reflected. *Wasn't exactlty common there, and Seijin Merlin was already odd enough without adding that to the equation. And it's not as if caffeine—or the lack thereof—has much effect on a PICA, either, so it wasn't like I needed the stuff to stay awake the way Nimue did when she had the bridge watch.*

"I told you and Cayleb that Sahbahtyno would be more useful alive than dead someday," Nynian replied with a decided note of triumph.

"I still say it would've been more satisfying just to kill the bastard."

"You see, that's the difference between us," Nynian told him with a twinkle. "You believe in brute force solutions, whereas I prefer more . . . subtle approaches. And unlike you, I understand that pleasure deferred is often much greater because of the wait. From where *I* sit, it's far more satisfying to put Master Sahbahtyno to work for us. Just think about his reaction when we finally do arrest him and explain exactly how he's been played!" She smiled seraphically. "The only thing better than that would be to find a way to send him home to report personally to Rayno and Clyntahn after they find out how we've used him but before *he* figures it out. I'm sure what they'd do to him would satisfy even someone as bloodthirsty as you and Cayleb!"

"Probably," he conceded. "But we're not giving up the opportunity to watch him hang right here in Siddar City when the time comes." He shrugged, his sapphire eyes far bleaker than his almost whimsical tone. "Sometimes tradition is important, and if anybody ever damned well deserved to hang, it's Sahbahtyno."

"I can't argue with you there," Nynian acknowledged, her own tone rather more serious than it had been. "But, all jesting aside, this is exactly why I argued against arresting him when we first identified him."

"And, as usual," Merlin turned smiled warmly at her, "you were right. Have I ever mentioned that you have a habit of being that way?"

"From time to time," she said, leaning closer to rest her head on his shoulder. "From time to time."

He tucked an arm around her and sipped cherrybean, then snorted a laugh.

"What?" she asked without lifting her head from his shoulder, and he chuckled.

"I was just thinking about Mahrlys and Rahool," he said. "I wonder if either of them ever expected this to turn out the way it looks like it's going to?"

"You mean in front of an altar?" It was Nynian's turn to chuckle warmly. "I doubt it, but it couldn't happen to two nicer people!"

"No, it couldn't. And I hope you don't mind that *Seijin* Aibram will always have a warm spot in his heart for Mahrlys."

"I'd be astonished if he didn't. She wasn't simply one of the most . . . accomplished young ladies in Madame Ahnzhelyk's employ, she was also one of the sweetest. And the smartest. There was a reason—besides Aibram's charming Silkiahan accent—that I suggested her for him that first night, you know. She always was one of my favorites."

"And with good reason," Merlin said with a fond smile. Then he sat back, sipping more cherrybean as the two of them watched the imagery from the SNARC remote on the ceiling of Airah Sahbahtyno's hotel room.

Even with the advantages the SNARCs conferred, and even with such talented hunters as Nahrmahn Baytz and Nynian Rychtyr, it had taken over four months to find and identify Sahbahtyno. They'd known he had to be out there somewhere, and together with Owl, they'd been back over every second of imagery from every single one of the hundreds of remotes seeded throughout Siddar City until they finally found him.

I suppose I should feel at least a little remorse that we hanged Samyl Naigail for Trumyn's murder, Merlin reflected. *On the other hand, he was definitely right there in the middle of the riot, and they found plenty of imagery of what that little bastard did in the Charisian Quarter two years ago.* The seijin's mouth tightened ever so briefly as he remembered reviewing some of that imagery. *Nobody in the universe ever deserved hanging more than he did. And the fact that we hanged him for it—and truly thought we were getting the guilty party, at the time—was probably a major factor in Sahbahtyno's conclusion that no one suspected him at all.*

It was painfully obvious that the Church's sudden acquisition of the open hearth steel process must have come from the briefcase which had been stolen from Zhorj Trumyn after his murder in that "spontaneous riot" in Tanner's Way. Unfortunately, there'd been far fewer remotes in Siddar City at the time, and that particular bit of violence had escaped their attention. Ultimately, that was probably for the best, though, because if they'd identified Sahbahtyno at the time, they would most certainly have executed *him* for it. And that, as Nynian had just pointed out, would have been a pity.

Or a waste, at least. Merlin couldn't quite convince himself to view Sahbahtyno's continued existence as a good thing, however useful he might have proved. In fact, he'd been all for bringing the bastard in and repairing the omission which had left him alive, and both Cayleb and Sharleyan had supported him strongly . . . until Nynian pointed out that after his success in acquiring the steelmaking information he must have absolutely established his reliability in the eyes of his masters in Zion.

Just leaving him in place while they studied his actions had told them a great deal about how Rayno and Clyntahn had reorganized their intelligence operations in light of Charis' lethally effective counterintelligence. Sahbahtyno had very carefully avoided creating any sort of network, any web of sources that could be penetrated and tracked back to him, and that explained a great deal about how he'd evaded detection in the first place. It had limited the reach of his information gathering, despite the unanticipated treasure trove which had fallen into his lap when he'd launched the riot in which Trumyn died, but it had also made him almost totally invisible, even to Nahrmahn and Owl. And he really was very, very good at his work, with exactly the combination of skill, acute observation, cool calculation, discipline, patience, and dash of recklessness a first-rate intelligence agent required.

The Inquisition had done an excellent job in establishing his basic cover, as well. He'd set up as an upscale rug merchant with a well-heeled clientele, importing his goods from both Chisholm and Tarot, and he turned a tidy legitimate profit. In fact, his business produced more than enough income for him to afford a room someplace like the Protector's Arms, and he clearly realized that the best place to hide was usually in plain sight. He'd made no effort to keep his activities—or, at least, the activities of his *public* persona—under wraps, and "furtive" was probably the last word anyone would have applied to him. After studying him for a few five-days, Nynian had realized he reminded her a great deal, in some ways, of Ahrloh Mahkbyth. She doubted he was as physically tough as the ex-Guardsman, and he definitely wanted to stay as far from any more "hands-on" work than he could possibly avoid. But he was perfectly willing to resort to violence when needed, as the Tanner's Way riot demonstrated, and he was probably just as smart as he thought he was. That was saying quite a lot—self-deprecation wasn't one of his outstanding qualities—and that suited her purposes just fine. A *smart* spy who didn't realize he was being manipulated was a priceless asset, she'd explained. Especially if his *superiors* knew how smart he was. They'd be far more cautious about accepting information from a *stupid* spy, after all.

And smart people could be counted upon to do smart things. Which meant that if one understood their motives and approached them properly, it was actually easier to predict how they would react than it would have been with someone who *wasn't* smart. That was a fundamental article of faith for her, and she'd set out to demonstrate its applicability in Airah Sahbahtyno's case.

Mahrlys Fahrno truly had been one of Ahnzhelyk Phonda's favorite courtesans in Zion, almost more daughter than an employee. She'd never been recruited by the Sisters of Saint Kohdy, but when Ahnzhelyk disappeared, she'd arranged independent routes by which each of her young ladies could escape Zion as well, if they chose. She hadn't expected the Inqusition to become suddenly and deeply interested in Ahnzyhelyk's past activities, but she hadn't been able to rule out the possibility, and so she'd given each young woman her own avenue out of the city without ever mentioning that she'd done the same thing for *all* of them.

In the event, no one in the Inquisition even seemed to have noticed Ahnzhelyk's disappearance, but the savagery of Zhaspahr Clyntahn's purge of the vicarate, following so closely on the closure of Madam Phonda's establishment, had made it easy for Mahrlys to make her choice. Few of Ahnzhelyk's competitors had been able—or willing—to provide the quality of client, the comfort, and—above all—the *safety* Ahnzhelyk had, and she'd personally known too many of the men Clyntahn had so brutally murdered. She'd known that whatever else they might have been, they definitely *hadn't* been the monsters the Inquisition claimed they had. She hadn't much thought about Reformism before that, but the shattering proof of the Group of Four's corruption had clarified her thinking remarkably, and Zion had been no place for a new, fiercely devoted Reformist. Besides, she'd been born and raised in Silk Town. That meant she'd had no family in the Temple Lands to hold her there, and she'd arrived on the doorstep of Aivah Pahrsahn's Siddar City townhouse less than three months later.

She wasn't the only one of Madam Phonda's ladies to flee the Temple Lands, and "Aivah" had quietly arranged comfortable livings for all of them. Those livings had meant none of them had to return to their previous careers, but Mahrlys had been different. She hadn't come seeking simple safety; she'd come seeking a way to strike back at Clyntahn and the others, and if she still didn't know about the Sisters of Saint Kohdy, she was as smart as she was beautiful. She'd quickly realized "Aivah" was deeply involved with the Reformist movement in Siddarmark, and it hadn't taken her long to deduce that *Ahnzhelyk* must have been just as deeply involved in it in Zion without Mahrlys ever suspecting a thing. Coupled with her own bitter disillusionment about the Church—or the Group of Four, at least—that had been more than enough for her to volunteer to join Aivah's efforts here in the capital.

She'd been very effective, too, especially after Aivah helped her establish herself in her old profession. Ahnzhelyk Phonda had never offered her guests in Zion anything so crude as simple prostitution. Her young ladies had been true companions, as well—highly decorative and skilled in the pleasures of the flesh, yes, but also intelligent, educated, and cultured, as accomplished in making witty conversation, critiquing the latest theatrical performance, discussing religion (in the days when that had been a safe topic), or enjoying a night at the opera, as they ever were in bed. It hadn't taken someone who'd been tutored by Ahnzhelyk very long to establish herself as one of the most sought-after courtesans in Siddar City.

Once they'd identified Sahbahtyno, they'd moved Mahrlys into the Protector's Arms. And once she'd been there for a few five-days, they'd arranged for Colonel Fhetukhav—a lonely widower, six years older than she, a logistics specialist on Daryus Parkair's personal staff who'd come up through the Quartermaster's Corps—to cross her orbit. Fhetukhav had been more than willing to play his part, especially after he set eyes on Mahrlys for the first time! And while he often took sensitive documents home to work on there, he was always scrupulous about securing them in the hotel's strongroom on the two nights every five-day he spent with Mahrlys.

They were both intelligent, warmhearted people who believed deeply in what they were doing and why. Merlin hadn't counted on it, but neither had he been surprised when their "cover" as lovers blossomed into a deep, genuine love for one another. He was happy for them, but he was even happier that Nynian—and Nahrmahn, who'd supported her strongly—had been right about Sahbahtyno. However careful he might have been to avoid any extended network that could be traced back to him, the temptation to spread his tendrils just a *little* wider had proved too much to resist when Nynian trolled Fhetukhav delicately under his nose. Especially given the fact that he'd long since realized that Charlz Ohbyrlyn, the Protector's Arms' senior night clerk, was an ardent Temple Loyalist. Ohbyrlyn had tried hard to conceal his personal fury at Greyghor Stohnar's decision to ally the Republic with Charis, but Sahbahtyno was very, very good at reading people.

Which, now that Merlin thought about it, probably made the genuine affection between Mahrlys and Fhetukhav an even better thing.

Within a month of Fhetukhav's first visit to the hotel, Sahbahtyno had been studying the contents of his briefcase whenever it was locked in the strongroom overnight. That didn't happen very often; Nynian and Nahrmahn were far too skilled for anything that crude. But when it did happen, every bit of information, every document in the briefcase, was completely genuine. Some of that information must have been quite valuable to the Temple, although most of it had been things they'd been confident would have eventually reached Zion anyway through one of Rayno and Clyntahn's other conduits. But coupled with Sahbahtyno's original triumph with Trumyn's notes, the fact that they'd never passed him one single piece of misinformation had probably turned him into Rayno's gold standard as an intelligence source.

There were times I thought you'd spent all this effort building the perfect asset we'd never use, love, Merlin thought, looking down at the top of Nynian's head with a smile. *You were right, though, bless your devious little heart—better to have it available and never use it than to not have it available when we needed it. And when* he *reports we're shifting so much of our available strength south to High Mount, Clyntahn—and Maigwair—will have to take the possibility very seriously, indeed.*

Merlin Athrawes could live with leaving him un-hanged a little longer to accomplish that.

Especially since they still had more than enough evidence to hang him in the end, anyway.

.V.
**Rhobair Duchairn's Office,
The Temple,
City of Zion,
The Temple Lands,
Republic of Siddarmark.**

That was delicious, Rhobair."

Vicar Allayn Maigwair wiped his mouth and laid the snowy napkin down beside the empty bowl before he sat back with a sigh of repletion.

"Thank you," Rhobair Duchairn replied with a smile. "I let Brother Lynkyn keep his cooks, but I extorted their clam chowder recipe out of them at knifepoint. I'm glad you enjoyed it, Allayn."

"Oh, I did. I did!" Maigwair shook his head. "In fact, I think I enjoyed it even more because I've rediscovered how much I prefer *simple* menus. There's something . . . honest about food like clam chowder. I never really enjoyed those fancified dinners we used to have before Zhaspahr got the wild hair up his arse about Charis. Although if I'm going to be honest," he smiled with a trace of bitterness, "that had less to do with menus and more to do with the fact that I knew the rest of you considered me the lightweight of our little group."

Duchairn opened his mouth, but Maigwair shook his head before the other vicar could speak.

"The main reason that bothered me was because I figured it was probably true," he confessed with a slightly broader smile. "On the other hand, it's occurred to me since that you can be smart as Proctor himself without having a lick of common sense. Our good friend Zhaspahr strikes me as a case in point. And then there's Zahmsyn."

"Good of you to leave me out of their company," Duchairn said wryly as Maigwair paused, and the Church's captain general snorted.

"I'm not going to propose *any* of us as geniuses, given the fucking mess we've managed to land the entire Church in! And ourselves; let's not forget that! But the truth is, you were the only one who even tried to put the brakes on. *I* sure as Shan-wei didn't!"

He scowled, reached for his beer stein, and finished its contents in a single long swallow.

"Keeps me up nights worrying, that does," he said in a much quieter voice. "I'm not looking forward to what God and Langhorne will have to say to me on the other side."

"None of us should be," Duchairn said in an even quieter voice.

He leaned back in the swivel chair on his side of the enormous desk—he and Maigwair were sharing yet another working lunch in his office—and contemplated the other man. They'd been forced into ever closer partnership as they coped with the rising flood of the Jihad's disastrous requirements. The fact that they knew Zhaspahr Clyntahn regarded them both with the utmost suspicion—and was undoubtedly simply waiting for the appropriate moment to act upon that suspicion—had only glued them more tightly together. And in the process, Duchairn had realized his own view of Maigwair as a slow, unimaginative plodder had been . . . less than fair. Or accurate. Allayn Maigwair might not be the most brilliant man he'd ever met, but he was a long, *long* way from the stupidest. And as he'd just pointed out, brilliance all too often ran a piss-poor second to common sense, and *that* he'd turned out to have in abundance. Yet for all the closeness with which they'd come to coordinate their plans and efforts, this was the first time Maigwair had ever expressed his own misgivings about the Jihad's origin—or probable outcome—quite so clearly.

"I don't think any rational human being would think God *wants* to see His children slaughter one another in His name," the Church's treasurer continued, his soft voice clearly audible against the muted backdrop of the blizzard howling outside the mystically heated comfort of the Temple. "Maybe it *is* necessary, sometimes, but surely it ought to've been a *last* resort, not the first one we reached for!"

"I know." Maigwair set his stein back beside his empty soup bowl and gazed down into it for a long moment. "I know." He looked back up at Duchairn. "But we're astride the slash lizard, and we've taken all of Mother Church there with us." His mouth was a grim line. "Until we've dealt with the outside threat, we can't risk trying to deal with any that might be . . . closer to home."

Duchairn nodded slowly, and his eyes were as dark as Maigwair's.

You're right, Allayn. Unfortunately, some outside threats are easier to deal with than others, he thought with a certain acid humor. *And then there's the little problem of timing. Supposing that we somehow miraculously "deal" with Charis and the Republic, what happens when Zhaspahr realizes we have? Just how are we supposed to "deal" with him if he has the two of us killed as soon as he decides he no longer needs us to keep his fat arse in the Grand Inquisitor's chair? That is sort of the heart of the question, isn't it?*

He thought about asking that out loud, but he didn't, and as he studied Maigwair's expression, he felt vaguely ashamed by the temptation. Because the truth was that he honestly didn't think Maigwair's first concern was over his own survival. Not any longer. And if it had taken the other vicar a little longer to reach that point, at least he *had* reached it. And the *Writ* itself taught that what mattered was the destination, not how long it took to get there.

Some things were best not said, however, even between just the two of them, and even here in his own office. If nothing else, it was dangerous to get into the habit of confiding too easily—or too openly, at least—when the Inquisition commanded so many spies, so many sets of ears. Maigwair had been given fresh proof of that only last June when Clyntahn summoned a dozen of the captain general's most trusted colleagues to receive their orders to betray him. Unfortunately for the Grand Inquisitor, the "Fist of God" had blown up the traitors—along with the Second Church of the Holy Pasquale of the Faithful of Zion—and Maigwair had moved with surprising speed to take advantage of the sudden vacuum at the top of the Army of God's hierarchy.

He'd been rather more careful about who he'd selected to fill those offices this time around. It was to be hoped he'd been careful *enough*.

And in the meantime, the treasurer reminded himself, *while winning the Jihad would be nice, we somehow have to see to it that we at least don't lose it. God knows I've heard of lighter challenges!*

"Well," he said out loud, cradling his own stein in both hands, "I think we've covered just about everything from my side, at least as far as current production plans are concerned. Is there anything else you think we need to discuss on that side, Allayn?"

"No." Maigwair shook his head and laid one hand on the fat looseleaf binder beside his tray. "I'm comfortable that we've come up with the best projections we can based on reports from the front and Brother Lynkyn's estimates." He shrugged. "I'd be lying if I said I was *satisfied* with those projections, because I'm damned well not, and I really don't like what meeting them is costing the Army in terms of personnel. But that doesn't mean we can come up with better ones."

"I wish we could cut you a little more slack on the manpower side," Duchairn said soberly. "Unfortunately, I need those men badly."

"Oh, I know that! And if it's a choice between putting them into uniform and having enough weapons to go around for the men we already have in uniform, I'm all in favor of letting you have them! It's just the caliber of the men in question. And then there's the little matter of how much more weight this makes us throw on Rainbow Waters and the Mighty Host." The captain general shook his head. "It's slowing the training process, too, and that means we'll be slower hitting our deployment targets this summer."

Duchairn nodded. The voracious demand of the manufactories supporting Mother Church's war effort was cutting into the personnel available to Mother Church's armies. There'd always been some competition in that regard, but it had gotten steadily worse—*far* worse—as the Church found itself confronting the floodtide of Charisian productivity. Duchairn's comb-out of the great orders had provided a huge upsurge in available hands two years ago, but much of that manpower surge had vanished like a prong buck sliding down a crusher serpent's gullet. Not because the hands the personnel requisition had provided weren't working harder than ever, but because the previous year's military catastrophes had required even more weapons—replacement weapons, as well as the newly designed and developed ones—than anyone had dreamed might be the case.

The production techniques Lynkyn Fultyn and Tahlbaht Bryairs had pioneered right here in Zion helped enormously, and Fultyn had assembled what he called his "brain trust" to push that process along. Duchairn knew the Chihirite monk was nervous about pulling so many of his more innovative thinkers together into a single group so close to Zhaspahr Clyntahn's personal eye, and the treasurer had been careful to point out in his memos to his colleagues how incredibly important that group's efforts were. That didn't keep him from worrying about the targets he and Fultyn had pasted onto those men's backs, but it was the best he could do, and they *needed* the "brain trust." They were not only Fultyn's primary problem solvers—the analysts he turned to whenever yet another new piece of Charisian technology was brought to his attention—but were also engaged in what Fultyn called "efficiency studies." They were specifically charged with studying the production techniques and processes being mandated and enforced across every single one of Mother Church's manufactories for the specific purpose of finding ways in which those techniques could become even more efficient.

Yet even with all the "brain trust" could do, Mother Church's productivity per man-hour remained drastically lower than that of Charis. There were times that seemed impossible when Duchairn looked at the thousands of artillery pieces—and the *hundreds* of thousands of rifles—pouring from her manufactories, yet it remained true. And, far worse, because the *capability* of those cannon and rifles remained inferior to that of the weapons in heretic hands, her defenders had no choice but to substitute quantity for quality. The Treasury had poured out a floodtide of marks building manufactories to make that possible, and that tide continued to flow, even though Duchairn had been forced to more and more desperate expediencies to sustain it. But manufactories needed far more than bricks and mortar, and money wasn't the only thing that had to be carefully budgeted to meet the Jihad's insatiable appetites.

More and more of the Temple Lands' women were moving into manufactory jobs and proving themselves equal or superior to the men who would normally have held those jobs, but that process was in its early stages and there simply weren't enough women—yet, at least—in the labor force to sustain the necessary production levels. Quite aside from the hands which could be taught the necessary skills "on-the-job," the steadily expanding numbers of manufactories needed hands which were *already* skilled. Even more critically, they needed *supervisors*, people who could teach those skills, who could implement the directives coming down from Fultyn's St. Kylmahn's offices.

That was why Maigwair had instituted a draconian manpower allocation policy within the Army of God. Experienced mechanics, and especially experienced *master* mechanics, who enlisted (or, increasingly, were conscripted) for the AOG, never saw an army parade ground. Instead, they became corporals or sergeants who were handed over to Duchairn and assigned wherever they were most badly needed. The numbers provided that way were lower than one might have thought, given the scale of the Army of God's rebuilding efforts, but they were a critical component of Duchairn's weapons production. Yet they would have been almost equally valuable to the Army's frontline maintenance commands, and even if that hadn't been true, their education, skills, and intelligence meant they represented a large supply of men who would have made excellent officers. Given the numbers of new formations Maigwair had been forced to stand up, the loss of so many potential officers was painful indeed.

"Allayn, if there was any—" Duchairn began, but Maigwair shook his head.

"I said I didn't think we could come up with better arrangements, and I meant it, Rhobair. The worst part is the delay in getting our new divisions trained up to something that can hope to face Charisians in the field. The number of experienced officers and noncoms we provided to the Mighty Host a couple of years ago is biting us on the arse in that regard, I'm afraid. But the delay means the Harchongians will have to carry even more of the load in the field longer than my people had originally projected." The captain general's expression was grim. "We'd hoped to have them ready for deployment by late November. It looks now like I *may* be able to get the first new divisions on their way by the end of *next* month. It'll be May, at least, and more likely June of even early July before we can get the bulk of them to the front, and I'll be honest with you, Rhobair. Even when we *get* them there, they'll still need a lot of additional training before I'd consider them suitable for anything much more demanding than holding fortified positions. They certainly won't be equal to Charisian mounted infantry in any sort of *mobile* battle, that's for damned sure! But there's nothing we can do to change that." He shrugged. "Sometimes your only choices are between bad and worse, I'm afraid."

"Been a lot of that going around for the last few years," Duchairn agreed sourly. "But it looks to me like Rainbow Waters has come up with the best way to use what we can give him."

"Assuming he can put his plans into effect without any more . . . elbow joggling from certain parties in Zion."

Maigwair's tone was even sourer than Duchairn's had been. But then the captain general shrugged again.

"The truth is," he told the treasurer, "he's got a lot better chance of pulling that off than anyone else would. And thank God he's got a brain that works!"

"From your mouth to Langhorne's ears," Duchairn agreed reverently.

Taychau Daiyang clearly intended to fight his own sort of campaign, and taking all of the known factors into account, his was almost certainly the best campaign plan available. As Maigwair had just said, sometimes it came down to a choice between bad or worse, but the Earl of Rainbow Waters clearly understood what was in play—not just on the field of battle, but in the foundries and manufactories.

Despite how steeply Mother Church's *total* production of weapons had grown relative to the Charisians over the last year or two, he was not at all confident about the outcome of *that* side of the Jihad. In fact, Duchairn had no doubt that curve was about to begin reversing itself, and not just because the Treasury was so close to outright collapse.

Both he and Maigwair were convinced Zhaspahr Clyntahn was holding back information the Inquisition had gleaned about the Empire of Charis' manufacturing capacity. That was ultimately stupid; the reality would become painfully evident on the battlefield sooner or later, and Duchairn couldn't decide whether Clyntahn was concealing things because he genuinely believed the Charisians were profiting from demonic intervention he didn't want spreading to Mother Church's own manufactories or if he was simply in what a Bédardist would have called "denial."

Given the way he'd twisted the Proscriptions into a pretzel any time he decided it suited his purposes, it was probably the latter.

Whatever else he might try to hide, however, the Inquisitor had been forced to admit that at least a half dozen additional major manufactory sites were about to come on-stream in the Empire of Charis. Three of them, in Old Charis itself, bade fair to eventually rival the sprawling Delthak Works which had spawned so many of the Church's military disasters, but that was scarcely the worst of it. The Maikelberg Works in Chisholm were also expanding at breakneck speed, and reports indicated that the Charisian Crown was using the windfall of the Silverlode Strike to finance additional works in Chisholm and Emerald, as well. There were even reports of two new manufactories breaking ground in Corisande—and another in *Zebediah*, of all damned places! And to make bad worse, the majority of Siddarmark's foundries and manufactories had always lain in the eastern portion of the Republic, which meant they'd been beyond the Sword of Schueler's reach.

Most of them were once again working propositions, and while there was no way they'd be matching Charisian levels of efficiency anytime soon, their productivity was still rising steadily . . . and at least as swiftly as anything Mother Church could boast.

And if the Imperial Charisian Navy succeeded in its quest to control the Gulf of Dohlar. . . .

The truth is that no matter what we do—no matter what we physically could *do, even if I had an unlimited supply of marks—we've lost the production race,* he thought bleakly. *They're not simply more efficient than we are in their existing manufactories, the number of their manufactories is increasing more rapidly than ours . . . and their rate of expansion's climbing like one of Brother Lynkyn's rockets. And despite everything Brother Lynkyn and people like Lieutenant Zwaigair can do, the weapons they're producing—especially their* heavy *weapons, like their artillery and those damned ironclad warships—are better than ours. And it looks like their rate of improvement's continuing to climb just as quickly as their manufactory capacity! At the moment, we're still producing more* total *weapons—a* lot *more total weapons—per month than they are, but by midsummer—early winter, at the latest—even that won't be true any longer.*

The tsunami coming out of Charis would simply bury the Mighty Host and the Army of God on the field of battle. That was obvious to both him and Maigwair, however resolutely Clyntahn might continue to insist that a man armed with a rock and the invincible spirit of God was superior to any rifle-armed heretic ever born. And since there was no hope of preventing the sprawling Charisian merchant fleet from delivering those ever-increasing numbers of weapons to their armies, Mother Church's only hope was to find a way to eliminate the armies themselves before the tidal wave destroyed everything in its path. Which, given the past record of the Army of God and its allies, would be a . . . nontrivial challenge, Duchairn thought mordantly.

"How likely do you really think it is that Rainbow Waters will be able to follow his campaign plan? His *actual* plan, I mean; not the one he's officially submitted for approval."

"Noticed that, did you?" Maigwair gave the treasurer a lopsided smile. "Careful to hide it all in the 'contingencies' section, wasn't he?" The captain general shook his head in admiration. "Just between you and me, I've never really liked Harchongese bureaucrats very much. Always seemed to me that they were even worse than *our* bureaucrats! But there are times when a good, bluff military man such as myself can only watch in awe and admiration as they dance rings around their superiors."

Duchairn chuckled, but Maigwair was right. Rainbow Waters—or *someone* on his staff, at least—obviously understood the fine art of obfuscation even better than most Harchongians, and the earl knew exactly what Zhaspahr Clyntahn wanted to hear. Duchairn was fairly sure he also appreciated the way Harchong's monumental loyalty to Mother Church inclined the Grand Inquisitor to put far more faith in a Harchongese commander than in anyone else. He'd certainly played to that inclination with consummate skill! His official dispatches were brimful of the offensive spirit, pointing out the way in which his fortifications and massive supply dumps would enable him to operate with far greater freedom once the weather permitted a general advance. And in the meantime, of course, they provided security against any sudden, unexpected move by the heretics.

What he very carefully *hadn't* pointed out was that he had absolutely no intention of ordering any of the general advances he'd laid out in such enthusiastic detail, supply base or no. His calculation of the military realities—which he'd shared privately with Maigwair, via an oral report delivered by Archbishop Militant Gustyv Walkyr—was that the sustained, rapid fire of the Charisians' new rifles and revolvers, coupled with their portable angle-guns and heavier artillery, would make any assault prohibitively expensive. He had the manpower to "win" at least some offensive battles simply by throwing bodies at the enemy, but the process would gut even the Mighty Host of God and the Archangels. And, given the Charisians' greater mobility, any assault he launched, however brilliantly it succeeded, was unlikely to prove decisive, since he couldn't prevent his enemies from slipping away and eluding pursuit.

He hadn't said a single word about that in any of his written reports. Acknowledging that Mother Church couldn't possibly take the war to her enemies and win wasn't something Zhaspahr Clyntahn wanted to hear, even out of a Harchongian. And despite his . . . pragmatic awareness of the realities he faced, the earl himself remained far from defeated, because he'd also calculated that those same realities favored the defense *whoever* happened to be doing the defending. Having faced that starting point squarely, he'd proceeded to throw away the rule book—even the brand-new one, devised by the Army of God—and created an entirely new operational approach. He'd even come up with a term to summarize his new thinking: the "tactical defense/strategic offense," he called it. And from Maigwair's description of it, it struck Duchairn as commendably clear and logical.

The earl had no intention of simply lying down and dying—or running away—whenever the Charisians finally put in their appearance. His "defense in depth" would slow their attack, bleed their forces, force them to use up manpower, weapons, and ammunition fighting their way through one fortified position after another. And then, at the moment they were fully extended, he would launch his *counter*offensive. With luck, the enemy would be caught off-balance and forced back, possibly even fully or partially enveloped and destroyed in detail. At the very least, his armies should be able to regain their original positions for a far lower price than that opponent had paid to push them back in the first place.

In fact, the difference in price tags might—*might*—be enough to offset the Charisians' preposterous ability to conjure new manufactories out of thin air. In his bleaker moments, Duchairn suspected that hope was whistling in the dark, but what he knew for certain was that it was the only approach which offered even a *possibility* of success.

No doubt if Rainbow Waters' strategy had been honestly explained to Clyntahn—which, thank God, no one had any intention of doing—the Grand Inquisitor would have denounced it as defeatist, since it conceded the offensive to the enemy. He might even have been right about that. The problem was that any other strategy would simply lead to Mother Church's far speedier collapse.

Duchairn winced as he used the noun "collapse" even in the privacy of his own thoughts, but there was no point pretending. He and his hideously overworked staff had done a better job of propping up Mother Church's finances than he'd ever dared hope they might. Yet despite every miracle they'd worked, they were only rearranging deck chairs as the ship foundered beneath them. Revenue streams were better than projected, and the initial response to his "Victory Bonds" had been far more favorable than anticipated, yet the civilian side of the ecnomy teetered on the very brink of collapse. He'd declared freezes of both wages and prices and instituted rationing—managed by the parish priests—of the most critical commodties, backed up by the full power of the Inquisition, but that had only succeeded in driving the price increases underground. Unless they were willing to equate black marketeering with treason to the Jihad and resort to the Punishment for violations—which he flatly refused to do—that was only going to get worse, and nothing he or the Inquisition did seemed able to halt the increasingly steep discount of the Temple's new, printed marks in favor of gold and silver. As of his last monthly report, the "exchange rate" was running at over sixty-to-one in favor of hard coinage, and despite the persistent (and accurate, unfortunately) rumors that the Temple's more recently coined marks had been adulterated, the differential continued to climb. The steadily approaching failure of his fiscal structure was inevitable, and the ever more drastic lengths to which he'd gone to stave it off as long as possible were only going to make the crash even more catastrophic when it finally occurred.

By the time the summer campaign season began in northern Haven and Howard, the Mighty Host would have just under two million men in the field. The newly revitalized Army of God, straining every sinew over the winter, would have almost eight hundred thousand new troops with the colors;

combined with its surviving strength from the previous year, Mother Church would have just over a million men of her own.

That meant Maigwair would deploy very close to three million men this year, exclusive of anything Dohlar and the Border States might be able to sustain. That would be a far greater troop strength—far better equipped and with far more artillery support—than Mother Church had ever had before, although as Maigwair had just pointed out, the new AOG divisions wouldn't be available before June or July. They would, however, be coming up behind the Mighty Host rapidly, which would provide a cushion against Harchongese losses in the earlier part of the campaign season. In fact, the combined strength of the Host and the new AOG formations would be at least four times as great as the Inquisition's worst-case estimate of the numbers of men Cayleb and Stohnar could throw against them. The sheer firepower that represented was awesome to contemplate, and it seemed incredible—impossible—that it could be shattered the same way the Armies of the Sylmahn and of Glacierheart had been shattered the year before, especially with Rainbow Waters' cool, practical brain in command.

Yet it *could* happen. Charisians were as mortal and as fallible as anyone, whatever Clyntahn might say about demonic intervention. What had happened to them in the Kaudzhu Narrows demonstrated that clearly enough! And if anyone could hand them another defeat, this time on land, that anyone had to be Rainbow Waters. Yet in Rhobair Duchairn's estimation, even he had only an even chance—at the very best—of pulling it off. And if he failed, if the Charisians destroyed the Mighty Host the way they had every other army they'd faced—or even if they only drove it back with heavy casualties and the loss of much of its equipment—the Jihad was over.

They might find millions more men prepared to die in Mother Church's defense, men willing to charge into the enemy's guns with no more than raw courage, sheer faith, and their bare hands. But bare hands would be all they'd have, because Mother Church simply couldn't replace the weapons of the armies she had in the field now. Not again. Win or lose, live or die, her purse was effectively empty. They were at the last stretch of her resources, and if those resources weren't enough, her defeat was certain.

"Well," he sighed, draining off the last of his own beer and setting the stein back on his desk, "I suppose we'll find out whether or not the Earl can pull it off soon enough. In the meantime, I wonder what the Desnairians are up to?"

"Nothing good," Maigwair growled.

"Well, they did get badly burned in Shiloh," Duchairn pointed out more judiciously. "What happened to them at Geyra Bay didn't make it any better, either. I'm sure—" the irony in his tone glittered like a bared razor "—they're doing their very best to get back into the field against Mother Church's enemies."

"And if you really believe that, I've got some bottomland to sell you," Maigwair said dryly. "Just don't ask me what it's on the bottom *of*."

"Oh, I agree they're planning on keeping their heads as far down as they can—up their own arses, actually, as far as I can tell," Duchairn replied. "They *are* still getting at least some of their tithes through, though. In fact, they've even turned up the wick. I'm not sure exactly how they're managing it, but they're actually eleven percent *ahead* of their tithe obligations, even on the new, steeper schedule. Not only that, the Desnairian crown's bought something like twenty million marks of the new bond issue, too." The treasurer shook his head. "Must be even more gold in those mines than I thought there was."

"Trying to buy off Zhaspahr's inquisitors, are they?"

"Pretty much." Duchairn nodded. "On the other hand, you know, it's remotely possible you and I are a little too cynical where they're concerned. Zahmsyn keeps telling me that, anyway."

"Zahmsyn's telling you anything he thinks will keep Zhaspahr from deciding he's expendable," Maigwair said cynically. "Especially because, frankly, he *is*. Expendable, I mean."

And that, Duchairn reflected, was brutally true. Vicar Zahmsyn Trynair, who'd once been the mastermind of the Group of Four that truly plotted Mother Church's course—whatever canon law might say—had become little more than a cipher. Of course, looking back, Duchairn had his doubts about the degree to which Trynair (and everyone else) had always *thought* he was the Group of Four's mastermind in the first place.

Over the last year or so, especially, the treasurer had come to realize Clyntahn had been heading towards the destruction of Charis long before Erayk Dynnys' supposed failures gave him the excuse he needed. The only question in Duchairn's mind was his motive for deciding Charis must die. It was always possible, given the Grand Inquisitor's blend of gluttonous hedonism and fanaticism, that he truly had distrusted Charisian orthodoxy. Yet it was equally possible—and, frankly, more likely—that he'd seen the Jihad— or at least *a* jihad—as the strategy which would finally give the Inquisition total and unquestioned control of Mother Church and the entire world from the very start.

He doubted Clyntahn had ever imagined Mother Church's inevitable victory would be as costly as the Jihad had already proven, far less that it might not be quite as inevitable as he'd thought, but the cost in blood and agony— in *other people*'s blood and agony—wouldn't have fazed him for a moment. If a few million innocent people had to die in order for the Inquisition—and

Zhaspahr Clyntahn—to secure absolute power, that would have struck him as a completely acceptable price.

If Duchairn was right, Clyntahn had been pulling the rest of the Group of Four's puppet strings all along. And whatever the Grand Inquisitor's secret agenda might have been, Trynair had depended upon the twin strengths of his control of Grand Vicar Erek XVII and his ability to orchestrate smooth, skillful diplomatic strategies and policies, both within and without the ranks of the vicarate. To the secular rulers of Safehold, he'd been the face of Mother Church's will in the world; to the rest of the vicarate, he'd been the suave diplomat who adroitly balanced one faction of prelates against another. Yet now even the Grand Vicar was too terrified of Clyntahn's Inquisition to defy him, and all those other machinations, all that diplomatic footwork, meant absolutely nothing. At bottom, diplomats operated on credit, and if there was anyone in the world who understood the limitations of credit, Rhobair Duchairn was that man. When diplomacy failed, when your bets and your hedges and bluffs were called, only raw power truly counted, and Trynair was no longer a power broker.

I guess the Group of Four really has become the Group of Three, because there are only three poles of power left: the Army that has to fight the Jihad; the Treasury that has to somehow pay for the Jihad; and the Inquisition that has to keep people willing to support the Jihad. So it comes down to Allayn, Zhaspahr . . . and me. But at least Allayn and I recognize—or are willing to admit we recognize, anyway— that there are limits to the power we control. I truly think Zhaspahr isn't . . . and what's going to happen when he finally comes face-to-face with the truth?

Rhobair Duchairn had asked himself many questions over the past five years.

Very few of them had filled his blood with as much ice as that one did.

.VI.
HMS *Eraystor,* 22,
Wind Gulf Sea.

There was no dawn.

Somewhere above the solid cliffs of lightning-shot cloud the sun had no doubt heaved itself back into the heavens. Below those cliffs, the midnight gloom simply grew marginally less dark and visibility increased to a slightly greater circle of wind-driven, tortured white. It was possible to see the oncoming wave crests loom up above the solid, seething surface of blown spray at least a little sooner, even without the stuttering flash of Langhorne's rakurai, but the jarring, bone-shaking impact as each furious mountain of water slammed home was no less vicious. Belowdecks, the stench from backed up heads and the vomit of desperately seasick men was enough to turn a statue's stomach, and green-gray water roared along the decks, seeking voraciously for any loose gear, clawing at the heavy gaskets of Corisandian rubber that sealed the casemates' gun shields. Some of that water spurted past the gaskets, spraying inboard in fans of icy brine and then sluicing along the decks until it found its way into the bilges where the humming pumps could send it back overside.

HMS *Eraystor* drove onward, climbing each thirty-foot wave in turn, lifting her sharply raked stem towards the heavens while water thundered green and white and angry across her foredeck, charged headlong down her narrow, gangway-like side decks, flowed in solid, angry sheets across her quarterdeck. Higher and higher she climbed, spray cascading from her flared bows like some demented waterfall until she reached the crest and her forefoot thrust free of the water. Then her bow came down once more in a fresh explosion of spray, landing like the hammer of Kau-yung, and she went charging down into the valley, while the smoke pouring from her single funnel vanished almost before it could be seen, torn apart by the sixty-mile-an-hour wind that screamed around her upper works like some lost demon, seeking its way home to Shan-wei.

"Thank God we didn't wait for the colliers, Sir!"

Dahnel Bahnyface, *Eraystor*'s third lieutenant, didn't—quite—have to shout in Zhaikyb Gregori's ear, but it was a near thing even in the shelter of the ironclad's conning tower. On the open bridge, conversation would have been flatly impossible.

"I hope they're well clear of this," Gregori agreed.

Bahnyface had been a little surprised to see the first lieutenant in the conning tower when he climbed up the ladder from below. Vyktyr Audhaimyr, *Eraystor*'s second lieutenant, had the watch for another—Bahnyface checked the bulkhead chronometer—seven glorious minutes, and Gregori wasn't the sort of worrier who typically checked up on his watch standers as if he didn't trust them.

On the other hand, this wasn't exactly typical weather.

At five-eleven, Gregori was tall for a native Old Charisian, and he was forced to bend slightly to peer through one of the conning tower vision slits. In calm conditions, that slot was forty feet above the ship's waterline; in the current conditions, a constant spatter of spray blew in through it on the fringe of the howling wind. Now he straightened, wiped his face, and shook his head, his expression grim.

"With any luck, they saw this coming in time to take shelter in Shepherd Bay," he said. "Just pray to God they weren't trying to round Hill Island when it hit!"

Bahnyface nodded soberly. Of course, while he was praying for the coal-laden galleons following in the squadron's wake, he might just have a word or two with the Archangels on *Eraystor*'s behalf, as well. Langhorne knew the four-thousand-ton ironclad was incomparably more survivable than the original jury-rigged *Delthak*-class or the shallow-draft riverine ironclads which had followed them. She'd been designed for blue water—or to survive crossing it between bombardment missions, at least—with a raised forecastle and a gracefully flared bow. At right on three hundred feet in length, her hull was an immensely strong iron and steel box, and the great, throbbing engines at the heart of her made her independent of any galleon's canvas.

Of course, if anything were to *happen* to those engines or the whirling screws they drove. . . .

Don't even go there, Dahnel, he told himself firmly as he settled the hammer-islander on his head and tied the strings tightly under his chin.

The waterproof headgear would be little enough protection, but its back flap might at least keep solid sheets of water from running down his neck. Like many professional seamen, Bahnyface favored the stiffened version made of heavily tarred canvas, although others preferred the softer oilskin version. Personally, he wanted as much protection against the force of the spray coming at him as he could get, although he had to admit the stiffer versions tended to catch the wind better. He'd had half a dozen of them blown away over the course of his career, no matter how tightly he tied their laces.

And if there'd ever been a wind suitable to blow away hats, this was it, he reflected glumly. He didn't normally envy Anthynee Tahlyvyr, *Eraystor*'s chief engineer. He didn't really understand Tahlyvyr's fascination with steam and coal and oil, and the noisy, vibrating clangor of an engine room under full power—with pistons, crankshafts, and Langhorne only knew what else whirring and driving in every conceivable direction while oilers squirted lubrication at all the madly spinning bits and pieces—struck him as a near approximation of hell. Nor did he envy the sweating, swearing stokers feeding the voracious furnaces, especially in weather like this, when just staying on one's feet, much less avoiding serious injury while heaping shovels of coal into a roaring firebox, became a serious challenge.

Today, he'd have changed places with Tahlyvyr in a heartbeat, however. Failing that, he would really have preferred to stand his watch from inside the conning tower. Unfortunately, visibility was far too limited from in here. Even more unfortunately, while the bridge lookouts would be rotated into the conning tower's protection every half hour or so, the officer of the watch—who would very shortly be named Dahnel Bahnyface—had no one with whom to rotate. And about the best anyone's oilskins could manage on a day like this was to limit the influx of fresh, *cold* seawater. The water already inside his foul-weather gear would gradually warm to something more endurable if he could only avoid fresh infusions.

Not a chance in Shan-wei's hell, he thought philosophically. *Still, a man has to hope.*

He finished fastening the hammer-islander and bent over the deck log, scanning it for any special notifications or instructions which might have been added. It was up-to-date, he noticed, checking the time chop on the duty quartermaster's most recent entry. He took special note of the damage report about the scuttle which had been stove in amidships. He'd have to keep an eye on it and make sure the repairs were holding . . . although he rather suspected that if they gave way and a solid stream of ocean water seven inches in diameter came roaring through the opening someone in the vicinity was likely to notice even without his keeping a wyvern's eye on it.

"Anything special I should keep in mind, Sir?" he asked, tapping the deck log and raising an eyebrow at the first lieutenant. Gregori shook his head.

"No. I just came up to take a look before the Captain and I sit down with the Admiral for breakfast."

One of the telegraphsmen made a soft, involuntary gagging sound, and the first lieutenant chuckled.

"Trust me, Symmyns," he said, "*Eraystor*'s like riding a kid's pony beside what a regular galleon would be doing in seas like this!"

"Oh, I know that, Sir!" Zhak Symmyns was a Chisholmian, with a pronounced Harris Island accent, and his family had been fishermen for generations. "Reason I joined the Navy, though, was to get away from *little* boats." He grimaced. "M' stomach was never up t' the fishing, really—no matter how many times m' Da beat me for it. An' Langhorne knows, he tried hard enough t' beat it out of me!"

The other duty telegraphsman chuckled. Symmyns' susceptibility to seasickness was well known throughout *Eraystor*'s company, and Bahnyface wasn't at all surprised it was giving him problems in *this*. On the other hand, the fact that he and his messmates could joke about it probably said volumes about their estimate of *Eraystor*'s ability to *survive* conditions like these.

"Well, anyway," Gregori said with the callousness of a man who enjoyed a cast-iron stomach as he clapped Symmyns on the shoulder, "I'm looking forward to a nice, greasy rasher of bacon, fried eggs sunny-side up, and a fresh pot of cherrybean to wash it down."

The petty officer looked distinctly green around the gills, and the first lieutenant laughed again, then shook his head.

"All right, Symmyns! I'll stop giving you a hard time. And in case you hadn't heard, the cooks are serving as much hot, sweet oatmeal as you can hold for breakfast. Maybe you'll be able to keep that down."

"Sounds better nor eggs an' bacon, an' that's a fact, Sir," Symmyns said fervently.

"Just make sure you eat *something*," Gregori said more sternly. "I know it's not the easiest thing in weather like this, but you've been at sea long enough to know it's as important to keep your belly filled as it is to keep a boiler stoked."

"Aye, Sir." Symmyns nodded, and Gregori glanced at Bahnyface.

"I'll leave her in your hands, Dahnel. Besides," he chuckled again, "I'm pretty sure Vyktyr's counting the minutes out there on the bridge wing waiting for you."

"I'm counting them, too, Sir. Just not with the same sort of enthusiasm."

"Dahnel, if you were *enthusiastic* about going out there, I'd be sending you to the Bédardists, not the bridge. Trust me on that."

He nodded and headed down the conning tower ladder. Using the *exterior* ladders to climb down the superstructure was . . . contraindicated in the current sea state.

Bahnyface watched him go, then drew a deep breath, nodded to the glum-faced lookouts waiting in their own foul-weather gear, and undogged the armored door to the starboard bridge wing.

The wind's howl intensified abruptly as it tried to turn the heavy door into a hammer and the bulkhead into an anvil, but he managed to control it and stay un-crushed. Then he bent his head and shouldered forward, leaning into the teeth of the storm like a man leaning against a wall.

Vyktyr Audhaimyr looked just as soaked, cold, miserable—and delighted to see him—as Bahnyface had expected.

"Langhorne!" The second lieutenant had to lean forward, his mouth inches from Bahnyface's ear. "Am I glad to see you!" he continued, as if he'd read Bahnyface's mind.

"I can imagine!" Bahnyface bawled back as he clipped his canvas safety harness to one of the rigged lifelines. Those normally weren't required on the bridge, but today wasn't normal, and Captain Cahnyrs was strict about things like keeping his crew both aboard and undrowned. "I checked the log! Anything else you need to pass on to me?!"

"Not really!" Audhaimyr turned and pointed to the northeast, water pouring from his outstretched, oilskin-covered arm like a cataract. "We lost sight of *Cherayth's* running lights about two hours ago, but she didn't seem to be in any trouble and we haven't seen any signal rockets! I figure she's out there somewhere and we just can't see her anymore!"

Bahnyface nodded in understanding . . . and hoped to hell Audhaimyr was right. There were almost two hundred and fifty men aboard each of the *City*-class ships.

"*Bayport's* still where she's supposed to be!" Audhaimyr continued, pointing aft this time, and *Gairmyn's* on station to starboard! Haven't actually seen *Riverbend* in an hour or so, but *Gairmyn* signaled about fifteen minutes ago and *Riverbend* was on station astern of her then!"

Bahnyface nodded again, even more vigorously. If four of the 2nd Ironclad Squadron's five ships had actually managed to remain in such close company in weather like this and after a night like the one just past it damned well proved miracles still happened. And Audhaimyr was almost certainly right about *Cherayth.*

Almost certainly.

"All right!" he shouted in his friend's ear. "I've got her! Go get something hot to eat and grab some sleep!"

"Best offer I've had all night!" Audhaimyr punched him on the shoulder, jerked his head at his own lookouts—who'd been waiting with as little obvious impatience as possible (which wasn't very much) after handing over to their reliefs—unclipped his own safety line, and headed for the relative protection of the conning tower.

I sure as hell wish Sir Dustyn had gone ahead with those enclosed bridges of his, Bahnyface thought glumly, trying to find a corner where the solid, chesthigh bridge face would shield him from at least the worst of the wind-driven spray flying aft from the plunging bow. He found one—after a fashion— and grimaced at the unmanned wheel in the opensided wheelhouse at the center of the bridge. The helmsman had moved to his alternate station inside the conning tower, and more power to him. The last thing they needed would be for the man on the wheel to get himself numbed into exhaustion by the weather conditions!

I guess I'm happy for him, but I could do with a nice, snug, glassed-in perch of my own right about now! Of course—he ducked, then spat out a mouthful of the solid bucket full of seawater which had just hit him in the face anyway— *it'd have to be pretty damned* thick *glass to handle this kind of crap!*

Well, he understood the *King Haarahlds* would have exactly that sort of bridge, and at fourteen thousand tons, they probably wouldn't care as much about the weather as *Eraystor* did in the first place.

Hah! he thought glumly. *It'll just mean Shan-wei needs to come up with worse storms to keep 'em occupied!*

He held on to a stanchion, watching twin geysers spurt skyward through the hawse holes every time the ship's bow came down, and marveled at the furious energy roaring all about him. There was nothing quite like a storm at sea to remind a man just how puny he was against the scale of God's creation, and he tried not to think too hard about the thousands of miles yet before them.

They'd left the Trellheim Gulf well astern after stopping at the coaling station Earl Sharpfield had established at Put-In Bay on Hill Island on his original voyage to Claw Island. Hill Island was little more than two hundred miles from the mainland across Heartbreak Passage, but the mainland in question was Trellheim, and the "corsairs" weren't about to dispute the Charisian Empire's possession of an island they'd never much wanted anyway. Besides, how valuable was a mountain of coal? It would be harder than hell to haul away, you couldn't spend it, you couldn't sell it to anyone else— you couldn't even *eat* it!—which meant no self-respecting corsair wanted anything to do with it.

And if that disinterest just happened to avoid pissing off the most powerful navy in the history of the world, so much the better.

That didn't mean Admiral Zhastro and the rest of the squadron hadn't been just a teeny bit nervous during the outbound voyage. The *City*-class ships' biggest weakness was their designed endurance of only a thousand miles. Even with maximum bunker loads—including countless bags of the stuff piled in every available passage below decks—they could reach only about seventeen hundred. So if it had happened that the coaling station wasn't there when they arrived, they would've been far up shit creek. To be sure, there were additional galleons loaded with coal following behind them, but the whole point of deploying the 2nd Ironclad Squadron was that it could make the trip far faster than any wind-dependent galleon. Sitting at anchor in Put-In Bay—which wasn't the most sheltered anchorage in the world at the best of times—while its ships waited would not be the best use of its time. And that assumed no one else was in possession to prevent it from dropping anchor in the first place.

Fortunately, the coal pile and the small, lonely Marine garrison and battery protecting it had been exactly where they were supposed to be. So now the squadron was midway between Hill Island and Apple Island, the southernmost of The Teardrops, the chain of islands two thousand miles westnorthwest of Claw Island. Assuming *that* coaling station was still there, they would have the ineffable joy of filling the ships' voracious bunkers entirely by hand yet again. After which, they would set out once more—not directly for Claw Island, which would still be several hundred miles outside their cruising range, but for Angel Wing Island, five hundred miles northwest of Green Tree Island. Where (if *that* coal was still available), they would refuel yet again before setting out on the last twelve hundred miles to Claw Island. Altogether, they had over thirty-seven hundred miles still to go, and even with the squadron's speed, that was going to take another thirteen days, not counting the time spent coaling.

On the other hand, they'd already traveled almost *seventeen* thousand miles since they'd received their orders in the Gulf of Mathyas. In fact, they were steaming twenty thousand miles east to reach a destination less than six thousand miles *west* of the point at which they'd begun, since there were unfortunate things like continents in the way of a direct trip. It would still have been seven or eight thousand miles shorter to go south, round the southern tip of Howard, and then steam northwest and up through the Strait of Quieroz, but for some odd reason, the Kingdom of Delferahk and the South Harchong Empire hadn't been very receptive to allowing the ICA to establish the coaling stations the short-legged *Cities* needed along their coasts. If it was a matter of seizing and then hanging onto tiny, isolated island coaling stations, it was better to reach out eastward from Chisholm than to try to go west from Charis, especially when typical South Ocean weather and the southern Sea of Justice were taken into consideration. It was currently summer in those waters, but it wouldn't have been when the coaling stations were established, and while passing through Schueler Strait or Judgment Strait wasn't *too* dreadful—normally—in summer. . . .

The *Cities'* limited operational range was the real reason the *King Haarahlds* had been earmarked to spearhead the Imperial Charisian Navy's decisive offensive into the Gulf of Dohlar. A *King Haarahld* had almost twelve times *Eraystor's* cruising radius; she could have made the trip direct from Tellesberg without refueling at all, and once she'd reached the Gulf, she'd have had far more freedom of action, not to mention a main battery capable of demolishing *any* fortifications she might face. But the disastrous Delthak Works fire had put the *King Haarahlds* on hold, and the ICN was accustomed to getting on with the job in hand, whether it had the most ideal tools for it or not.

Which was how Mahtylda Bahnyface's little boy Dahnel found himself smack in the middle of a Wind Gulf Sea winter storm, clawing his way towards an improvised naval base he hoped like hell would be there when they reached it.

Join the Navy and see the world, Dahnee, he told himself with biting humor. *That's what those grinning bastards told you. And, by God, you've seen a lot of it since!* Of course—he squinted up into the howling wind, solid sheets of rain, and spray—*they never warned you about just how miserable you were going to be while you were seeing it!*

.VII.
City of Zion,
The Temple Lands.

The sound of the doorbell startled Alahnah Bahrns up out of the sketch she'd been working on. The short winter day had ended hours ago, and heavy snow swirled down over the city streets. It was unlikely that the trolleys would be running much longer if the snow was as deep as it looked like being. All of which suggested there wouldn't be many visitors wandering around those same streets.

The bell rang again, and she felt a sudden tingle run down her nerves. A tingle, little though she wanted to admit it, of fear. A woman of twenty-five years shouldn't be *afraid* when her doorbell rang in the middle of God's own city! But there was so much uncertainty, so much fear. . . .

The bell rang a third time, and she gave herself a little shake. One thing it obviously wasn't was someone here to arrest her! If someone had come to do that, they'd hardly stand patiently in the hall and ring the bell again and again. The thought actually made her chuckle, and she crossed her apartment's small sitting room to open the security slide in the stout door. She peeked out onto the landing, and her eyebrows rose. Then she quickly unlocked the door and pulled it wide.

"Uncle Gahstahn! What in the world are you doing here at this hour?"

"Hello, Lahna," he said, using the childhood nickname that only he and Krystahl ever applied to her.

She opened her arms and embraced him, despite the snow clotted on the outside of his heavy coat. Then she caught him by one gloved hand and drew him into the apartment. She couldn't afford a very big fire, especially these days, but the room was well insulated and she'd hung heavy, warm blankets as extra curtains to cut down on the windows' drafts.

"Take off that coat. Let me make you some tea."

"I really can't stay, Lahna," he said, and her smile faded as his expression registered.

"What do you mean, you can't stay?" Her grip on his hand tightened. "You just came over ten blocks to get here on a night like this! Surely you can sit down long enough to let me fix you a cup of hot *tea!*"

"No, really." He shook his head. "I just . . . stopped by on my way."

"On your way where?" Her eyes narrowed. "Uncle Gahstahn, you're starting to frighten me."

"Oh, I didn't mean to do that!" He shook his head again, harder, and summoned up a smile. It was rather feeble looking. "I just . . . I just wanted to ask you if you've seen Krys in the last day or two."

"If I've what?" Alahnah blinked. Then her face tightened. "What do you mean if *I've* seen her? Are you saying she hasn't been home in *two days*?!"

For a moment, he looked as if he wasn't going to answer. But then his shoulders slumped and he nodded.

"I haven't seen her since Wednesday, right after mass," he said heavily. "She said she was going out to run an errand. That's the last I've seen of her."

Alahnah's fingers rose to her lips and her eyes were huge.

"You've checked the hospitals? Talked to the Guard?"

"Of course I have!" Concern for his daughter brought Gahstahn Bahrns' response out more sharply than he'd intended, and he laid his free hand quickly on her shoulder, his expression contrite.

"Of course I have," he repeated more quietly. "Nothing. It's like she disappeared into thin air. That's why I was hoping you might've seen her. Might have some idea where she went on that 'errand' of hers."

"Oh, Langhorne," Alahnah breathed.

"You *do* know where she went?" Gahstahn's eyes, the same hazel as his daughter's, widened with sudden hope.

"Uncle Gahstahn, she told me she was going to meet with friends." Alahnah released his hand to put both her own hands on his upper arms. "She said one of them was Sebahstean Graingyr. They were going . . . going to discuss a petition."

"A petition?" Gahstahn repeated sharply, but there was less surprise in his voice than Alahnah had expected. Or than she wanted to hear. "A petition to whom?"

"Vicar Rhobair," she said quietly. "They wanted . . . they wanted him to . . . look into their concerns about all the arrests the Inquisition's been making."

"Sweet Bédard." Gahstahn closed his eyes, his face sagging suddenly. "I knew she hiding something from me—I *knew* it!" He opened his eyes and managed another fleeting caricature of a smile. "I could always tell when one of you was up to something. But I told her—I *warned* her—that sometimes, in the middle of something like the Jihad, you can't just. . . ."

His voice trailed off, and Alahnah nodded slowly while tears welled at the corners of her eyes.

"We don't know—don't *know*—that . . . that anything *bad's* happened," she half whispered.

"When was the last time Krystahl didn't warn me if she wasn't going to be home?" Gahstahn asked bleakly. "At the very least she would've sent a message!" He shook his head. "She'd never have done something that would have caused me to worry this much—not willingly, anyway."

"What . . . what are we going to do?" Alahnah asked in a very small voice.

"*We* aren't going to do anything," her uncle told her sharply. "You're going to stay entirely out of this, young lady!" She opened her mouth to protest, but he shook her sharply by the shoulders. "Listen to me, Lanah! I don't want you doing anything that could get you in trouble, too. If . . . if Krys is already in trouble, you need to promise me you'll stay as far away from it as you can. I don't want anything happening to *both* my daughters!"

The tears broke free, rolling down her cheeks, and he gathered her into a fierce embrace.

"Then what are *you* going to do?" she asked in an even tinier voice, one that was almost inaudible over the wind blowing about the apartment building.

"I'm going to find Krystahl." His voice wasn't a lot louder than hers, but it was carved out of granite. "I've checked with the Guard, and I've checked the hospitals. I haven't checked with the Inquisition. Yet."

"But if . . . if—"

She broke off, unable to complete the sentence, and his expression was as granite-like as his voice.

"If the Inquisition's arrested Krys," he said unflinchingly, "it has to be a mistake. I can't even begin to imagine anything *she* could've done to get herself into that kind of trouble, but young Graingyr and his lot . . ." He tossed his head, his worried eyes touched with a flicker of anger. "I could see *them* doing something stupid, and if she was in the wrong place at the wrong time, the Inquisition might have taken her in for questioning." He swallowed. "Even if they did, they have to let me at least talk to her—that's the Inquisition's own law! And when I talk to them, explain that they must've made a mistake, I'm sure they'll release her as soon as they can."

Alahnah nodded quickly, although she was sure of nothing of the sort. Neither was he, she thought; he just wasn't going to admit that to *her.*

"You'll tell me what you find out?" The question came out as a command, but he shook his head.

"If I can. But if the . . . misunderstanding's more serious than I hope it is, I may not be talking to you for a while." His lips twitched another smile. "I'm sure we'll get it all straightened out eventually, but for now it would be best if I didn't get you involved in . . . anything."

She started to protest, then closed her mouth and nodded unhappily.

"Well," he said with forced brightness, "I suppose I'd better be going. If I'm lucky, I'll find Father Charlz in his office. We've known each other a long time, Lanah. I'm sure he'll be as shocked as I am by the notion that the Inquisition could have any reason to take *Krystahl* into custody!"

.VIII.

HMS *Fleet Wing*, 18,
Gulf of Dohlar,
and
Manchyr Palace,
City of Manchyr,
Princedom of Corisande,
Empire of Charis.

"A re you all right, Hektor?" Lieutenant Hahlbyrstaht asked quietly, and Hektor Aplyn-Ahrmahk looked up from his wineglass quickly.

The cabin provided to HMS *Fleet Wing*'s captain was tiny compared to similar quarters aboard larger ships, but it didn't quite seem that way tonight. The weather had been unseasonably warm for the last three days, so the broad, diamond-paned stern windows were opened wide on a beautiful view of the silver moon, just rising from the waters of the Gulf of Dohlar, and the wind scoop fitted to the skylight sent a brisk, cooling breeze through it. Hektor and his first lieutenant shared supper at least three times each five-day, catching up on all the innumerable decisions involved in commanding even the smallest warship, and this evening weather and breeze had combined to make it a far more pleasant meal than many. But Hektor had been noticeably distracted, and Hahlbyrstaht looked concerned.

"Hmmm?" Hektor's eyes were a bit blank for a moment, as if he'd been staring at something only he could see. Then he smiled quickly.

"Sorry, Zosh." He shook his head. "I'm afraid I'm just a little distracted at the moment. Thinking about Irys."

He smiled again, more broadly, and Hahlbyrstaht smiled back.

"I can understand that," he told his CO. "I may not be married yet, but Marzh plans to fix that as soon as I get home! And I have to admit there are times I find myself thinking about her . . . a lot. Besides," his expression sobered a bit, "it's just about time for the twins, isn't it?"

"Yes." Hektor nodded. "Yes, it is, and to be honest, that's a big part of the reason I'm thinking about her at the moment. I'm sure she's fine. Pasquale knows Daivyn's going to make sure he has the best healers in Corisande looking after his big sister! But I've discovered it's a lot easier for my head to feel confident about that than it is for the rest of me to go along with it."

"Probably be something wrong with you if it wasn't. And it's not like the two of you had a whole lot of time together before the Navy sent you back off to sea, either."

"I guess not," Hektor acknowledged, although both of them knew the Navy would have done nothing of the sort to any member of the imperial family, especially given the damage to his arm, not to mention the minor matter of just whom he was married to, if the family member in question had objected.

"Well, I think we're just about done, anyway," his first lieutenant said. "I can't think of anything important we haven't already covered, anyway. Can you?"

"No, not really." Hektor's smile turned crooked. "Of course, we just finished agreeing I'm a little distracted this evening."

"Fair enough. You deserve the chance to be a lonely husband every now and then." Hahlbyrstaht touched him on the shoulder in a display of affection he wouldn't have allowed himself in front of the crew. The captain's sacrosanct dignity must be maintained at all times, even in so small a ship. Possibly even *especially* in so small a ship. "Why don't you sit down and write her a letter or something while I discuss that sail survey with the Bos'un? If anything else occurs to you, you can always tell me about it later."

"Do you know, I think that might not be such a bad idea. Thanks, Zosh. And I don't care what anyone says about you—for a Chisholmian, you're not a bad fellow at all!"

"Just sucking up to the Captain, Your Grace," Hahlbyrstaht told him with something far more like a grin than a smile, and excused himself from the cabin.

Hektor smiled after him, then pushed back from the cabin table. He looked around the compartment, taking in its familiar confines in the light of the lamp swaying gently from the overhead, then walked across to the wide-open stern windows. Unlike larger vessels, *Fleet Wing* boasted no stern-walk, but he settled on one of the bench seats built across the windowsills and leaned back against the inward-curving hull that framed the schooner's oval stern. He thrust one leg over the windowsill and gazed out over his ship's bubbling wake, listening to the water laugh and gurgle around her rudder as *Fleet Wing* made good almost seven knots on a stiff topgallant breeze from broad on her starboard quarter. The wind scoop sent enough fresh, clean breeze through the cabin to ruffle the pages of the book lying open on his cot and pluck at his dark hair like a lover's gentle fingers, and the newly risen moon rode broad and bright on the horizon, like a polished silver coin, while its reflection danced on the moving mirror of the sea.

Anyone looking at him could have been excused for thinking he actually saw a single bit of it.

"I'm here, love," he said to the vista of the sea. "How are you feeling?"

"A little nervous, frankly," Irys Aplyn-Ahrmank replied from far distant Manchyr. She leaned back in an armchair, wrapped in a soft, warm robe, with her feet propped up and a carafe of hot chocolate at her elbow. The sky outside her bedchamber window glowed with the first faint brushstrokes of a tropical dawn, but she'd been up for the last two hours, timing the contractions.

"God, I *wish* I could be with you!" his voice murmured in her earplug. "I should've stayed, damn it!"

"We both agreed you needed to go with Sir Dunkyn." There was a trace of scold in her tone. "And I'm not some frightened little farm girl wondering if the sisters will get there in time, you know! Besides, with the exception of Alahnah, there's never been a pregnancy on all of Safehold that was more closely monitored than this one."

"And I'm still the father and I should still be there," he argued. Then he sighed. "Which doesn't change the fact that I can't be. Or that God only knows how many billions of fathers over the years haven't been able to be there, either. For that matter, I wonder how many hundreds of thousands of other Navy and Army fathers are in exactly the same boat right this minute?"

"Probably a lot. And there are probably even more who know they'll have a child they've never met waiting when they get home again, too."

"A child they've never even seen before." Hektor inhaled deeply. "At least I'll have one hell of a lot more than that," he continued, gazing up at the silver moon while his contact lenses showed him Irys' nod.

"Yes, you will. And if you can't be here physically, at least we've got this, too." She touched her ear and the invisible plug nestled deep within it and smiled a bit tremulously. "I can't even begin to tell you how much it means to hear your voice just now!"

"Well, of course you can, thanks to Zosh for being so tactful!" Hektor chuckled. "And to you for being so clever with the timing! If you get a move on, I'll be able to be with you for the actual birth."

"Get a *move on?!*" Irys glowered, then inhaled sharply as another spasm went through her abdomen. She paused, waiting out the contraction, then shook her head. "Listen, sailor—this is all *your* fault. Don't you go getting smart-arsed now that I'm stuck doing all the work!"

"Nothing smart-arsed about it," he said virtuously, with a lurking smile. "Just making a point. I've got maybe thirteen hours before Stywyrt's going to come banging on my cabin door with a pot of that horrible cherrybean he's gotten so besotted with."

Hektor shuddered fastidiously. He didn't have a formal steward—schooners *Fleet Wind*'s size didn't run to enough personnel for that—so Stywyrt Mahlyk had assigned himself to that duty, as well as captain's coxswain. And he'd turned out to have rather . . . robust ideas about what the job entailed.

"It's a good thing he makes you eat properly!" Irys scolded in a voice that was commendably stern, despite the twinkle in her hazel eyes. "I think it was wonderful of Sir Dunkyn to lend him to you!"

"Starting to look more like a permanent adoption," Hektor retorted. "But you're right; I'm lucky to have him," he acknowledged. "Which doesn't change the fact that once he decides it's time for wakey-wakey, I won't be able to sit staring soulfully up at any moons while I talk to myself and encourage myself to 'Breathe, sweetheart! Now *push!*' So, since I'd really like to be able to do just that, could you just speak to the children about possibly moving right along now?"

▼   ▼   ▼

"I don't want to sound impatient or anything," Irys Aplyn-Ahrmahk panted, "but I'd *really* like this to be over!"

She didn't look what anyone would have called her best just at the moment. Her dark hair was spiky with sweat, fatigue shadowed her hazel eyes, and pain tightened her mouth as the sun slipped steadily below the western horizon. She'd had a long, wearying day . . . and looked like having an even longer night.

"Of course you would, dear," Lady Sahmantha Gahrvai said, wiping her forehead with a damp cloth. "Now breathe."

"I am breathing—I *am* breathing!" Irys panted even harder. "I've been doing it for *hours* now! And while I'm thinking about it, this is a damned undignified way to go about this! Why hasn't someone invented a better one?!"

"Do you know, Mairah," Lady Sahmantha said, "she probably thinks she's the first one to think of that. Scary, isn't it?"

"I imagine it goes through most women's minds about the time they try motherhood for the first time," the tallish woman on the other side of Irys' bed said with a smile. Her golden hair and gray eyes marked her as a foreigner here in Corisande, but the Prince of Corisande's older sister clung tightly to her hand, gripping even harder whenever the labor pains peaked. "Of course, I wouldn't know from personal experience, you understand. Yet, at least. *I* was clever enough to marry someone who already had five children. Acquired an entire family without going through all of this . . . botheration."

Lady Mairah Breygart lifted her nose with an audible sniff, and Irys laughed. It was a rather breathless, exhausted laugh after eleven hours of labor, but a laugh nonetheless.

"And the fact that your husband's been off on the mainland for the last year has nothing to do with how you've continued to avoid all this 'botheration'?" she demanded.

"It does rather require the prospective father and mother to spend a certain amount of time in one another's company, Your Highness," Lady Sahmantha pointed out. She gave Mairah a look that combined humor and sympathy in equal measure. "And there's a certain degree of enthusiasm involved, as well. Of course, *some* of us seem to have more of that enthusiasm than others . . . judging from the results, at least."

"Oh, my! I see she knows you even better than I thought she did, you shameless hussy!" a beloved voice from the Gulf of Dohlar murmured in her ear.

"Oh! *Oh!*" Irys shook her head. "Don't you *dare* make me laugh . . . Lady Sahmantha!" she added a bit hastily.

"Best thing for you, actually, Your Highness," the Pasqualate sister standing beside her bed said pragmatically before anyone could notice the delay. "These youngsters have their own timetable. They'll get here when they get here, and anything that helps you pass the time while we wait is worthwhile."

"I'm glad everybody else can be so . . . prosaic about this, Sister Kahrmyncetah," Irys said a bit tartly. "It's just a little more exhausting from my perspective."

"Of course it is." Lady Sahmantha leaned closer to lay a cool hand on Irys' cheek. "As the Archangel Bédard said, 'That which we obtain too easily, we esteem too lightly.'" The hand on Irys' cheek stroked gently. "Trust me, you'll never esteem these children 'too lightly,' Your Highness. I promise you."

"I know." Irys reached out with the hand that wasn't clutching Mairah Breygart's. She gripped Countess Anvil Rock's free hand tightly, and Rysel Gahrvai's wife smiled down at her, the streaks of silver in her dark hair glinting in the steadily fading sunlight pouring through the chamber windows. "I know, and I'm so glad you're here!"

"I promised your mother I would be years ago, Irys. Just before she died, when we knew we were losing her. She'd be so proud of you, love. You and Daivyn both."

Tears welled in Irys' eyes for just a moment as Sahmantha dropped the formality she normally observed since Irys' return to Corisande, but then a fresh spasm went through her, and she grunted in pain and panted harder than ever.

"You're coming along exactly on schedule, Your Highness," Sister Kahrmyncetah said reassuringly. "Trust me. You're almost through transition now. I know it's exhausting, but it always takes a little longer with twins, especially for a first-time mother, you know. Everything looks just fine so far."

Irys nodded, even as she panted, and her hazel eyes glowed with gratitude for the reassurance.

The risk of complications with twins, she knew, was higher than with singleton births. Despite the deliberate limitations of the *Holy Writ*, however, the Order of Pasquale turned out superbly trained obstetricians and mid-wives. Pasqualate physicians might not know a thing about germ theory, but they knew all about the *Book of Pasquale*'s instructions for the consecration of hands and instruments with Pasquale's Cleanser (otherwise known as carbolic acid), alcohol, and boiling water and they were well taught on every conceivable complication. They also knew how to abstract the natural antibiotic in fleming moss and scores of other effective drugs from dozens of Safeholdian plants, many of which had been carefully genegineered by Pei Shan-wei's terraforming team for that very purpose. They even understood blood-typing and transfusions, and Pasqualate surgeons had at least as much knowledge of human anatomy as any pre-space doctor of Old Terra. There were still complications and conditions they couldn't cure, simply because they lacked the tools, but however short of advanced technology Safehold might be, deaths in childbirth were extremely rare, and the infant mortality rate compared favorably with Old Terra's mid-twentieth century. So when a Pasqualate midwife offered reassurance, she knew what she was talking about.

In this particular Pasqualate midwife's case, however, rather more than the *Book of Pasquale* was involved. Captain Chwaeriau was going to be very upset when she discovered Princess Irys had gone into labor less than ten hours after her own current undisclosed but undoubtedly important—and highly secret—errand had taken her away from Manchyr, yet Irys had accepted it philosophically. No doubt she missed the *seijin* assigned to watch over her brother and her—Nimue Chwaeriau had become at least a much a personal friend and member of her household as Mairah Breygart—but in this case, Sister Kahrmyncetah made a satisfactory substitute.

No one seemed entirely certain where the sister had come from, and Lieutenant Hairahm Bahnystyr, the head of Irys' personal protective detail, had made no secret of his initial qualms when she suddenly . . . turned up yesterday evening. It was obvious he would have felt much happier if Captain Chwaeriau had been there to vouch for her. Unfortunately, the captain hadn't been available and he'd had to settle for a mere archbishop's judgment.

To be fair, while Klairmant Gairlyng might not be a *seijin* and highly trained armswoman, he *was* the senior prelate of the Church of Charis in Corisande. That gave him a certain authority in the eyes of even the most suspicious bodyguard. Despite that, Lieutenant Bahnystyr might have felt a bit less reassured if he'd known Archbishop Klairmant had never met Sister Kahrmyncetah until six hours before the two of them turned up at Manchyr Palace.

By now, however, Gairlyng, like virtually everyone else in Corisande, realized there'd always been dozens of *seijins* working their hidden ways, discharging their hidden tasks, all about Safehold without anyone ever seeing them or, at least, recognizing them for what they were. Indeed, the archbishop had had rather more experience with *seijins* than most, and while *Seijin* Nimue hadn't been around to introduce Sister Kahrmyncetah to Lieutenant Bahnystyr, she'd at least warned Gairlyng the Pasqualate was coming. And she'd made it clear, without ever quite coming out and saying so, that Sister Kahrmyncetah might also legitimately have been called *Seijin* Kahrmyncetah.

Under the circumstances, Archbishop Klairmant had felt no qualms about introducing Sister Kahrmyncetah to Father Zhefry, Irys' attending physician. And if the sandy-haired, Siddarmark-born Pasqualate under-priest cherished any suspicions of his own about Sister Kahrmyncetah's origins, he'd kept them to himself. He'd cheerfully accepted her assistance, and it had quickly become evident that she was one of the finest midwives he'd ever encountered.

Which I darned well should be, Sister Kahrmyncetah thought, touching Irys' wrist lightly to monitor her pulse and respiration with an acuity even the best-trained, most experienced flesh-and-blood human being could never have equaled. *Unlike Merlin's*, my *high-speed data interface works just fine, and as good as the Pasqualates are, Owl's medical files are a hell of a lot better! Irys' pregnancy's been almost textbook from the beginning, but no way is the inner circle taking any chances with* this *delivery!*

"She's right, you know, sweetheart," another voice said in Irys' ear. "I think I had an easier labor with Alahnah than you're having, but there was only one of her, for Heaven's sake!" A soft, sympathetic chuckle came through the invisible earplug, and Irys smiled, despite the exhausting pangs of birth, as she listened to the voice only she and Sister Kahrmyncetah could hear. "I *wish* I could've stayed for this," Empress Sharleyan went on, "but you're doing wonderfully, and Sahmantha's right about how proud your mother would be of you. Of how proud *I* am of you!"

"I appreciate the encouragement," she gasped—to Sharleyan, as well as those who were physically present—as the current contraction eased. She sagged back, breathing hard and soaked with sweat. "It's just that no one warned me what hard *work* this was going to be!"

"Oh, nonsense!" Lady Sahmantha chided with a chuckle of her own. She disengaged her hand from Irys' grip to change the cool compress on the princess' forehead. "We did so warn you! You just didn't believe us."

"Did too!" Irys retorted, than grunted harshly as the next contraction hit. She panted hard, face tight with pain, and her fingers squeezed Lady Mairah's hand like a vise.

"You're doing *fine*, love!" Sharleyan said in her ear.

"She's right, sweetheart," Hektor agreed. "I'm *so* proud of you! Now just breathe!"

"And remember not to push yet," Sister Kahrmyncetah reminded her out loud. "I know you want to, but the babies aren't quite ready for you to start that yet."

Irys nodded convulsively, and one of the Pasqualate lay sisters began lighting the chamber's lamps as the sun dipped completely below the horizon beyond its windows.

▼   ▼   ▼

"Damn, I wish I could be there!" Hektor complained on a channel Irys couldn't hear. "I know I can't, but—"

He broke off, still sitting in the window, although the moon had long since disappeared. It wouldn't be that many more minutes until dawn, he thought, and once the first rim of the sun showed itself, Mahlyk was going to turn up with the pot of cherrybean. And when he figured out his youthful captain had been sitting up all night staring out the stern windows, he was going to want to know why.

"I guess I've said that a time or two already, haven't I?" he said ruefully.

"Just a time or two," another voice agreed.

"Well, I've only got another hour or two before Stywyrt starts knocking on the door. If the babies haven't put in an appearance by then. . . ." He shook his head.

"Stywyrt Maklyk's a very good man, Hektor!" Sharleyan scolded him. "And he's not going to take any nonsense when it comes to bullying you into taking care of yourself, either."

"No, Mother, he isn't," he agreed, never taking his attention from the images of a bedchamber in Corisande, projected onto his contact lenses. "But that doesn't mean he's not going to be a dead pain in the arse if he drags me away just about the time Irys is giving birth. I could love him like a brother and still want to drop him overside with a roundshot for company if *that* happens!"

Empress Sharleyan chuckled. It was late morning of the next day in Tellesberg, but the afternoon outside her chamber window was gray and overcast. A steady, drenching rain sifted down—not heavy, but with a patience that suggested it meant to linger for a while—and she sat gazing out those windows with a cup of hot chocolate cradled in her hands. The fresh smell of the rain blew in through the open window and Princess Alahnah lay sleeping peacefully on the rug at her feet, favorite blanket clutched in one small fist and surrounded by a landscape of blocks, stuffed animals, and picture books. A pot of chocolate stood on a small burner at Sharleyan's elbow, beside a plate of sugared almond cookies, and she'd informed her staff—including Sairaih Hahlmyn—that she would be enjoying a quiet day with her daughter. She took "working" time to spend with Alahnah only very rarely, and that staff—especially Sairaih and Sergeant Edwyrd Seahamper—could be counted on to guard her privacy like zealous dragons when she did.

It was deeply ironic, she thought, but it was actually far easier for one of the most powerful monarchs in the world to find a moment of privacy than it was for a mere navy lieutenant. Surely it should have been the other way around!

Unfortunately, it wasn't.

"We're all keeping an eye on her, you know," she said now. "And I hope you know how much we all wish you *could* be there with her in the flesh."

"Of course I do." Hektor smiled slightly, although his expression was rather more anxious than he'd allowed his voice to sound whenever he spoke to Irys. "And God knows I'm a hell of a lot luckier than any other sea officer in the same position! Doesn't make me wish I couldn't be there holding her hand, though."

"So do we all," Cayleb put in from the Siddar City breakfast table he was currently sharing with Aivah Pahrsahn and Merlin Athrawes. "And at least Numue's there to stand in for the lot of us!"

"Yes, I am," Sister Kahrmyncetah said a bit tartly, "although I'm just a *bit* occupied at the moment myself, you know!"

Unlike any of the other parties to the conversation, she had no need to speak aloud, thanks to her built-in communicator.

▼ ▼ ▼

"Oh, *my!*" Irys said suddenly, twenty minutes later, and Sister Kahrmyncetah smiled as she leaned forward to see the top of a tiny head.

"Father," she said, turning to look over her shoulder at the under-priest just coming back into the bedchamber, "I think you've timed it pretty well."

"Ah?" Father Zhefry crossed quickly and took his patient's hand in a light, comforting clasp. He glanced down and then looked back up, smiling as he met her weary eyes. "Sister's right, my dear," he said. "I *did* time that chocolate break well, if I do say so myself. And while I was away you went right on doing all the heavy work without me. Well done, Your Highness!"

"I didn't have a lot of choice, Father." Irys' voice was rough-edged and hoarse with exhaustion and more than a little pain, but there was still humor in it, and the Pasqualate nodded encouragingly. He'd expected the princess to handle the birth process better than most young first-time mothers, but she'd exceeded even his expectations. "I'll be just as happy to be done with it, though!"

"I imagine you will. But if you'll just reach down here. . . ." He guided the hand he held lower, laying its palm very gently on the scalp of the head just beginning to become visible.

"Ooooooh. . . ."

Her eyes went very wide, her pain-taut mouth relaxed in an enormous smile, and she looked up to meet Sister Kahrmyncetah's sapphire eyes. Then she gasped as a fresh contraction went through her. She took her hand from her baby's head to grip Lady Mairah's hand once more and gasped harshly, gritting her teeth and pushing hard, as she'd been taught.

"It's two steps forward and one step back for the next little bit," Father Zhefry said, "but you're making wonderful progress! This youngster will be along before very much longer, I promise!"

"And . . . then . . . I get . . . to go to work . . . on his . . . brother . . . or . . . sister!" Irys panted.

"Yes, you do, sweetheart," a beloved voice said in her ear. "But you'll do just as wonderfully with her as you're doing with him, and I know you won't believe this for a minute, but you've never been more beautiful in your life. I mean," the voice was rich with humor and deep with love, "fair's fair, and you look absolutely *awful* in a lot of ways, but *I* think you're the most beautiful sight I've ever seen. And it looks like you're even going to pull this off before Stywyrt comes barging in. Who says Corisandian girls are never on time?"

Father Zhefry had no idea why his patient should laugh suddenly, even through her contractions, but he approved entirely.

.IX.
Mistress Marzho's Fine Milliners,
City of Zion,
The Temple Lands.

That's your best design yet, Alahnah!" Zhorzhet Styvynsyn smiled in delight. "I especially like what you did with the slash lizard fur on the facing!"

"I'm glad you like it." Alahnah's answering smile was smaller and more fleeting. "Do you think Mistress Marzho will like it, too?"

"I'm *sure* she will." Zhorzhet tilted her head to one side. "What's worrying you, Alahnah?"

"Worrying me?" Alahnah laughed. It wasn't a very convincing laugh, and she knew it, but she shook her head quickly. "Nothing's worrying me, Zhorzhet. Well, nothing but whether or not Mistress Marzho's going to approve my design!"

"If that's really all that's worrying you, then you can stop right now," Zhorzhet told her. "Trust me, that's exactly what Vicar Tahdayus is looking for, and his wife will love it. It'll go perfectly with her hair and that new snow lizard coat he bought for her last month."

"Oh, good." Alahnah managed a slightly more genuine-looking smile. "I was really worried when she gave me the design commission. I mean, I knew she'd double-check everything and she wouldn't approve anything she didn't think would work, but it's still a big step from shopgirl to assistant designer."

"Oh, sweetheart!" Zhorzhet put an arm around her shoulders and hugged her quickly. "You've worked hard, and you've got a really good eye for colors and forms. I'm not a *bit* surprised Mistress Marzho's offered you the promotion. And you deserve every bit of it, too!"

"Thank you." Alahnah hugged her back. "That means a lot coming from you, especially, Zhorzhet."

"Just remember I'm never untruthful . . . except for occasionally with a client who has more money than is good for her and no designer sense at all!"

Alahnah surprised herself with a giggle, and Zhorzhet released her. From the look in the older woman's blue eyes, she wasn't remotely convinced their employer's approval or disapproval of Alahnah's design was the only thing on her mind. But she'd never been the sort to pry; that was one of the things Alahnah most liked about her. If Alahnah asked her for help, she knew Zhorzhet would give it in a heartbeat, but there were some things no one could help with.

And there are also things you don't involve friends in if you can help it, she reminded herself sternly.

She nodded to Zhorzhet and headed for the display window Mistress Marzho had asked her to rearrange before lunchtime. It was snowing again—heavily—and they didn't expect much walk-in business on a day like this, so she should have plenty of time to do it right. She would have preferred brighter sunshine outside the shop windows, though. The dull, grey daylight leaking in through the cloud cover and snow was going to mute and deaden the finer gradations of color.

Well, you can always rearrange it again when we finally get a day with actual sunlight for a change, she thought. *And in the meantime, it'll give you something to do besides worry.*

She bit her lip at that thought as she stepped into the window bay and began carefully taking down the current display of hats and mannequins. She told herself again—very firmly—that worrying never did any good. As Langhorne said, "Sufficient unto the day is the evil thereof, yet I tell you that that day will pass, as all evil passes. The worry within you will neither hasten or slow its passing, but rather put all fear from you and place your faith in God, Who will lift the burden of that uncertainty from you as He lifts all burdens."

Unfortunately, she'd always found that particular injunction a little difficult to obey at the best of times. After almost two full days of silence from Uncle Gahstahn—on top of whatever had happened to Krystahl—worry and, yes, *fear*, had become her constant companions. She considered sharing that fear with Zhorzhet, but only briefly. She'd never actually discussed Krystahl's concerns—or her own, for that matter—with Zhorzhet. She suspected the older woman would have offered a sympathetic ear, but that wasn't the sort of conversation you involved people in. You could never be *sure* how they'd react, or how—and to whom—they might repeat it. And even leaving that aside, it could be dangerous for whoever you talked to. If there was any real basis for her worry over her cousin and her uncle, it was probably because Krystahl had had exactly that sort of conversation with the wrong person, and she liked Zhorzhet far too much to involve her in anything that might get her into trouble.

▼　　▼　　▼

Zhorzhet Styvynsyn frowned as she updated the master ledger.

She had no idea what was preying on Alahnah's spirit, but one thing she did know was that it wasn't simple worry over whether or not Marzho Alysyn would approve the sketch design for Vicar Tahdayus' wife's hat. Oh, it was an important step for the younger woman, a commission that could go a long way towards establishing her as a premier designer in her own right. But Alahnah had known for years that it was a step she'd be taking eventually. The girl simply had too much talent for it to be any other way, and Marzho had always believed in grooming and supporting true talent.

Could it be a man problem? To the best of Zhorzhet's knowledge, Alahnah wasn't keeping company with anyone. She wasn't a flighty girl, and Zhilbert Ahtkyn, the young man to whom she'd been betrothed, had volunteered for service in the Army of God. He'd been assigned to the Army of the Sylmahn, and her last letter from him was over three months old. Given what had happened to that army, a girl like Alahnah wasn't going to be thinking much about other men—not yet, at least.

But *something* was obviously troubling her. On the other hand, God only knew there were troubles enough for anyone these days. She snorted softly at the thought. Some of those troubles were going to be worse for other people very shortly, and she'd take profound satisfaction in helping that happen. With any luck, and a little time—

The inner door to the shop's vestibule slammed open so violently it actually knocked the bell above it off its mounting arm. The bell landed with a discordant jangle and Zhorzhet's head snapped up.

Her eyes widened as two Temple Guardsmen crowded through the door, and then they darkened as an under-priest and a monk in the purple of the Order of Schueler followed them into the shop.

One hand rose to her throat and she swallowed hard. Then she wrapped her fingers around the locket on the fine chain around her neck. She pulled and popped it loose, concealing it in her palm as she stepped around the counter to greet the newcomers.

"Gentlemen," she said, inclining her head to the guardsmen, then bowed more deeply to the cleric. "Father. How can Mistress Marzho's serve you this afternoon?"

"I need a word with one of your employees," the under-priest said, and his eyes were very cold. "A Mistress Alahnah Bahrns. She *is* employed here, yes?"

"Of course she is, Father," Zhorzhet replied in a voice which was far calmer than she actually felt. "She's here right now, in fact."

"And how long has she been employed here?"

"For about two and a half or three years, I believe. I'd have to check Mistress Marzho's ledgers to be more definite than that."

"And have you ever had reason to question her fidelity to God and Mother Church?"

The question came out quickly, in a suddenly harder voice, and Zhorzhet stiffened.

"*Never*, Father!" She shook her head. "I've always believed Alahnah was a very pious young woman, truly devoted to Mother Church. I assure you, if I'd ever seen any evidence to the contrary I would have said something about it!"

"Would you?" He tilted his head, like a wyvern considering a rabbit who was about to become supper. "It's good to discover such a dutiful daughter of Mother Church. Especially these days."

"I've never been anything else, Father," Zhorzhet assured him, feeling sweat bead her hairline and wondering if he'd notice. Not that seeing a little sweat, even out of the most innocent, should be anything unusual for an agent inquisitor when he started asking pointed questions.

"I'm sure." He smiled thinly. "And where might I find Mistress Bahrns?"

"If you'll follow me, Father," she said, beckoning graciously with the hand which held the locket.

He stepped back half a pace to let him pass her, then fell in at her heels, and her pulse raced. The locket was getting sticky from her palm's perspiration, and that was probably good. It would help keep it stuck in place until she needed it. *If* she needed it. If God was good, she wouldn't, but she made herself draw a deep, cleansing breath and faced the possibility that she might.

"Excuse me, Alahnah," she said as the guardsmen and the agents inquisitor followed her to the display window. "There are some people here who'd like to speak to you."

"Oh?" Alahnah's back was to the shop as she worked on the display, and she turned with a pleasant smile . . . that vanished instantly when she saw the Schuelerite purple.

"*Oh!*" she gasped, stepping back involuntarily. Her back touched the display window's glass, and she stopped, staring huge-eyed at the inquisitors.

"Alahnah Bahrns?" the under-priest asked harshly.

"Y-y-yes," she got out. "I'm—I'm Alahnah Bahrns . . . Father."

"Come here, girl!" he half-snapped, pointing impatiently at the shop floor in front of him.

She stared at him a moment longer, trapped in the window bay, then her shoulders slumped and she obeyed the command. He waited until she stood directly in front of him, then crossed his arms and regarded her sternly.

"The Office of Inquisition has a few matters to discuss with you, Mistress Bahrns. Matters concerning your cousin and your uncle."

"M-m-my . . . ?"

She couldn't get the sentence out, and sudden fear—and grief—filled her brown eyes.

"Yes." His eyes were much harder than hers, glittering and cold. "They're in custody at the moment. I'm afraid I've been sent to fetch you to join them."

"In custody? Fetch *me?*" Alahnah shook her head. "No! There must be some mistake! Krystahl and Uncle Gahstahn—they're *good* people, Father! They *love* Mother Church and the Archangels! Truly they do!"

"In that case, they have nothing to fear . . . and neither do you," he told her in a voice which shouted exactly the opposite. "I'm sure we'll get all of that sorted out quickly enough. Now come along, girl."

Alahnah stared pleadingly at him. Then, against her will, her eyes flitted to Zhorzhet and she half-raised one imploring hand.

The under-priest's hard eyes narrowed, and his thin lips tightened. Then he glanced at the senior guardsman.

"Probably best to bring this one along, as well," he said. "It couldn't hurt, anyway, and if this conspiracy's as broad spread as we think it is, she may have something to tell us, too."

Zhorzhet Styvynsyn's racing heart seemed to stop.

"Father," she said carefully, "I don't know anything about any conspiracies. Frankly, I can't believe Alahnah does, either, but I can assure you that *I* don't."

"Then you have nothing to worry about," he told her, and twitched his head at the monk standing behind her.

She couldn't see the man, but she knew he was there, and her right hand shot towards her mouth as he reached for her. Her lips parted and her eyes closed in a quick, final prayer. Then her hand was at her mouth and—

Her eyes flared wide once more as the monk's fingers closed on her wrist. He'd been primed and ready for such an order, and his own hand had started moving an instant before hers. Now it stopped her fingers a fraction of an inch from her lips. She twisted desperately around to face him, clawing at his eyes with her free hand, fighting to wrench free and get the locket into her mouth, but he only turned his face away from her fingernails and twisted the arm he'd captured up and behind her. Something popped and tore in her elbow and she cried out in anguish and went to her knees, her face white with pain, then screamed through gritted teeth as he twisted even harder to keep her there.

"And what do we have *here?*" the under-priest said very softly, bending over her as one of the guardsmen caught her other arm, twisting it behind her as well and stilling her desperate struggles.

She stared up at them, panting hard, fear and defiance blazing in her blue eyes. There was no hope to keep those emotions company, yet she refused to look away, despite the awful pain in her ruined elbow as the monk forced her hand to turn palm-uppermost, his strength mocking her own, and pried her fingers apart. The under-priest reached out and peeled the locket from her palm, holding it up to the light, and his eyes flamed with triumph.

"So we've netted a rather bigger fish than I'd expected," he murmured, closing his fist around the locket and sliding it into his coat pocket. "Oh, I've wanted to meet one of *you* for a long, long time."

.X.
Allayn Maigwair's Office,
City of Zion,
The Temple Lands.

This is a bad idea, Allayn," Archbishop Militant Gustyv Walkyr said. "I can't begin to tell you how bad an idea I think this is, and Rainbow Waters is going to like it even less than I do."

"Then that makes three of us," Allayn Maigwair replied sourly. "Unfortunately, I don't see any way to avoid it."

Walkyr sat back in his chair, scowling so fiercely his thick beard seemed to bristle. One of the things Maigwair had always treasured about Walkyr was his willingness to speak his mind . . . to the captain general, at least. That—coupled with his sheer competence, energy, and personal sense of loyalty—explained how he'd risen from under-priest to archbishop militant in the six years since the initial disaster off Armageddon Reef. It was fortunate that he was also smart enough *not* to speak his mind in front of certain other ears, but this time he seemed furious enough Maigwair was actively concerned about his discretion.

"Listen, Gustyv," the captain general said, leaning forward slightly across the desk, "I need you where you are right now—*alive*, that is—so please don't express yourself quite this . . . frankly where it might get back to Zhaspahr."

Walkyr glowered at him for a moment, but then his shoulders seemed to relax ever so slightly and he nodded choppily.

"I understand," he conceded. "But this really is a bad idea."

"I agree it has definite shortcomings," Maigwair conceded, "and my initial response to it was about the same as yours. I've had some time to think about it since then, though, and the truth is that if the intelligence behind it holds up, it's not quite as insane as it looks on first glance."

Walkyr made a semi-polite sound of incredulity, and Maigwair snorted.

"I did say 'not quite,'" he pointed out.

He stood and crossed to the enormous topographic map hanging on one wall of the office. The known position of the headquarters of every Charisian and Siddarmarkian army was marked with pins, each with a tiny flag bearing that army's name, and his forefinger tapped the one indicating the Charisian Army of Cliff Peak's headquarters, located at the smallish Cliff Peak Province city of Halfmyn.

"According to the Inquisition's agents, all indications are that the Charisians are steadily reinforcing High Mount down here in Cliff Peak a lot more strongly than they are Green Valley up in New Northland or Eastshare in Westmarch." His finger swept over the other two armies' positions. "We're not as well informed about Stohnar." His expression was bleak as his finger tapped the city of Guarnak, which General Trumyn Stohnar had made his headquarters after his army completed the destruction of Bahrnabai Wyrshym's. "Indications are that he's definitely being strengthened, but we don't know by how much. We *do* know that at least three of the new Siddarmarkian rifle divisions are being sent to *High Mount*, though, not to Stohnar."

He indicated the Army of Cliff Peak's position once more, then returned to his chair, sat, and tipped it back, his expression serious.

"May I ask just how we 'know' that?" Walkyr's tone was skeptical.

"We *think* we know that because one of our spies in Siddar City got his hands on a copy of the actual movement orders and sent it off to us by messenger wyvern," Maigwair replied. "That's the strongest bit of evidence yet, but there are others. I wouldn't be inclined to put a huge amount of faith in any of them, given how effectively the other side's shut down our spy networks so often, but all of them together paint a convincing picture. And

Zhaspahr swears the agent who sent us the copy of those movement orders has never yet sent us false information. In fact, according to Zhaspahr, this is the spy who got us the plans for the new steelmaking methods."

Walkyr looked suddenly thoughtful at that, and Maigwair shrugged.

"Like I say. I wouldn't be in any hurry to jump at this sort of information in most cases. Chihiro, I'm not in a *hurry* to jump at it now! But nothing we've seen yet *contradicts* it, and at least some of the information we have comes from what certainly seems to be a reliable source. And if it's accurate, there has to be a reason they're reinforcing High Mount even at the expense of diverting additional *Siddarmarkian* troops to him rather than further strengthening Stohnar or standing up an entirely new, purely Siddarmarkian army to throw at us. Siddarmark's army was the best in the world for at least a century. It's got to be galling to take second place behind the Charisians at this point, however grateful the Republic may be to Cayleb and Sharleyan for saving its arse. I'm sure the Lord Protector's feeling a lot of pressure to establish major field armies under *Siddarmarkian* commanders, so the orders sending so many of his new divisions to High Mount probably don't represent some casual whim on his part. And the fact that High Mount's shifted his headquarters to Halfmyn doesn't make us any happier."

Walkyr frowned, contemplating the map from where he sat.

Halfmyn was over three hundred miles south of Aivahnstyn on the Daivyn River, where Cahnyr Kaitswyrth's Army of Glacierheart had met its doom, and High Mount's Army of Cliff Peak had been the primary pursuit force which had completed the Army of Glacierheart's destruction. At that point, he'd been well *north* of Aivahnstyn, so he'd actually moved something more like four hundred miles to his current position.

"What about Symkyn?" he asked, waving at the map which showed Ahlyn Symkyn's Army of the Daivyn headquartered at Aivahnstyn.

"Indications are that he's being strengthened, as well. Not as much as High Mount, but more than Eastshare on his northern flank," Maigwair replied, and Walkyr frowned some more.

"You think they're shifting the main weight of their attack *south*?" The archbishop militant's tone was slightly—*very* slightly—less incredulous.

"It seems possible, at any rate." Maigwair sighed and toyed with his pectoral scepter. "It's not what I expected out of them, and it would certainly represent a shift from their last year's strategy." He shrugged. "Last year—and the year before that, for that matter—they concentrated on destroying field armies. Did a damned good job of it, too, and it's a strategy that's been working well for them so far. Now they have to realize Rainbow Waters and the Host are both our strongest remaining field force and the most exposed, in a lot of ways. If they can push around behind him, the way they did to Wyrshym—I know that'd be a lot harder to pull off, especially in a summer campaign, but I'm not about to say it wouldn't be possible for those bastards—they could cut the Holy Langhorne. And if they managed *that*, the better part of two-thirds of the Mighty Host would lose its primary logistic link to the Temple Lands. Even if they can't get around behind him, they've got enough of a mobility advantage that I've been anticipating their trying to break his front at selected points, then exploiting to flank out his positions on either side of the breakthroughs."

Walkyr nodded. He'd shared Maigwair's analysis of the heretics' probable strategy. In fact, he'd helped formulate it.

Mother Church's enemies, and especially the Imperial Charisian Army, had given her defenders a pointed and extremely painful lesson in the virtues of mobility, starting with the destruction of the Army of Shiloh and culminating in the previous summer's crushing defeats on the Daivyn and in the Sylmahn Gap. The Army of God was attempting to offset at least some of that advantage in its newly raised divisions, a quarter of which were dragoons—mounted *infantry*, not lancers—although no one expected those new divisions to be as proficient, initially at least, as the far more experienced Charisians. The Mighty Host was more poorly placed than the AOG when it came to mounting its infantry for a lot of reasons, including the fact that serfs had always been . . . strongly discouraged from becoming proficient equestrians. Because of that, Rainbow Waters had been forced to convert existing cavalry units into dragoons if he wanted to increase his mounted infantry strength, and Walkyr was far from convinced the "conversion" was more than skin-deep for the majority of Harchongese cavalry officers.

Despite all efforts, however, Mother Church's armies were going to remain far less mobile than their opponents. That being the case, the logical thing for Cayleb and his generals to do was to continue to exploit that strength—and their successful strategy—and concentrate on destroying or at least crippling Rainbow Waters' Harchongians in the coming campaign. Piercing the Mighty Host's front at some carefully chosen point or points might well permit them to break loose mounted columns in Rainbow Waters' rear. If they managed that and were able to get in behind his fortified strong points before he could fall back, they might be able to cut his force up into disjointed detachments and crush them in detail.

That was the primary reason close to a quarter of the entire Mighty Host was earmarked as a strategic reserve, held well behind the Harchongians' "frontier positions" in order—hopefully—to counter any Charisian or Siddarmarkian breakthroughs.

"After Rayno brought the Inquisition's new reports about High Mount's reinforcements to my attention, I had Tobys and his analysts go over them," Maigwair continued, "and I asked him to look at anything we'd turned up, as well. It's all damnably 'hypothetical,' of course. Chihiro! I'd give one of my balls—maybe *both* of them—for spies as capable as Cayleb seems to have!" He glared at the wall map, then shrugged and looked back at Walkyr. "Hypothetical or not, though, there are definite signs they're weighting their left flank a lot more heavily than they ought to be if they plan on doing what we've all convinced ourselves is the smart thing for them to do. And much as I hate to say it, we don't exactly have the best possible record for out-guessing the bastards."

He did not, Walkyr noticed, point out that he and the Army of God in general had a rather better record than Zhaspahr Clyntahn did. If Maigwair had been free to make his own deployments and decisions without the Inquisitor General's interference, Cahnyr Kaitswyrth would have been replaced months before the Army of Glacierheart's destruction and Bahrnabai Wyrshym would have been allowed to retreat long before he was cut off and crushed. Whether even a replacement would have been able to prevent what the heretics had done to the Army of Glacierheart last summer was an unanswerable question, but no conceivable replacement could have done a *worse* job than Kaitswyrth had.

"At any rate," Maigwair continued, oblivious to the archbishop militant's thoughts, "it's certainly possible—conceivable, at least—that they've decided to capitalize on Hanth's successes against Rychtyr. In fact, according to Zhaspahr," he rolled his eyes, "that's obviously the reason they haven't reinforced Hanth more strongly."

"Excuse me?" Walkyr blinked, and Maigwair snorted.

"Zhaspahr's suggested that the reason Hanth isn't receiving as much new equipment and as many additional men as their other armies is to convince us Dohlar's a purely secondary theater in Cayleb and Stohnar's eyes. As he sees it, the fact that I've told him they obviously *do* regard Dohlar as a secondary theater, based on exactly that logic, only strengthens the possibility of it's all being an elaborate ruse. And one we've clearly fallen for, of course. We're supposed to discount the threat on our southern flank—just as I have—in order to 'concentrate disproportionately' in the north until High Mount's ready to punch through the Tymkyn Gap and either hook south to join up with Hanth and finish off Dohlar once and for all, or else continue southwest to Dairnyth."

"To Dairnyth," Walkyr repeated.

"Actually, that might not be as far-fetched as it looks at first glance," Maigwair said more soberly. "Oh, I'm not ready to sign onto the notion that they've deliberately starved Hanth of men and weapons as part of some deep-seated deception plan. Eastshare's too smart for that, and even if he wasn't, Cayleb and Stohnar definitely are." He waved one hand in a dismissive gesture. "But that's not to say they wouldn't be just as happy for us to come to the conclusion's Zhaspahr's suggesting if they really do have any ambitions beyond simply neutralizing Dohlar. Because the truth is that if they could surprise us there, and if High Mount *could* get all the way to Dairnyth, we might have some serious problems. Particularly given the situation in the Gulf."

Walkyr cocked his head, and Maigwair stopped toying with his scepter and let his chair come upright again so that he could brace his elbows on his desk and lean forward over it again.

"At the moment, their navy's still operating fairly circumspectly in the Gulf," he said. "Their commerce-raiders are inflicting a lot of pain, and the hit our logistics are taking is nothing to sneer at, but they haven't reacted as strongly to the Kaudzhu Narrows as I'd anticipated they would. Yet, at least."

"You think that's about to change?"

"I'll be Shan-wei-damned surprised if it *doesn't* change . . . and soon," Maigwair said grimly. "We've lost track of at least some of those ironclads they used on Desnair, for example, and Cayleb Ahrmahk's not the man to let what happened to his navy go unanswered. Taking back his people before they could be handed over for Punishment was a pretty emphatic first step in that direction, but I absolutely guarantee you that after what happened in Hahskyn Bay, those frigging ironclads are headed for the Gulf of Dohlar. If they haven't gotten there already, they'll be arriving soon. And when they do, what do you think will happen to the Royal Dohlaran Navy?"

"The term 'splinters' comes rather strongly to mind." Walkyr's tone was even grimmer than Maigwair's had been, and the captain general nodded sharply.

"Of course it does. Whatever Zhaspahr may think, Thirsk's navy will fight to the death. You and I both know that. I only pray to God and the Archangels that Rahnyld—or his Council, at least—has the sense to realize they can't fight those steam-powered ironclads and get their galleons the hell out of their way. But whatever they do, Charis is still going to control the entire Gulf. I don't even want to think about what that means for our logistics in the long term, but the short-term consequences could be just as catastrophic and a hell of a lot faster."

"I can see it's being inconvenient as hell," Walkyr said with a frown. "And I agree that it'd be a frigging disaster in the long run." He very carefully avoided words like "inevitable defeat" even speaking only to Maigwair, but they hung between the two of them. "I'm not sure I see the immediate catastrophe potential, though."

"No?" Maigwair showed his teeth in a thin smile. "Well, consider this scenario. We've been anticipating that the new troops being raised and trained in Chisholm would be deployed to their existing armies. But what if they send the new troops *east* from Chisholm, instead? What if they use their control of the sea to send a hundred thousand or so brand-new troops across the Gulf and through the Gulf of Tanshar to the Bay of Bess . . . just about the time High Mount's leading regiments take Dairnyth and offer them a city with damned good port facilities down on our southern flank? Usher and Jhurlahnk got hammered at Aivahnstyn last year, and they don't have anything like our ability to raise and equip new divisions. Much as I respect both Earl Usher and Prince Grygory, I think it's . . . unlikely their remaining militia could stand up to Charisian regulars."

Walkyr shuddered at the very thought, and Maigwair gave him a wintry smile.

"Right now, we've got Tayrens Teagmahn watching Tymkyn Gap, and Dohlar's still holding Alyksberg, but he and the Alyksberg garrison have barely a hundred and twenty thousand men between them. If High Mount got through the gap, they'd never be able to stop him. Especially since we still don't have Teagmahn's riflemen fully equipped with St. Kylmahns, far less all the artillery he's supposed to have. The first wave of new guns is on the way—or will be in the next few five-days—but they aren't there yet because we've been giving such priority to the northern lobe of the front."

"I know," Walkyr nodded. "But isn't Brydgmyn supposed to reinforce him?"

"As soon as he can, yes. Or that was the plan, anyway."

Bishop Militant Ahrnahld Brydgmyn was the designated commander of the Holy Langhorne Band. Among the other painful lessons the Imperial Charisian Army had taught its more backwards students was the advantage of organizing armies into corps. The use of that heresy-tainted term was, of course, anathema in the eyes of Zhaspahr Clyntahn and the Inquisition, so Maigwair and Rainbow Waters had settled on calling *their* corps "bands," instead. The Holy Langhorne Band consisted—or would consist, eventually— of a total of eight divisions, two of them mounted. Because AOG divisions were so much smaller than Charisian divisions, Brydgmyn's final strength would be around sixteen thousand men, plus artillery (when and as it became available), only about the size of a single Charisian division. That was still a powerful force, however, and about the largest Maigwair felt a single headquarters could realistically control at the operational level, given the AOG's current inexperience with the corps concept and the limits of its commanding officer's communications. So far, the new approach seemed to offer a lot of promise, but the Army of God was still figuring out how best to make the entire notion work. It was going to take a while for the new band commanders to master their responsibilities.

At the moment, only three of Brydgmyn's divisions were anywhere near ready for deployment: the reconstituted Holy Martyrs, Rakurai, and 1st Temple Divisions. That was barely fifty-seven hundred men, none of them mounted and less than ten percent of them experienced veterans. Just as bad, perhaps, Brydgmyn was almost as new to his present job as most of his men were to theirs. He was only thirty-two years old, and he'd been a major less than two years earlier. His meteoric promotion was one more consequence of the AOG's need to rebuild after its catastrophic losses in Cliff Peak and Mountaincross and an indication of how deep Maigwair was reaching for the senior officers he required.

Fortunately, Brydgmyn was smart, competent, and loyal, although he wasn't fully trusted by the Inquisition. It would appear Wyllym Rayno suspected—not without some reason, perhaps—that Brydgmyn's fierce loyalty to Mother Church was somewhat stronger than his loyalty to Zhaspahr Clyntahn. But however smart he might be, he was still very much in the process of learning his new duties. In fact, Maigwair had been almost relieved in some ways that his additional divisions would be slower than anticipated in joining him. The bishop militant could use that time very profitably learning to manage his present, considerably smaller force. At the same time. . . .

"The problem is that Brydgmyn won't significantly change the balance of forces," he went on. "And aside from a few other odds and sods—Parkair Gahrlyngtyn's band's actually going to be ready to deploy *earlier* than we'd expected, I think—we don't have anyone else to send right now. Worse, the weather in the south's going to permit serious campaigning well before that could happen farther north. So if there's anything at all to the possibility of a Charisian strike through Tymkyn Gap, Teagmahn's going to find himself really hard-pressed just to retreat in front of it, far less hold his ground."

"Can I ask if Earl Rainbow Waters has been consulted about this yet?" Walkyr asked after a thoughtful moment.

"He has. Unfortunately, we can only communicate by semaphore or wyvern, and that's never as satisfactory as a face-to-face discussion. After all, that's why I sent you to meet with him last winter."

Walkyr nodded. Of course, Maigwair hadn't mentioned that another sterling advantage of face-to-face discussions was that they left no paper trail for the Inquisition to . . . misconstrue. In the absence of direct discussion, correspondents needed to be circumspect in whatever they committed to paper.

"Having said that, I wouldn't exactly say the Earl's in favor of this," the captain general continued. "His current dispositions are all in accordance with what we—and he—had earlier agreed the heretics were most likely to do this summer. His officers and men have spent months preparing their positions, updating their maps, preplanning movements that might become necessary, and picking the best sites to emplace artillery and rocket launchers as they reach the front. He's not happy to see all that effort go to waste, and he's expressed the concern that putting a new commander and newly raised forces into Earl Silken Hills' current positions will weaken his own right flank. However good they may be, they won't have had the winter to learn their ground and they won't be as well integrated into his chain of command as the Southern Host is right now. Having said that, of course, he's prepared to defer to instructions from Zion."

My, Walkyr thought. *There's quite a lot of "circumspection" in that, isn't there?*

The archbishop militant pushed up out of his chair and walked across to stand closer to the map, studying its terrain. It didn't show a lot of detail, but he was amply familiar with smaller scale, more detailed maps of most of the terrain involved. And little though he still liked the idea, he had to admit it was less illogical—and considerably less stupid—than he'd originally thought.

However little Rainbow Waters might relish the thought of shifting a third of his total force even farther south, a potential attack through the Tymkyn Gap—especially with the prospect of Charisian naval control of the Gulf of Dohlar—could have serious consequences. And as Maigwair had just pointed out, Tayrens Teagmahn's Army of Tanshar would never be able to stand up to High Mount's Army of Cliff Peak in the open. As long as he could hold the chain of the Snake Mountains and avoid confronting High Mount's mobility, he could no doubt give a good account of himself. But while the Snakes' narrow passes and twisting secondary roads afforded all sorts of excellent defensive positions, the Tymkyn Gap itself was mostly open, rolling terrain. There were some patches of forest and hillside to slow an advancing army, but nothing like the mountain ramparts north and south of the Gap, and it was a hundred and ten miles wide. That was far too much frontage for him to cover with so few men.

But Earl Silken Hills had six times Teagmahn's strength, and the truth was that—especially after the last year of unmitigated disaster—the Mighty Host was better trained, better equipped, and more experienced than ninety percent of the current Army of God. If Silken Hill moved south to cover that flank, High Mount would find any effort to penetrate the Snakes far more difficult. In addition, Silken Hills' infantry and engineers had spent the last several months mastering the fortification techniques Captain of Horse Rungwyn had worked out. Walkyr had little doubt that the defenses *they'd* build across the Tymkyn Gap would give even High Mount pause . . . assuming they had time for it.

And, he admitted to himself, *they won't be taking the fortifications they've already built with them, will they? Most of the guns, yes, but the emplacements will still be there, and so will the trenches, the bunkers, and the redoubts.*

If Teagmahn shifted the Army of Tanshar north, he'd have—barely—enough men to man the most forward of the Southern Host's dug-in positions, and those were very *formidable* positions. By the time the weather improved enough for serious campaigning as far north as Westmarch and Tarikah, the bulk of the new AOG formations would be at the front or very close to it. If he'd been Rainbow Waters, he wouldn't have been at all happy about the thought of relying upon those new, potentially less than steady bands and divisions to cover his flank, but they'd be far more effective doing it from those prepared defenses than they'd be in an open field battle.

"I still don't like the idea," he said finally, turning back to his superior. "I have to admit I hadn't thought through everything you've just pointed out. In my defense, I didn't *know* about a lot of it, of course. But now that you've laid out the logic behind it, I'll concede that it's not the outright lunacy I thought it was."

"Not exactly a ringing endorsement," Maigwair observed dryly, "but I suppose I should take what I can get. Especially since Earl Rainbow Waters has made one . . . stipulation. I wouldn't exactly call it a 'demand,' but before he signs off on redeploying that drastically, he wants a voice in deciding who we'll assign to command the area Silken Hills is going to be handing over to us."

"Makes sense," Walkyr agreed, returning his eyes to the map as he thought back over his own face-to-face meetings with the Harchongese commander.

That was a smart, smart man. He'd want to be as certain as humanly possible of both the quality and the reliability of the AOG commander on his flank. Perhaps *especially* of that commander's reliability. Cahnyr Kaitswyrth's performance with the Army of Glacierheart couldn't have imbued him with boundless faith in the AOG's prowess, and the last thing he'd want would be a Temple commander whose competence might be in question and who might dispute his orders or, far worse, might . . . pull back precipitously under pressure.

"I'm glad you think so." Something about Maigwair's tone turned Walkyr back around to face him. The archbishop militant raised both eyebrows in question, and Maigwair smiled almost whimsically.

"He was rather insistent, actually," the captain general said. "In fact, there was really only one officer he cared to propose."

"And who might that have been?" Walkyr asked slowly.

"Why, you, Gustyv."

Maigwair smiled at Walkyr's expression, but then he shook his head and his own expression had turned very serious.

"I can think of a lot of reasons he might've preferred you for this," he said, "and all of them are good ones. The fact that you spent so much time with him before last summer's campaign has to be a part of it, of course. He had the chance to get a feel for the way your mind works, which means he can be confident you're not an idiot, like Kaitswyrth. Even more, though, you're the one senior commander we've got he can be certain understands his thinking and the strengths—and weaknesses—of the Mighty Host. But I'll be honest here. I think he has a few reasons he prefers not to discuss openly . . . and so do I."

"Such as?" Walkyr's tone was soft, his eyes dark.

"Whoever we send has to be smart, he has to be determined, and he has to be able to . . . 'think outside the box,' as Vicar Rhobair's become fond of putting it. But, most importantly of all, he has to be someone Earl Rainbow Waters—and I—can depend upon to do not simply what he's *told* to but what he knows he *needs* to, as well."

He held the archbishop militant's gaze levelly, and it was very, very quiet in his office.

.XI.
The Zhonesberg Switch
and
Town of Zhonesberg,
South March Lands,
Republic of Siddarmark.

It was raining, of course.

In this particular instance, it wasn't the depressing drizzle which had become entirely too familiar to anyone in the Army of Thesmar—or, for that matter, in the Army of the Seridahn—either. No, this was a hard, driving, icy rain, deluging out of a night sky darker than the underbelly of hell. The sound of it filled the universe: pounding, pattering, turning creeks into brawling rivers, blowing on the wind, and generally making every living thing miserable.

Except for Major Dynnys Mahklymorh's 1st Battalion, 2nd Scout Sniper Regiment, Imperial Charisian Army.

They thought it was lovely weather.

▼　▼　▼

Private Dynnys Ahdmohr dreamed wistfully of a nice, hot fire protected by sturdy, weathertight walls, where he could toast frozen toes and breathe without exhaling puffs of steam. For that matter, he would have settled for hunkering down under a scrap of tarpaulin which might keep the worst of the rain at bay while a small, miserable, smoky fire provided at least an illusion of warmth. Unfortunately, he had neither roof nor tarpaulin. And even if he'd had either of them, Sergeant Klymynty—who was not noted for his kind and gentle heart—frowned on sentries who made themselves too comfortable.

More to the point, the Army of the Seridahn had learned the hard way that sentries came to bad ends if they took liberties against the Army of Thesmar. So despite the weather, he hunched down inside his new oilskins—which, praise Langhorne, at least didn't *leak* like the ones they'd replaced—and walked his assigned section of 4th Company's perimeter as philosophically as possible.

That perimeter covered the central approach to the fortified position marked on the Army of the Seridahn's maps as the Zhonesberg Switch. The Switch wasn't the best defensive ground in the world, for a lot of reasons, including the scrubby, second-growth woodlot which crowded close upon it. It covered the vital road junction where the farm tracks from Byrtyn's Crossing, Zhonesberg, and Kharmych's Farm converged, however. It was much too far out on the Army's right flank to be heavily held, but the heretics had shown a truly fiendish talent for exploiting any unwatched spider-rat hole, which explained what Hyndyrsyn's Regiment was doing out in the middle of East Bumfuck in the Shan-wei-damned rain.

Stationary, sandbagged guard posts closer in to the main position actually did offer at least the illusion of overhead protection for which Ahdmohr longed, and more rudimentary—and much wetter and more miserable—posts formed a loose outer shell, as well. No one could put a solid wall of sentries across a frontage as wide as the Switch, however, especially with only four understrength companies. There had to be gaps, and Captain Tyrnyr believed in tying fixed positions together with mobile sentries as insurance. That was his policy at any time, but especially on a night when darkness conspired with driving rain to reduce visibility to zero and added a backdrop of sound that deadened all other noises, to boot. That policy had served him well, and since he was the senior officer in command of the Switch, his policies were the ones that mattered.

Ahdmohr understood that, and he wasn't about to argue with success. Despite that, the odds of any threat to a position over fifty miles from the Sheryl-Seridahn Canal materializing on a night like this weren't very high, in his opinion. For some reason, however, Sergeant Klymynty hadn't *asked* his opinion when he was handing out assignments. And, to be fair, the heretics had demonstrated a distressing tendency to do things most armies didn't. Including a nasty habit of creeping around on miserable, rainy nights for the express purpose of capturing any unwary sentry they could. The Army of the Seridahn had been slower to learn the value of offensive patrols and prisoner interrogation, but experience was a harsh instructor, and Dynnys Ahdmohr had no intention of finding himself the heretics' guest while they asked—

He approached the clump of brush which marked the boundary between his and Zhaif Truskyt's assigned circuits. He'd passed it at least forty times already. But this time was different, and unfortunately for Private Ahdmohr, the Imperial Charisian Army wasn't interested in interrogating him tonight.

An arm snaked around the private's head from behind. A hard, calloused palm clamped across his mouth and yanked his head back, a combat knife slashed his throat from ear to ear, and a spray of arterial blood steamed in the night's chill. The Charisian scout sniper and his partner dragged the twitching body back into the brush, then crouched down with their mates, waiting.

If the timing held, the other sentry should be along in four or five minutes.

▼ ▼ ▼

"What time is it?"

"Five minutes later than the *last* time you asked," Sergeant Ohmahr Swarez growled. Daivyn Mahkneel was not Swarez' favorite trooper at the best of times.

"I was only *asking*, Sarge."

The private was a past master at sounding aggrieved without sounding officially insolent . . . which was one of the things Swarez least liked about him. On the other hand, a sergeant was a practical sort of thing to be. His job was to manage the troops and take care of all those unpleasant little details officers lacked the time to deal with appropriately. To nip problems in the bud while they were still simple, before they had to be brought to the attention of higher, better paid authority, where things like fine shades of meaning and a carefully considered sense of justice might be important. Pragmatism was a vital military resource, when all was said, and it was the Army's sergeants who were the wyvern-eyed custodians of that precious commodity.

With that awesome responsibility in mind, Swarez chose his next words very carefully.

"Yeah, an' you've been asking every five minutes fer the last half hour, fer Langhorne's sake! Case it's missed yer notice, none of the other lads like bein' out here any more 'n you do, but I don't hear *them* bellyachin' 'bout the duty an' whining 'bout how soon we get t' go off watch. So, if you ask again before we're relieved, I'm gonna put a boot so far up your arse you'll taste leather for the next five-day. In fact, if I hear another word outa you *at all* 'tween now an' then, you'll get exactly the same answer plus—an' I absolutely guarantee this—three fucking five-days of picket duty. Now, was there somethin' *else* you wanted t' say?"

Someone chuckled loudly enough to be heard over the rain drumming on the canvas tent halves which had been laced together and stretched overhead to afford at least some protection. Given just how noisy that rain was, the chuckler had to have deliberately made sure Mahkneel—whose constant whining made him even less popular with his squadmates than with his sergeant—heard it.

Swarez smiled, gazing out into the rainy darkness as *he* heard it. It was unlikely Mahkneel would be able to keep his mouth shut, although he supposed it was remotely possible. The *Writ* promised miracles still happened, after all.

An' if the miserable prick insists on bein' a pain in the arse, the other lads'll sort his arse out with a little "counselin' session" next time there're no officers around. Prob'ly shouldn't be thinkin' that's a good thing, an' I hope they don't get too carried away, but the—

The sergeant's thoughts broke off, and his eyes narrowed. He cocked his head, trying to decide if he really had heard anything besides the splashing energy of the rain. It seemed unlikely, but he turned in the direction from which the possible sound had come, straining his eyes, and something tingled unpleasantly up and down his spine.

"What is it, Sarge?" one of the other members of the picket asked.

"Don't know," Swarez said tersely, but his hand groped for the signal flare, copied from a captured heretic signal rocket. "Thought I heard—"

▼   ▼   ▼

"*Now!*" Sergeant Ahrnahld Taisyn hissed, and two squads of 2nd Platoon, 1st Company, 1st Battalion, 2nd Scout Sniper Regiment, came to their feet in the muddy, rain-soaked scrub. "And remember," he added, totally superfluously, because it was his job to, "no *shooting*, damn it!"

The scout snipers were understrength, like every other unit in the Army of Thesmar, but 2nd Platoon was down only nine of its nominal fifty-seven men, and Lieutenant Abernethy had picked the squads for Taisyn's present mission with care. Not even a scout sniper could move through close, overgrown terrain in total darkness—and rain—without sounding like a draft dragon in a cornfield. But at least Abernethy and Taisyn could count on 3rd and 4th Squad to sound like *small* dragons.

The Charisians came out of the dark with bayoneted rifles at the ready and every safety set, sweeping through the gap they'd created by picking off Captain Tyrnyr's layered shell of sentries. Sergeant Swarez was a highly experienced veteran with well-honed combat instincts. That was why he had time to realize he truly had heard something, to find the signal flare with his right hand and reach for the primer tape with his left. His fingers actually found the tape and started to pull it . . . just as a fourteen-inch tempered steel bayonet rammed home at the base of his throat.

The unlit flare fell back into the mud as his hands pawed uselessly at the blood-spouting wound. He went down, gurgling for breath, trying to shout, and a muck-covered combat boot slammed down on his breastplate as the Charisian recovered his bayonet.

▼　　▼　　▼

"All right." Captain Zackery Wylsynn had to raise his voice over the rain and the sullen wind tossing the leafless branches around him. "Our forward squads have informed us they're at least theoretically where they're supposed to be. And Sergeant Major Bohzmhyn here—" Wylsynn twitched his head in the direction of the tallish, square-shouldered noncom at his elbow "—assures me the Temple Boys don't have a clue we're coming. I want you all to remember he gave us his word about that."

"Not exactly what I said, Sir." Unlike Wylsynn, who was an Old Charisian and an ex-Marine, Bohzmhyn was a Chisholmian who'd spent the better part of twenty years in the Royal Chisholmian Army before it became the Imperial *Charisian* Army. As such, he had a Langhorne-given responsibility to be the voice of reason for his Charisian CO. "What I said was that none of our lads fired a single shot and none of the pickets *warned* anyone we're coming. Doesn't mean somebody hasn't figured it out on his own."

"Ah, I see. I stand corrected." Wylsynn grinned at his company sergeant major. Then his expression sobered as he returned his attention to the youthful lieutenants standing around him while the rain battered their shoulders and bounced off their helmets.

"The point is that our people are in position, the engineers are out doing their jobs, and Colonel Maiyrs' lead elements should be closing up on our point teams right about now. In another—" he pulled his watch out of his tunic and tilted it to catch the narrow beam of light from the bull's-eye lantern Bohzmhyn cracked open "—eighty minutes or so, things're going to get lively. So," he closed the watch's case with a snap, "let's just get back and make sure no balls get dropped, shall we?"

▼　　▼　　▼

"Got an Alyksberg officer here lookin' for the Lieutenant, Sarge," Corporal Clyffyrd said.

Sergeant Taisyn looked up from the bayonet he'd been honing, then stood and saluted the sodden Siddarmarkian captain who stood dripping at the corporal's heels.

"Clyffyrd, yer an idiot," he growled, holding out the hand that wasn't full of bayonet to the officer. "Good to see you, Sir," he continued, still scowling at his corporal. "Sorry 'bout that 'Alyksberg officer' crap. Seems Clyffyrd here don't see too good in the dark."

"Not a problem, Sergeant." Captain Haarahld Hytchkahk chuckled as he clasped the noncom's forearm.

He and Lieutenant Ehlys Abernethy's platoon had worked together several times over the last few months, and they got along well. Which might, he reflected, have something to do with why Major Mahklymorh had chosen 2nd Platoon for this assignment.

"Hard to recognize anybody in weather like this. Or even *see* them in the first place . . . thank Chihiro!" he continued.

"Got that right, Sir," Taisyn agreed, and craned his neck, looking into the darkness beyond the captain. "Got your people up to the initial point, do you?"

"Just getting the last of them into position now," Hytchkahk confirmed.

"Damned good work, Sir." Taisyn's broad smile showed an elite soldier's approval of good field craft. "Never heard a frigging thing—begging the Captain's pardon."

"Coming from you, the boys'll take that as a compliment, Sergeant."

"And damned well should, Sir. Not the easiest thing t' move that many bodies in the dark 'thout somebody fallin' over a tree root—or his own two feet—an' lettin' the entire world know he's out there."

The sergeant slid the bayonet back into the sheath strapped to the outside of his right thigh, then turned back to Clyyfyrd.

"Go find the Lieutenant and tell him Captain *Hytchkahk's* here an' his men're assemblin' on the IP. An' fer Kau-yung's sake, *try* not t' get lost doing it."

"On it, Sarge." If Clyffyrd felt crushed by his platoon sergeant's lack of faith in him, it didn't show. "Captain," the corporal nodded to Hytchkahk and faded away into the rain.

▼　▼　▼

Sergeant Hairahm Klymynty slogged along the muddy trail, ankle-deep in rainwater runoff, with his head bent against the wind while his oilskin poncho flapped around his knees. He hated weather like this. He always had, and it was worse now that his knees had started to age along with the rest of him. The cold and wet weren't doing any favors for the shoulder which had stopped a Charisian bullet the year before, either. But he was pretty sure the men he'd detailed to stand watch out here were no happier about it than he was, and he wasn't going to lie around in a nice warm bedroll roll out of the rain—if such a thing actually existed anywhere in the world, a possibility he was coming to doubt—while he had men out here getting rained on.

Not that he had any intention of explaining that to them, of course. Just as he had no intention of mentioning the hot meal he'd arranged to have waiting when they came off duty. As far as *they* were concerned, those meals were going to be the company cooks' own idea . . . and the only reason *he* was out here was to carry out another "surprise readiness inspection." And, to be honest, making certain they were on their toes despite the miserable conditions was about as important as things came. Not that he anticipated any problems at his next stop. Ohmahr Swarez ran a tight squad. The possibility that any of his men were slacking off, no matter what the weather was doing, didn't really exist. Still—

Something moved at the edge of his vision, coming out of the brush beside the trail. He caught it from the corner of one eye, but he didn't really have time to react. He was, however, more fortunate than Sergeant Swarez had been; the rifle butt simply clubbed him to the ground, unconscious, with a concussion which would leave him seeing double for a five-day.

▼ ▼ ▼

"What the fuck d'you think he was doing, wanderin' around out here by himself?" Private Hynryk Ahzwald muttered as he and Tahdayus Gahsett dragged the unconscious Klymynty off the trail.

"Damned if I know." Gahsett shrugged. "Looks of things, he's prob'ly a sergeant. Might be he had it in mind to make sure his outposts were doin' their jobs."

"Kinda late fer that," Ahzwald said with profound satisfaction.

"Oh, yeah?" Gahsett snorted. "S'pose he'd come along five minutes earlier an' caught the engineers goin' in. Think Sergeant Ohflynn'd be just happy as a Temple Boy at a bonfire if we'd'a let *that* happen?"

"Pro'bly not," Ahzwald conceded after a moment.

He rolled the unconscious Dohlaran over and began tying him up securely, although that was probably unnecessary, given how hard he'd hit the poor bastard. The odds were at least even he'd never be waking up again, and if he did, it wouldn't be anytime soon.

If the other fellow had been a genuine Temple Boy, Ahzwald would have been inclined to simply slit his throat as the easiest way to make sure he wouldn't be posing any problems in the future. Regulations—and Major Mahklymorh—frowned on that sort of problem-solving. Still, Ahswald was a practical man . . . and the major wasn't here. But he'd developed a grudging respect for the Dohlarans. They seemed a lot less inclined towards "making examples" than the Temple Boys or the frigging Desnairians, and they were tough bastards. They'd given ground quickly when the Army of Thesmar first launched its counterattack, but surprise had never turned into panic. If there was an ounce of give-up in them *he* hadn't seen it, and there'd been nothing easy about the long advance from Evyrtyn. True, the Army of Thesmar had advanced better than two hundred miles since then, but the Army of the Seridahn had fought hard for every inch of that advance, and there'd been precious few atrocities on either side.

Under the circumstances, he was prepared to give a fellow veteran of that campaign at least the possibility of survival.

▼　▼　▼

"Last man, Sir," Platoon Sergeant Gyffry Tyllytsyn, 2nd Platoon, 115th Combat Engineer Company, 19th Combat Engineers Battalion, said quietly into Lieutenant Klymynt Hahrlys' ear.

"Confirmed the head count?" Hahrlys asked. Not that he doubted Tyllytsyn's assurance; the platoon sergeant didn't make that sort of mistake. But it never hurt to be doubly certain.

"Yes, Sir." Tyllytsyn smiled crookedly. "Double-checked it twice."

"Good enough for me." Hahrlys patted the sergeant's shoulder. "Now let's just make sure we don't trip over the fuse hoses, shall we?"

"Suits me right down to the ground, Sir. How're we doing for time?"

"That's a good question."

Hahrlys turned to face east, raising his arms to spread his poncho, and gestured to the private with the closed bull's-eye lantern. Raindrops hissed into steam on the lantern's hot case as the private leaned close and opened the tiny circular port set into the lantern's slide. The light spilling through it seemed almost blinding to their darkness-accustomed vision, but Hahrlys' body and poncho blocked its brilliance from any Dohlaran eyes as he held his opened watch in the small pool of brightness.

"Fifteen minutes ahead of schedule," he said with profound satisfaction.

▼　▼　▼

"Sure would feel better usin' signal rockets, Sir," Sergeant Pynhyrst muttered. "This doin' it all on a watch an' *hopin'* ever'one's where he's s'posed t' be. . . ."

He shook his head dolefully, and Haarahld Hytchkahk snorted. Pynhyrst was as reliable as the rocks of his native Snake Mountains, but he *did* have a talent for finding things to worry about. Which, Hytchkahk had to admit, was one of the things which made him so valuable as 3rd Section's senior noncom.

"If you have any concerns you want to discuss with Major Stefyns or

General Sumyrs, I'm sure they'll be happy to relay them to Earl Hanth," he said very quietly in the sergeant's ear.

"Just saying' I'd like a little more . . . control, maybe, Sir," Pynhyrst replied. "Waitin' around fer someone else t' open the ball's the sort of thing gets on a man's nerves."

"Now, there I can't argue with you, Adym," Hytchkahk conceded and thumped the sergeant lightly on the shoulder. "On the other hand, I'd rather be us than the engineers, wouldn't you?"

"Got a point there, Sir," Pynhyrst admitted. "Scout snipers've earned their pay tonight, too, come to that."

"That they have."

The two Siddarmarkians sheltered under the stretched canvas Ohmahr Swarez's picket no longer required. Its protection was purely temporary, and both of them were already so saturated that it was more symbolic than useful, but at least the rain which had already soaked them to the bone wasn't being constantly replenished by even colder reinforcements.

In most ways, Hytchkahk actually agreed with Pynhyrst. He would have preferred something more positive than "we're all supposed to be in position by now" himself. But he understood the logic, and the attack plan hinged on achieving surprise. In theory, the Temple Boys—although he supposed calling the Royal Dohlaran Army Temple Boys might be a tad unfair; they'd certainly massacred fewer prisoners than the "Sword of Schueler" or the Army of God's regulars had—weren't supposed to have a clue the 3rd Alyksberg Volunteers were anywhere close to them. Hopefully, they still thought they were dealing solely with patrols of the indefatigable Charisian scout snipers, and Earl Hanth had gone to some lengths to keep them thinking that way.

The Army of Thesmar had maintained the tempo of its patrols all across the Army of the Seridahn's front but those patrols continued to focus their main effort on the line of the canal, both as genuine probes of the Dohlaran positions and to create uncertainty about precisely what Earl Hanth had in mind for his next move. The Dohlarans had gotten much better at both offensive and defensive patrolling of their own, but when it came to that game, "better" was nowhere remotely close to "as good as" the Imperial Charisian Army. The Republic of Siddarmark had never been what anyone would have called incompetent when it came to scouting and reconnaissance, but Hytchkahk would have been the first to admit that even the RSA had learned an enormous amount from its Charisian allies.

At the moment, however, it was to be hoped Sir Fahstyr Rychtyr's attention was firmly focused on his main defensive line forty miles west of Fyrayth, where those patrols were doing their best to keep it fixed. The last place they wanted him worrying about was the security screen far out on his right flank in these miserable, rain-soaked woods.

No, Haarahld, he corrected himself. *In these beautiful, absolutely* gorgeous *rain-soaked woods! Langhorne, I love a good rainstorm!*

His lips twitched, but at the moment it was absolutely true. And—the nascent smile disappeared—he'd had entirely too much experience with Dohlaran defenders who knew he was coming. Surprise was a beautiful thing, which was why he was perfectly prepared to rely on runners and planned timetables until the moment came. Yes, he'd prefer to positively confirm everyone was in position with the addictive, convenient, far more *visible* signal rockets the Imperial Charisian Army had introduced to mainland warfare. But there'd be rockets and flares enough when the moment came, and if anyone screwed up and fired one of those off prematurely, where the wrong someone could see it, surprise would go out the damned window. And if *that* happened . . .

"I think the Colonel will get the word to us when he wants us to attack, Adym," he said out loud. "Should be pretty clear, really."

"Aye, Sir, that it will," Pynhyrst agreed in tones of grim satisfaction. "Can't come a minute too soon, either."

"That it can't," Hytchkahk agreed.

The Royal Dohlaran Army might not be the Army of God, but it still owed the Republic of Siddarmark—and especially the Alyksberg Volunteers—an enormous debt, and Haarahld Hytchkahk looked forward to collecting the next installment.

▼　▼　▼

"Runner from Major Ahtwatyr, Sir. All of the assault teams have reported in."

"Anything from the engineers?" Colonel Sedryk Maiyrs, CO, 3rd Alyksberg Volunteers, asked.

"No, Sir." His aide shook his head vigorously.

"Good!"

Maiyrs nodded in sharp satisfaction. Charisian combat engineers had a tendency to be where they were supposed to be when they were supposed to be there, and they damned well told someone if they weren't. It would never have done for Maiyrs to admit that he was almost as unhappy as Sergeant Pynhyrst about relying on timing and runners rather than more reliable signals, but he was confident the engineers would have informed him if they were running behind schedule.

He stood a moment longer, running over his mental checklist one last time. Then he drew a deep breath and turned to the youthful signalman at his elbow. Unlike Captain Hytchkahk, Maiyrs had all the signal rockets a man could want, and he was specifically authorized to use them when he was satisfied everyone was ready.

"Light the fuse," he said.

▼ ▼ ▼

"There's the signal, Sir!"

In addition to a last name which had forced him to endure an enormous number of so-called witticisms over the last several months, Private Zhames Dohlar possessed extraordinarily sharp eyes. That was why he was 1st Platoon's signalman. Not that particularly acute vision had been required to spot the signal rocket's brilliant green burst; it lit the clouds' underbelly like a fuming eye, touching the heavy rain with an eerie emerald glow.

"So I see," Lieutenant Zhaksyn, 1st Platoon's CO, replied in a tone whose mildness fooled no one.

Grygory Zhaksyn was a native Old Charisian who'd been a schoolteacher before his sister, her Siddarmarkian husband, and all three of their children were massacred by the Sword of Schueler. He'd embraced a new career, then, and he'd been a natural fit for the artillery. He'd commanded 1st Platoon for the past seven months, and if his men hadn't known at first quite what to make of his careful grammar and enormous trunk of books, they damned well did now. Dohlar smiled coldly at what he heard hidden in the depths of that calm response, and then Zhaksyn turned to Tymythy Hustyngs, 1st Platoon's senior noncom.

"I believe we can begin, Sergeant," he remarked.

"Yes, Sir!" Hustyngs slapped his chest in salute and wheeled to the twelve M97 mortars dug into their carefully leveled firing pits.

"*Fire!*" he barked.

▼ ▼ ▼

Captain Wyllys Rynshaw watched the rocket burst, then the mortars behind him coughed up enormous tongues of lurid fire, and he hoped like hell his crews had laid them in properly.

Surprise is great, he thought grimly, *but getting the artillery on target's even greater. Damn but I wish General Sumyrs had let me try at least a few ranging shots!*

▼ ▼ ▼

General Clyftyn Sumyrs watched the single signal rocket burst, vivid against the clouds. An instant later, lightning flickered along the horizon as the Charisian mortars opened fire.

"I hope we didn't get too clever for our own good," he said quietly, standing in the rain beside Captain Wylsynn. "By which, of course, I mean I hope *I* didn't get too clever for our own good, of course."

"Only one way to find out, Sir," the scout sniper replied. "To be honest, I think the bombardment's going to be less useful in the end than the illuminating rounds, but I could be wrong. And—" he bared his teeth "—I doubt like hell that it's going to *hurt* anything. On our side, anyway."

▼   ▼   ▼

Although Earl Hanth had received two complete batteries of mobile 6-inch heavy angle-guns, improved field guns remained a hope for the future. In the meantime, he had a campaign to fight while he waited, and he and Lywys Sympsyn had invested quite a bit of thought in ways to make the best possible use of the artillery—and especially the mortars—they had.

Captain Rynshaw's 2nd Support Company was the fruit of that thought. Sympsyn had combined two-thirds of the Army of Thesmar's total support platoons into support *companies*, each three platoons strong, that could be moved around and concentrated into "grand batteries" where they were needed. They had to get a lot closer to their targets than the angles did, but they were also one hell of a lot more mobile. That meant Rynshaw "owned" thirty-six mortars—in his case, all M97 4-inch weapons—and all of them had been carefully dug in and prepared for the night's fire mission. The only thing they hadn't been able to do was actually range the weapons in.

Be lucky to put half the rounds within five hundred yards of the target, Rynshaw thought grumpily.

In fact, however, he was grossly unfair to his gunners.

▼   ▼   ▼

"Stand to! *Stand to!*"

Captain Zhames Tyrnyr rolled out of his blankets as the urgent shout jerked him awake. He shot to his feet, as close to fully upright as the confines of his small tent permitted, automatically reaching for his boots even before his eyes were fully open.

"*Stand to!*"

He recognized Company Sergeant Wylsynn Stahdmaiyr's voice. Then the bugle started sounding, and he hoped like hell Stahdmaiyr was jumping at a false alarm. If the company sergeant was, it would be the first time Tyrnyr could remember, however, and he sat on the edge of his cot while he stamped his right foot into its boot.

He'd just reached for the left boot when confirmation that Stahdmaiyr still hadn't jumped at a false alarm arrived.

The first Charisian star shells exploded overhead with soft, almost innocuous popping sounds, and Tyrnyr swore vilely as the sodden canvas of his tent glowed under their furious incandescence.

Five seconds later, the first shrapnel bombs detonated.

▼　▼　▼

"Short!" Corporal Aizak Ohkailee shouted from his tree-branch perch thirty feet above the trail.

"You sure you're spotting First Platoon's fire?" Sergeant Yorak shouted back.

"Langhorne, Sarge!" Ohkailee shook his head. "Course I'm not! Got a red star shell at the right time, though."

"Well, I figure we'll find out if you know your arse from your elbow. How short?"

"Call it two hundred yards!"

"Two hundred," Yorak confirmed, and slapped Dynnys Bailahchyo on the shoulder. "You heard the man, Dynnys. Say it back, then send it."

"Two hundred yards short," Bailahchyo repeated, and reached for the sidemounted lever on his heavy, tripod-mounted signal lamp.

Ahlvyn Yorak grinned and shook his head, remembering all the care they'd taken to avoid showing even a single spark during the approach, as the shutters began to clatter and the light flashed back to Private Dohlar's waiting eyes.

Still, I guess the bastards've figured out we're out here by now anyway, Ahlvyn, he reflected.

▼　▼　▼

Colonel Zhaksyn Hyndyrsyn dropped his pen and jerked up out of his chair as the first mortar bomb exploded in mid-air above the four-company strong-point fifteen hundred yards northeast of his command post.

His regiment had been combined with Gylchryst Sheldyn's to form Sheldyn's Brigade. Hyndyrsyn hadn't approved of the arrangement when he first heard about it. His approval hadn't been required, however, and he'd changed his mind about it once the advantages made themselves apparent.

The idea had come from Sir Rainos Ahlverez' experiences with the Army of Shiloh, and little though he'd cared for finding himself under Sheldyn's command, Hyndyrsyn had to admit it had worked out well, especially with both regiments so badly understrength. Of the fourteen hundred men and officers he was supposed to have, he had just under *eleven* hundred, and if he was going to be stuck this far out on the Army of the Seridahn's flank, he was thoroughly in favor of having friends close to hand. Of course, if both regiments had been fully up to strength, they'd still have been less than two-thirds the size of a *Charisian* regiment, although they'd have been a bit larger than a Siddarmarkian regiment.

They weren't up to strength, however, and from the sound of things,

Captain Tyrnyr's detachment was about to get thoroughly reamed. And since Tyrnyr's companies held the road junction that was the key to the entire Zhonesberg Switch. . . .

"Messenger!" Hyndyrsyn ripped open his command tent's fly and bellowed at the sentry outside it. "I need a messenger right frigging *now!*"

▼   ▼   ▼

Zhames Dohlar read the dimly visible light as it blinked through the rain, then began flipping the shutters of his own lantern, repeating the signal back to confirm. Unlike Bailahchyo's lamp, it was at least remotely possible someone on the Dohlaran side would see Dohlar's, although he suspected they'd be a little too busy at the moment to pay much attention to rakurai bugs in the trees even if they could see them through the rain.

He finished sending, and Bailahchyo opened his lamp's shutters once again—this time in a single double-length dash of confirmation.

"Up two hundred yards, Sir!" he called down. "Confirmed!"

"Up two hundred," Lieutenant Zhaksyn repeated, as calmly as if he were still in his Tellesberg classroom, making certain of the correction.

"Yes, Sir!"

"Very well. Up two hundred, Tymythy," he told Sergeant Hustyngs.

▼   ▼   ▼

Captain Tyrnyr was in no position to appreciate the exquisite choreography General Sumyrs and his Charisian artillery support had arranged for him. Each of the platoons assigned to Rynshaw's support company fired separately to make it easier for the artillery support party assigned to it to spot its fire. In theory, one platoon was supposed to fire every ten seconds. In fact, of course, not even Charisians could keep to that sort of timing once the dance started. So each salvo included its own color-coded star shell as an identifier, as well. It wasn't a perfect system, since there were soon a *lot* of star shells floating above the Dohlaran positions, but it got the job done.

By the fourth salvo, Rynshaw's thirty-six mortars were putting over eighty percent of their rounds on target.

And in the meantime—

▼   ▼   ▼

"*Fire in the hole!*" Lieutenant Hahrlys called, and reached for the ring on the varnished wooden box as the first mortar bombs warbled overhead.

The Army of the Seridahn hadn't had the opportunity to profit from the Mighty Host of God and the Archangels' experiments in fortification building. It had, however, amassed an enormous amount of . . . experiential data on the same subject during its grueling fighting retreat up the Seridahn

River and then step-by-step back along the Sheryl-Seridahn Canal. Its men had discovered the beauty of the shovel and become almost as adroit at—and as fanatical about—digging in every time they stopped *anywhere* as the Imperial Charisian Army.

Given an hour, every single one of them had his own slit trench. Given three hours, and light breastworks crowned their fighting positions and their observation posts and any attached artillery were dug-in, with sandbags going up for additional protection. Given a full day, and communication trenches and rudimentary but serviceable dugouts made an appearance. Given a five-day, and blasting them out of their holes was Shan-wei's own piece of work.

As an engineer, Klymynt Hahrlys appreciated a good job of fortifying a position when he saw one, and the men charged with holding the Switch had done a very thorough job indeed. No one on Safehold had ever heard of barbed wire, but they understood all about constructing abatises out of tangled, interlocking tree branches. And the Dohlarans—in a trick they'd acquired from *Charisian* engineers—had taken to weaving their abatises together with wire vine whenever it was available, which made a very fair substitute for barbed wire. For that matter, they were fond of studding logs with old bayonets or even sword blades and adding them to the obstacles protecting their positions.

Enough mortar fire could blow gaps even through Dohlaran obstacle belts . . . eventually, and if the attacker was prepared to expend ammunition lavishly enough to get the job done. There were more efficient ways, however, towards which end Baron Seamount had incorporated Doctor Sahndrah Lywys' newly developed Lywysite into what an engineer from Old Earth would have called a Bangalore torpedo. The official name for it was the "Composite Demolition Charge, Mark 1," but the engineers equipped with it referred to it as "Sahndrah's Doorknocker" in honor of Doctor Lywys. By whatever name, it consisted of dynamite-loaded sections of lightweight pipe, each four feet long, which threaded together to produce a single, long demolition charge.

Watched over by protective teams of scout snipers and hidden by the darkness and pounding rain, Lieutenant Hahrlys' platoon had very quietly assembled forty of those sections into four forty-foot long tubes, sliding them forward and under the Dohlaran obstacle belt, four feet at a time, from well outside it. Then they'd connected the waterproof fuse hoses to them and unreeled hose behind them as they retreated back into the concealment of the rainy woods.

Now the lieutenant yanked the ring and the friction primer inside the box ignited. Its spitting spark raced furiously down the main channel to the junction point of all four fuse hoses, then split and sprinted towards the waiting charges, invisible inside the hoses which had protected the fuses from the wet.

Eight seconds later, all four Doorknockers detonated as one in a long, ripping explosion that tore straight through the obstacle belt.

▼　▼　▼

Captain Hytchkahk waited impatiently as the Charisian mortar fire savaged the Dohlaran position. The spectacular explosions were clearly visible from his vantage point, and he approved of them wholeheartedly. He'd felt even more satisfaction as the long, vivid pencil lines of the exploding Doorknockers ripped their way through the obstacles waiting for his assault force, however.

The scouts' reports and prisoner interrogation identified the local Dohlaran commander as Captain Zhames Tyrnyr, and Tyrnyr was supposed to be very good. According to those same reports, he had four of Hyndyrsyn's Regiment's six companies under his command—about seven hundred men—and Hyndyrsyn's Regiment had been part of the force Sir Rainos Ahlverez had taken with him to Alyksberg. By all reports, Hyndyrsyn's men were no more atrocity-prone than the rest of the Royal Dohlaran Army, but like every other man in his regiment, Haarahld Hytchkahk had lost men he cared about in Alyksberg.

That was the real reason Earl Hanth had assigned this attack to the 3rd Alyksberg Volunteers, and they were eager to be about it.

▼　▼　▼

"Second rocket now," Sedryk Maiyrs said almost gently, and an amber signal rocket streaked into the heavens. It exploded, and the mortars stopped firing HE and shrapnel rounds instantly. Star shells continued to erupt above the smoking, half-shattered Switch, but no more explosives rained down upon it.

▼　▼　▼

"Yes!" Hytchkahk hissed and raised his Charisian-designed flare pistol. He squeezed the trigger, and a brilliant red flare arced into the night.

▼　▼　▼

Captain Tyrnyr looked up from the dressing the healer was tying around his badly lacerated left thigh as the first red flare popped into the night. Even as he watched, another one blazed to life. Then a third . . . a fourth, raging like rainy curses in an arc around the Switch's left flank.

Of course there are four of them, he thought past the pain flaring in his wounded leg. *One for each of the lanes the bastards blew through the abatises. And if they turn our left, get between us and Zhonesberg. . . .*

He pushed himself to his feet.

"Sir, I'm not done!" the healer snapped.

"Yes, you are," Tyrnyr said distantly.

"Captain, you could *lose* that leg—assuming you don't just bleed out first!"

"Later," Tyrnyr said.

He took a step, his leg folded, and he started to fall, but a powerful arm caught him. He turned his head and saw Company Sergeant Stahdmaiyr.

"Healer's right, Sir." Stahdmaiyr's voice was pitched low, although it was clearly audible now that the portable angle-guns fire had stopped pounding them. "Let him finish, fer God's sake!"

"I know he's right." Tyrnyr smiled crookedly. "Unfortunately, I don't think we've got time right now, Wylsynn." He wrapped his left arm around the sergeant's shoulders. "Get me the rest of the way to the command post—*now*."

For an instant, Stahdmaiyr looked as if he was going to protest. But then he clamped his jaw and nodded, instead.

"Come with us," he told the Pasqualate lay brother as his CO started hopping towards the CP. "Might be you can finish tidying up once we get there."

▼   ▼   ▼

The last flare blazed to furious crimson life, spilling tendrils of flame down the rainy night, and the Siddarmarkian drums rolled. Then the rifle-armed Volunteers started forward, bayonets gleaming in the star shells' light, throwing back the bloody reflections of the flares, and the high, shivering war cry they'd adopted from their Charisian allies rose fierce and hungry into the downpour.

The 3rd Alyksberg Volunteers stormed forward into the sporadic rifle-fire of the stunned and shocked defenders behind a wave front of hand grenades.

▼   ▼   ▼

"*Stand your ground!* Stand and give 'em hell!" Lieutenant Kartyr Clymyns shouted. "Stand, boys—*stand!*"

Clymyns' 2nd Platoon held the line of trenches covering the Switch's left flank. The company hadn't been on its positions long enough to build the dugouts they really wanted, but the trenches—almost knee-deep with water in the rain—were chest-high and he'd laid out his firing lines with care. But no one had seen a single damned *thing* before the first star shell burst overhead, and then Shan-wei's own fury had ripped a gap straight through the obstacles in front of his lines. How the *hell* had they gotten that frigging close? And what had happened to the men he'd had out there to prevent them from doing anything of the sort?

A spasm of grief tore through him at the thought, sharp as a slash lizard's claw even through his desperate focus on the men around him, because he *knew* what had happened to those sentries.

"There, Sir!" Corporal Zhaikyb Sairaynoh, one of his runners shouted, pointing to the right. "Over there!"

"*Shit!*" Clymyns punched the muddy side of his trench as the assault came out of the dark into the glaring brilliance of the heretic star shells. That was no Charisian attack—it came forward in an almost solid mass, not in the individual waves the Charisians favored. That meant it was the Siddarmarkians, and—

"Alyksberg!" The deep-throated bellow sounded even through the rattle of drums and the crackle of the defenders' rifles, as if confirming his thoughts. "*Remember Alyksberg!*"

"Get back to the Captain, Zhaikyb!" he shouted in the corporal's ear. "Tell him they're hitting the junction between us and Captain Yairdyn's company!"

"Aye, Sir!" Sairaynoh slapped his breastplate in salute and vanished.

▼   ▼   ▼

"At a run, boys! Take 'em at a run!" Captain Hytchkahk shouted. "Take 'em at a run—*don't stop!*"

There was a time and a place for the Charisians' finely developed assault tactics, and he and his men had learned a great deal from their allies. But there were still times and places for the traditional, unstoppable charge of the Siddarmarkian pikes, too . . . even if it was made with bayonets and grenades instead of pikes these days.

Third Section stormed forward—four hundred men, roaring their fury, driving straight into the rippling flashes of the Dohlaran rifles. He was losing people, he knew, but not nearly so many as he might have under other conditions. The heavy rain wasn't doing the defenders' rifles any favors, and he knew were having their share of misfires. There weren't many of them, though, and shock and confusion were his men's strongest allies.

"*Go!*" he shrieked. "*Go for the fuckers' throats!*"

▼   ▼   ▼

"*Look out, Sir!*"

Clymyns' looked up as Adulf Wyznynt, his platoon bugler shouted the warning, and his eyes widened.

"Alyksberg! *Alykskberg!*"

A second Siddarmarkian column came storming in from the left on the wings of that shout, riding a tidal wave of exploding grenades. He heard the screams of wounded men—*his* men—as those grenades arced into their trenches and exploded among them. The front ranks of the column reached the outer trench line and its leading squads leapt down into the trenches, bayonets stabbing, while the ranks behind them simply hurdled the gap and kept right on coming in an obviously preplanned maneuver.

The lieutenant snatched at his double-barreled pistol with one hand and drew his sword with the other.

The 3rd Alyksberg Volunteers swept onward, each unstoppable column driving straight for its assigned objective, and the sudden violence and utter surprise was too much even for veteran troops. Dohlarans began to break from cover, started to fall back from the fury of grenades, the deadly gleam of bayonets gilded in the star shells' spiteful brilliance, and the terrible threat of that battle cry. Only by ones and twos, at first, but Clymyns could feel the fight going out of his men, and his eyes were wild with fury and grief as he vaulted up out of his trench.

"Sound the charge, Adulf!" he shouted, then glared at the two squads of his reserve, staring up at him from the trench he'd left.

"Come on, boys!" He stabbed his sword at that oncoming wave of death as the bugle took up the urgent call. "*With me!*"

He turned without another word, charging to meet the Siddarmarkians without even looking back.

Every single one of his men followed at his heels.

▼　　▼　　▼

"Second Platoon's gone, Sir!" Sergeant Stahdmaiyr said, and Zhames Trynyr swore. Fourth Platoon had already crumbled and 1st and 3rd were fighting for their lives. If 2nd was gone. . . .

"Anything from Captain Yairdyn?" he demanded.

"Nothin', Sir. But it don't look good," Stahdmaiyr said grimly. "Looks like the left's clear back t' the reserve line."

"Chihiro," Tyrnyr breathed. If Yairdyn had been driven back that far. . . .

"We can't hold them, Wylsynn." His voice was bleak, his face grim. "Go find Captain Zholsyn. Tell him it's time to get as many out as he can. We'll buy him as much time as we can."

"I'll send a runner," Stahdmaiyr promised.

"*No,* damn it! Go yourself, Make sure the frigging order gets through!"

"I'll send a good man."

"You'll take it yoursel—!"

"No, Sir," Stahdmaiyr said flatly. "I won't." He showed his teeth for an instant, white as bone under the star shells. "Happen you can court-martial me later, if you've a mind to."

Tyrnyr opened his mouth again, only to close it with a snap. There was no time . . . and he knew the sergeant wouldn't go, anyway.

"All right then, you frigging idiot," he said softly, squeezing the older man's shoulder. Then he cleared his throat. "You'd best get it off quickly, though."

"I'll do that thing," Stahdmaiyr told him, and Tyrnyr drew his pistol and checked the priming while the tide of battle rolled towards him in the staccato thunder of exploding grenades and the rattle of gunfire.

▼   ▼   ▼

"Message for Colonel Sheldyn! Where's Colonel Sheldyn?!"

The exhausted, mud-spattered courier half ran and half staggered into the Zhonesberg command post. He couldn't have been a day over nineteen, although the insignia of a lieutenant was visible through the liberal coating of mud, and he scrubbed fresh muck off his face as he stared around the dripping, poorly lit hut.

"Here!" Gylchryst Sheldyn straightened, turning away from the map table. The light was so bad he'd had his nose almost touching it and still found the smaller labels almost impossible to read. "What message? And who sent it?"

The courier swayed on his feet as he scrabbled in his shoulder pouch and found the hastily sealed letter.

"From Colonel Hyndyrsyn, Sir." Urgency burned through the hoarse fatigue of his voice. "The Switch's been overrun. Captain Tyrnyr's dead—we think—and no more than a hundred of his people got out."

Sheldyn's face tightened. He didn't need to be able to see any maps to understand what that meant.

The heretics had taken Byrtyn's Crossing just over a five-day ago, after driving the Army of the Seridahn out of Fyrayth in two five-days of heavy fighting. They'd obviously received a significant number of heavy angle-guns, and the heretic Hanth had used them to devastating effect on the Fyrayth defenses.

That was . . . unfortunate, since, Fyrayth had been the most important barrier, short of the border fortresses of Bryxtyn and Waymeet, against Hanth's advance into Dohlar itself. It had dominated the highest ground along the entire length of the Sheryl-Seridahn Canal, and that alone would have made its capture a critical loss. Worse, though, its loss had let Hanth out of the bottomless quagmire which had mired his every effort to repeat the short, flanking hooks which had driven the Army of the Seridahn back, step by bloody step, before the winter rains set in in earnest. Drainage west of the Fyrayth Hills was far better, the ground was firmer, and the network of small farming communities between Fyrayth and the border provided a network of roads. They were little more than farming tracks, but they still offered far better mobility for troops and supplies than anything *east* of the hills.

The heretics were out of the box, he thought grimly. Hanth wouldn't be sending any massive thrusts down any of those muddy farm roads, but he didn't need to. Sheldyn's present position at Zhonesberg was more than fifty miles south of the canal. There was no way General Rychtyr could hold a continuous front all the way from there to the canal with the sort of fortified positions needed to stop a determined heretic attack. The labor to build a line of entrenchments that long, even in this weather, *might* have been found, but he had too few troops to man something that enormous even if it had been available.

He'd fallen back thirty-five miles west of Fyrayth to his next main position, the fortified line of redoubts and entrenchments between the villages of Maiyrs Farm, north of the canal, and Stahdyrd's Farm, forty miles north of Zhonesberg, but that was the widest front he could hold in strength, and if even relatively light forces got loose in his rear, reached the canal and high road *behind* him. . . .

The terrain north of Maiyrs Farm was almost as bad as that east of Fyrayth, which gave his left flank a certain degree of security; at least there should be time to pull his left back if Hanth came slogging through the muck and mud to turn it. But the "road net" south and southeast of Stahdyrd's Farm was too widely spread for that. Instead, he'd fortified the towns and major farms and garrisoned them in company and regimental strength. No one thought those garrisons could stop any serious attacks, but what they *could* do was to slow the heretics down, impose enough of a road block Hanth would be forced to bring up the weight for those attracks—which would use up precious time—and warn General Rychtyr if his right was seriously threatened.

"How did they take the Switch so quickly?" he demanded.

"I don't know for sure, Sir," the swaying courier said hoarsely. "We saw signal rockets, then heard portable angle-gun fire." He shrugged helplessly. "Couldn't see or hear anything more than that through the rain before Colonel Hyndyrsyn sent me off to warn you, Colonel."

Sheldyn wanted to glare at the youngster, but it certainly wasn't *his* fault!

"What about—?" he began, then cut himself off.

No doubt Hyndrysyn's dispatch would tell him what in Shan-wei's name was happening . . . assuming the other colonel knew. But Hyndyrsyn's position was held by barely half the strength which had been assigned to Tyrnyr. It was little more than an observation post and communication point. It was unlikely to stop anything that could punch Tyrnyr out of the way so quickly.

"Find this man something hot to eat," he said curtly to his aides, moving closer to the lantern hanging from the hut's roof. "And find me some messengers. Three, at least."

"Yes, Sir!" someone responded, but Sheldyn was too busy slitting open the dispatch to notice who it was.

.XII.

The Temple,

City of Zion,

The Temple Lands,

and

Charisian Embassy,

Siddar City,

Republic of Siddarmark.

Zhaspahr Clyntahn snorted like an overweight doomwhale as the quiet chime sounded through his bedchamber. He rolled onto his side, pulling a pillow over his head, and the wide, comfortable bed surged under his weight. His current mistress stirred sleepily and rolled up against his back, wrapping her arms around him and nuzzling the back of his neck while her breasts pushed against his shoulder blades, and he smiled a half-awake smile.

But then the chime sounded again, louder and clearer. He shook himself and his eyes opened. One hand reached out and pawed at the dimly glowing circle on the bedside table and he squinted irritably at the clock. Its face was clearly visible in the mystic nightlight shining up from the tabletop in answer to his touch, and his face tightened with annoyance.

The woman—the girl, really—behind him clung tightly, urging him to turn towards her, but the chime sounded a third time, louder still, and he muttered a curse, threw back the light cover, and disentangled himself from her. He stooped to pick up the robe he'd discarded a few hours earlier and shrugged into it, tying the sash, then stomped towards the chamber door, waving one hand to bring up the overhead lights.

The door slid open at a touch on the plate set into its frame, and he glared at Brother Hahl Myndaiz, the nervous-looking Schuelerite monk who'd been his valet for the last six years.

"*What?*" he snarled.

"Your Grace, I apologize for disturbing you," Brother Hahl said so quickly the words seemed to stumble over one another. "I wouldn't have, I assure you, but Archbishop Wyllym is here."

"Here?" Clyntahn's eyebrows rose and surprise leached some of the anger out of his expression. "At *this* hour?"

"Indeed, Your Grace." The monk bowed, clearly hoping his vicar's ire had been assuaged . . . or directed at another target, at least. "He's waiting in your study."

"I see." Clyntahn stood for a moment, rubbing the stubble on his bristly jowls, then made the sound of an irate boar. "Well, if he's going to drag me out of bed in the middle of the night, then he can go on waiting for a few minutes. I need a shave and a fresh cassock. Now."

"At once, Your Grace!"

▼   ▼   ▼

Archbishop Wyllym Rayno came to his feet, turning towards the study door as it slid open. The Grand Inquisitor strode through it, immaculately groomed, carrying the fresh scent of shaving soap and expensive cologne with him, and his expression was not one of unalloyed happiness.

"Your Grace," Rayno bent to kiss the brusquely extended ring, then straightened, tucking his hands into the sleeves of his cassock.

"Wyllym." Clyntahn twitched his head in a curt nod and stalked past the archbishop to settle into the luxurious chair behind his study desk. He tilted it back, surveying the Inquisition's adjutant with a sour expression. "You do realize I'd been in bed for less than three hours—and gotten considerably less sleep than that—before you dragged me back out of it, don't you?"

"I wasn't aware of the exact time you retired, Your Grace, but, yes, I realized I'd be disturbing your sleep. For that, I apologize. However, I was convinced you'd want to hear my news as soon as possible."

"I find it difficult to think of anything short of a direct demonic visitation here in Zion that'd be so important it couldn't wait a few more hours," Clyntahn said acidly, but then his expression eased . . . a bit. "On the other hand, I doubt you'd be willing to piss me off this much over something you didn't think really was important. That being said," he smiled thinly, "why don't you just trot it out and find out if I *agree* with you?"

"Of course, Your Grace." Rayno bowed again, briefly, then straightened. "Your Grace," he said, "we've taken one of the so-called Fist of God's senior agents alive."

Clyntahn's chair shot upright and he leaned forward across the desk, eyes blazing with fierce, sudden fire.

"How? Where?" he demanded.

"Your Grace, I've always said that eventually the terrorists would make a mistake or we'd get lucky. In this case, I think it was mostly that God and Schueler decided to give us that luck. It was a routine visit by a parish agent inquisitor—Father Mairydyth Tymyns; he's distinguished himself in his pursuit of the heretic and the disaffected several times already—to collect and

question the cousin of a seditionist we'd taken into custody some days ago."
He shrugged. "The cousin we'd arrested had already been judged and condemned to the Punishment in closed tribunal, and it seemed likely from
Father Mairydyth's interrogation of her father that the rest of her family was
involved. When Father Mairydyth went by the second woman's place of employment, however, he observed that her supervisor appeared to be very
concerned about the interest the Inquisition was taking in her. And when
the cousin was informed she was being taken into custody, she obviously
expected—or hoped, at least—that her supervisor could do something to prevent that from happening. At that point, Father Mairydyth judged it best to
bring the supervisor along for examination, as well. And that was when she
betrayed herself."

"*She* betrayed herself?"

"Yes, Your Grace. It was a woman."

"And just how did she betray herself?" Clyntahn asked intently, his eyes
narrow.

"She attempted to take her own life, Your Grace. That would have been
enough to make us suspect a *possible* connection to the terrorists, regardless
of the means she used. In this case, however, she used poison—and Father
Mairydyth's report strongly commends Brother Zherom, one of our monks,
for reacting quickly enough to catch her wrist before she got the poison into
her mouth. Examination proved that it was identical to the poison capsules
we've found on the bodies of several dead terrorists." Rayno shrugged again.
"Under the circumstances, there can be little doubt she truly is an agent of
the 'Fist of God,' and it seems likely that the family which was already under
suspicion is also associated, perhaps less directly, with the terrorists."

"Yes, that *would* follow, wouldn't it?" Clyntahn murmured.

"Almost certainly, Your Grace. And there's another bit of evidence that,
I think, makes the connection to the terrorists crystal-clear." Clyntahn sat
back in his chair a bit once more, raising his eyebrows in question, and Rayno
smiled coldly. "I regret that I don't have the capture of *two* positively identified terrorists to announce to you," he said, "but clearly this was a well-hidden
cell of their organization. The proprietor of the milliner's in which both of
the prisoners were employed successfully poisoned herself while Father
Mairydyth and his guardsmen were breaking in the door to her apartment
above the shop."

"Excellent, Wyllym," Clyntahn murmured. "*Excellent!* I'd've been far
happier to take two of them, too, but that *does* pretty definitely confirm what
they were, doesn't it? I assume the premises have been thoroughly searched
for any additional incriminating evidence?"

"That search is underway at this very moment, Your Grace." Rayno inclined his head. "Given how elusive these people have been for so long, I'm

not as sanguine as I might wish to be about the likelihood of our discovering any such evidence, but they clearly didn't have time to destroy anything. If they had ciphers, codes, or any sort of written records, we *will* find them. And, in the meantime, I've instructed Bishop Zakryah—the shop is in Sondheimsborough, Your Grace—to make certain his agents inquisitor on-site are as visible as possible while they conduct the search."

"Is that wise?" Clyntahn frowned. "Won't informing the terrorists that we've taken at least one of them alive throw away any advantage of surprise?"

"It seems unlikely they wouldn't have become aware of that very soon," Rayno replied. "It's become painfully obvious that their organization is very tightly knit. They're certain to realize something's happened to this cell, and given the absolute importance of gaining full information from the terrorist we've taken, our interrogators will have to show extraordinary restraint. Frankly, from preliminary reports, I think it's unlikely she'll break quickly. Accursed and foolish though they may be, these terrorists are clearly fanatic in their devotion to their false cause, and this woman seems determined to protect her accomplices as long as possible. That being the case, I very much fear they'll have sufficient warning—and time—to take whatever precautions they can against the information we may obtain before we get it out of her. So I judged it more useful to make the arrests as public as possible, both as an example to any other seditionists who might be tempted to emulate the 'Fist of God' and as a step which might conceivably panic them into taking some action in response that could expose them to additional damage."

"I see." Clyntahn nodded slowly, his eyes slitted in thought. "I'm not certain I agree with you entirely," he continued after a moment, "but your analysis seems basically sound."

"Thank you, Your Grace. And I've also," Rayno flashed another of those cold razors of a smile, "officially announced that the shop's *proprietress* was also taken. I saw no reason to inform the terrorists she was dead at the time." The smile grew even thinner and colder. "If they think we have two information sources, the pressure on them will be even greater. And for the same reason, I've instructed the interrogators to allow the prisoner we do have to believe her friend is also in our custody."

"Very sound thinking," Clyntahn approved.

The Inquisition had learned long ago how to use a prisoner's concern for another against him or her, and the suggestion that someone else was already providing the information the Inquisition sought was often even more useful. Even the most obdurate enemy of God might break and yield answers to end the pain if he believed he was simply confirming something the Inquisition already knew. Why suffer the agony of the Question to protect information someone else had already divulged?

"Where have you sent her?" he asked after a moment.

"To St. Thyrmyn, Your Grace," Rayno replied, and Clyntahn nodded in fresh approval.

St. Thyrmyn Prison wasn't the closest facility to the Temple itself, but it belonged solely to the Inquisition. No one outside the Inquisition knew who'd disappeared into its cells . . . or what had happened to them after they did. It was also the site at which the Inquisition trained its most skilled interrogators, and the prison's permanent staff had been assigned to St. Thyrmyn only after proving their reliability and zeal in other duties. Bishop Inquisitor Bahltahzyr Vekko, St. Thyrmyn's senior prelate, had been an inquisitor for over half a century, and under his command, the prison's inquisitors had an outstanding record for convincing even the most recalcitrant to repent, confess, and seek absolution.

"Very good," Clyntahn said now, "but you're absolutely right that we have to get the fullest information possible out of this murderess." His expression hardened. "Thoroughness is far more important than speed in this instance, and I want every single thing she knows—*all* of it, Wyllym! Sift her to the *bone*, do you understand me?"

"Of course, Your Grace." Rayno bowed more profoundly.

"And tell Bishop Bahltahzyr to see to it that whoever he assigns to her interrogation understands that it's essential we get that information, including a public admission—in her own words in open court, mind you, Wyllym; not simply in writing!—that she and her accursed terrorists consort with demons. And it's essential—*essential*—she undergo the full, public infliction of the Punishment in the Plaza of Martyrs itself. This one *has* to be made an example! And even if that weren't true, her crimes and the crimes of her . . . associates merit the full, utter stringency of the Punishment."

His eyes were ugly, and Rayno nodded once more.

"Emphasize that to Bahltahzyr, Wyllym. Make it very clear! If this prisoner dies under the Question, the repercussions for whoever was in charge of her interrogation will be severe."

▼　▼　▼

"They're gorgeous babies, Irys," Sharleyan Ahrmahk said over the com from her Tellesberg bedchamber. "And so much more willing to sleep through the night than Alahnah was at their age!"

"They are beautiful, aren't they?" Irys said fondly, looking down in the early morning sunlight at the twin babies sleeping in the bassinet beside her bed in Manchyr Palace. "And they'd darned well better be," she added with a smile, "considering how hard I had to work for them!"

"I agree it's an unfair distribution of labor," Cayleb put in, gently swirling the amber whiskey in his glass in his study in the Charisian Embassy.

"Still, let's not completely overlook the male contribution to your handi-work, Irys."

"Oh, of course not, Father," Irys said demurely, hazel eyes glinting wick-edly, and Cayleb snorted. But he also smiled.

"I know you meant it as a joke," he told her, "and there was a time I would have flatly denied it could be possible, but I can't tell you how happy I am that you really are technically my daughter-in-law these days.

Irys' expression softened.

"Believe me, Cayleb, you couldn't possibly have found the idea more outlandish—or monstrous, really—than I would have. And I can't pretend I would have willingly paid the price to get to this moment. But now that I'm here, I wouldn't exchange it for anything."

"That's because you're an extraordinarily wise young woman," Phylyp Ahzgood told her gently. The Earl of Coris was alone in his office, working away steadily at the paperwork flowing across his desk even at so late an hour. "Really, you remind me more of your mother every day, and she was one of the wisest women I ever knew. I don't know how your father would feel about it, of course—not for certain. I know he'd want you to be happy, though, and I think he might be more . . . flexible about that than either of us would have believed, given what happened to him" The earl's mouth tightened. "After the way Clyntahn and those other pigs in Zion betrayed and murdered him and young Hektor, I strongly suspect that wherever he is, he's cheering Charis on every step of the way! Of course, it might still have been a bit much to expect him to be *enthusiastic* over your marriage." The tight lips relaxed into a small, think smile of memory. "He *was* a stub-born man. But I know Princess Raichynda would absolutely approve of young Hektor. And—" his taut mouth softened into a smile "—especially of her namesake and her brother!"

"I don't know about that, either—about Father, I mean," Irys said. "I know you're right that he'd want me to be happy, whatever else, but calling him 'stubborn' is a bit like calling a Chisholmian winter 'on the cool side.'"

It was her turn to smile in mingled memory and regret.

"But you're right about Mother," she continued more briskly after a mo-ment. "I think she'd adore Hektor, and not just because of his name! I only wish she could actually see the babies!"

"I expect she knows all about them," Maikel Staynair put in. "Of course," the Archbishop of Charis acknowledged with an impish smile of his own, "my vocation rather requires me to be optimistic on that point, I suppose."

"That's one way to put it," Aivah Pahrsahn acknowledged dryly. She sat on the small couch in Cayleb's study, shoulder to shoulder with Merlin Ath-rawes, each of them holding a glass of *Seijin* Kohdy's Premium Blend. "But let me get my own vote in for Most Beautiful Baby of the Year, Irys. While I fully agree that Raichynda's an absolutely adorable little girl, I've always had a weakness for handsome *men*, so I have to give my vote to young Hektor."

"You're a courageous woman to stake out an uncompromising position like that," Cayleb told her with a laugh. "As a ruling monarch, one who recognizes the necessity of handling important diplomatic questions with exquisite tact and delicacy, I'm far too wise to be so impetuous! That's why I officially decree that both of them are so beautiful it's impossible to pick between them and the award has to be shared equally."

"But only because Alahnah's no longer in contention for Most Beautiful *Baby* of the Year, of course" Sharleyan said rather pointedly.

"Do I *look* like I just fell off the turnip wagon?" her husband demanded. "Of course that's the only reason it's not a *three*-way tie!"

Laughter murmured over the link. Then Cayleb straightened in his chair.

"Since it's going to be at least another thirty or forty minutes before you can find some privacy in your cabin, Hektor," he said to his adopted son, standing on *Fleet Wing*'s quarterdeck under the bright—if somewhat chilly—afternoon sun of the Gulf of Dohlar, "I propose that we save the rest of this well-deserved lovefest and general baby-slobbering until you can join us."

Hektor snorted, then waved one hand dismissively as the helmsman looked at him with a raised eyebrow.

"It's nothing, Henrai," he told the seaman. "Just thinking about something His Majesty once said when he thought he was being clever. You know, his sense of humor's almost—*almost*—half as good as he thinks it is."

"Aye, Sir. Whatever you say," the helmsman said, grinning at his captain's dry tone, and returned his attention to the set of the schooner's sails.

"Oh, well handled, Hektor!" Cayleb chuckled. But then his expression sobered and he set his whiskey glass on the desk in front of him. "In the meantime, though, I really do want to discuss where we are with Countess Cheshyr. I'm pleased with how well the plan to slip her additional armsmen 'under the radar' is working out. By the way, Merlin, I've decided that's a *very* useful term. We just have to be careful not to use it with anyone else! But I'm still not happy about how focused Rock Coast is on slipping somebody onto her household staff. Sooner or later, either he's going to succeed or he's going to figure out that someone's warning her every time he tries to put an agent inside Rydymak Keep. When that happens, I think someone like him is likely to try . . . more direct measures."

"Not without profoundly pissing off his co-conspirators," Merlin pointed out. "They're not remotely ready to come out into the open yet, and assassinating Lady Karyl would risk doing exactly that. *Especially* if somebody's warning her, since that would imply that someone—probably more of those nefarious, devious *seijins*—already has at least some suspicions about what they're up to."

"That's true," Sharleyan agreed. "On the other hand, Zhasyn Seafarer's about as pigheaded, arrogant, and obstinate as a human being can be. If he thinks he won't be able to get what he wants, he's exactly the type to resort to smashing whatever he thinks is in his way and devil take the consequences."

"Agreed," Merlin began, "but—"

"Excuse me," a new voice said over the link. "I hate to interrupt, but something urgent's come up."

"Urgent?" Cayleb asked sharply, recognizing an unusual sawtooth edge in Nahrmahn Baytz' tone. "What kind of 'urgent'?"

"Owl's been monitoring our remote in Ahrloh Mahkbyth's shop," Nahrmahn said grimly. "What it's picking up isn't good."

.XIII.
St. Thyrmyn Prison,
City of Zion,
The Temple Lands,
Charisian Embassy,
Siddar City,
Republic of Siddarmark,
and
Zhaspahr Clyntahn's Office,
The Temple,
The Temple Lands.

The cell was small, dark, and cold. There was no light, only a dim trickle of pallid illumination spilling through the small, barred grate in the massive timber door. There was no bed, no furniture of any sort, only a thin layer of damp straw in one corner. There wasn't even a bucket or a chamber pot in which a prisoner might relieve herself.

She huddled in the corner, naked, crouching in the straw, her knees drawn up under her chin and her left arm—the only one that still worked—wrapped around them while she folded in upon herself. It was very quiet, but not completely so, and the distant sounds that came to her—their faintness somehow perfected and distilled by the stillness—were horrible. The sounds of screams, for the most part, torn from throats on the other side of heavy doors or so far down the chill, stone corridors of this terrible place that they were faint with distance. And then there were the closer sounds. The sound of a cracked, crazed voice babbling unceasing nonsense. Another voice, pleading helplessly—hopelessly—for someone to listen, to understand that its owner hadn't done whatever it was he'd been accused of. A voice that knew no one was listening, knew no one cared, but couldn't stop pleading anyway.

She knew where she was. Everyone in Sondheimsborough knew about St. Thyrmyn's, although only the truly foolish spoke about it. She'd known exactly where they were taking her and Alahnah from the instant they dragged them out of the shop into the snow and threw them into the closed carriage, and the knowledge had filled her with terror.

Alahnah had wept pleadingly, her pale face soaked with tears, begging to know what had happened to her cousin and her uncle, but of course no one had told her. Zhorzhet hadn't wept, despite her terror and the anguish pulsing in her crippled elbow. She'd refused to give her captors that satisfaction. And she hadn't said a single word, either, despite the monk who'd sat behind her holding the leather strap which had been fastened about her throat, ready to choke any sign of resistance into unconsciousness.

They'd chained both of them as well, of course, although that had scarcely been necessary in Zhorzhet's case. There'd been no way she could have fought them after the damage they'd already done to her right arm. Besides, they'd been armed and armored. She'd been neither, and even if she'd been able to fight, there was no way she could have provoked them into killing her. Not when the under-priest clearly knew exactly what sort of prize he'd stumbled upon.

Alahnah had moaned, shrinking in upon herself, seeming to collapse before Zhorzhet's eyes, when the carriage door opened on the courtyard of St. Thyrmyn Prison. She'd shaken her head frantically, bits and pieces of terrified protest spurting from her, but the priest who'd arrested them had only flung her from the carriage. She'd landed on her knees with brutal force, crying out in pain, then sprawled forward on her face, unable even to catch herself with her hands chained behind her, and a waiting agent inquisitor in the black gloves of an interrogator had jerked her back to her feet by her hair.

"Please, no!" she'd moaned, blood oozing from a split lip as he hauled her high on her toes. "It's a *mistake!* It's *all* a mistake!"

"Of course it is," the interrogator had sneered. "And I'm sure we'll get it all sorted out soon enough."

He'd dragged her away, and the arresting under-priest had looked at the monk holding the strap about Zhorzhet's neck.

"Be very careful with this one, Zherom," he'd said. "She has a great deal to tell us, and I'm looking forward to hearing all of it. Be sure you don't let her . . . slip away before Father Bahzwail's had the chance to make her acquaintance."

"Oh, no worry there, Father Mairydyth," the monk had assured him. "I'll get her delivered safe enough."

"I'm sure you will," the priest had said with a cold, cruel smile. Then he'd climbed down from the carriage himself and strode briskly across the courtyard without a single backwards glance, a man who was clearly eager to report his success to his superiors.

The monk watched him go, then twisted the strap hard enough to make Zhorzhet choke, her eyes widening as he cut off her air.

"Up you get, you murderous bitch," he'd hissed in her ear, his mouth so close she felt his hot breath. "There's a hot corner of hell for such as you, and you might's well start the trip there now."

She'd twisted, choking, fighting involuntarily for air as he strangled her, and he'd pulled her to her feet by the strap, then dragged her down the steep carriage steps and into the prison. At least he'd been forced to let her breathe along the way, but that hadn't been a kindness. Indeed, the kindest thing he could have done would have been to strangle her to death, and she knew it. But he hadn't. He'd only dragged her along endless corridors until, finally, he'd turned her over to another interrogator—a thick-shouldered, hulking giant of a man with blunt, hard features and merciless eyes.

"I'll take her, Brother Zherom," he'd said, and his voice had seemed to come from some underground cavern. It wasn't all that deep, but it was deadly cold, the voice of a man who no longer possessed any human emotions, and its *emptiness* was far more terrifying than any leering cruelty could have been.

"And welcome to her," Brother Zherom had said, passing over the strap. Then he'd reached out, capturing Zhorzhet's face between the thumb and fingers of his right hand, forcing her head around to face him, and he'd smiled.

"Don't reckon I'll be seeing you again . . . before the Punishment," he'd told her. "Might, though. There's more'n one way t' question a heretic bitch." He'd leaned forward and licked her forehead, slowly and gloatingly, then straightened. "Won't be so pretty by the time you hit the fire."

She'd only stared at him mutely, and he'd laughed, then tossed her head aside, turned, and walked away.

And then she'd been taken to her cell, but her new captor had paused at the door.

"You're one of the *priority* prisoners," he'd told her. "Understand you've already tried to kill yourself once." He'd shaken his head and spat contemptuously on the stone floor. "Don't know what your rush is. You'll see Shanwei soon enough! But we can't have you trying again, and I've seen people

198 / DAVID WEBER

hang themselves with things you'd never've thought they could." He'd smiled coldly. "Don't think *you'll* be doing that, though."

And then he'd stripped her naked, there in the cell doorway, before he'd removed her manacles and flung her into it, and she'd been wrong about his absence of emotion. There'd been more than enough leering cruelty in his eyes—in his groping hands—as he reduced her to fragile, naked vulnerability, and she'd never believed for a moment it was only to keep her from hanging herself with the hem of her chemise.

Then he'd laughed once, the door had crashed shut behind her, and he'd walked away, leaving her to the cold and the fear . . . and the despair.

▼   ▼   ▼

"You sent for me, My Lord?"

Father Bahzwail Hahpyr crossed the office quickly and bent to kiss the ruby-set ring Bishop Inquisitor Bahltahzyr Vekko extended across his desk.

"Yes, I did. Be seated. I think you'll be here a while."

"Of course, My Lord."

Hahpyr settled into his usual chair, his expression attentive. He and the bishop inquisitor were old colleagues, although he was little more than half Vekko's age. He was broad-shouldered, with dark hair and eyes, and a thin purse-like slit of a mouth, whereas Vekko was in his late seventies, with a frail, ascetic appearance. The white-haired, gray-eyed prelate looked like everyone's favorite grandfather with his full, snow-white beard. Until one looked *deeply* into those eyes of his and saw the curious . . . flatness lurking just below their surface like an opaque wall.

Bahltahzyr Vekko had been one of Zhaspahr Clyntahn's closest supporters for decades. Indeed, he'd been Clyntahn's mentor back in the Grand Inquisitor's seminary days. The student had long since outpaced the master, of course, yet he remained one of Clyntahn's closest confidants, and he'd played a major role in shaping the Grand Inquisitor's vision of Mother Church's future. In his more honest moments, Vekko acknowledged to himself that he would have lacked the iron nerve to embrace Clyntahn's strategy for *achieving* that vision, and he'd actually advised against his old protégé's . . . proactive attitude towards the Out Islands. Then again, he'd often thought his own caution was a failing in a true son of Mother Church. A servant of God with the steely spine of a Zhaspahr Clyntahn came along far too rarely, and Vekko could only thank Schuler—and envy them—when they did.

He knew he himself would never have dared to goad the Out Islanders to deliberately provoke a jihad, and there were times, especially when news from the battlefront was bad, when that timorousness of his made it difficult to sleep, worrying about the future. He'd never said as much to Clyntahn, but he knew the Grand Inquisitor had never imagined tiny, distant Charis could possibly survive the initial attack. Neither had Vekko, for that matter, and the fact that it had surely demonstrated Clyntahn had been right from the start. It could never have happened if Shan-wei *hadn't* been their secret mistress all along! And if there were times when his faith wavered, when it seemed the accursed weapons with which she'd gifted her minions must prove unstoppable, a little prayer always reassured him with the comforting knowledge that God would not permit Himself to be defeated. And the truth was that the ferocity of the Jihad—the stern measures required to meet its demands—had only further strengthened the Inquisition's position. Once the Jihad ended in God's inevitable victory, the Grand Inquisitor's control of Mother Church—and all of God's world—would be unbreakable.

Of course, first that victory had to be attained.

"I have a special charge for you, Father," the bishop inquisitor said, sitting back in his chair. "Father Mairydyth's brought us an unexpected prize."

"Indeed, My Lord?"

Hahpyr raised his eyebrows—in question, not surprise. As St. Thyrmyn's senior interrogator, he was accustomed to being handed "special charges," and his record of success was unbroken. There was a reason he taught all of the senior courses in interrogation technique, and many of the Inquisition's most successful agents interrogator had interned under him.

"Indeed." Vekko nodded, his normally kindly expression stern. "The Grand Inquisitor's made it clear that we need our best interrogator on this one. And you'll have to be careful, mind you! If she dies under the Question, Vicar Zhaspahr will be . . . most unhappy. Is that understood?"

"Of course, My Lord," Hahpyr murmured. He couldn't remember the last time he'd allowed a "special charge" to elude God's searchers in death.

"Very well. I know I can trust your intelligence is much as your efficiency, Bahzwail, but I want to be very clear with you about the needs of this particular interrogation, because its outcome is particularly vital to the Jihad. This isn't a simple heretic or seditionist—this is an outright rebel against God Himself, a true servant of Shan-wei and Kau-yung."

"I understand, My Lord."

"In that case, the first thing to consider—"

▼　▼　▼

She never knew how much time had passed before the door opened again—abruptly, without warning—and far brighter light streamed in through it. A man in a cassock and priest's cap stood silhouetted against the brightness, and her darkness-accustomed eyes blinked painfully against the light.

The faceless shape stood gazing down at her, the golden ring of an upper-priest glittering on one hand, then stepped back.

"Bring her," he said curtly, and two black-gloved inquisitors dragged her to her feet.

She thought about struggling. Every instinct cried out to fight desperately, but no resistance could help her now, and she refused to give them the satisfaction of beating her into submission. And so she walked between them, her head high, gazing directly in front of her and trying not to shiver in her nakedness.

It was a long walk . . . and it ended in a chamber filled with devices fit to fill the strongest heart with terror. She recognized many of them; others she had no name for, but it didn't matter. She knew what they were for.

Her captors dragged her across to a heavy wooden chair. They slammed her down in it and strapped her wrists and ankles to its arms and heavy front legs. Then she coughed as another strap went around her throat, yanking her head back against the rough timber of the chair back.

"Leave us," the upper-priest said, and his assistants sketched Langhorne's scepter in silent salute and disappeared, still without speaking a single word.

She sat there, still staring straight in front of her, and he settled onto a stool, sitting to one side, out of her line of vision unless she turned her head to look at him. He said nothing. He only sat there—a silent, predatory, looming presence. The silence stretched out interminably, until she felt her good wrist beginning to turn against its strap, struggling involuntarily as the terrible tension piled slowly higher and higher within her. She tried to make her hand be still, but she couldn't—she literally couldn't—and she closed her eyes, lips moving in silent prayer.

"So, this is what the 'Fist of God' looks like."

The cold, cutting voice came so suddenly, so unexpectedly, that she twitched in surprise. Her head started to turn automatically in the upper-priest's direction, but she stopped it in time, and he chuckled.

"Not very impressive, once you drag the scum out of the shadows," he continued. "You and your employer are going to tell me everything you know—everything you've *ever* known. Did you know that?"

She said nothing, only clenched her teeth while she continued to pray for strength.

"It's amazing how predictable heretics are," the upper-priest mused. "So brave while they hide in the dark like scorpions, waiting to sting the Faithful. But once you drag them into the light, not so brave. Oh, they *pretend*—at first. In the end, though, it's always the same. Shan-wei's promises won't help you here. *Nothing* will help you here, except true and sincere repentence and penance. Is there anything you'd care to confess now? I always prefer to give my charges the opportunity to confess and recant before the . . . unpleasantness begins."

She closed her eyes again.

"Well, I didn't really think there would be," he said calmly. "Not yet. But one thing we both have is plenty of time. Of course, ultimately, I have far more of it than you do, but I'm willing to invest however much of it is necessary to . . . show you the error of your ways. So why don't I just let you sit here and think about it for a bit? Oh, and perhaps you'd like a little company while you do that."

The stool scraped as he got off it and walked to the chamber door. Her eyes popped open again, against her will, and his path carried him into her field of vision and she saw him clearly at last. He paused and smiled at her—a dark-haired, dark-eyed man, broad shouldered and perhaps four inches taller than she was—and she closed her eyes again, quickly.

"Bring her in," she heard him say, and her hands clenched into helpless fists as she heard someone else whimpering hopelessly. Metal grated, clashed, and clicked, and then a hand twisted in her hair.

"I really must insist you open your eyes," the upper-priest told her. She only squeezed them more tightly together—and then someone shrieked in raw agony. "If you don't open them, I'm afraid we'll have to hurt her again," the inquisitor said calmly, and the shriek sounded again, more desperate and agonized even then before.

Zhorzhet's eyes jerked open, and she moaned involuntarily—not in fear, but in horror and grief—as she saw Alahnah Bahrns.

The younger woman was as naked as she was, but she'd been brutally beaten. She hung from chained wrists, welted and bleeding, her skin marked with at least a dozen deep, angry, serum-oozing burns where glowing irons—like the one in the hand of the hooded interrogator standing beside her—had touched. She was no more than half-conscious, and all the fingers on both hands were obviously broken.

"She didn't have a great deal to tell us," the upper-priest said. "I'm afraid it took some time for us to be fully satisfied of that, though."

He nodded to the hooded interrogator, and the other man gripped Alahnah's hair, jerking her head up, showing Zhorzhet the eye that was swollen totally shut, the bloody, broken mouth. He held her that way for several seconds, until the upper-priest nodded, then opened his hand contemptuously and let her head fall limply forward once more.

"At first, she insisted it was all a mistake, a misunderstanding, of course," the upper-priest told Zhorzhet conversationally. "That she knew nothing at all about your accursed organization. But after we'd reasoned with her for a bit, she understood how important to the soul confession is. She admitted you'd recruited her for the 'Fist of God,' although from how few facts she could tell us, she's obviously a new recruit. Still, I think it might be . . . instructional for both of you to spend a little time together before I get down to reasoning with *you*."

He released his hold on her hair, and then he and the masked inquisitor simply walked away and left them.

▼   ▼   ▼

"We have to do *something*." Aivah Pahrsahn's voice was tight, over-controlled. "We all know what they must be doing to them right this moment." She closed her eyes, her face wrung with pain. "That's terrible enough, but—God help me—what they *know* is even worse." She shook her head. "If they break—*when* they break; they're only human—they can do terrible damage."

"Forgive me," Nahrmahn Baytz said gently over the com link, "but the actual damage they can do is limited. You set up your organization too carefully for that, Nynian."

"If you're talking about details of other cells, you're probably right, Nahrmahn," Merlin said grimly. "But both Marzho and Zhorzhet know a great deal about general procedures, and Marzho, especially, had to know Nynian's overall strategy. At the very least, the information they have can give Rayno and Clyntahn a much better look inside how Helm Cleaver's organized. Not only that, Marzho definitely *does* know Nynian used to be Ahnzhelyk Phonda, and God only knows what Rayno's investigators could do with that bit of information! I don't think any of us will ever make the mistake of thinking they're *incompetent*, whatever else they may be, and they've got the manpower and the resources to investigate every single person who ever interacted with Ahnzhelyk. There's no way of telling where *that* might lead." He shook his head. "And if the Inquisition goes ahead and announces it's captured agents of the 'Fist of God' and produces them for the Punishment, it may go a long way towards undermining the aura of . . . inevitability Helm Cleaver's been building."

"Ahnzhelyk's not the only thing Marzho knows about that could cause serious damage, either." Aivah's voice was equally grim. "You're right, she does know I used to be Ahnzhelyk, but she also knows 'Barcor' used to be a Temple Guardsman . . . and that he's a shop owner in Zion. She doesn't know his real name, or what *sort* of shop, but that's enough to lead the Inquisition to Ahrloh Mahkbyth—especially if they put that information together with the fact that it was Ahnzhelyk who helped build his initial clientele—and if we lose Ahrloh, we lose the head of Helm Cleaver's action arm in Zion."

"He's already made plans to quietly disappear for a few five-days," Nahrmahn told her. "He's spread the alert through your organization in Zion—and composed a message for you, as well, although obviously he expects it to take five-days to reach you. In the meantime, he's been 'called away on business,' leaving that assistant of his, Myllyr, to mind the shop. It's an innocuous enough excuse that he can always come back if there's no sign that they suspect him. In the meantime, he'll be safely out of the Inquisition's reach."

"That's all well and good, Nahrmahn," Sharleyan's com voice said somberly. "And believe me, from a cold-blooded, strategic perspective, I'm deeply relieved to hear it. But completely aside from the damage their knowledge could do if the Inquisition gains it—and Merlin and Nynian are right; even if all they get is a better understanding of how Helm Cleaver's organized, they'll be far more dangerous—there's what we know is *happening* to them right now."

"I know," Merlin acknowledged, his sapphire eyes dark, his mouth a hard line. "I've met both of them—I *know* them. If I could do anything to get either of them out of St. Thyrmyn's, I damned well would, Sharley. But we can't. The prison's too close to those frigging power sources under the Temple for Nimue or me to stage a *seijin* jailbreak, and nothing else could possibly work. Helm Cleaver sure as hell can't break them out!"

"That's true." Cayleb's face was bleak, far older than his actual years. "But there are other forms of escape—like the one we'd've given Gwylym, if we'd only been able to figure out how."

"I know what *I'd* like to do," Nimue Chwaeriau said harshly. "You're right, Merlin—we can't rescue them. But if they're so eager to call you and me demons, I say we visit a little demonic vengeance on them."

"What do you mean?" Merlin asked, and the image Owl had projected into Merlin's vision showed her teeth.

"I mean we strap a two-thousand-kilo smart bomb onto one of the recon skimmers and drop it right down St. Thyrmyn's damned chimney!" she snarled. "We program it to use only optical guidance systems, so it's completely passive, without a damned thing for any sensors in the Temple to see coming, and we blow the entire prison to hell! At the very least, we spare Zhorzhet and Marzho a horrible death—yes, and every other poor bastard in the place, too. But just as important, I think it's time we gave these sick sons-of-bitches a little of Dialydd Mab's medicine closer to home. Let Clyntahn and Rayno try to explain why their precious Inquisition's just been hit by what has to be one of Langhorne's own Rakurai right in the middle of Zion!"

Agreement rumbled over the com, but Merlin shook his head.

"That *could* be a good idea," he said. "It could also be a very bad one, though. For instance, we couldn't possibly do that with a black powder bomb, and anything more advanced than that might very well cross some parameter in a threat file somewhere. We don't know whether or not there's anything under the Temple that would be capable of recognizing high explosives residue when it sees it, and the prison's so close anything like that would have

204 / DAVID WEBER

to get a sniff of the dust. Even if that weren't true, the law of unanticipated consequences worries me, because we don't know how Clyntahn and Rayno would spin that kind of an explosion. I'm inclined to think you're right, Nimue—a lot of people *would* think that it had to be a Rakurai strike, and that would almost have to be a good thing from our perspective. But there are other ways it could shake out. He might argue that it's clear proof we really *are* demons, for instance, and the people who're already inclined to believe him—and there are a hell of a lot of those people, even now— would probably accept that it was just that. Unless we're prepared to hit other targets the same way—a *lot* of other targets—he'll probably proclaim that we can't because the 'Archangels' have intervened to stop us, and I don't think we could do that without killing a hell of a lot of innocent people along the way. And from a purely pragmatic viewpoint, we couldn't be *positive*, even with the heaviest bomb one of the skimmers could lift, that we'd kill Zhorzhet and Marzho." His expression was unflinching. "Trust me, if I could be positive of that—positive we'd be sparing them the Question and the Punishment—I'd be a lot more inclined to say damn the consequences, and pull the trigger!"

"I think those are valid points." Maikel Staynair's voice was somber, heavy with grief. "And I think we should also bear in mind that whatever we do—or don't do—hasty decisions may have serious implications for the future. Merlin's right that the notion of unleashing 'Rakurai'—especially in Zion—is something we should consider very carefully before we act. And before we do, we should be very clear on when and where any of those *future* strikes might be in order. Particularly since we *can't* strike the Temple itself. As I understand it, that 'armorplast' covering it would stop almost any bomb we could throw at it?"

"That's true," Cayleb acknowledged heavily. "Mind you, I'm fully in favor of Nimue's bomb if that's the best possibility we can come up with, but you and Merlin are right. That sort of escalation could take us places we don't want to go . . . and we *can't* be positive it would save our people from the Question. I think we have to be careful our desperation to do *something* doesn't lead us into doing exactly the wrong thing."

Nimue looked rebellious, but she settled back in her chair in her Manchyr chamber without further argument.

For the moment, at least.

"The prison's just over the line into Sondheimsborough from Temples-borough, right on the edge of the safety zone you established, Merlin," Nahrmahn said after a moment. "Could we get a SNARC remote into it safely?"

"I don't want to actually see what they're doing to them, Nahrmahn!" Aivah said harshly.

"I wasn't thinking about that," he said, and shook his head, his expression gentle. "To be honest, monitoring their questioning so we know what may have been gotten out of them would be of critical importance, but I wouldn't expect anyone except Owl and me to actually view any of the take from the sensors. That wasn't what I had in mind, though—not really."

"Then what *were* you thinking about?" Merlin asked.

"I was thinking about the sabotage function." Nahrmahn's image frowned. "I remember something you said a long time ago, Merlin—something about the remotes' incendiary capability and how it could have been used to eliminate . . . someone."

The pause before the pronoun was barely noticeable, but Merlin understood it perfectly. And he also understood why, with Irys part of the conversation, the deceased Prince of Emerald didn't want to explain that the candidate for assassination in question had been her father.

"I remember the conversation," he said out loud. "You're thinking about penetrating St. Thyrmyn's, finding them, maneuvering a couple of the incendiaries into their ear canals, and setting them off."

Aivah looked at him with a horrified expression, and he reached out and took her hand in his.

"It would be quick," he told her quietly. "*Very* quick, especially compared to what they're already facing. In fact, it would almost certainly be faster and less painful than Nimue's bomb."

She stared at him for a long moment. Then she nodded, and a single tear trickled down her cheek.

"Unfortunately, Commander Athrawes," Owl's avatar said, "I compute that the prison in question is too close to the Temple."

"Why?" Cayleb asked. "We've sent remotes in closer than that before."

"Yes, we have, your majesty," the AI replied. "In all of those instances, however, the remote has been placed as a parasite on some individual or vehicle passing through the zone we wished to scan. It has been set for purely passive mode, and the telemetry channels have been deactivated until it leaves the dangerous proximity to the Temple once more."

"I see where he's going, Cayleb," Merlin said. The emperor looked across the study at him, and he shrugged heavily. "Placing the remotes accurately enough to do the job would require two-way communication. We'd have to actually steer them into place, which would be a ticklish maneuver at the best of times, and we'd have to be able to see where they needed to go while we were doing it." He shook his head. "Those remotes are pretty damned stealthy, but I'm afraid there's no way we could guarantee a telemetry link that close to the Temple wouldn't be detected."

"Oh God," Aivah whispered, and her pale face seemed to crumple, as if the dashing of Nahrmahn's suggestion had destroyed her final hope.

Merlin released her hand, to put his arm about her and drew her head down against his chest. She pressed her cheek into his breastplate, and one hand stroked her hair gently. They sat that way for several seconds, and then that hand paused and Merlin's eyes narrowed.

"What?" Cayleb asked sharply. Merlin looked at him, and the emperor twitched his head impatiently. "I know that expression, Merlin—I've seen it often enough! So out with it."

Aivah sat up, brushed the palm of one hand quickly across her wet face, and looked at him intently from eyes which held a fragile gleam of hope.

"*Have* you thought of something?" she asked.

"I don't know," he said slowly, "and even if I have, it's not something we'll be able to do instantly. But if it works," in that moment, his smile was Dialydd Mab's, "it should provide Clyntahn and Rayno with all the 'demonic vengeance' you could possibly hope for, Nimue."

▼　▼　▼

Zhorzhet Styvynsyn shivered uncontrollably and licked cracked and broken lips.

She sat once again in the horrible wooden chair, fastened in place, waiting for them to hurt her again, and felt the spirit—the faith—which had sustained her so far flickering, fading. Guttering towards extinction as it slipped from her desperate fingers.

So far, she'd told them nothing, and she clung to that knowledge, to that fierce determination. But that determination was beginning to fail, to crumble under the unceasing assault—under the pain, the hopelessness, the degradation. The carefully metered beatings, the rapes.

Alahnah had died, screaming, under the Question in front of her, *begging* her to tell the interrogators anything she knew to stop them from hurting her. Zhorzhet had sobbed, twisting in the chair, fighting her bonds, blinded by tears, but somehow—*somehow*—she'd held her silence while she watched her friend die.

She'd screamed herself, often enough, over the endless, terrible hours since Alahnah's death—begged them to stop hurting *her* when the red hot needles were used, when the fingernails and toenails were ripped away. But even as they made her beg, made her *plead*, she'd refused to speak the words that might actually have made them stop.

Yet she knew her defiance was nearing its end. Alahnah wasn't the only innocent they'd Questioned in front of her, and agony wasn't the only torture they'd used upon her. They'd left her in that accursed chair, keeping her awake endlessly, dousing her with buckets of icy water whenever she started to nod off—or touching her with a white-hot iron, just for a change.

They'd taken turns hammering her with questions, again and again—leaning close, screaming in her face, threatening her . . . and then hurting her horribly to prove their threats were real. They'd held her head under water until she was two-thirds drowned, mocked and degraded her. She'd refused to eat, tried to starve herself to death, and they'd force-fed her, cramming the food down her throat through a tube. And always—*always*—they'd come back to the pain. The pain she'd discovered they could inflict *forever*, in so *many* different ways, without allowing her to escape into death.

And soon, all too soon, they'd return to do that again. They'd promised her, and they'd left the brazier and the irons glowing ready in it to remind her.

Please, God, she thought. *Oh*, please. *Let me die. Let it* end. *I've fought—really I have—but I'm only mortal. I'm not an angel, not a* seijin, *I'm only me, and I can't fight forever. I just . . . can't. So please,* please *let me die*.

Tears trickled down her filthy, bruised face as she sat in the chair, staring at the irons, waiting, but there was no answer.

▼　　▼　　▼

No one ever saw the small, carefully programmed autonomous remotes that crept in through St. Thyrmyn Prison's barred windows, crawled quietly down its chimney flues, flowed under its doors. They were tiny, no bigger than the insects they were disguised to resemble, and they radiated no detectable emission signature. They only made their way to selected points, chosen from the most painstaking analysis of the prison's layout Owl's satellite imagery had allowed. And once they reached those points, they simply dissolved into inert, unremarkable dust and, in the process, released their cargoes.

The nanites which rose from those disintegrated remotes were still smaller, microscopic, their programmed lifetimes measured in less than a single Safeholdian day before they, too, became no more than dust. Yet there were millions of them, and they drifted upwards, freed from confinement, spreading in every direction. It took hours—far more hours than any member of the inner circle could have wished, just as it had taken too many days simply to design and fabricate them in the first place—but they spread inexorably, sifting into every nook and cranny, until they'd infiltrated the entire volume of that brooding, dreadful prison, found every living thing within those walls of horror.

And then they activated.

▼　　▼　　▼

Zhorzhet's eyes widened and she strained desperately, futilely, against her bonds as she heard Father Bahzwail's terrifyingly familiar stride coming down the corridor towards the torture chamber once again. She heard herself whimpering, hated the weakness, knew that all too soon the whimpers would once again become raw-throated shrieks.

The upper-priest appeared in the arched doorway, smiling at her, drawing the black gloves onto his hands.

"Well, I see you've been expecting me," he said chattily, crossing to stand beside the glowing irons. He stroked one insulating wooden handle, polished and smooth from years of use, with a slow, gloating fingertip, and his eyes were colder than a Zion winter. "Now, where *did* we stop last time, hmmm?" He drew an iron from the brazier, waving its glowing tip in a slow, thoughtful circle while he pursed contemplative lips. "Let me see, let me see. . . ."

She moaned, but then the Schuelerite blinked. He lowered the iron and raised his other hand to his forehead, and he looked . . . puzzled somehow.

Zhorzhet didn't notice. Not at first. But then *she* felt something, even through her shivering terror. She didn't know what it was, but she'd never felt anything like it. It didn't *hurt*—not really, and certainly not compared to the terrible, terrible things that happened in this dreadful chamber. But it felt so . . . strange. And then a gentle lassitude flowed into her—shockingly soothing after so much pain, so much terror. A soft, gray veil seemed to slip between her and the anguish throbbing through her body, and she gasped in unspeakable gratitude as she allowed herself to relax into its comfort. She had no idea what it was, how long it would last, but she knew it was the finger of God Himself. That He'd reached into her horrible, endless nightmare, to give her at least this brief moment of surcease. Her scabbed lips moved in a silent prayer of thanks and her head began to spin. No, it wasn't her head. The entire torture chamber—the whole world—was spinning *around* her, and she was spiraling down, down, down, as if the sleep she'd been denied so long was creeping up upon her at last. As if. . . .

▼ ▼ ▼

"What did you say?"

Zhaspahr Clyntahn stared across his desk at Wyllym Rayno, and for the first time the archbishop could ever remember, the Grand Inquisitor's florid face was paper white.

Of course, his own wasn't much better.

"Father Allayn's personally confirmed it, Your Grace," he said, wondering how his voice could sound so . . . normal.

"Everyone? *Everyone?*" Clyntahn demanded in a tone which desperately wanted the answer to be no.

"Everyone," Rayno replied heavily. "Every prisoner, every interrogator, every guard, Bishop Inquisitor Bahltahzyr, every member of his staff—*anyone* who was inside St. Thyrmyn's. All dead."

"But no one *outside* the prison?"

"No, Your Grace."

"But . . . *how?*" The question came out almost in a whisper, and something very like terror burned in Clyntahn's eyes.

"We don't know, Your Grace." Rayno closed his eyes for a moment, then raised one hand in a helpless gesture. "We have our own healers—members of the Order we can trust, not Pasqualates—examining the bodies even now. And as soon as they've finished, we'll dispose of them in the prison crematorium."

Clynthan nodded in understanding. The gesture was almost spastic. It would be far from the first time the crematorium on the prison's grounds had been used to hide the Inquisition's secrets. If it turned out that a prisoner wasn't suitable for public execution for whatever reason, it was simplest to just make sure they disappeared forever.

But it had never concealed a "secret" like *this* one.

"W-what have they found? The healers?" he asked now.

"Nothing, Your Grace," Rayno said heavily. "Just nothing at all. There are no wounds, no signs of violence, no indications of any known disease, no evidence any of them even sought assistance, assuming they had time for that. It's as if one moment they were walking around, going about their normal duties. And the next, they . . . they just *died*, Your Grace. Just died and dropped right where they stood. One of the lay brothers actually collapsed across the threshold as he stepped *out* of the prison. That was what drew the outside guards' attention so quickly."

"Oh, Sweet Schueler." This time, it truly was a whisper, and Clyntahn's hand shook as he gripped his pectoral scepter. "Pasquale preserve us."

Rayno nodded, signing himself quickly with the scepter, and his eyes were dark as they met the Grand Inquisitor's.

How did they do it? his brain demanded of itself. *How* could *they do it?*

He never doubted that it had to have been the false *seijins*—no, the demons who *pretended* to be *seijins!*—but how?

There's nothing like this in the records—not in The Testimonies, *not in the* Book of Chihiro, *and not in the Inquisition's secret files.* Nothing! *Never. Not at Shan-wei's hands or during the War Against the Fallen. Not even Grimaldi accomplished anything like this after his fall!*

He tried to push that thought from him, to concentrate on how the Inquisition must deal with this. At least it had happened at St. Thyrmyn's. With only a little good fortune, they could conceal it from the rest of Mother Church and her children, at least for a time. Pretend it had never happened—*deny* it had, if the false *seijins* and their allies spread the story. But *he* knew, and the Grand Inquisitor knew, and eventually more and more of their inquisitors would hear whispers, rumors, about what had truly happened.

St. Thyrmyn's was too central to the Inquisition, too vital a nexus for its operations, for the secret *not* to leak at least among the senior members of their own order. And once that happened, it would inevitably spread still farther. When it did, when they could no longer simply deny it, how did they address it, *explain* it?

He had no idea, but worrying about that was vastly preferable to facing the far more terrifying question beating in the back of his brain.

If the heretics' demon allies could do *this*, what *else* could they do?

.XIV.
St. Nezbyt's Church,
City of Gorath,
Kingdom of Dohlar.

I wish I was sure this was a good idea, Sir," Captain Lattymyr said quietly as the closed carriage turned into the courtyard behind St. Nezbyt's Church.

"*You* wish you were sure?" Sir Rainos Ahlverez laughed shortly. "This has the potential to turn into something very *un*-good, Lynkyn. That's why I should have put my foot down and refused to let you tag along!"

"Wouldn't have had much luck with that after all this time, Sir," Ahlverez's aide replied with a slow smile. "Besides," the smile faded, "I doubt it would've mattered in the end." He shrugged. "Been made pretty clear to me that the Army doesn't need my services at the moment any more'n it needs yours."

"And for that I'm truly sorry," Ahlverez said quietly.

"No, Sir." Lattymyr shook his head, eyes stubborn. "You did exactly what needed doing, and an officer of the Crown could be in a lot worse company."

"But not much more *dangerous* company," Ahlverez pointed out as the carriage drew up in the courtyard. "And this particular meeting's not likely to make that company any less dangerous."

"Maybe not, but I didn't have anywhere else I needed to be this evening, Sir. Might's well spend it watching your back." The tough, weathered-looking captain smiled again, briefly. "I'm getting sort of used to it, actually."

Ahlverez chuckled and reached out to clasp his aide's shoulder briefly before he reached down and unlatched the carriage door.

The driver—a solid, phlegmatic-looking Schuelerite monk with iron-gray hair and dark eyes—had already climbed down from the box. Now he unfolded the carriage's steps and stood holding the open door.

"Thank you, Brother Mahrtyn," Ahlverez said, climbing down, and the monk nodded.

"I'm happy to have been of service, General," he replied in a deep voice. There was a rasping edge to the words—from an old throat injury, Ahlverez suspected, looking at the scar on the side of the man's neck—and the monk bobbed his head in a respectful but far from obsequious bow.

Ahlverez nodded back and waited until Lattymyr had joined him. Then he raised an eyebrow at the monk in silent question.

"The side chapel, My Lord," the Schuelerite replied, addressing him with the courtesy due the general's rank no one had yet gotten around to formally taking away from him. "Langhorne's, not Bédard's."

"Thank you," Ahlverez murmured once more and led Lattymyr up the steep flight of stairs to the church's backdoor while Brother Mahrtyn climbed back up to the high driver's perch and drove the carriage back out of the courtyard.

This really could be an incredibly stupid idea, the general told himself as he opened the ancient wooden door at the head of the stairs. *Even assuming the son-of-a-bitch has something worth listening to, the mere fact that you're meeting him could be enough to get both of you handed over to the Inquisition.*

Yes, it could. And he'd never have accepted the . . . invitation if it hadn't been hand-delivered by Brother Mahrtyn. And, he admitted bleakly, if he hadn't had so much personal experience with arrogant, incompetent superiors who completely ignored their subordinates' advice—and reality. That had forced him to reconsider certain previously held views, and events since the Army of Shiloh's destruction had lent their own weight to his decision to come.

But it was still hard—harder than he'd expected, really.

He stepped through the door into the smell of incense, candle wax, printer's ink, leather bindings, and dust that seemed a part of every truly old church he'd ever visited. Saint Nezbyt's was older than many, and saw less use than most, though its parish had once been a bustling, thriving one, if never precisely wealthy. Located in the harbor district near the docks, that parish had lost members gradually for several decades as workers' homes were slowly but steadily displaced by commercial and Navy warehouses. Then the shipyards' tremendous expansion to meet the needs of the Jihad had accelerated that displacement enormously. In fact, Archbishop Trumahn and Bishop Executor Wylsynn had seriously contemplated closing Saint Nezbyt's entirely. In the end, they'd decided not to. Probably because Mother Church always hated closing churches—and, the more cynical might have added, depriving parish priests of their rectories—but also because Bishop Staiphan Maik and his staff had needed office space in his capacity as the Royal Dohlaran Navy's intendant.

212 / DAVID WEBER

None of that staff was present at this late an hour on a Wednesday, however. The nave and sanctuary were deserted, lit only by the gleam of presence lamps around the main and side altars, as Rainos and Lattymyr skirted the organ and the choir loft. A crack of light showed under the closed door to the side chapel dedicated to the Archangel Langhorne, and Rainos rapped lightly on the varnished wood.

"Enter," a voice responded, and Rainos' eyebrows rose in surprise as he recognized it. Despite the avenue by which the invitation had reached him, he hadn't really expected Maik to be personally present. Most churchmen would have avoided something like this like the plague, and the potential consequences for a bishop in Maik's position if things went badly didn't bear thinking upon.

The general opened the door and stepped through it into the lamp-lit chapel, Lattymyr at his heels. The aide closed the door behind them, and Ahlverez looked at the man who'd invited him here.

"My Lord," he said rather coldly.

"Sir Rainos," the other man said. "Thank you for coming. I know it couldn't have been an easy decision . . . for several reasons," the Earl of Thirsk added.

"I suppose that's one way to put it." Ahlverez twitched a brief smile, then bent to kiss the Staiphan Maik's ring. "My Lord," he said again, in warmer tones.

"I, too, thank you for coming, my son," Maik told him as he straightened. The silver-haired bishop's brown eyes were very steady. "As Lywys, I know it must have been a difficult decision. Unfortunately," it was his turn to smile, and the expression was sad, "many people face difficult decisions at the moment."

"Yes, they do, My Lord," Ahlverez acknowledged, then looked back at the Thirsk and raised both eyebrows in silent question.

▼   ▼   ▼

Lywys Gardynyr watched those eyebrows rise and murmured a mental prayer. There were more ways this meeting could go disastrously wrong than he could possibly have counted, and he was frankly amazed Ahlverez was here at all, given the bitter hatred between the Ahlverez family and himself. Maik had been openly dubious when Thirsk broached the possibility of the meeting, and the earl hadn't blamed him a bit. But he trusted Shulmyn Rahdgyrz' judgment as much as that of any man in the world, and Rahdgyrz had been Sir Rainos Ahlverez' quartermaster during the disastrous Shiloh campaign. His reaction when Thirsk cautiously sounded him out about Ahlverez had been . . . enlightening.

And, it would appear, judging by the fact that he's actually here, that Shulmyn had a point, the earl thought now. *Of course, I suppose it's always possible he only wants to hear what I have to say in hopes I'll come up with something so incriminating he can hand me straight over to the Inquisition.*

Given what he had in mind, the possibility certainly existed. Thirsk opened his mouth, but before he could speak, Bishop Staiphan raised his hand, his ruby ring glowing in the lamplight.

"Excuse me, Lywys," he said, "but as the host of this little meeting— or, at least, as the bishop providing a site for it—I think explanations to the General should come from me, first."

Thirsk hesitated for a moment, then inclined his head.

"Of course, My Lord," he murmured, and Rainos turned back to the prelate.

"The idea for this meeting was Lywys', Sir Rainos," he said. "Initially, he was hesitant to mention it to me, for reasons which are probably fairly evident. But he suspected he might need a suitable . . . intermediary to convince you to accept his invitation. And then, too, of course, it probably wouldn't have been very healthy for either of you if he or a member of *his* staff had contacted you. Especially after Mother Church's reaction to the suggestion that Admiral Rohsail's prisoners not be delivered to the Punishment." The bishop smiled fleetingly. "I realize the suggestion—which I also supported, as it happens—came from neither of you. I'm afraid certain . . . senior churchmen don't truly believe that, however."

He paused, head tilted, and Ahlverez nodded his understanding.

"I'm also aware of the long-standing . . . animosity between your family and him," Maik continued levelly. "I know the reasons for it, and I've had to deal with its consequences virtually every minute of every day since I was assigned to Gorath by Archbishop Wyllym." His eyes hardened. "I can tell you of my own certain knowledge that Lywys Gardynyr has never once, in all the time I've known him, made a decision out of personal pettiness or done a single inch less than his duty required of him. I know Duke Malikai was your cousin and the husband of Duke Thorast's sister. But I am as certain as I am of God's love that what happened off Armageddon Reef was *not* Lywys' fault. That he did all he could do to prevent it. And I strongly suspect, Sir Rainos, that you know the same thing, whatever Duke Thorast is willing to admit."

He paused again, waiting, and silence stretched out. Ahlverez' face was hard, his eyes dark. But then, finally, his shoulders settled ever so slightly and he seemed to sigh.

"I don't *know* that, My Lord," he said. "I have, however, been forced to come to *believe* it." He smiled bleakly. "It's not a subject I'm prepared to discuss over the family dinner table, you understand. But—" he looked squarely at Thirsk "—Faidel was always a stubborn man. And a proud one. He wasn't the type to allow anyone else to shoulder his responsibilities . . . or to rely on a subordinate whose authority might seem to challenge his own. Or, for that matter, to defer to a subordinate whose knowledge might underscore his *lack* of knowledge. It's not easy for me to say that, but I've had some experience standing in your shoes, My Lord. So, yes, I can believe you did your utmost to prevent what happened . . . and were ignored."

"Sir Rainos," Thirsk said frankly, "I think I know how difficult it must have been for you to come to that conclusion. And to be fair to your cousin, while I think what you've just said about him was accurate, it's also true that I had no more idea of what the Charisians—" he watched Ahlverez' eyes very carefully as he deliberately avoided calling them heretics "—were about to do to us at Armageddon Reef than he did. *No one* outside Charis had any clue about the galleons, the new artillery, the new tactics—*any* of it. Even if Duke Malikai had actively solicited my advice and taken every word of it to heart, Cayleb Ahrmahk still would have devastated our fleet." He shook his head. "He went right ahead and completely destroyed the portion of it under my direct command in Crag Reach, after all. I suppose what I'm trying to say is that simply because you feel you can't blame me for everything that happened, it would be the height of unfairness to blame your *cousin* for everything, either. I've done that, in the privacy of my own thoughts," he admitted. "More than once. And I've come to the conclusion that I felt that way at least partly to excuse my own failure, when it was my turn at Crag Reach. After all, if it was all because he hadn't listened to me, then none of it was *my* fault. But the truth is that however many mistakes he made, however stubborn he might have been, in the end we were simply beaten by a foe who was too powerful—and too unexpected—for it to have ended any other way, no matter what we did."

Ahlverez' nostrils flared. He hadn't expected that, and for a moment he felt a flicker of anger that Thirsk should think he could be flattered into some sort of sloppy-minded lovefest. But then he looked into the earl's eyes and realized he meant every word of it.

"I think that may have been as hard for you to say as it was for me to admit Faidel might have been more at fault than you, My Lord."

"Not so much hard to say as hard to accept in the first place," Thirsk said wryly, and Ahlverez surprised himself with a sharp snort of amused understanding.

"I can't tell you how relieved I am to hear what you've both just said," Maik said, smiling warmly at them. "I don't know you as well as I've come to know Lywys, Sir Rainos, but what I do know convinces me that both of you are good and godly men. That both of you are conscious of your responsibilities to God, the Archangels, Mother Church, and your kingdom . . . in that order."

The last three words came out deliberately, and he paused yet again, letting them lie in the chapel's stillness for several seconds before he inhaled sharply.

"This is a time of testing," he said very, very quietly. "A time of testing such as Mother Church and this entire world have never seen since the War Against the Fallen itself. As a bishop of Mother Church, it's my responsibility to recognize that test, to respond to it, to be the shepherd her children have the right to demand I be . . . and that's a responsibility I'm not convinced I've met." He shook his head. "I've done my best, or what I *thought* was my best, at least—as you and Lywys have—but I fear I've fallen short. Indeed, I've become *convinced* I've fallen short, especially since what happened to Lywys' family."

"That wasn't your fault, Staiphan. You did everything you could to protect them. You know you did!" Thirsk said quickly, his eyes distressed, but Maik shook his head again.

"Despite what you may have heard, Sir Ahlverez," the bishop said, his own eyes sad, "Commander Khapahr was no Charisian spy, nor did he attempt to murder Lywys when he was 'unmasked.' Indeed, he was the most loyal—and one of the most courageous—men I've ever been honored to know, and his death was a direct consequence of *my* actions."

Ahlverez' eyes widened, and Thirsk shook his head violently.

"It was *not!*" the earl half-snapped. "Ahlvyn was the bravest man I've ever known. He chose his actions, and if anyone's to blame for what happened to him, it's me. Because I knew what he'd do if he thought my girls, my grandchildren, were in danger. I *knew*, and I didn't try to stop him."

Thirsk's voice quivered, and Ahlverez realized there were tears in his eyes.

"You couldn't have stopped him, Lywys," Maik said gently. "That's the sort of man he was, and I knew it as well as you did." The bishop turned back to Ahlverez. "I summoned the Commander to a meeting, Sir Rainos, where I informed him, indirectly, that arrangements were being made to transport Lywys' family to Zion 'for their protection.' I didn't know, then, that he'd take unilateral action to smuggle them out of Gorath without informing Lywys but I did hope that he'd deliver my warning *to* Lywys. Except that he didn't, and when the Inquisition discovered his arrangements, he deliberately implicated himself as a Charisian agent to divert suspicion not simply from Lywys, but from me, as well. And when he shot Lywys, it was to provide the strongest 'proof' of Lywys' innocence he possibly could. *That's* the sort of man Ahlvyn Khapahr was."

Ahlverez swallowed, seeing the pain in Thirsk's face, the regret in Maik's eyes, and he knew it was true.

"All—" To his surprise, he had to stop and clear his throat. "All honor to him, My Lord. A man blessed with friends that loyal is blessed indeed. But why tell me about it?"

"For several reasons, my son. First, because I think it's further proof of the sort of man *Lywys* is." Maik allowed his eyes to flit briefly to Lattymyr, standing a pace behind Ahlverez. "A man doesn't inspire that sort of loyalty without earning it."

Ahlverez nodded slowly, and the bishop shrugged.

"A second reason to tell you is because his actions underscore the sacrifices good and godly men are willing to make for those they love and respect . . . and for what they *believe*." His eyes were back on Ahlverez now. "Neither side in this Jihad has an exclusive claim to honesty of belief, to devotion to God, or to courage, My Lord, whatever certain people may say. I think that's something any child of God needs to understand, no matter how mistaken he thinks his brother or sister may have become.

"And a third reason," the bishop's voice became no less measured, no less steady, but it was suddenly sadder than it had been, "is because the reason the Commander ran those risks, made that sacrifice, was that he understood *why* Lywys' family was to be transported to Zion . . . and that it had nothing at all to do with their protection. That the official reason for it was a lie, and that their 'safety' was the farthest thing from the mind of the men who ordered them moved."

Those steady brown eyes held Alverez' unflinchingly.

"But perhaps even more importantly," Maik continued in that same, un-wavering voice, "I told you so that you would understand what I'm about to say. Understand that this is no sudden, irrational conclusion on my part, but rather the result of a process it's taken me far too many months to work through. A conclusion which is the *reason* I summoned the Commander that night for the meeting which led to his death."

"What sort of . . . conclusion, My Lord?" Ahlverez asked as the prelate paused yet again.

"It's a very simple one, my son. One too many people—including me—have failed to reach . . . or to remember. And it's merely this: Mother Church is not the mortal, *fallible* men who happen to choose her policies at any given moment. The Archangels are not the servants of men who think they know God's will better than God Himself. And God is not impressed by mortal pride, overweening ambition, or the narcissism which makes a man like Zhaspahr Clyntahn seek to pervert all that Mother Church was ever meant to be—to drown the world, all of God's creation, in blood and fire and terror—in the name of his own insatiable quest for power."

APRIL
YEAR OF GOD 898

A t least it wasn't snowing.

In fact, he thought as he stepped down from the carriage to St. Kylmahn's Foundry's paved courtyard, it was a beautiful morning. Cold, but crystal-clear, with a sky of polished lapis and only the merest hint of a breeze.

It was, in fact, the sort of day April sent to lull the citizens of Zion into the false hope that spring might be upon them soon.

No doubt there's an allegory in that, he thought dryly, and turned to the commander of his mounted escort as the door to Brother Lynkyn Fultyn's office opened and the bearded Chihirite stepped out into the cold. The lay brother's breath rose in a cloud of steam, touched to gold, like a frail echo of the sacred fire which had crackled about the Archangels' brows. Under other circumstances, Rhobair Duchairn would have preferred to walk, enjoying the sunlight and the opportunity to make personal contact with the people whose spiritual shepherd he was supposed to be, but Major Khanstahnzo Phandys, the commander of his personal bodyguard, had refused to permit it. In this instance, given some of the rumors floating about the Temple, Duchairn wasn't at all certain the major didn't have a point where his personal safety was concerned. On the other hand, he wasn't supposed to know Wyllym Rayno had personally ordered Phandys to be certain Duchairn had as little contact with his sheep as was humanly possible. That was a new twist, and the Church's treasurer suspected it might actually confirm some of the wilder "rumors" which had come his way.

He put that thought temporarily on hold and beckoned Phandys closer.

"Yes, Your Grace?" the major said, just as attentively as if he hadn't been the Inquisition's spy.

"We'll probably be here at least an hour or two, Major. In fact, I think it's entirely possible we'll be here through lunch. I think you should see about getting your men under cover and arranging a meal for them if we do stay through midday. Should I speak to Brother Lynkyn about that?"

"Thank you, but no, Your Grace. That won't be necessary. I'll arrange a rotation to keep anyone from being out in the cold too long, and Brother

Zhoel and I have worked out standing arrangements to feed the men if we're here through mealtime."

"Good," Duchairn said, and walked across the courtyard to Fultyn, extending a gloved hand. The Chihiro bowed to kiss the vicar's ring through the leather, but a wave of Duchairn's other hand stopped him.

"Consider that all courtesies due my lordly rank have been duly offered and received, Brother," he said with a breath-steamy smile. "We don't need your lips getting frostbite!"

"It's not cold enough for that, Your Grace." Fultyn gave him an answering smile, but obeyed the injunction. "It is, however, cold enough that I'm sure you'd rather get into the warmth than stand out here talking," the foundry's director continued, and stepped to one side, beckoning the vicar through the door he'd just emerged from. "Vicar Allayn's already here."

"I saw his carriage." Duchairn nodded at the other vehicle standing in the courtyard, its paired horses well rugged against the sunny cold. "Has he been here long?"

"Only twenty minutes or so, Your Grace." Fultyn followed the vicar through the door into his office vestibule. "He and I have already discussed Earl Rainbow Waters' request that we expedite manufacture of his land-bombs."

Duchairn nodded again, more soberly this time. The Inquisition-prescribed term for the infernal device in question was certainly accurate, although he personally found the Army of God's original name for it much more appropriate. They truly were the very spawn of Kau-yung, and the Order of Pasquale's hospitals were all too crowded with men who'd lost limbs to them. Still, he wasn't surprised Zhaspahr Clyntahn had opted to "discourage" the troops' chosen label, especially when his own inquisitors had taken to calling the terrorists here in Zion "the Fist of Kau-Yung" . . . at least where they didn't expect their words to get back to the Grand Inquisitor's ears. And whatever *he* might think of them, he could scarcely fault Rainbow Waters for responding in kind to a weapon which was going to cost him so many men in the coming campaigns. And now that the Inquisition had signed off on the production of the Charisian-introduced "percussion caps," at least Brother Lynkyn's foundries could provide him with the things, whether they were called "land-bombs" or "Kau-yungs."

"Will you be able to meet the quantities he's requesting?" the treasurer asked, unbuttoning his heavy coat as they crossed the vestibule and entered the outer office. Fultyn's clerks rose, bowing deeply to the vicar as he passed through, then diving back into their never-ending paperwork as soon as he waved them back onto their stools.

"Of course not." Fultyn smiled crookedly. "He knew that when he submitted the request, Your Grace. I doubt we'll be able to manufacture more than a third of the numbers he's asking for—especially if we mean to get them to him in time for the beginning of the campaign."

Duchairn snorted in understanding. Frankly, he doubted the Church could have *paid* for all of the land-bombs the Mighty Host of God and the Archangels' commander desired, and he was pretty sure Rainbow Waters knew it. But he understood exactly why he'd asked for them anyway. By requesting three or four times as many as could possibly be manufactured and shipped in the available time, he established his own opinion of how production capabilities should be allocated. The earl and the treasurer had come to understand one another quite well, and in the process, Duchairn had picked up a few new wrinkles on how to manipulate a bureaucracy.

There truly were some skills in which Harchongians had no peers.

"Well, we'll just have to come as close as we can," he said as Fultyn reached past him to open the inner office's door. He stepped through it, and Allayn Maigwair turned from the courtyard window from which he'd watched his arrival and extended a hand to his fellow vicar.

"Beautiful weather, isn't it?" he said, and Duchairn nodded.

"I think it's the best we've seen since the end of October," he agreed, clasping forearms with Maigwair. "I hope no one's stupid enough to think it's the beginning of the spring thaw, though!"

"No one outside the Inquisition," Maigwair said dryly. Duchairn's eyes widened, and he flicked them sideways to Fultyn, still half a stride behind him and to one side, but Maigwair only grimaced. "Brother Fultyn's not going to misunderstand me," he said. "He knows I was simply referring to the Inquisition's . . . impatience to resume operations as soon as the weather makes it humanly possible. Or, preferably, even sooner than that! Don't you, Brother?"

"Of course I do, Your Grace," Fultyn replied imperturbably . . . and exactly as if he truly meant it.

"I see." Duchairn gave Maigwair's forearm a tighter squeeze than usual, then stepped back to allow Fultyn to walk around him to the chair behind the desk. The Chihirite started past him, then paused as Maigwair raised a forestalling hand.

"Yes, Your Grace?"

"I completely forgot that I wanted to ask Brother Sylvestrai and Master Bryairs to sit in on our discussion today, Brother." The Church's captain general smiled apologetically. "There are a couple of points about the new shells and their fuses I wanted their opinions on. Would it be too much trouble to ask you to invite them to join us?"

Fultyn's eyebrows twitched, as if they'd begun rising in surprise. If they had, though, he stopped them immediately and nodded.

"Of course, Your Grace. I'm sure Brother Sylvestrai is in his office, but

I believe Tahlbaht may be out on the manufacturing floor. I'll probably have to hunt for him. I hope a ten-minute or so wait will be acceptable?"

"Ten minutes will be just fine, Brother. I'm sure Vicar Rhobair and I can find something to talk about until you get back."

"With your permission, then, Your Graces," Fultyn murmured, bowed, and withdrew from the office, closing the door behind him.

"He really is a remarkably perceptive fellow, isn't he?" Maigwair said dryly as the door shut.

"Being disciplined by the Inquisition for questioning perceived wisdom when you're only nineteen has that effect on people," Duchairn replied, unwrapping his thick, soft muffler and slipping gratefully out of his coat in the office's warmth. He hung the coat on Fultyn's coat tree and turned back to Maigwair, smoothing his cassock.

"He's about the farthest thing from an idiot you're likely to meet, too," he continued. "That means he's staying as far away as possible from offering the Inquisition an excuse to 'discipline' him again . . . which isn't all that easy, now that I think about it, given what he's doing for the Jihad." The treasurer's lips twisted bitterly for a moment, then he shook himself and looked Maigwair in the eye. "Which brings me to why you've sent him off on an errand any one of his clerks could have discharged equally well. Should I assume it has something to do with St. Thyrmyn's? Or, rather, with the obviously utterly baseless *rumors* about St. Thyrmyn's which are currently swirling about the Temple's rarefied heights?"

"You should, indeed," Maigwair said grimly, and in a considerably lower voice. He twitched his head, inviting Duchairn to join him once again by the window . . . which happened to be the farthest point in the office from its door and whose frosty panes happened to let them see if anyone's ear just happened to be pressed against them.

"Have you heard anything beyond rumors?" Duchairn asked, equally quietly, his shoulder less than two inches from his fellow vicar's.

"No." Maigwair shook his head. "But they're so damnably persistent I'm positive there's at least something to them. And Tobys agrees; he's been making some very quiet inquiries of his own, and the very things his sources in the Inquisition aren't telling him convinces him that something—something *serious*, Rhobair—went wrong at the prison."

Duchairn nodded almost imperceptibly and pursed his lips, clearly considering what Maigwair had just said. Bishop Militant Tobys Mykylhny was probably Maigwair's most trusted subordinate after Archbishop Militant Gustyv Walkyr, himself. Maigwair and Mykylhny had attended seminary together, although Maigwair had been two years ahead of him at the time. In fact, he'd been the younger man's assigned mentor until his own consecration, and Mykylhny had been a senior officer in the Temple Guard before it gave up so many of its personnel to the newly formed Army of God. For the last several years, he'd functioned as the captain general's senior intelligence officer. As such, he'd been forced to establish his own contacts in the Inquisition and create a working relationship with them which was at least civil. Duchairn never doubted that Wyllym Rayno was fully aware of who those contacts were, but the Inquisition's adjutant clearly understood that Maigwair needed the ability to cross check at least some of what the Inquisition told him about Charisian capabilities. For that matter, Rayno—unlike Clyntahn—probably understood that Maigwair needed access to at least some of the information the Inquisition deliberately *didn't* share with him.

Of course, those "contacts" of Mykylhny's have to know Rayno's keeping a very close eye on them, the treasurer reflected. *That's probably what Allayn meant about "aren't telling him"—if they've got working brains, anyway! The question is what I tell him. . . .*

"I think you're right," he said after a long moment. "And whatever it is, it scares the hell out of Zhaspahr."

"Really?" Maigwair rubbed his chin. "I admit, I thought he looked a little . . . squirrely at our last meeting. I couldn't decide whether it was because of whatever happened at St. Thyrmyn's or the way Hanth's driving Rychtyr back into Dohlar." He shook his head. "He didn't even gloat at me over how that 'confirms the heretics' are positioning themselves for their southern strategic shift."

"I was a bit surprised by that myself," Duchairn admitted. "On the other hand, however pleased he may be by the evidence that his 'Rakurai' brought us good information, he's still unhappy as Shan-wei about the Dohlaran situation." The treasurer shrugged. "On the one hand, he thinks it proves he was right; on the other, we're still only in the early stages of the redeployment, and he's afraid they're going to succeed before we can get all the pieces moved around. I think he's feeling some serious doubts about how . . . firmly committed to the Jihad, let's say, Dohlar is. In fact, I'm surprised he hasn't already taken Thirsk completely off the board, especially now that the Inquisition's lost its . . . leverage with him. I expect he would've, if he wasn't so worried about how the Dohlaran Navy might react. They're not too happy about what happened to their commanding admiral's family already, and only the ones too dumb to pour piss out of a boot haven't figured out the real reason his daughters and grandchildren were being sent to Zion 'for their own safety.'"

Both vicars grimaced in matching distaste.

"But Dohlar isn't what has him running scared," Duchairn continued. "I don't know exactly what happened at St. Thyrmyn's, but I do know you're right that it must've been disastrous, whatever it was."

"You *know* that?" Maigwair turned his head to look at his fellow vicar. "How?"

"I'm sure you've realized by now that I don't keep Major Phandys around just because I'm so fond of him," Duchairn replied a bit obliquely, his tone dry, and Maigwair snorted.

"I *am* still the Temple Guard's official commanding officer," he said. "And, as a matter of fact, I know *exactly* why Major Phandys was assigned to your detail, since I was the one who signed off on that assignment when Rayno 'suggested' it." He actually looked embarrassed for a moment, then shrugged. "He doesn't report directly to me anymore—hasn't in quite a while, actually—but I don't doubt for a moment that he's still Zhaspahr's dagger inside your staff, Rhobair. I trust you're keeping that in mind?"

"Since my brain still functions, at least on odd-numbered days, yes, I am." Duchairn's tone was even drier than it had been. "On the other hand, every so often the Major can be worth having around." Maigwair arched his eyebrows in polite disbelief, and Duchairn chuckled harshly. "Oh, not because he *means* to be! Although, to be fair," he added judiciously, "I think he's perfectly prepared to keep me in one piece against threats that don't come out of the Inquisition. And against those sorts of threats, he's actually a very competent fellow."

Maigwair nodded, and Duchairn shrugged.

"Anyway, I've discovered I can use him as a sounding board in some ways. His poker face isn't quite as good as he thinks it is, and his reactions to things I say sometimes offer me an insight into what Rayno's been discussing with him. And every so often some little tidbit of information oozes out of him without his realizing it. And because it does, I know—or at least strongly suspect—something Zhaspahr hasn't seen fit to share with us."

"About what happened in the prison?" Maigwair asked intently.

"Not directly." Duchairn shook his head. "But what Zhaspahr hasn't told you or me—or even Zhasyn, for that matter—is that his agents inquisitor took a member of the 'Fist of God' alive a couple of five-days ago."

"*What?*" Maigwair's eyes widened. "Are you sure about that?"

"Almost positive," Duchairn said firmly. "Of course, the Inquisition might be wrong about their suspicions, but that's certainly who *they* thought they'd caught. It was that arrest in Sondheimsborough—the milliner and her staff."

"Mistress Marzho?" Maigwair's tone was equal parts incredulous and disgusted, and it was Duchairn's turn to arch an inquiring eyebrow. "My wife's been one of her clients for the last ten years." The captain general shrugged. "That's probably true of a quarter of the vicarate, for that matter! I'd assumed that was one reason Rayno's publicized the arrests so energetically. I'm sure everyone on her client list is looking over his shoulder, peering into his closet, and going feverishly over all his correspondence for the last thirty years or so to see if there's anything *he* needs to worry about. Langhorne knows she'll denounce anyone Zhaspahr wants denounced in the end." He shook his head, his eyes dark. "They always do . . . just like they always confess. And if they don't, Rayno and his bastards will lie about it, just like they did about Manthyr."

Duchairn nodded, although he was a bit surprised by Maigwair's frankness—and, especially, the specific mention of what had happened to Gwylym Manthyr—even now. The fate of the Charisian prisoners Dohlar had surrendered to the Inquisition must rankle even more with the other vicar than he'd realized.

Well, whatever else he may be—or may have been—Allayn's a soldier at heart and always has been. Of course that had to rankle. And you've already figured out he's not as stupid as you always liked to think he was. Maybe you shouldn't be so surprised that he's ashamed when Mother Church tortures honorably surrendered prisoners to death . . . and the "heretics" don't.

"That's not why they were arrested," he said softly.

"Oh, don't tell me *Mistress Marzho* is a heretic!" Maigwair looked as if he wanted to spit on the office floor. "I've *met* the woman, Rhobair! If *she's* a heretic, then *I'm* Harchongese!"

"I don't know about the state of her soul, but according to a minor indiscretion on Major Phandys' part—one which would probably get him toasted over a slow fire if Rayno knew about it—both she and her assistant were agents of the 'Fist of God.'"

"That's ridiculous!" Maigwair snapped, but his expression was suddenly more troubled, and Duchairn shrugged.

"I didn't say the Inquisition was right about that; I only said that's what they were *arrested* for. Of course, we both know Zhaspahr and Rayno aren't exactly noted for granting anyone the benefit of the doubt these days, but I'm about as confident as I could be without a signed memo from Zhaspahr that that's exactly what they thought they had on their hands. Apparently, there's some actual corroborating evidence this time, too. Something about one of them trying to poison herself when the Inquisition turned up at the shop."

"Langhorne," Maigwair murmured, his eyes more troubled than ever, and Duchairn nodded slowly.

That's right, Allayn. Think about it. I never met this Marzho, but you obviously thought she was a good and godly woman. So if she really was a member of the "terrorists" killing our fellow vicars, what does that say about the rest of them? Or, for that matter, for just how well—and where—that "rest of them" might be hidden?

"At any rate, Zhaspahr had both of them taken off to St. Thyrmyn's, where he could be positive of his security. And, probably, be confident you and I wouldn't get wind of his accomplishment until he was ready to spring it on us at a time and a place of his own choosing."

"That's exactly what he *would* do, isn't it?" Maigwair granted sourly.

"Of course it is. But that's why I'm sure something truly disastrous must've happened at the prison. He's had them in custody for the better part of four five-days, and he hasn't called us in to crow about it yet."

"Maybe he doesn't have anything *to* crow about yet," Maigwair suggested.

"Allayn, if there was any connection at all between these women and *anyone* Zhaspahr's put on his 'needs killing' list, we'd've heard about it by now. Do you really think anyone could spend that long under the Question without giving up something Zhaspahr could at least spin to suit his purposes?"

"No," Maigwair shook his head, his expression grim. "No, of course not."

"Well, he hasn't released them, the Inquisition hasn't publicly confirmed why they were arrested in the first place, and according to a couple of my lay brother clerks in the Treasury—we're responsible for St. Thyrmyn's operating expenses, so there's some contact between my people and theirs—no one's seen Bahltahzyr Vekko or that poisonous bastard Hahpyr in at least a five-day. When I heard that, I asked a few quiet questions of my own. Nothing heavy-handed, of course, but I 'accidentally' ran into Rayno day before yesterday and, while we were chatting, I mentioned that I needed the monthly spreadsheets from St. Thyrmyn's for February and March. It's a fairly large budget item, probably the Inquisition's second or third single largest expense, and they frequently get behind on their accounting and need a little nudge, so it's hardly the first time I've mentioned it to him. Usually, he rolls his eyes and promises to look into it, but it still takes a five-day or two to get me the numbers. *This* time he just brushed it off, though, so I offered to have my people contact Vekko's staff directly. He didn't like that idea at all. He didn't *say* so, but Wyllym's not quite as good at fooling me as he thinks he is, and he was just a bit too hearty about assuring me he'd *personally* see that I got the needed paperwork."

He shrugged again.

"Given his reaction, Zhaspahr's continued silence about one of his greatest triumphs, and Vekko and Hahpyr's . . . non-appearance, I'm forced to conclude that something nasty must have happened to the prison. Something nasty enough Zhaspahr's decided to keep it completely quiet. Oh, and by the way—the spreadsheets arrived in my offices that very afternoon, over Vekko's signature. But, you know, Treasury's *very* good at detecting forgeries."

"It wasn't his signature? That's what you're saying?"

"Not unless he's taken to making both 'k's in his last name the same height. Since he hadn't done that a single time in the last seventy years or so—I checked against an expense voucher in his file that goes all the way back to 856, as well as more recent examples of his signature—it seems unlikely he should suddenly change now. I spent five years in Treasury's forgery division as an under-priest, you know. Or maybe you didn't," he acknowledged, recognizing the surprise in the other man's expression. "It's been quite a while, and no doubt I'm a little rusty, but I can still recognize a falsified signature when I see one. It's not a big thing, but I'm positive someone else signed the documents with his name. Which, coupled with the fact that they arrived so promptly. . . ."

He shrugged, his eyes cold.

"Langhorne," Maigwair said again, clasping his arms across his chest while he stared out the frosty window. "But what *could* have happened?" he murmured, as much to himself as to Duchairn. "I never met Hahpyr—I'd heard about him, of course—and I'm just as happy I haven't. But I know Vekko. Always makes me feel like there's fresh dog shit on the sole of my shoe when I'm in the same room with him, but he's a tough old bastard, and unlike certain inquisitors you and I could name, he's always seemed more concerned with the Inquisition's mission than its powerbase. God knows I won't miss either of them if something *has* happened to them, but what could cause both of them to suddenly disappear?"

"Now *that*, Allayn, is an excellent question. And while you're pondering it, you might want to consider another minor point, too."

"And what would that be?" Maigwair asked, regarding the other Vicar warily.

"The St. Thyrmyn's crematorium's been awfully busy the last few days," Duchairn said very, very quietly. Maigwair's nostrils flared, and it was Duchairn's turn to turn away, gazing out the window. "You and I both know the Inquisition's used that crematorium to dispose of a lot of . . . inconvenient mistakes over the years. One heap of ashes is very like another, after all. But it's been operating steadily for almost a full five-day now, and my people at Treasury just got a supplemental invoice for an *awful* lot of fuel. One hell of a lot more than they'd need to get rid of two or three women who'd been arrested by mistake."

"You're suggesting everyone on the prison staff is *dead*?" Duchairn suspected Maigwair would have preferred to sound rather more incredulous than he did.

"I don't know what happened any more than you do, Allayn. But *something* sure as hell did, and Zhaspahr's not frothing at the mouth and demanding something be done about whatever it was, either. Instead, he and his pet viper are pulling out all the stops to sweep it under the rug. And whatever's happened, it's put the fear of Shan-wei into our good friend the Grand Inquisitor. I doubt it'll keep him knocked off stride for very long—he's a resilient, arrogant son-of-a-bitch who's absolutely convinced things will work out the way he wants them to in the end, and I suspect a good Bédardist would find him a *very* interesting subject—but for right now, he's had the *shit* scared out of him."

"The question, of course," the treasurer added with an almost whimsical smile, "is whether what's scared the hell out of *him* should be scaring the hell out of you and me, too."

.II.
Battery St. Thermyn,
Basset Island,
HMS *Eraystor*, 22;
HMS *Destiny*, 54;
and
HMS *Hurricane*, 60,
Saram Bay,
Province of Stene,
Harchong Empire.

W hat's that, Sir?"
Captain of Spears Thaidin Chinzhou looked up from the cup of tea cradled in his gloved hands at the question. Sergeant Yinkow Gaihin stood on the rampart, pointing out across Basset Channel. The early morning sun gilded Battery St. Thermyn in chill golden light, spilling down from a sky that was crystal-clear to the south and east but layered with steadily spreading, dramatic cloud coming down from the northwest. Chinzhou was a native of Stene Province, and he could almost smell the late-winter snow hiding in those clouds. It wouldn't be that many more five-days before spring actually put in an appearance, but winter obviously wasn't giving in without a fight.

He shook that thought aside, handed the teacup regretfully back to the private with the straw-wrapped demijohn of hot tea, and climbed the steps to Gaihin's side.

"What's what, Sergeant?"

He really tried not to sound testy, and Gaihin had been with him for the better part of a year now. He was also more than ten years older than his section commander, and he only twitched a shoulder apologetically and pointed again.

"*That,* Sir," he said, and for the first time, the concern in his voice registered with the youthful captain of spears.

Chinzhou's sun-dazzled eyes saw nothing for a moment and he stepped behind the sergeant, peering along the outstretched arm and pointing finger, shading his eyes with one hand. Still he saw nothing . . . but then he did, and his spine stiffened.

"That's *smoke*, Sergeant," he said very, very softly. "And it's moving."

▼   ▼   ▼

A hand knocked sharply on the cabin door, and Admiral Caitahno Raisahndo looked up from his plate with a frown. He *hated* interruptions during breakfast. Especially during *working* breakfasts, which this one most assuredly was. The rumors about heretic shipping movements were enough to make anyone nervous . . . and especially the "anyone" who happened to have inherited command of the Western Squadron, the Kingdom of Dohlar's sole remaining forward-deployed naval force in the Gulf of Dohlar. That squadron had been heavily reinforced since the Battle of the Kaudzhu Narrows, which was a good thing. But those rumors suggested the heretics had been reinforced even more heavily, and that could be a very *bad* thing.

Unfortunately, while the heretics' spies and intelligence sources were clearly fiendishly—he tried very hard not to use the word "demonically" even in the privacy of his own thoughts—good, his own were . . . less good. All he had to go on were those rumors.

So far at least.

"Yes?" he called in response to the knock.

"Flag Lieutenant, Sir!" the sentry outside his day cabin announced, and Caitahno glanced at Commander Gahryth Kahmelka. Kahmelka was his chief of staff—and Raisahndo didn't give much of a damn whether or not anyone approved of his adoption of the "heretical" Charisian term; it was too frigging useful a description *and* a function which had become self-evidently necessary—and the commander normally had a finger on the pulse of anything to do with the entire squadron. In this case, however, he only shrugged his own ignorance.

Fat lot of help that *is*, Raisandho thought, and raised his voice again.

"Enter!" he said, and a short, slender officer stepped into the cabin.

"Message from Captain Kharmahdy, Sir," Lieutenant Ahrnahld Mahkmyn said, and extended an envelope.

"A *written* message?"

"Yes, Sir. It just came out from dockside in a boat."

"I see." Raisahndo accepted the envelope and looked at Kahmelka again, one eyebrow raised.

"No idea, Sir," Kahmelka replied to the silent question. "Must be some reason he didn't use signals, but damned if I can think of one."

"Not one we'll like, you mean," Raisahndo said sourly, and Kahmelka's answering snort was harsh. There'd been a lot of messages neither of them had liked in the months since the Kaudzhu Narrows action, and with Sir

Dahrand Rohsail invalided home minus an arm and a leg, responsibility for dealing with those messages had devolved on one Caitahno Raisahndo.

The admiral looked down at the canvas envelope, addressed in Captain Styvyn Kharmahdy's clerk's handwriting, stitched shut, and secured with a wax seal.

Kharmahdy commanded the Dohlaran shore establishment: not simply the Dohlaran manned batteries protecting the immediate base area, but also its warehouses, dockyards, service craft, powder magazines, sail lofts, and everything else associated with keeping the Squadron in fighting trim. Under other circumstances, he would have been accorded the title of "port admiral" and given the rank to go with it, but Duke Fern had decreed otherwise in this case. Apparently the First Councilor had worried it might offend their Harchongese hosts in Rhaigair. But if Kharmahdy remained a mere captain, he was also a very capable—and levelheaded—sort of fellow. It wasn't like him to go off into fits of anxiety or panic, but this envelope was far heavier than usual. Obviously, the commodore's clerk had tucked a handful of musket balls into it before he handed it to the messenger. That was a security measure designed to carry it to the bottom if it strayed out of authorized hands, and Raisahndo's sense of trepidation sharpened as he wondered why that had seemed necessary.

The most probable answer was that Kharmahdy was relaying a message from Dohlar which had just arrived by coded semaphore or messenger wyvern, and if it was important enough to send by itself rather than waiting for the regular afternoon mail delivery, it was unlikely to contain good news. Which, given what had happened to Earl Thirsk's family a few months ago—and how it had happened—was more than enough to send his heart down to somewhere in the vicinity of his shoe soles.

Stop procrastinating, he told himself. *Sooner or later, you have to open the damned thing!*

He exhaled, picked up the cheese knife, and slit the envelope's stitches. Then he laid the knife down, extracted the single sheet of paper, and unfolded it.

His face tightened, and he made himself reread the brief, concise note a second time.

At least it's not an announcement that the Earl's been arrested, Caitahno, he thought. *Be grateful for that much! Not that this is any better.*

"Well, I suppose I understand why he didn't use signals." His tone was dry, but his brown eyes were very dark as he looked up at Kahmelka and extended the message. "No point spreading panic any sooner than we have to. But it would appear the question of the heretics' intentions has just been answered."

▼　▼　▼

"Finger Cape off the starboard bow, Sir," the lookout called, then bent over the pelorus mounted on HMS *Eraystor*'s bridge wing and peered through the aperture in the raised sighting vanes. It was another of the plethora of new devices coming out of Charis these days, and he measured the angle carefully against the lubber line before he looked back over his shoulder.

"Seventeen degrees, relative, Sir."

"Very good," Zhaikyb Gregori said and turned to the bridge messenger at his elbow.

"My respects to the Captain and Admiral Zhastro," he said. "Inform them Finger Cape is now visible from the bridge, a point and a half off the starboard bow. I estimate we'll be abreast the battery there in approximately forty minutes."

▼　▼　▼

Captain of Swords Raikow Kaidahn stood in the observation tower atop Battery St. Thermyn, gazing through the tripod-mounted spyglass at the bizarre-looking vessels making their way steadily—and with complete disregard for wind or current—through South Channel into the broad waters of Saram Bay. He'd waited for the last half hour, holding his followup reports to Rhagair until he had something more definite than smoke to report. Now he did, and he wished to hell he didn't. Or that he could have done something more *effective* than sending in reports about them, anyway.

Unfortunately for anything he might have done, however, those ships were at least seven miles from his battery's site on the very tip of the long, thin ribbon of Finger Cape. Known with very little affection to its occupants, who deeply resented being given their current assignment, as "the Finger" (after the hand gesture which expressed much the same meaning it once had on Old Terra), the cape projecting into the channel from Basset Island was over ten miles long, but less than a mile and a half across at its widest, and its highest elevation was little more than forty feet above sea level at high tide. That made things . . . interesting when heavy weather blew up the channel and sent seas crashing clear across it. In fact, in Raikow Kaidahn's considered opinion, the Finger was a miserable, waterlogged sandbar at the best of times . . . which winter in Stene Province wasn't. Just building a battery on it had required more than a little ingenuity out of the Imperial Harchongese Army's engineers.

And keeping *the damned thing here's required a hell of a lot more*, he thought moodily.

The winter's storms had not been kind to him or his gunners—they'd had to evacuate the battery twice, and each time repairs had amounted to effectively rebuilding it afterward—and he couldn't really understand why Lord of Horse Golden Grass had stuck them out here in the first place. They hadn't even been equipped with any of the new rifled artillery pieces, since the navigable channel between the Finger and Saram Head was almost fourteen miles across. No one was coming into range of Battery St. Thermyn unless he was one hell of a bad navigator or wind and weather gave him no choice. For that matter, the channel was literally impossible to defend at all; there was simply no place to put the guns that might have engaged an intruder.

On the other hand, you're in a good position to warn Rhaigair they're coming, aren't you? Not that they're being particularly stealthy. For that matter, it's hard to see how those . . . smokepots could sneak up on Rhaigair, whether we were sitting out on this Shan-wei-damned sandspit or not!

He sighed, straightened his back, and turned to the anxious-faced young captain of spears at his elbow.

"I make it five of the bastards, Thaidin. I don't see any topsails tagging along, but I'm sure they're out there somewhere. I imagine their galleons'll keep their distance unless the wind shifts to favor them." His lips twitched under his pencil thin mustache. "Not like these fellows will need them anytime soon."

Captain of Spears Chinzhou's face tightened. For a moment, Kaidahn thought the younger man would accuse him of defeatism. Young Chinzhou was a very devout fellow, who spent too much time with the local inquisitors, in Kaidahn's opinion. After a moment, though, the captain of spears nodded unhappily.

"I suppose not, Sir," he acknowledged. "May I?"

He gestured at the spyglass, and Kaidahn nodded and stepped back to let him look through it. His shoulders tightened as the image of the smoke-spewing heretic vessels swam into sharper focus, and Kaidahn didn't blame him. They were huge, easily two or three hundred feet long, and the enormously long guns protruding from their stepped-back, armored superstructures were enough to strike a chill in any heart.

Especially if the possessor of that heart had read the reports of what those same guns had done to the Desnairian fortifications at Geyra Bay.

Chinzhou gazed at them for at least two minutes before he stood back, shaking his head.

"What do you think Admiral Raisahndo will do, Sir?"

"Whatever he can," Kaidahn said. "I've never met him personally, but I understand he's a brave and determined man, so I have no doubt of that. As to *what* he can do against something like this—?"

He gestured at the columns of smoke steaming steadily past their position, and Chinzhou nodded somberly.

I know what he damned well ought *to do, though,* Kaidahn thought. *The wind's fair for all three channels, and unless those heretic bastards have enough of these things to cover all of them, I'd damned well be getting my ships the Shan-wei out of their way. Of course, the heretics probably have some of their armored galleons waiting out to sea, but I'd a hell of a lot rather take my chances with* them *than face these things inside the bay.*

He considered what he'd just thought for a moment, then smiled grimly.

Maybe young Thaidin would've had a point about my "defeatism." But—any temptation to smile disappeared—*in Raisahndo's shoes, I'd really like to keep at* least *some of my men alive.*

"Well, all we can do is see to it that he's as well-informed as possible," he said out loud, and looked at the signalman standing respectfully by the tower rail. "Signal to Admiral Raisahndo, General Cahstnyr, Captain Kharmahdy, and Baron Golden Grass."

"Yes, Sir," the signalman replied, pencil poised above his pad.

"'Have confirmed five—repeat, five—heretic steam ironclads entering Saram Bay. Present position—' be sure to insert the present time, Chyngdow '—approximately seven miles due south of Battery St. Thermyn. Estimated speed ten—repeat, ten—knots.'" He paused a moment, considering whether or not to add something more, then shrugged. "Read that back," he said.

"Yes, Sir," the signalman said, and read it back word-for-word.

"Excellent. Get it off immediately."

"Yes, Sir!"

The signalman bowed in salute and headed for the observation tower's stairs and the signal mast at the far end of the long, narrow battery. Kaidahn watched him go, then drew a deep breath and turned back to the spyglass.

▼ ▼ ▼

"I don't suppose anyone's come up with any brilliant ideas in the last couple of hours?" Caitahno Raisahndo asked, smiling with very little humor. Captain of Swords Kaidahn's message, relayed by the semaphore stations on Basset and Shipworm Island, lay on the chart table aboard HMS *Hurricane*.

His 60-gun flagship was the lead ship of the most heavily armed class of galleons the Royal Dohlaran Navy had ever built, fitted with the new 6-inch shell-firing smoothbores. That made her one of the most powerful warships in the world . . . and meant absolutely nothing against the threat steaming towards them.

"I'm afraid not," Admiral Pawal Hahlynd replied heavily. His armored screw-galleys had been the decisive factor in the Kaudzhu Narrows, but like

Hurricane, they were utterly outclassed by the Charisian ships which had demolished the fortifications at Geyra. And these *had* to be the same ships.

Unless, of course, the bastards have managed to build even more of the Shan-wei-damned things, Raisahndo reminded himself grimly. *Don't forget that delightful possibility.*

"Sir," Commander Kahmelka said in a very careful tone, "the Squadron can't fight them. I mean, it literally *can't*." He looked at the far more senior officers hiding their thoughts behind faces of stone. "If the Harchongians are right about their speed, not even Admiral Hahlynd's screw-galleys could hope to maneuver with them. And according to the reports from Geyra, their guns have a range of at least ten thousand yards. With all the courage in the world, our ships would never live to get into our range of them."

"We can't just run away, Commander!" Captain Bryntyn Mykylhny said sharply. "And the bastards have to get into the bay in the first place before we start worrying about how we get at them!"

Mykylhny commanded HMS *Cyclone*, *Hurricane*'s sister ship, and he'd stepped into a dead man's shoes to take command of one of Dahrand Rohsail's divisions at the Kaudzhu Narrows. His promotion to acting commodore had been confirmed by Rohsail as one of his last actions before he went into hospital in Rhaigair, and he'd always been one of Rohsail's favorites. Raisahndo tried not to hold that against him, reminding himself—again—that however big a pain in the arse Rohsail might be, the supercilious, arrogant, aristocratic son-of-a-bitch had always been one hell of a fighter. And the same was true of Mykylhny . . . including the arrogant, aristocratic attitude.

"I'm not advocating 'running away,' Sir," Kahmelka said in an even more careful tone. "I'm simply pointing out that if we try to engage them ship-to-ship, we won't be able to. We'll be *physically* unable to, Sir. And, frankly, I don't think the batteries will keep them out of the inner bay, either." He shook his head, his expression grim. "I know they'll give a good account of themselves, but based on the reports from Geyra—and even more on our own analysis of *Dreadnought*—I don't think they can hope to get past the heretics' armor before ships this fast sail right past their muzzles. If they had more elevation, if they could shoot *down* at their decks, where the armor's almost certainly thinner, they might be able to inflict some serious damage. But firing directly into their thickest armor?"

He shook his head again.

"They're coming through, Sir. One way or another, unless we want to assume they won't have the guts to try, they'll be off Rhaigair by this time tomorrow."

He paused, looking around the cabin, but it was obvious no one cared to suggest anything that damned silly where *Charisians* were concerned. After a moment, he shrugged and continued.

"Under other circumstances, we might do some good by anchoring to help cover the channel exits." That was, in fact, precisely what the Western Squadron had intended to do in the event of an attack by more conventional opponents. "In this case, I doubt we'd accomplish anything except bringing them into their range of us even sooner. And much as I hate saying this—and, believe me, I *do*—just one of those ships could easily destroy the entire Squadron . . . and they have *five* of them." He shook his head a third time. "Captain, no one has more respect for the courage and the determination of our officers—and men—than I do. But this isn't about courage or dedication, or even about devotion to God. It's about the fact that the Squadron represents sixty percent of the Navy's entire remaining strength . . . and that if we stand and fight—*try* to fight—against the ironclads that destroyed Geyra as a port, we'll lose it in return for nothing."

Mykylhny glared at him, and Raisahndo frowned. Kahmelka had been one of Ahlvyn Khapahr's close friends, and Mykylhny, unfortunately, knew that. He wasn't quite ready to accuse Kahmelka of guilt by association—Khapahr had had a *lot* of friends in the Navy, and they couldn't *all* have been traitors—but the captain was undeniably . . . less confident of Khamelka's fighting spirit than he'd been before Khapahr was unmasked as a Charisian spy.

Personally, Raisahndo wondered if Mykylhny suspected that his admiral's chief of staff—and his admiral, for that matter—had never believed for a moment that Ahlvyn Khapahr, of all people, could have been a traitor to the flag officer he'd served so long and well. They'd never specifically discussed it, but Raisahndo was fairly positive Kahmelka shared his own suspicions about what Khapahr had really been doing—and the reason someone who'd supposedly been a hired assassin had shot Earl Thirsk in the shoulder, instead of the heart.

And a hell of a lot of good it did in the end, he thought harshly. *That bastard Clyntahn still ordered the Earl's daughters hauled off to Zion. And then the goddamned ship blew up!* He shook his head mentally. *God knows they—and the Earl—deserved better than that. In fact, I'm pretty damned sure God knows exactly that . . . whatever that fat fornicator in Zion thinks. And I'm not the only Dohlaran sea officer who thinks that!*

He made himself back away from that dangerous thought and focused on Mykylhny, instead.

"I don't like it either, Captain," he said quietly, "but Commander Kahmelka's right."

A silent sigh seemed to circle the cabin as he said it. Mykylhny's glare didn't abate, but it took on a different edge, the edge of a man who knew that what he was hearing wasn't going to change, however much he might want it to.

"What do you propose we do instead . . . Sir?" he asked after a moment.

Raisahndo felt a flicker of anger, but he suppressed it. The pause before Mykylhny's last word hadn't been one of disrespect, and he knew it. Bitterness and disappointment, yes, but not really disrespect . . . mostly, anyway.

"From what you're saying—and I can't really argue with it, however much I'd like to," the captain continued, "we'll *never* be able to fight these miserable fuckers. In that case, what's the point in preserving our ships?"

"Well," Raisahndo was surprised by the almost whimsical edge which crept into his own voice, "I suppose I could point out that preserving the men who *crew* those ships would probably be worthwhile." Mykylhny's face darkened, and the admiral raised a placating hand. "I know what you meant, Captain, and I'm really not trying to be flippant, but our trained manpower represents a vital military resource. Preserving them for the future service of the Crown and Mother Church, whether that's afloat or ashore, is a legitimate consideration."

He held Mykylhny's eyes steadily, and after a moment, the captain nodded. He even had the grace to look a little abashed.

"More to the point, perhaps," Raisahndo continued, "while we don't know how many of these . . . powered ironclads the heretics have, I think it's unlikely they have a *lot* of them. Against their conventional galleons—even their ironclad galleons, like *Dreadnought*—we've demonstrated we have a fighting chance. So unless and until they do have enough of these damned things to be *everywhere*, our ships are still valuable if only as a threat—a fleet in being, if you will—to inhibit the freedom of action of the heretics' *other* ships—their 'conventional' warships', I suppose you'd say." He grimaced. "I don't like the thought of becoming as passive as the Desnairians were before the heretics went into the Gulf of Jahras after them, but if that's the only service we can perform for the Jihad, then we'll damned well perform it!"

Mykylhny's frustration was obvious, and more than a few of the other officers in the cabin clearly shared it. But they also nodded in unhappy acknowledgment of the admiral's point.

"So what *will* we do, Sir?" Mykylhny's tone was much less confrontational.

"The outer batteries report light heretic units scouting the channels from outside their range," Raisandho replied. "We don't know for certain how many galleons they have out beyond our spotters' horizon, but they've got two passages to cover—North Channel and Basset Channel. I imagine—" he produced a wintry smile "—they probably assume their ironclads have

South Channel covered. Although," he added, "I suppose we might be able to work our way around them overnight. Frankly, though, I doubt we could manage it without being spotted.

"One possibility would be to split our own units, send some of them through North Channel and some of them through Basset Channel, but that would simply beg to be defeated in detail. So I propose to sortie with the entire Squadron concentrated. We have two galleons and a screw-galley in dockyard hands and we won't be able to get them back in time, so Captain Kharmahdy will tow out into the harbor and fire them to prevent their capture."

His expression showed his unhappiness at that thought, but he continued unflinchingly.

"The rest of the Squadron will get underway within the hour. If I were the heretics, I'd anticipate that anyone trying to evade my ironclads would choose North Channel, because it's closer to Rhaigair and farther from South Channel. In addition, there's that damned battery of theirs on Shyan Island. It couldn't stop us from getting through Basset Channel any more than St. Thermyn or St. Charlz are going to stop the heretics, but it would still be a factor in my thinking.

"The wind's almost dead out of the northwest, so it'll serve equally well for either, and the channel mouths are over eighty miles apart. They may have opted to hold their main strength in a central position off the Shipworm Shoal and used light units to watch both channels and whistle up their galleons when someone finally emerges from one of them. That's what I'd've done in their place, but the sighting reports indicate they have at least some of their galleons far enough forward in both channels to support their scouts. That means they can't have their *full* strength covering either of them. So we'll use *Basset* Channel, and hope they've gone all logical on us and weighted their right flank more heavily than their left. We can't know what we'll run into, but whatever it is, it'll be the best odds we can find."

▼   ▼   ▼

Sir Dunkyn Yairley, Baron of Sarmouth, stood on HMS *Destiny*'s sternwalk in a thick, warm duffle coat, chin buried in a soft, woolen muffler as he leaned forward, both gloved hands braced on the carved railing, and gazed out over the cold, windy blue water of the Gulf of Dohlar.

At the moment, *Destiny* lay hove-to thirty miles northeast of Broken Hawser Rock at the eastern tip of the Shyan Island Shoal, moving a little uneasily in the offshore swell but well beyond visual range from any Harchongese battery. Thirty other galleons kept company with her, and long chains of schooners were busily relaying signals to her from the scouts closer in to the mouths of Basset Channel and North Channel. He knew some of his captains thought he'd chosen his station poorly, although they were, of course, far too tactful to say so. He was perfectly placed to intercept anyone coming through Basset, and he was far enough out to let the Dohlarans get too far from safety to retreat without a fight before he pounced. But he was also over a hundred miles from *North* Channel, and he'd stationed only a single six-ship division to support the schooners watching *that* avenue of escape.

In theory, he should have sufficient warning to intercept the Dohlarans well out into the gulf even if they chose the northern route . . . assuming the scouts managed to maintain contact while whistling up the rest of his squadron. Theory had an unhappy habit of failing in real life, however, and he couldn't blame the captains who thought he should have chosen a more central position rather than risk letting the Dohlarans slip away under the cover of darkness or heavy weather in the event that he'd guessed their intentions wrongly.

Of course, none of those captains knew that even as he stood on the sternwalk, gazing thoughtfully out over the water, the SNARC remote perched on the chain supporting the lamp above the table in Caitahno Raisahndo's day cabin was transmitting every word the Dohlaran admiral said to his earplug.

The real reason he'd disposed his force as he had was that Raisahndo's galleons were twice as far from North Channel's mouth as *Destiny* was. Sarmouth had always rather expected Raisahndo, who was no one's fool, to opt for the less blatantly obvious Basset Channel route. Even if he'd been wrong about that, however, the SNARCs would have given him ample warning to "change his mind" and move his main body to cover the northern route well before Raisahndo and his galleons ever hove into sight of his waiting schooners.

It's not really fair, he thought as Owl projected schematics of Saram and Rhaigair Bay—and the exact position of every Dohlaran vessel in either of them—onto his contact lenses. It was like peering down over God's own shoulder, and Raisahndo had about as much chance of eluding Sarmouth's observation as he would have had hiding from the Archangels.

Assuming the Archangels had ever existed, that was. Which they hadn't.

Unhappily for Admiral Raisahndo, the Imperial Charisian Navy—and Sir Dunkyn Yairley—*did* exist.

Well, maybe it isn't fair . . . but it's a damned poor excuse for a flag officer who worries about "fair" when it comes to keeping his people alive and making the other fellow's people do the dying.

Truth be told, he wasn't that eager for *anyone* to die, but he rather doubted Caitahno Raisahndo was going to meekly haul down his flag when he ran into the Imperial Charisian Navy at sea. Which could be very unfortunate for the Western Squadron, given the powerful reinforcements Tymythy

Darys had delivered to Claw Island even before Zhaztro's arrival. Unlike Sir Dunkyn Yairley, the officers and men of HMS *Lightning*, *Seamount*, and *Floodtide* were eager to kill as many of Raisahndo's ships—and men—as they could. They especially wanted any of the ships which had been present in the Kaudzhu Narrows and taken their sister ship *Dreadnought*, but any unit of Raisahndo's squadron would do in a pinch.

Well, they'll get their chance, he thought grimly. *I don't suppose it'll hurt my reputation for smelling my way to the enemy, either. For that matter,* he snorted, *I guess it* shouldn't. *After all, I did figure out what Raisahndo was most likely to do even before he was kind enough to confirm it to the SNARCs. Fortunately, I'm far too modest a fellow to gloat at the doubters' awestruck admiration of my strategic brilliance once it's vindicated.*

He chuckled and shook his head, then straightened and tucked his hands behind him. Under current wind conditions, Raisahndo could make a good perhaps seven knots—what would have been six knots, back on Old Earth—at which rate it would take him over forty hours to clear Basset Channel. That was on the direct route from Rhaigair, however, and it was very unlikely he'd take that route with Zhaztro loose inside the bay. No, he'd circle wide—heading east, hugging the north shore of the bay and hopefully disappearing from sight before Zhaztro came into range of Rhaigair. The Western Squadron was far slower than the ironclads, but Zhaztro's smoke would be visible to a galleon's masthead lookouts well before anyone aboard his own low-lying ships spotted its topsails. With only a little luck, Raisahndo should be able to successfully play hide-and-seek with the invaders . . . especially since Zhaztro had no interest in chasing him. Immediately, at least. The 2nd Ironclad Squadron would deal with the Western Squadron if it was unwise enough to enter its reach, but first things first. Hainz Zhaztro's primary business was with Rhaigair, and unlike Sarmouth, he was unable to eavesdrop on Raisahndo's intentions and movements. He was perfectly content to leave Sarmouth and his galleons to keep the Dohlaran force penned up inside the Bay while he got on with demolishing their base and its fortifications. If Raisahndo avoided action by turning back from the Gulf when he sighted Sarmouth, there'd be plenty of time for the ironclads to hunt him down then.

But assuming Sarmouth had properly assessed the Dohlaran's choice of courses, eluding Zhaztro would add another fifty miles, easily, to his route. Which meant he'd present himself in the waters between Shyan Island and Shipworm Shoal about this same time day after tomorrow.

Just in time for lunch, he thought. *I can work with that.*

He clapped his hands together, breath steaming before it whipped away on the wind, and smiled a small, cold smile as he discovered he was just a bit less blasé about personally delivering a little retribution to the victors of the Kaudzhu Narrows than he'd realized.

.III.
HMS *Eraystor*, 22,
and
Battery St. Charlz,
Main Ship Channel,
Rhaigair Bay,
Province of Stene,
Harchgong Empire.

"Enter!"

The chart room door opened and a tallish young man with fair hair and gray eyes stepped through it.

"Second Lieutenant's respects, Sir." He touched his chest in salute to Sir Hainz Zhaztro. "*Trident*'s just signaled. She reports no sign of the enemy . . . except for a few columns of smoke that are probably from ships on fire."

There was a pronounced edge of satisfaction in the last fourteen words, Admiral Zhaztro noted without surprise. Despite his coloration—inherited from his "imported" Siddarmarkian mother—Midshipman Paitryk Shawnysy was a native Old Charisian. His accent was straight from Tellesberg, but his attitude towards the Group of Four and all its works came from what had happened to his mother's family when the Sword of Schueler struck the Republic.

"Thank you," the admiral replied. "My compliments to Lieutenant Audhaimyr. And instruct him to relay a 'Well done' to *Trident* from me."

"Aye, aye, Sir. Your compliments to Lieutenant Audhaimyr, and relay 'Well done' to *Trident*," Shawnysy replied. Zhaztro nodded at the confirmation, and the midshipman saluted again and withdrew.

"Well, that's disappointing, Sir," Captain Cahnyrs observed as the door closed behind him. "I've been looking to something a tad more . . . energetic than that. I *hate* to miss a party I've been counting on."

"'A few' columns of smoke hardly indicate Raisahndo's burned his entire squadron just to evade us. And the fact that *Trident* didn't see anyone doesn't mean they aren't there," Zhaztro reminded his flag captain. "Her lookouts' maximum range can't be more than twenty miles, even assuming conditions are as clear for them as they are for us, and you know how patchy the weather can be this time of year. Even if she's got brilliant sunlight and crystal blue skies, there's plenty of room for them to be hiding from her somewhere deeper into the bay."

"Of course there is." Cahnyrs nodded. "But if I was Raisahndo and I thought the Imperial Charisian Navy was about to come calling, I'd have my warships up close enough to support my fortifications."

"You might. Or you might think about it and decide it would be smarter to keep them as far out of those nasty Charisians' range as you possibly could."

"Either they're going to stop us short of the city or they aren't, Sir." Cahnyrs shrugged. "If they aren't, it doesn't matter where their ships are. Sooner or later we'll find them, and when we do, they'll be dead meat. At the same time, we know they've been reinforced with some pretty powerful galleons. It's at least possible those ships could make the difference as to whether or not we get past the shore batteries, and everything we know about Raisahndo suggests he's the sort who'd recognize that." The flag captain shook his head. "No, Sir. If he was still inside Rhaigair Bay, he'd be anchored on springs to support the batteries or at least hovering close enough to the channels to see if he'd be needed. And if he was that close *Trident* would've seen his mastheads. If she didn't, he's not there. Which means he's gotten away from us."

"Only from *us*, even if you're right, Alyk. I expect Baron Sarmouth's people will have a little something to say about his travel plans if you are, though."

"Assuming the Baron's guessed right."

"That's very small-minded—and mercenary—of you," Zhaztro scolded, and Cahnyrs grinned. The flag captain was an old friend of Dunkyn Yairley's, and he'd bet the baron five gold marks that he *hadn't* guessed right.

"Oh, I'm sure Dunkyn'll catch up with him in the end, Sir. I just think it's going to take a little longer than he thinks it will."

"Well, in the meantime, we have our own fish to fry," Zhaztro said, returning his attention to the large-scale chart on the table between them.

"I just hope the *seijins* are right about those 'sea-bombs' of theirs," Cahnyrs replied, his humor fading noticeably. "I hate the very idea of those damned things! Hell of an unfair weapon."

"Excuse me, Sir," Commander Lywys Pharsaygyn cocked his head, "but isn't the idea behind *any* weapon to give you an 'unfair' advantage over the fellow who doesn't have it? Which, by the way, if memory serves, is something you sneaky Charisians have been doing for years now!"

"Point, Commander. A very good one, actually." Cahnyrs nodded. "I guess what truly pisses me off is that the Temple Boys and their friends came up with the idea first."

"I've noticed Old Charisians have a certain . . . youthful enthusiasm for coming up with things first, Sir," Zhaztro's chief of staff observed with a smile. "I almost said that they take a *childish pleasure* in it, but that probably would have been disrespectful."

"Grossly so," Cahnyrs agreed. "Especially because it would be so accurate," he added with a cheerful nod, and Zhaztro chuckled.

Like himself, Pharsaygyn was an Emeraldian, and he'd been with Zhaztro for six years now, ever since Darcos Sound, where he'd served in *Arbalest*—as a common seaman, of all things. Of course, he'd been a rather *uncommon* sort of common seaman, however the muster book had described him. The younger son of a prominent Eraystor merchant family with powerful Church connections, he'd been destined for seminary and a career with Mother Church. In fact, one of his uncles was a Schuelerite upper-priest serving in the Inquisition in Zion itself, and Pharsaygyn had offered his services to the Emeraldian Navy as a clerk because he'd genuinely believed what his uncle had told him about Charis and the reason Mother Church was supporting Hektor Daykyn's war against the island kingdom.

Zhaztro had heard about him from one of his own cousins, a Manchyr importer who'd done business with the Pharsaygyn family, and grabbed him before anyone else realized he was available. He'd never regretted it. Pharsaygyn had served with distinction and courage as Zhaztro's flag secretary throughout that short, disastrous war . . . and his disillusionment when he discovered the truth about the Inquisition's allegations had been brutal. Instead of leaving naval service, however—which he would have been fully entitled to do, as a short-term volunteer—he'd sought Zhaztro's assistance in obtaining a commission when the Emeraldian Navy was folded into the Imperial Charisian Navy. He'd passed the competitive examination with absurd ease, although he was scarcely the finest *shiphandler* in the world. Then again, Zhaztro wouldn't have applied that label to himself, where galleon command was concerned, either.

More to the point where his present duties were concerned, Pharsaygyn had never really wanted command. He'd been a born staff officer who'd enjoyed Zhaztro's total confidence and he'd transitioned from secretary to flag lieutenant the instant his Charisian commission came through. And then, last year, following a well-deserved promotion, he'd moved directly to the position of 2nd Ironclad Squadron's chief of staff. Zhaztro had offered to help him find a command of his own, instead, but he'd turned that down flat.

"I'm not a *real* officer like you, Sir," he'd said with a smile. "God help the poor seaman stuck in a galleon under *my* command the first time we hit a real blow! Let's face it, Sir—I'm just around till the job's done. Better to steer a career officer into a positon like that. He needs it on his resume a lot more than *I* do."

That "not a real officer" was a gross disservice to his accomplishments and value, but Zhaztro had decided he was probably right. Personally, the admiral would have offered even odds Pharsaygyn would seek ordination in the Church of Charis once the Group of Four was defeated, but until then, the commander was fully focused on bringing about that defeat.

"The truth is, Sir," he said to the flag captain now, "that sea-bombs are the sort of weapon that's going to appeal to the weaker navy. They'd be an ideal way to deal with something like this squadron, too. In fact, if they *did* have them, they'd have put them right damned here."

He tapped the chart with the index finger of his mangled left hand— he'd lost the last two fingers at Darcos Sound—and his expression had turned much more serious, but then he shrugged and shook his head with a smile.

"As for coming up with things first, if it makes you feel any better, I'm willing to bet Baron Seamount *did* come up with the idea well before any Temple Boy did. It's the sort of thing that would occur to him—a way to achieve an enormous economization in force while denying a more powerful enemy fleet passage through defended waters. And it's also exactly the sort of thing Admiral Lock Island or Admiral Rock Point would've told him to stick in the very bottom of his seabag and forget about." He shook his head again, his smile even broader. "The last thing *they* would've wanted would've been to suggest the idea to someone like Dohlar before Thirsk thought of it on his own!"

"I hate it when he turns all logical, Sir," Cahnyrs complained.

"Unfortunately, it's one of the reasons I keep him around," Zhaztro said just a bit absently, frowning down at the chart.

South Channel lay two hundred miles behind *Eraystor,* and her true target, Rhaigair Bay, at the mouth of the Rhaigair River, lay before her. And while Rhaigair was far smaller than Saram Bay, it was also a much more difficult objective.

There were four passages through the islands which guarded the Rhaigair approaches, but only two of them really mattered.

Sand Passage, the westernmost channel, between the mainland and the twin islands the Harchongians called The Sisters, was suitable only for light craft and shallow draft fishing boats. That completely disqualified it for his purposes.

Broad Channel, the next possibility to the east, between The Sisters and Sharyn Island, was—as its name suggested—the widest approach. It was also shallow, although the soundings showed sufficient depth for a *City*-class ironclad . . . if she was careful and chose the right stage of the tide. Unfortunately, the Harchongians had spent a year or so after Gwylym Manthyr's foray into Gorath Bay driving a double line of pilings across the eight-mile-wide channel. The Lywysite-equipped dive teams which had been sent out to Earl Sharpfield could probably have cleared the barrier, but not without investing five-days in the effort . . . and risking serious loss of life along the way, given water temperatures at this time of year.

The rather unimaginatively named East Channel—farthest to the east, between East Island and Knobby Head, the closest point on the mainland—was normally more than deep enough for his ships, but it was also subject to silting from mud carried down the Rhaigair River. His best information on its current depth of water was . . . problematical, and he had a pronounced aversion to reprising HMS *Thunderer*'s role from last July.

And that, unfortunately, left only the even more unimaginatively named Main Ship Channel, between Sharyn Island and East Island. It was the deepest of the entry channels, and the combined tidal patterns and set of the river's current scoured it, rather than silting it up. It offered plenty of depth, and while it was narrow, it was *less* narrow than the northern end of East Channel.

It was also, however, the most predictable route, if only by process of elimination . . . and the best defended.

All of Rhaigair Bay's entrances had been fortified for well over two hundred years, and the Harchong Empire and Kingdom of Dohlar had cooperated to overhaul, modernize, and improve those fortifications once the Royal Dohlaran Navy decided to station its forward naval strength in Saram Bay. Rhaigair, by far the largest city on the bay and one of the two or three largest cities in all of Stene Province, had been the logical place to homeport those ships, and the Harchongians—who'd already begun investing in the upgrade of Rhaigair's defenses—had responded enthusiastically to the proposal to turn the city into the Western Squadron's forward base. Not surprisingly, since it had offered the opportunity to finish updating those defenses—and to a much more powerful level—with Mother Church picking up the tab.

Given the city's current importance to both Harchong and Dohlar, its batteries had received high priority for the new rifled artillery, too. Most of the inner defensive batteries had been thoroughly rearmed, including Zhaztro's current main cause for concern: Battery St. Charlz, the small spot on the chart Pharsaygyn had just tapped.

Located a good forty miles from the city, Battery St. Charlz was actually an artificial island in the throat of the Main Ship Channel. The entire island—which had been built up a hundred and ten years ago by thousands of Harchongese serfs dumping Hastings only knew how many tons of granite onto the single shoal in the entire channel—was little more than a mile and a half long, and less than half that wide. It was, however, one huge fort. Aside from a single stone quay, well covered by artillery embrasures, there were exactly zero landing spots, which ruled out any notion of taking it by assault. Its onetime masonry walls had been replaced with modern earthen berms, and the Harchongese engineers—made wise by others' misfortunes—had mounted its weapons in individual masonry bays, well buried inside those berms. They'd also provided its garrison with thick-roofed, shell-proof dugouts from which to wait out any angle-gun bombardment, and its dozens of heavy rifled guns faced matching batteries on the islands to either side of the channel.

The passage east of Battery St. Charlz was wider than the one to the west . . . which was exactly why the pestiferous Dohlarans had sunk barges and old galleons to block it. There were rumors the powerful currents had shifted some of those blockships, but even if that was true, they hadn't been moved far enough to clear the way for a *City*-class like *Eraystor*. On the western side, where the path was still open, the channel was barely two miles wide and it was less than five miles from St. Charlz's guns to those in the batteries on East Island. That was barely 8,500 yards, and given the reported 9,000-yard range of the Temple's newest and heaviest Fultyn Rifles, any ship trying to attempt that passage would be forced to run an eight-mile gauntlet while under heavy fire from both sides.

Well, that's why you've got all this nice armor, Hainz, he told himself. *And just hope to Langhorne the* seijins' *information about the sea-bombs is* right.

"I'm inclined to think you're probably right about what Raisahndo would've done if *he'd* thought the batteries could stop us, Alyk," he said out loud. "Of course, the fact that he doesn't seem to think they can doesn't mean they actually can't, but given how quickly we'll be past them, they won't have very long to work on us. These 'Fultyn Rifles' are a lot more dangerous than the Desnairians' forty-pounders were at Geyra, but the latest spy reports to Earl Sharpfield suggest they won't be *enough* more dangerous to stop us.

"To be honest, the one thing that really does worry me is that the *seijins* might be wrong about those sea-bombs, because Lywys is dead right. If these people *do* have them, this is sure as hell the place they'd use them," he continued, tapping Battery St. Charlz's position on the chart himself. "I genuinely don't think they do, but difficult as it may be for you two to believe this, I've been wrong once or twice in my life."

He smiled quickly, briefly, then stood back from the chart table.

"So we'll proceed as planned, except for one small change. Lywys," he looked at the commander, "please draft a signal to Captain Gahnzahlyz. Inform him that *Bayport* won't be leading the column after all."

"She won't be, Sir?" Pharsaygyn didn't seem especially surprised, Zhaztro noted. Well, they'd been together for a while now.

"No. *Cherayth* will take the lead."

"Of course, Sir."

No, the chief of staff definitely hadn't been surprised, Zhaztro thought, and turned to Cahnyrs.

"Please go ahead and clear for action now, Captain," he said, rather more formally than he normally addressed his flag captain. "I'd like to proceed while we have the tide with us."

"Yes, Sir." If Cahnyrs was perturbed by the change, it didn't show. "With your permission, Sir," he continued, "I'd like to make our speed about six knots when we engage the batteries. I know we'd originally planned to make the run at ten knots, and the slower speed would mean they could hold us under fire for roughly a half hour longer, but it would also make our return fire more accurate. I think that would probably pay a dividend for us on our own way through, and anything that lets us knock out more of their guns has to be helpful to the rest of the Squadron when it's their turn."

And it will also give your lookouts a marginally better chance of spotting the buoys of any sea-bombs the Dohlarans may have planted, Zhaztro thought. *That probably wouldn't be a huge help, but you're the sort of fellow who plays for* anything *that might keep your men alive a little longer, aren't you, Alyk?*

"She's your ship, Captain," he said simply. "How you fight her is your decision."

▼　▼　▼

"It would appear the heretics have made up their minds."

Lord of Foot Kwaichee Bauzhyng stood on the outer platform, just in front of the sandbags protecting the observation tower at the south end of Battery St. Charlz, gazing down-channel through a spyglass while his orderly held the parasol to keep the sun off his head. Given the fact that the temperature was only a little above freezing—and that the wind had strengthened and the oncoming clouds threatened to do a far better job of blocking the sun than any parasol—that struck Major Ahdem Kylpaitryc as an even more useless affectation than usual.

"So I see, Sir," Kylpaitryc agreed out loud.

His own spyglass was far less ornate, without a trace of the gold and silver inlay glittering from Bauzhyng's—which must have cost at least two hundred marks, just for the inlay work—but he suspected the lenses were actually better. Dohlaran spyglass makers were more concerned with what someone could see through one of their instruments than with how beautiful it looked.

What Kylpaitryc could see through his at the moment, however, was distinctly *un*beautiful: a single heretic ironclad steaming implacably towards its rendezvous with St. Charlz's heavy artillery. Columns of smoke beyond it showed where its consorts followed, apparently waiting to see what happened, and he wondered if the heretics had learned about the newly designed sea-bombs and chosen to send one ship ahead to test the waters for the others. More thick, black smoke poured from the leader's flat-sided, slab-like smokestack, a broad furrow of white rolled back from either side of a sharply raked prow, a huge battle standard flew from its single mast, and the long, slender barrels of its guns were trained out on either broadside.

All in all, it looked remarkably unperturbed by the challenge awaiting it, he thought glumly, silently counting the seconds as the intruder crossed between the ranging marks Admiral Raisandho had ordered erected in the shallows on either side of the Main Ship Channel. They weren't enough to give an exact estimate, of course—not at that distance—but. . . .

"I make it about six or seven knots, Sir," he said finally, lowering his glass.

"Approximately that, yes," Bauzhyng agreed calmly.

It was a pity Baron Golden Grass had decided to inflict a Dohlaran "liaison officer" on Battery St. Charlz, the lord of foot reflected, still gazing at the heretic vessel. No doubt the politics had made it inevitable, and he supposed Kylpaitryc was at least minimally less uncouth than most of his barbarian countrymen. He hadn't attempted to interfere unduly in Bauzhyng's decisions, at any rate, and he'd actually come up with a handful of useful recommendations when the new artillery first arrived. But still—! Bauzhyng could almost smell the turnips every time the man opened his mouth.

"Bit surprised they aren't moving faster'n that, Sir," Kylpaitryc continued. "All the reports indicate they should be able to hit at least *ten* knots, even against the current." He shook his head, his expression unhappy. "Seems to me they'd want to get through our fire zone quick as they can."

"Clearly they have great confidence in the efficacy of their armor." Bauzhyng shrugged ever so slightly. "It would seem the moment has come to . . . disabuse them of that confidence, Major."

"Aye, it has that, Sir."

Kylpaitryc smiled, for once in complete agreement with Battery St. Charlz's dapper, foppish CO. He didn't much like Kwaichee Bauzhyng, for a lot of reasons. For that matter, he didn't like *most* Harchongian officers he'd met. Every single one of them acted as if he'd smelled something bad as soon as a *Dohlaran* officer walked in the door. He didn't like that, and he especially didn't care for it given the monumental incompetency he'd seen in so many of those disdainful Harchongians. As a matter of fact, that disdain seemed strongest in the very officers least entitled to it. Of course, that described at least three-fourths of the Harchongese officer corps, when a man came down to it. In Kylpaitryc's considered opinion, the best that could be said for most Harchongese officers was that they were at least a step up from Desnairians, which was damning with about the faintest praise possible.

That wasn't really fair in Bauzhyng's case, however. Whatever else might be true of the lord of foot, he took his duties seriously, and he'd drilled his men ruthlessly on the new artillery. He'd even arm-wrestled the mark-pinching Harchongese bureaucrats into providing sufficient of the new shells for twice-a-five-day live fire exercises and asked Kylpaitryc to arrange for Admiral Hahlynd's screw-galleys to tow barges past the island to give his gunners practice against moving targets. Kylpaitryc couldn't resist tweaking the haughty Harchongian by addressing him as "Sir" rather than the "My Lord" he obviously preferred, but overall, he knew he'd been more fortunate than the majority of the Dohlaran officers assigned to liaise with their Harchongese "hosts."

Of course, he'd probably get even better performance out of his gunners if he treated them like people instead of two-footed animals that simply know how to talk. I guess it's unreasonable to expect him not to think of them as serfs, though—especially since most of them were serfs before they enlisted. And he's not actually all that brutal, compared to some of the real bastards here in Harchong. Still, I can't help thinking that flogging the gun captain with the lowest score after each drill isn't the very best way to build the men's morale.

"How soon do you intend to open fire, Sir?" he asked.

"I would prefer to allow the range to drop to no more than perhaps five thousand yards," Bauzhyng replied, lowering his own spyglass at last. He handed it to another aide in exchange for a steaming teacup and sipped contemplatively. "We have the benefit of stable, unmoving gun platforms, and one would normally assume that would give us a substantial advantage over a warship underway. In this instance, however, I prefer to make as few assumptions as possible. We shall wait until they open fire or the range falls to five thousand yards."

He shrugged ever so slightly, eyes distant as he considered the upcoming engagement.

Depending on how well Battery St. Charlz's berms stood up to the heretics' fire, he might well hold fire until the range fell to his own chosen range regardless of when they opened fire. He had great confidence in the power of his guns against most targets, but after studying the reports from the Kaudzhu Narrows, he rather doubted that shells—even the three-hundred-pound cylindrical projectiles of his new 10-inch guns—would pierce the heretics' armor. It seemed unlikely these ships were less well armored than the heretics ironclad galleons, and the Dohlarans' 10-inch smoothbores had never even come close to penetrating HMS *Dreadnought*'s side armor. Of course, even their solid shot had weighed little more than half as much as one of his shells, so comparing their relative performances was probably suspect. Still, he was distinctly unoptimistic about shells, especially at longer ranges, where they would strike at a lower velocity. A solid shot from one of his guns, on the other hand, weighed half again as much as a shell—three times the weight of the Dohlaran shot at the Kaudzhu Narrows—since there was no cavity for gunpowder. That decreased its destructive power if it actually penetrated the target yet gave it a greater chance of penetrating in the first place. The heavier shot also had a shorter range, however; the best any of his gunners had achieved with it was on the order of seven thousand yards to first strike, little better than three-quarters of their maximum range firing shell. They'd trained diligently to use ricochet fire to extend their range, skipping the shot across the water from its initial point of impact, but there seemed little chance of a shot which had lost that much energy penetrating an armored vessel if it finally hit it. Unarmored galleons, yes; steam-driven ironclads, no.

No, he thought. I'll wait until they come as close as I can get them before engaging them. And when I do, he smiled thinly, *they may enjoy the experience far less than they think they will.*

▼ ▼ ▼

"Coming up on your specified range, Captain," Petty Officer Wahldair Hahlynd announced, straightening from the voice pipe.

Hahlynd was *Eraystor*'s senior signalman, but he wasn't passing a signal from another unit of the squadron at the moment. That voice pipe connected him to an instrument atop *Eraystor*'s armored superstructure. The product of yet another fruitful collaboration between Admiral Semount, the Royal College of Charis, and Ehdwyrd Howsmyn's endlessly inventive artisans, it was called a "rangefinder." Alyk Cahnyrs had read the documentation by Doctor Zhain Frymyn, the College's optics specialist, but he still had only the vaguest notion of how the thing—it looked like a double-headed version of one of the *Rottweiler*-class galleons' angle-glasses, but with the upper lenses at the ends of an 18-foot crossbar—worked. What was important was that it *did* work and that its readings were accurate to within a hundred yards at ten miles.

In some ways, that information was of purely academic interest, since no moving ship could possibly hit another ship at over seventeen thousand yards. Even assuming its gunners could see the target, ship's motion would guarantee they missed it when they fired. In other ways, however, accurate range numbers could be extremely important. Even highly experienced gunners could misestimate ranges, and *knowing* the range—as opposed to simply guessing—allowed his gunners to set their sights accurately. That was still one hell of a long way from guaranteeing hits, but it took at least one of the variables out of the equation.

At the moment, however. . . .

"Pass the signal to *Bayport*," he said, then blew down another voice pipe to sound the whistle at its far end.

"Gundeck, Third Lieutenant," a voice announced.

"This is the Captain, Dahnel. Do you have the target in sight?"

"Yes, Sir. St. Charlz is in First Division's field of fire."

"Excellent. Unfortunately, I'm not going to be able to bring Third Division's guns onto the target for a while."

"Understood, Sir." Something suspiciously like a chuckle came up the voice pipe. "I imagine young Paitryk can amuse himself with the batteries on Sharyn Island in the meantime if he has to."

"As long as we're not just wasting ammunition," Cahnyrs replied.

Eraystor's armament was divided into divisions on the basis of their fields of fire. The ironclad's heavily armored casemate formed a lozenge-shaped superstructure, like two blunt-ended triangles set base-to-base and stepped just far enough back from the side of the hull to mitigate the wave action which would have washed far up over the gun ports of a ship like the original *Delthak*-class in a seaway. All of her weapons were broadside mounts, but the five forward guns in each broadside could fire only at targets no more than thirty degrees abaft the beam, while the five after-most guns could train no farther forward than thirty degrees *before* the beam. That formed a logical basis for dividing them into numbered divisions: First and Second division, forward, and Third and Fourth division, aft. But she mounted a total of *eleven* guns in each broadside. The center weapons, located at the broadest points of the lozenge, could bear almost as far forward as First or Second Division and almost as far aft as Third or Fourth Division. As a consequence, those weapons were allocated to both divisions on their side of the ship, with control passing to whichever division could offer it a target.

Dahnel Bahnyface was *Eraystor's* Gunnery Officer as well as her third lieutenant, a new position which placed a commissioned officer between the ship's captain and the Chief Gunner, who was traditionally a warrant officer. The former Chief Gunner was now simply the Gunner, and served as the Gunnery Officer's chief assistant and advisor, and in action, each division of the armament was assigned to one of *Eraystor's* other commissioned officers. Or, in the case of Third Division, to a passed midshipman who remained two years shy of legal age for a lieutenant's commission.

"I don't think we'll be wasting any, Sir," Bahnyface told the captain now. "Not from the after divisions, anyway."

"Are you confident of engaging St. Charlz from this range?" Cahnyrs asked.

"Reasonably, Sir." Cahnyrs could almost see Bahnyface's slight shrug. "The roll's not bad, and it's not like we'll be shooting at a moving target. I don't guarantee very *many* hits from this range, but we'll score you at least some, Sir!"

"In that case, you may open fire, Master Bahnyface."

▼ ▼ ▼

"My Lord!"

Major Kylpaitryc had deliberately looked away from the heretic ironclad. At a range of over four and a half miles, the smoke-spouting thing was still tiny with distance, but there was something undeniably . . . ominous about its steady, unwavering progress. Perhaps it was because it was moving directly into both current and wind, its smoke banner blowing dead astern. Or perhaps it was that dense, unnatural smoke itself.

Or perhaps, he'd thought grimly, *it's the fact that it's steaming directly into the converging fire of over fifty heavy guns and it doesn't seem to give a spider-rat's arse about it.*

Whatever it was, he'd found other things to do than peer through his spyglass at it, which meant he was looking in the opposite direction when the lookout shouted to Lord of Foot Bauzhyng.

Now he spun around, eyes widening in surprise, as a dense, brown eruption of gunsmoke billowed from the ironclad. It was still almost bows-on to Battery St. Charlz, but it had slewed enough to starboard to bring its forward larboard guns to bear. It was also so far away that the thunder of those guns hadn't yet reached his ears when six 6-inch shells came sizzling down out of the heavens ahead of the sound of their passage.

▼ ▼ ▼

"Not bad at all, Alyk!" Zhaztro commented as the shells impacted. He had to raise his voice—a lot—to be heard through the thick earplugs protecting *Eraystor*'s crew's hearing from the artillery's deafening thunder.

Three of Lieutenant Bahnyface's shells threw up tall, white columns of water—all of those had landed short—but three more erupted in dark, fire-hearted explosions that ripped into Battery St. Charlz's berm. He doubted they'd done much damage to anything—or anyone—on the far side of that berm. Unless they scored a direct hit on one of the gun embrasures—and the odds of that at this range were effectively nonexistent—they weren't going to seriously injure the heavily protected battery. One of the sail-powered bombardment ships might well actually have been more effective than *Eraystor*'s higher-velocity, lower-elevation broadside weapons, since the bombardment ship could have dropped its fire into the battery's interior without worrying about its berm. Unfortunately, with wind and current both against them, working one of the bombardment ships into position would have been a time-consuming and potentially risky proposition. And whether or not they were inflicting actual damage at this range, it was at least likely to give the enemy commander "furiously to think," as Emperor Cayleb might have put it.

I'd really like to get the bastard to return fire while we're still as far out as possible,
he thought, standing on his flagship's exposed bridge wing with his double-
glass to his eyes. *Getting a feel for their range and accuracy before we get too close
would come under the heading of a Good Thing. And I'd like a better feel for how
likely those new "Fultyn Rifles" are to actually punch through our armor.*

He grimaced at that thought without lowering the double-glass, because
he was less confident on that head than he'd been prepared to admit to any
of his officers, including Alyk Cahnyrs. He wasn't *unconfident* . . . exactly,
but he'd had enough experience with flagships getting pounded into wreckage to last him the rest of his life.

"Not bad," Cahnyrs agreed from beside him, watching through his own
double-glass. "Dahnel can do better, though."

"And he will," Zhaztro replied. "The guns are cold, the range is long,
and his gun captains need to get a feel for her motion." He smiled thinly.
"And at least *Eraystor*'s a hell of a lot steadier than any galleon."

The ironclad's guns bellowed again,

▼　▼　▼

That's got to be eighty-five hundred yards, Major Kylpaitryc thought as the dirt
and debris thrown up by the nearest shell pattered back down around him.
Most of that debris was fairly small, but a few larger chunks thudded down
onto the heavily sandbagged roof of his observation post. *I didn't really expect
them to open fire from that far out. Or to be that accurate when they did, either!*

He raised his spyglass, capturing the lead ironclad's image once again as
the huge, dense clouds of brown gunsmoke rolled astern. Part of that was the
wind, which was already beginning to shred the cloud bank, but part of it
was also the armored ship's steady forward progress. The long, black fingers
of its guns hadn't recoiled at all, as far as he could see, and even as he watched,
they belched huge, fresh bubbles of fire.

Langhorne! Something cold settled in the vicinity of his stomach. *The
reports from Geyra said they could fire those things quickly, but I didn't expect them
to be* that *fast! It couldn't have been more than thirty seconds!*

Battery St. Charlz's Fultyn Rifles—especially the huge 10-inch weapons—
could never hope to match that rate of fire. They'd be doing well to get off
one shot every couple of minutes! Of course, the battery had many more
guns than any single ironclad could bring to bear, but not all of St. Charlz's
weapons could be brought to bear on the same target, either. And unlike an
ironclad, the battery wasn't going to be moving.

And we don't have to worry about an *ironclad; we've got to worry about* five *of
the frigging things!*

He didn't like how powerful the heretics' shells appeared to be, either.
According to the Desnairians, who'd actually measured one of the heretics'

shells which had failed to explode at Geyra, the ironclads' broadside weapons fired only 6-inch shells, considerably smaller than the ones fired by their bombardment galleons. If that was accurate, however, then the Imperial Charisian Navy had managed to build a 6-inch shell which seemed to carry a bursting charge at least as big as anyone else's *10*-incher.

That's going to hurt when they start registering a lot of hits, he thought grimly, lowering his spyglass and ducking involuntarily as four more dazzlingly white columns of water—tinged mud-brown at their bases—erupted from the Main Ship Channel. Two more shells burrowed deeply into the protective berm before they exploded, and fresh showers of debris came pelting down.

▼   ▼   ▼

Eraystor forged onward, the range dropping steadily. She'd taken Battery St. Charlz under fire at a range of 8,400 yards—still 12,000 yards from Battery St. Rahnyld on the eastern end of Sharyn Island and 10,500 from Battery St. Agtha on East Island's Cut Bait Point. That put her well beyond the effective range of the other batteries, although the range to St. Agtha dropped just as steadily as the range to St. Charlz.

At six knots, she'd need an hour to reach her shortest range to St. Charlz, at which point—assuming she held her intended course—she'd be less than *one* thousand yards from the muzzles of the Harchongese guns. It was a sobering thought . . . especially since those guns had yet to fire a single round.

"Signal *Bayport* to reduce speed!" Admiral Zhaztro ordered. "Captain Gahnzahlyz is to open the interval between her and *Eraystor* by at least a thousand yards."

"Aye, aye, Sir. *Bayport* to reduce speed and open the interval to *Eraystor* by at least a thousand yards," the signalman repeated. Zhaztro nodded, and the signalman and his assistant started pulling signal flags out of their bags.

The ironclad's guns fired again, the shock of recoil hitting the soles of Zhaztro's shoes like a hammer and Captain Cahnyrs leaned close to shout in the admiral's ear in the—relatively—quiet interval between shots.

"Buying a little more time for Lynkyn to look things over before it's his turn, Sir?"

"Couldn't hurt," Zhaztro shouted back with a shrug. "Can't pretend I won't be happier when the bastards shoot back and give us a better feel for what they've got!"

▼   ▼   ▼

Major Kylpaitryc coughed and spat out a mouthful of grit, then dragged a watch from his pocket and peered down at its face.

Thirty minutes? He shook his head, feeling like a prizefighter who'd taken too many punches to the body. *It has to be more than half an hour!*

But he knew it hadn't been, whatever it might *feel* like.

The ironclad's side disappeared behind a fresh eruption of flame-cored brown smoke and two 6-inch shells came screaming across the top of the eastern berm. One of them slammed into the inner face of the western berm, blasting a huge divot out of the masonry backing the thick earthwork.

Brick shattered, men screamed, and Kylpaitryc cursed. Each of Battery St. Charlz's guns was mounted in its own, individual bay—a vaulted chamber built out of thick, solid brickwork and then buried under as much as twenty feet of solid earth. Those bays were impervious to anything short of a direct hit . . . which was exactly what that Shan-wei-damned shell had just scored. Worse, the hit had come in from the bay's *rear*, where it was open to St. Charlz's small parade ground. The 8-inch Fultyn Rifle lurched drunkenly sideways, spilling from its fortress carriage and crushing one of its crew to death before the entire bay collapsed and buried him and half his companions.

Shouted orders brought more men on the run, ignoring the heretics' fire as they dashed from their own protected positions to help the gun crew's survivors dig frantically for their buried fellows, and Kylpaitryc shook his head, trying to clear his thoughts.

There was something more than a little terrifying about the ironclad's remorseless, unflinching approach. The range had fallen from over eight thousand yards to barely *three* thousand, and the hellish ship had turned to present its full broadside to St. Charlz. Now eleven guns bellowed from it three times every minute, driving their merciless fire brutally into the earthworks, filling the air with smoke and dust.

How much longer was Bauzhyng going to wait? The heretics were already well within his five-thousand-yard range, and *still* he simply stood there, gazing out through the vision slit at the channel! Dust and dirt speckled his immaculate uniform and his face bled freely where a fragment of brick had flown in through the slit and opened an inch-long cut just below the cheekbone. Yet his expression was calm, almost contemplative, and Ahdem Kylpaitryc had discovered that he felt a deep admiration—almost a sense of affection—for the arrogant, fastidious "fop" who commanded Battery St. Charlz.

Another heretic broadside thundered, blasting into the fortifications outer face, and more screams arose, faint to Kylpaitryc's brutalized ears. The ironclad was close enough now, firing rapidly enough, that its fire had finally started to shred even those high, thick earthen ramparts. Surely Bauzhyng had to—

"All batteries will open fire now!" Kwaichee Bauzhyng said.

▼   ▼   ▼

"The bastards *do* have guns in there, don't they, Sir?!" Alyk Cahnyrs demanded in tones of profound exasperation.

"I'm sure they do!" Zhaztro replied. "And sooner or later, they'll *have* to shoot back!"

After thirty minutes' steady firing, he felt as if he'd been hammered out on a flat rock and left to dry in the sun. So far, *Eraystor* had fired almost four hundred 6-inch shells into Battery St. Charlz. She carried only a hundred and twenty shells per gun, so that represented fifteen percent of her total ammunition supply . . . and almost a quarter of her total supply of standard shells. And *still* the Harchongians hadn't fired a single shot in reply!

Whoever the hell's in command over there is one tough-minded bastard, Zhaztro thought with the grim admiration of one tough-minded bastard for another. *Son-of-a-bitch must be determined to get us in as close as he possibly can before he opens up.*

The admiral raised his double-glass, peering through the lenses—and the swirling clouds of smoke—and smiled bleakly as a solid line of explosions ripped into the fortifications. He could scarcely see it clearly in the current visibility—or lack thereof—but he'd be astonished if a single shot had missed. The range was down to barely a mile and a half, and even if the gunners' vision was badly obscured by the torrents of gun and funnel smoke, their target was unmoving and they knew exactly where to find it. At such a short range, their shells drove even deeper into the earthworks protecting the Harchongese guns and the whirlwind of fire opened deep gouges in the battery's battered berm. Zhaztro didn't care how *thick* that berm was. Sooner or later, those guns had to open fire or simply find themselves buried in their ramparts' collapse, and—

The entire face of Battery St. Charlz belched a rolling cloud of flame as thirty-four heavy rifled guns fired as one.

▼　　▼　　▼

"*Yesssssss!*" Ahdem Kylpaitryc heard someone scream . . . and realized it was himself.

Every gun on St. Charlz's southeastern front vomited fire and smoke. There were three dozen Fultyn Rifles on that face of the battery, although one of them had been dismounted by a direct hit and another was unable to fire because the rampart above its bay had collapsed across its embrasure.

Twelve of those guns were "only" 8-inch weapons, firing hundred-pound solid shot. Kylpaitryc hadn't really expected very much out of the 8-inchers, given their target's thick, armored hide . . . but he also hadn't expected the heretics to come within twenty-five hundred yards before St. Charlz opened fire, either. At this range, even their shot might just penetrate, and their rate of fire was thirty percent higher than the 10-inch weapons could manage.

On the other hand, there were *twenty-two* of the 10-inch rifles. Their shot weighed over four hundred and fifty pounds apiece . . . and only three of them missed their target.

▼　▼　▼

It was like being inside the world's biggest bell, Sir Hainz Zhaztro thought. Or perhaps more like being inside one of Ehdwyrd Howsmyn's boilers while a hundred maniacs with sledgehammers pounded on its surface.

Whatever else it might be like, it was nothing *at all* like the fire *Eraystor* had taken at Geyra. Even at the very end, when he'd closed to four hundred yards of the Geyra waterfront, the defenders had scored very few hits—largely because he'd completely shattered their defensive works before he ever came into their range. But even then, the heaviest shot to actually hit his flagship's armor had come from one of the Desnairian *40-pounders*. Now *Eraystor* rocked as just over four and a half tons of solid iron slammed into her in a single wave.

It wasn't all concentrated in a single spot—and thank God for it! He and Captain Cahnyrs and the rest of the bridge crew had retreated into the conning tower's protection when the range fell below two miles, which was just as well. Zhaztro was peering through one of the vision slits when a three-hundred-pound solid shot ripped into the open bridge at an angle almost exactly perpendicular to the hull's centerline. Wood and steel shattered, spraying the face of the conning tower with fragments which would have shredded anyone still in the open, and the incredible cacophony as dozens of heavy projectiles slammed into the casemate armor was indescribable.

Three of *Eraystor*'s gunners who'd been in direct contact with that armor were bowled over, hurled effortlessly from their feet as one of those 10-inch shot sent a savage concussion straight through the tough, face-hardened steel. Two of them were simply stunned; the third drove headfirst into the breech of his own gun and the impact smashed his skull like an eggshell.

Two of St. Charlz's shots went high, punching contemptuously through the ironclad's funnel. She'd hoisted out her boats to tow astern to protect them from blast damage, but both larboard lifeboat davits and the steam-powered boat crane fitted to her mast were shattered in that tempest of screaming iron, and one of the 8-inch shot went home forward of the armor belt, punching through the relatively thin steel hull plating and into her cable tier.

None of Battery St. Charlz's shot actually penetrated *Eraystor*'s armor, but the casemate face and her belt armor were dimpled and scarred. Here and there the outer face was actually broken, although the tough, flexible inner layers of the Howsmynized plate held, and Zhaztro's face tightened. Charis' spies had reported that Lieutenant Zhwaigair, the infernally inventive fellow who'd come up with the screw-galley concept for the Earl of Thirsk, had proposed a way to attack armor that couldn't actually be penetrated. He called it "wracking," and the idea was simple: get in as close as possible with the heaviest possible gun and pound that armor again and again and *again* until its securing bolts or even the supporting frames behind it shattered. Zhaztro hadn't been particularly impressed when he first read those reports. Now, as his flagship heaved under that massive impact, he found himself wondering if Zhwaigair might not just have hit upon something.

▼　▼　▼

Battery St. Charlz's gun crews swarmed over their pieces with the urgent, disciplined speed Lord of Foot Kwaichee Bauzhyng had drilled so ruthlessly into them. There was more to it than simple training, though. That accursed ironclad had pounded their fortress for over half an hour, increasingly accurate, scoring ever more hits, killing and wounding men they knew— friends—and they'd been refused permission to reply. Now it was *their* turn, and they bent to their guns with a will.

The heretics fired again before the slower muzzleloaders were ready, and another of the 8-inch weapons disintegrated as a 6-inch shell screamed directly into its embrasure and reduced it—and its entire crew—to broken wreckage. Despite the wind, the dense gunsmoke—from St. Charlz, as well as the ironclad—welled up in an impenetrable veil. But the ship's funnel and mast were visible above the rolling banks of smoke, and that was enough.

The guns were reloaded, with a speed that owed nothing at all to the threatened flogging awaiting the most tardy crew, and then St. Charlz belched smoke and fire again.

▼　▼　▼

A three-hundred-pound shot smashed directly into the rotating shield of number three larboard 6-inch gun. The shield held, but the impact deformed it badly. It jammed in place, the gun no longer able to train, and its gun captain cursed in savage frustration as he realized what had happened.

More shot hammered home, carrying away ventilator mushrooms, cutting stanchions and chain railings, punching more holes in the smoke-spewing funnel. The exposed rangefinder atop *Eraystor*'s bridge vanished in a swirling cloud of wreckage, and the bridge signal locker disintegrated, sending signal flags flying like terrified wyverns. A four-foot section of the starboard leg of the ironclad's tripod mast simply vanished, but that was another shot that went higher than intended.

The Harchongians were deliberately shooting low, trying to get their iron shot into the ship's side . . . or to land just *short* of the side. Earl Thirsk's people had carefully analyzed the placement of HMS *Dreadnought*'s armor.

That was what had suggested the "wracking" tactic to Lieutenant Shwaigair, who'd paid special attention to how the armor plates were secured. But the lieutenant had also noted that while the ship's armor extended below the waterline, it was by only about three feet at her normal load waterline, and Lord of Foot Bauzhyng had taken that analysis to heart. His primary purpose was, indeed, to "wrack" the heretic's armor as Zwaigair had recommended, but if his gunners missed her armor, he wanted their fire to come in *low*, not high—at an angle which might just hole the ironclad's thin hull plating below the protection of her armored belt.

It wasn't likely they'd land *many* hits there, but it was certainly possible. And even the best armored ship had to sink if someone stopped trying to make holes above the water to let air *out* and managed to punch enough holes below the waterline to let water *in*.

▼　　▼　　▼

Kylpaitryc's eyes streamed tears as he coughed explosively on harsh, sinus-raping smoke. St. Charlz's rate of fire had slowed—after twenty-five minutes of furious action, the gunners were beginning to tire badly, but even more to the point, they'd *had* to reduce fire as the guns heated dangerously. Two of the 8-inchers had already burst, although—Praise Langhorne!—close to their muzzles and nowhere near as catastrophically as they could have, and he was frankly amazed they'd held up as well as they had. St. Charlz had been equipped with older, iron Fultyn Rifles (not that *any* of them were all that old), which had a much worse reputation for bursting than the newer, steel guns did.

But the Harchongians had never faltered for a moment, despite the risk of failing guns, and he felt a swell of vast, ungrudging pride in them. Perhaps it owed something to that phlegmatic, stoic endurance—that stolid ability to survive anything their masters did to them—for which Harchongese serfs were famed. But perhaps it didn't, as well.

Kylpaitryc knew *he'd* never imagined such a tempest of fire and iron, of smoke and battering waves of overpressure. The torrent of heretic fire was a solid wall of hate, scourging the battery's earthworks like the hammer of Kau-yung, and six more guns had been destroyed by direct hits or silenced by avalanches of earth and masonry, plunging down to block their firing embrasures. It must be as evident to Bauzhyng's gunners as it was to the lord of foot's liaison officer that if the rest of the heretic ironclads joined the battle, St. Charlz *had* to be wrecked from one end to the other by the time they were done.

It took more than resignation, more than fatalism, to face *that* sort of holocaust, and he recognized raw, unbending courage when he saw it.

The ironclad forged onward—taking fire from both sides now, as Battery St. Agtha joined the battle at a range of 7,500 yards. St. Agtha was sited farther above water level, with a better angle downward at the heretics' decks, where both logic and the Dohlaran analysis of HMS *Dreadnought* said the armor had to be thinner. But the longer range, the smoke, and the 6-inch shells shrieking back into its gunners' faces negated any advantage its gunners might have enjoyed. On the other hand, the ironclad was now under fire from over a hundred heavy guns. A lot of them were missing, judging by the continuous, tortured geysers of white water all about the ship. But a lot of them *weren't* missing, too.

It was impossible to make out details through the walls of smoke, the ear-battering thunder of the guns, the explosions of the heretics' shells, but it seemed to Kylpaitryc that their fire had decreased. They weren't firing any more slowly, but they seemed to have fewer guns in action, and he bared his teeth at that thought. If they could inflict enough damage, cripple the lead ship, the heretics might break off the attack . . . and realistically, that was the best Rhaigair Bay's defenders could hope for.

▼　▼　▼

"Three inches of water in the bilge, Sir!" Lieutenant Tahlyvyr reported to Alyk Cahnyrs over the conning tower voice pipe. "Pumps're handling it no problem . . . so far."

"Understood," Cahnyrs replied. "Stay on it, Anthynee."

"Aye, Sir," *Eraystor*'s engineering officer replied, and Cahnyrs let the voice pipe flap close and looked at Zhaztro, standing at his shoulder.

"Bastards are getting more of them in under the belt," the flag captain said grimly.

"Not enough to make a difference . . . yet," Zhaztro said, and Cahnyrs nodded.

"Yet," he agreed.

It was almost impossible for them to hear one another as the bedlam roared and bellowed around the ship. The Harchongians were firing at least some explosive shells now, and the pounding of shell splinters—and pieces of decking, breakwaters, bridge faces, and Langhorne only knew what else—battered the conning tower's armor like Shan-wei's hail. The range was coming down on nine hundred yards, and the savagery of the engagement seemed to redouble with every yard *Eraystor* steamed. Four of her guns were out of action, now. Damage to her ventilators and funnel had reduced the draft to her boilers, reducing steam pressure accordingly. Everything above decks—everything not protected by armor—had been swept away as if by some fiery hurricane, yet she drove on through the heart of holocaust, firing back, her shells scourging the batteries.

It was impossible to make out details through the smoke, flame, spray, and dust—the conning tower's vision slits were almost useless, and even the three angle-glasses protruding through the tower's roof were three-quarters blind—but it seemed to Zhaztro that St. Charlz, in particular, was losing guns. There was nothing wrong with the courage and determination of the men *behind* those guns, but even though *Eraystor* was now in the field of fire of every gun on the battery's western face, it seemed to him that they were actually being hit less frequently . . . from larboard, at least. Battery St. Agtha was larger, with more guns, and despite the longer range, it was scoring a *lot* of hits on *Eraystor*'s starboard side. But there were definitely fewer coming in from St. Charlz, so either the Harchonians were having more trouble finding their target through the blinding walls of smoke—which, he admitted, was a distinct possibility—or else Lieutenant Bahnyface's gunners were dismounting and crippling their guns.

I hope to hell we are, anyway. Unless something totally unexpected happens, Eraystor's going to clear the batteries' fire in the next twenty minutes or so, but God only knows what kind of shape she'll be in after she does. And then there's the rest of the squadron. Not to mention the little problem of how we get the galleons and the other support ships into the bay if we can't silence these frigging batteries! Even a Rottweiler would have trouble living through this kind of fire—there's no way anything without armor could—and any galleon in the world would've been dismasted in the first ten minutes. So nothing besides the Cities is getting through if we can't take these bastards out.

He gave himself a mental shake. Of course they'd silence the batteries eventually—one way or another. He wasn't about to let these bastards stop him from doing *that*! But this sure as hell wasn't Geyra over again. If the Desnairians had shown this kind of discipline, this kind of accuracy. . . .

▼   ▼   ▼

"*Shit!*" Kylpaitryc said bitterly.

Whatever might have happened to the lead ironclad's weight of fire had just become unfortunately irrelevant. The second ironclad in line, steaming relentlessly forward and almost invisible beyond the rolling banks of smoke, had just opened fire on Battery St. Charlz.

"Another of the bastards coming up astern of the second one!" Lord of Foot Bauzhyng's signalman announced. He had to shout to be heard, and he never raised his head from the tripod-mounted spyglass focused on the signal mast above Battery St. Rahnyld, on the eastern end of Sharyn Island, whose garrison's view of the oncoming heretics was unobscured by the torrents of smoke.

As an enemy report, it was more than a little . . . informal, specially from a Harchongese noncom to a lord of foot. But Kwaichee Bauzhyng only nodded. And then—

"Thank you, Seargeant!" he shouted back.

Under other circumstances, Kylpaitryc might have blinked in surprise. Under these, he only felt his mouth try to twitch in harsh, ironic amusement. But any amusement vanished as fresh strings of shells exploded, scourging St. Charlz's already gouged and torn flanks. More than a quarter of the battery's guns had been put out of action, although most of them could have been restored to service quickly if only the heretical sons-of-bitches stopped *shooting* at them.

But the ironclads coming on behind the lead heretic promised that that wasn't going to happen. Not unless the defenders' last ditch ploy worked, anyway.

▼   ▼   ▼

"*Buoy dead ahead!*" the lookout on the larboard angle-glass shouted suddenly, and Alyk Cahnyrs grabbed the handles of the forward angle-glass, training it onto the indicated bearing.

"Multiple buoys!" the lookout amplified, and Cahnyrs' shoulders tightened.

"At least a dozen of the things, Sir," he grated, turning from the angle-glass to Zhaztro. "Probably more I can't see through the smoke. They're damned well marking *something* right in the middle of the frigging channel, though."

"Maybe the *seijins* were wrong about the Dohlaran sea-bombs after all." Commander Pharsaygyn's expression was taut, his tone grim.

"If they were, we'll sail right into the middle of the goddamn things unless we change course in the next four minutes, Admiral," Cahnyrs said flatly.

▼   ▼   ▼

Wonder if the bastards will even see *the buoys?* Kylpaitryc wondered.

There was no way of telling, or even of knowing if the heretics would be looking for buoys in the first place. For that matter, they didn't *know* the heretics had discovered sea-bombs' existence in the first place, but it struck him as unlikely they hadn't. If there was one thing they'd demonstrated, over and over again, it was that their spies were fiendishly capable and *every* damned where. So, yes, they almost certainly knew at least something about the new weapon.

That was why he'd suggested laying the buoys to Bauzhyng. Somewhat to his surprise, the lord of foot had grabbed the idea and run with it. He'd planted a veritable forest of the things, and unless Kylpaitryc was much mistaken, the ironclad would be entering that forest sometime in the next few minutes.

The question, of course, was what they'd do when they did—assuming they *realized* they'd done it. It could be very . . . interesting, because those buoys had been placed with malice aforethought. The logical course to evade them would be to turn *away* from Battery St. Charlz, not towards it, and that course would just happen to lead the ironclad onto a spur of the shoal upon which St. Charlz had been built. At the same time the false sea-mine buoys had been laid, the navigation buoys marking that spur had been *removed*, in hopes of repeating what had happened to the heretics on Shingle Shoal the preceding year. If the ploy succeeded and the defenders had just a little luck, the ironclad would hit hard enough to rip out its bottom. Even if it avoided that, a ship aground—no matter how well armored it might be— would inevitably be pounded apart by all of the guns St. Charlz and St. Agtha could bring to bear upon it.

And if it doesn't *turn—if it just keeps going and those other ironclads follow it through—we're fuck*ed.

▼   ▼   ▼

Hainz Zhaztro looked at his flag captain, his jaw tight, his face like iron.

True or false? he thought harshly. *Real sea-bombs, or just a bluff? And which way does Alyk veer if he avoids them? There's a goddamned shoal out there some-where, and in all this smoke and other shit, how the hell do we avoid it if we start taking evasive action in the middle of a frigging duel with a couple of hundred heavy rifles?!*

The thoughts flickered through his brain like chainlightning, hammering the weight of command down on his shoulders as nothing had since Darcos Sound. He saw Cahnyrs' expression, knew the captain wanted to swing wide of the danger zone. The admiral didn't blame him at all, and how he fought his ship was his decision, wasn't it?

Yes, it was. But whatever he decided would have huge implications for the rest of the squadron. And even if it was Cahnyrs' *decision,* that made it someone else's *responsibility.*

Hainz Zhaztro drew a deep breath and looked his flag captain squarely in the eye.

"Damn the sea-bombs, Alyk," he said flatly. "Hold your course and go ahead."

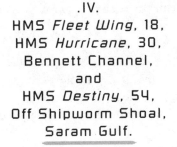

.IV.
HMS *Fleet Wing*, 18,
HMS *Hurricane*, 30,
Bennett Channel,
and
HMS *Destiny*, 54,
Off Shipworm Shoal,
Saram Gulf.

Must be nice to be able to read minds, Sir," Zosh Hahlbyrstaht remarked as he stood beside Hektor Aplyn-Ahrmahk gazing northwest into the wind at the low-lying cloud of weather-stained canvas plowing steadily down Basset Channel. "Is that something just any admiral can do, or do you have to be a baron?" He shook his head. "Either way, I do admire a man who can predict what the other fellow's going to do so far in advance! How is he at picking baseball teams?"

"Well," Hektor said dryly, gazing through the double-glass braced on Stywyrt Mahlyk's shoulder; he had trouble supporting even a double-glass, much less a regular spyglass, for very long with only one hand, "I don't know whether or not he can read just anybody's mind, and he's never picked a winning team that *I* know of. But I will say that as a midshipman in *Destiny* I had ample evidence he could read the mind of anyone under his command!" He straightened, lowering the double-glass with a nod of thanks to Mahlyk. "Never saw a single seaman sneak something past him—and they *tried,* believe me; it was almost like a game they played with him! Didn't matter what I had on *my* conscience, either. He always knew about it. Usually before *I* did!"

"Works that way for cox'ins, too, if you don't mind m' saying so, Sir," Mahlyk observed, and gave his youthful commander a rather sharp glance. "Seems to be the sort of gift a Pasqualate'd call 'contagious,' now I think on it."

"Well, since no one ever accused *me* of mind-reading, I'm sure I don't have the least idea what you're talking about," Hektor returned, but his expression was absent as he resettled the double-glass strap around his neck without ever taking his eyes from the loom of those oncoming sails, etched against the late-afternoon sunlight. Neither of his companions understood just how well he could actually see them, of course.

He stood that way for the better part of another minute, then shook himself and looked back at Hahlbyrstaht.

"Send Lawrync up to the crosstrees for another count. We're damned well not seeing *all* of them from here, but I want the numbers we *can* see confirmed as definitely as we possibly can. Then I think we'd best send Sir Dunkyn another note while there's still light for *Sojourner* to relay our signals."

▼   ▼   ▼

"Lad's got a talent for this, doesn't he, My Lord?" Captain Lathyk observed, looking down at the written signal. "To the point, tells you what he knows, and tells you what he knows he *doesn't* know, too." He looked up, shaking his head. "I know captains three times his age who don't bother with that last bit!"

"Well, I suppose he got a *fairly* competent grounding in his profession's responsibilities in his previous ship," Admiral Sarmouth acknowledged with a wry smile. He stood gazing down at the chart on the desktop between them while the lamps swung gently on their overhead chains. "Always nice when the other fellow seems to be doing what you want, too."

"I guess you could call it that," Lathyk said a bit sourly, then waved the signal. "Doesn't seem to be showing a lot of imagination, though. Just sail straight down the channel to us?" He shook his head. "Best way *I* can think of to get a lot of his own fellows killed."

"Fair's fair, Rhobair," Sarmouth chided, tapping the chart with a pair of brass dividers. "It's not like he's got a huge number of options. Unless *you'd* like to be the galleon skipper who finds himself dancing with Sir Hainz?"

Lathyk's expression made his opinion of any such goings-on abundantly clear, and the baron snorted.

"That's what I thought. And don't forget that all he's seen so far are schooners keeping an eye on him." Sarmouth shrugged. "He's got to assume the rest of us are out here somewhere, but he doesn't have any proof of that, he can't know exactly what our numbers are, and he doesn't know *where* 'out here' we might be. For all he *knows*, he could smack into us in the next quarter hour . . . or we could be running a bluff and those schooners are just pretending to be talking to a squadron of galleons which are really somewhere else doing something entirely different. Wouldn't be so different from what you and I did to the Desnairians before the Markovian Sea, now would it? I'll guarantee there were some red faces when *that* got out! You don't suppose Thirsk and Raisahndo haven't bothered to study their opposite numbers' records, do you?"

The admiral smiled, and the flag captain chuckled and shook his head.

"Not bloody likely, My Lord. If they were *that* stupid, the kraken'd already be flying over Gorath!"

"Exactly," Sarmouth said. "I don't think he believes for an instant that that's what we're actually doing, but he has to at least bear the possibility in mind, especially when the entire world knows we did it before . . . and he damned well *does* know where the ironclads were when he left port. And even though we have the advantage of all-coppered hulls and he still doesn't, the difference between our speed and his has to be a lot less lopsided than the difference between sailing galleons and steamers. Unless he simply chooses to scuttle them without ever leaving harbor, he has to take his galleons *somewhere*, Rhobair. Without knowing where we've placed our major strength, about all he can do is pick an escape route and hope he's guessed right. And the *last* thing he could afford to do was to vacillate until those ironclads rolled into range of his anchorage. Better to bash on—try to fight at least some of his squadron through to Gorath, even if it means taking on this entire squadron in confined waters—than try to avoid action and find himself caught *between* us and Sir Hainz."

"Well, put that way, I suppose he isn't being quite as . . . unimaginative as I might've thought," Lathyk admitted. "I think I'd still've tried to time things to make it out to sea in darkness, though, Sir."

"Now there you may have a point. On the other hand, he *will* clear the Cutfish Narrows before dawn, and that's the narrowest part of his entire passage. He'll still have to weather Broken Hawser Rock before he reaches the Gulf, and if I were in his boots, I might prefer to have darkness for the last eighty or ninety miles of that run on the theory that it would be easier to give our schooners the slip in the dark with that much more open water to work with. But it's not an easy choice. Does he try to evade us in daylight on this side of the Narrows *after* he clears the channel, or does he worry about our jumping him *here* in the dark?"

Sarmouth tapped the chart again, the points of his dividers on the Cutfish Narrows, between Tybor Rock, at the southern tip of Shipworm Shoal, and the northeastern arc of Shyan Island Shoal.

"What he'd really prefer would be to get through the channel and out to sea—and home to Gorath—without ever sighting a single one of our galleons. There's no way he could believe that's going to happen, though, and if he has to fight his way past us, he'd probably prefer to fight at the shortest possible range. Which is a pretty fair description of any action in the Narrows, when you come down to it. They're only about fifteen miles wide, even at high water, which I expect his screw-galleys would like. They're designed to get to knife-range as quickly as possible, not fight ships like *Lightning* and *Seamount*—or *Zhenyfyr Ahrmahk* and *Iceberg*, for that matter—in open water when we've got a wind to work with. So, yes, it could work out for Hahlynd and his boys if we were foolish enough to take him on there, especially in the dark. But those same tight quarters mean he wouldn't have a lot of room to evade us, and his ability to control his ships would be a lot poorer in the dark. Nobody would be seeing any signal flags, that's for damn sure! And don't forget how badly the Temple Boys and their friends have gotten hurt in night engagements in the past. Like, oh . . . the Markovian Sea, for example."

The baron's smile was much colder this time.

"Still, I think he'll figure tight quarters—like the Narrows—and poor visibility would cramp our maneuverability as much as it would his, and that means it would give him the best chance if he actually has to *fight* us. That's why he's making his approach so late in the day and passing through them in the dark. I suspect one reason he's timed his passage this way is to offer me the opportunity to sneak in under cover of darkness and 'ambush him' in the hope I'll take it.

"*Our* options are different, of course. If we didn't have entirely coppered bottoms—and if Hektor and the other scouts weren't keeping such a close eye on him—I might well try to jump him there, daylight or not, to keep the cork in the bottle and keep him from breaking out into the Gulf and making us chase him. But he's not getting away from us even if, by some miracle, he *does* make it to the Gulf. Given that, I'm not in all *that* big a hurry to finish the business—unlike him we've got all the time in the world to do this right—and frankly, there's no way in hell I want to tangle with those screw-galleys in the dark. They've never managed to use one of Zhwaigair's 'spar torpedoes' on us yet, and damned if I see any reason to give them the opportunity to use one now!"

"Fair enough, Sir." Lathyk nodded. "So what *do* we do next?"

"A reasonable question."

Sarmouth dropped the dividers and stood back, folding his arms and frowning. In fact, he was looking at a rather different chart, projected onto his contact lenses and showing the precise current positions—with movement vectors—of every ship in a hundred-and-fifty-mile circle centered on *Destiny*.

At the moment, Raisahndo and his forty-three galleons, twelve screw-galleys, and eleven brigs and schooners, were the better part of ninety miles from Sarmouth's chart table. The Dohlaran's speed had dropped a bit as the wind moderated, but he hadn't cracked on additional sail, which confirmed that he held to his determination to pass the Narrows in darkness. As Sarmouth had just pointed out to Lathyk, however, not all of Raisahndo's hulls were coppered.

In fact, the Imperial Charisian Navy remained the only navy in the world which coppered *all* of its vessels. Even ICN-owned transports and freight galleons were coppered, and the ironclads were wooden sheathed below the waterline so copper could be attached without galvanic action dissolving the iron fastenings. It was expensive as hell, but until the Royal College got around to inventing antifouling paints—which wouldn't happen anytime soon—it was the only way to protect a submerged hull against borers and weed. And however resistant to *borers* an iron hull might be, it certainly wasn't immune to the drag effect of weed and encrusted shellfish. Just over a quarter of Raisahndo's galleons lacked that advantage, however, and if they'd been in the water any length of time, that would cost them at least a knot or two—maybe even more—compared to a Charisian galleon of the same size and sail power.

He can't run—not with everyone—if things go badly for him . . . and they're going to go very *badly, unless I manage to screw up by the numbers. But just like I told Rhobair, he's caught in one hell of a trap. The only way out's through, and we're the only people he has a prayer of fighting his way past.*

Except that's not going to happen.

For a moment, he felt a pang of pity, but he suppressed it sternly. Caitahno Rausahndo might be—indeed, he was—an honorable and a decent man. But so was Earl Thirsk . . . and that hadn't prevented what had happened to Gwyllym Manthyr and his men. Nor did it change the fact that the Kingdom of Dohlar had been the Group of Four's most effective proxy from the very beginning.

There's a price for that sort of thing, he thought grimly. *I may not like being the one sent to collect it, but I by God* will *collect it!*

"I think we want to be right about *here* around breakfast time tomorrow," he said finally, unfolding one arm to tap an index finger on a spot thirty miles north-northeast of their current position. "That's far enough out to prevent anyone on Shipworm Island from reporting our position to him, and assuming Hektor and his friends are their usual efficient selves about maintaining contact overnight, we'll be well placed to run down on him for a meeting engagement sometime around midafternoon."

His flag captain craned his neck, looking down at Sarmouth's fingertip, then nodded.

"Yes, My Lord," he acknowledged. "Shouldn't be a problem."

▼　▼　▼

"I wish the bastards would go ahead and show themselves, Sir," Captain Trahvys said quietly.

He and Caitahno Raisahndo stood on HMS *Hurricane*'s quarterdeck, faces dimly lit by the backwash of the binnacle light, as the flagship made her cautious way into the Cutfish Narrows. Now the flag captain grimaced, folding his hands behind him and rocking on his heels as he looked away from the compass into the moonless dark. Faint starlight glimmered on his ship's canvas, but every other light had been doused, aside from the binnacle and the single blue lantern each galleon showed to her next astern for guidance and stationkeeping. Every gun was loaded and run out, with the crews sleeping—or trying to sleep, anyway—beside their pieces, despite the cold. It was about as quiet as things ever got aboard a sailing vessel underway, and Raisahndo wondered if Trahvys' nerves were as tightly wound as his own.

"Assuming they intend to show up at all," Trahvys added. "And somehow," his grimace deepened, "I don't see them being quite so obliging as to just wave as we sail past to Gorath."

"Neither do I," Raisahndo acknowledged. "Just between you and me, I'll spend the odd hour or two on my knees thanking Langhorne if we *do* sneak by without Sarmouth's ever getting a galleon in range of us." He wouldn't have admitted that to just anyone, but Trahvys only nodded. "Unfortunately," the admiral continued, "that's the one thing I'm sure *isn't* going to happen."

"Can't disagree, Sir," the flag captain said grimly, and Raisahndo shrugged.

"The best we can do is the best we can do, Lewk, and I'm sure that's what the lads will give us. But you're right, if we *have* to fight, this would be the perfect spot, especially for Admiral Hahlynd's screw-galleys. They might even get a chance to use those damned torpedoes for something besides training!"

Trahvys nodded, Pawal Hahlynd's screw-galleys had armed the percussion detonators on the spar-mounted three-hundred-pound charges of powder and then raised the spars into the vertical position. Assuming they got the chance, the spars would be lowered to project forty feet ahead of their stubby bowsprits, like an old-fashioned cavalry lance. If they could get close enough in the dark, ram one of *those* into a Charisian's side, all the armor in the world wouldn't save their victim!

"Even without the screw-galleys, getting in close would be our galleons' best chance to hurt them, too. Of course, it'd be frigging impossible to exert any sort of *control* over an unholy brawl like that, but confusion usually helps the fellow trying to run more than the fellow trying to *stop* him from running, and let's be honest here. I know what I told the others, but the truth is we're not looking for a battle under *any* circumstances, no matter how 'good' they might be. We're looking for an *escape*, and for that, we need as much sea room as we can get before we run into them. If Sarmouth's considerate enough to present his squadron in the next couple of hours and let us fight him here, on the best terms we can get, I sure as Shan-wei won't complain! In fact, I've done my dead level best to convince him to do just that. But if I were him and he was me?" He shook his head. "I'd sit somewhere ahead of us, knowing we'd *have* to come to him, and I'd stay the hell out of any night battles while I waited for daylight."

Trahvys made a wordless sound of agreement, and it was Raisahndo's turn to grimace under cover of the darkness. He must be even more nervous than he'd thought he was. He hadn't just told the flag captain all those things he already knew for *Trahvys'* benefit; he was still trying to convince *himself* they had at least some chance to pull this off. But the truth was that any engagement—daylight or dark—was unlikely to be a happy experience for the Western Squadron, and there wasn't one damned thing he could do about that. A competent admiral could usually find ways to defeat an adversary—or at least cope with it—if his fleet was more powerful than his opponent's *or* if it was faster.

Unhappily for the Western Squadron, it was neither.

"Well, it'll be dawn in about three hours," he pointed out, breath-steam gleaming in the chill night as it caught the binnacle's reflection. "Assuming the bastards persist in not showing up between then and now, it probably wouldn't be a bad idea to feed the men early, just in case."

▼　▼　▼

"Still with us, I see. Nice of them to be so punctual!" Lieutenant Hahl-byrstaht observed as the sunrise slanted sharply across the waves to gild the distant topsails with gold. He shook his head. "And right where you said they'd be. Sort of reminds me of that business in the Fern Narrows last year."

"We're not supposed to talk about that, Zosh," Hektor reminded him, and Hahlbyrstaht nodded.

"Point taken, Sir," he said rather more formally, then grinned. "It's still an impressive trick, though, Skipper, and I'm not the only man aboard who thinks that. Is this ability to smell the enemy something His Majesty taught you?"

"No, but I sometimes think it might be something Sir Dunkyn taught Cayleb back when *Cayleb* was a midshipman." Hektor smiled as someone in far-off Siddar City snorted an imperial sort of chuckle over his com earplugs. Then he shrugged. "Actually, it wasn't all that hard to figure out where they'd pretty much have to be under these conditions."

"Maybe not, but staying close enough to see them at first light without blundering right the hell into those two fellows in the dark was just a *tad* more challenging," Hahlbyrstaht countered, and pointed at the topsails of a pair of Dohlaran brigs less than four miles clear of *Fleet Wing*. The closest galleons were at least eight miles beyond them. "*I* found it a little worri-some, anyway. Of course, I realize two-to-one odds are a mere nothing for seasoned Charisian seadogs like us!" He snapped his fingers with fine dis-dain. "Still, it could've gotten lively."

"Which is why I knew I could rely on our 'seadog' lookouts to do such a good job." Hektor smiled again. This time, actually, it was more of a grin. "The Admiral always told me caution can be a great motivator and that a little honest fear does more to keep a man on his toes than any amount of confidence." He shook his head, his grin fading. "I sometimes wonder if he really realizes how much . . . moral authority it takes to say something like that to a ten- or eleven-year-old midshipman."

"'Moral authority'?" Hahlbyrstaht snorted. "*That's* something the Baron has in spades!"

"Oh, I think you could say that," Hektor agreed. Then he turned to look to the northeast, shading his eyes with his good hand as he gazed into the sun. "I assume *Sojourn's* up there where she's supposed to be?"

"Yes, Sir. Last time we looked, anyway." Hahlbyrstaht chuckled sourly. "Of course that was before we had the damned sun shining right into our eyes. I imagine she'll be able to read our signals just fine, but seeing her confirmation hoists'll be just a bit tougher."

"Well, if she's up there, I suppose we should update Commander Cupyr and ask him to pass it along to the Admiral." Hektor grimaced. "We should be able to see his confirmation sometime in the next, oh, hour or so."

.V.
Off Shipworm Shoal,
Gulf of Dohlar.

I don't suppose anyone mentioned where the delay was, Master Zhones?" Lathyk asked, gazing at the time chop on *Fleet Wing's* original dispatch.

"No, Sir. I'm afraid not," Passed Midshipman Ahrlee Zhones replied. The sandy-haired, bespeckled midshipman—he wouldn't be legally old enough to receive his ensign's commission for another ten months—had become Baron Sarmouth's acting flag lieutenant with the Duke of Darcos' departure from *Destiny*.

"I could send back an inquiry, if you'd like me to," he continued, although *he* manifestly didn't want to do anything of the sort, and the flag captain's lip twitched. Not so very long ago, Zhones had been HMS *Destiny's* signals midshipman. It would appear his tribal loyalties were alive and well.

"No, don't bother, Master Zhones," he said. "Probably nothing serious. But," he added, looking up from the dispatch at Sarmouth, "we should've had this at least forty-five minutes ago, My Lord."

"In a perfect world, yes." Sarmouth was bent over his chart table again, busily swinging dividers while he measured distances. "In the real world," he laid the dividers aside and gave Zhones a quick flicker of a smile, "as I believe the Emperor's said upon occasion, 'shit happens'. In this case, somebody probably had to wait for the sun to get out of his eyes." He shrugged.

"It's not as if it was all that time-critical, Rhobair. The important point is that we've got it now, and—assuming Raisahndo's maintained speed and heading—we're about sixty miles north-northeast of him. And, of course, that the wind seems to be veering in our favor," he added with pronounced satisfaction.

"Yes, My Lord," Lathyk agreed, looking down at the chart with him.

"Then I want us underway on a south-southeast heading as soon as possible." Sarmouth ran his index finger across the chart in a flattened crescent that swept about twenty miles south before it angled back to the west. "If everything works perfectly—and as we just pointed out, in the real world it doesn't—we should find our Dohlaran friends right about here."

He tapped a spot thirty miles south of Shipworm Shoal and about fifty miles west of Shyan Island, and Lathyk frowned, running mental calculations for a moment. Then the flag captain nodded.

"About fifteen o'clock, I make it, My Lord," he said with a faint edge of admiration. "Plenty of daylight left to work on them."

"That'll depend on how soon they see us and what they do when they do." Sarmouth twitched a shrug. "Actually bringing them to action could be trickier than we'd prefer, but at least we'll have plenty of sea room to do it in!"

Lathyk nodded again. A lot of flag officers would have immediately altered course to intercept Raisahndo as soon as possible. Sarmouth, on the other hand, had made it clear to all of his captains that he wanted to entice the Dohlarans as far out to sea as he could. A running battle at sea would play to the Imperial Charisian Navy's strengths, not the RDN's, and the heavy swell farther out would limit the Dohlaran screw-galleys' utility. The waves were no more than six feet tall at the moment, but the wind looked like freshening once more as it veered slowly but steadily eastward, and even six feet would be a much bigger problem for the low-lying and *fragile* screw-galleys than for blue-water galleons. It might not make a great deal of difference, but Sarmouth was the sort of flag officer who thought about things like that.

Besides, once they had the Western Squadron well out to sea, it would have a hell of a time crawling into another hidey hole before they laid it by the heels.

"Yes, My Lord," the flag captain said. "Master Zhones and I will just go and start passing the signals."

▼   ▼   ▼

"Watch your head, Sir!"

Hektor Aplyn-Ahrmahk hurled himself backwards as Stywyrt Mahlyk grabbed the back of his tunic and heaved. An instant later, the heavy block—streaming two or three feet of tarred hemp—crashed to the deck with skull-crushing force, right where he'd been standing, and bounced high into the air.

"Thanks, Stywyrt," he said, but he never looked away from the clouds of smoke rising from the Dohlaran brig.

Most of that was gunsmoke, but there was woodsmoke, as well, pouring up out of her midships hatch. At least a third of her crew were desperately fighting the flames, but the rest of her people had other business, and even as he watched, half a dozen more red eyes winked from within the cloudbank streaming from her gunports. Unlike *Fleet Wing's* last duel with a Dohlaran brig, the range was short enough for this one to get her carronades into action, and white columns of spray rose around his schooner as the smoothbore shells hit the water.

Only one of those shells had hit *Fleet Wing* so far . . . thank God. It was fortunate her captain's cabin was stripped, its furnishings bustled below, whenever she cleared for action, or else he'd need new furniture. Not to mention a new portrait of Irys. But he'd gladly have traded all his possessions for what that bursting shell had cost him. It had left three dead, four wounded, half a dozen shattered planks, and a pair of badly damaged deck beams in its wake, and it had been touch and go for several minutes for the firefighting parties.

But *Fleet Wing* had given as good as she'd gotten and then some. Even with the SNARCs' remotes, it was hard to be certain amid all of this smoke and confusion and artillery thunder, but it looked like the Dohlaran's people were losing ground on *her* fire. Hektor was astonished she was still in action at all, after being hit by no less than three 30-pounder and a pair of 14-pounder shells, but they were made of stern stuff, those Dohlarans. Their ship might be on fire, they might be outgunned, and water might be rising slowly in their bilges, yet they were *still* trying to fight their way past *Fleet Wing* to get a better count on Baron Sarmouth's squadron. He liked to think he'd be as persistent—and as gutsy—in their place, but—

The brig *Sword of Justice* disappeared into an expanding ball of fire as the flames finally reached her magazine.

▼   ▼   ▼

"So much for unsolved mysteries." Caitahno Raisahndo tried not to sound bitter as he stood under his cabin skylight. He also tried not to think about the price his scouting units had paid to buy him the information—the *fragmentary* information—Gahryth Kahmelka had just marked on the chart. He'd have preferred a more complete report, but that was more than flesh and blood could have given him.

And what he did have was bad enough.

At the moment, Kahmelka stood at his shoulder and Ahrnahld Mahkmyn stood on the other side of the chart table, signals pad and pencil poised. Of the two, the flag lieutenant looked less concerned, although Raisahndo suspected appearances could be deceiving. Mahkmyn was too smart not to realize how bad things were . . . but he was still too young—and too junior—to feel comfortable being obvious about it in front of his flag officer.

The sunlight streaming down through the skylight illuminated the chart's markings pitilessly while *Hurricane* creaked gently about them. Raisahndo listened to the ship's quiet voice and found himself wondering if she realized what was about to happen to her.

He hoped not. Almost as much as he wished his own imagination didn't already hear the shrieks—from splintering wood, not simply bleeding flesh and blood—which would replace that quiet all too soon.

You can still scatter and order them to run for it, he reminded himself. *You've got a good twenty miles to work with, his fleet speed can't be more than a knot or two faster than yours even with all that frigging copper, and he's got the smaller squadron. He doesn't have the numbers to chase* all *your people, so at least some of them would almost have to make it clear.*

Unfortunately, the directions available for running were limited.

Unless he wanted to flee back the way he'd come—which would simply be a slower version of suicide, given what had to have happened to Rhaigair by now—the only directions his ships could run with any hope of avoiding the enemy were east or southeast.

The toe of Shyan Island Shoal prevented him from turning south . . . unless he wanted to risk ending up embayed in the forty-mile-wide sheet of water bitten out of the shoal between Mussel Shell Ledge and Broken Hawser Rock. As it happened, he very much *didn't* want to end up there—there was a reason the local fishermen called that deceptively welcoming water Drowned Man's Sound—but the wind had continued to veer. It was not only freshening but blowing roughly from the north-northeast, now—a good six- or six-and-a-half-point shift since the day before. Barring a miracle (and those seemed to be in short supply for Mother Church's defenders) it was going to go on veering, and if it did, Sarmouth would be easily able to cut him off before he rounded Broken Hawser.

And finding himself in Drowned Man's Sound on a lee shore with the wind and sea getting up *and* a hostile squadron lurking up to windward would be . . . unpleasant.

He couldn't escape to the north or northeast, either. Shipworm Shoal was squarely in the way to the north. He couldn't run away *through* it, and he didn't much fancy cramping himself *between* it and a more powerful fleet.

The northeast was out because he'd have to sail almost directly into the wind. His schooners and the screw-galleys might be able to do that, assuming it veeered no farther; his squareriggers couldn't possibly come close enough to the wind.

And at this particular moment, Baron Sarmouth's squadron was perfectly placed to the east of him, blocking any escape due east and ready to cut him off whichever direction he tried to run.

All of which meant that however widely he scattered, his ships couldn't—literally *could not*—evade interception. All he'd accomplish by trying to scatter and run for it would be to transform his squadron into a mob of fugitives, incapable of supporting one another when the moment came.

It'd be Armageddon Reef all over again, with me as Malikai this time around, he thought harshly.

On the other hand, his bleeding scouts' best estimate was that the Charisians had no more than thirty galleons—thirty-five at the outside—to his own forty-three. True, at least one was a sister of the captured *Dreadnought*, and where there was one, there might be *more* than one. And it seemed likely that at least some of the others were more of the Charisians' damnable "bombardment ships," with far more powerful armaments than even *Hurricane* boasted. But a forty percent advantage in hulls was still a forty percent advantage, especially if he was able to keep them under firm tactical control, at least until the action became general. And that didn't even consider the possibilities Hahlynd's dozen screw-galleys presented.

You're not going to find better odds, no matter what you do, and you aren't going to evade him. Time to bite the bullet and use your numbers, he told himself . . . and tried not to think about the numerical advantage Duke Malikai had enjoyed off Armageddon Reef.

"All right," he said out loud, looking up from the chart, "at least we outnumber them damned near two-to-one, counting the screw-galleys. According to our spies, they should have at least half a dozen galleons our scouts aren't reporting, though. It's always possible—likely, really—that they're there and we just haven't seen them yet, but it's also possible they're still up watching North Channel. If they are, we need to hit them as soon as we can, before they whistle up any reinforcements. If we can punch through and get fifty or sixty miles farther east, we'll clear Broken Hawser whatever the wind does. Give us that, darkness, and maybe a little heavy weather, and at least some of the lads are likely to be able to break for home."

Kahmelka nodded, his expression tight but his eyes steady.

"I don't think this is a time for finesse," Raisahndo went on grimly. "If he wants to close with us, then I'm willing to close with *him* . . . and the sooner the better." He switched his gaze to Lieutenant Mahkmyn. "We'll have a general signal, Ahrnahld."

"Yes, Sir?"

"To all galleons, 'Make all sail to topgallants. Course northeast-by-east.' To Admiral Hahlynd, 'Screw-galleys conform to previous orders.' And to all ships, 'Prepare for battle.'"

▼　▼　▼

"He's made up his mind, My Lord," Lathyk said, standing beside his admiral on *Destiny*'s quarterdeck as they watched the Western Squadron's distant canvas swing to the northeast, turning to sail close-hauled on the larboard tack. *Destiny* and her consorts, on the other hand, had the wind broad on their starboard beams, which was very nearly a galleon's best point of sailing.

At the moment, anyway.

"Unless I miss my guess, he'd 'made his mind up' about what he'd do in a situation like this before he ever left Rhaigair," Sarmouth replied. "I won't pretend I haven't done everything I could to encourage him to do just this, but he knew what his options were when he set out." He shook his head. "Reminds me of Thirsk a lot, really. Good men, both of them." Then his expression hardened. "Too bad they couldn't find an equally good cause to serve."

He gazed around the quarterdeck. The wide, holystoned expanse of planking looked pristine and pure in the bright, chill sunlight, he thought. By evening it might look very different.

He shook that thought aside and looked up at the rigging, instead. The masthead pendant stood out boldly, not yet starched stiff by the wind but partly extended and flapping over its entire length. Between twenty-five and thirty miles per hour, his experienced eye estimated, but even with his additional sail, Raisahndo's speed wasn't going to be much above four or five knots, now that he'd brought his squadron so close to the wind. He was obviously bidding to keep Sarmouth from getting up to windward of him before they engaged. It was unlikely he thought he could *evade* Sarmouth that way, since Shipworm Shoal lay squarely across his path on his present course. But taking the wind gauge—if he could—was the right gambit for the Dohlaran.

Whether it would work or not was another thing entirely, but it looked like being a close run race, and if he somehow managed to *win* it. . . .

If Sarmouth pointed high enough to contest the wind gauge, he'd have to come starboard, moving the wind forward of the beam for his own ships as he put them close-hauled on the *starboard* tack, sailing the longer leg of an isosceles triangle towards the point where their courses crossed. If he *didn't* contest it, though, and Raisahndo managed to get to windward of him *and* avoid Shipworm Shoal, the Dohlaran might actually be able to avoid action— immediately, at least—after all. With the advantage of their copper and their loftier rigs, Sarmouth's ships could manage a good knot—at least—better than the Dohlarans under the same press of canvas . . . but he also had farther to go if *he* wanted the wind gauge, and he nodded crisply to himself.

"All right, Rhobair. If he's in such a hurry to make our acquaintance, it's only courteous to meet him halfway. Let's get the topgallants on her and come to west-northwest."

▼　　▼　　▼

"Why do I feel so small and insignificant, Sir?"

Zosh Hahlbyrstaht and Hektor Aplyn-Ahrmahk stood shoulder to shoulder at *Fleet Wing*'s taffrail. The pumps worked steadily, although fairly slowly, and hammers, saws, and adzes sounded behind them as the schooner's carpenter and his mates dealt with her damages. Hektor had just come from visiting his wounded. He was going to lose two of them, and that thought tightened his mouth with a pain worse than any physical injury, yet he knew *Fleet Wing* had been unreasonably fortunate. Much more fortunate than *Sword of Justice*, at any rate. *Fleet Wing* had plucked the Dohlaran brig's survivors—all seventeen of them—from the icy water, and three of them had already succumbed to their savage burns.

He shook that thought aside . . . for now. He already knew it would come back to visit him in his dreams. But he found it easier to evade at the moment as he and Hahlbyrstaht gazed out at a spectacle fit to strike awe into any seaman.

Eighty galleons forged towards one another, like two huge, floating islands or distant, snow-capped mountain ranges. Canvas gleamed under the chill midday sun: pewter, or weathered tan or gray, or—here and there—the pristine white of newly replaced sails. Banners floated in brilliant splashes of color against the blue sky and the steadily thickening banks of dark-bottomed white cloud rolling down upon the wind. That same wind sang in the rigging and plucked at uniform tunics and hats, and gulls and wyverns wheeled and plunged, crying to wind and wave as they followed the warships moving through the water with a deliberate, terrible majesty both young men knew was doomed to disappear into history.

That was preposterous in, oh, so many ways, Hektor thought, yet it was also inevitable. Barely seven years ago, those would have been fleets of galleys, closing on oars to ram and board and settle the business with cold steel. Now they were stately castles, driving through the freshening swell under towers of canvas, spray bursting white from their cutwaters, while row upon row of hungry cannon snouted from their gunports.

The difference in raw destruction and carnage those seven years had made was astonishing, even to an officer—or possibly *especially* to an officer— Hahlbyrstaht or Hektor's age, who'd lived through the breakneck fury of that change. And yet even as those two massive fleets, without a single unit more than six years old between them, manned by thousands of men and carrying thousands of guns, sailed slowly into the crushing embrace of destruction, Sir Hainz Zhaztro's steam-powered ironclads must be completing the devastation of Rhaigair two hundred and ninety miles to the north. And the only reason the Dohlarans had accepted battle here rather than staying put at Rhaigair to defend their fortified anchorage was because their galleons—*anyone's* galleons, however big, however powerful—couldn't have lived ten minutes in combat with one of the *City*-class ships.

And whether the Temple Boys know it or not, something one hell of a lot worse than the Cities *is coming on behind,* he thought now, grimly.

"You probably feel small and insignificant because *Fleet Wing's* only a schooner and she *is* pretty damned small and insignificant against this," he said out loud, waving at the panorama of sails with his good arm. Then he lowered his hand and shook his head.

"We won't see something like this ever again," he said softly. "Oh, there may be a little cleaning up around the edges, but aside from Thirsk's Home Squadron, this is the last fleet the Group of Four's got, Zosh, and Thirsk won't be coming out to meet us when we finally move on Gorath. Not after what Admiral Zhaztro's probably finished doing to Rhaigair." He shook his head with an edge of sadness. "Galleons are about to become as obsolete as crossbows. Nobody's going to be building another fleet of them after the war's over."

"I know." Hahlbyrstaht sighed. "And I guess it's pretty damned stupid for anyone who's ever served aboard a galleon in heavy weather to get all nostalgic over them. Hard to think of any experience more miserable than that! And it's not like they've got some sort of centuries of naval tradition behind them, but . . . Damn it, Sir! I'm going to *miss* them."

"A seaman's life is a stone-cold bitch as often as not," Hektor agreed, "but a galleon's a hell of a lot prettier than any steamer ever designed—yet, at least. Of course, given his choice between going aloft in a hurricane and down to shovel coal in a nice, dry stokehold, I know which any *sane* seaman's going to choose!"

"That's so . . . pragmatic of you," Hahlbyrstaht complained.

"What Charisians do, Zosh." Hektor shrugged, his eyes dark with mingled pride and regret. "Be pragmatic, I mean. It's what we do best."

▼   ▼   ▼

The opposing squadrons drew together with the slow, dreadful inexorability of sailing men-of-war. Even on converging courses, their closing speed was barely ten miles an hour. That left plenty of time to turn any man's bowels to water, Sir Dunkyn Yairley reflected.

Somewhat to his surprise, his own palms were dry and his pulse was almost normal, and he wondered why that was. Fatalism seemed an unlikely answer after all these years of pre-battle butterflies. Was it that this time he understood the reasons—the *real* reasons—he was out here risking the perfectly serviceable life which was the only one God had given him? Or was it simple duty? Or the realization that, one way or the other, this was almost certainly the last fleet action of the war against the Group of Four?

Maybe it's even simpler than that, he mused, pacing slowly, steadily, up and down the weather side of *Destiny's* quarterdeck. *Maybe it's just that this time I know where every single bastard on the other side is. I'm sure there'll be plenty of the "fog of war" once the guns open up, but for now—for the first time in any major engagement I've ever fought—I know exactly what the stakes are, exactly who's coming to the dance, and exactly where to find the other side when I want it. Won't keep a stray cannonball from taking off my head, I suppose, but at least this time that head won't be wondering what the hell is going on when the round shot arrives!*

He chuckled at the thought and never noticed the way the midshipman of the watch relaxed ever so slightly at the evidence of his admiral's amusement.

▼   ▼   ▼

"They're going to take the weather gauge, Sir," Captain Trahvys observed unhappily.

"They're more weatherly, they're faster, and their damned chain of scouts must've been telling Sarmouth where we were ever since we entered Basset Channel." Raisahndo shrugged. "Given all those advantages, it'd've taken a drooling idiot to *lose* the weather gauge."

Trahvys arched an eyebrow at him, and the admiral barked a laugh.

"Oh, I fought hard enough for it, Lewk! Would've taken it in a heartbeat if he'd let us have it, too. But when was the last time you saw a Charisian flag officer do something that stupid?"

"Don't believe I've *ever* seen a Charisian flag officer do something *that* stupid, Sir," the flag captain replied after a moment, and Raisahndo nodded.

"I rest my case."

He stood, gazing at the long, stately lines of ships. There must be five thousand guns aboard those ships, he thought, and Langhorne only knew how many officers and men were sailing so steadily—so *deliberately*—into the waiting furnace. *Raisahndo* certainly didn't know the answer to that question . . . but he no longer needed a spyglass to pick out details, and Sarmouth's formation made his intentions easy enough to understand.

The Charisian was coming at him in a single long column. Every ship in it looked big and powerful, but it was the two leaders who worried him most. The Charisian practice of painting every ship in the same stark colors—black hull, striped with white along the gunports—could make it difficult to identify individual ships, especially at any sort of distance. The Charisian leaders showed only a single row of gunports each, however, and that almost certainly made them ironclads like *Dreadnought*.

Not too surprising he put the two of them up front, Raisahndo thought grimly. *Haigyl showed what just* one *of them could do, without any supports at all, and these fellows've brought along plenty of friends to watch their backs. I'd feel happier if I knew for sure there weren't any* more *of the frigging things farther back in that column of his, though!*

Clearly, Sarmouth intended for his vanguard to take the initial brunt and smash hell out of anything that got in its way, and if there was any reason he shouldn't be confident of doing that, Caitahno Raisahndo didn't know what it might be!

"You know," he said slowly, eyes narrowing, "I think the time's come to let them *have* the weather gauge."

"I beg your pardon, Sir?"

"I said it's time to let them have the weather gauge," Raisahndo repeated, turning to face the flag captain squarely. "We can't keep him from taking it anyway, but he's pointed quite a bit higher than I thought he would. I don't know if he misestimated our heading or simply wanted to make sure he'd have plenty of maneuvering distance between us when he finally turns to close the range, but he may have given us a little more wiggle room than he intended to."

Trahvys looked at him for a moment, then back at the Charisian line, and then he began to nod.

▼　▼　▼

"Midshipman of the watch, My Lord," Sylvyst Raigly, Sir Dunkyn Yairley's valet and steward, announced, stepping out onto *Destiny*'s stern gallery.

As always, whenever the possibility of combat presented itself, Raigly was liberally equipped with pistols, swords, dirks, probably a grenade or two, and God only knew what other lethal, pointy objects.

Thank God I got Stywyrt into Fleet Wing *to watch Hektor's back*, the baron thought wryly. *If he and Sylvyst were in the same place when a shell went off, God only knows how many dozens of people the flying knives, guns, and brass knuckles would take down with them!*

"Thank you, Sylvyst," he said out loud, straightening from where he'd stood, leaning on the railing as he watched HMS *Empress* sail steadily up *Destiny*'s wake. He turned away from the rail and made a beckoning motion with the fingers of his right hand, and the valet vanished back the way he'd come, then reappeared with a brown-haired, brown-eyed midshipman.

"Master Ahbaht," Sarmouth said as the youngster came to attention and touched his chest in salute.

"My Lord," the fourteen-year-old replied. "Captain Lathyk's respects, and the enemy's changing course. The Captain said to tell you you were right."

The youngster seemed a little puzzled by the last sentence, but Sarmouth only shook his head.

"Don't worry about it, Master Ahbaht," he advised. "My compliments to Captain Lathyk and tell him I'll join him on deck directly."

"Aye, aye, My Lord. Your compliments to the Captain, and you'll join him on deck directly."

Sarmouth nodded in confirmation, and Ahbaht saluted again and withdrew.

The baron stood a moment longer, gazing out at the stupendous line of galleons following in *Destiny*'s wake, listening to the seagulls and sea wyverns as they swooped and darted around his ships. They'd disappear soon enough when the guns began to roar, he thought grimly. Then he shook himself and followed the midshipman, stepping from the stern gallery into what had been his cabin until the galleon cleared for action. Now the entire ship was one long, wide wooden cavern, every dividing bulkhead struck below for storage, its planked floor covered with sand for traction and dotted with tubs of water for swabs and firefighting. A cave with gunports gaping at regular intervals to let in wind and sunlight and let *out* the blunt, hungry muzzles of her artillery. He felt the wind plucking at his hair with invisible fingers and the sand crunched under the soles of his shoes as he strode past the waiting gunners, posed like martial statuary around their weapons—rammers, swabs, and worms in hand, cutlasses and pistols at their sides, bayoneted rifles racked ready if they should be needed—and the men of his flagship's crew bobbed their heads respectfully as he went by.

He emerged onto the quarterdeck and Lathyk greeted him.

"They're doing it, My Lord," he said.

"Of course they are." Sarmouth shook his head. "Once it was obvious they couldn't take the weather gauge, it was really the only move open to them."

"Oh, I know that, My Lord." Lathyk smiled crookedly. "It's just that you pegged when they'd make it almost to the minute. I was sure they'd hold on longer."

"That's because you underestimate Admiral Raisahndo. There's nothing wrong with that man's brain, Rhobair, and he's just demonstrated he has the moral courage to do the right thing even if it risks getting him labeled 'defeatist' by the Inquisition."

The baron crossed to the larboard rail and looked out across four miles or so of seawater. The head of the Dohlaran line had swung around, altering course from northeast-by-east to almost due southeast, curling around inside his own line. The rest of the enemy line followed, turning in succession as each galleon reached the same point, taking the wind on her larboard beam and shaking out more canvas.

Raisahndo had timed it reasonably well, Sarmouth thought, but he should have ordered a *simultaneous* turn. If he'd turned his entire squadron onto the wind simultaneously, he'd have bought his rearmost ships a much greater margin of safety. Sarmouth knew why he hadn't done it, though. Maneuvering forty-odd galleons as a single, cohesive force was akin to driving a herd of wild dragons through the middle of Tellesberg at midday . . . only harder. Once an admiral had them in line ahead, he *really* didn't want to break up that line any sooner than he had to, because as soon as he did, he'd lose control of it. Visibility-limited signals simply weren't up to coordinating a line of ships ten miles long, especially with gunsmoke to obscure flag hoists, but trying to control the same number of ships maneuvering independently of one another was immeasurably more difficult. Maintaining a line-ahead formation made control far simpler; it became a huge, deadly serious game of follow-the-leader, where what really mattered was no longer the ability to communicate but simply the iron courage to hold to the ship ahead of yours while all the world dissolved in fire, smoke, terror, and death.

But if a line was easier to *control*, it was also far less *flexible*. Raisahndo wanted to maintain as tight a tactical control as he could because he recognized the danger of disintegrating into a disorganized mob. Yet in his place, Sarmouth would have ordered the simultaneous turn, accepting that it was likely to reduce his line to a confused mass, at least until his captains could sort things out, as the price of getting the biggest head start he could.

Of course, once they turned to run—and every one of those captain would know that was exactly what they were doing; running—getting them to stop running and reform might not be the very easiest thing in the world, either. They're brave men, most of them—God knows there were no cowards in the Kaudzhu Narrows!—but every damned one of them knows their navy's up shit creek. Preventing a withdrawal from turning into a rout . . . ?

He shook his head, wondering how he'd react in their place. Easy to think about someone *else* losing his nerve, but what if *he'd* been the one in their shoes?

Fortunately, I'm not, he thought, and turned back to Lathyk.

"About another . . . fifteen minutes, I think, Rhobair. Let's let them get properly committed first."

"Aye, My Lord." Lathyk nodded, then snapped his fingers at the twelve-year-old midshipman standing at the mizzen halyards with his part of signalmen.

"We'll have that signal to Admiral Darys bent on, Master Rychtyr," he said, and smiled thinly. "We'll need it shortly."

"Aye, aye, Sir!"

▼   ▼   ▼

Caitahno Raisahndo watched the Charisian line and fought against letting himself hope.

Maneuvering a fleet at sea in sight of its enemies was like a dance where everyone knew the steps. Both admirals knew precisely what the other admiral's options were at any given moment, and assuming they'd accurately assessed one another's intentions, surprises were hard to come by.

In Sarmouth's position, Raisahndo would have realized the Western Squadron had no option but to break back south once it became evident the Charisians would take the weather gauge. The only real question in the Charisian admiral's mind should have been *when* Raisahndo would make his break, since it was obvious the only smart thing for him to do was to avoid action. The only way he could hope to do that, now that it was clear he couldn't get to windward of Sarmouth's line, was to turn and take the wind broad on his beam while he ran as fast and as hard as he could to *leeward*. He could do that now, assuming Sarmouth allowed him to, because the two squadrons' maneuvers for the weather gauge had carried them far enough east that a southeasterly heading would weather Broken Hawser Rock with at least a few miles to spare. That was the other reason he'd fought so hard for the windward position. Now if he was very, very lucky—and if Sarmouth suffered a sudden stupidity attack—he *might* get enough of a head start to squeak around the southern end of the Charisian line, between its rearmost galleons and Broken Hawser. And if he managed *that*, he might just manage to stay away from the Charisians until dark, too.

Some things were more likely than others, however.

Yet even as he thought that, the massive Charisian battle line—there were a couple more ships in it than he'd expected, but obviously at least half a dozen of them were, indeed, somewhere else—continued plowing towards the west-northwest. It was as if Sarmouth hadn't even noticed his course change!

If he doesn't alter pretty soon, he'll lose his chance, Raisahndo thought almost incredulously. *He can't turn the entire line and overtake us, copper bottoms or not, if he doesn't make his move in the next . . . ten minutes.*

Of course, when he realized Raisahndo was slipping away he could always order a general chase. The chance of any Charisian admiral being brainless enough to do that, however, was about on a par with the chance that Langhorne would return in glory sometime in the next five minutes. A general chase—with every captain maneuvering independently as he raced to catch up with the enemy—would certainly let Sarmouth's faster ships overhaul Raisahndo's compact, mutually supporting line of battle. They'd be disordered and out of mutual support of one another when they did, however . . . at which point they would discover what happened to the hunting hound that caught the slash lizard. No. A flag officer of Sarmouth's experience wouldn't make *that* mistake, especially against a fleet which outnumbered him as substantially as the Western Squadron did. His ships, and especially the ironclads, might be far more powerful than any individual unit on the other side, but if he was stupid enough to feed them into Raisahndo's well-organized, tightly controlled line in dribs and drabs, where discipline and numbers came into their own. . . .

▼   ▼   ▼

"Now, I think, Rhobair."

"Aye, aye, My Lord. Master Rychtyr!"

"Aye, aye, Sir," Trynt Rychtyr acknowledged, and the colorful bunting which had been bent on to the signal halyards a quarter of an hour earlier soared to the yardarm. A flick of the signalman's wrist broke the signal and the flags streamed on the wind.

▼   ▼   ▼

"Signal from the Flag, Sir!" Lieutenant Fraid Stedmyn said sharply. "With *our* number," he added rather pointedly, and glared up at the midshipman perched in HMS *Lightning*'s mizzen top.

"Indeed?" Doniphan Cumyngs, *Lightning*'s first lieutenant, raised an eyebrow and joined the flag lieutenant in glaring up at the mizzen top. "Odd that no one else noticed it," he continued, loudly enough to ensure the midshipman would find it difficult to pretend he hadn't heard.

That luckless youth snatched up his spyglass and peered through it at the distant flags, and Tymythy Darys felt his lips twitch with an utterly inappropriate temptation to smile. There really wasn't anything particularly amusing about it, the admiral supposed, but at the same time, there was. Stedmyn had been a signals specialist himself before Darys tapped him as his flag lieutenant. He was an efficient, hard-working young man, and almost as smart as he thought he was—no one could have been *quite* as smart as Fraid Stedmyn thought he was—who found it extraordinarily difficult to delegate anything.

Not that this particular duty was his to delegate in the first place, since *Lightning*'s signals department was Captain Sympsyn's and Lieutenant Cumyngs' responsibility, not the flag lieutenant's.

Which wouldn't save Midshipman Braiahn's youthful arse when Cumyngs had the opportunity to 'discuss' it with him. First lieutenants didn't take kindly to midshipmen who embarrassed them in front of flag officers. Especially not in front of flag officers they would probably be facing across the breakfast table sometime quite soon now. The fact that Cumyngs and Stedmyn thoroughly detested one another was only icing on the cake.

"The Division's number, Sir," Braiahn called down. Clearly he would have preferred not to offer that particular bit of information, given Stedmyn's rather pointed comment. Unfortunately, the ICN's standard signals procedures left him no choice. "Number 80 and Number 59!"

His assistant at the foot of the mast flipped pages swiftly in the signal book, very careful not to look at anything—or anyone—else in the process. Then he cleared his throat and looked up from the book.

"'Execute previous orders,' Sir, and 'Southwest-by-South.'"

"Thank you, Master Sellyrs," Cumyngs said frostily, and turned to Captain Sympsyn, who'd been observing the operation of his ship's communications department with an interested expression. "Execute previous orders, course southwest-by-south, Sir."

"Thank you, Master Cumyngs."

Despite an admirably grave tone, there might have been a slight twinkle in Sympsyn's eye as he repeated Cumyngs acknowledgment to young Sellyrs. If there was, it disappeared instantly as he looked at Darys.

"I heard," the admiral said, and showed his teeth. "Looks like the Baron was right. Very well, Captain Sympsyn. Let's be about it!"

▼　　▼　　▼

"Sir—!"

"I see it, Lewk," Raisahndo said, and slammed a fist down on the quarterdeck rail, swearing with silent eloquence as the Charisian formation changed at last. The last eight galleons in Sarmouth's line were altering course sharply, yards swinging with mechanical precision as they came all the way from west-northwest to southwest-by-south, and his teeth grated together as he recalled his earlier thought about dance steps.

He raised his spyglass, peering through it, and his face tightened as he got his first real good look at the division which had formed the rear of the Charisian line. Apparently the two ships leading Sarmouth's line weren't the only ironclads in his squadron after all. Either that, or they'd been bombardment ships, instead. Which was certainly possible, especially if Sarmouth had intended this all along. Whatever *they* might have been, however, the pair of ships leading the abbreviated line which had just turned southwest also showed only a single line of gunports, and he was closer to these. His spyglass showed him the streaks of rust where wind and weather had scoured away their black paint.

And beyond *them*. . . .

"Signal to Admiral Hahlynd," he said, never lowering the glass.

"Yes, Sir?"

" 'Engage the enemy to windward.' "

▼   ▼   ▼

"All right, Ahlfryd," Pawal Hahlynd said grimly. "It looks like we get to try it a second time."

"One way to put it, Sir," Captain Ahlfryd Mahgyrs said as the screw-galley *Sword* turned towards the enemy.

The deck quivered as her cranksmen bent to the pair of long, belowdecks crankshafts spinning her propellers. Speed was as important as maneuverability today, and she heeled to the press of her canvas, as well. Spray burst back from her cutwater, glittering like diamonds in the sunlight before it pattered across the decks, drenching every exposed surface, and both of them knew they were driving her too hard for safety. The screw-galleys were surprisingly good seaboats, but the weight of their guns and armor was really too much for their frames. They were fragile vessels, and more than one member of the ship's company had to be remembering the day they'd watched one of her sisters simply break up and disappear in less than twenty minutes in seas no heavier than today's.

"I didn't much enjoy it the first time, really," Hahlynd's flag captain continued, much too quietly for anyone else to hear him over the noise of wind, water, and shouted orders. "And, frankly, this time around the odds suck, Sir."

"Always such a way with words," Hahlynd replied with an off-center smile. Then he shrugged. "Wish I could disagree. But look at it this way— assuming we get past these people, we've still got the entire Gulf to cross before we get to Gorath. Given normal weather for this time of year, that's got to be at least as much a challenge as this, don't you think?"

"That's a strange way to encourage someone, Sir."

"Best I can come up with, I'm afraid," Hahlynd replied, and raised his spyglass, studying the Charisian galleons as his screw-galleys charged to meet them in a buffeting rush of ice-edged wind and pitching explosions of spray.

▼   ▼   ▼

"Now those have to be some unhappy people, Sir," Captain Sympsyn said, and looked up at the set of his ironclad galleon's canvas, studying it as if considering some way it might be tweaked.

"I'm sure they are," Tymythy Darys replied.

The admiral wasn't looking at his flag captain at the moment; he was still peering through the raised angle-glass bracketed to the inner face of HMS *Lightning*'s seven-foot armored bulwark. He had to angle it almost parallel with the ship's keel, because the screw-galleys were taking advantage of their weatherly rig and screws to come at his flagship head-on. Now he straightened and rubbed his chin thoughtfully.

"I'm sure they are," he repeated, "but I don't think that's going to slow them up very much. And it's pretty clear what Raisahndo's up to."

Sympsyn nodded, his own expression less than delighted. With their screws to supplement their sails, the screw-galleys were faster than the Dohlaran galleons, despite their smaller size. The seas were approaching ten or eleven feet, and the galleons' bigger, deeper—not to mention more strongly built—hulls ought to have allowed them to make considerably more speed than the small, frail screw-galleys. Their commander was driving them dangerously hard, however, despite the sea conditions. He was clearly prepared to run some serious risks in the execution of his portion of the Dohlaran battle plan.

And they obviously *had* a plan.

"They're trying to get across our line of advance," the admiral continued, speaking to himself as much as to his flagship's commander. "The question in my mind is whether they plan to stay clear until they can take up firing positions on our disengaged side after their galleons get to grips with us, or if they're going to try to get in close and hit our rigging, slow us down *before* we get to grips."

"Might be a little of both, Sir," Sympsyn offered. "If I was them, I'd see about putting some shot through our masts and spars while I waited for the galleons to catch up." He shrugged. "Might not achieve anything, but you never know till you try. And if what happened in the Kaudzhu Narrows is any guide, they'll probably try to swarm in once the action's general and go for our rudder."

Darys nodded, still rubbing his chin. The rescued handful of survivors from Kahrltyn Haigyl's crew all agreed that the screw-galleys had gotten in close on *Dreadnought*—close enough to be out of the play of her guns—and then hung off her quarters, pounding steadily away at her rudder, and that persistent pounding had ultimately paid off. He didn't doubt they'd try to repeat the performance here . . . if they could. But there was a world of difference between a single, unsupported galleon—no matter how well armored she might be—and what the Dohlarans faced this afternoon.

In fact, there was an even bigger difference than they might yet realize.

"I think that's exactly what they'll try to do," he agreed. "Although," he added judiciously, "I also doubt they'd mind a bit if we decided to avoid the threat by breaking off and letting their galleons by us."

"They'd probably drop dead of heart failure, Sir," Sympsyn said dryly. "I suppose that'd be *one* way to take them out without firing a single shot."

Darys chuckled, but his flag captain had a point. A very good one, in fact. Whatever else might be true, the Royal Dohlaran Navy and the Imperial Charisian Navy had come to hold one another's tenacity in lively respect.

Not a whole lot of quit in either of us, I guess, he thought. *And of course, in our case, there's the minor matter of what Dunkyn would have to say to me.* He snorted. *Come to think of it, I'd rather face the round shot!*

▼   ▼   ▼

So much for the best possible outcome, Pawal Hahlynd thought with a certain bitter amusement.

In the months since the Kaudzhu Narrows, some of Risahndo's officers had expected—or claimed to expect—the Charisians to refuse to expose unarmored galleons to his screw-galleys now that they'd demonstrated how dangerous they were. They'd argued the Charisians' regular galleons would back off, opt to hold the range open, whatever their ironclads might do. The more optimistic had even suggested the screw-galleys' threat might be enough to strip the unarmored ships away entirely, leave the ironclads to take on the entire squadron by themselves. Hahlynd, on the other hand, hadn't believed that for a moment—that wasn't the way Charisian seamen were built—but he'd been willing to concede at least the possibility that they'd be . . . more tentative after the Narrows.

Until now, of course.

The Charisians had turned, all right, but only to open their broadsides. The range was little more than twenty-four hundred yards now, but his screw-galleys would do well to mark a target at much over six hundred under these conditions of wind and sea. The Charisians were far larger, heavier ships—twice the length of his own, with a beam to match—which made them much steadier gun platforms. Coupled with their rifled guns, that equated to a major advantage in effective range, and he watched the lead ship's outline shifting, lengthening from a narrow, bows-on silhouette to show its full long, lean length . . . and gunports. Her next astern followed her around, showing an identical profile, and his jaw tightened as the *third* Charisian turned. She had none of the telltale rust streaks visible on the two leaders, marking the spots where wind and the weather had worn away their armor's protective paint, but—

"Signal to Admiral Raisahndo," he said.

"Yes, Sir?"

"'Confirm two leading galleons are ironclads,'" Hahlynd dictated. "'Estimate at least two three-decked ships in company.'" He heard someone suck in sharply at that, but he never lowered his glass or looked away from the Charisian ships.

"Add one more signal," he added.

"Yes, Sir?"

" 'Engaging.' "

▼　▼　▼

"So they are going to try to use the screw-galleys as their battering ram, My Lord," Captain Lathyk said.

He and Sarmouth stood side-by-side in *Destiny*'s mizzen rigging, each with an arm looped through the shrouds for safety's sake while they peered through their double-glasses.

"I think at least part of this is Hahlynd exercising his discretion," the baron said now. "Raisahndo's still trying to run; he's too smart to do anything else. I'm sure he'd be delighted if he managed to inflict damage on us, but Hahlynd's primary mission was to kick the door open for their galleons and then hold it open as long as he could. Engaging Tymythy and tying him up, forcing him to maneuver against the screw-galleys rather than letting them get in close the way they did against *Dreadnought*, would be one way to do that. For that matter, it's even possible they thought they could bluff him into breaking off and letting them through rather than risk a repeat of the Narrows."

"Never going to happen, My Lord," Lathyk said flatly.

"Of course it wasn't . . . and they knew it as well as we did." Sarmouth never lowered his double-glass. "Doesn't mean they didn't have to try. And if they'd pulled it off it would've been worth losing every one of his screw-galleys. I suspect they thought they had a better chance of that than they really did, too. Unless I miss my guess, Hahlynd's only just now realized what Tymythy has with him."

Lathyk made a wordless sound of agreement, and Sarmouth wondered exactly what was going through Pawal Hahlynd's brain at this moment.

The Dohlaran admiral understood the odds, the actual balance of combat power, as well as anyone on the Charisian side. And he also had to know this day was effectively the Royal Dohlaran Navy's death ride. He'd seen *Dreadnought* up close, seen her in action. After that experience, he could have had no illusions when the first *steam-powered* ironclad turned up in the Gulf of Dohlar. He was one of the Dohlaran admirals who'd made a point of using his brain from the very beginning and, like Raisahndo, he was one of Earl Thirsk's closest allies. For that matter, Greyghor Whytmyn, who was married to Thirsk's younger daughter, Hailyn, was Hahlynd's nephew by marriage. And, like his friend the earl, Hahlynd could have been under no illusions about why his nephew had been summoned to Zion. He knew—he *had* to know—the Group of Four was losing and that the Kingdom of Dohlar was about to pay a terrible price for its loyalty to the Temple. Yet there was no more give, no more surrender, in Pawal Hahlynd than there was in Lywys

Gardynyr. He would do his duty, however grim, to the very end, without flinching.

Damn, I wish *we didn't have to kill men like that just to get to scum like Clyntahn,* the baron thought bitterly. *Not enough for that fat son-of-a-bitch to murder God only knows how many millions of innocent 'heretics,' himself. Oh, no! He's got to put us in the position of killing good, honorable men if we want to stop him.*

And now it's time for me to go kill a few thousand more of them.

He lowered his double-glass but his gaze stayed on the suddenly tiny sails of the screw-galleys, driving unwaveringly to meet Admiral Darys' division.

"I believe it's time for the rest of us to join the party, Rhobair," he said.

"Yes, My Lord. I'll have the signal made."

▼　▼　▼

"They're coming down on us, Sir," Captain Trahvys said harshly, and Caitahno Raisahndo nodded.

"It's what Sarmouth had in mind from the beginning," he replied. "He's taking a hell of a chance, but unlike us, he's got an entire navy left even if he loses his whole squadron. And if it works. . . ."

He stood on *Hurricane's* quarterdeck, watching the incredible panorama as the two enormous fleets flowed towards one another. Sarmouth had broken the rest of his line at last, turning each division in it simultaneously. Now four short, compact columns forged down upon Raisahndo, ready to turn back to form a single line of battle to windward *or* leeward, whichever seemed best when they overhauled him, and he knew exactly what the Charisian admiral had in mind.

He sucked me as far up to windward as he could, and he was willing to risk losing the wind gauge to do it. Not that there was ever much chance of that, really, I suppose. But that's why he was in that long, single line from the beginning—specifically so he could detach his last division and swing it directly across our only escape route. He couldn't have known he'd get the opportunity, but he had it ready from the start in case he did. Why else put such heavy firepower at the rear of his line? If Pawal's right—if those frigging ironclads really do have three-deckers in company—this is his Wednesday punch. He's throwing a haymaker straight into our teeth, risking what we might accomplish against it in isolation before he catches up with us, because we don't have any choice but to fight our way past it. And that slows us. Just maneuvering against it would do that . . . and anyone who takes damage aloft in the process is dead meat, no matter what else happens, unless I'm willing to abandon the cripples. And he's faster, anyway. If that division in front of us can slow us down for an hour— Shan-wei, half an hour!—he'll be right in among the rear of the Squadron. And when that *happens—*

"General signal, Lewk." His voice was hammered iron. "'Make more sail. Engage the enemy more closely.'"

▼   ▼   ▼

"It looks like being a little different today, Sir," Lieutenant Commander Kylmahn said quietly. "I don't think those damned screw-galleys are going to enjoy this one bit."

"No, they aren't," Sir Bruhstair Ahbaht agreed, never looking away from the Dohlaran squadron.

There was an ugly edge in his chief of staff's voice, he thought. An edge of vengeful anticipation. He couldn't really blame Kylmahn for that—not after the Khadzhu Narrows. Yet he was a bit surprised to discover that he didn't share that sense of anticipation. Or perhaps he did. But if so, he was more aware of what the men aboard those screw-galleys must be thinking as they charged headlong into such a massive weight of guns.

No cowards over there, he thought. *No butchers, either . . . not really. Only men. Men with families, with wives and daughters and sons too many of them will never see again. And men who are no more going to turn away from their duty than my men did at the Narrows.*

He lowered his double-glass and looked up at the set of *Floodtide*'s canvas. The ironclad led Baron Sarmouth's Second Division—*Floodtide* and the sixty-eights *Dynzayl Tryvythyn, Turbulent, Vindicator, Sand Point,* and *Bruxtyn*—steadily southwest. If it worked the way Sarmouth had hoped it might, that powerful division would come crashing in about the time Raisahndo's lead galleons became closely engaged with Admiral Darys' even more powerful squadron. And while that was happening, Sarmouth would lead his own division completely across the Dohlarans' rear and come ranging up from leeward.

It might not work, he thought. But for it to fail, Raisahndo had to somehow break past Darys without being drawn into a melee. . . .

And that's not going to happen, Sir Bruhstair Ahbaht thought with grim, curiously regretful satisfaction. *Not going to happen in a million years.*

▼   ▼   ▼

"Fire!"

The long line of massive cannon hurled themselves inboard in a crashing bellow of thunder, and HMS *Lightning*'s tall, black side disappeared behind a wall of flame and smoke. Astern of her, her next in line, *Seamount,* followed suit, and thirty-two heavy shells went wailing across the waves.

▼   ▼   ▼

"Make a note in the log," Captain Trahvys told *Hurricane*'s duty quartermaster. He pulled his watch from his pocket, opened the case, then snapped it shut once more.

"The enemy opened fire at seventeen minutes past sixteen o'clock," he said.

▾   ▾   ▾

Pawal Hahlynd saw the leading Charisian galleons vanish into the huge, volcanic gush of dark-brown smoke. None of the other ships in front of his screw-galleys had fired. No doubt they were well supplied with shells, but he'd gotten a good look at all them now, and any one of them was at least as powerful as any galleon in the Royal Dohlaran Navy. Aside from the ironclads, not a one of them could mount fewer than sixty guns, and at least two of them were units of a class no Dohlaran officer had ever seen. He knew what they had to be—the Inquisition's agents had learned at least some details of the *Zhenyfyr Ahrmahk*-class—but most of the *Zhenyfyr Ahrmahks* had been earmarked for conversion into ironclads, cut down to a single gundeck because they'd offered the only hulls big and strong enough to carry the massive weight of the *Rottweilers*' armor.

These hadn't been, and each of them showed three complete gundecks, counting the carronades on their spar decks. Ninety-eight guns, that was how many a *Zhenyfyr Ahrmahk* carried. The thought of facing that holocaust was enough to turn any man's stomach into frozen lead. Intellectually, Hahlynd knew the ironclads were even more dangerous, but those tall-sided galleons, sides throwing back the spray like black-painted cliffs while better than forty guns grinned hungrily from their open ports, screamed "*Danger!*" even more shrilly than the low-slung, evil-looking ironclads.

Yet whatever instinct might say, the three-deckers obviously mounted the standard 30-pounder smoothbores of the ICN, not the rifled 6-inchers of a *Rottweiler*, and the range was still at least a mile. No, they'd reserve their fire until someone was unfortunate enough to come deeper into their reach. Once someone *did* enter their range, though, that many shells would reduce any target to broken, flaming wreckage in mere minutes.

The only Doharan ships with any chance at all of surviving that kind of fire were Hahlynd's screw-galleys. If they waited for the conventional galleys to close enough to support them, they'd only be bringing their consorts into a vortex of destruction they could never survive. The likelihood that even the screw-galleys might was probably little better, but at least their armor would give them *some* chance.

And that was precisely why he *couldn't* wait, whatever his original instructions might have been.

The ironclads to break our teeth . . . and the three-deckers to break our bones. That's what Sarmouth means for them to do, and unless I can get in close enough fast enough—

That massive double broadside crashed into the sea, throwing up thirty-foot pillars of water whiter than snow. They rose like a forest of titan oaks, tall and terrible, all around the screw-galleys *Arrow* and *Javelin*. The small ships clove the icy waterfalls, cranksmen bending desperately to their duty even as their ships leaned to the dangerous press of their canvas. Every man aboard those screw-galleys knew it was insanely risky to drive them so hard through such seas, that their hulls hovered on the brink of failure even before the enemy inflicted a single hit, yet they never hesitated. They sliced through the waves at almost twelve knots, clawing their way across the envelope of their enemies' longer range, lying so far over to the press of the wind their lee rails were awash in a smother of white. Yet even at their speed, they'd need six minutes to bring the ironclads into their own reach, and in that time the superbly trained gunners of the Imperial Charisian Navy could fire as many as ten more broadsides.

▼　　▼　　▼

"Gutsy bastards," Zosh Hahlbyrstaht said quietly.

Fleet Wing's position, well to the northwest of the Dohlaran main body, put her safely beyond Caitahno Raisahndo's reach. It also meant she was too far away to see a damned thing from deck level. Which was why Hahlbyrstaht and Hektor had climbed to the schooner's maintop.

The first lieutenant wasn't very happy whenever his CO went up the mast, although he knew better than to say anything of the sort. And the truth was that, even with only one working arm, the Duke of Darcos was nimble as a monkey lizard. He'd been scooting up and down warships' rigging since he was ten years old, he'd always been blessed with an excellent head for heights, and that single arm of his had grown amazingly muscular since he'd lost the use of the other.

Hahlbyrstaht knew all of that. But he also knew the old sailor's aphorism: "One hand for the ship, and one hand for yourself." In his opinion, it would be just a little difficult for someone with one hand—period—to put that into practice if the ship pitched suddenly.

From their lofty perch, however, their double-glasses let them see only too clearly, and Hektor's expression was bleak as they watched the screw-galleys' charge.

"Nobody ever said they weren't gutsy," he said as fresh torrents of brown smoke burst from the ironclads' sides. It rolled across the ships, driven by the wind, spreading away to leeward. "All the guts in the world aren't going to get them out of this one, though." He shrugged. "In their place, I probably would've pulled the screw-galleys back, slowed them down and gone in with the galleons for support. I can see arguments for doing it this way, though, and Raisahndo obviously intended for them to maneuver independently of the galleons all along. In a lot of ways, this only speeds that up, and if he can get them far enough into Admiral Darys' face before the rest of his squadron gets there, the distraction quotient might be enough to—"

He broke off, his bleak expression turning to stone as HMS *Javelin* ran headlong into a pair of 6-inch shells. All of Sir Dunkyn Yairley's ironclads and bombardment ships had been issued the "armor piercing" ammunition Admiral Seamount and the Duke of Delthak had developed for their rifled guns. It was intended more for drilling deep into stone fortifications than for killing warships, but it worked just fine against those, too.

Both shells punched cleanly through *Javelin*'s armor and exploded deep inside her hull. She was unreasonably fortunate in at least one sense, because her magazine didn't explode right along with them. But the sudden, savage explosions were too much for a hull already driven to and beyond its limits.

Her back broke, and the combination of her whirling screws and the massive wind pressure on her sails drove her bodily under.

There were no survivors. Even if anyone had made it into the icy water, hypothermia would have killed them long before anyone could rescue them.

Forty seconds later, *Arrow* staggered sideways, rolling madly, as a shell hit her, as well. It missed her armor completely, and it didn't even explode. But it *did* strike her mainmast ten feet above her deck, and eight feet of the heavy spar disintegrated in shrieking splinters. The mast collapsed instantly under the weight of its rigging and the fierce strength of the wind.

The screw-galley almost capsized, and the wrecked mast toppled overside, still fastened to her by the shrouds, pounding her hull like a captive battering ram. Axes and cutlasses flashed as her crew hacked frantically at the rigging, fighting to free their ship from its lethal embrace, and HMS *Flail* and *Catapult* swerved to avoid her as they continued their own headlong charge.

▼　　▼　　▼

"The rest of their galleons are setting their royals, Sir!" Captain Sympsyn shouted in Admiral Darys' ear.

The admiral turned to look at him, and Sympsyn pointed up to the lookout in the maintop through the smoke swirling across *Lightning*'s deck.

"All of them?"

"Yes, Sir," Sympsyn confirmed, and Darys inhaled a deep, smoky lungful.

I sure hope Dunkyn was right about how close on these bastards' heels he'll be, he thought. *If he's very far behind them, this could get . . . dicey.*

"Trying to pile in on us, make it a general melee. They want to break our line and swarm in close enough to board," he said grimly, and Sympsyn nodded.

"Current range?" The admiral tapped the angle-glass at his side and smiled without humor. "I can see damn-all through the smoke from deck level."

"Their van's about two miles behind the screw-galleys," Sympsyn said. "According to my man up there—" he pointed at the maintop again "—and he's a good, experienced man—that interval's increasing because of how fast the screw-galleys are going, and their main body's as much as a mile behind that." The flag captain shrugged. "Sounds like Raisahndo's trying to close with us as fast as he can, but they've still got a long way to go."

Darys frowned, brain whirring like one of Rhaiyan Mychail's spinning jennies while he considered distances and wind speeds. If Raisahndo was setting his royals in this freshening wind, he was clearly willing to court damage aloft, even knowing any ship with crippled rigging would become easy prey. That could turn around and bite him, and even with the royals set, he'd be considerably slower than the screw-galleys.

Call it ten knots in these conditions with the wind where it is, he decided, *and three miles from us to their van. Twenty minutes before they can reach us, and six minutes or so more for their main body. So that means. . . .*

"We'll finish dealing with the screw-galleys," he told his flag captain. "Tell the gunners they've got fifteen minutes. Then we turn downwind."

"Yes, Sir."

▼   ▼   ▼

Pawal Hahlynd's face was an iron mask as HMS *Halberd* staggered. For a second or two, it seemed she'd shake off the blow. Then the Charisian shell detonated and she heaved madly. Her mast snapped, thundering down across her deck, crushing and maiming her people, but that wasn't all that had happened. She began losing way almost instantly, far more quickly than a screw-galley should have, and Hahlynd's jaw clamped.

Took out the cranks, he thought, trying not to picture the carnage in the cramped space below decks where the cranksmen stood literally shoulder to shoulder, laboring to drive their vessel through the water. An explosion in that confined space must have ripped the crewmen to pieces and painted the planking with their blood.

Well, they'd already had plenty of company. *Arrow* was still afloat, although it looked as if she was slowly foundering. That wreckage must have beaten in her planking like a hammer on wickerwork before her people managed to cut it away. *Flail* was also afloat . . . barely, and not for very much longer; there was no question that *she* was going down. *Arbalest* had blown up in a spectacular ball of fire, and *Saber*'s armored citadel had been gutted by a pair of 6-inch shells that had slammed through her bow armor and exploded almost simultaneously. *Cutlass* had been driven out of action while she fought a losing battle against the flames consuming her, and if *Dirk*'s citadel remained intact, her starboard broadside had been hideously maimed by the explosion which had ripped her flank like some slash lizard's furious talon. He could see the blood flowing from her scuppers as proof of the casualties she'd taken, and though she continued to fight her way through the waves with heartbreaking courage, her combat value had to be . . . dubious.

With *Halberd*, that was seven of his twelve screw-galleys gone, and he'd been wrong about how long the three-deckers would hold their fire. They weren't using their lower deck guns, but like Raisahndo's *Hurricane*, they had heavy rifles in pivot mountings on their *upper* decks. But whereas *Hurricane* showed a pair of 8-inch Fultyn Rifles, each of the Charisians was big enough to mount three, and they were longer and slimmer than the Dohlaran guns—long enough their muzzles projected far beyond their bulwarks when they were trained out on the broadside.

They also fired far, far faster than his own 150-pounders. In fact, they fired at least twice as rapidly as their own ironclads' broadside guns. Breechloaders—they had to be, like the ones in their accursed armored steamers—and they were fiendishly accurate. Thank God there were only six of them!

Smoke erupted from *Mace*'s bows, and bared his teeth as all three forward guns fired as one. Her captain had obviously decided to disregard the safety restriction that prohibited firing all of those massive guns simultaneously. That restriction had even more point than usual in the current sea conditions, but Captain Clymyns clearly calculated that there was no tomorrow for his ship, whatever happened. The ironclad had denied him the quartering approach he'd wanted, maneuvering with the impeccable skill of the Imperial Charisian Navy to force him to approach through the very heart of her broadside firing arc, instead. Yet even though they'd held him under fire the whole way, he'd done it, Now he was end-on to her, barely ninety yards clear, presenting only his bow armor to her guns while he blazed away. His gunners were good . . . and just as determined as their captain. Not a shot missed. Hahlynd could actually *see* the massive round shot strike her target's armor . . . and rebound. The trio of 10-inch projectiles shrieked away, baffled. One of them shattered into at least five pieces.

And then four of the ironclad's guns fired back.

Mace disintegrated in a bubble of fire and smoke. Pieces of debris arced across the sky, trailing lines of smoke, rising as much as three hundred feet before they spiraled back down into the icy water in feathers white, and Hahlynd heard Ahlfryd Mahgyrs swearing viciously beside him.

"Clymyns deserved better," he heard his own voice saying, and wondered why. It wasn't like anything he could possibly say at this point was going to matter, but he went right on speaking. "I think we'll be in range in about two more m—"

The 6-inch shell from HMS *Zhenyfyr Ahrmahk*'s forward pivot gun punched through HMS *Sword*'s frontal armor like an awl through butter. It detonated, the ready charges for her 10-inch smoothbores erupted in sympathetic detonation, and the forward forty feet of Pawal Hahlynd's flagship shattered in a cloud of smoke, debris, and spray.

▼ ▼ ▼

"They're changing course, Sir," Captain Trahvys said heavily. Caitahno Raisahndo only looked at him, and the flag captain shrugged. "They're coming onto the wind, Sir. Not making any more sail, but—"

He shrugged, and Raisahndo nodded.

Of course the ironclads were coming onto the wind. They'd delayed long enough to deal with Hahlynd's screw-galleys—only two of them were left, and he didn't blame their skippers for spending more effort trying to evade the ironclads' fire than trying to close. It was clear they weren't going to *damage* the damned things, whatever they did. About the best they could hope to do now was to delay the bastards, convince the Charisians to spend a little more time on their own destruction in hopes their more conventional consorts could get to grips with the blocking force.

But that wasn't going to happen. The ironclads and their division mates were turning to run in front of the rest of his squadron, timing the move with consummate professionalism. They weren't even making any more sail, because they didn't want to stay away from him forever. They only wanted to stay clear until the rest of Sarmouth's squadron, coming up steadily behind Raisahndo's formation, arrived to close the trap.

And there wasn't one damned thing *he* could do about it.

The columns coming up astern were overtaking him rapidly, even with his royals set, and they were close enough his lookouts had been able to confirm that neither of the ships leading the original Charisian line had been ironclads after all. The Dohlaran admiral's mouth twisted bitterly. *Just like the sneaky bastards to convince me bombardment ships were ironclads in order to drive me into the real ironclads—not to mention those damned three-deckers. Not that it's going to matter very much.*

And, of course, there was the fact that the ship leading the closest Charisian division *was* another ironclad.

They're going to shove that division into our backs like a dagger while their friends in front of us hold us for the kill. And their third *division's coming up fast on our lee quarter. We're like a kraken in a net, waiting for the axe.*

"General signal to reduce sail," he told Trahvys. The flag captain looked at him, and he shrugged. "We've lost the race, Lewk, and we're driving so hard our line's started to scatter. Time to reduce to fighting sail and get ourselves reorganized. No point taking any more damage aloft than we have to, and the bastards will have to come into our range if they want us."

"Yes, Sir." Trahvys' voice was level, almost as if he didn't realize what Raisahndo's decision truly meant.

"And while we're doing that, bring the Squadron to north-northwest," Raisahndo continued, and smiled thinly. "Let's see how long it takes those frigging ironclads to catch up with *us* for a change."

"Yes, Sir." Trahvys saluted, then raised one hand, beckoning for a signal-man, and Raisahndo turned to Commander Kahmelka.

"Go below," he said quietly. "Take Ahrnahld with you, and make sure all our confidential papers and codes go overside with a grapeshot or two to keep them company."

"Yes, Sir." Kahmelka's eyes were unflinching. "They won't find anything useful, Sir. I guarantee it."

"I know, Gahryth. I know." Raisahndo patted the commander's shoulder. "And while you're at it, ask Father Symyn to join me on the quarterdeck." He smiled bleakly. "I think we need someone to put in a good word for us."

.VI.
Royal Palace,
City of Gorath,
Kingdom of Dohlar.

Well, this is a frigging disaster!" Aibram Zaivyair snarled, waving the dispatch, then hurled it down on the council table so hard the staple ripped out and the pages scattered. "Do you want to explain how *this* one happened, *My Lord?*"

Lywys Gardynyr sat in his own chair, across the table from the man who was his superior . . . nominally, at least. Aibram Zaivyair was the Duke of Thorast, effectively the Kingdom of Dohlar's Navy Minister, and the senior officer of the Royal Dohlaran Navy. Of course, he hadn't been to sea in almost thirty years, and even when he had, he'd been a "navy" officer in a navy which still thought assigning *army* officers to command ships and fleets made sense.

And he hasn't learned one Shan-wei-damned thing about the difference between armies and navies since, the Earl of Thirsk thought coldly. *No reason he should, really. He's got the birth and the political allies to* pretend *he knows his arse from his elbow where ships are concerned. And the son-of-a-bitch's been in Clyntahn's hip pocket from the minute this whole rolling disaster started.*

"Well?" Thorast snapped. He'd been even more belligerently antagonistic since Thirsk had returned to limited duty. Probably, the earl thought, because the "death" of his family—and its circumstances—suggested to him that the patronage which had supported and protected Thirsk was about to disappear. Assuming it hadn't already completely vanished, that was.

"I asked you a question, Earl Thirsk!" he barked now, and Thirsk cocked his head slightly, as if considering some minor source of annoyance. There was no point pretending anything he did could *placate* the duke, after all.

"I realize that, My Lord." Thorast's face turned darker, his expression thunderous, at Thirsk's cool reply. "I assumed it was a rhetorical question, since the reports we've received from the Harchongians make it abundantly clear how it happened. The heretics sailed into Rhaigair Bay aboard the same ironclads that blew Geyra apart and did exactly the same thing to us. Exactly the way Admiral Raisahndo and I had been warning they were almost certain to do, sooner or later, if we left the Western Squadron exposed in such proximity to Claw Island. Given that they sailed straight through the fire of a couple of hundred heavy guns—a lot of them the new Fultyn Rifles—and completely demolished Rhaigair's waterfront, the dockyard, and every defensive battery without losing a single ship, I would've thought you'd understand what happened."

"Listen, you goddamned—!"

"That's enough, Aibram!"

The three words weren't all that loud, but they cracked like a whip, and Thorast reared back in his chair, staring at the man who'd spoken. Samyl Cahkrayn, the Duke of Fern and Dohlar's first councilor, glared right back.

"Our situation's too grave for me to indulge you," Fern said. "Everyone in Dohlar knows how much you hate Earl Thirsk. But this isn't about him, and it isn't about you. It's about what just happened to our Navy and what's going to happen next to the entire damned Kingdom! If you can't get that through your head and contribute something *constructive* to this discussion, I suggest you go find something else to do while the rest of us get on with it."

Thorast's eyes went wide. Then they narrowed, blazing with fury, and he leaned aggressively forward once more. His index finger stabbed the tabletop, and he opened his mouth, but another voice intervened before he could speak.

"His Grace may not have phrased himself as . . . diplomatically as he might have, Duke Thorast," it said. "He does have a point, however. At this moment, trying to fix fault for something that happened three thousand miles from here isn't going to help decide what to do about it."

The navy minister shut his mouth, and his face turned into stone.

"I . . . beg your pardon, Your Eminence," he said after a long, tense moment. "In my opinion, understanding the towering degree of incompetence—if not outright treason—which allowed this to happen is essential if we're going to prevent it from happening again. That's the only reason I've . . . pressed the point as warmly as I have."

"No doubt."

An unbiased observer might have been forgiven for concluding from Bishop Executor Wylsynn Lainyr dry tone that he was less than convinced by Thorast's last sentence. The duke's eyes flickered, but he forbore any direct response, and Lainyr reached out to rest one hand on his own copy of the report. His ruby ring of office gleamed in the lamplight, and he turned his gaze to Thirsk.

"I'm sure we all understand why Duke Thorast, as the councilor responsible to His Majesty for the Navy, should be concerned about . . . procedural matters, My Lord. And no doubt a formal board of inquiry needs to be assembled, in the fullness of time, to consider all of the decisions and policies which led to the current situation. At the moment, however, I'm rather more concerned with what we do about it. May I ask for your thoughts on that?"

Thirsk gazed back at the tallish, black-haired Langhornite who was Mother Church's effective day-to-day administrator for the entire Kingdom of Dohlar. Archbishop Trumahn Rowzvel might actually occupy the see of Gorath Cathedral, but Lainyr was his executive officer and, like all bishops executor, he knew far more about the actual operations of his archbishopric than its archbishop did.

He was also a consummate professional, highly skilled in the management of the Church bureaucracy. Unfortunately, he was very much a part of the Church establishment, as well. He was far more concerned with keeping her up and running—with maintaining the Church's continuity and authority, and his own personal power as part of that—than with addressing her possible faults. And he'd been sent to Gorath as Bishop Executor Ahrain Mahrlow's successor, upon Mahrlow's death, because he could be relied upon as a loyal and obedient cog in Mother Church's machinery for fighting the Jihad.

Thirsk wasn't surprised Thorast was nonplussed by Lainyr's intervention in his favor. He and the bishop executor had been at loggerheads, to put it mildly, ever since Lainyr's arrival in Gorath. The prelate made little secret of his . . . impatience with Thirsk's unwillingness to hew to Mother Church's version of events when she twisted the truth—or even manufactured new truths out of whole cloth—to serve Zhaspahr Clyntahn's purposes. Yet despite that, he'd never seemed to actively hate Thirsk the way Father Ahbsahlahn Kharmych, Archbishop Trumahn's intendant, clearly did. Kharmych—a Schuelerite, like all intendants—made no secret of his distrust for Thirsk's zeal in Mother Church's service and he'd been furious at the very suggestion that prisoners captured by Thirsk's navy might not be transported to Zion to suffer the full rigor of the Punishment. Only Staiphan Maik's reports, with their stress on how badly the RDN needed his expertise and leadership, had delayed the Grand Inquisitor's decision to move against him and his family as long as it had, and Thirsk knew Kharmych's reports to his superiors in the Inquisition had only fed Zhaspahr Clyntahn's distrust and venomous hatred for him.

Which made Kharmych's absence from this meeting even more interesting. Thirsk had wondered about that, when he arrived and realized the intendant wasn't attending, but he hadn't been prepared for Lainyr to take his part against Thorast, one of the Jihad's strongest Dohlaran supporters.

He must be even more scared than I thought, the earl thought dryly. *It sounds as if he wants actual advice, not just more sycophancy. That's novel.*

"Your Eminence, what we do—what we *can* do—really depends on our ability to understand what happened. We can't devise an effective defense against a threat we don't understand. That's something which has been demonstrated with unfortunate frequency over the course of the Jihad."

Thorast's expression could have curdled fresh milk, but Lainyr nodded.

"And do you think you *do* understand what's happened, my son?"

Of course I do, you idiot, Thirsk told him silently from behind a gravely thoughtful expression. *Exactly what I just* said *happened.*

The reports were still far from complete and conclusive, and he felt bitterly certain he was going to learn that far too many of the officers he'd groomed to command the navy he'd built were among the dead. At the moment, they had no casualty lists from the Western Squadron itself, only from the garrisons of Rhaigair and its protective batteries. But they did know not a single one of Caitahno Raisahndo's galleons had escaped the debacle he supposed would be known officially as the Battle of Shipworm Shoal. Three of Raisahndo's brigs had contrived to somehow elude their Charisian counterparts, and one of them—hotly pursued by a pair of Charisian schooners—had managed to reach Fairstock Bay and take cover under the city of Fairstock's batteries. The dispatch from HMS *Sea Dragon*'s traumatized captain was less than complete—or fully coherent, for that matter. Of course the man was only a lieutenant, scarcely one of Raisahndo's senior officers, and he'd been through a lot. For that matter, he'd performed a minor miracle in simply escaping the Charisians himself! It was understandable that his report might be less than perfect. It was, however, the closest thing to an account of the battle they were likely to get for quite some time, and they were damned lucky to have that much information.

And the fact that we got it demonstrates that at least their damned schooners can't just wade into our defenses and pound them into garbage, he thought bitterly.

That clearly wasn't the case for the armored steamers which had attacked

Rhaigair. According to Lord of Horse Golden Grass, the channel batteries had stood their ground unflinchingly and given the Charisian ironclads the hardest fight they'd had yet. Golden Grass was a Harchongian, of course, and the reports of Harchongese authorities who'd gotten caught with their pants down were normally suspect, in Thirsk's experience. It was amazing how persistently they and their forces had fought with desperate gallantry, despite any temporary tactical withdrawals . . . even if the "temporary withdrawals" in question had looked suspiciously like mad, panicked flight.

But in this case, General Cahstnyr, the commander of the Dohlaran naval base's garrison and the Dohlaran-manned batteries defending the anchorage itself, fully supported Golden Grass' assessment. It was possible Cahstnyr was trying to cover his own arse, but he had a reputation as an officer in the Fahstyr Rychtyr mold. Perhaps even more to the point, Captain Kharmahdy, who Thirsk knew personally as a solid, reliable, and *trustworthy* man, concurred.

If all three of them were correct, the lead Charisian ironclad had resembled nothing so much as a foundry scrapyard when it arrived off the Rhaigair breakwater with its consorts. The heavy guns protecting the main ship channel had battered it almost beyond recognition. Its smokestack had been completely demolished, as had every other unarmored portion of its superstructure, and there'd been signs, according to Kharmahdy, that the after portion of its armored carapace had suffered significant fire damage.

Of course, Kharmahdy had also pointed out with scrupulous honesty that the apparent fire damage might be just that—apparent. Soot from the ironclad's truncated smokestack could have accounted for much or all of the blackening, and while Kharmahdy had personally seen evidence that the ship's pumps were working steadily, it was obvious it had never been in any danger of sinking. For that matter, despite its battered and broken outer appearance, it had participated in the bombardment of Rhaigair's outer batteries right along with its consorts.

"Your Eminence," the earl said, "it's going to take us a long time to fully understand what happened. Some points strike me as fairly evident, however."

He sat straighter, raising his right hand with its fingers folded. His left hand remained resting in his lap. He'd recovered more of his left arm's range of motion than he'd expected, but the residual pain in his shoulder discouraged its use.

"First," he said, raising his index finger to count off his points, "the Harchongese batteries tried hard but couldn't prevent the steam-powered ironclads from penetrating Rhaigair Bay effectively at will. From all reports—and I believe those reports are accurate, Your Eminence—" he paused ever so slightly, holding Lainyr's eyes until the bishop executive nodded in recognition of the "this time" Thirsk had carefully not said out loud "—the

Harchongians stood to their guns with enormous steadiness and courage. According to General Cahstnyr, the heretics had to close to within less than three hundred yards of Battery St. Thermyn to suppress its fire. We don't have anything like a complete casualty list—for our people, far less the Harchongians—but apparently Lord of Foot Bauzhyng fought until his last gun was dismounted. In fact, according to Major Kylpaitryc, our liaison officer in the battery, the Lord of Foot was personally laying and firing his final gun when a heretic shell exploded directly inside the gun's bay and killed him along with three-quarters of his gun crew.

"Second," he raised his second finger, "and the reason I made a point of how determinedly the Harchongians stood to their guns, those guns don't appear to have even come close to actually *stopping* the heretics. That's significant because Battery St. Thermyn, in particular, had been given high priority for the new artillery and had been completely reequipped with Fultyn Rifles with bores as great as ten inches, and the ironclads' close approach allowed them to attempt Lieutenant Zhwaigair's proposed 'wracking' attack on their armor. From the scanty information available to us, they inflicted far more damage than the Desnairians did at Geyra. Unfortunately, it wasn't enough. Clearly, even well-served guns firing ten-inch solid shot at three hundred yards range—or less—were unable to penetrate the heretics' armor."

"Forgive me, my son," Lainyr said, "but didn't Baron Golden Grass' message suggest the heretics' armor *had* been penetrated?"

"It did, Your Eminence," Thirsk acknowledged. "At least the lead ironclad's hull must have been holed below the water line—or possibly the 'wracking' attack succeeded in producing at least some leaks—because it appeared to be pumping a constant, low-volume stream from its bilges. Perhaps what I should have said is that even ten-inch solid shot at three hundred yards was unable to inflict crippling damage." He shrugged ever so slightly. "The distinction is probably real, but it really doesn't affect my analysis. And that analysis is that the heretics could penetrate equivalent defenses any time they care to."

He paused to let that sink in, then raised a third finger.

"Third, in the face of that level of threat, I fully endorse Admiral Raisahndo's decision to take the Western Squadron to sea and attempt to fight his way through to Gorath. I realize some may feel the Admiral should have stayed at Rhaigair and used his galleons to defend his anchorage. That, however, would have been a *serious* mistake."

Thorast shifted in his chair, his shoulders tight and his eyes hot, but Thirsk kept his own eyes focused on Lainyr's face, refusing to look in the duke's direction.

"Shellfire capable of silencing heavy guns protected by modern earthen berms would have made short work of any unarmored wooden vessel in the world. By the same token, armor capable of surviving the fire of heavy Fultyn Rifles at such short range would have been impenetrable by any gun we currently have afloat." He twitched another tiny shrug. "I don't like saying that, Your Eminence, but my likes or dislikes don't affect whether or not it's true. If Admiral Raisahndo had turned his ships into floating batteries in Rhaigair's defense, they would simply have been destroyed at anchor."

"And how, exactly, did taking them to sea produce a different outcome?" Shain Hauwyl, the Duke of Salthar, was ten years older than Thirsk and while he was less likely to be driven by prejudices and jealousy than Thorast, he was undeniably more comfortable with Thorast than with Thirsk. That was probably inevitable, since he and Thorast were kinsmen . . . and since Salthar was also a firm supporter of the Jihad.

"I didn't say it did, Your Grace," Thirsk replied. "What I said was that it was the proper decision, not that it produced the result we all obviously wish it had. He didn't succeed in breaking out of the trap, but it was the only option which offered even the possibility of getting our galleons—and their crews—home for further service in the Jihad. And I might also point out that according to *Sea Dragon*'s dispatch, Admiral Raisahndo and his people managed to inflict heavy damage on at least some of the heretic galleons which engaged them. In fact, had it not been for the ironclad galleons in the heretics' order of battle, they might well have succeeded in reaching Gorath after all. Whatever else anyone may think," the earl's voice hardened slightly but was clearly discernibly, "the Western Squadron fought— and *died*—hard, My Lords. No one broke, no one ran, and I could not be prouder of our officers and men."

This time, he did turn his head and meet Thorast's fiery gaze levelly, steadily . . . and very, very coldly.

"That's all well and good," Salthar said, and waved one hand in a half-apologetic gesture when Thirsk glared at him. "I'm not trying to downplay or denigrate the courage and determination they showed, My Lord. If it sounded that way, I apologize."

To his credit, Thirsk thought, he sounded as if he meant it. Which Thorast never would have.

"What I meant to get at," Salthar continued, glancing at Lainyr, "is that however hard they may have fought, they lost. And my understanding is that with the destruction of Admiral Raisahndo's ships, we no longer have a Navy."

"That's not entirely correct, Your Grace," Thirsk disagreed respectfully. Salthar looked at him incredulously, and the baron smiled a lopsided smile.

"We still have approximately forty galleons and at least thirty screw-galleys in commission. We're short on trained manpower for them, but we've got the ships, and we should commission the first of the new, heavier screw-galleys within the next four or five five-days. Unfortunately, if any of them—including the new screw-galleys, I'm afraid—run into one of these steam-powered ironclads of the heretics, they'll have no chance of survival. I know no one seated at this table wants to hear that, and believe me when I say that I absolutely hate having to *say* it, but it's the unvarnished truth."

"So you just want to give up and crawl under the table and hide?" Thorast more than half sneered.

"No, I don't." Thirsk's quiet, almost courteous tone was a distinct contrast to Thorast's fleeting contempt. "What I said is that our galleons and screw-galleys can't fight the heretics' ironclads—especially their *steam-powered* ironclads—and live."

"Forgive me, my son," Lainyr said, "but doesn't that imply that we can't fight them anywhere?"

"Your Eminence, I'm not going to pretend we're not looking at a disastrous situation." Thirsk shook his head, his expression unyielding. "In fact, you may not have realized just how disastrous it truly is.

"The good news is that these steamers appear to be relatively short-legged. In fact, I'm morally certain that that short range is the real reason the heretics have been prowling around Trove Island. I strongly suspect they want to base at least some of their steamers there, and if they do, they'll be within fifteen hundred sea miles of Gorath. That's probably still too long a reach for them, judging by what we've seen so far. It would, however, put them in a position to interdict the Mahthyw Passage, the Trosan Channel, and the Hilda Channel. In effect, to interdict all traffic from Dohlar proper to any point in the Gulf. Which, obviously, would include the Gulf of Tanshar, with all the implications for General Rychtyr's logistics and our ability to support the southern lobe of the Mighty Host."

"Are you saying the heretics can shut down all of our support for the Jihad?" Lainyr looked and sounded badly shaken, and Thirsk didn't blame him.

"Probably not completely, Your Eminence," the earl said almost compassionately. "First, the Mahthyw Passage is the next best thing to two hundred miles wide. For that matter, the Trosan Channel's over *three* hundred miles wide, and the heretics clearly don't have an unlimited supply of these things. However fast and powerfully armed they may be, each of them can still cover only a single circle of seawater no more than fifteen or twenty miles across. Their masts aren't tall enough for them to see much if any farther than that. In fact, I'd be surprised if they could see twenty miles even in perfect visibility. That limits their ability to spot targets. In addition, the smoke from their furnaces is likely to be visible to a sailing vessel long before a sailing vessel's top-hamper is visible to them. A ship doesn't have to be faster than they are to escape them if she can alter course and simply *avoid* them without ever being spotted." The earl shook his head. "No, Your Eminence. The real threat they'd present at Trove Island would be that they'd make it effectively impossible for us to retake the island or deprive their conventional light cruisers of their forward base."

"And what's to keep them from . . . leapfrogging from Trove to someplace closer to Gorath?" Lainyr asked. "Dragon or Lizard islands, for example?"

"Not a great deal at this time, Your Eminence," Thirsk replied unflinchingly, with a surprised sense of respect for the question. It would appear Lainyr *did* have an imagination . . . when he chose to turn it on. "I'm sorry, but I'd be derelict in my duty if I suggested anything else. The Navy's prepared to do everything we can to defend the islands, but the truth is that we'll be desperately hard-pressed just to defend the Kingdom's major ports."

"Then you think you *can* defend them?"

"We certainly intend to try, Your Eminence." Thirsk showed his teeth.

"Truly? How?"

"We're in the process of mounting as many of the 'superheavy' Fultyn Rifles as we can in our port-defense batteries. The most powerful of them will fire a twelve-inch solid shot, although I've been promised a *fifteen*-inch weapon. Even if St. Kylmahn's can actually deliver a fifteen-inch rifle, though, they aren't going to be able to provide them any time soon, especially if the heretics succeed in cutting the shipping routes across the Gulf of Tanshar. We already have quite a few of the twelve-inch weapons, however. Most of them are Dohlaran-built—I'm afraid the proposed fifteen-incher's beyond our present capabilities, which is why we were relying on St. Kylmahn's to deliver them to us—and the foundries assigned to the Navy are producing more of them on a crash basis. We've given priority to mounting them in the Gorath Bay fortifications, and as more become available, we'll deploy as many as possible to the other major ports. My own preference would be to cover a few ports, the most important ones, as heavily as possible rather than spreading them about in tenth-mark-packets. To be effective, their fire will have to be concentrated, not dispersed, because even though they hit with one hell of a lot of authority, if you'll pardon the phrase, they're individually slow-firing."

Lainyr nodded his understanding, and Thirsk shrugged.

"In addition to the artillery, Lieutenant Zhwaigair's been adapting the new rockets into harbor defense weapons. We won't have a real way to measure their effectiveness until we get a chance to fire them at the heretics, but they're designed to attack at a very steep angle—as steep as any angle-gun could provide—and they'll carry heavy 'warheads,' to use Brother Lynkyn's terminology. Their trajectory means they'll be targeted on the ironclads' decks, which have to be more weakly protected than their side armor, and they'll hit like very heavy shells. Almost like shot, really; the Lieutenant's designed an entirely new 'warhead.' It's so heavy it reduces range considerably, but it's based on the 'armor piercng' shells we found in *Dreadnought*'s shot lockers."

"All right. I can see that."

"Again, I can't *promise* the Lieutenant's rockets will constitute an *effective* defense," Thirsk said with the air of a man being painstakingly honest. "I can only say that they have the chance to be one . . . and that if they are, we can manufacture more of them far more rapidly than we can cast new cannon. And if we can get the new sea-bombs produced and placed to protect the approaches, then cover the sea-bombs in turn with direct fire from the St. Kylmahns and the rockets, we'll have a far more effective defense than Rhaigair had. In fact, if the heretics realize what the sea-bombs are and that we have them, they'll probably feel constrained to operate much more cautiously. As I say, the evidence suggests they don't have a great many of those armored steamers of theirs. They aren't going to lightly risk losing one—or more—of them. And I can definitely say that even if the defenses I've described are less effective than I believe they'll be, they'll constitute the best defense humanly possible."

Lainyr's eyes flickered ever so slightly at the adverb "humanly," and Thirsk kicked himself mentally for having used it. He wasn't about to make it worse by trying to unsay it, however.

"In the meantime," he continued, "even if they do base their steamers on Trove, they seem to still be short of light cruisers of their own. Given the amount of damage *Sea Dragon*'s report indicates they took from Admiral Raisahndo, they're probably going to be short on full-sized galleons for at least the next couple of months and possibly longer. And that means we should still be able to get the majority of our freight traffic through to its destination for the immediate future."

Lainyr's expression eased just a bit, and he nodded.

"That sounds more hopeful, my son!"

"I'm glad, Your Eminence," Thirsk replied.

Of course, it's also what they call "whistling in the dark," he reflected. *But that probably wouldn't be the best thing to tell you at the moment.*

"As I said, Your Eminence, there's no point trying to pretend we aren't in serious trouble at the moment, and I can't promise to work miracles. The Navy's crewed by mere mortals, when all's said and done. But this I *can* promise you—the Royal Dohlaran Navy is prepared to die where it stands in defense of its Kingdom and the Jihad. If the heretics succeed in attacking our home ports, it will be over the sunken ships—and the floating bodies—of my Navy."

.VII.
The Temple,
City of Zion,
The Temple Lands.

I am getting so *frigging* sick and tired of 'courageous defenses' that don't accomplish squat," Zhaspahr Clyntahn said harshly. The Grand Inquisitor glared around the sumptuously furnished council chamber and slapped one beefy hand on the table. "And the fact that that gutless wonder Thirsk plans to just *sit* there behind his guns and his 'sea-bombs' instead of doing something *proactive* sticks in my craw sideways." The hand slapped again, harder. "By his own admission, he's prepared to surrender control of the entire Gulf of Dohlar—*and* the Gulf of Tanshar—without firing a single shot! The man's a traitor to the Jihad!"

"With all due respect, Zhaspahr, I disagree," Allayn Maigwair said flatly. Clyntahn's eyes flamed, but the Captain General met them squarely. "It says a tremendous amount for Dohlaran—yes, and Earl Thirsk's—*loyalty* to Mother Church that they're still fighting at all. The heretics' Army of Thesmar is across their border into Reskar now. The Dohlaran Army is fighting on its own territory, destroying its own roads and canals, burning its own farms and villages and towns, to slow the heretics down, Zhaspahr! You're the one whose spies warned us Cayleb and Stohnar may be planning to drive south instead of north this summer. Well, without the fight Dohlar's putting up, that would be one hell of a lot easier for them! You've seen the sorts of casualty rates they're suffering while they do it, too, and half the entire Dohlaran *Navy* just went down fighting. I don't have complete casualty numbers for that yet, but I already know they're going to be high—very high. I do have confirmation from my liaison officers in Stene that all but one of their screw-galleys and at least nine of their galleons went down bodily or blew the hell up, Zhaspahr. That's a third of their entire fleet *sunk*, not captured or surrendered, and your own Inquisition reports also indicate they sank at least one heretic galleon and that the heretics themselves burned two or three more ships after the battle because they were too badly damaged to be repaired! That means they put up one hell of a fight even after their entire forward operating base was blown out from under them by ironclads that sailed right through the fire of a couple of hundred heavy cannon without apparently losing a single man. And after all that, Thirsk is still proposing ways to defend Dohlar's harbors as effectively as possible! You want to compare that to what *Desnair* did after the Kyplyngyr Forest and Geyra?!"

Clyntahn's hands curled into white-knuckled fists on the tabletop, and Rhobair Duchairn held his breath. Clyntahn's hatred for Lywys Gardynyr had grown only more intense since the death of the earl's family, and the Treasurer suspected fear was at least part of the reason it had.

It would appear that even Zhaspahr can grasp that a man whose entire family died because of him isn't likely to be one of his greater fans. I doubt that bothers him as much as the fact that the loss of Thirsk's entire family took away the only real lever we had to use against him, though.

"You can say whatever you want, Allayn," Clyntahn half snarled. "I don't trust the son-of-a-bitch. I *never* trusted the son-of-a-bitch, from the moment he screwed up off Armageddon Reef. I want him removed from command. In fact, I want him right here in Zion to explain his . . . dubious decisions in person!"

"Zhaspahr, removing the most effective single naval commander we've got—the most effective naval commander we've ever *had*—isn't likely to encourage the *rest* of his navy to go on fightingt!" Maigwair shot back.

"I don't give a—" Clyntahn began furiously, but an unexpected voice intervened.

"Zhaspahr," Zhasyn Trynair said, "Allayn's right."

The Grand Inquisitor's mouth snapped shut and he turned on Trynair with fiery eyes, but the Church's Chancellor continued with unaccustomed resolution.

"I'm not speaking about Thirsk's personal reliability," he continued. "I haven't seen any evidence that he *isn't* reliable, but the Inquisition may very well have information I don't that fully justifies your distrust of him. But my own sources in Dohlar tell me there's a lot of fear and uncertainty—fear and uncertainty that could flash over into panic entirely too easily—and that Fern, Thirsk, and Salthar are doing everything humanly possible to defend the Kingdom. And, more to the point, perhaps, King Rahnyld's subjects *know* they're doing it. They regard Thirsk as the architect of the Kingdom's only chance of survival, and if we remove him at this moment, when things are so . . . unsettled, we really could see a repetition of what's happening in Desnair."

By rights, Clyntahn's glare should have incinerated the Chancellor on the spot, but Trynair met it without flinching, almost as if he were still a member of the Group of Four, and Duchairn cleared his throat. The Grand Inquisitor's eyes snapped to him, glaring like a slash lizard at bay, and he shook his head.

"Zhaspahr, you head the Inquisition. Ultimately, decisions about spiritual and doctrinal loyalty reside with you. At this momen, however, Allayn and Zhasyn are right. You know I've never really agreed with your concerns about Thirsk's possible disloyalty, and to be honest, I don't now, either. But even assuming you're absolutely right about him, the policies and defensive measures he and Fern are proposing are the strongest, most effective ones possible. Maybe they won't be enough, and maybe Thirsk is a weaker reed than any of us might prefer. But nobody could do more—it's not physically *possible* to do more in this situation—and removing the man responsible for doing it, the man whose resolution underpins his entire navys, can only weaken those measures."

It was his turn to meet Clyntahn's incandescent eyes, and he sat very still as he waited for the Grand Inquisitor's explosion.

▼　　▼　　▼

"—and *then* the gutless, puking cowards told me that if I thought I could come up with someone who could get *more* out of the goddamned Dohlarans I should tell them who it was!"

Wyllym Rayno stood in Zhaspahr Clyntahn's enormous office, watching his superior pace furiously back and forth across it. The Grand Inquisitor's cassock swirled with the fury of his stride, and his jowly face was dark. He might have allowed himself to be dissuaded from dragging Thirsk back to Zion, but Rayno knew the signs. He was working his way into . . . reconsidering that decision. Which might be unfortunate in too many ways to count.

And not just for the Jihad.

"Your Grace," he said carefully, "my own reports would tend to support those Vicar Zhasyn has received."

Clyntahn stopped pacing and whirled to glare at him, but the archbishop only shrugged, ever so slightly, his expression calm. It was, perhaps, just as well that the Grand Inquisitor couldn't see the way his hands had tightened on one another in the concealment of his cassock's full sleeves.

"What did you say?" Clyntahn said icily.

"I said our reports, including Bishop Staiphan's, tend to corroborate Vicar Zhasyn's analysis. I don't defend anyone who's allowed his faith to falter, Your Grace. I'm simply saying there's a great deal of . . . uncertainty and fear. Understandably, I think, among members of the laity who have to be terrified by this fresh evidence that Shan-wei is loose in the world once more."

"So you're saying I should just roll over for this? That I should let this traitorous, cowardly son-of-a-bitch stay right where he is, in command of his precious navy, even if that means he'll just sit at anchor and let the frigging heretics do whatever they want out on the Gulf of Dohlar?" The Grand

Inquisitor showed his teeth. "I might point out that that means they'll be able to do whatever they want along the *coasts* of the Gulf of Dohlar . . . and the Sea of Harchong, for that matter. I don't think your fellow Harchongians will be very happy when the rest of their cities start burning like Rhaigair. Of course, Chiang-wu is *inland*, isn't it?"

"Your Grace, I have kinsmen in Tiegelkamp and Stene, not just Chiang-wu." Rayno met Clyntahn's eyes. "I don't want to see any Harchongese cities burning—I don't want to see *any* cities burning. But in the face of the heretics' presence in the Gulf and what's happened to Rhaigair, it's especially important that the man the Dohlaran man in the street trusts to do everything possible in defense of the Kingdom be left where he is, at least for now. If he provides proof, or even strong circumstantial evidence, that he *isn't* doing everything possible, you'll have grounds enough to justify taking him into custody in *anyone's* eyes. And—" the archbishop allowed himself a very small smile "—this state of panic won't last forever. One way or the other, it will ease as God and Schueler show us the path forward. It will be time to summon Thirsk to Zion when that happens. In the meantime, whether we trust him or not, let's *use* him as effectively as we can."

"And if he bites us on the arse in the meantime?" Clyntahn demanded, although he seemed at least marginally calmer than he had been.

"I think we'll simply have to trust in God—and Bishop Staiphan's vigilance—to prevent that from happening, Your Grace," Rayno replied, and saw Clyntahn relax a tiny bit more at the mention of Staiphan Maik.

The auxiliary bishop had been the Grand Inquisitor's personal choice as Thirsk's intendant, and Clyntahn retained a great deal of confidence in him. From the beginning, Maik's reports had emphasized Thirsk's competence and loyalty to the Dohlaran crown but acknowledged Clyntahn's concerns about the earl's spiritual reliability. Although Maik had never seen any signs of *un*reliability, he'd clearly kept a king wyvern's eye out for it. Rayno had admired the skillful way the intendant had maneuvered within Clyntahn's antipathy for the Dohlaran admiral, and he'd even taken it upon himself to . . . adjust certain of Ahbsahlahn Kharmych's more poisonous reports to support Maik's efforts. Whatever Clyntahn might have thought, they truly had needed Thirsk where he was.

Unfortunately, it was evident to Rayno him that the intendant had become a much closer ally in Thirsk's confrontations with Thorast. That had probably been inevitable, if Maik was going to do his job, but over the last several months, and especially since the death of Thirsk's family, Rayno had begun to sense a *personal* closeness between the admiral and his intendant.

That was worrisome, yet if he informed Clyntahn he'd become suspicious of *Maik's* ultimate loyalties, the Grand Inquisitor would insist on personally reviewing all the relevant correspondence. That could be . . .

inconvenient, since the raw files wouldn't mesh perfectly with what Rayno had reported to him. Normally, that wouldn't have worried him all that much. Clyntahn had known for years that his adjutant occasionally "massaged" information, and because the Grand Inquisitor had been confident of Rayno's loyalty—and total dependence upon him—he'd been willing to have that information flow managed. Indeed, a part of him had recognized that he *needed* someone to manage it to protect him against the consequences of his occasional fits of rage.

But those fits of rage had become ever more frequent. How he might react *now* to the discovery that Rayno had "concealed evidence" of Thirsk's—and possibly even Maik's—potential treason wasn't something the archbishop cared to contemplate.

Better not to mention how deeply involved Maik's been in the formulation of Thirsk's defensive strategy, either, he thought. *The way he's feeling right now, there's no telling what that might touch off. At the very least, he's likely to insist Maik come back to Zion for a debriefing. And what happens if Maik refuses?*

Rayno didn't like that possibility at all . . . almost as much as he didn't like the single, unsubstantiated report indicating that Thirsk and *Ahlverez*, of all people, had met clandestinely on at least two occasions. Letting *that* fall into Clyntahn's hands would have precipitated the worst explosion since the destruction of Armageddon Reef, and it was not only unsubstantiated, it was *suspect*, since it came from Kharmych who hated both men with a blinding passion and was perfectly willing to fabricate evidence against them. After all, the Inquisition routinely fabricated evidence against people it knew were guilty rather than pursue the long, hard investigation to acquire the actual proof, and Kharmych had been an agent-inquisitor for over twenty years before his present post. He knew how the game was played, and Rayno knew he was quite capable of using the same tactics out of personal choler and spite. That was why he hadn't passed along Kharmych's report at the time. And because he hadn't passed it along *then* it would be extraordinarily dangerous to pass it along *now*, when Clyntahn would almost certainly see the delay as proof Rayno had concealed evidence of Thirsk's disloyalty well before the Battle of Shipworm Shoal.

And then there was the minor worry of what would happen if it turned out, against all odds, that there'd been something to Kharmych's report after all. If Clyntahn summoned Maik to Zion and he refused to go and Thirsk and Ahlverez *protected* him, the consequences might be deadly. Unless the Inquisition in Dohlar was able to take all three of them into custody almost instantly, the best outcome they could hope for would be either a civil war or a repeat of what had happened in Desnair. The *worst* outcome would be to create a new, even more dangerous Corisande—or even Siddarmark—right here on the mainland.

Deep inside, Wyllym Rayno felt a growing dread that the Jihad was lost, yet he saw no way forward except to fight to the bitter end, trusting in the intervention of the Archangels. And after what had happened at St. Thyrmyn Prison, he was far less confident of the Archangels' intervention than he might once have been.

No, that wasn't quite true, a small still voice, all but inaudible in his heart of hearts, told him. He remained completely confident of the Archangels' intervention to prevent the triumph of evil.

He was simply no longer confident they'd intervene on the side of the Group of Four.

.VIII.
HMS *Gwylym Manthyr*,
Howell Bay,
and
Tellesberg Palace,
City of Tellesberg,
Kingdom of Old Charis,
Charisian Empire.

The stupendous vessel swept across the dark blue water like one of Langhorne's own *rakurai*. She was enormous, the biggest mobile structure ever built on Safehold: over four hundred and fifty feet between perpendiculars—four hundred and thirty feet long on the water line; twice the length of even a *Zhenefyr Ahrmahk*-class galleon or a *Rottweiler*-class ironclad—and seventy-eight feet across the beam. Her 10-inch guns—four of them, mounted in pairs fore and aft—were the heaviest ordnance ever sent to sea, and they were backed by no less than fourteen casemated 8-inch guns, with another twelve four-inch guns behind shields in deck mounts. She displaced over fourteen thousand tons at normal load, and the vast white furrow of her bow wave turned back on either side of her sharply raked prow as she sliced across Howell Bay at twenty knots . . . with at *least* another five knots in reserve.

The wind was out of the southwest, but it was little more than a light breeze, not enough to break the day's heat or raise much in the way of a sea . . . and scarcely even a zephyr compared to the wind generated by her passage. The thick banner of black coal smoke pouring from her twin funnels hung heavy above the water, shredding only slowly. It lingered far behind her, like an airborne mirror of her broad, white wake, and Captain Halcom Bahrns stood on the open wing of her navigating bridge, both hands on the bridge rail in front of him, his uniform tunic pasted to his chest—the sleeves fluttering—as the wind of her passage swept back across him.

My God, he thought, *she's real. She's really, really* real! *Deep inside, I never believed she was—not truly—even when I came aboard.*

He'd been devastated when they told him to hand *Delthak* over to Pawal Blahdysnberg and return to Old Charis. Despite his deep initial doubts, he'd come to love every bolt, every plank, of his unlovely, ungainly command, and she'd never refused a single thing he'd asked of her. After everything he and his ship's company had been through, it seemed bitterly unfair to be summoned home with no explanation at all. Zherald Cahnyrs, *Delthak's* second officer, had been ordered home with him, and although the lieutenant was too disciplined and professional to say it, Bahrns knew he'd been just as disappointed.

But only until they reported to Admiral Rock Point—not at Tellesberg, or Lock Island, or even King's Harbor, as they'd expected, but at Larek, at the mouth of the Delthak River—and found out *why* they'd been recalled.

He'd stood on the deck of HMS *Destroyer*, Rock Point's flagship, staring at the enormous vessel moored at the fitting out dock, her decks and upper works aswarm with workmen, and he'd been unable to believe what he was seeing.

"Bit of a surprise, is it, Captain?" the one-legged high admiral had asked with a crooked smile.

"Oh, yes, My Lord," Bahrns had replied fervently. "In *so* many ways! I never imagined I might be considered to command one of them! And even if I had—!"

He'd broken off, shaking his head, and Rock Point had snorted. The sound had been harsh, but it had also contained amusement. And possibly something almost like . . . satisfaction.

"After the Delthak Fire, I'm not surprised you're surprised," he'd said. "And hopefully Clyntahn, Maigwair—and Thirsk—will go right on thinking what you thought. We've certainly done our damnedest to *help* them do that, anyway!"

"I can understand why you'd do that, My Lord, but does that mean the fire was actually less destructive than the rumors said?"

"Unfortunately, no." If there'd been any amusement in Rock Point's voice a moment earlier, it had disappeared. "In fact, it was even worse than we first thought, especially given the need to continue producing the Army's artillery. Frankly, little though anyone in Navy uniform would like to admit it—I know *I* sure as hell didn't want to!—equipping the Army's even more important than equipping *us*, at the moment. I imagine—" he'd given Bahrns a very sharp look "—you probably understand that better than most, Captain."

"Yes, My Lord, I do." Bahrns' expression had tightened. "Earl Hanth's been working miracles, but his people're paying in blood for him to pull them off. Mind you, there's not a man in this world who could do a better job than the Earl, and all of us know the price'd be even higher under anyone else. But I *know* those people, My Lord. They're *real* to me, not just names in dispatches or newspaper articles. I'm in favor of anything that knocks that price down."

"As it happens, Captain, so am I." Rock Point had rested a hand on Bahrns' shoulder. "And to be honest, the way you've coordinated with the Army so well—starting with the Canal Raid and continuing straight through the Seridahn Campaign—is one reason your name jumped the queue when we found ourselves looking for a skipper on short notice."

Bahrns had felt his face heat, but, fortunately, the high admiral had continued before he had to try to come up with some sort of a response.

"At any rate," he'd said more briskly, taking his hand from the captain's shoulder and turning back to *Destroyer*'s rail, "between the damage to the Delthak Works and the need to provide the Army's artillery, it's going to be at least four more months before we're able to complete the armament for the class. But by taking the two undamaged ten-inchers from the works and combining them with the proofing guns, we were able to put together the main battery for one *King Haarahld*-class—*this* one." He jutted his chin at the enormous vessel. "Duke Delthak tells me she'll be ready for trials in three five-days."

"But surely a captain had already been assigned, My Lord? For that matter, captains must've been assigned to *all* of them. Wouldn't it make more sense to give her to someone who's been associated with the building program from the beginning?"

"Yes, we'd assigned captains. We didn't exactly pick them at random, either, and we'd given this one to Zhorj Mahlrunee. I believe you know him?"

"Yes, My Lord, I do. Very well, in fact." Bahrns had frowned. "He was first officer in *Sea Shrike* when I was a snotty. May I ask why he isn't *still* assigned to her? He's one of the finest officers I know!"

The concern in his voice had been obvious, and Rock Point had sighed

"I'm sorry, Captain—I thought you knew. Captain Mahlrunee was called home to Chisholm. It wasn't an easy decision for him or for us, but his wife was killed in an accident."

"Ahnalee is *dead*?" Bahrns had stared at the high armiral. Ahnalee Mahlrunee was the widow of a brother officer; she and Zhorj had been married for less than two years, and they had three young children, two of them hers by her previous marriage.

"I'm afraid so," Rock Point had confirmed. "Just one of those stupid things. But you probably know he'd moved his parents to Chisholm after his marriage?"

The high admiral had cocked an eyebrow, and Bahrns nodded, Mahlrunee's mother and father were quite elderly, and his only living sibling was also a Navy officer. Since both of them had been constantly at sea, Ahnahlee had insisted their parents move to Chisholm where she could care for them.

"He was devastated by the news," Rock Point continued, "and his brother's at sea in Baron Sarmouth's squadron, so there was literally no one else to care for his family. Under the circumstances, he requested relief and went on inactive duty—with my complete support. Some duties take priority over anything else, and this is damned well one of them! But it left us with a bit of a personnel problem, and when I asked him to recommend his relief, he picked *you*. To be honest, we'd already ordered you home to give you one of the new *City*-class, so I wasn't inclined to accept his recommendation at the time. It was only after you were in transit that Duke Delthak's people completed their damage survey and determined we had the artillery to complete one *King Haarahld*, after all. Their Majesties picked this one, and that meant she needed a captain fast."

Bahrns' expression had shouted the question he'd been unable to ask, and Rock Point had chuckled sourly.

"As it happens, Captain, the ship's construction was at least as advanced as any of the others'. The only one they might have picked instead was *King Haarahld VII*, and her boilers are . . . less than satisfactory, let's say." The high admiral had shrugged. "It doesn't happen often with the Delthak Works, but even Duke Delthak's people occasionally screw up. In fact, we'd already discovered we had to rip them out and start over again, and getting that done had dropped in priority when we didn't think we'd have the guns for any of them. We hadn't made much progress on that little chore when we found out we *could* complete one, so there really wasn't another candidate. After all," he'd showed Bahrns his teeth, "we don't want anyone in the Gulf of Dohlar . . . misconstruing our message."

"No, My Lord. I can see that," Bahrns had said, his eyes on the name emblazoned in golden letters on the cliff-like side of the enormous ship's bow.

"HMS *Gwylym Manthyr*" those letters had said.

▼   ▼   ▼

"Well, Captain?"

The man standing at Halcom Bahrns' side had to raise his voice over the sound of rushing wind and water, and Bahrns turned to him courteously.

"Should I assume she passes muster?" he continued with a slight smile, and there was nothing at all *slight* about Bahrns' answering smile.

"Oh, I think you can assume that, Your Grace!" he told the recently ennobled Duke of Delthak. "Langhorne! I thought *Delthak* was incredible when you and High Admiral Rock Point gave her to me, but this—!"

He waved one arm in a wide arc, taking in the long, lethal barrels of her guns, the white water bursting away from either bow, the wind of her passage humming in the signal halyards, and the broad deck—vibrating to the throbbing pulse beat of her mighty engines, yet steady as a rock underfoot, despite her headlong charge across the bay—and shook his head.

"I can understand why the details were so closely held," he continued, "but I never would've imagined what they really were. This ship—this *single* ship—is more powerful than every other warship in the entire world!"

"That might be a *little* bit of an exaggeration," Ehdwyrd Howsmyn said judiciously. "And she's not designed just to engage other navies, either. To be honest, I suspect that's another reason Baron Rock Point thought you'd be the proper man to command her. I believe you're intended to be what His Majesty calls 'Earl Sharpfield's Doorknocker' when it's time to . . . go calling on Gorath."

"And I'm looking forward to the visit, Your Grace," Bahrns said much more grimly.

"We all are," Delthak assured him. "I knew Gwylym Manthyr." He rested a hand on the bridge railing and looked out across the endless waters of the bay for a moment. "A lot of us have been waiting for his namesake's voice to make itself heard. Do us proud, Captain."

"We will, Your Grace." Bahrns met his gaze levelly. "*Depend* on that— we will."

▼   ▼   ▼

"If I'd realized Master Tahnguchi would shave three full five-days off his own best estimate, I might've delayed our visit to Rhaigair until she arrived, Ehdwyrd," Dunkyn Yairley said, studying the recorded satellite imagery of HMS *Gwylym Manthyr*'s final acceptance trials. "A lot of people who're dead now might not've been if I had, too."

"As I recall, Dunkyn," Cayleb Ahrmahk put in from his Siddar City study, just a bit tartly, "*Lewk Cohlmyn* is our overall commander for the Gulf of Dohlar. Forgive me if I'm wrong, but doesn't that mean *he* got to pick the timing?"

"Well, yes, Your Majesty. But I could have argued instead of getting behind and pushing. And if I'd known she'd be available, I damned well *would* have!"

"Dunkyn, it could've been argued either way even if you'd known exactly when *Manthyr* was going to commission," Domynyk Staynair said. "Every day we'd delayed would've been one more day for the Dohlarans to get their damned 'sea-bombs' into production and deployed, and not even a *King Haarahld* has an armored *bottom*. Then there were Zhwaigair's coast-defense rockets, and those frigging twelve-inch rifles Duchairn and Maigwair had earmarked for Golden Grass and Cahstnyr. The first of Zhwaigair's rockets would've arrived yesterday morning, and the first twelve-inch battery was less than a five-day behind them, I believe?"

Sarmouth nodded, if perhaps a bit unwillingly, and Rock Point shrugged.

"The *King Haarahld*s aren't magic. I think it's unlikely any of that could have significantly damaged *Manthyr*, but I might be wrong—especially about the rockets. When we designed her deck armor, we weren't thinking in terms of plunging fire from two-hundred-pound warheads, you know. If you'd waited, there'd've been time for all of those to get into play before you hit Rhaigair."

"I think there's a certain point to that argument," Merlin put in. Sarmouth looked at the image projected onto his contact lenses, and Merlin shrugged. "Let's not forget how beaten up *Eraystor* was by *ten*-inch guns by the time Zhaztro finished running the batteries."

"All right," Sarmouth said after a moment. "I'll grant that. But I really, *really* wish I'd been able to send *Manthyr* in—alone, even—to deal with Rhaigair while Hainz and his squadron waited for Raisahndo's galleons off Shipworm Shoal. Hell! Even somebody as stubborn as Raisahndo might've surrendered when he saw *that* waiting for him!"

Merlin chuckled bleakly and Cayleb snorted, although Sarmouth definitely had a point. The RDN's Western Squadron had simply ceased to exist after the Battle of Shipworm Shoal; not a single ship heavier than a twenty-gun brig had escaped. But the Royal Dohlaran Navy had lived up to its own tradition. By the time Caitahno Raisahndo's surviving galleons struck their colors, only eleven of them had still been in action. For that matter, only twenty-six of them—and only one of his crippled screw-galleys—had still been afloat.

His flagship had not been among them.

Yet they hadn't died alone, those ships. If the Charisians had wanted to get into their range of him, they'd had to let him into *his* range of *them*, as well, and only three of their ships had been armored. The carnage wooden ships armed with shell-firing guns could wreak upon one another was incredible. Two Charisian galleons had simply blown up. Four more had foundered as the hungry sea poured into breached and shattered hulls, and another five had been too badly damaged to return to service. Sarmouth had burned one of them on the spot rather than attempt to nurse the broken, leaking wreck back to Claw Island. The other four had returned to Claw Keep to be stripped of their guns and useful fittings before they, too, were burned.

As recently as a year or two earlier, at least two of them probably would have been repaired, but there'd been no point now. With the Western Squadron's destruction, the Imperial Charisian Navy's only remaining opposition was the squadron under Thirsk's personal command in Gorath. Even the Desnairian privateers had become only a ghost of their onetime menace. Sir Hainz Zhaztro's message to Geyra had inspired Emperor Mahrys and his councilors to . . . reconsider their support for that strategy. Or for anything *else* which might conceivably inspire another visit from the ICN.

Zhaspahr Clyntahn had been livid when he learned that the Desnairians who'd already deserted the Jihad's land war had quietly done the same at sea, as well. Fortunately for Mahrys, Desnair the City was out of the Grand Inquisitor's reach, unless he wanted to risk the even worse possibility of ordering the emperor's arrest and discovering the Inquisition couldn't carry it out! Clearly, that was one more risk than even he was willing to run . . . at least until he'd dealt with Charis and her allies. After *that*, of course, he'd look at things differently, and all the world knew that Zhaspahr Clyntahn had a long, long memory.

That must leave Mahrys just a tad . . . ambivalent *about the Jihad's outcome*, Merlin reflected with a certain nasty sense of pleasure.

But the upshot was that, after so many years of explosive expansion, the ICN had more ships—a *lot* more ships—than it actually needed. And thanks to the introduction of steam, steel hulls, and rifled artillery, virtually all those ships were at best obsolescent. There was little point repairing badly damaged galleons which would only be retired and broken up within the next two or three years.

"You know," Nynian Rychtyr said from where she sat on the arm of Merlin's chair, "I've been meaning to ask this for a while, but why in Kohdy's name did you people decide to build something like the *King Haarahlds*?" She shook her head, her expression quizzical. "Oh, I understand you needed Cayleb's 'doorknocker,' and I understand the *Cities* don't have the operating range you'd really like to have. But they did just fine at Rhaigair, and Sir Dunkyn's clearly demonstrated he and his Marines can seize islands for forward coaling stations anytime he feels like it. So why build something so big? And so *fast*, for that matter! Captain Bahrns' had it up to twenty-six knots, and wasn't even straining its machinery when he did."

"Had *her* up to twenty-six knots, please," Merlin said with a pained expression and shuddered delicately. "*Her*, Nynian! You really want to be careful about how you offend a Charisian's sensibilities with that sort of loose language."

"*Sure* I do." She rolled her eyes and smacked him across the top of his head. "But my question stands. I'd never heard of 'overkill' until I fell into my present evil company, but to be honest, these ships strike me as a pretty clear example of exactly that. And you've diverted an awful lot of resources into them."

"The resource cost is probably the strongest argument against them," Earl Pine Hollow said before Merlin could reply. The imperial first councilor sat comfortably propped up in bed with an open book in his lap and his evening cup of chocolate on a bedside table. "On the other hand, you have to remember when they were first put into the pipeline, Nynian." He shrugged. "We'd already begun work on them before Clyntahn's 'Sword of Schueler' ever hit the Republic. At that point, the Navy was still our primary focus, since there was no way we were going to be able to invade the Mainland out of our own resources anytime soon. By the time the Army's needs took center stage, we were already well launched on the program and, frankly, the Army didn't need armor plate, steam engines, or most of the rest of what was going into the ships. So the resource diversion aspect of it actually isn't nearly as clear-cut as it might appear."

"All right, I'll grant that," Nynian conceded, but she rallied gamely. "On the other hand, you could've built—what? Ten *Cities* for each *King Haarahld*?"

"Yes, we could," Sharleyan acknowledged from her own Tellesberg bedchamber. "And we considered doing just that. But I'm a little surprised, Nynian."

"Surprised?"

"Yes. You, of all people, should be accustomed to long-term strategic thinking."

Nynian's eyebrows arched, and Sharleyan chuckled.

"It was your idea, Merlin. Why don't you explain it?"

"All right." Merlin leaned back in his chair and smiled up at Nynian. "Of course, there's always the problem of getting such a land-bound ignoramus to understand the finer points so glaringly obvious to us subtle sea creatures."

She glared down at him, raising one mock-ferocious fist, and he lifted his hands in a gesture of surrender.

"Sorry!" he told her while laughter sounded over the com channel. "I couldn't resist. But," his expression sobered, "Sharley's put her finger on the real reason I backed Dustyn so strongly when he and Ehdwyrd first came up with the notion. I almost argued against it, really—for all the reasons you just cited. But then another aspect of their proposal occurred to me."

"What sort of aspect?" she asked, lowering her fist, her own expression more serious as his tone registered.

"What's our end strategy, Nynian?" he countered, and she frowned.

That was a question which the Inner Circle's members had discussed often enough, both before and after she'd become a member of it, she reflected. And while *parts* of it were simplicity itself to answer, others were anything but.

Initially, *Charis'* overriding objective had been simple survival, although Maikel Staynair's quest for freedom of conscience had run a close second. Of course, Charis' survival had required the Group of Four's defeat, and as the jihad grew increasingly bitter and ever bloodier, that priority had broadened as all Charisians, aside from the dwindling number of diehard Temple Loyalists, had come to demand a complete separation from the Church of the Temple, coupled with the destruction of the Inquisition's power. And that—hard though many Charisians, including a great many of the most ardent Reformists, had fought against accepting it—meant more than simply defending Charis against the immediate threat of invasion and conquest. It meant the Church itself had to be beaten into submission on the field of battle, because that was the only way a Zhaspahr Clyntahn could be forced to abandon that effort.

But those were the strategic imperatives all Charisians knew about—the same imperatives that operated for the Republic of Siddarmark, following Clyntahn's brutal assault upon it. They were not *Nimue Alban's* overriding imperative, and Nimue's imperative—which had become that of the Inner Circle—was the outright *destruction*, not simply the defeat, of the Church of God Awaiting. It was her task, her mission—the burning purpose for which the original Nimue Alban had *died*—to overturn the Proscriptions, proclaim the truth about the 'Archangels,' liberate the human race from the anti-technology shackles Eric Langhorne had fastened upon it, and—above every other priority in the universe—prepare it to face the peril of the Gbaba once again.

"Ideally," Nynian said finally, "the end game's to compel the Group of Four—well, Group of *Three* now, I suppose—to surrender and give us possession of the Temple so we can get at whatever's in the basement." She grimaced. "Of course, as we've all agreed, the chance of pulling that off ranges between slim and none."

"Exactly." Merlin shrugged. "And even if they were willing to let us into that basement, it might not solve our problem. We realized even before Paityr brought us the Stone of Schueler that we couldn't just waltz into the Temple and start shutting off power switches." He smiled very thinly. "Leaving aside the probability that someone as paranoid as Chihiro and Schueler would've left safeguards to prevent anybody from deliberately—or accidentally—shutting *anything* down, we know that at least one 'Archangel' left at least *one* booby-trap down there. God only knows what somebody else may've left! And how would every believer in Zion react if all the Temple's 'divine' environmental services, lighting, and repair-mech 'servitors' suddenly go down? Since 'every believer in Zion' happens to be the same thing as 'every living human being in Zion,' that's a not-minor consideration.

"And would *any* vicarate, even one that somehow deposes Clyntahn and the others, be willing to let us 'heretics' profane the Temple, whatever happens? I suspect they'd balk at that. They might be reduced to offering *passive* resistance, but I could see the truly devout among them standing on the Temple steps to block our access unless we were willing to use physical force to move them, and the last thing we want to do is to physically invade the Temple. At the moment, we're totally undermining Zhaspahr Clyntahn's moral authority. Of course, he's our best ally in that endeavor, but if we landed 'heretical' troops in Zion to violate the precincts of the Temple. . . ."

He shrugged again, much less nonchalantly, and his sapphire eyes were darker and deeper than the sea.

"I can't think of a single thing more likely to provoke fanatical resistance. The kind of resistance where children with bombs strapped to their backs run straight into the machine guns and parents *encourage* them to do it. God knows we've seen enough of that sort of fanaticism, and not just on the Temple Loyalists' side. Look at some of the things that happened in Glacierheart and Tarikah and Hildermoss." He shook his head. "That's the largest city on Safehold, Nynian. The body count could well be in the millions, even if we 'won' in the end . . . and that assumes the bombardment platform isn't programmed to protect the physical integrity of the Temple by automatically taking out any attacking army or fleet, which I suspect it damned well is. Hell, *I'm* not a crazed, mass-murdering lunatic, and that's how *I'd*'ve set it up!"

"But if we can't invade Zion," Cayleb said quietly, drawing Nynian's gaze to him, "then the chance of our being able to . . . undo the *Holy Writ* just because we defeat the Group of Four goes from 'unlikely as hell' to completely impossible. When we started this—once the 'Inner Circle' really understood what was at stake, at least—we were willing to settle for driving the Church back, breaking the Inquisition's kneecaps, and creating a situation in which the Church of Charis *gradually* destroyed the Church's authority. We were thinking in terms of decades, even generations, of slowly undermining the *Writ* and the Proscriptions through example and gradual reinterpretation. And we were willing to take however long we needed to take to find a solution to the bombardment system. But then Paityr brought us the Stone . . . and Schueler's promise of the 'Archangels' return.' And that gave us a deadline we hadn't known we faced."

Nynian nodded, her own expression somber. None of that was new to her, although this was really the first time she'd been inside the gradual evolution of her Charisian allies' thinking. By the time she'd become aware of them—and they'd become aware of her—that evolution had already completed itself.

"We don't know for certain that the 'Archangels' are actually going to return at all," Merlin said. "And if they do, we don't know *how* they'll return. One possibility would be for PICA 'Archangels' to suddenly emerge from vaults under the Temple. Frankly, I don't think that's likely, because if they'd prepared a stack of PICAs in the first place, they'd probably also have continued to interact with the flesh-and-blood population of Safehold. We had the capability to build a single PICA out of the resources in my cave, once Owl and Nahrmahn figured out how to do it. It's for damn sure Chihiro and Schueler had that capability after Langhorne's death. Oh, they might've needed to do the same research Owl did, although I think it's more likely they would've already had the necessary information. But they certainly could've done it before or during the War Against the Fallen if they'd wanted to, and if they had, they could have had clearly superhuman 'Archangels' and 'angels' leading their armies in the field instead of relying on mortal *seijins*, like Kohdy. Think how that would have cemented the Church's authority—especially if the same 'Archangels' or their 'angelic' successors were *still* available to be the Church's public face." He shook his head. "No, if they'd been willing to go the PICA route, then when Nimue Alban woke up in a PICA here on Safehold, her entire mission would have been flat out impossible instead of simply *damned near* impossible."

Nynian nodded again, suppressing an inner shiver as she thought of the nightmare Merlin—Nimue—would have faced under those circumstances.

"So, if they're 'returning,' it has to be in some other fashion, and, frankly, I don't have a clue what that might be. For that matter, as I say, we don't know they're really going to 'return' at all. There's nothing in the *Writ* about it, nothing in *The Testimonies* or *The Commentaries*. For that matter, there's nothing in the message Schueler left. So unless there's something in the Church's secret archives that not even Paityr's father ever heard so much as a *hint* about—which strikes me as unlikely, to say the least—the only evidence that they're going to come back is the oral tradition passed down in the Wylsynn family, theoretically from Schueler himself but independent of the message he personally recorded."

Merlin grimaced, the expression as frustrated as it was worried.

"Taking all of that together, I'd be very tempted to simply brush the whole thing off as a myth that self-started somehow over the last several hundred years. Unfortunately, Paityr tells us there are veiled allusions to the return in Wylsynn family diaries that date from within twenty years of the War Against the Fallen. So if it's a self-starting myth, it self-started pretty damned early. And, leaving that aside completely, deciding there's nothing to it would be the sort of wrong assumption we only get to make once."

"Agreed," Nynian said. "But that's why we're pushing so hard to 'get the genie out of the bottle,'" she smiled faintly as she used the phrase Merlin had introduced her to. "Right?"

"Exactly." Merlin nodded. "We're looking at a binary solution set here, in a lot of ways. Either there's going to be some sort of return of the 'Archangels,' or there isn't. Even if there isn't, we still need to figure out how to neutralize what's under the Temple and/or the bombardment system eventually. Actually, now that I think about it, there's no 'and/or' in it—we need to neutralize *both* of those to be sure something really, really bad doesn't happen. We're just under a lot more time pressure to get it done if they *are* coming back somehow.

"We may or may not be able to accomplish that, but unless we can manage that and get the industrial plant in Nimue's Cave up and running and replicating itself—with at least a decade or so to spare—we're still screwed. If we could pull that off, and if we had that decade to work with, we wouldn't really *care* if the 'Archangels' decided to put in an actual physical reappearance of some sort." He smiled coldly. "Give me four or five years of open Federation-level tech to work with, and I will guarantee that anything the 'Archangels' bring with them gets blown to hell and gone. And I can think of very few things that would give me more personal satisfaction!

"But if we can't do that, we have to play for the possibility—the *probability*, I hope!—that whatever turns up calling itself an 'Archangel' isn't quite as lunatic as Langhorne was when he pulled the trigger on the Alexandria Enclave. I have to think they wouldn't be coming back at all if they didn't want to make sure the human race survives. And killing the human race themselves wouldn't strike me as the best way to do that, which is why we want the 'genie out of the bottle.' Spreading the violation of the Proscriptions—of their *purpose*, the thing they were supposed to *achieve*, at least—as broadly as possible, even if their word was still technically observed was always part of our gradualist strategy. But Paityr's warning's lent that strategy a lot more urgency, because if we can spread the new technology broadly enough that it would require a planet-wide application of *'rakurai'* to eradicate all the threats to Langhorne's grand plan, then anyone *but* a raving lunatic would realize that plan's failed. We're in no position to predict how he might react, but I think it's likely any non-lunatic would see no option but to engineer as soft a landing to the Proscriptions' collapse as possible.

"That's why the economic implications of Ehdwyrd's railroads and of steam-powered maritime trade are far more dangerous to the Church in the long term than any warship or artillery piece. But let's be honest—it's always possible for someone to cut off his economic nose to spite his face on religious grounds. God knows it was done often enough back on Old Earth! The ultimate consequences would be disastrous, and any realm that chose to do that would be a complete political and economic nonfactor within a generation. But that doesn't mean they won't do it, and I can easily imagine a reactionary 'counterreformation' throwing up all sorts of obstacles to stretch the process out even farther. Quite possibly for longer than we have before that return visit we're worrying about.

"Enter the *King Haarahlds*."

He leaned back in his chair again, raising both hands in the gesture of someone who'd just completed his revelation, and Nynian frowned.

"What are you talking about?" Her tone suggested she was on the cusp of understanding and knew it but hadn't quite made the leap.

"A single *King Haarahld* is—as Captain Bahrns told Domynyk—more powerful than every other warship on the face of the planet put together, Nynian," Sharleyan said. "Faster, bigger, more dangerous than anything she could conceivably face . . . and impossible to build without embracing—*fully* embracing—Ehdwyrd's innovations. At the moment, the Temple's support-ers can argue that nothing we're using against them is completely beyond their capabilities. They may not be able to produce weapons that do what ours do as effectively and efficiently as ours do it, but they're in a position to convince themselves that theirs come *close enough* for an army equipped with enough of them to survive against an army equipped with Charisian new-model weapons."

Nynian nodded slowly . . . and then her eyes widened and understand-ing flowed across her beautiful face.

"I knew you'd get there, love," Merlin said, tucking an arm around her.

"They're . . . they're *technology demonstrators!*" she said.

"That's *exactly* what they are," Cayleb agreed in a tone of grim, profound satisfaction. "Mind you, I really would like to sail them into Temple Bay, but I've known all along we can't, whatever I've suggested to people who don't know what this war's really about. But when *Gwylym Manthyr* steams right through anything that gets in her way without even slowing down, when she steams all the way from Tellesberg to Claw Island at twenty-plus knots with only a single refueling and shows she's twice as fast as any gal-leon ever built, and when she steams into Gorath Bay and blows its fortifi-cations into *gravel*, it isn't going to be just the retribution Sharley and I promised ourselves—that we promised *Gwylym*. It's going to be that, and Sharley's going to make that point for our people before she ever sails. And it's also going to be an object lesson to Zhaspahr Clyntahn and any other bloody-minded bastard who thinks the way he does. A warning about what will happen to anyone else who butchers our people or hands them over to be butchered by someone else. That's a lesson we damned well mean to drive home to the *bone*, Nynian—as Emperor and Empress of Charis, not just members of the Inner Circle.

"But it's going to be a different sort of object lesson, too, and no ruler who's smarter than a rock is going to be able to miss its point. Without equivalent technology, no realm can survive against anyone who adopts it, and no one out there—from Mahrys of Desnair, to Rahnyld of Dohlar, to Emperor Waisu's bureaucrats—hell, to that idiot Zhames in Delferahk!—is going to decide to trust that none of *his* enemies will build it. For that matter, they'll know damned well *we're* going to—that we already *have*—and even Greyghor, here in Siddarmark, is going to have to worry about the possibility that some perfectly legitimate dispute will someday arise between the Republic and us.

"So that's what the *King Haarahld*s are, Nynian," the Emperor of Charis said levelly, meeting her eyes across the study. "They'll do the job at Gorath—that's for damn sure—but just like you said, so would the *Cities*. They're not Earl *Sharpfield's* doorknockers; they're Merlin's, and the 'door' he has in mind is a hell of a lot more important than Gorath."

.IX.
Rock Coast Keep,
Duchy of Rock Coast,
Kingdom of Chisholm;
and
Manchyr Palace,
City of Manchyr,
Princedom of Corisande,
Empire of Charis.

With all due respect, Father," Zhasyn Seafarer, the Duke of Rock Coast, said sharply, "I'm getting pretty tired of waiting for Father Zhordyn to get off the tenth-mark! We need to know exactly when—or, for that matter, Schueler help us, *if*—Lady Swayle's going to agree to our strategy!" He glowered, dark eyes fiery. "I thought all of that had already been agreed, frankly. Black Horse and I have certainly been proceeding on that basis, and we've got firm pledges of loyalty from almost all the key men here in our own duchies. And now we can't get a firm commitment out of her?" His expression was not a happy one. "*She's* the one who contacted *us*—and she did it through Father Zhordyn. If she's changed her mind, we need to know it. And if she *hasn't* changed her mind, we need to know *that*, too!"

"I realize you need better communications, Your Grace." Father Sedryk

Mahrtynsyn raised a placating hand. "And I lnow it's impossible to make concrete plans without knowing what your allies have in mind. But Father Zhordyn is a passionate and loyal son of Mother Church, just as Countess Swayle is a loyal daughter. Surely there's no reason to fear their resolution has flagged!"

"It's not their 'resolution' I'm concerned about, Father!"

The duke erupted from his chair and strode to the window, glaring out into the gray afternoon's chill, windy rain while he worked to get his temper back under control. A spray of sleet rattled against the glass, and he turned back to the priest.

"What I'm concerned about is their willingness to *do* anything," he said in a rather calmer tone. "Well, that and the fact that at this point we don't really know what she's been able to arrange—or not arrange—with Holy Tree or how those contacts of hers with Earl Mandigora have gone. If he's willing to come in with us, he'd give Dragon Hill a secure northern frontier, and between them he, Dragon Hill, and Holy Tree could probably squeeze Greentree into joining us as well . . . or neutralize him, if he refuses."

He scowled in frustration and walked across to the new model-cast iron stove heating his office. He opened the door, tossed in a couple of lumps of coal, and stalked back to the window.

"I think you'll agree it's pretty important to know whether or not we can count on support that far east," he growled, looking back out into the rain. "And Dragon Hill's not saying squat to *me*! He's made it pretty clear he thinks I'm 'overly enthusiastic,' but if Rebkah and Father Zhordyn can get a firm commitment out of him, that would be huge. And if they can convince Mandigora and Holy Tree to do the same thing—and if I can bring in Mountain Heart and Lantern Walk—we'd effectively control all of the southwest outside the Crown Desmene. That's more than a quarter of the entire Kingdom! There's an enormous difference between that and what Black Horse and I can accomplish on our own. But if they won't even tell us what they're doing—or what they're *willing* to do—Pait and I can't make any definitive plans of our own, and it won't be very many more five-days before White Crag and Kahlyns start counting noses on the troops to send to the mainland. When they send them off, we'll have a window—a narrow one, only a few months wide, at the outside—before that sorry bastard Kahlyns trains up an entire fresh army of replacements. That means we have to be ready to act as soon as that window opens. And for that to happen, we have to make plans *now* based on what our 'allies' are or aren't willing to *do*. It's that simple, Father."

Mahrtynsyn nodded, and not just to calm the other man down. There were times Zhasyn Seafarer could act like a petulant teenager who wanted his way *now*, and damn the consequences. This wasn't one of those times, however, and the Schuelerite shared his frustration to the full.

Which didn't keep him from understanding why Rebkah Rahskail, the Dowager Countess of Swayle, and Father Zhordyn Rydach, her confessor, were hesitant to give Rock Coast the firm commitments he wanted. And there were aspects of the kind of communication Rock Coast was demanding which made *him* distinctly nervous, as well. But whatever his own concerns, and however understandable their hesitation, the duke had it exactly right. The problem was what Mahrtynsyn did about it.

And whatever anyone else—including Zhasyn Seafarer—might think, it was *his* job to make this work. His superiors back in Zion had been very clear about that, and they wouldn't be very happy with him if he *didn't* make it work.

Of course, if I don't, I doubt the Archbishop and the Grand Inquisitor will have the opportunity to express their displeasure to me. He grimaced mentally. *Sharleyan and her executioners will probably make sure of that.*

At forty-seven—although he looked considerably younger—Sedryk Mahrtynsyn had served the Inquisition for almost thirty years. His youthful appearance could have been a handicap in a parish priest, who needed to project an aura of mature wisdom and judgment. It had, however, served him well as a young agent inquisitor who'd specialized in infiltrating suspect groups. He also had fair hair, blue eyes, and a guileless face—one which habitually wore an expression of gentle, bemused surprise that was as deceiving (and useful) as his apparent youth. It had taken him years to perfect that mask, and by now displaying it was second nature to him. At the moment, however, it was notable mostly for its absence and the sharp intelligence behind those normally innocent blue eyes was focused and obvious as he frowned in thought.

He was willing to admit Rock Coast wasn't the most patient and meticulous of conspirators. There were, in fact, sound reasons to keep him on a short leash, and in this instance it was scarcely surprising that his reputation for . . . impetuosity worried the countess and her confessor. But they were moving into the stage where zeal became a virtue, not a liability, and one of the reasons he'd been sent to Rock Coast Keep was to be Zhaspahr Clyntahn's voice of caution in Rock Coast's councils.

He was confident he'd be able to restrain any rashness on the duke's part and, truthfully, Rock Coast had shown far more self-discipline than he'd expected. The duke seemed to grasp the notion—intellectually, at least—that this time Sharleyan and Cayleb Ahrmahk would crush any rebellion ruthlessly and for good. A part of him clearly still cherished the notion that his high birth and family connections would protect him from the worst if things went awry, as they had in the past, but deep inside, he knew that if he and his fellows launched an open rebellion and failed, Sharleyan would leave very few heads attached to their owners' necks.

But if they were going to succeed, they needed to share information and make firm plans. Mahrtynsyn agreed completely with that point. His concern—and, he admitted, it was a serious one—had nothing to do with whether or not the duke should have that information or begin solidifying a comprehensive plan. It was the fact that he was a great believer in the proposition that successful conspiracies were always planned "under four eyes," as the Desnairians called it. Face-to-face conversations, with no unfortunate witnesses, were the only truly secure way to communicate, and he hated the very thought of writing down anything that might fall into unfriendly hands.

Unfortunately, there was no practical way—or plausible pretext—for Lady Swayle to journey all the way to the Duchy of Rock Coast at this time of year. Or the other way around, either. True, she and Rock Coast were first cousins. But only the most pressing emergency could justify a sixteen-hundred-mile journey by road through the ice, snow, and sleet of a typical Chisholmian April. Simply visiting a kinsman, however much one might love the kinsman in question, scarcely constituted that sort of emergency. And given the long-standing tension between Rock Coast and the Crown—and the fact that Colonel Barkyr Rahskail, Rebkah's husband and the recently deceased Earl of Swayle, had been executed for treason—any open contact between Rock Coast Keep and Swayleton was dangerous.

The problem was that Mahrtynsyn knew too much about what the Inquisition could do with written messages, however well encoded they might be, to be happy about having *them* traveling back and forth, either. It was true that the Inquisition had more experience dealing with ciphers and codes than almost anyone else. It was also true, however, that the heretics' spies seemed to be even better than Mother Church's. The possibility that they owed their efficiency to demonic intervention couldn't be overlooked. Yet troubling and frightening as that thought was, and dire as the religious implications might be, it was the practical consequences which concerned him most.

And there was also the not so minor concern that if Rock Coast wasn't noted for subtlety or thinking things through, the same could be reasonably said of his cousin. Lady Swayle hated Sharleyan Tayt Ahrmahk and her husband with every fiber of her being, and while Rock Coast was a man of faith, the countess went beyond simple faith to a zealotry even Mahrtynsyn found worrisome. The service of God required the exercise of intelligence, not simple, unthinking fervor. That was something the Inquisition understood, and just as Mahrtynsyn had been tasked with restraining Rock Coast's enthusiasm, Father Zhordyn Rydach had the unenviable task of moderating Lady Swayle's. The fact that he'd succeeded was greatly to his credit, but it seemed that having once put the brakes on Rebkah Rahskail's impulsiveness, Rydach was understandably hesitant about encouraging her to give anything that might be construed as a blank credit draft to her headstrong cousin.

But in this instance, the Duke's right and Zhordyn's wrong, Mahrtynsyn thought. *If we're going to move forward with any real chance of success, it's time for everyone to put his or her cards on the table and start making some firm commitments and hard plans.*

He didn't really like that conclusion, yet this was a moment he'd always known would come . . . just as he'd always known it would be one of the most dangerous moments of his entire mission to Chisholm.

"Your Grace," he said finally, "I understand what you're saying, and I share your concerns. More than that, I agree it's essential we . . . solidify your plans as soon as possible, in order to be ready the instant General Kahlyns sends Duke Eastshare's reinforcements out of the Kingdom. If there were any way for you and Lady Swayle to meet face-to-face without drawing unwelcome attention, that would clearly be the ideal solution. Unfortunately, I can't think of one. Can you?"

"No," Rock Coast growled.

"In that case, we're left with the danger involved in written messages, and I understand exactly why the Countess and Father Zhordyn are hesitant to write down anything that might fall into the heretics' hands. Perhaps I might serve as your communication link? I'm far less visible than you or Lady Swayle, so finding some pretext for me to make the journey to Swayleton, to serve as your personal messenger, would probably be feasible. There'd still be *some* risk, of course, but I could bring back oral answers to any questions you might wish to pose, and she and Father Zhordyn might well be the more comfortable with that."

"Father," Rock Coast said in a much warmer tone, "I'd trust you implicitly as my messenger—and my representative and advocate, for that matter. But I'm not the only one involved, and simply knowing what *they* intend isn't sufficient. We need to put together a complete plan, one that orchestrates their efforts and ours into a single strategy instead of going off in our own separate directions and inadvertently getting in each other's ways. Or even working at cross purposes because we didn't know what they meant to do. A lot of the pieces of any strategy will have to be *executed* independently, if only because of the distances involved, but they have to be *coordinated*. And they also have to be executed *simultaneously*, because success will depend on achieving our initial objectives quickly, before the other side can react. A lot of our longer term planning will depend on how well the initial stage goes, and once we've established a firm base of control in this part of the Kingdom and our initial success begins attracting more supporters, we'll have more flexible options going forward. The situation will be in a state of flux at that stage, as well, with both the opportunities and the threats changing rapidly, so it would actually be a mistake to try to make definitive plans—tactical plans, at least; we need full agreement on the ultimate outcome of all this—beyond that point. The problem's *getting* to that point, and that requires us to discuss what we're doing. Not just agree to cooperate, but agree on *how* to cooperate. And that's going to require two-way communication."

He shook his head and looked back out into the rain.

"I'm afraid it would be difficult for you to carry sufficient of the details for that level of communication in your memory, Father. I'm eternally grateful that you're willing to undertake the journey, but what we really need is a way to exchange those very written messages—*plural,* I'm sorry to say—that we both wish weren't necessary. And, that being the case, I'd prefer not to risk you as a simple courier. I have reliable men who could take care of that for me, and my relationship with Rebkah's close enough that exchanges of written messages, even at this time of year, wouldn't seem too noteworthy. For that matter, once she's agreed, we won't need couriers; we can use messenger wyverns. *If* she's willing to correspond with me at all."

He did not, Mahrtynsyn noted, say, "If you can convince that infuriatingly overcautious priest to *let* her correspond with me." The thought had come through pretty clearly, though, and the duke proceeded to make it even clearer.

"What I need from you, I think, is your support in urging her—and Father Zhordyn—to give me confirmation of what she's prepared to do or not do, and when, and how her 'negotiations' with Holy Tree—and Mandigora, assuming she really is talking to him—are proceeding. I need that sort of information as an absolute bare minimum, and I also need to know what *she* knows about what's happening in Maikelberg. Despite what happened to Barkah, she still has better contacts there than I do, to be honest." The duke shrugged. "But in addition to all that, we've got to concert our plans on when and how we'll strike."

Mahrtynsyn contemplated what the duke had just said glumly, wishing he could disagree with any of it. Unfortunately. . . .

"Very well, Your Grace," he sighed. "I can't pretend I'm happy about the necessity, but I can't deny that it *is* a necessity. Choose your courier. I'll draft a message to Father Zhordyn and, once you've approved it, I'll put it into cipher."

▼　▼　▼

Well, how very good of you, Father, Nimue Chwaeriau thought.

At the moment, she was standing post outside the Manchyr Palace nursery while the ruling Prince of Corisande, his First Councilor, and the head of his Regency Council spent an hour or so admiring their niece and nephew and godchildren, respectively.

Prince Daivyn still seemed a little in two minds about the twins' durability. The very thought of holding one of them was enough to induce something very like a panic attack, although he'd summoned all his will and courageously allowed his sister to place his nephew in his lap once he was safely seated in an outsized chair where he'd find it difficult to drop a baby on its head with no doubt fatal consequences. Then he'd sat absolutely motionless, obviously afraid that if he breathed, young Hektor would somehow spontaneously explode.

Nimue found that rather touching. Possibly that was because she'd had a somewhat similar initial reaction. The citizens of the Terran Federation had stopped producing children by the time Nimue Alban was a teenager, so she'd had very little experience with infants.

Earl Coris and Earl Anvil Rock, on the other hand, were old hands at dealing with babies and the sometimes interesting contents of their diapers. As she stood outside the nursery door, the head of the Regency Council was busily singing a lullaby—badly—to Prince Hektor Merlin Haarahld Aplyn-Ahrmahk while the aforesaid prince complained loudly about the universe's state of affairs and the princedom's first councilor helped his mother change Princess Raichynda Sharleyan Nimue Aplyn-Ahrmahk's diaper.

It was, perhaps, as well that none of Prince Daivyn's more dignified great nobles were present to observe the disgraceful spectacle.

Nimue fully intended to do her own singing—and burping, and even diaper changing—later that evening. For now, her attention was split between her bodyguard responsibilities and the SNARC imagery which had just been automatically downloaded to her. Owl and Nahrmahn were undoubtedly studying the same data at the same moment, but Nimue liked to be hands-on, and she'd programmed the SNARC remotes watching over Rock Coast Keep to alert her when their filters picked up certain keywords or phrases.

Looks like it's time for the "seijin network" in Chisholm to report in to White Crag and Sir Ahlber, she reflected. *If Mahrtynsyn's really ready to start writing things down, it would be churlish of us not to allow him to share his literary efforts with us. Besides, I want to check in with Lady Karyl and see how she and her new armsmen are getting along.*

Now how do we account for Captain Chwaeriau's absence this time . . . ?

.X.
HMS *Gwylym Manthyr,*
City of Tellesberg,
Kingdom of Old Charis,
Empire of Charis.

W
ell, Zhames?" Halcom Bahrns raised his eyebrows at Lieutenant Commander Zhames Skaht, his chief engineer.

"As well as it's going to get, Sir," Skaht replied cheerfully.

At fifty-one, he was seventeen years older than his CO, and he'd been a naval officer for barely a year. Normally, that would be far, *far* too little "time in grade" for his rank, far less his position in *Gwylym Manthyr's* command structure. Yet the very brevity of his naval service was precisely what accounted for that position . . . and for his captain's confidence in him. What he'd been instead of an officer in the Crown's service was a master artificer in Ehdwyrd Howsmyn's employ. He understood the machinery aboard *Gwylym Manthyr* better than any naval officer who'd grown up with galleys or galleons possibly could. He'd helped *design* it, and the engineering "officers" assigned to the other *King Haarahlds* had very similar pedigrees.

Knowing that was an immense comfort to Halcom Bahrns as he contemplated the task before them. But what truly mattered to him at this moment was that if Zhames Skaht thought his ship was ready for service, then—mechanically, at least—she damned well was.

And we're going to be making the rest of it up as we go along, he thought, then snorted. *Nothing new there! We did exactly the same thing with* Delthak *. . . although, she* was *just a tiny bit smaller—by no more than, oh, twelve, thirteen thousand tons or so.*

He sat back in his chair in his enormous day cabin—*everything* aboard his new ship seemed built on a stupendous scale to someone who'd first gone to sea in the cramped confines of an old-fashioned galley—smoking his pipe and gazing out the open scuttle at the gaslit Tellesberg docks, while he considered the task he and his officers and men still faced.

There were seven hundred of those officers and men, and all of them were still in the process of learning their jobs. Fortunately, his gunners had been thoroughly trained on the complexities of their new mounts in the shore establishment Duke Delthak and Baron Rock Point had established. The Urvyn Mahndrayn School of Gunnery was the very first formal school ever established to teach the art of gunnery ashore. That wasn't the same thing as training at sea, with the ship moving under them, but the "art of gunnery" had changed far too fundamentally to be taught "on the job" any longer . . . and *Manthyr* was going to be a hell of a lot steadier gun platform than any other ship in the world.

In fact, he was completely satisfied with his people's training, even though the notion of acquiring that training in special schools was as revolutionary as anything else the Imperial Charisian Navy had embraced in the last decade. It was just that there was a difference between individually trained seamen, stokers, gunners, and oilers—however *well*-trained they might be—and a crew which had been thoroughly worked up as a unit.

Don't borrow trouble, he told himself. *Sea officers have been combining gaggles of experienced seamen,* inexperienced *seamen—and* landsmen—*into actual* crews *for as long as there've* been *sea officers. Not a lot of difference there. Well, aside from the fact that you're about to deploy the next damned best thing to fourteen thousand miles and still get only five five-days of training time out of the entire voyage! Hardly seems fair, somehow.*

He snorted again, then blew a smoke ring towards the overhead. He watched it drift upwards, then looked back at Skaht.

"Well, in that case, I suppose I should tell the High Admiral we're ready to leave, shouldn't I?"

▼　　▼　　▼

My God, that's a beautiful ship, Sharleyan Ahrmahk thought as she descended from the carriage into the golden flare of trumpets and the massed, deafening thunder of her waiting subjects. She started down the double line of saluting Imperial Guardsmen towards the waiting platform, Edwyrd Seahamper at her heels even here, but her eyes clung to the ship lying to a single anchor off the Tellesberg seafront, and she knew she'd never seen a more magnificent vessel.

It was true, although *Gwylym Manthyr's* beauty was quite different from that of the galleys which had preceded her or the galleons dwarfed by her stupendous presence. It was an angular, severe beauty—rearing out of the water like a floating cliff. Or like an island crowned by fortress walls and towers. Her single mast thrust up with only one yard, intended solely to display signal flags, not to carry canvas. The fat pod of the lookout's position was over a hundred feet above water level, and her funnels rose with the clean, arrogant severity of a great dragon's spinal plates. Unlike the traditional stark black of the ICN's galleons or the earlier ironclads, her hull and gunshields were painted a dark blue gray while her upperworks and funnels were painted in what Ahlfryd Hyndryk and Ehdwyrd Howsmyn called "haze gray," although the funnel caps and her mast were an unrelieved black. Probably because that was the color her funnel smoke was going to leave them anyway, in the end.

The guns in her barbettes, thrusting from her casemates, or in their shielded deck mounts promised unyielding death and destruction, yet they, too, had their own beauty—the beauty of function, of purpose. And so did her long, graceful sheer, the sharply raked prow and flared bows, the way she sat in the water, a living creature in her own element.

The Tellesberg sky was a blue dome bounded by dramatic banks of cumulus cloud. They piled against the southern and eastern horizons, rolling slowly, almost imperceptibly to the northwest, brilliant white above and shadowed gray below. The harbor's seabirds and wyverns rode the breeze, calling to one another, diving for particularly tempting bits of flotsam, and small craft bobbed around the waiting warship, keeping a respectful distance and yet somehow like the harbor's winged citizens.

Twin columns of smoke rose from *Gwylym Manthyr*'s funnels, and steam plumed white against it as relief valves vented. She was ready—eager—to go, Sharleyan thought as she ascended the platform's steps.

Makel Staynair, his brother, and Halcom Bahrns—the last two in dress uniform, dress swords at their sides—were already there. They bowed profoundly to her, and then it was her turn to kiss the archbishop's ring.

She straightened, turning to face the crowd that packed the waterfront, and stillness radiated out from the platform as the spectators closer to it shouted for those farther from it to be still and listen.

She let that stillness settle, then held out one hand to Syaynair.

"If you would, Your Grace," she said into the stillness, and the archbishop moved forward to stand beside her and raised his hands.

"Let us pray," he said, and a stir rippled through the crowd as caps were remove and heads were bowed.

"Oh God," he said then, his voice rising clear and clean against the sound of the wind, the pop of the platform's banners, the distant cries of gulls and wyverns, "we come to You this day to ask Your blessing upon this ship, upon her crew, and upon her mission. We know how You must weep to see Your children shed the blood of any of Your other children, yet we also know You understand the test to which we have been called. You know the task before us, and we thank You for having been with us so far, walked at our side in our battle for survival, our struggle to serve Your will as You've given us to understand it and to defend those who the corrupt, vile men in Zion would torture and murder in Your name, just as they tortured and murdered the man for whom this ship is named. We ask You to walk with us for the rest of our journey, as well, and we beseech You to keep, guard, guide, and protect these, *our* protectors, in the five-days and months to come. Be with them in the furnace, give them victory, and grant that—*in* that victory—they do not forget that even their mortal foes are also Your children and *our* brothers. Let no unnecessary bloodshed, no cruelty, mar their actions, and preserve them from the hatred that can poison even the cleanest soul. We ask this as You have taught us to ask, trusting in Your goodness as we would trust in the love of any father. Amen."

"Amen!" the response came back from the crowded quay and the streets behind it like a grumble of thunder, and Sharleyan took one more stride forward, resting her hands on the platform's flag-draped railing, while hats and caps were replaced amid a brief, fresh susurration of conversation. But that conversation faded quickly as all eyes turned attentively, expectantly, towards her. She let the stillness settle once more, let the anticipation build—waited until the vast crowd was ready—and then squared her shoulders.

"Charisians!"

Her voice was far sweeter—and lighter—than Maikel Staynair's. Yet it had been trained from childhood for moments just like this one and it rang out with astonishing clarity. Even so, those farthest from her couldn't possibly hope to hear her. The crowd which had come to witness *Gwylym Manthyr's* sailing stretched for hundreds of yards along the waterfront, thrust tendrils up the approach streets. No one's voice could have carried to its fringes, but the highly trained priests and lay brothers the archbishop had seeded throughout it were prepared to relay her words to those distant ears. She would have to time her delivery, leave spaces for those repetitions, but that, too, was something in which she'd been trained since girlhood.

"Charisians!" she repeated. "Three and a half years ago, four ships of the Imperial Charisian Navy fought to the death against impossible odds. Crippled by storm damage, facing a squadron—a *fleet*—which outnumbered them many times over, they chose not to surrender unharmed, but to *fight*. To fight against those impossible odds to protect their undamaged consorts who might yet avoid destruction . . . but only if those four ships fought and died to buy them the time they needed. And so those ships fought—fought just as *every* ship in our Navy fights to protect *every* Charisian, every child of God who defies the savagery and the arrogance and the ambition of the men who have perverted all Mother Church means and is."

She paused to let her words be repeated . . . and to let them sink in.

"We've remembered those ships in memorial masses every Wednesday in each month of September since that day . . . and we will remember them in every September to come. We will remember HMS *Rock Point*, HMS *Damsel*, HMS *Avalanche*, and—especially!—HMS *Dancer* for as long as there is a Charisian Navy, a Charisian Empire, and a Church of Charis, because the men aboard those ships—your brothers, your husbands, your fathers, your *sons*—fought for *us*, for every single one of us. And when they'd fought their ships into sinking wrecks, when three-quarters of them had fallen in combat against an entire *fleet*, the wounded, bleeding survivors surrendered honorably to their foes."

She paused once again, waiting while the repeaters relayed her words, and her voice was hard when she resumed.

"Yes, they surrendered . . . but their captors ignored the very laws recorded in the *Holy Writ* to prescribe the treatment of prioners taken in open combat, captured in time of war. They were treated as *criminals*—as *worse* than criminals—and after they'd surrendered, after they'd been denied the rights and protections the *Writ* itself guarantees to prisoners of war, after they'd spent a bitter winter in captivity aboard prison hulks in Gorath Bay—denied winter clothing, blankets, an adequate diet, or even minimal healers' care on the direct orders of the Intendant of Dohlar—after a quarter of them had died, the survivors of *that* ordeal were delivered into the hands of the butcher who calls himself Mother Church's Grand Inquisitor. They were delivered to Zion, where three-quarters—*more* than three-quarters—of those who'd managed to survive that far were brutally tortured to death. Where the pitiful handful who'd survived battle, survived cold, survived starvation and illness and exposure, survived the brutality of their journey to Zion, survived even the Inquisition's savage torture, were given to the Punishment—*burned* to death, after all else they had suffered. And lest they denounce their torturers, lest they proclaim the *truth* of why they'd fought and of what had been done to them, their tongues were cut out before they faced the flame!"

She paused once again, and her eyes were brown fire as the distant voices of the repeaters came through the ringing silence. A silence so deep, so profound the distant cries of gulls and wyverns came clearly through its crystal heart.

"*That* is why we remember them," she said then, and even her superbly trained voice wavered around the edges, frayed by remembered pain and present grief while tears blurred her vision. "That is why *I* remember them. Why I will tell my daughter the story of their courage, of their devotion, of their *sacrifice*. Why I will teach her to never—*ever*—forget what those husbands, brothers, fathers, and sons did for each and every one of us."

Again, the repeaters carried her words to the farthest fringes of the crowd, and here and there in that vast stillness single voices were raised in agreement. She waited until they'd faded, and when she spoke again, the tears in her voice had become steel.

"And that is why we will never forget or forgive what was done *to* them," she told her subjects. "There is a price for what was inflicted upon them, what they suffered. A penalty for those who would turn their hands to such acts—who would *acquiesce* in them! A penalty which goes beyond simple vengeance for those we've lost, those who have been so foully and brutally murdered. One which goes even beyond *justice*. A penalty which will serve not simply to avenge them, but to teach the world that no one will ever—*ever!*—torture and murder Charisian subjects with impunity. That there will be a *reckoning* for anyone who would commit such actions. That the Empire of Charis will come for them—that we will *always* come for them, whoever they may be, wherever they may hide—and that we will not rest until they pay for their actions. The men who ordered and carried out the Ferayd Massacre have already learned that lesson; the inquisitors with the Group of Four's armies have learned that lesson; now the time has come for those in Gorath who supinely yielded our sailors, our Marines—our brothers, fathers, and sons—to the Butcher of Zion to learn it. And, in the fullness of time, *Zhaspahr Clyntahn* will learn it!"

The shouts of agreement were sharp-clawed with anger this time. There weren't very many, and yet the fury in them swelled like the sea. They were the first tremors, the earthquake's precursor shocks, and they cut off instantly when she leaned over the rail towards her audience once more.

"Every one of you knows what's happened in the Gulf of Dohlar since the Battle of the Kaudzhu Narrows," she told them. "You know that *this time*, our Navy rescued the men who'd been destined for murder in Zion. You know Earl Sharpfield, Baron Sarmouth, Admiral Zhaztro have *annihilated* the squadron which hurt us so badly in the Narrows. And you know that now—today—*this* ship—" she thrust out an arm, pointing at the enormous vessel floating in the harbor behind her "—departs for the Gulf, as well. Departs to join Earl Sharpfield and Baron Sarmouth. She will make that voyage in less than *one month*, and when she arrives, they will move against the Kingdom of Dohlar itself.

"Charisians, there's a *reason* this ship bears the name she does! There's a reason she will be our Navy's spearhead—and the hammer that reduces the City of Gorath's walls to *rubble*. There's a reason her very name will *terrify* Zhaspahr Clyntahn and every single one of his butchers!

"My friends—my brothers and my sisters—" tears fogged her voice and she could barely see, yet somehow her words rang clear, each one of them forged of steel and fire, of grief and pride, and of the fierce, unyielding purpose which made Sharleyan Ahrmahk—and the people of Charis—what they were "—the murderers who tortured and killed our people, our friends, our warriors and protectors, may have cut out their tongues. They may have silenced them before the hour of their deaths. But today—*today*—we give them back their voices! Gwylym Manthyr will speak again in Gorath, and the words we will give him—the words he will deliver for us, and for himself, and for his men—will echo far beyond Gorath, far beyond the borders of Dohlar. They will echo in Zion itself, within the walls of the very Temple of God! And the men who hear the thunder of those words will know the day is coming very soon when, as God is our witness, we will come for *them*, as well!"

The earthquake broke free at last. It rose above the city of Tellesberg, and it was the voice not just of a crowd, not just of a city, but of an *empire*. Of an entire realm—a *people*—for whom she'd found the words, the promise, to speak not just what was in their hearts, but what was in their *souls*.

By rights, Zhaspahr Clyntahn should have heard that fierce, hungry, *implacable* roar even in Zion.

.XI.
Seventy-Foot Hill,
Cahrswyl's Farm Road,
Duchy of Thorast,
Kingdom of Dohlar.

Sweet Bédard. If I didn't see it with my own eyes, I wouldn't believe it!" Rohsyndo Mylyndyz said almost prayerfully.

"See what?" Corporal Ahskar Mahkgyl, section leader of 4th Platoon's first section, demanded irritably. No one was shooting at them for the moment, and the corporal had been hunkered down in his lizardhole—what the Imperial Charisian Army would have called a "foxhole"—trying to gnaw his way through a particularly well petrified piece of hardtack. So far, success had eluded him.

"That."

Mylyndyz pointed down the southwestern slope of the hill upon and around which 2nd Company of Colonel Mahryahno Hyrtatho's sadly battered infantry regiment was dug in. Mahkgyl sat up in his lizardhole and shaded his eyes against the steadily setting sun with a filthy hand as his gaze followed the private's pointing hand. He squinted against the brilliant horizon for a moment, and then his eyes widened.

"Schueler's bones," he muttered. "I see it and I *still* don't believe it! How in Shan-wei's name did he manage *that*?"

"I don't know, but I'm sure as hell not going to complain!" Mylyndyz replied almost prayerfully.

"For a worthless city boy from Gorath, you do get it right once in a while," Mahkgyl told him.

The hill was scarcely a towering mountain—according to the maps, its crest rose a whole seventy feet above its surroundings, although Mahkgyl figured that was an exaggeration—but it passed for a commanding height in these parts. The hill three miles to the northwest, where Wahlys Sahndyrsyn's 4th Company was dug in, was half again as tall, but despite its less lofty height, "Seventy-Foot Hill" was actually the steeper of the two.

Now Mahkgyl and Mylyndyz watched the black silhouettes of the eight-man party struggling up the slope. The silhouette at its head was huge, at least six feet tall, and wore the kilt of a Salthar mountaineer. There was only one man that size in 2nd Company, and the kilt was a dead giveaway of his identity. Besides, there was also only one man in the entire company who could have organized the miracle they saw approaching them.

It took that miracle quite a while to arrive, since the hill's western face was even steeper than the eastern side. That was unfortunate for several reasons, the biggest of which was the little matter of who lay hidden beyond the scrub woods on the eastern side . . . and who'd made three determined attempts in the last two days to come up *that* side of the hill. Several dozen of those who'd made those unsuccessful attempts still lay out on the slope, stiff and stark, and the sickly smell of decay wafted up the hill on the gentle easterly breeze. From behind the hill, an occasional salvo of angle-gun shells landed in those woods at random intervals. Not because any heretics were visible at the moment, but to discourage them from massing for yet another attack.

Mahkgyl had his doubts about how effective that would be if the heretics decided to make another serious try, especially since they seemed willing enough to put snipers into the woods, despite the harassing fire. On the other hand, it sure as Shan-wei couldn't hurt!

Second Company—and, in particular, 4th Platoon—was here to keep the road from Cahrswyl's Farm to the Saiksyn Farm open, although calling that sandy, unpaved country track—suitable (barely) for farm wagons—a "road" was a bit of a stretch. That unprepossessing dirt lane had acquired an importance far beyond its grubby appearance, however, when the heretic advance cut the high road between Bryxtyn and Waymeet eight days ago. Scuttlebutt had it that in the last five-day they'd also taken the town of Mahrakton, thirty-plus miles northwest of Bryxtyn *and* cut the Sairhalk Switch Canal south of Waymeet, as well. That made the miserable strip of dirt running up the southern end of 4th Platoon's hill the only lateral connection north of Kettle Bottom Swamp between the Waymeet-Fronzport High Road and the Bryxtyn-Shan High Road, and if the heretics really were sweeping around the fortresses' flanks. . . .

Neither Mahkgyl nor Mylyndyz really liked to think about that, although it did explain their present position. Colonel Mahryahno Hyrtatho's regiment had been ordered to dig in hard to hold the road. It had done just that for the last three days, and at least the heretics in front of it seemed almost as exhausted as its men were. Unless Mahkgyl missed his guess, the heretics were moving up fresh troops beyond those damned woods, though. In theory, an entire fresh regiment was on its way to relieve Hyrtatho's Regiment, as well, but Ahskar Mahkgyl would believe that when he saw it.

In the meantime, half the regiment was deployed farther north along the road, leaving 2nd Company to hold Seventy-Foot Hill while Captain Tybahld Hwairta's 1st Company and Captain Daivyn Sebahstean's 3rd Company held Cahrswyl's Farm and anchored Hyrtatho's right flank. Their companies were even more understrength than 2nd Company, which was why they'd been brigaded together under Captain Hwairta to hold the farm. Well, the fact that Captain Sebahstean had been carried to the rear on a stretcher before the sixty remaining men of his command were handed over to Hwairta probably had a little to do with it, as well, Not that 2nd Company was in much better shape; 4th Platoon was down six of its thirty-seven men, but that still made it 2nd Company's strongest platoon. In fact, Hyrtatho's entire regiment had been badly mauled during its fighting withdrawal from the Stryklyr's Farm–Atlyn line.

General Rychtyr had fought hard to hold that line, the last strong position before the Dohlaran border, but the heretic engineers had blown a path through the obstacles directly along the canal bed under cover of their damnable artillery. Then a Siddarmarkian assault had carried the breach while a simultaneous flanking attack by mounted Charisian infantry and a regiment of Siddarmarkian dragoons curled around Atlyn. With its front broken and its right flank crumbling, the Army of the Seridahn had been forced to give ground yet again, falling back for forty miles into the Duchy of Thorast— onto *Dohlaran* soil for the first time in the Jihad—until it had managed to stand once more.

It would have helped if the new "line" offered better defensive terrain, but the need to hold the connection between the high roads into Bryxtyn and Waymeet left the general no option but to hold here. If the heretics took the two fortresses, they could advance up either high road far more readily than they could using country roads like the one 2nd Company was charged with protecting. They'd be out of the straitjacket to which the Army of the Seridahn's slow, stubborn retreat had so far confined them, with all sorts of maneuver advantages they hadn't had before.

That would be . . . bad.

But however well Mahkgyl and Mylyndyz grasped the reasons they were stuck on their miserable hill, it struck them as grossly unfair that the detail struggling up its steepest side couldn't use the road they were guarding. It would have offered a much easier ascent, but the heretic snipers still floating about in the scrubby, tangled trees to the east had shown a nasty tendency to take the road under fire at unpredictable intervals. True, the light wasn't very good, even for heretic snipers, and it was getting worse rapidly. There hadn't been any firing anywhere along 2nd Company's line for the last couple of hours, for that matter, and Mahkgyl and Mylyndyz had watched a mounted courier gallop by without drawing so much as a single shot less than thirty minutes ago. Maybe the harassing artillery fire was actually working for a change. On the other hand, the fact that they weren't firing at the moment didn't mean they weren't lying there, watching the road over their rifle sights, waiting for a richer prize . . . like a group the size of the one picking its way up from the west.

It took the eight-man detail over twenty-five minutes to climb what wasn't a particularly high hill, but only partly because of its steepness. The four large, covered kettles suspended from the shoulder-carried poles at the center of the detail accounted for most of the delay. And given what they were almost certain those kettles contained, Mahkgyl and Mylyndyz approved wholeheartedly of their fellows' disinclination to spill them.

The sun had disappeared below the horizon and dusk was setting in by the time they reached the top of the hill, crossed its highest point, and clambered cautiously down to 1st Section's lizardholes. The first pale stars showed in the eastern sky, but the sky to the west still glowed, and Mahkgyl was careful not to silhouette himself against it as he greeted the man at the small column's head.

"When you said you were gonna see about some food, I thought you meant more of *this* crap, Sarge," he said, waving his gnawed-at bit of hardtack at the kilted giant. "I didn't realize you meant like . . . well, like *food* food!"

"Listen, boyo," Brahdryk Clahrksyn, 4th Platoon's senior noncom, had the deep, rolling accent to go with his kilt, "I'm a man of my word. Remember when you saved my life last five-day? Well, I swore I'd pay you back, didn't I?"

"Yeah, you did." Mahkgyl loosened the retaining clip on one of the kettles, lifted the lid, and inhaled deeply. "Oh, Sondheim, that smells good!" He replaced the lid as carefully as he'd loosened it and looked back at Clahrksyn. "Sarge, you've done a hell of a lot more'n just pay me back! Not quite ready to take a bullet fer you, but I might take a chance on throwing back a hand-bomb for you!"

Clahrksyn grinned.

"Hah! I expect this gratitude'll last *just* about until the next time I need someone to dig latrines."

"Maybe even four or five minutes longer," Mahkgyl said solemnly.

"I'm deeply touched," Clahrksyn told him, then nodded to the members of his detail, who were still breathing heavily after their climb. "Take it on to the CP and start organizing a chow line," he told them. "I'll be along in a minute."

"Gotcha, Sarge," a corporal Mahkgyl and Mylyndyz didn't know, with a quartermaster's armband, replied. "And don't forget, I need these kettles back!" He chuckled. "If I *don't* get them back, it's gonna take a lot more'n one bottle of booze to make Lieutenant Tuhtyl happy with us!"

"Complaints, complaints!" Clahrksyn shook his head. "First, it was *good* booze. And, second, I promised we'd get your kettles back. What's the matter, you don't trust m—"

The 4.5" mortar bomb which burst almost directly above Clahrksyn's head had a lethal zone ninety feet in diameter. Mylyndyz and two of the quartermaster detail actually survived it.

▼   ▼   ▼

Captain Hovsep Zohannsyn slid his watch back into his pocket and cocked the flare pistol's hammer. Fourth Company's platoons had been briefed to follow the short, savage mortar bombardment as closely as possible, but he'd commanded the company for almost two years now. None of *his* men were going to charge into that holocaust until Hovsep Zohannsyn was certain it was over. If the support companies were their usual, efficient selves, the bombardment would end exactly when it was supposed to. That didn't always happen, though, and the captain watched the explosions walking back and forth across the hilltop.

The last light in the western sky was fading quickly, and he grimaced in mingled satisfaction and unhappiness. Night attacks were a perfect recipe for confusion, chaos, and loss of tactical control, which accounted for his unhappiness. That was true for the defender, as well as the attacker, however, and the Imperial Charisian Army—and, especially, the Army of Thesmar—had made night attacks a specialty, with a tactical doctrine far better suited to that sort of chaotic encounter than almost anyone else's. Fourth Company's attempt to take the hill in daylight had failed painfully, but the Dohlarans dug in along its military crest hadn't yet had time to do the sort of thorough job the Army of Thesmar had come to dread, and Zohannsyn was fully in favor of not giving them that time. If this worked half as well as Major Edmyndsyn expected it to—or *said* he expected it to, anyway—then—

The torrent of explosions and air bursts stopped abruptly. Not instantly, of course. A half-dozen tardy antipersonnel bombs burst in midair, pounding the hilltop with a final downpour of shrapnel. But then there was silence while the vast pall of dust and smoke spilled upwards to blot away the newborn stars.

Zhohannsyn counted slowly to ten, waiting to see if any additional laggards would happen along. Then he squeezed the trigger.

▼   ▼   ▼

"Where the hell is Clahrksyn?!" Lieutenant Ahmbrohs Tyrnyr shouted, trying to make himself heard through the rolling thunder as he crouched in his
command post trench.

His CP was on the hill's reverse slope, the far side of its crest, and most
of the heretic angle-gun bombs were landing on its eastern slopes. Despite
that, dirt and debris pelted down all around him, and deeper, angrier explosions thundered behind him as the heretics far heavier angle-guns laid the
lash of their fire across the Dohlaran angles which had been harassing the
woods in 4th Platoon's front. He felt some of the airborne trash bouncing
from his steel helmet, and he coughed harshly as the dust and smoke caught
at the back of his throat.

"*What?!*" Sergeant Ahntohnyo Bahndairo shouted back, leaning closer
until his mouth was barely a foot from Tyrnyr's ear.

"I said, where the hell is—" Tyrnyr bawled, using his cupped hands as
a megaphone. And then, almost as abruptly as it had begun, the bombardment stopped.

"—Clahrksyn?!" he finished.

Bahndairo flinched a bit from the shout in his ear, and the sudden quiet
was almost more frightening than the explosions had been. It wasn't a *silence*, however. Bits and pieces of debris continued to patter down for a good
five seconds, and the screams of wounded men could be heard only too
clearly. Most of those screaming men were Tyrnyr's, and a pain that had
nothing to do with physical hurt went through the youthful lieutenant. But
there were other screams, as well, fainter, perhaps, but just as shrill and coming from the flanks of the hill, where the company's other platoons had
been hammered almost as brutally.

"Dunno where he is, Sir," Bahndairo said against that backdrop of wailing anguish. The sergeant was 4th Platoon's standard bearer, its second
ranking noncom. He and Brahdryk Clahrksyn were extremely close, and his
voice was harsh as he pulled back the hammer on his rifle and capped the
lock. "Said he was going to arrange some hot chow for the boys. Last I saw
of him, he was headed off to discuss that with Lieutenant Tuthyl." Despite
his tension, Bahndairo actually twitched a smile. "Took my last bottle of
rotgut with him when he went. Told me to tell you he'd be back in time for
supper. I think he figured if you didn't know what he was up to, you'd be
able to tell the Captain you didn't know a thing about any quartermaster
bribes if it happened as how he asked."

Tyrnyr snorted harshly. That sounded like the platoon sergeant.
Clahrksyn was the one who'd taught an ignorant young lieutenant how

important hot food really was, especially for men facing the energy-devouring terror of combat. And, in many ways, those "little comforts" civilians took for granted meant even more *between* bouts of combat for the same reason food was a traditional part of wakes and funerals. The simple act of eating was a sort of promise that life went on.

But now a much older and bitterly wiser lieutenant's face was stone as he listened to those screams and wondered how many more of his men had just discovered the falsity of that promise under the savage pounding of the heretics' portable angle-guns.

"Go find Captain Ahndairsyn," he told Bahndairo. "Tell him we got hit hard and we're damned well going to need reinforcement if the heretics follow up."

"You go, Sir," Bahndairo disagreed. "I'll take Hainz and go sort out—"

"You'll damned well go where I told you to go, Sergeant!" Tyrnyr snapped. "I need somebody I can count on to get it straight. And someone the Captain'll know knows what he's talking about! Besides, they may not even—"

A crimson flare burst in solitary splendor above the scrub woods on the far side of the road and Tyrnyr punched the sergeant savagely on the shoulder.

"*Go*, damn it!" he shouted.

Bahndairo looked back at him for a moment. The lieutenant could scarcely see him—the darkness was all but complete now, and the smoke and dust didn't help—but he knew what he'd have seen in the standard bearer's eyes if the light had been better. Bahndairo hesitated for one anguished second longer, listening to the pain sounds of the men of Tyrnyr's platoon. Then he nodded viciously.

"Yes, *Sir*," he grated, his voice ugly.

"Now!" the lieutenant snapped, and the noncom vaulted out of the trench and went racing towards the company CP.

Tyrnyr watched him go and smiled crookedly. He knew why Bahndairo's tone had been so harsh, because he'd learned the same illogical lesson.

He gazed after the sergeant he'd very probably just ordered to survive, then climbed out of the trench himself and beckoned to Corporal Hainz Dyrwynt. The fourteen men of Dyrwynt's section had been due to relieve Mahkgyl's in another four hours. Now it looked like they'd be doing that a bit earlier than scheduled.

"Let's go," Tyrnyr said flatly, and Dyrwynt's men climbed out of their individual lizardholes and started up and over the crest at his heels.

▼ ▼ ▼

Lieutenant Pyaitroh Ahldyrs came to his feet as Captain Zohannsyn's flare blossomed overhead. The men of his 1st Platoon had filtered very quietly forward through the stunted trees and scrubby undergrowth to the very edge of the Cahrswyl's Farm Road two hours earlier. They'd taken a half-dozen casualties in the process, but blind harassing fire was never as effective as it might look to the casual observer, and the fact that Dohlaran fuses remained less than fully reliable meant their antipersonnel air bursts tended to explode too high—or too low, after they'd already hit the ground. That had made it no less nerve-racking, however, and the signal flare came as a distinct relief. First Platoon was a veteran outfit. Its men weren't stupid enough to look forward to close combat, but if they had it to do, they'd just as soon get it done. Now, as their lieutenant stood, they climbed to their feet, as well, and Ahldyrs heard the quiet whisper of clicks as rifle safeties were released all around him. He drew his revolver, swung out the cylinder, and slid a cartridge into the chamber which normally rode empty under the hammer, and nodded to Platoon Sergeant Sahbahtyno.

"Let's go, Zhulyo," he said grimly.

▼　▼　▼

Rohsyndo Mylyndyz pushed his face up out of the dirt at the bottom of his lizardhole and made himself climb to his feet. He'd seen Mahkgyl go down, and he'd seen enough dead men over the last year to know he was now in charge of whatever remained of 1st Section.

That wasn't going to be a lot of men . . . and they weren't going to be alone on Seventy-Foot Hill for long.

"Stand to!" His voice sounded faint and frail even to his own ears after the cacophony of portable angle-gun bombs. "Count off and *stand to!*"

▼　▼　▼

Lieutenant Tyrnyr scrambled towards the crest of the hill, cursing the dark—and the dust and smoke—as he stumbled across the uneven terrain. There were lizardholes for his entire platoon on the eastern face of the hill, but they'd never been meant for permanent occupancy. Heretic infantry could call down portable angle-gun fire on any target it could see with hellish accuracy and the Royal Dohlaran Army had learned not to offer up any more targets to heretic artillery than it had to. He'd needed a picket on the east side of the crest line, far enough down the hill to be able to see the terrain at its base—and to avoid silhouetting itself against the sky—but the rest of the platoon had been safely dug in beyond the crest, waiting to come forward only when an actual attack was imminent.

His deployment had worked well against the three previous attacks. The section with the picket duty had been able to alert his reserve section and call it up to reinforce the defensive line well before the heretics had been able to cross the dead ground between the hill and the woodlot.

So you damned well should've expected them to try something different *next time!* he told himself savagely. *The one thing the heretics aren't is* stupid!

"Straight for your holes, boys!" he shouted to the troopers panting their way up and over the top with him. "Straight for your holes!"

Somebody actually gasped out an acknowledgment, and Tyrnyr grunted in satisfaction. They would have done that anyway, he knew. Each man had his own assigned lizardhole, the specific spot Tyrnyr and Clahrksyn had selected as part of their defense's mosaic, and they'd practiced getting to their positions until Clahrksyn had been satisfied they could do it in the dark, blindfolded. But they'd practiced without the screams and moans from 1st Section's wounded and dying men. The human need to stop to help ripped and torn comrades was a distraction they couldn't afford tonight.

Something inside the lieutenant cringed as he used the term "distraction," even if only in the privacy of his thoughts, but he went right on scrambling, steeling his own heart against what he knew he'd see on the way to his own lizardhole.

▼   ▼   ▼

First Platoon went up the hill like a silent, murderous tide. There was a time and a place for the Charisian warcry; this wasn't it.

Lieutenant Ahldyrs nodded in satisfaction as the first illuminating rounds plopped to brilliant light above the hill. He glanced to his left. Lieutenant Phylyp Claityn's 3rd Platoon had that flank of the attack, and he could just see Claityn's extreme right. Third Platoon was angling slightly away, bearing farther south to interpose between the base of Seventy-Foot Hill and Cahrswyl's Farm to intercept any counterattacks from the Dohlaran infantry dug in around the big stone farmhouse and its outbuildings. On the extreme right, Lieutenant Faidryko Vahalhkys' 4th Platoon was supposed to be cutting between Seventy-Foot Hill and Hundred-Foot Hill, three miles farther to the northwest. And Lieutenant Dahnahtelo Dragonsbane's 2nd Platoon, on Ahldyrs' immediate right, was already climbing up the hill as quickly and purposefully as his own men.

The scout snipers said there was only a single Dohlaran platoon on the hilltop itself, although there were what looked like two or three more platoons deployed to cover its base, especially to the north, where the road headed towards the Saiksyn Farm. That was 4th Platoon's worry at the moment, though, *Ahldyrs'* concern was the hilltop itself, and its defenders had handled the three previous attacks harshly.

Should've taken time to organize them properly, Ahldyrs thought, trying to make sure he didn't put his foot into a rabbit hole in the dark. *Bastards had time to get set before we hit 'em and we damned well know what dug-in rifle-*

men perched on a frigging hill can do to anyone stupid enough to come up it after them!

He was right . . . and he knew Aikymohto Mahkgavysk's 3rd Company had had no choice but to launch those attacks anyway. The Army of the Seridahn was finally out in the open, forced to give ground in dry weather and terrain that favored the ICA's mobility. The last thing Earl Hanth needed was to let Sir Fahstyr Rychtyr regain his balance, settle back into prepared defenses. Keeping him on the move, denying that chance to catch his breath, was worth taking a few chances . . . or losing a few men, however much it hurt.

But 3rd Company had carried the brunt of 4th Battalion's advance ever since the Dohlaran positions around Atlyn had collapsed. Mahkgavysk's casualties had been significant over that fifty-mile distance, so when the Dohlarans on that hill demonstrated that they meant to be difficult, Major Edmyndsyn had pulled 3rd Company back and given the job of clearing it to Captain Zohannsyn.

So now it's our *turn,* Ahldyrs told himself as he reached the base of the hill himself and started up it, fifteen yards behind his leading squad.

▼　　▼　　▼

Rifles began to flash and crack in the darkness as Lieutenant Tyrnyr slid into his waiting lizardhole. He doubted like hell that any of his riflemen could actually see what they thought they were shooting at, but they might be able to. And at least those barking rifle shots demonstrated that some of 1st Section's men were still alive and in action.

"*Give 'em hell, boys!*" he screamed. "Give 'em hell! Twenty minutes—we have to hold them for *twenty minutes!*"

He might as well have asked for twenty *years,* he told himself bitterly. The regimental reserve was supposed to reach 2nd Company's positions within twenty minutes of a serious heretic attack, but that was in daylight.

And when there are no Shan-wei-damned heretics in the way, he added bitterly as he heard a sudden outbreak of riflefire from his extreme left.

He stood upright in his lizardhole, craning his neck, and cursed viciously as the blinding *rakurai* of muzzle flashes swept across the roadway north of Seventy-Foot Hill. More riflefire flared and flashed farther down the hill, its deadly beauty marking the firing lines of 2nd Company's other platoons, but the heretics had already cut the road. Now that flank of their attack was wheeling *away* from the hill. The bastards were settling in between 2nd Company and the rest of the regiment, and—

Something sizzled past his left ear and he dropped back down into the hole, punching its side with a despairing fist. If the heretics succeeded in cutting that road, or even simply prevented the reserve from using it. . . .

▼　　▼　　▼

First Platoon swept up the slope in a grim, purposeful wave without firing a single shot to pinpoint its men in the dark.

Unlike any other army—even the RDA, which had become one of the best armies in Safeholdian history—the Imperial Charisian Army very seldom told its junior officers how to do their jobs. It trained them exhaustively, taught them a common doctrine, put them through the most demanding field problems it could come up with. But when it came to actually using that training, it told them *what* they were supposed to do, not *how*. They were responsible for understanding their superiors' intentions and then accomplishing them. In the process, they were supposed to think for themselves and be perfectly willing to adapt, improvise, and overcome as they went along, and those same expectations extended downward to their sergeants, corporals, and even privates.

That was why the ICA was prepared to attack even in darkness, when no other army could risk the loss of cohesion—the loss of *control*—night attacks entailed. Few of their opponents—not even Allayn Maigwair, who'd turned out to be a far better military thinker than anyone in Charis would have believed before the Charisians encountered the Army of God—truly understood that. To them, loss of control equaled chaos, and the Temple Guard had understood long before anyone ever heard of the Army of God that no organized force was ever outnumbered by a disorganized mob. But 1st Platoon, 4th Company, 8th Regiment, 4th Infantry Brigade, Imperial Charisian Army, *wasn't* disorganized. It was simply *decentralized* into its individual squads . . . and the farthest thing from a mob imaginable.

"Keep moving! *Keep moving!*" Corporal Zherald Tohmys bellowed as the blinding blink lizards of Dohlaran riflefire sparkled against the black backdrop of the hillside. He reached out, grabbed Haarahld Kyngsfyrd's web gear, and dragged the stumbling 3rd Squad private back up off his knees. "*Climb* the frigging hill, damn it! Don't *kiss* it!"

Ahead of him, the first grenades exploded.

▼　　▼　　▼

"On the left!" someone screamed. "*They're coming up on the—!*"

The warning died, turned into a keening wail of agony in the earshattering explosion of a heretic hand-bomb.

The hillside was a hellscape of darkness stabbed through by lightning bolts of riflefire, thunderclaps of grenades, shouts of warning, or command, or simple fury.

Second Platoon was dying, but it was dying hard, and Ahmbrohs Tyrnyr swung towards the warning shout, bringing up the revolver he'd taken from a dead heretic in a two-handed grip and cocking the hammer. He had only twenty cartridges for it, but while they lasted . . .

There! He saw movement, a shape silhouetted against the flickering glare of explosions and muzzle flashes. A shape that was moving, when every one of his men knew to stay put in his lizardhole in the dark—that the rest of the platoon would assume anyone who *wasn't* in his hole was a heretic.

The revolver roared, and he'd remembered the first rule of a firefight in the dark and closed his eyes the instant before the trigger broke to avoid the blinding eruption of his own muzzle flash. He opened them again, just as quickly, and saw another shape moving to the left of the first. Or maybe it *was* the first, and he'd missed. It didn't matter. He swung the muzzle, cocked the hammer, squeezed. The revolver thundered again, and he reopened his eyes, searching desperately for another target, knowing his muzzle flashes had marked his position for any heretic in the vicinity.

Something moved at the corner of his vision. He twisted towards it, bringing the revolver around, lifting the muzzle, and grunted in explosive agony as the fourteen-inch bayonet drove all the way through his left shoulder. He slammed back against the rear wall of his lizardhole and squeezed the trigger.

The range was less than three feet. The bullet struck its target with almost eight-hundred-foot-pounds of energy, and a deeper, more personal darkness smashed the lieutenant under as the man he'd just killed toppled into the lizardhole and a steel helmet hit him in the face like a piledriver.

.XII.
Army of the Seridahn HQ,
Kraisyr,
Duchy of Thorast,
Kingdom of Dohlar.

How bad is it, Fahstyr?" Pairaik Metzlyr's voice was very quiet. He stood with Sir Fahstyr Rychtyr, Colonel Ahskar Mohrtynsyn, and General Clyftyn Rahdgyrz in the office Rychtyr had appropriated from the town of Kraisyr's mayor, staring down at the map covering the mayor's desk. There was no one else in the office—at the moment—but urgent voices could be heard through its open door and no doubt another of the general's clerks would turn up momentarily with fresh tidings of disaster.

"I'm afraid it's about as bad as it gets, Father," Rychtyr said heavily.

He kept his own voice down, for the same reason his intendant had, but his gray eyes met Metzlyr's gaze without flinching. Then he straightened, running one hand through his graying, sandy hair and sighed.

"They've not only cut the road, they've taken both the Saiksyn Farm and Cahrswyl's Farm," he said, his worn face grim. "That gives them control of the road from Cahrswyl's to Kraisyr . . . and of the only solid ground between the road and the swamp." He shook his head. "I can't put the front back together, Father. Not before they cut the Waymeet-Fronzport High Road, anyway. And according to Brigadier Byrgair, their right flank's less than ten miles from the Bryxtyn-Shan High Road right now."

"It may be that close, Sir, but it hasn't reached the damned road yet," General Rahdgyrz rasped. The one-armed general's eyes—well, his *left* eye; the right one was covered by a black eye patch—was very dark in a lean, strong-nosed face.

"No, no it hasn't, Clyftyn," Rychtyr agreed, smiling at the tall, narrow-shouldered general whose long black hair spilled down his back in a thick, old-fashioned braid. That braid was matched by a flowing beard that covered his chest, as if a stained-glass *seijin* from the War Against the Fallen had returned to take up his sword once more, and the image was more than skin deep.

Rahdgyrz had become Rychtyr's ranking subordinate after Sir Ohtys Godwyl's death in a Charisian bombardment, and Rychtyr had been prayerfully grateful for him more than once since then. They'd known one another for twenty-five years, since long before the Jihad, and if there was a braver man in all the world—or one more fiercely devoted to Mother Church—Sir Fahstyr Rychtyr had never met him. Rahdgyrz had been one of the first to volunteer for the initial, disastrous naval campaign, and he'd lost his right leg five inches below the knee aboard the galley *Saint Taitys*, fighting under the Earl of Thirsk in the battle of Crag Reach. That would have been sacrifice enough for most, but not for Clyftyn Rahdgyrz, who'd returned to field service as soon as he'd adjusted to his peg leg. He'd bulled through every objection, pointing out that he could still ride as well as he ever had and a general had no business fighting on foot, anyway! He'd gotten his way—he generally did . . . and lost his left arm above the elbow under Sir Rainos Ahlverez at Alyksberg. He'd only been invalided for about three months that time, rejoining the field army before Thesmar just after Ahlverez marched off to Desnairian-engineered disaster in the Kyplyngyr Forest, and he'd fought like a great dragon when Hanth counterattacked out of Thesmar. And, as always seemed to happen, he'd been wounded yet again. This time, he'd been out of action for less than a month . . . but he'd returned to his command without the vision of his right eye.

And to Sir Fahstyr Rychtyr's knowledge, he'd never complained a single time about the wounds he'd sustained in God's service. There was a reason

Rychtyr's army called Clyftyn Rahdgyrz "the Slash Lizard," and the general had never failed him.

"The heretics haven't reached it yet," Rychtyr said now, "but they're damned close." He tapped the map with his forefinger. "Brynygair's brigade's done incredibly well to slow them as much as it has, and I know he's got some terrain to work with. But it's only a matter of time, and not much of that."

"I've already sent Gairwyl and Klunee to support Brynygair," Rahdgyrz said stubbornly, and it was his turn to tap the map with his remaining hand. "You're right about the terrain, too. I know the woods aren't all that thick, and most of the rivers are barely creeks, now that we're into summer. But the Chydor's still running deep, and Brynygair has the fords covered. Once Gairwyl, especially, closes up to the river, he'll squeeze every ounce of advantage out of anything he has to work with, and I can have two more regiments up to support them within . . . six hours, at the outside."

"I know you can—I know you would, and you'd be standing at their heads, sword in hand." Rychtyr squeezed the general's shoulder. "Just like I know your men would fight like dragons for you. But I need them—and *you*, you old slash lizard!—*alive*. I know every one of you would die in your tracks, but the best you could do would be to slow them down for *maybe* two days. Every hour more than that would require a separate miracle, and you know it."

"But—" Rahdgyrz began, his expression mulish, but Metzlyr raised a hand, and the general closed his mouth on whatever he'd been about to say.

"If you can't keep them from cutting the road, what do you intend to do now, Fahstyr?" The intendant laid one hand on Rychtyr's forearm. "I'm not trying to paint you into any corners, my son, and I know right now your thoughts have to be with your men. But I've come to know you pretty well, and I'm sure you were already thinking about your options in the face of this sort of disaster."

"There's only one thing we *can* do, Father," Rychtyr told him with bleak honesty. "We have to fall back, and not just a few miles this time. The terrain along the canal between Waymeet and Shandyr's too open, too flat, and the heretics are too mobile. For that matter, there are too many of these damned farm roads, and Langhorne knows their mounted infantry's too damned good at finding its way along them. I need to fall back far enough to build a defensible front again—probably between Duhnsmyr Forest and Kaiylee's Woods."

Metzlyr nodded in understanding, although his expression was deeply troubled. Rychtyr was talking about a sixty-mile retreat, and the thought of giving that much ground was . . . unpleasant.

But the general wasn't done yet.

"And," he added unflinchingly, "I need to evacuate Bryxtyn and Waymeet . . . assuming there's still time."

"*Evacuate?*" Rahdgyrz' eye widened. "Those are *fortresses*, Sir! We can't just hand them over to the heretics!"

"We can't keep the heretics from simply *taking* them anytime they decide to, Clyftyn," Rychtyr replied. "For that matter, they don't even need to take them. Waymeet blocks the junction of the Sheryl-Seridahn Canal and the Sairhalik Switch Canal, but now that the heretics have Canal Bank Farm—" he tapped another point on the map, thirty-five miles south of Waymeet "—they've already cut the Switch. Besides, they aren't using the damned canals now, anyway! Holding the city won't deprive them of any significant strategic or logistic advantage, and Bryxtyn isn't even on one of the canals. Yes, they're both fortresses, but they were designed against the old-style *Siddarmarkian* army, against someone without new model Charisian artillery or Charisian logistics. In terms of importance to the Jihad, they're really only names on a map now. But General Iglaisys has seven thousand men in Bryxtyn and General Symyngtyn has ten thousand in Waymeet. Between them, that's seventeen thousand, and we were down to barely *forty-five* thousand before the heretics' most recent attack. If we leave them where they are, they're useless to the Jihad. If Iglaisys and Symyngtyn pull back— if they *can* pull back, get out before the heretics cut the high roads behind them—they'll increase our available field force by almost forty percent." He shook his head. "Believe me, they'll be a lot more valuable to the Jihad in the field with us than sitting behind old-fashioned stone walls that won't last two five-days against Hanth's artillery."

"Sir, I swear we can *bleed* them before they cut the high road!" Rahdgyrz' tone was respectful, but his dismay was obvious and his expression was almost desperate. "You're right, my boys'll die where they stand if I ask 'em to! And if we can't stand and fight for major fortresses, where *can* we stand?"

"Clyftyn, we *will* fight—we *are* fighting," Rychtyr said. "A wise man doesn't pick a fight he can't win, though, and when they broke our front, they broke our lateral communications *behind* it. That means they can transfer forces, shift their weight, faster than we can. Shan-wei! They could do that *before*, given how many mounted infantry and dragoons have reinforced Hanth! They can just do it even faster now, and from Brynygair's dispatch, they'd started doing exactly that even before they cut the Cahrswyl's Farm Road."

Rychtyr shook his head, his eyes unhappy but his expression resolute.

"Yes, we can bleed them before they actually cut the high road. And with you in command on that flank, we could probably inflict a lot more casualties than we took, especially in that kind of terrain. But they have the men to *absorb* those casualties; we don't. It's that simple. And that's the very reason I need to pull those garrisons out, add them to our field strength. Our best guess is that Hanth has close to eighty thousand, maybe even ninety thousand men, and he's got more mounted strength than we do even proportionately, much less in absolute terms. I need the additional manpower, and I need someplace I can anchor my flanks on natural obstacles again. And that's *here*."

His forefinger stabbed a point west of the city of Shandyr.

Rahdgyrz glowered down at the map, and Metzlyr gripped his pectoral scepter as he stepped up closer beside the general and gazed down at it, as well. But then, finally, the intendant inhaled sharply and looked back up once more.

"I very much fear you're right . . . again, my son," he told Rychtyr. "I don't like giving so much ground, especially when your army's fought so magnificently this long. But neither do I want to see that army cut down in a battle that can't stop the heretics, anyway. Godly men should always be prepared to die in His service . . . but not when they know their deaths will accomplish nothing."

"You'll support the evacuation of Bryxtyn and Waymeet, Father?" Rychtyr asked softly, and Metzlyr nodded.

"Even that, my son." He produced a rather twisted smile. "I suspect a few people in Gorath won't be very happy with us, but your logic's compelling. In fact, if you concur, I'll recommend that as many troops as possible be combed out of the Kingdom's other fortresses and sent to us, as well. As you say, they can accomplish little sitting behind stone walls the heretics can either avoid or blast to pieces."

Rahdgyrz' single remaining eye was desperately unhappy as he looked back and forth between his commander and the intendant, and Rychtyr squeezed his shoulder again.

"I know you don't agree with me on this one, Clyftyn, but I need you to go back out there and fight like Chihiro himself for me again. Buy me as much time as you can. You said you could bleed them? *Do it!* Cost them every casualty you can, slow them up any way you can think of. Hold that road open until Iglaisys and the Bryxtyn garrison can break clear, but don't get yourself tied down in a fight to the finish! I'm not sure Iglaisys can get his men out of the city and join us at this late a date anyway, and if he can't, I don't want to lose your men—or *you*—reinforcing failure. You've got to promise me you won't set your teeth into the heretics and hold on too long. Can you do that for me? *Will* you do that for me?"

"Of course I will, Sir." Rahdgyrz' voice was hoarse, but he met Rychtyr's gaze levelly. "You can count on me and my boys. As Langhorne's my witness, we'll still be standing on that damned road when Iglaisys' rearguard marches past us!"

"I'm sure you will be, Clyftyn." Rychtyr gripped both of the taller Rahdgyrz' shoulders and shook him gently. "I'm sure you will. Just be damned sure you get back to me without losing any more body parts, understand?"

"I'll put that on my list, Sir," Rahdgyrz told him with a glint of true humor. Then he stood back, touched his chest in salute, and limped out of the office with a grim, determined stride.

"He doesn't like it, Sir," Mohrtynsyn said quietly, and Rychtyr sighed.

"No, he doesn't," he told his chief of staff, then glanced at Metzlyr. "*I* don't like it. But if there's a man alive who can do it for us, that man just walked out of this office."

▼ ▼ ▼

"—so we're moving up to the Chydor," Clyftyn Rahdgyrz said. "I need at least three more regiments. Find out who's closest and get them moving."

"Of course, Sir!" Colonel Mahkzwail Mahkgrudyr, Rahdgyrz' senior aide, nodded sharply. "How soon can Sir Fahstyr send additional troops to our support?"

"He won't," Rahdgyrz said heavily, and Mahkgrudyr's eyes widened. The colonel was cut very much from the same cloth as his general, but Rahdgyrz held up his hand before the other officer could protest.

"I don't like it, either. And, neither does Sir Fahstyr," Rahdgyrz added. "But our job is to hold the high road open until General Iglaisys can evacuate Bryxtyn."

"Evacuate," Mahkgrudyr repeated in the voice of a man who couldn't quite believe what he'd just heard. Or who didn't *want* to, perhaps.

"You heard me," Rahdgyrz said a bit roughly. "He's decided—and Father Pairaik agrees with him—that we need the Bryxtyn and Waymeet garrisons with the field army more than we do locked up in fortresses behind the heretics."

"But I thought the idea was to stand and fight *somewhere*, Sir," Mahkgrudyr said bitterly.

"That's enough!" Rahdgyrz half-snapped, rubbing the patch over his blind eye while he glared at his aide with the other one. "We've got our orders, and we'll carry them out. Right?"

"Of course, Sir," Mahkgrudyr said after only the briefest hesitation. Then he shook himself. "I'll go start the clerks drafting the movement orders."

"Good, Mahkzwail. Good!" Rychtyr patted the colonel's back. "I have a note of my own to write while you do that."

"Of course, Sir," Mahkgrudyr repeated, his tone closer to normal as he came back on balance. He saluted, turned, and left, and Rychtyr settled into the folding chair in front of his field desk. He opened the drawer, extracted a sheet of the thin paper used for messenger wyvern dispatches, and dipped his pen into the inkwell.

It was, perhaps, as well that Colonel Mahkgrudyr couldn't see his expression at the moment, and he sat for several seconds, his remaining eye dark with a pain that had nothing to do with the physical wounds he'd suffered in Mother Church's service. And then, slowly—reluctantly—the pen began to move.

My Lord Bishop, it is with a heavy heart and profound regret, only after many hours of prayerful meditation, that I take pen in hand to inform you—

MAY

YEAR OF GOD 898

.I.
Swayelton,
Earldom of Swayle;
Rydymak Keep,
Earldom of Cheshyr;
Rock Coast Keep,
Duchy of Rock Coast,
Kingdom of Chisholm,
Empire of Charis,
and
Nimue's Cave,
The Mountains of Light.

Thank you for agreeing to see me, Milady."

The tall, dark-haired man had gray-green eyes, dramatic silver sideburns, and a strong, distinguished face. He was well dressed and elegantly groomed, though clearly not of noble station, and looked every inch what he was: a skilled craftsman, confident in his competence and accustomed to the respect due a senior member of the Gunmakers Guild.

And those gray-green eyes were dark and bitter as he straightened from kissing Rebkah Rahskail's hand.

"You are most welcome, Master Clyntahn. Please, be seated," the Dowager Countess of Swayle replied, and waved the hand he'd just released in a graceful gesture at the comfortable chair facing her own across the cast-iron stove ducted into what had been a massive, old-fashioned, and hideously inefficient fireplace.

It was the month of May, but May was often the cruelest month in Chisholm, and the weather had turned vile again. A nasty mix of sleet and snow rattled against the solar's glass, and her visitor's boots were wet. He settled into the indicated chair with only a hint of uneasiness at sitting in the presence of a noblewoman to betray his commoner origins and the countess studied him thoughtfully and unobtrusively.

Anger radiated off of him in waves even stronger than the heat rolling off the stove, but she suspected it was so obvious to her only because of the matching hatred radiating from *her*. She rather doubted his motives were the same as hers, yet that scarcely mattered. What *mattered* was that in addition to a name which had become increasingly unfortunate here in Chisholm, he carried the burden of a trade which was about to disappear, taking not simply his wealth but his status with it.

Zhonathyn Clyntahn had been narrowly defeated for the office of Master of the Gunmakers Guild in Cherayth three years back. He hadn't enjoyed that defeat, but he'd actually taken it fairly well, especially when the Crown offered him one of three supervisor's positions at the Maikelberg Rifle Works. As a supervisor, working directly with Styvyn Nezbyt, the Old Charisian manager of the Maikelberg Works, he'd earned almost twice his previous income, although it might have been a bit less than he could have earned as an independent contractor, given the incredible press of orders for firearms. Of course, there weren't very many of those "independent contractors" anymore, and as Maikelberg hit its stride, there would be even fewer of them. That had quite a bit to do with Clyntahn's presence here in Swayleton on this icy May afternoon.

"With your permission, Master Clyntahn," Rebkah said now, "I'll dispense with the customary circumlocutions and cut straight to the heart of the matter. I understand from our . . . mutual friend that you're less than enthralled with the state of affairs here in the Kingdom."

She watched him narrowly as she deliberately used the word "Kingdom" instead of "Empire." A flicker of alarm warred with the deep-seated anger in his eyes, but it was a brief battle.

"You understand correctly, Milady." He lifted his chin, meeting her gaze as anger won. "And *I* understand from our 'mutual friend' that you're a lot less 'enthralled' with it than I am. Although, much as it pains me to disagree with a man of the cloth," he smiled thinly, "I find it a little hard to believe that *anyone* could be less enthralled than I am at the moment."

"Perhaps that would be true for most people." More than a hint of frost crept into Rebkah's voice. "But *most* people didn't see their husband hanged like a common criminal by that traitorous bitch on the Throne."

The words came out evenly, almost conversationally but for that edge of ice, yet all the more potent for her restraint, and Clyntahn's face tightened.

"I beg your pardon, Milady. That wasn't meant to sound churlish or uncaring. If it did, I do most humbly apologize."

"No apologies are necessary, Master Clyntahn. And if I gave the impression that they were, that was never my intention. It's just that . . . some wounds cut deeper than others."

"I can understand that." Clyntahn shook his head. "I haven't suffered the same loss, so I'm sure I can't truly appreciate the depth of your pain, but I've always been cursed with an active imagination."

Rebkah nodded, but she also reminded herself of Father Zhordyn's warning. Despite his last name, Clyntahn was far more sympathetic to the

Reformists than to the Temple Loyalists. His dissatisfaction with Sharleyan and Cayleb Ahrmahk had much less to do with religious conviction than with the wave of disruptions sweeping through Chisholm's social fabric.

But that's all right, she told herself. *A true daughter of God can build with whatever bricks He sends her.*

"At any rate," she said more briskly, "I was most interested when our mutual friend suggested you and your friends in Cherayth might have more in common with us than I'd realized. Of course, the deplorable state to which the Kingdom's being reduced would be enough to give anyone of goodwill deep concern at this moment."

"Absolutely, Milady." Clyntahn nodded sharply. "I suppose some people would find the notion of an . . . alliance between the Kingdom's nobility and commoner craftsmen such as myself unlikely, but there's order and balance in everything. It's taken centuries for Chisholm to reach the level of prosperity—and decades for it to reach the state of peace and security—we enjoyed before this accursed jihad. Bad enough that men and women should be slaughtering one another in God's name, but the damage being done to the very fabric of our society is simply impossible to overestimate. Every professional and economic relationship is being disrupted, broken—thrown away like so much garbage!" His eyes glittered hotly. "It's unnatural. It's *worse* than unnatural! It's going to open the door to the sort of Leveler madness they scream about on the streets of Siddar City! And as if *that* weren't enough, the effect these new child labor laws and all the rest of that crap will have on the order God decreed for the family will be absolutely disastrous. I can understand getting them out of these accursed *manufactories* and away from all that insane machinery, but abolishing the guilds' control of their own apprenticing practices? Insisting we open our crafts to just *anyone*? And then denying our ancient right to set our own journeyman and apprentice salaries, as if we were no more than—!"

Rebkah nodded gravely as she listened to his onrushing tirade, although it was difficult to keep her lip from curling as Clyntahn exposed the true reasons for his visit. Rebkah Rahskail liked social disruption no more than the next woman, but what really drove Clyntahn was the realization that his guild's privileged position—and *his* position, as a member of that guild—was in the process of becoming totally irrelevant.

I wonder if it's the money or the prestige he'll miss the most? I'd bet it's the prestige more than the income. He looks like that sort of man. But I don't really care why he's willing to serve as our go-between with the other craftmasters.

She very much doubted that Clyntahn and his associates had any clear notion of exactly what her cousin Zhasyn had in mind for them and all of their other "uppity" commoner friends after the Crown's overweening power had been broken to bridle. That didn't matter either, though, and Rebkah cared very little about what might happen then. Her purpose, the only one left to her, was to destroy Sharleyan Ahrmahk. It was only too likely that the murderess herself would escape Rebkah, hiding with her apostate husband in Old Charis at least until Zhaspahr Clyntahn and Mother Church dragged them out for the Punishment. Rebkah was realist enough to recognize that long ago. But that was fine. In fact, in some ways it would be even better. Dying would be an easy out for the bitch; watching the demolition of every single thing to which she and her father had dedicated their lives, though. *That* would be hard.

And if we can't manage that, we can damned well make her slaughter enough people in the process of putting us down that the Crown will never rest easy on her head again. After all, when you come down to it, we're the legacy of King Sailys' war on the nobility. By the time I'm done with her, that apostate whore's hands will be so bloodstained her great grandchildren will be seeing plots under every carpet, courtesy of "Sharleyan the Butcher's" reign of terror.

She made herself sit calmly, listening attentively to Clyntahn's diatribe, and schooled her expression to show no sign of her own volcanic fury. Not even Father Zhordyn recognized the true depth of her hatred. She knew that, from many of the things her confessor had said to her. And she intended to keep it that way. If she could restore Chisholm to Mother Church and God's true plan for Safehold, then she would, and rejoice in the accomplishment. But the truth was that Mother Church's victory was secondary. If the cost of Sharleyan Ahrmahk's destruction was Rebkah Rahskail's immortal soul, she would pay it in an instant and spend eternity laughing as she stood in hell at Shan-wei's shoulder.

". . . so I spoke with the others—carefully, of course," Clyntahn said, winding down at last, "and they agreed that I should accept Father Zh—ah, our mutual friend's—invitation to . . . exchange views with you, Milady."

"I'm honored by your trust," Rebkah said, exactly as if she'd actually been listening to him rather than dwelling in her own thoughts. Of course, she hadn't really needed to listen. Father Zhordyn had briefed her fully on Clyntahn and his motivations. "And I hope you're prepared to go beyond a mere exchange of views."

"I can't commit the others until I know more about your plans, Milady." Clyntahn met her gaze levelly. "For myself, I'd made up *my* mind before I climbed into the coach to come speak to you. I don't know how much good I can do you if the others decline to commit themselves, but whatever I *can* do, I will. You have my word on that."

"Yes, I believe I do," she said slowly, smiling at him with the first true warmth she'd felt since he'd entered the solar.

She sat for a moment, listening to the rattle of sleet and the moan of wind, feeling the warmth radiating from the iron stove—the *Charisian* iron stove—while the coal burned in its belly like an echo of the rage burning in her own. Then she inhaled sharply.

"What we propose to do," she began crisply, "is to overthrow the tyranny of the House of Tayt once and for all. We don't expect it to be easy, but we have powerful allies in this. I'm not in a position to name names any more than you are, but I can assure you that they include some of the most powerful nobles in the entire Kingdom. Unfortunately, their lands—and thus their power base—lie outside Cherayth or the lands immediately around it. When we raise the standard of defiance, we'll have an extensive base of operations in the western part of the Kingdom—a springboard for additional expansion which will also be compact enough to be easily defended at need. What we won't have is the same reach into the eastern fiefdoms or into the towns and cities. You craftmasters, on the other hand, dominate the town and city councils. As respected members of your town and city governments, you have exactly the sort of reach our western allies lack."

Clyntahn paled so slightly at her devastating frankness, but his expression never flinched, and she felt a fresh flicker of approval as he nodded gamely.

"Obviously, we have to be concerned about the Army," she continued, "but most of the newly raised troops have already departed for Siddarmark or will board ship within the next few five-days. The training cadres will remain, but they're overwhelmingly concentrated in Eastshare, Cherayth, Lake Shore, and Port Royal. By the time they could be combined to mount an expedition against our allies in the west, we'll have consolidated our positions there. Indeed, all indications are that since we'll be the ones choosing the time and place to proclaim our defiance and strike, we may well . . . neutralize many of those training cadres before they realize what's happening.

"I'm sure your position in the Maikelberg Works makes you even more aware than most of the advantages of the new-model weapons. I assure you that *we* are, at any rate. Because of that, I've used some of my late husband's contacts in the Army. Not everyone's forgotten him or Duke Halbrook Hollow or the price they paid for their principles. One of those who remember, in the Quartermaster Corps, has arranged to divert several thousand rifles to our use. They aren't the very latest weapons. They're what he calls 'Trapdoor Mahndrayns,' and he's been very forthright in his warning that they don't fire as rapidly as the newer rifles. They're enormously better than nothing—or muzzleloaders—however, and he should be able to provide nearly enough of them to offset the weapons remaining in the hands of the Army's training cadres. And, of course, there's also the possibility that at least two or three of the training regiments will join us, given all of my husband and Duke Halbrook Hollow's remaining friends in the Army. After all," she bared her teeth in a humorless smile, "they've been left home because they're 'tainted' by their past friendships and not fully trusted in the field."

Clyntahn nodded, his eyes intent, obviously reassured—to some extent, at least—by her calm, confident manner.

"We intend, assuming you and your friends decide to join us, to have several hundred of those rifles 'misplaced' in Cherayth itself. We don't want you to go anywhere near them until and unless we're in a position to threaten the capital. Then—*then*, when every man they have is mustered and sent out to meet us in the field—you and your friends will arm yourselves, seize the capital, and close its gates against the Army until we've destroyed it in battle. We're confident we can take Cherayth in the end, with or without friends inside the walls, but it would obviously be easier—and many fewer innocent civilians would be injured or killed—if someone else takes control of it for us while we deal with the Army."

She paused, then sat back in her chair with her hands folded in her lap.

"Those are only the bare bones, of course. Should your friends be interested, I can provide the detail to put flesh and muscle onto them. Trust me, we've given this a great deal of thought over the last several years, and none of us are interested in glorious failures. We intend to *succeed*, Master Clyntahn, and I'm confident we will.

"So, tell me. Do you think 'your friends' will want to hear more?"

▾　▾　▾

Oh, I'm sure they will, Milady, Merch O Obaith thought, listening through the remote on the flu of Lady Swayle's stove as she guided the recon skimmer towards Rydymak Keep. *And thank you ever so much for drawing them out into the open for us! I'll be interested to see how many of Master Clyntahn's "friends" Sir Ahlber's already identified. I'm willing to bet Nahrmahn and Owl have most of them, even if he doesn't, but you can never ID too many of the rats in the woodwork when it comes to spotting traitors.*

There were moments when she actually felt a little guilty for taking such shameless advantage of Owl and the SNARCs. But those moments were few and far between. She'd become just as fierce a partisan of Cayleb and Sharleyan Ahrmahk—and all their friends—as Merlin Athrawes ever had, and, like Merlin, she didn't much care for anyone who wanted to murder the people she loved.

She wondered, sometimes, if Nimue Alban's personality had always been that . . . direct, and she simply hadn't realized it because all of her attention had been so focused on the hopeless, losing war against the Gbaba. Or was it the ultimate futility of that war—the knowledge that it could end only one way, whatever she might do—which had *made* her so direct?

Of course, Lady Swayle was going to be in for a few unhappy surprises.

For example, Colonel Brekyn Ainsail, that friend of hers who was supplying her with the Trapdoor Mahndrayns out of the goodness of his heart and loyalty to her husband's memory. Ainsail was actually just a bit more mercenary than that, and Duke Rock Coast's marks spoke much more convincingly to him than any appeal to loyalty, whether to a friend's memory or to the Temple. And he didn't realize the ghost of a dead Emeraldian prince and an electronic being who'd never breathed had carefully tracked every payment, every piece of forged paperwork, every diversionary order, and every shipment of arms. They knew exactly where every rifle was, where it had come from, and how it had gotten there. Explaining *how* they knew in open court might be just a tad awkward, but she suspected Ainsail would be more than willing to help out. Once they showed him proof of his complicity, he'd accept any deal the Crown offered just as quickly as he could get the words out of his mouth. He'd be just *delighted* to show the investigators exactly where all of those weapons caches were, which would neatly solve the question of how the Crown had found them.

Now that's *going to leave a mark on someone,* Merch thought with an unpleasant smile. *And if it should happen that a bunch of traitorous bastards turn up to collect their rifles and find a platoon or so of infantry waiting for them, won't that be sad?*

There were still a lot of ways this could go south, she reflected as the Sunset Hills appeared below her. Given her own preferences, she'd pounce the instant they had enough evidence to identify the key players, but Sharleyan had other plans. Merch understood the empress's thinking, and she agreed it was time to draw out the traitors in Sharleyan's nobility and . . . eliminate them once and for all rather than deal with a fresh crop every ten or twenty years. She just couldn't help worrying about how many innocent people might get hurt in the process.

That concern explained her presence here this evening, actually.

▼   ▼   ▼

The weather was marginally better in Cheshyr than in Swayle. But it was only *marginally* better, and coal cost more in Rydymak than in Swayleton. Or, rather, the citizens of Rydymak had far fewer marks in their pockets when it came time to pay for it.

Things had gotten a little better of late, though. No one had any more money, but Lady Cheshyr had managed to get some of the coal originally destined for the steamers in the Gulf of Dohlar diverted to Cheshyr Bay. She might not have much money, but she clearly still had friends in Cherayth, and she'd made that coal available to her people for barely a tenth of its market price. Unless they couldn't afford even that much, of course . . . in which case, it was free.

There was a reason the people of her earldom loved Karyl Rydmakyr.

Sergeant Major Ahzbyrn Ohdwiar understood that. He'd known Lady Karyl—Lady K, she'd been to the entire regiment, then—for the better part of thirty years. Ohdwiar was a muscular, dauntingly fit forty-five-year-old, with black hair, very dark brown eyes, a scarred cheek, and a limp. He'd been born with the first two; the scar and the limp he'd acquired fighting under Styvyn Rydmakyr in King Sailys' army. Twenty-six years he'd given the Army, until the training accident that finally retired him. He'd drifted then, until he washed up here, in Rydymak, where his old CO's widow had taken him in, put a roof over his head, and found him a comfortable semiretirement as an "armsman," even if he was to crippled up to be much good.

Of course, he reflected as he pushed himself through the two hundredth push-up, there was crippled and then there was *crippled*.

He went right on pumping, lowering himself smoothly—spine absolutely straight—until his nose just touched the floor, and then pushing himself equally smoothly back up again. Despite his limp, he really preferred jogging for cardio exercise—one of his cousins was a Pasqualate healer who'd helped design his own personal exercise program over a decade ago—but that was out of the question after his "training accident." And so, like most of the other "crippled" armsmen who'd drifted into Rydymak, he did his exercising in private.

Fortunately, despite its draftiness, Rydymak Keep had indoor plumbing and Chisholmian winters guaranteed that its communal bathhouse was efficiently heated. Well, it had been *designed* to be efficiently heated, anyway, since that was the only way to keep it from freezing solid four months out of the year, and with the influx of good, Glacierheart coal it was heated once again.

He finished his exercises and came to his feet, stretching carefully as he cooled down and already contemplating the bathhouse's welcome. This late at night, he'd have it all to himself, unless Clairync Ohsulyvyn or Dynnys Mykgylykudi—both of whom he'd known for the better part of twenty years—drifted in. Zhaksyn Ohraily, on the other hand, was a mere babe in arms, barely thirty-eight years old. Because of that, he got the late-night duty outside Lady K's chamber door, while the creaky old bones of his elders got a good night's sleep.

Ohdwiar chuckled and opened the door from his small sleeping chamber into the barely larger sitting room attached to it, reaching for the towel he'd hung across his single chair before beginning his nightly calisthenics. He'd just—

"Looking for this, Sergeant Major?"

Ohdwiar froze at the totally unexpected soprano question. Then he stepped through into the sitting room and reached out to accept the towel from his equally unexpected guest. He gave her a less-than-approving look, but she only smiled impishly, and her blue eyes—even darker than Dynnys Mykgylykudi's—twinkled mischievously.

"I'd not like to sound like I was complaining or anything, *Seijin* Merch," he said ever so slightly repressively, "but there're reasons a man's quarters have doors. Doors with *locks*, now that I think on it."

"Well, of course they do, Ahzbyrn. I wouldn't have anything to *pick* if they didn't!"

Ohdwiar sighed. Estimating any *seijin's* age was probably pointless, but he was reasonably certain Merch O Obaith was a very *young* example of the breed. He'd known too many young smart arses not to recognize one when he saw it.

For that matter, he'd seen it looking out of his own mirror at him for far too many years, now that he thought about it.

"I suppose that's true," he said rather than any of several rather pithier utterances which suggested themselves to him, and toweled his sweaty, graying—and *thinning*, damn it—hair dry. "And would it happen you've not dropped by *just* to practice picking my lock?"

"Aren't you happy to see me, Ahzbyrn?" She managed to put an edge of wistful longing into her tone. For that matter, it looked as if she'd actually gotten her lower lip to quiver.

"As a mist wyvern in springtime, lassie," he assured her.

"That's better, then," she said with such earnest relief that, despite himself, he chuckled.

It had been her companion, *Seijin* Cennady, who recruited Ohdwiar and the others for their present duty, but ever since they'd arrived here in Cheshyr Bay, *Seijin* Merch had been their primary contact with the *seijin* network which served Their Majesties. He had no doubt she was death incarnate on two feet. That was true of every *seijin* ever born, as far as he could tell. But she did remind him of his long dead wife. Not physically—Mahrglys had been a tall woman, towering at least five inches higher even than *Seijin* Merch, who was scarcely a midget, with golden hair and gray eyes. But under the skin . . . there the two of them were so much alike it hurt sometimes.

"Seriously, My Lady," he said, using the honorific he knew irked her, and not simply *because* it irked her. She was a *seijin*, for Langhorne's sake! "I'm guessing there's more to it than a social call?"

"Yes, there is," she acknowledged, hopping up to sit tailor-fashion on his rickety desk. He regarded the arrangement with trepidation, having discovered some time ago that *Seijin* Merch was just as solid and muscular as she looked. "I'm here mainly to visit with Lady Karyl, really. I have a couple of messages for her from Her Majesty, and another from Earl White Crag.

While I was here, though, I thought I'd check in with you and the other gray lizards."

Ohdwiar snorted. He wasn't sure which of the *seijins* had dubbed him and his companions the "gray slash lizards," but the truth was, he approved. It was the sort of backhanded compliment an old soldier appreciated.

"There's not much to report since your last visit," he said after a moment. "We've kept a sharp eye out, and it's a good thing we'd that note of yours." He shook his head, expression disgusted. "Rock Coast seems a right slow learner."

"It's not like he doesn't have plenty of other potential spies where the last one came from," *Seijin* Merch pointed out. "He figures that sooner or later he's bound to get someone onto Lady Karyl's staff if he just keeps trying. After all—" she grinned at Ohdwiar "—everyone knows she's a notoriously soft touch for taking in stray puppies and gray lizards."

Ohdwiar snorted again, rather more harshly.

"How difficult was it to discourage the most recent candidate?" the *seijin* asked.

"Not so difficult as all that." Ohdwiar returned her grin with a nasty little smile. "Strangest thing happened. When Lady K was interviewing her, Zhorzhyna came in to announce that the silver salt cellar had disappeared out of the kitchen while the young lady was waiting to see the Mistress. Turned out it was in her bag. No clue how it got there."

"Oh, that was *wicked*, Ahzbyrn! I like it."

"Well, it might be the lass was a miserable treacherous spy, but the lads and I didn't have the stomach to go breaking her kneecaps. So it seemed best all round. Besides, you've reminded us often enough to keep a low profile. Hard to do that when you're tossing young women off the battlements every other five-day."

"I imagine it would be, yes." Merch nodded gravely, blue eyes sparkling. She *did* like Sergeant Major Ohdwiar. He reminded her forcibly of a couple of tough-as-nails Terran Marine sergeants she'd known a thousand years ago.

"Well, in addition to making sure you aren't tossing any dishonest, salt cellar–stealing maids off any battlements, and besides dropping in on Lady Karyl for a cup of tea, I did have one other thing on my mind."

"And what might that be?" Ohdwiar asked warily.

"It's just that I hope you've found that hiding place we were talking about last time I was here, because in about two five-days, a fishing boat's going to turn up here in Cheshyr Bay. The only 'fisherman' aboard will be a fellow named Dagyr Cudd, so he'll need a little help to get his catch ashore."

"And what sort of catch might we be speaking of, if you don't mind my asking?"

"Oh, a few crates of rifles. A few more crates of ammunition. That sort of thing," she said with an airy wave of her hand. "Oh! And I think Dynnys will be especially happy. Unless I'm mistaken, there should be two or three mortars, as well." She smiled seraphically at him. "I do hope you boys will take proper care of your toys, Ahzbyrn."

▼   ▼   ▼

"Have you deciphered the letter, Your Grace?" Sedryk Mahrtynsyn asked.

"Just finished, Father," Zhasyn Seafarer replied, sitting back in his chair before the roaring fire. He tilted the several sheets of paper to catch the lantern light as he read back over them in silence for several minutes. Then he looked up from them with a smile.

"I can't really thank you enough for agreeing to serve as our messenger, Father," he said warmly. "Rebkah asked me to tell you she appreciates your services just as deeply as I do. We understand the risk you're running for us."

"With all due respect, Your Grace, I'm not running those risks solely for *you*," the under-priest pointed out with a slightly crooked smile. "Mind you, it's my honor to assist you, but I'm not certain I'd be quite so eager to run them for any merely mortal reward."

"No one could argue with that," Duke Rock Coast said simply.

"May I ask if Lady Swayle's written good news?"

For his own safety, Mahrtynsyn never knew the contents of the encrypted letters he carried back and forth. As far as he knew, they were simply the correspondence of the cousins for whom he was honored to deliver them. That was his story, and if he didn't know their content, he couldn't be tricked into betraying himself by revealing that knowledge under interrogation.

"Quite a bit, actually. I'll keep most of it back, I'm afraid. It's not my information to reveal without her permission, but she's confirmed that Holy Tree's climbed down off the fence."

"That's wonderful, Your Grace!" Mahrtynsyn exclaimed.

The Schuelerite had wondered which way Sir Bryndyn Crawfyrd would jump in the end. He was only in his late thirties and he'd never been very active in resisting the Crown's power. Nor was he an especially fervent Temple Loyalist. He was, however, concerned by the social changes he saw sweeping towards him, and his status as the current Earl of Swayle's future brother-in-law had probably been the decisive factor. If he brought his duchy into the conspiracy, it would cover Swayle's eastern border and extend their territorial reach another three hundred miles towards Cherayth. Perhaps even more to the point, it would outflank the Earldom of Saint Howan, trapping it between Holy Tree and Swayle to the north and the Duchy of Black Horse to the west, and they could absolutely rely upon Sir Dynzayl Hyntyn, the

Earl of Saint Howan's loyalty to Sharleyan Ahrmahk. He was the Chancellor of the Treasury, after all.

"Yes, it is good news," Rock Coast acknowledged. "But there may be better."

"Better, Your Grace?" Mahrtynsyn's eyes glowed, and Rock Coast smiled.

"First, while you were away, I hosted a snow lizard hunt. Lantern Walk was part of the party, and he and I had a long talk sitting in one of the hunting blinds."

"Has the Duke agreed to join us, Your Grace?" Mahrtynsyn asked eagerly.

"Not *quite* . . . yet, at any rate. He's a careful sort, you know. I suspect he's been involved in more than one earlier attempt to . . . restrain the Crown, but no one's ever been able to prove anything of the sort. So it's not too surprising that he hasn't rushed to fling himself into our arms."

Mahrtynsyn nodded. Calling Sir Bahnyvyl Kyvlokyn "a careful sort" was a massive understatement. He was in his early forties and remarkably untrammeled by anything approaching a fundamental principle. He did have some concerns about the erosion of aristocratic privilege, but he was willing to accept that . . . so long as he wound up on top of whatever system replaced it.

"I don't know if we'll be able to involve him fully, but at least he's prepared to declare his 'neutrality' when we make our move. Under the right circumstances, I believe he'll do more. He's been in contact with both Lady Swayle and Black Horse, as well as with me, without reporting any of us to Zhustyn or Stoneheart."

"Your Grace!" Mahrtynsyn looked alarmed, but Rock Coast waved it away.

"It's not like any of us have said anything outwardly actionable in front of anyone else, Father. And none of us have committed anything to Bahnyvyl in writing. So even if he'd been inclined to betray us, there's no evidence he could hand over, and hearsay evidence has never been enough to convict a peer of the realm, even under Sailys and Sharleyan. Besides, he may be under more pressure to join us than he thinks when the time comes."

"Why, Your Grace?"

"I've spoken very cautiously with Mountain Heart. He's burned his fingers a couple of times before, so he's more than a little cautious about going back for another try, especially now that that bastard Cayleb's been added to the mix. He pointed out that even if we succeed in taking the entire Kingdom, Sharleyan can always borrow an army—or at least a navy—from her husband and come back for another try. Of course, if we succeed and disband the current army, I'm sure we can produce one of our own big enough to give any number of Marines more than they want to handle. More to the point, I think Mountain Heart suspects Black Bottom's agreed to join us this time."

Mahrtynsyn nodded slowly. Sir Vyrnyn Atwatyr, the Duke of Black Bottom, was an aristocrat of the *very* old school. He'd avoided any previous plots against the Crown, however, because he'd had a lively respect for the Royal Army and no desire to see it marching across his lands. But he was also seventy-eight years old, and unbeknownst to the majority of his fellow aristocrats, he was secretly a fierce Temple Loyalist. More than that, both his sons and his only grandson had predeceased him, which made the current heir to his duchy a grandnephew he didn't particularly like, and his health was declining rapidly. He felt the cold wind of mortality on his spine, urging him to make his peace with God, and this time around he had very little to lose in *this* world.

"Well, I sort of intimated to Mountain Heart that Lantern Walk's more . . . enthusiastically committed to us than he actually is at the moment. Mountain Heart's too cautious an old wyvern to go bleating to Lantern Walk about it, and Lantern Walk's too cautious to ask Mountain Heart which way he's leaning. So at the moment, both of them are inclined to believe the other one's already signed on with us. And that, obviously, gives each of them multiple borders to worry about. Lantern Walk already had Swayle and Holy Tree on his frontier; if Mountain Heart and Black Bottom both come in, he'll be surrounded on three sides. As for Mountain Heart, if Lantern Walk comes in, he'll have Black Bottom to the southeast, Cheshyr—one way or the other—on the south, and me right on the other side of Lake Land. Once upon a time, I'd've counted on Lake Land's support, but that was before old Symyn died last year. After the way Paitryk stabbed us in the back in Tellesberg—and the way he's been sucking up to Sharleyan and Cayleb ever since—things have changed, unfortunately. I could be wrong about Paitryk now that he's formally inherited the title and started dealing with the realities of Sharleyan's tyranny, but I'm damned sure not saying a word to him ahead of time! On the other hand, he's got less than a third of the population I have and no more than twenty or thirty armsmen, courtesy of Sailys' damned restrictions. I, on the other hand, have close to a thousand of them training out in the back of beyond. If I have to, I'll go through his duchy like shit through a wyvern, and he—and Mountain Heart—both know it."

Mahrtynsyn nodded slowly, and his respect for Rock Coast went up another notch. No one would ever call the duke a brilliant man, but he clearly meant business. The under-priest was impressed by the sheer focus he'd brought to the task, and this time around he'd taken remarkably few missteps.

"But the other bit of good news from Lady Swayle is that she's been in contact with Elahnah Waistyn."

"Was that wise, Your Grace?"

Waistyn found himself wondering abruptly if he'd been overly optimistic about missteps. Elahnah Waistyn, the Dowager Duchess of Halbrook Hollow, was Empress Sharleyan's maternal aunt by marriage. She was also the Duke of Eastshare's *sister*. To be sure, her husband had been convicted of treason after his death, so she and Rebkah Rahskail had that much in common. More, their husbands had been close friends for many years. But venturing into the complex stew of Elahnah's understandably conflicted loyalties did *not* strike him as a prudent move.

"Oh, don't worry! First, Elahnah contacted Rebkah, not the other way around. They hadn't actually spoken since Barkah's execution, so she was a little surprised by the invitation to visit Halbrook Hall. And she didn't say a word about any conspiracies while she was there. But Elahnah made it quite clear that she would 'look favorably' upon the restoration of Mother Church's proper authority here in Chisholm. I'm sure she's still in a great deal of pain over Byrtrym's death, and especially over the way he died. But her faith's solid, and if we approach her properly when the time comes, there's an excellent chance she'd lend us at least her passive support. And Sailys is the spitting image of Byrtrym in more than one way. You know he shared Byrtrym's beliefs, and there's been very little contact between him and Sharleyan since his father's death. I know which way his heart will pull him, and if it looks like the entire West is coming over to us—and if his mother pushes him just a bit—I don't think it will matter a lot which way his *head* pulls."

Mahrtynsyn breathed a surreptitious sigh of relief. He wasn't as convinced as Rock Coast that the young Duke of Halbrook Hollow's heart was that thoroughly with the Temple Loyalists, but he could be wrong. Halbrook Hollow's proximity to the Crown had made him far too dangerous for any of the Inquisitor General's agents to contact, so Mahrtynsyn had no personal impression one way or the other. But it was certainly possible Rock Coast had a point, especially if, as he said, it looked like the entire southwest was falling into line. And if Halbrook Hollow *did* join them, it would be huge.

It was already clear that Ahdem Zhefry, the Earl of Cross Creek, would never join them willingly. Bad enough he'd always staunchly supported Sharleyan and the monarchy in his own right, but Earl White Crag, who'd become the kingdom's First Councilor after Baron Green Mountain was crippled by one of Zhaspahr Clyntahn's assassins, was his brother-in-law! Yet if Holy Tree, Lantern Walk, and Halbrook Hollow all came in, not only would Cross Creek be hemmed in on three sides by hostile territory, but so would three-quarters of the Duchy of Tayt eastern border.

It really looks like Rock Coast's going to pull this off, the Schuelerite thought almost wonderingly.

He'd worked towards that end for over two years, yet he'd never really believed it was going to happen. He'd been willing to make the effort, despite the dangers, for at the end of the day he was not simply a man of the Church, but a man of deep and abiding faith. A man had to know what he was willing to die for, and Sedryk Mahrtynsyn had decided that the day the Jihad officially began. But only now did he truly realize that he'd never actually expected it to work.

Not until this very day.

"Your Grace, I'm deeply impressed. Especially that this is all coming together now. Surely it's an indication of God's approval that this should be happening at the very moment that General Kahlyns is in the process of sending all the new regiments to the front!"

"Of course it is," Rock Coast agreed. "But let's not forget that God and the Archangels help those who help themselves, Father! No matter how many people we can recruit before we strike, we'll represent only a minority of the Kingdom, at least to start. I've discussed it with Black Horse, and we're in agreement that what we need is for the two of us to declare our defiance of the Crown first and then bring the others in in a sort of rolling cascade. Have them make it clear to everyone that they're responding to the inherent justice of our demands only after we've made them rather than part of some preconcerted plot. It shouldn't take more than a five-day or so for all of them to make their 'decisions of conscience,' and doing it that way will create a wave of momentum in our favor."

"I can see that, Your Grace," Mahrtynsyn said, impressed yet again.

"So far, Black Horse and I have boiled it down to five principal points," Rock Coast continued, unlocking an iron-reinforced desk drawer and extracting a single sheet of paper. "I've discussed most of these with you, at least in principle before, but we've hammered it into a semi-final shape and I'd like your opinion."

"Of course, Your Grace." Mahrtynsyn leaned back in his chair, tucking his hands into the arms of his cassock and cocking his head attentively.

"First," Rock Coast said, glancing down at his sheet of notes, "we begin by declaring that Sharleyan's marriage to Cayleb is null and void because it was patently illegal, since the House of Lords' ancient and customary right to approve the betrothal or marriage of the heir to the throne was flouted. Langhorne! It wasn't simply *flouted*; it was completely *ignored*! She simply stood up in Parliament and told us all what she'd already decided!

"Second, since the merger of the two kingdoms was a part of the illegal and hence void marriage contract, it was also illegal, which means Chisholm's never *legally* been a part of this Charisian Empire abortion.

"Third, not content with flouting the constitution through an illegal marriage and merger, Sharleyan and Cayleb have conspired to further curtail the ancient rights and privileges of the peers of the Realm, continuing the process King Sailys began illegally by brute force of arms all those years ago.

"Fourth, this illegal mockery of a marriage has involved the Kingdom in a needless war against Mother Church, leading directly to the deaths of thousands upon thousands of Sharleyan's subjects who need not have died. And, even if it be granted that Mother Church—or some of her vicars, acting in her name—have been guilty of crimes of their own, the commission of still *more* crimes is no way to address the problem! Certainly not before first seeking redress through the ecclesiastic courts provided by the *Holy Writ* and the blessed Archangels themselves for that very purpose.

"And fifth, Sharleyan and Cayleb, in order to whip up support for this entire illegal, obscene edifice they've constructed, are encouraging the dregs of society—not just peasants and the rabble of the street but actual ex-serfs—to combine in an unholy alliance against the stability and property rights of the Kingdom, creating a . . . a mobocracy, for want of a better term, that pits their base-born 'allies' against not simply the nobility, but also against the small property owners, the shopkeepers, and the skilled craftsmen who, along with our farmers, have always been the true bone and sinew of Chisholm."

He folded the sheet of paper and handed it across to the under-priest.

"I'm sure it needs a little polish, Father, and I'm much more comfortable with actions than with words. But at least it's clear, and at least it's a starting point. And between you and me," he met Mahrtynsyn's eyes levelly, "a man could die for a lot worse principles than these."

▼   ▼   ▼

"If you think those are principles worth dying for, Your Grace, I've got a nice little floating island in Hsing-wu's Passage I'd like to sell you for a summer vacation home," Nahrmahn Baytz said sourly. "Of course, you'd better get it built before it melts!"

At the moment, he was "visiting" in Owl's main CPU. The AI had enabled the link as part of the support he—Owl had decided he definitely preferred the masculine pronoun—provided to maintain Nahrmahn's incomplete gestalt. Since the two of them had become so . . . intimately connected, Owl had built what amounted to a guesthouse for Nahrmahn's virtual personality, and the two of them conducted quite a bit of their intelligence analysis there in hyper heuristic mode.

"I have observed that humans historically have been capable of embracing any number of illogical 'principles worth dying for,'" Owl observed now. "I believe Duke Rock Coast's are no more foolish than a great many others."

"Now there, Owl, I'm afraid you may have a point," Nahrmahn admitted. "Of course, I may be just a bit prejudiced, since *I* was never so foolish as to decide to die for a principal."

"My analysis suggests that that was simply because you never had to choose whether or not to do so," Owl corrected gently. "Although, I will concede that when you did choose to die, it was for something rather more important than an empty, self-serving political 'principle.'"

"There wasn't a great deal of 'choosing' to it, really. It was more a matter of automatic reaction."

"And, looking back, would you have chosen any other way?" Owl challenged with a smile.

"No," Nahrmahn acknowledged. He rested one electronic hand on the AI's equally immaterial shoulder and shook him gently. "No, I wouldn't have. So I suppose you win this one."

"When it is a matter of logic and analysis, I almost always win," Owl pointed out. "Unfortunately, dealing with humans, logic and analysis are usually the last resort of scoundrels."

"A joke!" Nahrmahn laughed delightedly. "I'm corrupting you, Owl! Next thing, you'll be producing *puns!*"

"At which point I trust Commander Athrawes will be compassionate enough to order a complete memory purge," Owl replied.

Nahrmahn laughed again, then returned his attention to the task at hand.

Quite a bit of written correspondence was passing back and forth as the conspirators moved into the end game. They didn't have much choice about that, although most of it was being conscientiously burned after it was read by its recipient. The SNARCs' remotes got solid imagery of almost all of it before it was consigned to the flames, and the people who'd burned it were going to be dreadfully surprised when perfect replicas of it turned up as evidence against them. Not *all* of it, of course—only the most incriminating bits. And only when there was a convincing way to explain—to someone else, at least—how it might have come into the prosecution's hands. Which meant, among other things, that it had to be correspondence no witness had seen burned.

It's really fortunate that most traitors prefer to dispose of the really incriminating evidence in splendid solitude, he thought now. *That's going to make it just a little difficult for Rock Coast and his friends. It's not as if it's going to make things a lot better for them if they announce we can't possibly have that evidence because they destroyed it, since the fact that they destroyed it confirms it once existed, anyway. For that matter, destroying it in the first place would constitute admission of guilt, wouldn't it?*

He chortled quietly to himself as he contemplated the potential law masters' arguments. The possible consequences for Safehold's jurisprudence might be . . . interesting. Not that it was going to matter much in the end.

They'll have open, scrupulously fair trials before we hang them, he thought. *Which*, his expression darkened, *is one hell of a lot more than they're planning on giving anyone on the other side.*

And meanwhile, it was time for the mysterious *seijins* to write up their latest discoveries. He sat back in a virtual chair, leafing through his notes while he decided which sections to put into which *seijin's* handwriting.

It was almost worth having died to be able to play the Great Game at this level, he decided.

.II.
Mahkbyth's Fine Spirits and Wine,
Mylycynt Court,
City of Zion,
The Temple Lands.

The bell over the door jingled.

"Good afternoon, Sir. How may I serve you?"

Zhak Myllyr's voice registered only vaguely with Ahrloh Mahkbyth. If Zhak hadn't been there to promptly greet whoever had just entered the shop, *that* would have registered sharply and immediately. The sound of things going the way they were supposed to, on the other hand, was poor compensation for the fact that he couldn't figure out where an entire case of Yu-kwau brandy had gone.

He glowered at the inventory list. Paperwork was his least favorite part of owning his own business, but he was usually good at it. Misplacing something that big—and expensive—was unlike him. And, of course, he had to have done it now, when the Charisian commerce-raiders swarming about the Western Gulf of Dohlar guaranteed there wouldn't be any replacement shipments from the Bay of Alexov anytime soon. If Zhak Myllyr hadn't been a scrupulously honest sort—aside from a single understandable shortcoming—he'd have wondered if pilferage could explain it. But that was ridiculous! It was more likely Langhorne would return in glory than that Zhak Myllyr would steal from his employer. And the truth was that there'd been enough other—and more pressing—matters on his mind of late to produce a *dozen* errors no worse than this one. No, it was here *somewhere*; he just had to find it. And once he did, by God, he wouldn't let it slip away ag—

"Good afternoon," a voice answered Zhak. "I wonder if you might have a bottle of *Seijin* Kohdy's Premium Blend?"

Yu-kwau brandy was abruptly the last thing on Ahrloh Mahkbyth's mind.

He made himself stretch in a casual yawn without ever so much as glancing at the front of the shop. Then he shrugged, carefully wiped the nib of his pen and set it in the stand, and stepped around his standing desk to glance—casually, casually—at the customer who'd just spoken.

The man was well dressed and very tall, with gray eyes, sharply receding fair hair, and a full beard and majestic mustache. He looked up, as if he'd just realized Myllyr wasn't alone in the store, and glanced casually at Mahkbyth over Myllyr's shoulder, then returned his attention to the clerk.

"As a matter of fact, we do, Sir," Myllyr was saying. "In fact, I think we're one of the few shops here in Zion to stock it. I'm afraid it's a little too peaty for the majority of Temple Lands connoisseurs, although I'm quite fond of it myself."

"As am I," Mahkbyth said. He walked forward, extending his hand to the customer. "It's good to see you again, Master Murphai. I wasn't aware you favored *Seijin* Kohdy's?"

"Master Mahkbyth." Murphai smiled warmly, accepting the proffered hand and clasping forearms with him. "I was recently introduced to it at a friend's. She spoke very highly of it, and I found it . . . palatable. As your assistant here says, it's a bit peaty, but it does settle well, doesn't it?"

"Yes, it does." Mahkbyth glanced at Myllyr and grimaced. "Zhak, I'll take this one."

"But—" Myllyr began, and Mahkbyth shook his head.

"Don't be silly, man! It's coming up on time for your lunch, anyway. And I'm no closer to finding that Shan-wei-damned case than I was yesterday! My eyes are crossing going over those inventory lists, and I need a break from them."

"If you're sure, Sir."

"Of course I'm sure." Mahkbyth reached into his breeches pocket, extracted a silver tenth-mark, and flipped it to the clerk. "If you're going to feel guilty about sticking me with this incredibly difficult task, bring me back some fish and chips from Zhantry's. With extra vinegar and at least two of those big pickles, mind!"

"Yes, Sir!" Myllyr caught the coin neatly out of the air with a grin, then nodded to Murphai and reached for his coat. "Have a good day, Master Murphai."

"Thank you," Murphai responded pleasantly.

Myllyr shrugged into his coat, flipped his muffler around his neck, and headed out the door. It was mild enough he scarcely needed either of them, but only a crazed optimist would assume that would remain true for more than an hour or two in a row here in Zion. The month of May had scarcely begun, and while the sun might burn down brightly at the moment, that was subject to change. In places where that bright sun reached the ground, the remnants of the most recent snowfall were thin and patchy, crusty where they'd refrozen overnight but disappearing quickly under the city's foot traffic. In places where the sun didn't reach, however, it still lay mid-calf deep, and the heaps where the snow removed from sidewalks and shop entrances had been piled by the removal crews were still head high. And whatever that deceitful brightness might promise, the ice on Lake Pei had only just begun to break up, and nasty weather could roll in off Temple Bay—or over the lake, when the wind was in the west—on a bit less than no notice at all.

Murphai watched Myllyr's departure, then turned to Mahkbyth as the door closed behind him.

"It *is* good to see you, *Seijin*," the shop owner said then in a very different tone. "Have you come from Arbalest?"

"Not directly." Murphai's voice was far more somber, as well. "I have been in contact with her, though. And I apologize. I wish I could've gotten here sooner, but Arbalest felt—and I agreed—that it would probably be best to limit contact with you until we were reasonably confident you weren't under suspicion."

"So you *are* 'reasonably confident' of that now, I take it?" Mahkbyth tilted his head, his smile painfully tart, and Murphai snorted softly.

"I may be a *seijin*, Ahrloh," he said, using Mahkbyth's given name rather than his Helm Cleaver codename, Barcor, "but I'm not omniscient. That said, I do have better sources than most, and none of them have seen any sign you're being watched. And, frankly, you're too big a fish to let you swim free in hopes you'd lead them to someone even more important. If Rayno or Wynchystair had a clue about who you really are, you'd've been arrested the instant you came back from that 'business trip' of yours. Which, I'd like to add, took one hell of a lot of guts."

"Maybe." Mahkbyth shrugged. "It was the only way to be sure, and it's not like I didn't make my peace with the Archangels the day Arbalest recruited me. Oh, I'm not quite *that* blasé about it," he added as Murphai raised one eyebrow, "and I'm not in a tearing hurry to make any personal reports in Heaven, either. But I decided then it was worth risking my life, and I haven't changed my mind since. Mind you, I'd just as soon avoid the Question or the Punishment."

His expression wasn't simply grim. It had turned cold and vicious with his last sentence, and he shifted his left hand slightly, catching the light on the opal-set golden ring he wore on it.

"I don't know how the bastards got to Bracelet and Castanet before they could poison themselves, but they'll find it a right bitch to stop *me*."

"I'd just as soon it didn't come to that, if that's all right with you," Murphai said. "Leaving aside the fact that Arbalest is very fond of you, we can't really afford to lose you. Especially after the hit we've already taken."

"I passed the word as soon as I heard they'd been arrested," Mahkbyth said heavily. "I didn't have time to see whether or not everyone got it. For that matter, if any of us were under suspicion, talking to the others wouldn't have been the very smartest thing we could've done."

"No, it wouldn't have. And, as of last five-day, all but two of Bracelet's cell have reached their safe houses in Tanshar. I'm pretty sure—" in fact, he knew for certain "—that those two are en route. They had farther to go, and the weather was against them."

"Thank Langhorne," Mahkbyth half-whispered, closing his eyes briefly, and his shoulders sagged as if someone had just lifted an enormous weight from them.

"You got them out in time, Ahrloh." The *seijin* rested a hand on Mahkbyth's shoulder.

"And Bracelet and Castanet held out long enough for me to do that." Mahkbyth's voice was hoarse around the edges, and his eyes gleamed with unshed tears when he opened them again. "Langhorne and Bédard grant them peace and comfort."

"Amen," Murphai said softly, and despite his own feelings where the "Archangels" were concerned, he was totally sincere.

Silence lingered for a moment, and then the *seijin* cleared his throat.

"We've heard some fairly incredible rumors about what happened here in Zion after they were arrested. We're inclined to think there has to be at least some truth to them, but as to how much—?" He shook his head.

"If they're the same ones I've been hearing, 'incredible' is putting it mildly," Mahkbyth told him.

"Tell me what you've heard, and I'll tell you what *I've* heard," Murphai invited.

"Well, for starters—"

▼　▼　▼

In fact, Mahkbyth's version of events was seriously inaccurate, Murphai decided. Or, rather, *incomplete*. He had the most essential part of it straight, but exactly *how* everyone inside St. Thyrmyn Prison had died was another matter. Murphai listened gravely, nodding occasionally, then inhaled deeply at the end.

"Yes, they're the same rumors," he said then. "I can assure you, however, that it wasn't Dialydd Mab or any of the other *seijins* marching through the prison dispensing justice. Not because we wouldn't like to, you understand, but unless we're prepared to confront the Inquisition openly here on the streets of Zion, we can't be quite that . . . proactive. And I can also assure you it wasn't Grimaldi attacking the Inquisition in Shan-wei's name, either.

Although," he conceded thoughtfully, "that's actually not a bad move on Rayno's part."

"So you're pretty sure he's the one behind that particular story?"

"I can't say for certain, but it has the right smell to be something of his. And it's more subtle than Clyntahn tends to be." Murphai stroked his beard thoughtfully. "The first line of defense is to say nothing and deny that anything happened for as long as they possibly can. The second line of defense is to strengthen their own people's spines by spreading the story among the Inquisition's own that it was a demonic attack by Grimaldi against the champions of Mother Church. And they know damned well that version of it will 'leak' no matter how hard they stress the need to keep it confidential. Even inquisitors are human, and human tongues wag when you hand their owners a juicy enough story. And I'm fairly sure the third line of defense—and after the 'truth' about Grimaldi's involvement's had time to leak out and spread nicely—will be to inform all of Mother Church's children here in Zion that the Inquisition kept what happened secret while it investigated thoroughly. After all, who better to determine the truth of a demonic act than the guardians of the *Holy Writ*?"

"I'm sure you're right, but do you really think he's going to be able to sell that one?" Mahkbyth asked skeptically.

"You've lived in Zion longer than I have," Murphai pointed out. "How do you think the average Zionite would react?"

Mahkbyth frowned thoughtfully for several seconds. Then the frown segued into a grimace.

"You're right," he sighed. "Those who're already inclined to doubt anything that comes out of Clyntahn's mouth won't believe it for a moment. There are more of those than there used to be, too, but they're still a minority. And for those who don't disbelieve anything simply because *he* said it, there's going to be a real need to have *some* sort of explanation, especially with all the bad news leaking out in those mysterious broadsheets." He eyed Murphai speculatively. "In fact, I'm a little curious about why they haven't already reported the entire mystery. You wouldn't happen to know anything about that, would you, *Seijin* Murphai?"

"Me?" Murphai looked back innocently. "*I* haven't been in Zion since the last time you and I spoke, Ahrloh."

"That's not exactly an answer," Mahkbyth observed. "On the other hand, it's probably as close to one as I'm going to get, isn't it?"

"Probably," Murphai agreed. "On the other hand, if I *were* the one posting those—which, of course, I'm not—I'd probably wait to spread the truth until I knew what the truth *was*. My understanding is that they've been so effective in large part because they've never contained anything that wasn't both true and *accurate*." The *seijin* shrugged. "With something as . . . fantastic as this, I'd think they'd need to be *very* sure of their facts—and probably of how the Inquisition plans on spinning things once the story comes out. For that matter, I wouldn't be surprised—although you understand, of course, that I can't say for certain—if whoever makes the call on their content isn't experiencing the occasional mild glow of enjoyment while they think about how . . . unhappy Clyntahn and Rayno probably are while *they* wonder when it's going to hit the broadsheets. I imagine it's giving those two the odd sleepless night, don't you?"

Mahkbyth snorted a harsh chuckle of agreement. But then he stopped chuckling and stared out the shop windows into the street. Days were still short in Zion in May, even when the weather didn't decide to roll in on the city, and the western side of the square was already deep in shadow.

"Zhak will be back with my fish and chips soon," he said. "He may be an informant for the Inquisition, but he's a hard worker. Should I assume you'll be dropping by the house tonight in your usual inconspicuous fashion to continue this conversation?"

"Probably," Murphai said again. He turned casually to look out the windows at Mahkbyth's side, alert for Myllyr's return. "In the meantime, though, Arbalest didn't send me just to check in with you. She's got a mission for you."

"She does?" A sudden, bright light glowed in his blue eyes. "*Rayno?* Can I finally go after that sick son-of-a-bitch?!"

"No, not Rayno." Murphai shook his head regretfully.

"With all due respect, Arbalest needs to let us take him down," Mahkbyth said passionately. "There's nothing we could do that would hurt Clyntahn worse—aside from killing the fat bastard himself—and we need to send a message to the entire Inquisition. They may be keeping a lid on what happened inside St. Thyrmyn, but every agent inquisitor, from the newest lay brother on the streets to the borough bishops inquisitor, knows they took two of us alive. That's done a lot to undermine the . . . inevitability we'd acquired in their eyes."

"I can understand that, but it's really not the first time you've lost people," Murphai replied. "Are you sure you're not being influenced by the fact that this is so personal for you? You knew Bracelet, and Castanet may not have known who Barcor was, but she knew Ahrloh Mahkbyth."

"Of course it's personal. It's *all* personal, or I'd never have joined Helm Cleaver in the first place! That doesn't make me wrong, though. Tell Arbalest I *need* to take Rayno down and pin a note to his cassock telling the entire Inquisition it's retaliation—and justice—for what he did to two of our sisters. Let the fucking Inquisition deal with *that!*"

"I'd love to see it," Murphai said frankly. "Unfortunately, I think Arbalest is right. We still need him where he is. It may not seem like it, but he's actually a moderating influence. God only knows what Clyntahn would do if we took him off the board, but I'm willing to bet it would be a blood-bath." The *seijin's* lips twisted. "In some ways, that might not be a bad thing from the perspective of defeating the Group of Four. If he orders a purge as . . . promiscuous as the one he'd demand if the Fist of God eliminates Rayno—especially without Rayno to warn him against overreacting—it would have to further undermine the Inquisition's legitimacy in the eyes of almost all Zionites. But think of the number of other Bracelets and Casta-nets we'd create along the way."

"I'll grant you that," Mahkbyth said unflinchingly. "But sooner or later, we'll have to do it. And I'm serious when I say we need to hit the Inquisi-tion back—hard—to undercut the boost their morale's gotten out of this."

"Ultimately, what happened at St. Thyrmyn—even the *rumors* of what happened at St. Thyrmyn—will do all the undercutting you could want, Ahrloh," Murphai pointed out. "But that's not to say Arbalest doesn't agree it's time to 'send a message' to Clyntahn. She just doesn't want that message to be named 'Rayno.' Not yet. She's saving that one for a special occasion."

"So what 'message' *does* she have in mind?" Mahkbyth's eyes had nar-rowed. "It must be fairly special to send you personally to arrange it."

"Oh, believe me, she didn't have to *send* me for this one," Murphai told him. "For this one, I volunteered. In fact, it was something of a toss-up for a while as to whether I'd get to deliver it or Merlin would."

"Really?" The light was back in Mahkbyth's eyes—not quite as bright as it had been, but bright enough.

"Oh, *really*," Murphai said. "Apparently the Grand Inquisitor's still rattled by whatever actually happened at St. Thyrmyn, and he's decided he has to turn up the wick under everyone else. Just between you and me, I think he's almost at the point of making examples at the very top. In fact, in my ideal outcome, he'd decide to make an example out of *Rayno* so we didn't have to. It wouldn't exactly break my heart to see the good Archbishop in the Plaza of Martyrs."

"I'll bring the potato slices."

"That's what I thought. But that's not going to happen tomorrow. On the other hand, it seems the situation's getting bad enough in the Border States that Inquisitor General Wylbyr's been summoned to Zion for a per-sonal 'conference' with Vicar Zhaspahr."

"Arbalest thinks Clyntahn's going to send *Edwyrds* to the Punishment?" Mahkbyth sounded skeptical, and Murphai didn't blame him.

"Killing off the man he hand-picked to return Siddarmark to the fold would be a little demoralizing for the rank-and-file, I imagine," Murphai acknowledged. "He may be a lot closer to that point than he was a month or so ago, but, no. I think it's entirely possible he does plan to give the

Inquisitor General a significant tongue lashing and send him back to ginger up his inquisitors in the Border States and Tarikah and Westmarch. Their enthusiasm seems to have waned under Dialydd's tender ministrations."

The smiles they exchanged would have done any kraken proud.

"That's not what's going to happen, though," the *seijin* said then. "As it happens, we have a source which will give us Edwyrds' itinerary. We'll know exactly when, where, and how he'll arrive in Zion, and when he does, Helm Cleaver will be waiting for him."

"We get to take down Edwyrds?" Mahkbyth repeated very carefully, like a man making sure he'd heard correctly.

"You get to take down Edwyrds," Murphai confirmed. "Not only that, Arbalest wants it done *here*—in Zion itself, not out in the Border States or in the Republic where Dialydd Mab would receive credit for it. No questions about who's responsible for this kill, Ahrloh. And that note you wanted to leave pinned to Rayno's cassock? I think it wouldn't be . . . inappropriate to pin it to the Inquisitor General's, instead."

.III.
Lake City,
Tarikah Province,
Republic of Siddarmark.

The silent, efficient servants removed the dessert dishes and Earl Rainbow Waters' wine steward poured brandy into his and his nephew's snifters with the careful attention the ritual required. Then he stood back, decanter at port arms, raising one eyebrow at his master. A slow, thoughtful wave of the tulip-shaped snifter under aristocratic nostrils, a nod of approval, and a flick of Rainbow Waters' fingers indicated where he should set the brandy decanter—at the earl's nephew's elbow—and banished him to follow the other servants.

The wine steward bowed himself out, and the earl smiled indulgently as Baron Wind Song pulled out his pipe and raised his own eyebrow.

"Yes. Yes!" Rainbow Waters shook his head. "If you insist on destroying the palate of such an excellent brandy with tobacco, by all means do so."

"It doesn't *destroy* the palate, Uncle," the baron replied. "It *enhances* it."

Rainbow Waters snorted, because it was an old, familiar dance. And, while the earl would never have admitted it, even under torture, he rather enjoyed the scent of Wind Song's tobacco.

The baron did treat himself to a luxurious sip of his own brandy before he carefully filled the foamstone bowl. He tamped the tobacco, and then slipped a hand into his pocket for one of the "lighters" Harchongese artisans had begun to craft from the samples which had been captured from the heretics. Of course, the heretics' version were plain, unadorned—undoubtedly stamped out on some clumsy machine by one of their uncouth mechanics with dirty fingernails somewhere in one of their smoky, smelly manufactories—whereas the Harchongese version was exquisitely adorned, crafted of the finest materials by highly paid artists of the most impeccable sensibilities in a studio with perfect lighting and (probably) a harpist playing softly to aid its master's pursuit of his creative muse. Wind Song's, for example, bore a traditional hunting motif in bas-relief, with a magnificent prong buck, its eyes crafted from tiny chips of ruby, rearing as it was surrounded by the baying hounds.

And for the same cost and the same number of man-hours, the heretics would have produced at least two hundred of them, he reflected as he spun the wheel. The wick burst into flame and he lit his tobacco slowly and carefully. *Of course, it would never do to point that out. God forbid anyone back home should pay attention to Uncle Taychau's pleas to forget about luxury and start thinking about survival!*

"So," Rainbow Waters said as the younger man got his pipe properly alight and sat back in his chair, "what did you think of Bishop Merkyl's explanation of the Inquisitor General's travel plans, Nephew?"

That was coming to the point rather quickly, Wind Song thought. And the fact that Rainbow Waters called him "nephew" suggested he wasn't asking in his official capacity as the Mighty Host of God and the Archangels' commanding officer. Or not *solely* in that capacity, at least.

"I thought it was accurate in so far as it went, but probably . . . less than complete, Uncle," he replied after a thoughtful moment. The small beckoning motion of Rainbow Waters' left hand invited expansion, and he shrugged.

"I'm sure the Grand Inquisitor truly does need to confer with him about the Inquisition's affairs in the Republic. And, for that matter, in the Border States, now that he's been given authority in that area, as well. And, strictly between the two of us, I wouldn't be a bit surprised if Inquisitor General Wylbyr gets . . . quite an earful about the conduct of the inquisitors in Mother Church's camps in the Republic. On several points."

Rainbow Waters snorted, then sipped his own brandy with an expression that mingled disgust, unhappiness, and a certain bitter amusement.

Despite the best efforts of the inquisitors in charge of evacuating Mother Church's holding camps, more than two-thirds of those camps had been seized—liberated—by the advancing heretics over the previous summer. And, also despite the best efforts of the inquisitors in charge, the truth about how those seizures had occurred had gotten out. The fact that so many of the Inquisition's loyal servants had been less than zealous about obeying

Zhaspahr Clyntahn's orders to massacre the camps' inmates rather than allow them to be freed had not been calculated to soothe the Grand Inquisitor's feelings. True, much of that disobedience had been laid at the feet of the Army of God guard forces, but Rainbow Waters' sources in Zion reported that at least a half-dozen senior inquisitors had been severely punished—to the level of the Punishment, in at least two cases—for their failures. Or, perhaps, for failing to *conceal* their failures.

The fact that the Inquisition had found it necessary to make examples of some of its own boded ill, he thought. And it did put an interesting twist on Wylbyr Edwyrds recall to Zion.

I wonder if that fool is feeling just a little nervous? The possibility that he was brought Rainbow Waters a modest glow of pleasure.

"I expect you're correct about that," he said, gazing down into his snifter for a handful of seconds. Then he looked back up at his nephew.

"And what do you make of the rumors we're hearing out of Zion?" he asked much more softly.

Wind Song drew deeply on his pipe, filling his mouth with aromatic smoke. He held it for a moment, then blew a perfect smoke ring and watched it float upwards. The icy wind blustering about the eaves as another spring snowstorm dumped its burden on Lake City's roofs and streets made a fitting background to that silence, but as the smoke ring kissed the ceiling and disintegrated, he lowered his gaze to his uncle once more.

"I don't know *what* to make of them," he admitted. "The fact that there's been no mention of them in those broadsheets doesn't make me feel any more inclined to doubt them, however. It should, I suppose, but the whispers are too persistent, and they're coming from sources which are too highly placed to be readily dismissed. And, to be honest, our . . . friends in Zion seem too frightened by them." He inhaled deeply. "We've seen enough evidence—those broadsheets are a case in point—that whether they're truly demonic or not, these '*seijins*' aiding the heretics are capable of what one can only call superhuman feats, Uncle. If something like that's happened in the middle of Zion, then I fear much worse is to come *outside* Zion."

Rainbow Waters nodded gravely. It was the first time he'd asked Wind Song's opinion of the frightening rumors so frankly, and he was pleased by the boy's willingness to answer honestly—at least in private. More than that, he shared the baron's conclusions.

"I fear you have a point," he said. "And I've also received some additional, very private reports, both on events in Zion and in Dohlar, which have disturbed my sleep of late." Wind Song's eyes narrowed, but Rainbow Waters shook his head. "No, I'm not going to share them with you, Nephew, or even with Silken Hills. First, they contain no information truly relevant to our responsibilities to the Mighty Host. Secondly, it will be far better if you can honestly tell anyone who asks that you've never heard of the individuals providing those reports to me." He smiled, very briefly and without a trace of humor. "I promised your lady mother I'd try to get you home in one piece. I would prefer to have to worry only about the *heretics* where that promise is concerned."

The eyes which had narrowed widened as Wind Song considered the implications of that last sentence. It wasn't as if either of them had any doubt about the consequences if they failed Mother Church—or Zhaspahr Clyntahn, at least—but it sounded as if his uncle was becoming even more cautious.

Is it that, Wind Song wondered suddenly, *or is it something else? What do those "reports" say? And who are they from? I can't believe Uncle Taychau would ever actively conspire against the Inquisition or even Vicar Zhaspahr. Whatever else they may be, they speak with the full authority of* Mother Church*! I know how little he cares for the . . . aristocratic excesses Mother Church so often condones back home, if only by her silence, but he could never challenge the will of God's Own bride on Safehold! Unless. . . .*

A chill which had nothing to do with the snowfall outside the comfortable dining room went through him. Was it possible, he wondered, that his uncle was beginning to question whose side God was truly on?

"Well," Rainbow Waters said more briskly, "there's little we can do about matters in Zion, and Langhorne knows we have more than enough to concern ourselves with closer at hand. I've read your summary of Earl Silken Hills' progress on the handover to Bishop Militant Tahrens. I could wish he was in a position to take more of his own artillery south with him, but I suppose road conditions would make that difficult even if the Bishop Militant had enough guns of his own to cover his new positions. There are a few points where I no doubt need to see the actual numbers and sketch maps from his original reports, but overall the movement seems to be going well. From your memo, I take it that's your conclusion, as well?"

"It is," Wind Song concurred. "The spring thaw will come more rapidly on our southern flank, of course. Indeed, as I mentioned in my summary, the Earl had anticipated that the heretics in Cliff Peak were likely to move against his forward positions in the next several five-days. That's one reason he was so unhappy about handing them over to the Army of God on such short notice. On the other hand, he knew the terrain would still be bad for them, especially in light of the thoroughgoing destruction of the canals and high roads in his front, and he's arranged for his local commanders to brief their Army of God reliefs very carefully before they pull out. He's also had complete duplicates of all of his maps made for Archbishop Militant Gustyv and his staff.

"He's obviously concerned that if the heretics realize he's shifting so much of his strength south they may choose to move even sooner than he'd expected. Of course, if our spy reports are correct about the heretics' actual intentions—and none of his own patrols have picked up anything to challenge those reports—they have no intention of attacking the frontage he's handing over to Bishop Militant Tahrens, and the weather in western Westmarch and Sardahn isn't a great deal better just now than it is here." The baron waved the pipe in his hand to indicate the wind howling around the eaves and grimaced. "They're getting more rain and less snow than we are, but he doubts the heretics will be able to exert a great deal of pressure upon Bishop Militant Tahrens until the ground dries and their mounted infantry is once more capable of free movement off the high roads. I'm afraid he also believes they've accomplished more in the way of repairing their communications behind their own front over the winter, however, and if he's right about what they've managed opposite his current positions, it seems likely they've accomplished still more farther south. So once the ground does dry, they'll be in a better position to bring *heavy* pressure to bear upon him— and the Bishop Militant—than we'd hoped."

The baron shrugged ever so slightly.

"I won't say the Earl's delighted by his orders, nor do I think he's completely convinced the heretics truly are looking to the south, but I don't believe anyone could fault the fashion in which he's carrying those orders out."

His eyes met his uncle's levelly, and, once again, Rainbow Waters nodded. He couldn't really fault Silken Hills' skepticism, but while the intelligence reports available to him remained less complete than those the heretics' spies appeared to be able to provide to *their* field commanders, all of the Inquisition's sources supported the same conclusion.

Or all of the intelligence sources the Inquisition's seen fit to share with me, at any rate, he reminded himself. *Would that I could convince myself Vicar Zhaspahr's learned the consequences of . . . restricting the information he makes available to his own field commanders!*

Unfortunately, he couldn't, Still, there was no *conflict* between the Inquisition and his secular sources. That was an improvement in many ways. Now if only the conclusions they supported were more palatable!

The heretics were still reinforcing their armies in the northern provinces, but they were reinforcing their southern armies, as well. In fact, they seemed to be reinforcing them much more strongly than he'd anticipated when he created his original deployment plans, which certainly tended to support the conclusions coming out of Zion.

On the other hand, it was always possible he'd been right the first time around, wasn't it?

And if this business was simple, anyone could be a successful general, he thought dryly.

"Their troop movements would appear to suggest Vicar Allayn's read their intentions—their *immediate* intentions, at any rate—correctly," he observed out loud, although he and his nephew both knew Allayn Maigwair remained rather less strongly convinced of those intentions than certain other parties in Zion. "Mind you, they've demonstrated often enough that becoming too enamored of our own cleverness can have painful consequences," he continued. "And what happened to the Army of Shiloh suggests we should be particularly wary of convincing ourselves that we've positively identified where their troops truly are, as opposed to where they'd like us to *think* they are."

"Agreed, Uncle." Wind Song drew on his pipe again, then shook his head. "Despite everything, though, it still seems to me their armies could be most usefully employed in the north." He expelled another jet of smoke on an unhappy sigh. "I recognize the threat in the south, but surely we have greater strategic depth there . . . aside from Dohlar. And to be honest, I'm concerned about Earl Silken Hills logistics south of Usher. Given recent events in the Gulf, I fear his supply line from South Harchong is in serious jeopardy, and Dohlar has nothing to spare from its own production to make up the loss."

"Now there, Medyng, you are unfortunately correct."

Rainbow Waters allowed himself another sip of brandy, then leaned back in his chair, resting his head against the cushioned back.

In the wake of the Imperial Charisian Navy's crushing defeat of the Royal Dohlaran Navy's Western Squadron, their light-commerce raiders had swarmed into the Malansath Bight and effectively closed the entire central Gulf to Mother Church's shipping. The limited quantities of weapons and food still reaching the Mighty Host from South Harchong all now had to funnel through the Sherach Canal, down the Altan River, across Hankey Sound, and all the way up around the Dohlaran coast to Dairnyth before it could ascend the Fairmyn River to the Charayan Canal or flow down the Dairnyth-Alyksberg Canal to the garrison still holding Alyksberg. Unfortunately, the Sherach Canal could handle no more than ten percent, at the outside, of the freight which could have been shipped across the Gulf but for the Charisian presence. Just as bad, the coastal route forced upon Mother Church by the loss of the Sheryl-Seridahn Canal cut deeply into the Church's increasingly limited supply of cargo ships. It was a simple enough equation: if it took twice as long for a galleon to complete a round trip, that was the same as having only half as many galleons.

But there was worse to come, because it couldn't be very many more five-days before those accursed commerce-raiders began operating in the Gulf of Tanshar and even the Bay of Bess, as well. When that happened, the entire Kingdom of Dohlar—and everything south of it, including anything still getting through from South Harchong—would be cut off from the rest of the mainland.

Which, he acknowledged, might well lend point to Clyntahn's predictions of a major southern offensive. I'd expected them to settle for . . . neutralizing Dohlar while they threw their main weight against me here in Tarikah and Westmarch. They wouldn't need to encompass Dohlar's outright conquest for that, and I expect they'll encounter their own difficulties in suppressing local resistance, now that they're getting into more densely populated areas of the kingdom. The need to hold down guerrilla movements will soon begin dissipating their manpower, just as it dissipated the Army of God's in Siddarmark. So why incur the expense in casualties and resources to force its formal surrender? Especially if it diverts them from the destruction of the Mighty Host? Surely we remain the primary threat to the Republic, at least until the Army of God can finish rebuilding after last year!

He chose not to dwell on the likelihood that the heretics' policy of religious tolerance might defuse a great deal of that resistance. Nor did he dwell upon the fact that the example of *Zhaspahr Clyntahn's* policies in Siddarmark might well have done even more in that respect in the end. Besides, that was neither his affair nor his responsibility.

But I hadn't really considered their navy, had I? He shook his head mentally, chiding himself for that blindspot. *If anyone in the world has ever demonstrated that he understands how to blend land and seapower into one strategy, that person has to be Cayleb Ahrmahk. I have no idea even now if he truly intends to conquer Dohlar this year or not—the fact that he continues not to reinforce Hanth as strongly as his other armies may well indicate he doesn't—but then again, he doesn't need to if the Inquisition's spies are correct. Given how far back Rychtyr's been forced, a naval presence in the Bay of Bess would completely sever Dohlar from the rest of the Jihad, anyway. And they can land troops there directly from Chisholm. . . .*

He sighed. His instincts all still insisted the heaviest attack would come in the north, under Green Valley and Eastshare, yet he couldn't ignore the steadily accumulating evidence in favor of the southern strategy. And whatever *he* might think, the directives coming out of Zion were clear enough.

And it's not as if moving Silken Hills leaves your right flank naked, Taychau! Of course you'd rather have your own troops covering Talmar and Selyk, but at least Teagmahn's command's had almost a full year to train. The rest of this new "Army of the Center" will be greener than grass, but Teagmahn's made a solid enough start on replacing Silken Hills. And Walkyr will assume overall command next five-day. It's hard to think of an AoG commander who could do a better job of fitting the newer divisions into place as they come in. Things could be far worse, and you know it. Of course. . . .

"Unfortunately," he said, his voice rather grimmer than he normally allowed it to become, "the situation in the Gulf of Dohlar also makes the Holy Langhorne absolutely vital as the only direct waterborne connection between the Temple Lands and the Mighty Host. That's the main reason I feel confident they'll be calling on us here, as well as in the south, as soon as weather permits."

Wind Song nodded in stonefaced acknowledgment . . . and agreement. Neither of them chose to mention the fact that the Holy Langhorne Canal might not have been quite so essential if the Imperial Charisian Navy hadn't demonstrated the year before that it could completely dominate Hsing-wu's Passage, as well. At the moment, supplies were still being sledded in to the detachments watching the Mighty Host's extreme northern flank across both the Passage's ice and the high road that paralleled it. Once that ice melted, however, spring floods would make even the high road unusable for at least three or four five-days . . . and the Passage's waters would become a high road for the *heretics*. And as the Charisian Empire had demonstrated, its navy and army understood "amphibious operations" better than anyone else in the world.

Not surprisingly, the baron reflected, unaware of how his thoughts mirrored those of his uncle. *It's obvious they understand everything about these hellish new weapons and . . . questionable devices better than anyone else does!*

Well, perhaps they did. But his uncle clearly understood the new realities better than any other field commander they'd yet faced. It only remained to see whether or not he understood them well *enough*.

He'd better—*we'd* better, Wind Song told himself. *Because if Dohlar does fall, and if Silken Hills is pushed back from the Snake Mountains, they'll damned well try to push up north through Jhurlahnk and Usher to hit the Holy Langhorne from that direction. That means we have to inflict defeats—or at least decisive* checks—*on both flanks, because if we don't, if they're able to reach the Holy Langhorne from* either *direction, we'll have to fall back so rapidly we'll never be able to pull out all our men, far less all our artillery and other supplies. The ring around the Temple Lands and North Harchong would become unbreakable, even if we managed to retreat with some semblance of order. And if that happens. . . .*

He busied himself tamping the tobacco in his pipe bowl and decided not to think about that too deeply.

The three men seated at one end of the vast, richly polished table looked up as someone knocked sharply on the chamber door. The door opened and a tallish, brown-haired man in his early fifties stepped through it.

"Bishop Executor Wylsynn and Father Ahbsahlahn are here, Your Grace," he said quietly.

"I see." Samyl Cahkrayn, the Duke of Fern, glanced across the table at his companions, then back at the man in the doorway. "Thank you, Lawrync," he said. "Please, escort them in."

"Of course, Your Grace."

Lawrync Servahntyz had been Fern's personal secretary for almost eighteen years. During those years, he'd seen a great deal, and very few things could disturb his monumental aplomb. Yet there was an unusual edge of something very like anxiety in his brown eyes as he bowed to his patron. Whatever it was, it seemed to have vanished by the time he straightened, stepped back a pace, and closed the door once more.

It opened again, twenty seconds later, and all three of the men at the table rose as he reappeared, followed by Bishop Executor Wylsynn Lainyr and Father Ahbsahlahn Kharmych.

"Your Grace, Bishop Executor Wylsynn and Father Ahbsahlahn."

Few introductions had ever been more superfluous, and Fern stepped forward to kiss Lainyr's extended ring.

"Your Eminence," the Dohlaran first councilor murmured as he straightened. "You honor us with your presence."

"It's my honor to be so courteously received by such loyal defenders of Mother Church," Lainyr replied.

The dukes of Thorast and Salthar came forward to kiss Lainyr's ring in turn, and Fern waved the bishop executor to the seat of honor at the far end of the gleaming table. The tallish Kharmych—Lainyr was above average in height, but the intendant was both seven years younger and a head and a half taller—took the chair at his superior's right elbow. Servahntyz opened the rollup top of the desk in one corner and started to seat himself, prepared to take notes, but Lainyr's raised hand stopped him. Duke Fern raised one eyebrow in polite interrogation, and the bishop executor shook his head ever so slightly.

"Thank you, Lawrync," Fern said after only the briefest of pauses. "I don't believe we'll need notes for today's meeting."

"Of course, Your Grace," Servahntyz replied. He closed the desk once more, then bowed to Lainyr and Kharmych. "Your Eminence, Father," he murmured, and withdrew, closing the ornately carved council room door silently behind him.

Silence hovered for a second or two, then Lainyr cleared his throat.

"Thank you for seeing me on such short notice, Your Grace," he said to Fern.

"Your Eminence, you're Bishop Executor of Dohlar," Fern observed a bit dryly. "We can usually make a little time in our busy schedules when you think you need a word with us."

"I know." Lainyr smiled briefly. "I also know that isn't always easy, though, because you truly do have very busy schedules, all of you. That's true at any time, but I'm painfully well aware that it's even truer at this moment. Indeed, I wouldn't intrude on you if a matter of some considerable importance hadn't been brought to my attention."

"What sort of 'matter,' Your Eminence?" Fern asked obediently as the bishop executor paused, clearly inviting the question.

"I've received a letter," Lainyr replied. "It arrived last five-day, and I spent the last six days in prayer and meditation, trying to decide what to do about it."

Fern nodded, his expression attentive, although his own sources suggested the "prayer and meditation" had actually been a case of waiting for a response from Zion. The duke didn't know what Lainyr's urgent semaphore transmission had contained, but both of Fern's discreetly—and expensively—bribed sources in the Church-administered semaphore office confirmed that the bishop executor had dispatched a lengthy coded message to the Temple, addressed collectively to Zhaspahr Clyntahn, Zahmsyn Trynair, and Allayn Maigwair. That was sufficient grounds for concern, but scarcely so unusual as to rise to the level of worrisome, given the fact that Mother Church *was* at war . . . and losing. Unfortunately, Lainyr's message had been accompanied by an even lengthier one from Ahbsahlahn Kharmych which had been addressed solely to the Grand Inquisitor, and *that* had elevated the duke's reaction from simple worry to outright alarm.

The fact that it had taken at least three days for those messages' recipients to decide upon a reply didn't make Samyl Cahkrayn feel one bit less alarmed.

"Having prayed and meditated," Lainyr continued somberly, "I've decided my proper course is share that letter's contents and concerns with you."

"With me, specifically, Your Eminence, or with all of us present, collectively?"

Another unnecessary question, Fern thought, *since you specifically asked for all three of us to be here. I wonder if you get as tired of this diplomatic song and dance as I do, Your Eminence?*

"Most immediately, with you and Duke Salthar." Lainyr nodded in Salthar's direction. "Under the circumstances, however, it does touch upon Duke Thorast's legitimate concerns, as well, I believe."

"Then please tell us how we can be of service."

"Thank you, Your Grace."

Lainyr reached into the breast of his cassock and removed two folded sheets of handwritten paper. He unfolded them carefully and laid them on the table in front of him, running the heel of one hand across them, as if to smooth out the fold marks, then looked up once more.

"Your Grace, this is a letter addressed to me from Sir Clyftyn Rahdgyrz. It wasn't an easy letter for him to write, and I'm afraid that, after much prayer, I've concluded parts of it must be treated as falling under the seal of the confessional." The bishop executor shook his head slowly. "Sir Clyftyn was obviously deeply troubled by his decision to write me at all, and it's my belief the portions of it which deal directly with his spiritual concerns are best left between him, Mother Church, and God. I trust you'll respect that decision on my part."

"Of course I will, Your Eminence," Fern assured him, just as seriously and soberly as if he'd had an actual choice in the matter.

"Thank you."

Lainyr smiled again, fleetingly, but then his nostrils flared and he sat back in his chair, squaring his shoulders.

"Your Grace, I'm sure you know—I know Duke Salthar does, at any rate—that Sir Clyftyn and Sir Fahstyr Rychtyr have been close friends for many years?"

Fern nodded, and Lainyr stroked the letter in front of him.

"The reason I mention their long friendship is because I believe it lends added point to Sir Clyftyn's concerns. I think it best to remind all of us that this is the letter of a *friend* and a man of honor and deep conviction, not of a personal enemy, political opponent, or anyone with what you might call an ax to grind. In other words, he would never have said anything . . . potentially damaging about a friend of such long-standing if he hadn't believed he had an overriding responsibility to God and the Archangels to do so."

The bishop executor paused, and Fern glanced at the other two. Then he turned back to Lainyr.

"Should we assume this letter is somehow . . . critical of Sir Fahstyr, Your Eminence?" he asked in a careful tone.

"I'm afraid it is." Lainyr's expression was grave, but he raised one hand in an almost placating gesture. "Mind you, it doesn't criticize Sir Fahstyr's devotion to God, Mother Church, or his Kingdom in any way. If anything, it extols his devotion. At the same time, however, Sir Clyftyn has concerns—*deep* concerns—over certain of Sir Fahstyr's recent decisions. I believe he feels fatigue, which I'm sure is completely understandable given the terrible burdens the Jihad has laid upon Sir Fahstyr's shoulders, is beginning to affect those decisions."

"I see."

Fern leaned back in his own chair, and his mind raced. He did, indeed, know about the close friendship between Rahdgyrz and Rychtyr, and he would never have expected Rahdgyrz to provide such potentially lethal ammunition against Rychtyr to the Inquisition.

But he didn't, really. Or he wouldn't see it that way, at any rate, so maybe you should have seen this coming. *You've always known how . . . aggressively devoted to Mother Church Rahdgyrz is. If there's one man in the entire Kingdom who'd be constitutionally incapable of questioning Zhaspahr Clyntahn's version of reality, it would have to be him. And the way the Jihad's been going has to be like acid eating his soul. He thinks we're failing God, and that's unacceptable. But he also believes Mother Church is still the clean and dutiful Bride the* Writ *describes, not captive to someone like Clyntahn. So he wouldn't see this as betraying his friend to the Grand Inquisitor. If he'd wanted to do that, he'd've written to* Kharmych, *not* Lainyr! *No, he's a dutiful son of Mother Church bringing his concerns to her senior shepherd here in the Kingdom, and he truly believes she'll listen compassionately, not judgmentally.*

"Which of Sir Fahstyr's decisions are causing General Rahdgyrz distress, Your Eminence?" he asked after a long, still moment. He stressed the military title very slightly, and Lainyr's eyes seemed to flicker.

"*Sir Clyftyn,*" the bishop executor's tone recognized—and rejected—the duke's implication that, as an officer in the Royal Dohlaran Army, Rahdgyrz' concerns might more appropriately have been expressed to his secular superiors, "is concerned that Sir Fahstyr's exhaustion is affecting his readiness to stand and fight. I should point out that Sir Clyftyn expresses the opinion that if, in fact, General Rychtyr is . . . disinclined to engage the heretics in a fight to the finish, that hesitation owes far more to the thousands of casualties his army has suffered than to any trace of physical or moral cowardice on his part. Sir Clyftyn agrees Sir Fahstyr is a good and godly man, Your Grace, and a brave soldier, but he's also a very tired one. An officer who's seen far too many of his men viciously slaughtered by the heretics. If, in fact, that's the case—if grief for all of the *other* brave soldiers who've died under his orders is affecting his judgment—that would be totally understandable. Indeed, given how long he's held his command, and the pressure under which he's operated for so long, it would be remarkable if a man of Sir Fahstyr's caliber *wasn't* affected—to some extent, at least—by the casualties his regiments have taken."

You're trying much too hard, Your Eminence, Fern thought. *If you really thought so highly of Rychtyr—or if your superiors did, anyway—it wouldn't have taken six days for you to bring this to us. Of course, that does rather raise the question of why it did take so long. And of why that lunatic Clyntahn isn't already frothing at the mouth for us to send Rychtyr off to Zion!*

"I'm sure General Rychtyr *has* been under a great deal of stress, Your Eminence," he said out loud. "And the *Book of Bédard* warns us about the many ways in which fatigue and stress can affect our judgment. Could you, perhaps, be a bit more specific about the aspects of his recent decisions that cause you—and Sir Clyftyn, of course—to think that might be true in his case?"

"I should think the decision to simply surrender Bryxtyn and Waymeet to the heretics without so much as a fight might be a case in point, Your Grace," Kharmych said a bit sharply, speaking up for the first time.

The intendant was only in his mid-thirties, brown-haired and with a very fair complexion. A native of the Episcopate of St. Cehseelya on the shore of Hsing-wu's Passage, he found Dohlar's hotter summers difficult. That wasn't the only thing he found difficult about his present assignment, however, for he was a man of strong passions. He wasn't what anyone might have called a tolerant man, either, nor was he always a tactful one. Lainyr gave him a dirty look, but the kingdom's intendant seemed unfazed.

"Neither fortress had even been *attacked* when he ordered their garrisons to evacuate," he continued. "Surely they could have tied down considerable numbers of the heretics' forces if they'd resisted until they could be relieved!"

"Is that the opinion Sir Clyftyn expressed?" Fern inquired after a moment.

"It was one of the decisions that concerned him, yes, Your Grace," Lainyr said before Kharmych could respond, and this time the intendant wasn't able to ignore the sharp glance that came along with the words.

"Did Sir Clyftyn believe Bryxtyn or Waymeet could have held out for an extended period?" Duke Salthar asked, leaning forward slightly in his chair.

"No, Your Grace—not for an *extended* period." Lainyr appeared unhappy about that concession, but he gave Kharmych another stern glance when the intendant shifted in his chair.

"And, in answer to the . . . difficulty which you see with Father Ahbsahlahn's analysis," the bishop executor continued, looking back to Salthar, "Sir Clyftyn didn't suggest it would be possible to relieve either fortress in anything *less* than an extended period. He did, however, feel they might have held up the heretics long enough to permit General Rychtyr to establish a new front between, say, Kraisyr and the Bryxtyn High Road. As he points out, a labor force sufficient to throw up fresh entrenchments at that point was readily to hand. Given as much as another five-day or two, that labor force could have erected defensible earthworks. In Sir Clyftyn's opinion, at least."

"I see." Salthar sat back once more and stroked his flowing mustache with a thoughtful air. "No one in the world has more respect or a greater admiration for Sir Clyftyn's courage and tactical skill, Your Eminence," he said then. "He's demonstrated both of those far too conclusively to ever doubt them. However, I think it might be well to point out that the distance from Kraisyr to the Bryxtyn High Road is just over ninety miles as the wyvern flies. At the time Sir Fahstyr—and Father Pairaik—ordered the evacuation of the two fortresses, the Army of the Seridahn's effective strength had fallen to approximately thirty-eight thousand men. That would have given him about four men per yard of frontage if he'd attempted to hold a line that long."

"Sir Clyftyn wasn't suggesting holding that entire distance in a single fortified line, Your Grace." Kharmych's sharp tone was that of a man who couldn't keep himself from responding, despite the bishop executor's glare.

"I'm sure he wasn't, Father," Salthar replied. "But that's still the density Sir Fahstyr would have had to cover the distance. I'm afraid this is something he and I had discussed earlier, well before the heretics crossed out of the South March. If you'd like, I can share the correspondence with you and the Bishop Executor. To summarize, however, the sense of our conversation was that to generate sufficient density to hold an extended line like that would require him to adopt a 'nodal' deployment. He couldn't have enough men in any one spot to resist a heretic attack without splitting his army into numerous smaller forces and stringing them out like beads in a necklace. But he simply can't afford to parcel his men out into isolated fortified positions, like that, unable to offer one another mutual support. He was outnumbered by the heretics by very close to three-to-one. If he'd dug in in the necessary nodal positions, Hanth would have found it absurdly simple to drive forces between them to isolate them from one another and then bring overpowering strength to bear on each of them in turn. The entire Army of the Seridahn would almost certainly have been destroyed within five-days."

Something flickered in Kharmych's eyes, and Fern kept his expression very carefully neutral as he saw it.

"There might well have been risks involved in such an attempt, Your Grace, but he could still have compelled the heretics to deploy against him," Lainyr pointed out before Kharmych could speak. Salthar cocked his head politely, and the bishop executor shrugged. "He's done that several times since his retreat from Thesmar. Indeed, that's how his strategy was explained to Mother Church from the beginning. The entire idea was to compel the heretics to bring up the 'overpowering strength' necessary to crush his for-tified positions because they would expend precious time doing that before he slipped away and required them to do it all over again. Was that not the way *you* understood it, Your Grace?"

His tone was a bit more pointed, although still considerably less sharp than Kharmych's had been.

"Yes, Your Eminence, that's exactly the way I understood his proposed strategy from the beginning. And as we pointed out to Captain General Al-layn, without more manpower—and the weapons for them—that was the only strategy available to us. But for it to work, he needs to find positions that are relatively compact and where he can establish something like firm flanks. And, I should point out that the dryer ground and the flatter terrain west of the border strongly favor the heretics' greater mobility. That puts them in a far better position to flank any line he establishes—or to break through between nodes and crush them in isolation—than they were over the winter while he had them pinned against the canal in the bad ground east of the border. And that, I'm afraid, securing his flanks means finding terrain that significantly restricts their mobility. Unfortunately, he couldn't have done that on the line you're saying—if I understand you correctly, at least—Sir Clyftyn advocated."

Lainyr nodded, although his expression was that of a man who didn't much care for where the conversation was going. And, of a man who hadn't expected the Duke of Salthar to be the one taking it there.

Fern kept his own expression merely politely attentive, but it was diffi-cult. What he really wanted to do was to beam at Salthar in approval. The other duke would never see seventy again, and he'd have been utterly out of his depth trying to actually manage a battle using the new model weapons Charis had introduced to the world. But the first councilor had always known he was a long way from stupid. He might not be anything like adequately versed in the new style of warfare's *tactics*, but he understood *strategy* just fine. On the other hand, he'd always been one of the Jihad's strongest supporters. He might have been willing, upon occasion, to question some of Mother Church's tactical decisions, but he'd been firmly devoted to achieving her victory at any cost. He'd been one of the voices in King Rahnyld's Council upon whose support Lainyr and Kharmych had always been able to depend. The possibility that this time might be different obviously didn't make the bishop executor very happy.

Of course, he hasn't known Shain as long as I have, Fern thought dryly. *Yes, he's a loyal son of Mother Church, but the problem with a man of faith is that he's a man of faith. If you push him beyond the limits of his beliefs, his own understanding of God's will, bad things can happen . . . especially when you crank in a dash of des-peration. And he is feeling the desperation. For that matter, you know damned well that desperation's playing a part in* your *thinking, now don't you? What was it Cay-leb's supposed to have said? Something like 'When a man knows he's going to be hanged in a five-day, it concentrates his thoughts wonderfully' or something like that, wasn't it?* The first councilor snorted silently in harsh amusement. *Man may be a heretic—for some definitions of the word, anyway—but he* does *have a way with words!*

Lainyr wasn't the only person at the table who looked unhappy with Salthar's analysis.

"But sooner or later, *somewhere*, he has to actually *stop* the heretics, Your Grace!"

Kharmych's tone was hotter than an upper-priest should use to the duke who commanded Mother Church's only army currently in contact with the enemy, Fern thought. This time, however, Lainyr showed no inclination to call his attack dog to heel.

"After all," the intendant continued, "every mile they advance leaves still more of the faithful children of Mother Church in heretical clutches!" The corners of the intendant's eyes strayed towards Thorast. "They're already over a hundred miles deep into the Kingdom, a third of the way across Thorast. And when General Rychtyr abandoned—I mean, declined to defend—Shandyr, he handed Hanth the largest city in eastern Thorast! If he wasn't prepared to stand in defense of that city, where *will* he stand?!"

This time he looked straight at Thorast, clearly inviting his contribution to the argument, and the duke shifted in his chair.

"Believe me, Father," he said gravely, his expression troubled, "I under-stand what you're saying, and the thought of my people in the grip of heresy, however temporarily, weighs heavily upon me."

Kharmych's eyes gleamed, and he couldn't quite keep an edge of triumph out of the glance he shot Fern and Salthar. But Thorast wasn't quite done yet.

"Despite that," he continued in that same grave tone, "as a military man, I find myself in unhappy agreement with Duke Salthar. General Rychtyr's done brilliantly in slowing the heretics as much as he has, particularly after the . . . rash fashion in which the Army of Justice was hazarded—and lost—in the Shiloh Campaign." He shook his head. "With all the other heavy charges upon the Kingdom—especially those of the Navy, with which I'm particularly familiar—it hasn't yet been possible for us to reconstitute the strength we lost in Siddarmark. We have well over five and a half thousand miles of coastline, Your Eminence, whereas our entire land border frontier runs less than a thousand miles north-to-south, and after the Western Squad-ron's destruction, the heretic navy's in a position to threaten every single mile of that coast." He shrugged ever so slightly. "It's our responsibility—*my* re-sponsibility, as a servant of the Crown and a member of the Royal Council—

to protect *all* of His Majesty's subjects, not just my own duchy. Beset by threats from so many directions, we have no choice but to spar for time while we rebuild the strength to take the battle to the heretics. Until we've done that, the best we can hope to do is to continue General Rychtyr's delaying tactics. In time—when our own forces are stronger, or when the results of Mother Church's other armies have forced the heretics to rethink their posture here in the south—not only will we stand and fight, we'll retake the offensive and drive the Jihad through to final victory. Until then, however, I believe General Rychtyr's strategy is the best available to us. And I also think the Army of the Seridahn as a whole has a great deal of confidence in him. If we were to relieve him at this time, the damage to the army's morale might be severe."

Kharmych sat back in his chair, his thunderous expression one of mingled anger, frustration, and surprise, and Fern hid a tart smile.

Didn't see that one coming either, did you, Father? he thought. *Wouldn't have, either, if Shain and I hadn't worked on him for a couple of hours first! Probably wouldn't have brought him around in the end, anyway, if he realized* Thirsk's *the one who wrote that analysis he just delivered instead of Shain! Or if most of the wealth in Thorast wasn't in the west, closer to Erekston and Lake Sheryl, for that matter. Aside from Shandyr the only things eastern Thorast has are farmers and forests, and those don't pay much in the way of taxes. But he did come through nicely in the end. So now what do you do?*

The first councilor kept his eyes on Kharmych, but his attention was actually focused on Lainyr. The intendant was probably a better barometer of Zhaspahr Clyntahn's attitude, but Lainyr would offer a far better measure of the Group of Four's actual policy.

"Your Grace," the intendant said, rallying and leaning forward once more, "while I know you speak from the heart, surely—"

"A moment, Ahbsahlahn," Lainyr said.

The bishop executor's expression was stony, his eyes hard, but he placed a restraining hand on Kharmych's arm and inclined his head ever so slightly in Fern's direction.

"Your Grace, I see you and your colleagues have, indeed, thought these issues through." He showed his teeth in something that wasn't quite a smile. "While I might . . . differ with certain of your conclusions, Dohlar is your Kingdom. The spiritual welfare of King Rahnyld's subjects is the duty of Archbishop Trumahn, Father Ahbsahlahn, and myself, but the burden of their *secular* welfare rests rightfully upon the King's shoulders and in your hands, as his servants. Certainly no one could fault the energy and devotion Dohlar's brought to the Jihad from the very beginning. If it seemed in any way that I'd suggested differently, I assure you that was never my intention. If you, as the secular authorities here in Dohlar, are satisfied with General

Rychtyr's strategy, then certainly *I* am! It was never a question of his devotion to God or Mother Church. I believe Sir Clyftyn may well have a point about his mounting fatigue, and as one of his spiritual shepherds, I beg you to keep watch upon him. Don't drive him beyond his breaking point or lay burdens upon him which may be too heavy for his weary shoulders. Beyond that admonition, I leave the conduct of the battle against the heretics here in Dohlar in your capable hands."

Well, someone *in Zion's developing a case of nerves,* Fern thought. *I wonder who? It's got the feel of Trynair's touch, but Clyntahn must be more . . . anxious than I'd thought, too. Maybe even he can figure out how badly he got his fingers burned here in Dohlar with that whole business with Thirsk's family?*

Whatever it was, the decision not to push if King Rahnyld's ministers declined to relieve Rychtyr had clearly come from Zion, not from Archbishop Trumahn or from Lainyr. That was interesting. In fact, that was *very* interesting.

They're afraid we'll become another Desnair and they obviously need us more than they needed the Desnairians. But this goes farther than that. We're in deep trouble, but we're not exactly on the brink of collapse yet. But I have to wonder about this . . . reasonableness on Clyntahn's part. We're not simply anchoring their southern flank right now, we're also a lot closer to Zion and the Temple Lands—for that matter, to the Mighty Host!—than Desnair. That give them a bigger stick in our case, so, logically, they should be less concerned about us deciding to . . . opt out of the Jihad. And if they're worried about I anyway, why the velvet glove? Where are Clyntahn's decrees and demands? The command *that we recall Rychtyr . . . and the veiled—and not so veiled—threats like the ones he used against Thirsk if we decided to be obstinate about it? Could he be becoming less confident about the Inquisition's power here in Dohlar? Or is there something else in play? Something about this summer's campaign they haven't told us about?*

"Your Eminence," he said out loud, "I never thought for a moment that you questioned Sir Fahstyr's courage or devotion." He shook his head with a smile. "No one who knows him could question either of those! But it's certainly fair for others, especially friends like Sir Clyftyn, to worry about the strain of the burden he's carried for so long. The fact that he expressed those worries to you, and that you—as the acting shepherd of the entire archbishopric—brought them in turn to us speaks well for the regard in which Sir Fahstyr is held by all those who know him."

The first councilor of Dohlar smiled again, bending his head in a graceful nod of thanks.

"I assure you, Your Eminence," he continued, "we'll be mindful of both the burdens we ask him to bear and of the responsibility *we* bear, as you've just reminded us, for the secular welfare of all of King Rahnyld's subjects."

.V.
Protector's Palace,
Siddar City,
Republic of Siddarmark;
and
Claw Island,
Sea of Harchong.

Congratulations, Cayleb!" Greyghor Stohnar, Lord Protector of the Republic of Siddarmark, extended his hand with a huge smile as Cayleb Ahrmahk entered the conference room with Aivah Pahrsahn at his side and Merlin Athrawes at his heels. "I've just been reading the copy of Baron Sarmouth's dispatches you forwarded to us. We don't use decadent things like patents of nobility here in the Republic, of course, but if we did, I'd say that man deserves promotion to some title *way* beyond a mere *baron!*"

"Yes, he has done rather well by us, hasn't he?" Cayleb responded, clasping the Lord Protector's forearm firmly. "On the other hand, I'm not too sure he'd actually like being known as 'Earl *Shipworm*,' you know!"

Stohnar laughed in acknowledgment, but then Cayleb grimaced.

"He got hurt worse than we could wish, but you're still right. I hate losing even one man we don't have to, but in cold-blooded terms, the elimination of Raisahndo's squadron was worth every drop of blood it cost. And neither he nor Earl Sharpfield like to let the grass grow under their feet."

"I have to admit I spent a rather pleasant evening last night—with a good bottle of Chisholmian whiskey, as a matter of fact—contemplating what his activities have to be doing to Silken Hills' logistics," Daryus Parkair, the Republic of Siddarmark's seneschal, said with a wicked smile as he bent to press a kiss of greeting on the back of Aivah's hand. "Especially after the way they're weakening themselves along the Sardahn Front, thanks to Aivah's devious little notion."

He bestowed another kiss on the back of her hand and beamed at her, and she smiled in gracious acknowledgment of the compliment. Someone from a cave hidden in the Mountains of Light made a rude sound in her earplug, but she ignored it. Someone had to be the public face of the strategy, and they couldn't exactly credit a prince who'd been dead for several years.

"It's been obvious from all our reports that they'd on shipping in an awful lot of the support he'll need covering the Snakes and protecting Tymkyn Gap," Parkair continued in a tone of profound satisfaction. "This means

Teagmahn—and Walkyr, now that he's reached Glydahr—will have to share their part of the overland supply route with him. So he's going to be short of the material support he'd anticipated, and Walkyr won't be able to build up as rapidly or as strongly as *he'd* hoped, either. We've always been a land power, and I don't think I ever fully appreciated how valuable seaborne logistics could be. Which is probably because no one's ever fought a war on this scale before. But you Charisians have shown me a thing or three, and I think the lesson Baron Sarmouth's just taught the Temple Boys is a lot more painful than *my* lessons've been."

"Fair's fair," Cayleb said. "We Old Charisians never had an army to speak of, but even Sharleyan's Chisholmians had a lot to learn about mainland logistics—especially canals—from you people."

"That's probably true," Parkair conceded. "With both sides trashing canals as they retreat, though, that seaborne side of things is even more important. And when the ice melts in the Passage and your slash hounds get loose again in *those* waters, those Temple bastards—*all* those Temple bastards— will find themselves between the proverbial rock and a hard place."

"Yes, they are," Cayleb acknowledged with an answering smile. But then, as Merlin pulled out one of the heavy chairs at the conference table and seated Aivah in it, that smile faded a bit around the edges.

"They are, but that simplifies the strategic equation for them, as well as for us. The only way we can come at them is from the front, and they know it." He grimaced. "The decision to move Silken Hills south helps from our perspective, but those damned fortifications of his are still going to be there. Walkyr may not be as well-equipped to defend them as the Mighty Host would have been, but his men will be a lot more effective—and kill a lot more of *our* men—fighting from them than any of us is going to like.

"I have to admit, I'd almost prefer to let Walkyr get himself thoroughly settled while we very quietly pulled troops back to the Passage coast on Baron Green Valley's right. If we did that and combined them, the Army of the Hildermoss, and some of the new drafts from Chisholm, we could put together a tidy little amphibious force to drop on the *Temple Lands* coast the same way we got around behind the Corisandians in Manchyr. They couldn't pull enough men to stop us back from the Host without uncovering the Holy Langhorne, and now that they're basically sending every man the Army of God has forward to cover Rainbow Waters' right flank they wouldn't have a reserve that could stand up to us any more than General Gahrvai did in Corisande."

"That would be sweet, wouldn't it?" Parkair murmured, a speculative light gleaming in his eyes, but Cayleb shook his head.

"First of all, we can't count on their sending *everything* forward to Walkyr. As you just pointed out, what's happening in the Gulf of Dohlar's going to force them into some fairly fundamental logistic reconsiderations, and they may decide it's more important to move artillery and ammunition than manpower. More importantly, though, the Mountains of Light are just a *bit* more of a barrier than the Dark Hills were, and unless we could simultaneously cut the Holy Langhorne behind then—which would mean we'd still have to punch through their front somewhere—we couldn't starve the Host out the way we could General Gharvi's army. If we couldn't finish them off in the field before winter—or at least link up with Green Valley through the Mountains of Light so *our* people didn't starve over the winter—we'd have to pull them back out, and that would be a copper-plated bitch."

"I agree it would be a decisive stroke, if we could pull it off," Stohnar said soberly, sinking into his own chair. "But you're right. Too much could go wrong. Sometimes it's better to stick with the frontal approach, even if you know it's going to be costly, if you're confident it will still work. And barring the sort of miracle those bastards in Zion sure as hell don't deserve, this *will* work, Cayleb."

"I think it will, too," Cayleb acknowledged, taking his chair at the other end of the table, with Merlin at his shoulder.

"That doesn't mean it's not going to be bloody as hell, though," the emperor continued more bleakly. "It would help a lot if Rainbow Waters was as incompetent as Kaitswyrth."

"Although I realize Duke Harless would tend to disprove what I'm about to say," Parkair said dryly, "no one has any right to expect two opponents as toweringly incompetent as Kaitswyrth in a single generation, far less the same war."

"I'm afraid that's true," Samyl Gohdard, the Republic's keeper of the seal, agreed sourly.

"Then let's be grateful for the ones we've been given," Aivah suggested.

"And the fact that we *have* been given more than one of them would seem to further underscore whose side God is truly on," Archbishop Dahnyld Fardhym put in. "Of course, I'm probably a little biased on that subject."

A mutter of laughter ran around the table, and Stohnar grinned.

"I think we all find ourselves in agreement on that point, Dahnyld," he told the archbishop.

"Absolutely," Cayleb said firmly. "And, sort of on that head, there's another bit of news I'd like to deliver before we get into discussing our most recent status reports from Duke Eastshare, Baron Green Valley, and General Stohnar."

"More evidence God's on our side?" Stohnar leaned back and crossed his legs. "That sort of thing is always welcome, Cayleb!"

"Well, this is actually more Aivah and Merlin's news than mine." The emperor waved one hand in an airy gesture. "More of that devious, under-handed, sweaty spy stuff Daryus has just been talking about, you understand."

"Only too well, Your Majesty," Henrai Maidyn, the Republic's chan-cellor of the exchequer and spymaster, said feelingly.

He remained astonished and perplexed—in a pleasant but nonetheless worrisome fashion—by the incredible efficacy of Charis' *seijin*-backed spy networks. For the present, he was delighted by that efficacy, but even the closest of allies would need to keep an eye on their friends once the war against the Group of Four ended and the more usual game of thrones re-sumed. If the *seijins* continued to support Charisian intelligence efforts when that longed for day arrived. . . .

"Madam Pahrsahn?" Stohnar invited.

"Our agents report that the Dohlaran Council—or at least its two most important members, Fern and Salthar—are being . . . less than totally sub-servient to the Group of Four's demands," Aivah said. "There's nothing overt we can point to, and they certainly aren't *defying* the Temple. But Clyntahn, at least, would clearly like to see Rychtyr removed from the Army of the Seridahn in favor of a more aggressive commander, and Fern and Salthar have declined to do anything of the sort. Not only that, they appear to be sitting on Thorast in that regard, despite the fact that Earl Hanth is well into Thorast's duchy."

"I suppose I'm happy to hear Fern and the others may finally be grow-ing big enough balls—you should pardon the expression, please, Aivah—to stop licking Clyntahn's hand like obedient little puppies," Stohnar said. "On the other hand, I'd *love* for them to put someone 'more aggressive' in com-mand of Rychtyr's army! Earl Hanth would eat him for breakfast!"

"True," Aivah agree with a smile. "But that's only one straw in the wind. A significant one, perhaps, but not as significant as some of our other reports. There are indications—and I stress that at this point they're *only* indications—that Earl Thirsk and General Ahlverez may be thinking in terms of . . . a Dohlaran exit strategy completely independent of anything Fern may have in mind."

Stohnar came upright in his chair and Parkair's eyes widened abruptly.

"You're serious, aren't you?" the Lord Protector said after a moment. Aivah nodded, and Stohnar frowned. "I realize you said you had only indications, but how strong are they?"

"We can confirm that they've held several meetings now," she said. "Given the enmity between them prior to the Shiloh Campaign, that would be informative enough in its own right, I think. Anything that could bring the two of them together—my destiny, especially with Ahlverez still under such a cloud in the Church's eyes and what just happened to Thirsk's family, would have to be pretty important. In this case, however, the individual who's brokered those meetings may be even more significant."

"Really?" Maidyn leaned forward with an intent expression. "And who would that individual be?"

"Staiphan Maik," she said simply, and Parkair muttered an incredulous oath.

"Thirsk's *intendant* is . . . facilitating secret meetings between him and Ahlverez?" Stohnar said in the tone of a man who wanted to be very sure he'd understood correctly.

"That's exactly what he's doing." Aivah nodded. "It appears that what happened to Thirsk's family was something of a tipping point for Maik, as well." Her tone was somber. "The man may be a Schuelerite, but evidently his order hasn't managed to amputate his conscience the way it's done for so many of Clyntahn's other hand-picked representatives."

"And on top of what happened to Thirsk's family," Merlin put in, "Maik has what certainly looks like a genuine sense of pastoral responsibility. Not just for the Dohlaran Navy, either. I think he's worried about what will happen to the entire Kingdom if this goes down to the bitter end."

"And he damned well should be," Parkair said in a considerably harsher tone. The Charisian side of the table looked at him, and the seneschal shrugged, his earlier amusement vanished. "Let's not forget where a goodly chunk—the most *effective* chunk!—of the Army of Shiloh came from. Or, for that matter, what Rychtair did in South March and Ahlverez did at Alyksberg. That was a pretty sharp dagger they planted in our back. As your lady wife said in that splendid speech that's appeared in all the newspapers, Your Majesty, there's a price for actions like that."

"I can't deny that," Cayleb said, after a moment. "But I also think we'd all have to admit that whatever their other faults, the Dohlaran Army—and its Navy, for that matter, despite what happened to Gwyllym and the others—have fought a hell of a lot 'cleaner' war than the Army of God or Desnair."

He ended on a slightly rising note and quirked an eyebrow at the seneschal.

"There's a difference between 'cleaner' and *clean*," Parkair growled. But then his nostrils flared as he inhaled deeply. "Still, you have a point. And as you said a few minutes ago, I don't want to lose a single man we don't have to lose. If there's an acceptable . . . arrangement that takes Dohlar out of the war, then I suppose we probably have to be reasonable about accepting it."

"It's not a decision we'll need to make tomorrow, whatever happens," Aivah pointed out pragmatically. "But it is something to consider. And I think it's especially important to consider the broader impact a Dohlaran exit would have."

"Broader impact?" Gahdarhd's tone suggested he already saw where she was headed, and she nodded to him.

"Precisely. After Baron Sarmouth's victory at Shipworm Shoal—and especially after *Gwylym Manthyr* reinforces Earl Sharpfield and Baron Sarmouth's squadron shifts farther east—Dohlar will be as effectively neutralized as Desnair. From a practical viewpoint, Earl Hanth could stop at Shandyr and adopt a defensive stance and Dohlar—and South Harchong, for that matter—couldn't do a single thing to affect what happens in Tarikah or Cliff Peak this summer. That may not be all that apparent to anyone else if Dohlar's still formally in the jihad, but what happens if Dohlar *withdraws* from the jihad? I think we're all in agreement that our minimum requirement would be a *formal* withdrawal, one which is officially acknowledged and not just another unilateral 'we're not going to fight anymore' *in*formal arrangement like Desnair's."

She looked around the table, saw agreement on every other face, and shrugged.

"That sort of formal withdrawal—a *surrender*, really, whatever it's called—by a Mainland realm would have an enormous impact on morale in the Border States, North Harchong, and even the Temple Lands. We all know Clyntahn will rant, rave, and thunder anathemas, and I don't doubt he'll make 'examples' of any Dohlaran he can possibly accuse of 'complicity' in the 'betrayal of Mother Church.'" Her beautiful face twisted in an expression of distaste. "I'm sure the certainty he'd do exactly that would be a hard pill for Thirsk and Ahlverez to swallow, too. But no matter how he tries to spin it, he won't be able to hide the fact that the Church's most effective ally—a *Mainland* ally, not just another of those barbarian Out Island realms, *and* the one whose navy the Group of Four's own propaganda's held up as their counterweight for the ICN—has abandoned them. And if, as I'm sure would happen, Thirsk, Ahlverez and, possibly even Maik, denounce Clyntahn and the Group of Four as the corrupters of Mother Church they actually are. . . ."

Her voice trailed off, and Stohnar nodded firmly.

"You're right," he said. "I'm with Daryus where the price for Dohlar's earlier actions is concerned, but we're hardly alone in that. And if they're willing to formally and officially denounce Clyntahn and his friends, that would be a pretty hefty installment on the debt, as far as I'm concerned."

"I know that's not an easy thing to accept," Cayleb said quietly. "Truth to tell, it won't be an easy choice for me and Sharleyan, either. And it's not one we'll have to make until and unless Thirsk and Ahlverez decide they have to act, come up with a plan, and actually make it work. Trust me," his tone turned grim, "if they try and *fail*, the price Clyntahn will exact from the entire Kingdom's likely to be a lot higher than either of us would ever have asked for."

"Absolutely, Your Majesty," Fardhym said. The archbishop's expression was troubled—not by doubt, but by his concern for the lives of any of God's children. "I trust no one will be offended if I spend a few Wednesdays praying for them, as well as for their success."

"I'm sure Maikel will be doing exactly the same thing in Tellesberg, Your Grace," Cayleb assured him. "For that matter, I don't have the same sort of . . . access you two have, but I may find myself spending a little time on my own knees over them."

Silence fell again, lingering for several seconds until Stohnar straightened in his chair again and inhaled.

"That was certainly some of the best *potential* news I've heard in a long time," he said briskly. "However, we have a few more immediate concerns right here in the Republic, and I think we'd better get back to those status reports from the northern front if we want to finish in time for dinner. Cayleb, the first point I'd like to consider is the Army of Tarikah's supply position. I know Baron Green Valley's said he's satisfied, but—"

▼　　▼　　▼

Quite a few of the spectators crowding the batteries and steadily expanding quays seemed to have trouble believing their eyes, Earl Sharpfield thought dryly. That was fair enough. *He* was having a little trouble in that regard.

HMS *Gwylym Manthyr* had waited until full light to make her way across Shell Sound and then through North Channel into Hardship Bay. She'd taken North Channel because it was wider and quite a bit deeper than Snake Channel, and Halcom Bahrns obviously had no intention of putting his magnificent new command onto a sandbar. For all her size, *Gwylym Manthyr's* normal draft was actually only three feet deeper than a *Rottweiler*-class ironclad's, but it seemed impossible, looking at her, that that could be true, and he didn't blame Bahrns one bit for his caution.

Saluting guns boomed from the battery, and *Manthyr* replied with a timed ripple of smoke from her larboard four-inch breechloaders. The cheers rising along with the salute were deafening, and it was a bit difficult for Sharpfield to remember his dignity and not join them. Not that anyone would have held it against him, under the circumstances.

The enormous, gray-hulled monster moved across the harbor's tiny waves with preposterous, majestic grace, gliding through the water, turning back a thin mustache of white and leaving a brief, glassy smoothness in her wake. Not a man watching her could doubt that he looked upon the final doom of the Royal Dohlaran Navy. Sharpfield was no different in that respect, but in some ways he was actually happier to see the columns of smoke following her out of North Channel.

There were four of them, each rising from a ship barely twenty feet shorter than *Gwylym Manthyr* herself. They weren't warships. In fact, those tall, boxy, slab-sided hulls weren't armed at all. Their only defense was the fact that no hostile warship in the world could possibly *catch* one of them, but in their own way, they were even more dangerous to Charis' foes than *Manthyr*.

"Victory ships." That was what Emperor Cayleb had christened them when the Duke of Delthak—only he'd still been simple Master Ehdwyrd Howsmyn at the time—first proposed them, and that's precisely what they were: the first steam-powered, ocean-going cargo vessels in the world. These four, like the eight sister ships still completing behind them, had steel frames and wooden planking. The next flight were already well into construction, however, and they'd be steel-hulled, as well as framed. They'd also be at least a little faster, but Sharpfield wasn't about to complain about what he had. Each of those four ships could carry just over ten thousand tons of cargo, five times as much as the largest galleon in the world, for ten thousand miles at a constant speed of almost thirteen knots, regardless of wind conditions, on a single bunkerload of coal.

He didn't have a complete list of their present cargo, since—like *Manthyr*—they'd far outrun any dispatches. He did know, in general terms at least, what was *supposed* to be aboard them, however, and he smiled thinly at the thought.

Manthyr slowed still further as Bahrns reversed power. She was barely ghosting through the water now, and a fountain of white erupted as her anchor plunged into the harbor.

And now, Sharpfield told himself, starting down the stone stairs to the launch bobbing at their feet, *it's time for me to go inspect my new toy. And it's not even God's Day!*

He chuckled at the thought, but then the chuckle stopped and he frowned thoughtfully.

Well, maybe that's not really true, he reflected. *It won't* formally *be God's Day until July, but the* Writ *teaches that every day belongs to Him, and just this minute, He's in the process of showing those bastards in Zion whose side He's really on, isn't He? Because when* Manthyr *turns up in Gorath Bay, the message will be pretty damned clear.*

I *really* don't like what we're hearing about those damned rockets. Kynt," Ruhsyl Thairis said quietly. The Duke of Eastshare and Baron Green Valley rode through the chill afternoon along Dahltyn Sumyrs Way, the slushy central road across the sprawling complex of Camp Mahrtyn Taisyn, towards Green Valley's headquarters block. "If they're as good as the *seijins'* reports suggest they are, we're going to get hurt a lot worse this year than last."

"Yes, we are," Green Valley replied unhappily, his breath steaming faintly in the cold. "But, let's be honest, Ruhsyl. We already knew that was going to happen. This'll only push the price a little higher than it would have been anyway. And at least we know about them, so we can take them into consideration."

"And at least Duke Delthak's given us our own rockets," Eastshare acknowledged with a sharp nod.

"That he has. And this latest cold snap'll give us at least another few five-days to get them to the front."

"Well, *that's* a case of finding a bright side to look upon if I ever heard one!" Eastshare laughed sourly.

" 'We can't change the weather, only curse it'," Green Valley responded, quoting a Chisholmian proverb. "And if the damned winter wants to drop four or five feet of late snow on us, I might as *well* find something good about it!"

"Can't argue with that."

They reached their destination and their escort drew up around them. There was quite a lot of that escort, actually. The Imperial Charisian Army wasn't in the habit of taking chances with its general officers, and the last effort to assassinate Eastshare had occurred barely three months ago. The last attempt on *Green Valley's* life, on the other hand, was well over a year old. The Inquisition could still find zealots willing to carry out suicidal missions, but it had become evident Green Valley's security was simply too good. No one had gotten within a hundred yards of him in so long even Wyllym Rayno had decided his assets could be better expended someplace they had a chance of succeeding.

The two generals dismounted, once the escort commander had given his gracious approval, and handed their reins to waiting orderlies and started up the short flight of steps to the covered snow porch that fronted the HQ block. As they did, Captain Bryahn Slokym, Green Valley's aide, opened the door and stepped out onto the porch, came to attention, and saluted.

"Captain," Eastshare acknowledged, returning his salute, then smiled and patted the younger man's shoulder. "Congratulations on the promotion."

"Thank you, Your Grace." Slokym smiled and nodded to the red-haired, slightly built major following at Eastshare's heels. "There seems to be quite a bit of that going around. I understand that happens to people who spend a lot of time around generals."

"No, does it really?" Major Lywys Braynair said, rounding his eyes as he clasped forearms with Slokym.

"That's what I've heard, anyway, Sir."

"You obviously don't keep him trimmed back to size, Kynt," Eastshare observed, scowling ferociously at the captain.

"And you *do* keep Lywys pruned back, is that it? You'll have to show me how that works sometime," Green Valley said innocently.

"Well, I suppose as long as they keep doing their jobs—and have plenty of hot chocolate or that barbarous cherrybean ready—I'll let them keep their ill-deserved promotions," the duke replied.

Slokym opened the door again, holding it for his superiors, then followed them into Green Valley's office. Where, by the strangest coincidence steaming carafes of both hot chocolate and cherrybean tea were ready and waiting. With fresh donuts, no less.

"Passable, I suppose," Eastshare observed as the generals shed coats, hats, gloves, and mufflers. He blew into his cupped palms for a moment, then settled into a chair while Slokym poured hot chocolate into a cup for him. "Passable."

Green Valley snorted in amusement, then settled into his own chair.

In a lot of ways, today's meeting was a pure formality. Eastshare had been kept fully briefed on his plans, and the duke had suggested more than one useful improvement. There'd been plenty of time—more time than any of them wanted, really—to tweak those plans. And Rainbow Waters had compelled them to do more of that tweaking than Green Valley would have preferred.

Still, there was no true substitute for face-to-face discussions. Even the most carefully written dispatch could be misconstrued, and without that face-to-face conversation, there was no opportunity for the sort of feedback that might correct the misunderstanding. That was something Ruhsyl Thairis understood bone-deep, and Green Valley felt yet another surge of admiration for his superior. Eastshare wasn't a member of the inner circle. He had access to neither the SNARCs' reconnaissance capabilities—certainly not in real time, although it was true that the "*seijins*' reports" he regularly received helped a great deal in that respect—nor to the real-time *communication* capabilities of the inner circle. Green Valley enjoyed both those advantages, yet Eastshare's performance was at least as good as his own. In his personal opinion, it was actually *better*, in fact.

And because Eastshare understood the value of personal conferences, he'd made the wearisome circuit of his broadly deployed army commanders. Which, in the middle of a mainland winter, was scarcely a trivial undertaking. Camp Taisyn was his final stop, however. He'd head back to his more central position in Glacierheart as soon as they were finished, and even with canal ice boats, Safeholdian high roads, and snow lizard-drawn sleds, he was looking at three solid five-days of travel just to get there.

So maybe those extra five-days will come in handy after all, the baron reflected.

He tipped back in his chair with a cup of cherrybean in one hand and a donut in the other and contemplated the large, detailed wall maps. There was a lot of information on them. Any Inquisition spy would cheerfully have sacrificed an arm for an hour or two to look at them and take notes, and Green Valley's smile grew hungry as his eyes drifted towards the southern end of the long front stretching from Hsing-wu's Passage all the way to the Gulf of Dohlar.

Nahrmahn Baytz' deception plan had borne better fruit than even the rotund little dead Emeraldian, who was no more addicted to modesty in death than he'd been in life, had dared to predict.

Green Valley had a great deal of respect for Gustyv Walkyr. The archbishop militant wasn't simply an intelligent man or a smart commander; he was also a man of compassion whose heart had been sorely tried by the kind of war he'd been ordered to fight. In fact, Green Valley had decided it spoke rather better for Allayn Maigwair than he'd ever expected that a man like Walkyr was so obviously devoted to the Church's captain general on a *personal* level. Especially when Walkyr so obviously knew Maigwair had to be in Zhaspahr Clyntahn's sights.

He expected Walkyr to make the best use anyone could have of his advantages of position, his fortifications, and his artillery and rocket launchers. But Earl Silken Hills would have done the same thing, and however good Walkyr might be, the caliber of his men didn't come close to that of Silken Hills' men. Those Harchongese serfs had spent the better part of two years learning to outpace their tutors, acquiring a set of military skills no "Temple Boy" army had ever possessed. There were still holes, they were still . . . unsophisticated, and their units weren't as capable of thinking for themselves as the best of the original Army of God divisions had been. They were immensely better at it than any *current* Army of God division, however, and their sheer toughness—especially their cohesion—made them extraordinarily tough opponents. They possessed a deep and abiding faith in themselves, their weapons, and—astonishing in any Harchongese army, and an enormous tribute to Rainbow Waters—in their *officers*. They were tough-minded, tenacious, and unlikely to give in easily, whatever happened, but they were also pragmatic and realistic.

Green Valley would have been happier if the men of the Mighty Host had been supremely confident of victory. That kind of assurance could be turned against an army. A crushing victory—like his own, when he'd arrived in the nick of time to stop Bahrnabai Wyrshym from breaking through the Sylmahn Gap—did far more damage to the morale of an overconfident army than to one with a realistic grasp of the task before it.

The Mighty Host of God and the Archangels was too realistic for overconfidence . . . but it was also a long way from expecting to lose. One of Rainbow Waters' most impressive achievements—and God knew he'd managed one hell of a lot more "achievements" than Green Valley would have preferred!—was his ability to produce an army which still believed it could win, even though it knew it would confront enemies with better weapons and more experience. That would have been more than bad enough from Green Valley's perspective, but Rainbow Waters hadn't stopped there. He'd also used the example of Sir Fahstyr Rychtyr's success in slowing Hauwerd Breygart to inculcate an understanding that even a *retreating* army could accomplish its most important mission. That the simple fact that the Host might be forced to give ground didn't mean it had been *defeated* as long as it maintained its cohesion, continued to fight, and withdrew in good order to the next point at which it could stand. He'd convinced his men that as long as their army existed, so long as they were still fighting—still represented a formed force in the field—they were accomplishing their mission in God's defense.

I wish to hell he'd never come up with his damned realization that a tactical defense could be the best strategic offense, but it probably would've been expecting too much for someone as smart as he is not to realize that. I can actually accept that. But did the insufferable pain in the arse really have to be able to convince his entire damned army of that? That's just a little much.

Whatever else might happen, the new-model Mighty Host was most unlikely to simply shatter. It was far more probable that it would conduct a tough, resilient fighting withdrawal along the routes Rainbow Waters' commanders had already surveyed and marked on their maps. The kind of fighting withdrawal that would get a lot of Charisians and Siddarmarkians killed. Kynt Clareyk couldn't help admiring a commander who could overcome the prejudices of his birth—and the inveterate, hard learned distrust of serfs who'd been abused for centuries by people from families just like his—sufficiently to create that kind of fighting force out of the functionally illiterate men who'd been conscripted for the Mighty Host, but he sure as hell didn't need to like the consequences.

And that was why he was so happy Nahrmahn's suggestion appeared to have worked out so well. By the time the Allied offensive actually kicked off, Gustyv Walkyr's AOG divisions, supported by perhaps a hundred and fifty thousand Border State levees, would have sole responsibility for almost nine hundred miles of the Church's front, from the southern end of the Great Tarikah Forest all the way to the northern end of the Black Wyvern Mountains. His men would be "corseted" on either side by Harchongians, but they represented an undeniable soft spot in the Church's defenses. One the Allies thoroughly intended to exploit, and he felt a powerful surge of eagerness to be about it. He fully expected the upcoming campaign to be the bloodiest—from the Charisian side, at least—they'd yet fought. But he also expected it to be decisive, despite the worst Taychau Daiyang could do, and if it wasn't, it wouldn't be because he and his fellows hadn't planned for every contingency they could think of.

The canals were thawing, the ICN's ironclads—including the original *Delthaks*—would soon be free to operate along the rivers and canals in the armies' rear, and the first steam-powered canal barges would be available as soon as the ice melted. Hsing-wu's Passage would be navigable within another three or four five-days, as well, and the Navy was waiting impatiently. Both its galleons and another half dozen *City*-class ironclads were ready to push into the Passage the instant they possibly could with orders to take, burn, or destroy any attempt to move seaborne supplies. And when there weren't any of those supplies to interdict, they could amuse themselves raiding the Temple coastal shipping cowering under the threadbare protection of the protective batteries in the larger bays and inlets along the Passage's flanks.

Like Eastshare, he was thoroughly unhappy about the new rockets Lynkyn Fultyn had devised to supplement the Church's artillery. For that matter, he was less than enthralled by the proliferation of field guns, angle-guns, and first-generation mortars appearing in the Mighty Host of God and the Archangels' artillery parks now that the Church's foundries were producing good quality steel in quantity. Still, his own artillery was stronger—in absolute terms, certainly and probably even relatively in comparison to the Temple's—than the year before, and the small arms situation was highly satisfactory. Virtually all of his Charisian infantry had been equipped with the M96 magazine-fed rifle, and over half of the Republic's infantry had been reequipped with Trapdoor Mahndrayns, a third of which had been converted right here in Siddarmark. Sandarah Lywys Composition D-filled shells were actually a little ahead of schedule, although he still wouldn't have them in time for the campaign's opening moves, and almost a third of his infantry's rifle ammunition was now smokeless, which would probably come as a nasty surprise to the Temple.

The Republic's manufactories had recovered almost completely from the dislocations of the Sword of Schueler, and their production was climbing nicely, as well. Siddarmark-built versions of Charisian-designed weapons— and even innovations which owed nothing at all to Charis—were beginning to make their way onto the battlefield in ever increasing numbers. Green Valley was delighted by the increase in weapons production, but he was even more delighted—for a lot of reasons—that Siddarmark was clearly catching what Merlin called the "innovation bug." And in this case, one of those reasons was Ahntahn Sykahrelli.

Sykahrelli, an artificer in a Midhold Province manufactory before the Sword of Schueler, had enlisted in the Republic of Siddarmark Army before the first Charisian Marine's boot ever touched a Siddar City dock. Since then, he'd risen from the enlisted ranks to the rank of major and put his technical background to good use as an artillerist. He'd seen a lot of action in the process. He'd been only a sergeant in the Sylmahn Gap Campaign, but he'd also assumed acting command of his battery after every one of its officers had been killed or wounded, and that battery had been the lynchpin of the final gun line which had held the line at Serabor with its teeth and fingernails until Green Valley could move to Trumyn Stohnar's relief. He'd commanded the remnants of no less than three batteries, with almost enough men to have fully crewed *one*, by the end of that bloody night, and he'd come out of it with a battlefield promotion to captain and the Cross of Courage, the Republic's highest award for valor.

It wasn't too surprising that a man with his experience had understood the implications immediately when he was briefed on the new Temple rockets. But he'd also been inspired, and—taking advantage of the better propellants and, especially, the Lywysite his Charisian allies could provide— he'd produced a man-portable rocket of his own. The initial version was actually light enough to have been shoulder-fired, if there'd been some way to protect its user from the back blast. Green Valley felt confident a solution to that problem would be found eventually—if Sykahrelli didn't come up with one, no doubt the Delthak Works would be "inspired" to—but in the meantime, he'd up-sized it a bit and turned it into a crew-served weapon whose portability and devastating punch offered all sorts of possibilities. It would also be available in quantity, if not in the numbers Green Valley would have liked, and neither the Temple Boys nor the Harchongians were going to like *that* one little bit.

No, he thought, bringing his eyes back from the maps to his superior, *they aren't. They won't like the Balloon Corps or some of our other surprises, either. And I don't give a* damn *what the other side's come up with. End of the day, our boys will kick their arses up one side and down the other. We may lose a lot of good men along the way, but this year, by God—this year—we end this frigging war.*

"All right, Bryahn," he told his aide. "Now that you've got us properly ensconced, cups in hand, august posteriors parked in our chairs, donut crumbs covering our tunics, why don't you begin with a quick overview of our current deployment? After that, I think a detailed review of Rainbow Waters' most recent adjustments at Ayaltyn and Sairmeet are probably in order."

He cocked an inquiring eyebrow at Eastshare, and the duke nodded.

"That sounds like an excellent place to start," he agreed. "But first, I understand your patrols have brought back some examples of a new footstool the Harchongians have deployed?"

"Yes, they have," Green Valley confirmed rather less cheerfully. "It's actually more of a foot stool crossed with a sweeper though."

"A sweeper?" Eastshare cocked his head. "From the initial reports, I was thinking they were more like fountains," he said, using the ICA's term for the "bounding" mines Charis had fielded a couple of years earlier, and Green Valley scowled.

He'd hated the fountains even when Charis had held a monopoly on them, but they'd been too useful not to be utilized at a time when the ICA was so desperately outnumbered.

"I can see where you might've gotten that impression," he said, "but they don't seem to've figured out how to make them launch themselves. Instead, they've come up with a sort of domed footstool with a hundred or so old-style musket balls embedded in a 'roof' of pitch and resin. When the charge goes, it sprays the musket balls directionally in a cone. It might be more accurate to call the pattern a hemisphere I suppose, though, now that I think about it." He shrugged. "Either way, the things are going to be a major pain in the arse."

Eastshare made a less than delighted sound of agreement. Like Green Valley, he'd always recognized the consequences of introducing a weapon like the footstools. He'd even considered objecting to their use, but no commander worthy of his men could refuse to embrace such a potentially effective weapon when those men were going to be outnumbered a hundred-to-one . . . or more. And they'd been enormously useful. In fact, they'd probably been the decisive factor—or at least *one* of the decisive factors—in his ability to stop Cahnyr Kaitswyrth's advance after Kaitswyrth massacred Mahrtyn Taisyn and his men. But the wyvern he'd worried about seemed to be coming home to roost, although at least Green Valley had insisted on devising a doctrine for dealing with footstools—*sweeping* them, he called it—at the same time he'd come up with one to employ them offensively. It was a slow and dangerous process, however, and that, unfortunately, would favor the Mighty Host more than the Allies in the upcoming campaign.

Anything that clogged Allied mobility—and especially the mobility of Charis' mounted infantry—had to be considered a good thing from Rainbow Waters' perspective.

"Well, I can't say I'm happy to hear that," he observed. "We knew it was coming eventually, though. And at least your boys've made sure it doesn't surprise us. That's something. In fact, that's a lot! Your scout snipers brought it in, Kynt?"

"Yes." Green Valley nodded, then smiled. "I can't help suspecting Rainbow Waters probably didn't want them laid quite this early. He knows how active our patrols are, and he's too smart to not want to surprise us with it."

"A local commander trying to be sure he gets them in before you jump him, you think?"

"That's exactly what I think."

In fact, Green Valley *knew* that was what had happened. And while he was grateful for the warning, he could wish Rainbow Waters hadn't engendered enough independence of mind in his frontline commanders to make something like this possible. The *"seijins"* could have "discovered" the new weapon's existence in ample time to plan for the upcoming campaign. In fact, the report had already been written when the scout snipers quietly dug up an actual example and brought it in for examination. In a lot of ways, he would have preferred to rely on the *seijins* rather than face an army whose officers had learned the value of initiative . . . and who weren't afraid of their superiors' wrath if they got caught *exercising* that initiative, even against orders.

"Well, thank Andropov for small favors!" Eastshare said philosophically, then leaned back in his chair and waved a donut with a bite taken out of it at the captain standing, pointer in hand, in front of the huge map of Tarikah Province.

"I apologize for the interruption, Captain Slokym," he said. "I'll try to keep my mouth shut until you get through your initial briefing." He smiled crookedly. "And I'll also try to remember how much *I* always hated being interrupted by monumentally senior officers when it was my turn to do the briefing."

"I promise you, Your Grace," Slokym said solemnly, "that such an ignoble thought would never cross my mind."

"Junior officers who lie to generals come to bad ends," Eastshare remarked to no one in particular, his eyes carefully fixed upon the ceiling.

"I believe I've heard that, Your Grace," Slokym said and laid the tip of his pointer on the town of Ayaltyn.

"To begin, Sir," he said in a much more serious tone, "the Harchongians have been thickening the overhead cover on their bunkers here at Ayaltyn, and if they're doing it here, they're probably doing the same thing everywhere else, as well. We suspect that's the result of more of those tests

Captain of Horse Rungwyn and Lord of Foot Zhyngbau have been conducting." He grimaced. "Whatever inspired it, it's going to make them harder artillery targets when we launch our attack. Unfortunately, we're still going to need the river line, and that means dealing with Ayaltyn somehow. That's why we've moved the Fourth Mounted around to the west and given Brigadier Tymkyn two extra battalions of M97 field guns and a hundred or so of Major Sykharelli's new rockets, plus a company of mounted engineers with demolition charges and the new flamethrowers. In addition, we've—"

His pointer moved again as he spoke briskly, confidently, without ever consulting the notepad in his pocket, and High General Ruhsyl Thairis, Duke of Eastshare, cocked his head and listened intently.

JUNE

YEAR OF GOD 898

The Wednesday wind blowing sharply off Lake Pei spread the voices of Zion's thousands upon thousands of bells all across the City of God on Safehold. They sang their ageless song of God's love for His creation and His children on this, His day, and that song was more welcome than ever in these times of worry and despair. It promised His people comfort and ultimate victory, whatever temporary reverses His servants here in the world might suffer. It would be God's Day, the highest holy day of the year, in only two more five-days, and the entire city was already bedecking streets and buildings with banners, spring flowers, and icons of the Archangels and Holy Martyrs while its hundreds of churches and cathedrals purified and reconsecrated themselves in anticipation of that joyous celebration. After April's terrible news from the Gulf of Dohlar and May's dreary, late-spring snows, His people needed that promise, that confirmation that they truly were *His* and that He would never forget them.

The wind spreading that joyous music across the city was brisk enough to strike a chill even in the bright June sunlight, but the picked bodyguard of Temple Guardsmen and agents inquisitor made a brave show as they waited on the immaculate, marble-faced quay consecrated to the Temple's use, like an island of snow-white sanctity on the bustling Zion waterfront. Polished armor and the silver-plated heads of the halberds the Guard still carried on ceremonial occasions flashed back the sun, which gleamed less brilliantly from the burnished barrels of far more businesslike rifles and pistols. Banners snapped above them—Mother Church's green-and-gold and the flame-badged purple of the Inquisition.

Wyllym Rayno had been scheduled to join them, but the Grand Inquisitor had decreed otherwise at the last minute. Probably, Rayno thought, watching through a parapet-mounted spyglass from the Temple Annex roof, because for all the pomp and ceremony, Zhaspahr Clyntahn was less than pleased with the man those guards were there to escort directly to his first audience. Rayno couldn't be certain that was why his own agenda had been changed. He only knew his new instructions had been waiting when he'd emerged from the Temple side chapel dedicated to the Archangel Schueler after celebrating his own Wednesday mass. On the other hand, he *did* know it would have been like his superior to "send a message" to the Inquisitor General by deliberately changing Rayno's itinerary to snub Edwyrds only after making certain the Inquisitor General had received his own copy of it. After all, if he hadn't received his copy first, he wouldn't have known he was *being* snubbed, would he?

Petty of Zhaspahr, but it does get his feelings across, doesn't it? the archbishop mused, deflecting the spyglass from the bodyguards to the vessel still the better part of two miles out from the waterfront. Like so much else of the Temple, that spyglass was a holy relic, finer than anything mortal hands could make, with lenses that were water-clear and powerful. Now he turned the focusing knob until the boat leapt into crystalline clarity, only an arm's length away despite the distance, and smiled as he saw spray bursting white on the purple-bannered schooner's weather bow.

It must be chilly out there—among other things—in the boat bouncing in the steep, choppy waves. The thought amused him, since Inquisitor General Wylbyr's vulnerability to motion sickness was well known and he wasn't exactly basking in the esteem of the Inquisition's adjutant at the moment, either.

Of course, Rayno thought, moving the spyglass slowly and delicately in hopes of finding a green-faced Edwyrds leaning over the lee rail, *we'll have to project all of that approval and brotherly love very publicly before we send him back. What I'd like to do is to replace him with someone with a clue, but that would mean someone who'd recognize the need to . . . moderate the enforcement of Zhaspahr's directives, and that probably wouldn't work out any better in the end. Somebody willing to do that might actually at least slow the bleeding, but he'd be lucky to last three five-days before Zhaspahr yanked him home to face the Punishment himself.*

The frown that crossed the archbishop's face was far more worried than he would have permitted himself in front of witnesses. Clyntahn was digging in ever more deeply on his demand that the least sign of heresy be immediately punished. He might still recognize the need to show at least some moderation here in Zion and in the Temple Lands generally, but even that was eroding as he became more and more determined to yield not a single inch more ground. And whatever he was willing to concede here, he insisted upon a complete crackdown on anything that even *might* be a sign of heresy in the portion of Siddarmark still occupied by Mother Church's forces and even—or perhaps *especially*—in the Border States, where the looming threat of heretic invasion, with its suggestion that the heretics might actually be winning their blasphemous war, threatened the faith of Mother Church's children.

Rayno could understand his need to do *something* to stop the heretics, yet their own agents inquisitor's reports clearly indicated that the Inquisitor General's repressiveness actually fueled Reformist fervor. Even some of those with no desire at all to become part of a heretical, schismatic church had begun to question whether God could truly approve of the Inquisition's ferocity. There was a reason people even here, in Zion, whispered prayers every night that the Inquisition would at least . . . moderate its severity.

Yet Clyntahn refused—more adamantly than ever, in fact—to admit that too much severity was actually as bad—or *worse*—than too little firmness.

It was *fear*, Rayno thought. Clyntahn would never admit it—not in a thousand years—but that was the reason he refused to relent. The worm of fear ate its poisonous way deeper into the Grand Inquisitor's heart with every passing day, and his response was to lash out at those whose weakness—whose *failures*—fed his fear and made it strong. It was a worm Wyllym Rayno was coming to know only too well, one he'd found hidden in his own heart. Yet there was a difference between his fear and Clyntahn's. Rayno liked it no more than the next man, yet at least he was willing to acknowledge it was fear he felt. Clyntahn wasn't, and he was building a bubble about himself—a bubble in which it was still permissible to discuss how the Inquisition might respond most effectively to its enemies, or even ways in which *specific* reverses might be addressed, but no underling dared to suggest Mother Church's triumph over each and every one of those enemies might conceivably be anything but inevitable.

Whether the Grand Inquisitor would allow even Duchairn or Maigwair to discuss the military situation with anything like frankness at this point was an open question in Rayno's mind. What *wasn't* a question was that even if he would for the present, the time was coming when he no longer would, and what happened then?

We need a miracle, God, he thought, still gazing at the Inquisitor General's approaching schooner, remembering the celebrants' reverent, rumbling liturgical responses in the mass he'd celebrated. Treasuring the chanted scripture and the soaring harmonies of the hymns. On a day like this, a Wednesday when he was freshly come from God's own Presence, when God's Day loomed so close upon the calendar, he could truly believe miracles were possible. *You've given enough of them to the heretics. Now we need You to give one to us. Something to show we truly* are *Your champions, that You* haven't *deserted us. That—*

He stiffened in shock, his eyes flaring wide, as the schooner disintegrated into a boil of fire and smoke that filled his field of view. He actually saw two of the men on deck, both Schuelerite under-priests, simply *disappear* as the blast of fury snatched them into its maw and devoured them.

He leapt back from the spyglass and the ball of flame was suddenly tiny with distance, but that distance did nothing to dispel his horror as he watched broken debris—debris he knew included the shredded flesh of the priests he'd seen vanish into that searing wall of flame—arc upwards in dreadful silence while the bells sang sweetly, sweetly behind him.

Just over nine seconds later, the explosion's rumbling thunder rolled over that golden song like Shan-wei's own curse.

▼   ▼   ▼

Zhozuah Murphai watched the same column of fiery, spray-shot smoke. His waterfront-level vantage point was rather different from Archbishop Wyllym's . . . and so was his reaction. The brisk wind began to twist the column into a shredding spiral, bending it so that it loomed towards Zion, standing up from the surface of Lake Pei in a sign visible to every citizen of the city, and satisfaction blazed within him like the heart of a star.

Ahrloh Mahkbyth had been bitterly disappointed when he learned Helm Cleaver wouldn't be able to reach Wylbyr Edwyrds upon his arrival after all. Security was simply too tight for his people to penetrate—no doubt because of the record of successes the Fist of God and Dialydd Mab had already run up. Mahkbyth's people might have been able to get to Edwyrds before he *left* Zion, but the odds were overwhelmingly against it. So Murphai had volunteered to see to that part of the mission. After all, a PICA, had no need to breathe. Given that, it had made far more sense for Murphai to attach the charge—an Owl-provided charge of explosives not even Sahndrah Lywys would be able to duplicate for decades—to the keel of Edwyrds' schooner while it waited for Edwyrds' canal boat at Brouhkamp, the capital of the Episcopate of Schueler on the far side of Lake Pei. He'd rather enjoyed the irony of planting the charge in the episcopate named for the Inquisition's patron "archangel."

He'd trudged across the bottom of Brouhkamp's harbor to see to that minor detail two days earlier. The truth was that he could easily have delegated that task to one of Owl's remotes if he'd so desired. But he'd witnessed entirely too much of Edwyrds' bloody handiwork over the last two years to let *anyone* else plant that particular charge.

This afternoon, however, he was a mere spectator. He'd been sure to pick a good vantage point, well clear of the Temple but with an excellent view of the waterfront, while the other teams worked their ways into position. Nahrmahn and Owl had watched over them through the SNARCs, waiting until everyone was in place, and only then triggered the explosion through a SNARC relay.

In many ways, Murphai wished Mahkbyth could have been with him to share the moment. A man couldn't have everything, though, and if Mahkbyth had been unhappy to lose that particular kill, the modifications he'd suggested to Murphai's original plan more than compensated.

Besides, the ex-Guardsman wasn't the spectator type. He was the sort of man who preferred to be more . . . hands-on.

Especially for some things.

▼   ▼   ▼

Bishop Zakryah Ohygyns had just kissed his wife, hugged his children, collected his personal Guardsmen, and started back down his front walk to return to his office when he heard the explosion. Of course, he didn't know it was an explosion; he simply knew it wasn't a sound he should be hearing in Zion on a sunny Wednesday afternoon.

He also knew how bitterly his wife resented the hours he worked. In her opinion, a bishop of Mother Church ought to be able to spend at least an occasional Wednesday with his family. But, no! Not *her* husband! *He* had to race home from mass, bolt down Wednesday dinner, and then turn around and head straight back to the office. She would never dream of complaining, especially in the middle of a jihad. But *this* Jihad had been going on for *years* now. It was long past time the Inquisitor General found someone else to carry some of Ohygyns' load, at least on Wednesdays, and the fact that she would never complain about it in so many words—and certainly never to anyone else—didn't keep her from making her feelings abundantly clear to *him*. Nor did it keep him from feeling guilty. Yet there was nothing he could do about it until the Jihad was won.

Maybe then *I can convince Archbishop Wyllym I've earned a vacation,* he thought, stopping on the sidewalk, one foot on the carriage's running board as he craned his neck, trying to decide where that thunder had come from on such a cloudless day. The six men of his protective detail stopped with him, as puzzled as he was, and the driver on the coach's high seat half stood, as if he thought he could actually see its source from his higher vantage point.

Maybe we could take the kids to visit her brother in Malantor, his thought ran on even as he tried to determine what he'd heard. *God knows the beaches are nicer—and a lot* warmer*—in Tahlryn Bay than they are on Lake Pei or Temple Bay! And it's been* years *since we had a real family vacation. Besides, she has a point. The* Writ *itself says a man's duty to his family comes—*

"For our sisters!" a voice said.

Ohygyns was still turning towards it when the trio of Composition D-charged hand grenades, with Delthak Works proof marks, exploded. There were two survivors from the men clustered around the carriage.

Zakryah Ohygyns was not among them.

▼   ▼   ▼

Father Mairydyth Tymyns looked up from his copy of the current *Decrees of Schueler* with a muttered oath. It was *Wednesday,* for Schueler's sake! Surely on this day, of all days, a priest could spend a little time re-dedicating himself to his holy purpose without being disturbed?

"What's all that racket, Zherohm?" he demanded irritably.

There was no answer, and he swore again as he laid the *Decrees* aside and pushed up out of his chair. It sounded like Zherohm Slokym had just dropped something in the vestibule, but that wasn't like him. The grizzled, thick-shouldered monk had been with Tymyns for years now, and for all his muscular bulk, he was as sure-handed as he was reliable. He was also just as passionate as Tymyns himself about ferreting out heretics. They suited one another, and the monk served as Tymyns' combination personal bodyguard and batman/valet, as well as the senior member of his detail in the field.

"Zherohm!" he said in a louder voice, then cocked his head as what sounded for all the world like a peal of thunder rattled the windows of the modest house the Order had assigned to him.

Now *what?* he wondered exasperatedly. *It can't be thunder—not on a day like this! But in that case—*

CRAAACK!

His library door's latch splintered under the straight, savage kick of a heavy boot. The door flew wide, slamming explosively back against the wall, and Zherohm Slokym hurtled in through the opening. But he hadn't arrived in response to Tymyns' summons. And he wasn't going to be explaining anything, either—not with his throat slashed from ear to ear. He hit the floor with a dull, meaty thud, and blood spread in a thick, hot pool across the carpet.

Tymyns was still staring at the body, smelling the strong, coppery stench of blood and stunned into utter immobility, when more solid, muscular men charged into the room in Slokym's wake and strong, angry hands seized him.

There were four of them, he realized. All of them were masked, and they wore aprons—the heavy, full-length aprons butchers wore. They ought to have looked ridiculous, a corner of his mind thought, but they didn't. Not with the bright spatters those aprons had already intercepted when Slokym's severed carotid sprayed blood.

Of course, that same corner thought. *They wanted to keep Zherohm's blood off their clothes. They'll just take off the aprons and leave them behind when they blend into the crowds and simply walk away from—*

His shock-numbed thought processes stuttered back into life as he realized what *else* those men had come to do, and he opened his mouth to cry out as two of the intruders wrenched his arms agonizingly behind him as expertly as any agent inquisitor. He writhed frantically, fighting to pull away, but a third man twisted his fingers in his hair, yanked his head back, and crammed a thick wad of cloth into his mouth.

The Schuelerite's desperate, belated shout for help was muffled, smothered into inaudibility, and his eyes went huge with terror as the fourth man—the one with the bloody dagger in his hand—reached inside the bib of his apron and removed an envelope. He dropped it on Slokym's body, and then that featureless, masked face turned towards Tymyns.

"We have a message for you from our sisters, Father," Ahrloh Mahkbyth said coldly, and Tymyns gurgled frantically, bulging eyes pleading for the mercy he'd never shown another, as his head was wrenched even farther back, arching his throat for the knife.

▼   ▼   ▼

"Of course it wasn't the 'Fist of God'!" Zhaspahr Clyntahn snapped, glaring around the council chamber. "How in Shan-wei's name *could* it have been? That schooner belonged to the Inquisition! Its crew consisted entirely of agents inquisitor and Schuelerite lay brothers, all sworn to the Order, and Bishop Wylbyr's personal guards went over it inch-by-inch before they ever allowed him to board!" The Grand Inquisitor's jowls were dark, his eyes fiery. "Are you suggesting that somehow a pack of murderous fanatics got a bomb big enough to do *that* much damage past its entire crew and all of that security?!"

Rhobair Duchairn and Allayn Maigwair were careful not to look at one another. Zahmsyn Trynair, fortunately for him, was out of Zion on diplomatic business, although he'd undoubtedly have been sitting in his corner emulating a mouse if he hadn't been.

"I'm telling you, this is just the lying bastards taking credit for something they had *nothing* to do with!"

Clyntahn slammed back in his chair, staring at them, and the crackling silence stretched out as his furious scowl dared them to disagree with him.

"I understand what you're saying about the security around the Inquisitor General," Maigwair said at last, his tone that of a man picking his words with extraordinary care. "And I'll readily admit that *I* don't see any way assassins could've gotten through it, either. But they obviously got to at least half a dozen other servants of the Inquisition right here in Zion, and *something* happened to Bishop Wylbyr, Zhaspahr. His boat blew up in plain sight of anyone on the waterfront, and the fact that he was returning to Zion was pretty widely known. Not only that, his escort was waiting down at the docks." The captain general shook his head. "We can't pretend he wasn't aboard when the damned thing went up! And that means we need some sort of statement, some sort of explanation for how that could've happened if it *wasn't* the 'Fist of God.'"

"It was obviously an accident," Clyntahn snapped, leaning forward again to slap one meaty palm on the conference table for emphasis. "For that matter, we don't know for certain it was even the 'Fist of God'—" the three words came out like a curse "—that murdered Ohygyns and the others!"

Maigwair couldn't keep his eyes from rolling, and Clyntahn's lips tightened.

"All right," he grated. "I'll grant you that *that* almost had to be the frigging terrorists. But it's only a fluke those murders came so close to the explosion! I'll admit it's one hell of a coincidence—and the timing sucks—but that's all it *can* be, damn it! They're trying to make something that was pure serendipity look like it was all part of a single, coordinated operation because that will make them look so much more dangerous than they really are. But it couldn't have been! They're trying to take advantage of a completely separate *accident!*"

"An accident?" Maigwair repeated, and Clyntahn slapped the tabletop again, harder.

"Yes, damn it—an *accident!* The Inquisitor General's guard detail had its own weapons along, which means they were carrying ammunition. Besides, the boat itself had cannon! There had to be powder and shot in its magazine for *those*, didn't there? Obviously a spark must have set it off somehow!"

Maigwair's jaw tightened, and Duchairn clamped his own teeth together, remembering another explosion, at a place called Sarkhan, which Clyntahn—and Wylbyr Edwyrds, for that matter—had flatly *denied* could have been a "coincidence." And there'd been one hell of a lot more gunpowder aboard that canal barge to explain the accident, too. The "cannon" aboard Edwyrds' pint-sized schooner had consisted of a total of six wolves: half-pound swivel guns, purely antipersonnel weapons that were effectively outsized smoothbore muskets. He had no idea how much powder it would have had in its magazine—he was pretty sure Maigwair did, which probably explained the incredulity the captain general couldn't keep out of his eyes—but it certainly hadn't been enough to produce *that* explosion. Divers had already confirmed that the schooner's wreckage was spread over two hundred yards of lake bottom, and its midsection had simply disintegrated. The shattered bow and stern lay almost forty yards apart at the heart of the debris field, totally severed from one another. No powder supply for half a dozen wolves was going to accomplish *that*.

"I suspect quite a few people will find a spontaneous magazine explosion less believable than a successful assasination," Maigwair said after a moment with what Duchairn privately thought was foolhardy courage. Clyntahn's lips drew back, but the captain general continued before he could speak. "I'm not saying it couldn't have happened that way, Zhaspahr. I'm just saying that even if it's precisely what *did* happen, some people will find it difficult to accept."

"And your point is?" Clyntahn demanded harshly.

"My point is that those who find it difficult to accept may begin to wonder if we're not trying to sell them a falsified cover story because we're afraid to admit what really happened." Maigwair met the Grand Inquisitor's glare steadily. "I'm not saying that's what it *is*, Zhaspahr; I'm saying that's what the more . . . fainthearted may *think* it is."

"The Inquisition knows how to deal with 'faintheartedness'!"

"I don't doubt it, but dealing with it *after the fact* doesn't strike me as the best approach, especially if we can be more . . . proactive. I'm only suggesting that there was already a great deal of concern in the city, especially after the news of Rhaigair Bay. And word of the other murderers has already spread all across Zion. Even if the terrorists hadn't said a word, anyone who puts the explosion together with the obvious—and *simultaneous*—assassinations is going to leap to the conclusion that they were coordinated, part of the same terrorist attack. It's only human nature to think that way unless it can be *proven* differently, Zhaspahr! My question is whether or not we want to give the appearance that we're trying to deny something they'll be naturally inclined to believe *has* to be the truth. Half of Zion was down on the lakefront, enjoying the first sunny Wednesday in over a month. They *saw* the explosion, and if anyone here in the city decides Mother Church is lying to them about something they saw with their own eyes, it could undermine the credibility of *anything* we tell them from here out. Especially if the heretics give them a different story, the way the terrorists are doing right this minute."

Clyntahn started to snarl a response, but then, miraculously, he stopped himself. He braced the heels of his hands on the edge of the massive table, instead, thrusting himself fully back into his chair, and his expression was as ugly as Rhobair Duchairn had ever seen.

"So what d'*you* suggest we do?" he demanded after a long, smoldering moment.

"I'm afraid I'm suggesting that allowing the terrorists to claim credit for Bishop Wylbyr's murder along with the others—even if we absolutely agree that they didn't actually have a thing to do with it—may be the lesser of two evils."

"I won't give them the satisfaction!"

"Zhaspahr, they're going to claim it, anyway. Langhorne! They already *have*! And there are some people in the city whose faith is weak enough they'll *believe* that claim whatever *anyone* else tells them. So what's your alternative? Even if we tell everyone it was gunpowder in the boat's magazine— and even *if* they believe us—they're going to wonder how it came to explode at exactly the right moment for the terrorists, and how that sort of explosion could inflict that much damage. And if they start wondering that, Zhaspahr, and if they decide it wasn't the terrorists, it's only a very short step to assigning credit to . . . a more than mortal agency *helping* the terrorists. Do we want them thinking it was demonic intervention? Demons working directly with the terrorists this close to Zion—barely *two miles* from the Temple itself?!"

This time the silence was deathly still, and Duchairn breathed a short, silent prayer for his fellow vicar as Clyntahn stared at him with pure murder in his eyes. Yet Maigwair refused to back down, and as the silence stretched out, Duchairn realized his argument might actually be getting through.

Because it's a very pointed argument, isn't it, Zhaspahr? the treasurer thought. *You don't like it, and it scares the shit out of you, but Allayn's got one hell of a point! Especially since this isn't the first time a "more than mortal agency" seems to've acted right in the heart of Zion. Don't want to admit that to anyone, do you?*

Clyntahn resolutely refused to confirm what had happened at St. Thyrmyn Prison, even now and even to the other two members of the Group of Three. For that matter, the Inquisition refused to acknowledge that *anything* had happened there. By now, though, Duchairn and Maigwair had confirmed that every single individual in the prison had mysteriously and suddenly died—confirmed it through multiple, independent sources both of them trusted implicitly. Worse, garbled versions of the same event had spread throughout the city, despite the Inquisition's best efforts to stop them.

And now this.

Duchairn hadn't yet officially seen the manifesto from the Fist of God which had gone up all across the city, obviously through the same mysterious avenue as those heretical broadsheets Clyntahn had never been able to stop. He wasn't about to suggest he *had* seen that manifesto—or breathe one single word about those broadsheets—to Clyntahn at this moment, either. But whether or not he had any *official* knowledge, he'd already seen a copy, and he knew exactly what it had said:

> *To the Grand Fornicator:*
>
> *Greetings! We thank you for summoning Bishop Wylbyr home so that we might send him along with Bishop Zakryah, Father Mairydyth, Brother Zherohm, Father Charlz, Sister Tyldah, and Brother Hahnz to render a long overdue accounting for their actions before God and the Archangels. We doubt they took pleasure at the final rendering of their accounts, yet their debts were only a tiny fragment of yours.*
>
> *The Inquisition has much for which to atone before the Throne of Langhorne. Most grievously of all, it must answer for its willingness to serve the human-shaped corruption which profanes the office of Grand Inquisitor. Mother Church's rod of correction was never created to become the whore of an arrogant, egotistical fornicator who sets his personal, unholy ambition above the will of God Himself. You have seen fit to torture, starve, and murder countless children of God in the name of that ambition, turned the Holy Inquisition into your accomplice in the service of that arrogance, and, in the process, become the greatest butcher since the War Against the Fallen itself.*

The Fist of God has sworn to stop you, and we will neither halt, nor rest, nor pause until you pay the last, full measure of your debt to God and the Archangels whose true will you defile and pervert with every breath you draw.

You have chosen to torture and kill those dear to us—our sisters Zhorzhet and Marzho. They are only two more deaths among the millions whose blood stains your hands, and their souls are already with God. But unlike those other, nameless dead, Zhorzhet and Marzho have champions. They have avengers. We will not defile ourselves before God by lending ourselves to torture out of hate and love of cruelty, as you do, but we will balance the scale of justice as Schueler and Langhorne require, and so we begin by taking from you Wylbyr Edwyrds and the others struck down this day. We take them in recompense not only for our sisters, but for the millions of innocents Edwyrds has murdered in the Republic of Siddarmark and in the Border States in your service. In your *service—never God's!*

We begin with these names, but we will not end here. In the fullness of time, we will come for you, as well, murderer of innocence. And know this: there is no threat you can levy, no bribe you can offer, no plea you can utter which will turn us from our purpose . . . and there is no place you can hide from us. Whatever lies you may tell, you know, as we do—as the inquisitors of St. Thyrmyn Prison learned—whose side God is truly on, and the day will come when He delivers you into our hand, as well.

No wonder Clyntahn wanted so desperately to deny the Fist of God's involvement in Edwyrds' assassination! Yet Maigwair was right. Perhaps some *would* believe his denial . . . but many, many more would not. Not with the other deaths associated with it. And when they rejected the truth of *one* claim, then the truth of every single fresh lie would become suspect.

They couldn't prevent that from happening in the long term, whatever they did. Not unless the Charisians and their allies suffered a major reverse— or something that could be spun as a major reverse—to offset the endless chain of disasters which had befallen the forces of Mother Church. The City of Zion—the entire Church—had sunk deeper and deeper into what Duchairn could describe only as a "fortress mentality." More and more of Mother Church's children were hunkering down, hunching their shoulders under the lash of one defeat after another. They might endure those lashes without admitting open despair, even to themselves. Might even continue to believe victory was possible. But they no longer believed it was *inevitable.* They *expected* more defeats, more reverses, and more and more of them were coming to the view that stopping the "heretics" short of Zion itself would require the direct intervention of God and the Archangels.

He and Maigwair realized that; Clyntahn chose to deny it, yet he, too, had to know the truth deep inside.

432 / DAVID WEBER

But he'll never admit it, the treasurer thought sinkingly. *Never. He can't—he literally* can't—*because he knows the Fist of God is telling him the exact truth in at least one respect. After all the death, all the destruction, all the torture and murder handed out by the Inquisition in Mother Church's name, her defeat—no,* our *defeat—can end only in his death. However fiercely he may deny that to others, he can no longer deny it to himself, because his millions of victims demand nothing less. And for all the faith he professes in God, he can no more divorce his own survival from the survival of Mother Church than he could bodily ascend to Heaven from the Temple's dome. Whatever he may say, the entire world ends with* his *death, and it would never occur to him in a million years to sacrifice himself for anyone else, no matter what the Writ says. And since that's the case, he has nothing to lose . . . and no reason not to pull the rest of the world down with him.*

"All right," Clyntahn said finally, and his voice was like crushed glass. "It *wasn't* the 'Fist of God,' Allayn. Whatever else they may have done, this *couldn't* have been them. But in this case—*in this case*—you may have a point. Perhaps it will be better to allow the lying sons-of-bitches' claim to stand rather than give any credence to the possibility that they're receiving demonic aid here in God's own city. But there's a difference between allowing it to stand and *confirming* it! The Inquisition's official position on the cause of Bishop Wylbyr's death will be silence. We will neither confirm nor deny that it was an act of murder, and if we're asked, in the fullness of time, we'll say only that it's impossible for us to know exactly how that explosion occurred. We'll concede that it could—*could*—have been the work of the same impious, bloody-handed assassins who struck down so many other blameless sons and daughters of God this day. But we'll also point out that it might have been the spontaneous, accidental explosion of the boat's magazines, instead, and that all the evidence available to us suggests that that's precisely what it was. If that's not going far enough, then fuck you!"

The final sentence came out in a venomous hiss, and Duchairn drew a deep breath. If he'd ever doubted for a moment that Allayn Maigwair was already a dead man in Zhaspahr Clyntahn's eyes, he would have doubted no longer. Yet the captain general only nodded, and his own expression was calm, almost serene.

"Yes, Zhaspahr," he said, "that's enough to allay most of my concerns, for the moment, at least. It's not perfect, but that's my point. There *isn't* a perfect reponse for this one. For that matter, there's not even a *good* one. But that answer will stand, at least for a time—hopefully, until the Mighty Host achieves a significant victory. When that happens, when the heretics suffer a clear, unambiguous defeat—which will be even more disheartening to them and more *en*heartening to the Faithful, after this string of reverses— the internal dynamic here in Zion will change and the man in the street won't be so damned inclined to think some bit of news is accurate only if it's *bad* news."

The Grand Inquisitor snarled something unprintable, shoved himself violently up out of his chair, and stalked out of the conference chamber like a thunder cloud.

Maigwair and Duchairn gave him a few seconds to storm down the hall, then stood rather more sedately and followed him out the door. Neither wanted to be too close on his heels, nor was either of them foolish enough to say anything where other ears might hear. But neither of them needed to, because both of them knew what Maigwair had really said, underneath all the spin needed to buy even that grudging, disgusted acceptance from Clyntahn.

It wasn't a matter of "until' the Mighty Host achieved a "significant victory." It was a matter of "if" . . . and the chance that Earl Rainbow Waters could produce one looked more and more threadbare with every passing five-day.

.II.
St. Haarahld's Harbor,
White Rock Island,
The Dohlar Bank,
Gulf of Dohlar.

I hate to interrupt breakfast, Father, but I think you'd better hear this."

Sir Hahndyl Jyrohm looked up from his scrambled eggs and frowned. At seventy-six, he preferred not to have his creature comforts interfered with any more than he could possibly avoid, and his son Lainyl knew that better than most. On the other hand, Lainyl *did* know that, so it followed that he wouldn't have burst into the breakfast parlor without a damned good reason.

The thought of the sort of "good reason" which might have brought his son calling was enough to kill Sir Hahndyl's appetite rather abruptly.

"Hear what?" he asked.

"I've got Ahndru and Zhilbert Ashtyn waiting in my office. They say they've seen the heretics' ironclads." Sir Hahndyl's face stiffened, and Lainyl nodded glumly. "They say they've seen *all* the heretics' ironclads, Father. From the sound of things, they're talking about that big bastard we've been hearing rumors about, not 'just' the ones operating out of Chelmport."

"In your office, you say?" Sir Hahndyl was already pushing back his chair. "Have you sent word to the Major, too?"

"Of course I did . . . for all the good it's going to do," Lainyl said gloomily.

▼   ▼   ▼

Major Samyl Truskyt climbed carefully down from the carriage and fitted his forearms into his crutches' arm cuffs.

The sun shone brilliantly, although the air remained cool and morning fog still clung to the waters of St. Haarahld's Harbor. That weren't uncommon on the Dohlar Bank this time of year, at least on calm mornings, or so he'd been told. This was his first spring here on White Rock Island, but he was willing to take the locals' word for that. And he'd seen enough of those fogs by now to know this one would be burning off within the next hour or so, assuming the breeze didn't come up and disperse it first.

Truskyt was what his wife Mahtylda called—with less than total approbation—"a morning person." She, most emphatically was not, but Truskyt loved the early morning, especially right after dawn, and once upon a time, he'd been a notable equestrian—the sort who treasured brisk canters through the dawn and who would never have taken a stuffy carriage on a glorious morning like this one. That had been before a heretic grapeshot removed both legs at the knees in the abortive assault on Thesmar, however. That had been a spider-ratfuck if he'd ever seen one, and he'd been more than a little bitter about the whole thing. Still was, for that matter, although he'd come to the conclusion that that worthless Desnarian piece of shit Harless might actually have done him a favor . . . of sorts, at any rate. At least he'd missed the even worse spider-ratfuck in the Kyplyngyr Forest.

Only one other officer and six enlisted men of his infantry company's original two hundred and thirty had come home from the Kyplyngyr with General Alvarezh. So maybe Mahtylda had been right all along that the loss of his legs hadn't been the worst thing that could have happened to him. He still had the occasional day when it was difficult to maintain his emotional detachment about the whole business, though. The fact that he routinely used a carriage now, instead of one of the horses he loved, normally made that even more difficult than usual, but that was scarcely front and center in his concerns this morning.

Sergeant Pahrkyns climbed down from his place beside the driver and ostentatiously didn't hover while the major got his crutches squared away. Zhozaphat Pahrkyns had been with Truskyt for a long time. In fact, he'd been the major's company sergeant, and he, too, had been seriously wounded at Thesmar—mostly because he'd been too busy dragging his commanding officer back to safety to stay out of the line of fire himself. At least he hadn't completely lost any body parts, although he retained only limited use of his left arm, and Truskyt had managed to hang on to him while they both convalesced. Neither would've been much good in the field any longer, however. That was how Truskyt had wound up transferred to the artillery and assigned as the senior officer here on White Rock Island, and Pahrkyns was still with him as his battery sergeant major and self-appointed bodyguard. "Nursemaid" might have been nearer the mark, Truskyt often thought, not that either of them would ever have been so crass—or honest—as to use the word.

Neither of them had known a damned thing about artillery before the transfer, but they'd worked hard on making up their knowledge deficit since. They'd had time for that, as it happened, since their new post was scarcely one of the Kingdom of Dohlar's most demanding assignments. But it still needed filling, the fishing wasn't bad, and at least he'd be home for his and Mahtylda's third child sometime in August. She tried not to be too obvious about her gratitude that she'd gotten him back more or less in one piece— and, he thought, with a fond smile, still . . . functional—and he couldn't pretend *he* wasn't glad, too.

And at least he could release an officer with two sound legs for service with the Army of the Seridahn. That was something.

He stumped up the crushed-shell walkway to the neatly whitewashed town hall. The town of St. Haarahld's—more of a glorified village, really, in Truskyt's opinion—had all a small town's civic pride, and the town hall was actually on the ostentatious side for a community of barely three thousand souls. On the other hand, it also housed the White Rock Island office of the Fisherman's Guild, and Lainyl Jyrohm was the guild master, as well as Mayor of St. Haarahld's. Truskyt had never been able to figure out whether he'd become guild master because he'd been elected mayor, or if he'd been elected mayor because he was the guild master. In either case, the fact that his father was the largest landowner on the island—which, admittedly, wasn't saying all that much; the entire island was barely eighty miles across at its broadest point and measured just under a hundred and fifty miles north-to-south—probably explained both offices. Although, to be fair, Lainyl had worked the fishing fleet for over ten years before his promotion to guild master and he was a hard-working, conscientious fellow who took both sets of duties seriously.

Pahrkyns stepped around the major and up the shallow steps to open the door, and Truskyt nodded his thanks as he climbed those steps more laboriously in his wake. Lainyl had just stepped out of his office to greet him, leaving the door partially open, as the two of them entered the vestibule. He produced a somewhat strained smile of welcome, and as Truskyt glanced past him through the door, he saw Sir Hahndyl and old Ahndru Ashtyn and his son Zhilbert waiting for them.

"Sorry to drag you out for something like this, Major," Lainyl said.

"It's what I'm here for." Truskyt shrugged with a crooked smile. "Not too sure what either of us is supposed to *do* about it, though!"

"Aside from worrying like hell and passing the word on to someone on the mainland, I don't know what we're supposed to do, either," Lainyl said frankly, then snorted. "On the other hand, you're the official Army representative. That probably means I can get away with sliding the whole thing off on you!"

"Always nice to deal with a quick-thinking fellow," Truskyt said dryly, swinging along on his crutches at Lainyl's side. "With a mindset like that, you'd've gone far in the Army. Of course, you might want to think about the fact that as the official Army representative, I get to write the official reports. Sort of gives me the inside track on assigning responsibilities for the record."

Lainyl chuckled, then pushed the door fully open and ushered Truskyt into his office.

"Sir Hahndyl," Truskyt greeted the elder Jyrohm.

"Major Truskyt." Sir Hahndyl rose to clasp forearms with him once he'd disentangled his right arm from the cuff of his crutch.

Technically, Sir Hahndyl was also the island's senior noble. Actually, he was its *only* noble. What that meant was that he got to hang "baronet" on the back of his name on formal occasions. It also explained why the old man had been officially named "Governor of White Rock Island" when the Crown of Dohlar and the Harchong Empire agreed King Rahnyld's government should have undivided responsibility for—and legal authority over—the entire Dohlar Bank at least for the duration of the Jihad. It was a thankless task, but it had also been little more than a formality . . . until recently. Which had been just as well. Truskyt liked Sir Hahndyl quite a lot, and he was a nice old dodderer, but he was scarcely a decisive man of action.

"So," Truskyt continued, turning to the elder of the Ashtyns. "I understand we have you to thank for this little meeting, Ahndru?"

"Wasn't rightly *my* idea, Major!" Ashtyn, a wizened, weathered sixty-year-old, had a powerful, thickly calloused grip after five decades spent hauling in nets. His son, Zhilbert, was only thirty-six, with a cap of thick, curly hair as black as his father's had been before it turned snowy white. He shared his father's hazel eyes, as well, and he was just as physically tough as the old man. A life in the boats tended to do that for a man.

"No, I know it wasn't your idea, but Sir Hahndyl and I have to write up a report for Gorath on what it was you saw, so it's probably best if we get down to it. Why don't you tell me about it?"

"I can do that," Ahndru said. "Course, it'll go better—and faster—with a wee dram to oil the words, as it were. Might help after that wicked-cold fog out there in the harbor, too!" The old man shivered dramatically, and Zhilbert rolled his eyes.

"Why am I not surprised?" Lainyl sighed, then opened a desk drawer and started extracting whiskey glasses. "Fortunately, after so long dealing with fishermen, I'm prepared. But only one glass of the good stuff until you're done, Ahndru! Clear?"

"You've a way of encouraging a man t'come t'the point," Ashtyn chuckled, then took a slow, savoring sip. He let it roll down his throat and sighed blissfully. But then he turned back to Truskyt, and his expression had sobered.

"We seen 'em just about sunset yesterday, Major," he said. "Zhilbert and me, we were out in the *Zhaney Su,* helping old Hairahm check his buoys along the Lobster Pot. Traps needed respottin', some of 'em, after that blow we had Wednesday."

Truskyt nodded in understanding. The Ashtyns were fishermen—their family operated a total of four boats—not lobstermen. But the White Rock fishing community's members tended to help one another out, and Lobster Pot Bend, the northeastern arc of the confused mass of shoals and mudbanks known as the Dohlar Bank, teemed with lobsters and spider crab.

"Anyway, that was where we seen them," Ashtyn went on. "Five of 'em there was, and one of 'em drat near twice the size of t'others. Got two of them smokestacks, too, not just the one." He shook his head, and there was more than a trace of fear in his eyes. "Biggest damned guns I ever did see, Major. Don't think anybody's going t'be happy t'see *this* bitch coming his way!"

"Doesn't sound like it to me, either," Truskyt said, sipping from his own glass. "Yesterday evening, you said?"

"Yep." Ashtyn nodded. "Headed in soon's we seen 'em. Figured they weren't s' likely t' come calling in the dark, so we figured t' get the jump on 'em." He shrugged. "Wind died just as we was roundin' Tobys Head, so we dropped th' hook clear of the channel an' left Zwan an' Hektor t'keep an eye on things an' we rowed in in th' dinghy t' let Lainyl—I mean, the Mayor, o' course—" despite his obvious worry, Ahndru flashed a grin at the craft master he'd known his entire life "—know what we seen."

"That was good thinking," Truskyt approved sincerely. "On the other hand, I doubt they'll be interested in St. Haarahld's Harbor." He shrugged and opted not to mention that there would have been damn-all St. Haarahld's Harbor's six 25-pounders could have done about it if the Charisian Navy *had* been interested in St. Haarahld's. "I know the water's deep and it's a decent anchorage, as long as the weather's not out of the northeast, but they've already got Chelmsport over on Trove. I wouldn't think they'd be looking for—"

"Master Mayor! Sir Hahndyl!"

The office door flew open as Lainyl's town clerk burst through it. Truskyt looked up in surprise at the interruption, but the other man had actually grabbed Lainyl by the sleeve and was physically dragging him towards the office window.

"What do you think—?!" Lainyl had begun as he was hauled across his office when the waterfront bell which normally summoned the St. Haarahld's Harbor lifeboat burst into urgent life.

"Look! *Look!*"

The clerk was pointing out the window. Lainyl's eyes followed the gesture and the mayor froze in mid stride. Truskyt could actually see the color draining out of his face as he struggled to his own wooden feet. Pahrkyns was there in an instant, his good arm lifting the major powerfully upright. Under normal circumstances, Truskyt would have resented the assistance—or, at least, the way that assistance emphasized the fact that he needed it in the first place. Under these, he only muttered a word of thanks and swung across to the window on his crutches as quickly as he could.

"What is—?" he started urgently, then stopped.

A breeze *had* come up, a corner of his mind noted, rolling away the fog, and it would appear he'd been guilty of a slight miscalculation.

▼　▼　▼

"Well, they've seen us now, My Lord," Halcom Bahrns remarked dryly as the last of the offshore fog dissipated.

He was happy to see it go, although St. Haarahld's Harbor was remarkably commodious and its bottom dropped off with cliff-like steepness, as if some enormous doomwhale had taken a bite out of the mudbanks and shoals on the Dohlar Bank side of the Fern Narrows. According to the charts, they had almost six fathoms even at low tide to within a thousand yards of the town itself.

That was ample depth even for *Gwylym Manthyr* . . . which hadn't made Bahrns a lot happier about approaching White Rock in the dark. Fortunately, he hadn't had to, and *Manthyr* and her consorts had marked time, steaming at no more than a knot or two in the narrows, out of sight from the mainland, while they waited for the fog to lift.

"I believe you can probably take that as a given, Captain," Sir Dunkyn Yairley said, even more dryly. He stood beside Bahrns on the starboard wing of *Manthyr*'s tall navigation bridge, outside the glassed-in pilot house, gazing through his double-glass at the three-mile distant waterfront which had just become visible. "We're not exactly the easiest sight for someone to miss, after all."

Bahrns snorted a laugh, and Baron Sarmouth lowered the double-glass he really hadn't needed and turned to look back past *Manthyr*'s mast and funnels at the four *City*-class ironclads steaming along in her wake. The Victory ships *Barcor* and *Iron Hill* kept them company, and *Gairmyn*, the fifth of Hainz Zhaztro's ironclads, tagged along astern, keeping a wary eye on the five galleons filled with good Glacierheart coal.

Sarmouth turned back to St. Haarahld's Harbor—*And what an appropriate name that is!*—with a smile of his own. The SNARCs gave him a wyvern's eye view of Lainyl Jyrohm's office, and the mayor's response was well worth watching. So was Major Truskyt's, and the baron's smile faded into an expression that was almost more grateful than satisfied as he realized Truskyt was too levelheaded to do anything stupid. He'd hoped that would be the case when he'd decided to exercise the discretion Earl Sharpfield had granted him and move the squadron's forward base from Trove Island to St. Haarahld's Harbor.

With the bulk of the Dohlar Bank in the way, it was over seven hundred miles from Chelmsport to the Fern Narrows, whether a raiding squadron went north or south. That wasn't an issue for a galleon or a schooner; it simply meant they took a little longer reaching the hunting grounds. But it definitely was an issue for the short-legged *Cities*. Until he'd known Zhaztro was coming—officially, that was, without any embarrassing explanations about inner circles, SNARCs, and personal communicators—Sarmouth couldn't have justified recommending White Rock over the decision to base on Trove. He'd pointed out White Rock's many advantages in his report to Sharpfield, but until Raisahndo's squadron had been dealt with—and until the armored steamers became available—trying to seize an island in such close proximity to the Dohlaran coast—and the powerful squadron based on Gorath Bay—had been out of the question.

But things have changed, he thought, watching the distant harborfront grow larger.

Astern of him, the first Marines were already going down the boarding nets into the landing craft bobbing alongside *Barcor* and *Iron Hill*. Those landing craft had been fitted with steam-powered paddle wheels which had been sent out aboard the Victory ship *Iron Spine* for installation at Claw Island. In many ways, Sarmouth would have preferred screw propulsion, but paddle wheels were easier to install and ate up less of the landing craft's internal volume. And, he conceded, the boats were less likely to lose a paddle wheel than a propeller if they grounded unexpectedly. He had two complete battalions aboard the steamers, and the other two battalions of their regiment were aboard transport galleons accompanying *Gairmyn* and the colliers. Four thousand Charisian Marines constituted a pretty severe case of overkill for an island whose entire garrison numbered less than two hundred men, but Sarmouth was all in favor of overkill. He was in favor of anything likely to inspire the sort of sanity Truskyt was showing at the moment.

Yes, things have changed, he told himself. *And I can hardly wait to see how they react to this in Gorath. Of course, they'll have some other news to react to pretty damned soon, too, won't they?*

"Nothing," he said out loud when Captain Bahrns raised a politely inquisitive eyebrow at his sudden chuckle. He couldn't really tell the captain of his new flagship. He was looking forward to watching that reaction in real time.

"Just a passing thought, Captain," he said. "Just a thought."

.III.
Shandyr Bulge,
Duchy of Thorast,
Kingdom of Dohlar.

I t's time, Sir."

Sir Hauwerd Breygart's eyes popped open as the hand on his shoulder shook him gently. He'd be fifty years old in another seven days, and he'd recently begun feeling his age. The habits of a thirty-year military career didn't disappear just because a man had torn a few more sheets off the calendar, though, and he still woke quickly, almost instantly.

He sat up, swung his legs over the edge of the cot, and stood. He stretched, then massaged the small of his back with both hands. That was one of part that seemed to be aging somewhat more rapidly than the rest of him, and he missed the comfortable bed he'd become accustomed to at his headquarters in Shandyr. But he needed to be closer to the front for this, and at least he had a proper headquarters tent, which was a far cry from the hand-to-mouth, desperate days defending Thesmar.

In more ways than one, he thought with grim satisfaction.

The once threadbare, cobbled-together Army of Thesmar had been reinforced to almost eighty thousand well-fed, well-equipped men . . . exclusive of its artillery. And that artillery had been heavily reinforced, as well, with the promised 6-inch angle-guns and even a single battery of the newer and even more powerful 10-inch angles, based on a squat, sawed-off version of the *King Haarahld*-class' main gun tubes. Those were actually too much gun for field use; even with double teams of dragons, they weren't exactly highly mobile once they got off the high road. They did get around better than one might have anticipated out of weapons that weighed seventeen tons in firing position, however, and they packed one hell of a whallop.

Lieutenant Karmaikel held out a steaming mug of cherrybean and the earl accepted it with a nod.

"Thank you," he said, and took a large—but cautious; it was hotter than the hinges of Shan-wei's hell, the way he liked it—sip. Then he set the mug on the camp table by his cot and sat back down while he reached for his boots.

"I'm assuming that if any last-minute disaster had hit you'd already have told me about it, Dyntyn?"

"Probably not before you'd had your first cup of cherrybean, My Lord," Karmaikel replied straightfaced, and the earl snorted as he shoved his right foot into its boot.

"Seriously, My Lord," Karmaikel continued, "things have gone almost too well. Everything seems to be exactly on schedule, and I tend to worry when things go that well."

"Sometimes, Lieutenant Karmaikel, things actually do go according to plan," Hanth observed. "Mind you, it's better to operate on the assumption they won't. You get surprised a hell of a lot less often that way . . . and some of your surprises are actually pleasant ones."

"Exactly, Sir."

Hanth stamped into his other boot, stood, collected his cherrybean, and followed his aide out of the small, screened off section of the HQ tent set aside for the commanding general's cot. A dozen other aides—not to mention a few dozen clerks and messengers—came to attention as Karmaikel held the flap for him to pass under it, and he waved his mug.

"Stand easy," he growled and crossed to the enormous map while he sipped more of the hot cherrybean.

There was a lot of detail on that map, most of it garnered by his own patrols, although quite a bit had also been assembled from reports from the network of informants the *seijins* seemed to be able to put together anywhere on the face of the world. He'd lost more than a few scout snipers filling in that detail, and he didn't like that any more than the next commander would have, but the price those men had paid was going to save one hell of a lot more men's lives in the next few days. A few items remained a little . . . amorphous, but overall he was reassuringly confident of both the terrain and the Army of the Seridahn's current dispositions. He wasn't entirely *happy* about those dispositions, but at least he knew where the bastards were.

Sir Fahstyr Rychtyr had been busy as Shan-wei over the five five-days since he'd broken contact. He'd fallen back to his current position, where the Sheryl-Seridahn Canal and the high road passed between Duhnsmyr Forest and Kaiylee's Woods, and dug in hard. Breaking contact had cost him close to four thousand men—over half of them POWs, not dead or wounded—from the rearguard he'd been forced to leave behind. The fact that so many Dohlarans had been willing to surrender said some interesting things about the RDA's current morale, in Hanth's judgment, and Rychtyr couldn't have been happy with how many men he'd lost. Still, the earl was fairly certain the Dohlaran CO thought the prize had been worth the price. He'd certainly made damned effective use of the time, anyway!

A solid line of entrenchments, redoubts, dugouts, and—unfortunately—footstools stretched across the twenty-mile-wide gap between the two forests, with its flanks anchored on the tiny canalside village of Tyzwail in the north and the large Zhozuah Farm to the south. Most of that line had been awaiting his arrival, built by the enormous labor gangs who'd been assembled for the task, but he'd gone right on improving them from the moment of his arrival.

He'd established similarly formidable positions covering the gap between Kaiylee's Woods and the appropriately named "Forty-Mile Wood" farther south of it. And, for that matter, between Forty-Mile Wood and Moon Shadow Forest, just over a hundred miles southwest of his Tyzwail-Zhozuah Farm line. Those labor gangs had built two additional fallback positions behind his main line of defense, as well, the rearmost of them—still under construction at the moment—a good sixty miles behind his present front line, and every little fold in the ground between the major defensive lines had been surveyed by his engineers and marked on his army's maps. His subordinates knew exactly where to find the best terrain for delaying actions if his front broke, and, in many cases, the most defensible ground had been provided with at least rudimentary trenches and breastworks, as well.

A competent opponent is a genuine pain in the arse, Hanth reflected moodily. *And being told I can't go ahead and attack as soon as I'm ready—and before the miserable Dohlaran bastard has time to dig his arse in—doesn't make it any better. Damn it, Cayleb knows better than to screw around with his field commanders this way! I ought to send that young man a dispatch that gives him a good piece of my mind!*

He snorted in amusement as he imagined how his emperor would respond to any such note. And, however much he might grumble, he understood exactly why he'd been ordered to wait. For that matter, it even made sense, on the grand strategy level, however painful it was going to be for the Army of Thesmar. He just hoped the Navy was ready to hold up *its* end of the timing.

Of course it is, Hauwerd, he told himself. *You just want something to think about besides the number of men who're about to get killed. On* both *sides.*

In addition to digging in like a rabid trap lizard, Rychtyr had been reinforced himself, and not just with the garrisons the overly capable bastard had pulled out of Bryxtyn and Waymeet, ether. The spies' latest estimates were that he had about sixty thousand men suitable for field service and another twenty thousand or so odds-and-sods armed with whatever Duke Salthar had been able to scare up. Most of that twenty thousand were occupied holding down positions in the flanking redoubts. They were little more than militia and unlikely, to say the least, to stand up to a heavy new-model attack. But if their morale held, they'd give a better account of themselves from fortified positions than one might have expected out of hastily levied troops . . . and they freed up twenty thousand veterans Rychtyr would otherwise have been forced to fritter away covering those same positions. He still had to split his field force between the Tyzwail-Zhozuah Farm line and the redoubts and entrenchments covering the gap between Kaiylee Woods and Forty-Mile Wood, however. That gave him a combined frontage of damned near thirty-five miles, and sixty thousand men turned into a much smaller number when they were spread that thin. Rychtyr's well-designed and laid-out field works allowed him to economize on manpower, yet Hanth was confident he could break the front at any point of his choosing. He could simply concentrate too much artillery and infantry for it to be any other way.

Which doesn't mean it can't still end up costing like Shan-wei, he reflected grimly.

At least those same spy reports confirmed that Rychtyr hadn't received any of the new Temple Boy rockets. Apparently, every rocket Dohlar could produce was earmarked for the kingdom's coastal defenses while Temple Lands rocket production was all going to the Mighty Host of God and the Archangels. That wasn't going to make things any easier for Baron Green Valley and Duke Eastshare—or for Earl Sharpfield and Baron Sarmouth, for that matter—but Hanth couldn't pretend he wasn't happy *his* boys weren't going to be facing them.

He gazed at the map for another few minutes, then pulled out his watch, opened it, and checked the time.

"Why don't we take this outside, gentlemen?" he said with a wintry smile as he snapped the case shut again. He took another sip of cherrybean, and nodded at the tent fly open on the Dohlaran night. "I expect the light show to be pretty spectacular."

▼ ▼ ▼

It was a beautiful night, for certain values of the word "beautiful." If one was an admirer of moonlight and clear, starry skies, then that would not have been the word one would have chosen. If, on the other hand, one was a combat engineer charged with clearing a path through a field of footstools—what a denizen of Old Terra would have called landmines—it was gorgeous. Not that it didn't have certain drawbacks even from that perspective.

Lieutenant Klymynt Hahrlys crawled forward on his belly, inching through the warm, humid darkness and coated in sweat that owed nothing to the overcast night's closeness. Well, perhaps a little bit, he reflected as he paused to lay down his prodding tool, swipe at the sweat glazing his carefully blackened face, and blot his palm dry on the leg of his trousers. Then he picked the probe back up and began edging forward again, prodding gently and cautiously at the ground before him in a carefully planned and practiced arc.

He really ought to be leaving this to his noncoms and enlisted personnel while he stayed back and supervised, and he knew it. He also knew Captain Maizak was going to rip a strip off his hide when he found out how 2nd Platoon's CO had spent the evening. It had been drummed into him that an officer's true duties were managerial. He was supposed to run his platoon efficiently, make sure its training was up to snuff, that its men were healthy and well fed, and that they understood—and accomplished—whatever tasks they were assigned. That had damn-all to do with things like gallantry, and—as Captain Maizak had pointed out a bit acidly after the Zhonesberg attack—the inspirational value of leading his men from the front wouldn't be especially useful if he managed to get himself blown up in the process.

On the other hand, he also knew Maizak's heart wouldn't really be in it. For that matter, if he was *truly* lucky, Maizak was out doing exactly the same thing he was on this fine, cloudy night.

The Imperial Charisian Army had determined that the Royal Dohlaran Army's version of its own footstools were both larger than its own and made of wood. Their wooden construction made them more susceptible to leaks and rot, so it was unlikely they'd last as long as the Charisian versions once they'd been emplaced. Probably a quarter of the footstools out here were already inoperable, thanks to the last five-day's rain, and their larger size made each of them a larger target for detection, too.

Neither of which things made him feel one bit better at the moment.

Somebody's got to do it, Klymynt, he reflected. *And in the Army, "somebody" is usually the poor bloody engineers.*

He would vastly have preferred to be doing this in daylight . . . if not for the minor drawback that a Dohlaran sniper would almost certainly have blown his brains out. As it was, the clouds along the eastern horizon had begun to show the very faintest hint of gray behind him, which made the darkness in front of him even blacker. That didn't make his present task any easier, but in another twenty or thirty minutes that eastern sky was going to be far brighter. That *would* make it far easier to spot any footstools. Unfortunately, it would also make it far easier for that Dohlaran sniper to spot *him*.

Actually, the odds were substantially in his favor at the moment, despite—or perhaps *because of*—the darkness. He knew that, but he also knew at least some of his men were going to crap out. Sooner or later—and probably sooner—one of them was going to detonate a footstool rather than detect it with the curved tip of his five-foot probe. Hahrlys didn't like that, and he knew Colonel Sylvstyr, the 19th Combat Engineer Battalion's CO, didn't like it, either. That didn't change the fact that somebody had to do it or that one of the unpleasant truths about armies was that they suffered casualties. The object of a *good* army was to suffer as few of them as possible, and Hahrlys and his highly trained, veteran engineers were going to take a hell of a lot fewer than a couple of infantry battalions attacking across an uncleared field of footstools would.

Yeah, but those *casualties wouldn't be* my *people,* he thought grimly. *And, for that matter—*

He swung his probe to the right once more, a precisely metered eighteen inches and brought its curved tip down again.

Thunk.

He froze as he heard the unmistakable sound of steel on wood.

"Got one," he whispered very, very quietly, and a hand pressed his right bootheel in acknowledgment.

Corporal Fhranklyn Sygzbee, 2nd Platoon's runner—known, more or less affectionately, to his platoon mates as "Clumsy"—had kept his mouth shut when he learned his lieutenant intended to crawl around in the dark along with the rest of the platoon and had nominated *him* as his partner, but his expression had been eloquent. Hahrlys couldn't quite decide whether Sygzbee's . . . limited enthusiasm had more to do with the possibility of being blown up or the possibility of seeing *Hahrlys* blown up and then returning to face Platoon Sergeant Tyllytsyn.

The lieutenant chuckled softly at the thought. Then he pressed himself as closely as possible to the ground and moved the probe again, very gently, trying to find the dimensions of the damned thing. After several seconds of careful probing, he was reasonably confident he had the footstool located, and he drove the probe firmly through the soil covering it and into the wood of its case, anchoring the curved, sharply pointed steel tip.

He crawled towards it very carefully, following the shaft of his probe, using it to position himself. When he was within arm's reach of the probe's tip, he ran his hand forward along the shaft and felt for the footstool's case—or detonator or tripwire—with gentle fingertips.

Funny. The night hadn't gotten any warmer, but he was absolutely saturated with sweat as those fingertips found the telltale mounded earth. Fortunately, the Dohlarans' doctrine for footstool use was still in the developmental stage. They weren't as careful about leveling the ground when they emplaced them as they ought to be—not that Klymynt Hahrlys had any intention of complaining!

He and his men had spent hours playing with inert copies of the Dohlaran footstools which had been brought back by the Army of Thesmar's scout sniper patrols. There were two main versions, and Hahrlys' fingertips quickly identified this one as a Type I: a wooden case approximately fourteen inches wide, ten inches from front to back, and six inches deep, filled with black powder under a layer of old-style musket balls. The Type II was nastier, in a lot of ways: a wooden case topped with a built-up dome formed out of pitch as a matrix to hold sixty-five musket balls. It was designed to throw them in a hemispherical pattern, almost like one of the ICA's "sweepers," and its lethal zone was considerably wider than the straight-up cone of a Type I even though its directional pattern was more limited than a sweeper's.

If it was a Type I, then the detonator ought to be . . . right about. . . .

There! His fingertips found the raised bridge of the pressure switch. The Type I used an internal percussion lock for detonation, but the trigger was a rectangular plate that was pulled up and turned through ninety degrees to arm it. And that meant. . . .

"Type I," he told Sygzbee softly. "Got the bridge. Pass me a wedge."

He reached back with his left hand, never taking his right off of the pressure switch. The last thing he needed now was to lose the damned thing in the dark and have to find it all over again.

Something pressed his left hand, and he closed his fingers on one of the precisely shaped wooden wedges from Corporal Sygzbee's backpack. It was awkward to squirm around on his belly to get both hands on the footstool, but he managed and held his breath as he very, very gently slid the wedge under the raised bridge. He pushed it firmly home, careful to exert steady pressure rather than jam it into place, then exhaled the breath he hadn't realized he was holding.

"Flag," he murmured, and Sygzbee passed him the four-inch-long orange pennant fastened to the thin eighteen-inch steel pin. He pushed the sharp end of the pin into the ground right next to the footstool, then rolled onto his side, leaning on one elbow to look back at the corporal, only dimly visible even to his darkness accustomed eyes, despite his proximity.

"Charge," he said, and Sygzbee handed across the modified hand grenade for Hahrlys to nestle into the dirt covering the footstool.

The corporal had attached the grenade to the strong length of quick match which had been unreeling from the spool clipped to his web gear. There were already fourteen grenades spaced out behind them, all connected by the same quick match, and Hahrlys made sure the match was spiked firmly to the ground between the fifteenth grenade and the length still unreeling behind Sygzbee. In theory, when the time came, the quick match would be lit and each of the grenades strung along it would detonate, taking its footstool with it. Assuming that failed, the flag should alert any advancing Charisian infantryman to the footstool's presence. And assuming *that* failed, the wedge should prevent the bridge from being depressed and setting the damn thing off even if some poor sod stepped right on top of it.

Now if there's just not a tripwire backup that I missed finding, we're golden, Hahrlys thought.

"All right, I guess we've rested long enough," he whispered.

"Seems that way to me, anyway, Sir," another voice observed softly, barely audible above the quiet sigh of the wind, from the darkness to their left where Corporal Ahlvyn Ahdahmski and Private Zhon Vyrnyn were assigned to clear the northern flank of their lane. "Don't want to sound like I'm complaining," Ahdahmski continued, "but you and Clumsy're making an awful lot of racket."

"That's because some of us are actually finding the Shan-wei-damned things," Hahrlys whispered back a bit pointedly, and Sygzbee chuckled sourly. "Don't tell me you're going to let an *officer* find more of them than you do!"

"Does seem unnatural, doesn't it?" Ahdahmski acknowledged.

"Damned right it does. And I think we're getting close enough it'd probably be a good idea to keep your mouth shut, Ahlvyn."

"Good point, Sir." Ahdahmski's whispered response was the next best thing to impossible to hear, even from a distance of less than twenty feet, and Hahrlys grunted in soft approval as he began crawling slowly ahead once more. The admonition *probably* hadn't been truly necessary . . . yet, at least. By his calculations, they were still at least two hundred yards from the Dohlarans' most advanced listening posts. But it was always possible his estimate was wrong . . . or that they'd decided to move their pickets forward, just to be difficult. It was the sort of thing the irritatingly competent bastards were likely to do, although they wouldn't want to get too far out into their own footstools.

Well, if the gun dogs are on schedule, they'll have something else to be listening to any minute now, wherever the hell they are, he reflected. *And when that happens—*

His probe touched something, and Lieutenant Klymynt Hahrlys had just under two seconds to realize he'd found another footstool before the tripwire he'd snagged detonated the Type II and a storm front of musket balls killed him instantly.

▼   ▼   ▼

"Somebody in the Kau-yungs!" Private Yaisu Rahdryghyz shouted as the brilliant explosion flared in the darkness.

The private was part of a three-man picket from 2nd Platoon of Captain Ahbaht Mahrtynez' company of Colonel Efrahm Acairverah's infantry regiment. It was the third night in a row he'd had the duty, and he'd been looking forward to going off watch in another couple of hours. He could think of very few things which simultaneously produced so much nervous tension and boredom as sitting here in the dark, staring out into more dark, for five-days on end with absolutely nothing happening. If not for the heretics' nasty habit of sneaking their damn scout snipers all the way across the defensive zone to cut some poor damned sentry's throat, boring was *all* it would have been.

Frankly, Rahdryghyz would have been simply delighted to be bored.

Not happening tonight, he thought, straining his eyes as the explosive crack of the detonating Kau-yung rolled over him and he peered towards the afterimage of its blinding flash.

There'd been a few of those detonations over the last couple of five-days. A lot of them had been stray livestock or local wildlife, but three of the heretic scout snipers had been killed in 1st Platoon's area night before last. So this *could* be something a lot more important than another unlucky grass lizard or prong buck. He was still blinking his eyes against the flash, trying to decide exactly where it had been, when someone slid into his lizard hull with him.

"Where was it?" Corporal Ahndru Nohceeda asked.

"Hard to say," Rahdryghyz replied. "Wasn't looking right at it when it went off, but it looked like it was maybe a hundred, a hundred and fifty yards out."

"Think it was another prong buck?"

"Now, how in Shan-wei am I supposed to know that?" Rahdryghyz demanded. "It's blacker'n Shan-wei's boots out there! If it was a prong buck, though, it got through a hell of a lot of other Kau-yungs before it set one off!"

"Got a point," Nohceeda conceded. He put two fingers into his mouth and whistled. "Raidahndo!"

"Yo!" Private Ahbsahlahn Raidahndo acknowledged from his own lizardhole, fifteen yards behind Rahdryghyz' position.

"Get back to the CP. Tell Lieutenant Ulysees we just saw—"

Dawn came early in a rolling crescendo of thunder.

▼   ▼   ▼

The single rocket burst in crimson splendor against the moonless sky two miles behind the Army of Thesmar's front lines. It blazed there for long seconds, floating slowly down under its parachute. The night seemed to hold its breath as the fuming red eye slid down it, and then the massed artillery which had awaited its presence spoke.

The heavy angle-guns had been in place for almost a month, preparing for this moment. Each battery had been allowed to range in one gun, determining deflection and elevation for each of its assigned targets. There'd been no heavy bombardments to warn the Dohlarans of what those targets were, and the ranging shots had been hidden as "random" harassing fire. Now that carefully prepared artillery—deployed in a gun line almost ten miles long—opened fire. The eruption began in the center, running out towards either end, and hundreds of heavy shells painted streaks of fire across the night.

Fifteen seconds later, the mortar companies just behind the Charisian frontline positions joined the holocaust. Airburst antipersonnel mortar bombs exploded like brief, hateful suns, sending their deadly showers of shrapnel down to search every fold and hollow.

The torrent of fire arced across the ground between the armies' front lines, a canopy of thunderous flame above the engineers still picking their careful way through the defensive fields of footstools.

Beneath that canopy, Platoon Sergeant Gyffry Tyllytsyn gently closed his lieutenant's eyes. He looked down at the dead young man he'd followed so far, looked after so long, for fifteen or twenty seconds, his face carved out of stone in the reflected fury of the bombardment. Then he drew a deep breath and patted Hahrlys once on the chest.

"All right!" He had to clear his throat twice to get it out, but that was all right. His voice could barely be heard over the steadily swelling bellow of the guns, anyway. "We've got a job to finish for the Lieutenant, so let's get to it!"

▼   ▼   ▼

"Get your heads down! *Get your heads down!*" Lieutenant Ulysees shouted, and heard Platoon Sergeant Gyairmoh Sahlazhar repeating the order.

Here and there, someone cried out in alarm as the shower of heretic angle-gun shells grew from a thunderstorm's first, scattered raindrops into the catastrophic downpour of a fiery typhoon. For the most part, though, his men responded with almost instant, wordless discipline. They were veterans, every one of them, and they went deep in their individual lizard-holes or rolled into one of the deep, heavily sandbagged bunkers.

His pride in them swelled fiercely, but there was an arsenic-bitter edge to that pride. They'd fought so hard, so tenaciously. Taken so much pride in their long, fighting retreat—in knowing they were the one army the heretics had fully engaged which had survived the experience. The Army of the Sylmahn, the Army of Glacierheart, the Army of Shiloh . . . the heretics had utterly destroyed each of them. But the Army of the Seridahn had fought them every step of the way, over seven hundred miles from Cheryk to the Tyzwail Line, without ever once breaking. It had been close a time or two, perhaps, but the men had always remembered who they were, rallied again and again.

And now, at last, that spirit, the tenacity which had carried them so far, was beginning to erode. Ulysees wasn't supposed to know about the whispers, the quiet discussions where no inquisitor's ears were likely to hear. Wasn't supposed to know some of them had come to refer to this as "Clyntahn's War," and not the Jihad. Wasn't supposed to know how his men had reacted to the news about Earl Thirsk's family. And he wasn't supposed to know about the steady, ominous corrosion of his men's confidence as one disaster after another rolled in from the Gulf of Dohlar—disasters made ever so much worse in the wake of the RDN's victory in the Kaudzhu Narrows.

No, he wasn't supposed to know his men felt that way, harbored those thoughts, sensed the tremors of ultimate defeat sweeping towards them. And he wasn't supposed to feel that way, harbor those thoughts, or sense those tremors himself, either.

He flung himself into the command post bunker, crouching just inside the entrance to count off the other members of his command section as they tumbled through it behind him, and the ceiling-hung lantern began to sway and dance as 6-inch and 10-inch shells rumbled down the sky like sledge-hammers of flame.

▼　▼　▼

The first phase of the Charisian bombardment lasted forty-five minutes. Forty-five minutes in which hundreds of angle-gun shells and thousands of mortar bombs hammered the Dohlaran fortifications. They were shooting blind, those guns, but they had a very large target. Not all of their shells could miss, and when a 6-inch or—especially—a *10-inch* shell scored a direct hit on even the deepest bunker, the consequences were lethal.

In addition to the deluge of explosive shells and the airburst shrapnel shells pitilessly probing every nook and cranny, sending their deadly rain down into lizardholes and communication trenches, the infernally inventive Charisians introduced the Army of the Seridahn to yet another innovation. A quarter of the mortar bombs slicing down out of the heavens were packed with a mix of saltpetre, coal, pitch, tar, resin, sawdust, false silver and sulfur that spewed out an incredibly noisome cloud of blinding smoke. Dohlar had received reports—fragmentary, unfortunately, like so much else from the Inquisition—about the smoke shells the heretic Eastshare had employed against the Army of Glacierheart the previous year. Very few of the AOG troops who'd experienced them had escaped to describe their effectiveness, however, and the Army of the Seridahn was sadly unprepared for its own introduction to them.

The artificial generation of smoke hadn't received a lot of attention from Safeholdian armies, probably because gunpowder-armed armies normally had too *much* smoke, not too little. In this case, however, the reeking, choking cloud rolling steadily westward on a Charisian wind had two effects. One was to blind sentries like Private Rahdryghyz and Corporal Nohceeda who might otherwise have observed the combat engineers as they completed their sweeps and started back to their own lines. The second was to infiltrate dugouts and entrenchments, choking and suffocating their inhabitants. The smoke cloud wasn't actually poisonous, but that was a minor distinction for General Rychtyr's troops. The stench was indescribable, it was certainly capable of asphyxiating a victim under the right circumstances, and the discovery of yet another infernal Charisian innovation didn't do a thing for the Army of the Seridahn's morale.

But then, after only forty-five minutes, the bombardment trickled off, although the smoke rounds continued to fall.

▼ ▼ ▼

"Out!" Lieutenant Ulysees shouted. "The bastards'll be right on the heels of their damned artillery, boys! Man your positions!"

The men of 2nd Platoon didn't need to be told twice. They were veterans, and they knew how closely Charisian infantry followed its artillery in an attack like this. They scrambled out of their dugouts, sat up in their lizard-holes, spread out along the firing steps of their trenches.

All along Acairverah's Regiment's front—all along the entire Tyzwail Line—other companies, other platoons, followed suit. Riflemen settled into firing positions, capping their locks, making sure their bayonets were securely fixed, laying out hand bombs. Healers in green armbands marked with Pasquale's caduceus took advantage of the opportunity to scurry from lizard-hole to lizardhole, searching for wounded, dragging them back to the aid stations in their own deep bunkers. The enormous craters left by the new 10-inch shells had obliterated entire bunkers and the sections of trenches which had connected them, but determined squads of Dohlaran infantry settled into the craters themselves, using them in place of the entrenchments they'd demolished.

Within ten minutes, the entire front line bristled with ready and waiting riflemen, coughing on the noxious smoke, peering into it with slitted, tear-streaming eyes, waiting to greet the attackers with a withering curtain of fire.

▼ ▼ ▼

"All right," Admiral Lywys Sympsyn said grimly. He snapped his watch's case shut and slid it deliberately into his pocket. "Phase two."

"Yes, Sir!"

Another crimson rocket soared upwards to burst in the bright morning sunlight.

▼ ▼ ▼

That's funny, Lieutenant Ulysees thought between violent, sinus-tearing sneezes. *Where the fuck are they? The one thing they* don't *do is give somebody time to get set! I guess even Charisians can screw up their timing sometimes, but this isn't like the Thesmars!*

He was grateful, of course. On more than one occasion, the heretic infantry—especially their accursed scout snipers—had crept to within no more than thirty or forty yards of an isolated Dohlaran picket under cover of darkness, then swept in behind a merciless shower of grenades. Even when that didn't happen, they hit hard and with as little warning as possible. This time, he'd been given time to get his entire platoon into its assigned positions, reinforcing the pickets, and the heretics would regret giving the Army of the Seridahn time to get set.

But something about the unnatural calm, broken only by the dull, ongoing thuds of the incoming smoke shells, made his skin crawl. It wasn't right. Langhorne knew, the heretics were better than this! If they weren't already storming the forward trench lines, there was a reason for it, and—

▼ ▼ ▼

Spider webs of flame raced forward from the Army of Thesmar's positions like fiery serpents, following the lines of quick match the combat engineers had strung across the footstool field during the night. The modified hand grenades strung along the quick match exploded in rapid succession, belching fountains of dirt, musket balls, and still more smoke as the Dohlaran footstools went up in sympathetic detonations.

A few Dohlarans trying vainly to see through the choking fog of smoke heard the explosions. Some of them recognized the sound of exploding footstools, although not even they truly realized what they were hearing. They assumed the deadly devices must be exploding as enemy infantry stormed through the protective fields and shouted in warning. The alert passed up and down the frontline positions, and the defenders settled more solidly into position. Whatever had delayed the heretics this long, they were on their way now!

But no Charisian or Siddarmarkian riflemen came out of the smoke.

Yahkeem Ulysees heard a sound like the world's largest sail ripping in half, and his heart seemed to freeze as he realized what it was. Realized what was about to happen.

No wonder they gave us time! he thought. *They wanted us back up out of the bunkers before—*

The 6-inch shell whose arrival he'd heard exploded three hundred yards to his right. That one did very little damage. But it was only *one* shell, and the

Army of the Seridahn had done precisely what Hauwerd Breygart had expected it to do when the barrage lifted. It had raced to man its defensive positions . . . just in time for the *renewed* bombardment to catch its men in the open.

"*Back!*" Lieutenant Ulysees screamed. He came to his feet, standing upright and waving madly to the men who couldn't hear him in the sudden renewal of thunder but might *see* him, instead. "Back into the bunk—!"

One of the new 10-inch shells exploded almost directly on top of his position.

His body was never identified.

.IV.
Symyn's Farm
and
Village of Borahn,
Duchy of Thorast,
Kingdom of Dohlar.

S ir, you've *got* to fall back!" Colonel Mahkzwail Mahkgrudyr said fiercely. "This line's *gone!* Sir Fahstyr's going to need you at Borahn!"

"Like hell he will!" Clyftyn Rahdgyrz snarled back. "He needs me right the fuck *here*, turning these sorry-arsed bastards back into frigging *soldiers!*"

"Sir, there's a reason he built the Borahn Line in the first place! He needs you back there directing the troops into the right pos—"

"No, he doesn't." This time Rahdgyrz' voice was flat, with an iron tang, and Mahkgrudyr shut his mouth and stared appealingly at Father Ahntahn Rahdryghyz.

Rahdgyrz' intendant looked back at the general's senior aide, then glanced at Rahdgyrz from the corner of one eye. His face tightened, and then, almost imperceptibly, he shook his head.

Mahkgrudyr's jaw clenched, yet inside he'd already known his appeal would fail. He was certain Father Ahntahn agreed with him, but the Schuelerite had been with Rahdgyrz for a long time now. He knew as well as Mahkgrudyr that the general wasn't about to listen to anything except his own conscience . . . and God.

"All right, Sir," the colonel sighed finally. "All right. But for Langhorne's sake, at least let me put together some cavalry to keep an eye on you!"

"You can put together whatever you want, Mahkzwail, but they're going to have to catch up."

Mahkgrudyr opened his mouth in fresh protest, but Rahdgyrz had already put the spurs to his horse. It thundered down the unpaved dirt track of the Symyn's Farm Road in a shower of churned up clods of earth. Father Ahntahn was right on the general's heels, and Mahkgrudyr spat an ugly curse before he gave his own horse the office and went galloping in pursuit.

▼   ▼   ▼

Clyftyn Rahdgyrz leaned forward over his horse's neck, urging his mount to greater speed while desperation ate at his soul. In only eight days of fighting, and despite all of Rychtyr's painstaking preparations, all his troops' determination, the heretics had driven the Army of the Seridahn back for over twenty-five miles. The heretic Hanth had disdained the flanking movements which had been his hallmark ever since he launched his counter-offensive out of Thesmar. Instead, he'd driven directly at the center of the Tyzwail Line, straight into the heaviest defenses the Army of the Seridahn could build.

The massive weight of his initial bombardment—and the diabolical timing which had drawn the defenders back out into the open to be slaughtered—explained much of his initial success. He hadn't done it just once, either. He'd done it to them twice more, as well. Little wonder the traumatized defenders had been slower rushing back to their positions the *fourth* time . . . when the attack truly did come crashing in upon them. It hadn't helped that his troops had proven far more adept at clearing lanes through the Kau-yungs than anyone in Dohlar's service had anticipated, either. Shattered and demoralized by a heavier bombardment than any of them could possibly have imagined, the troops in what remained of the forward trenches and bunkers had been totally unprepared for the assault which had come out of the choking wall of smoke almost the instant that bombardment finally ended.

The defenders had captured a handful of heretic prisoners. According to interrogations, their assault troops had probably taken at least five percent of their casualties from their own artillery. That was how close behind the final, withering wave of the bombardment they'd been, waiting for it to lift. And however much Rahdgyrz might hate and despise them for their apostasy, he was confident taking those losses—being that close on the artillery's heels—had reduced their total casualties by at least half.

Their assault parties had swarmed out of the smoke, advancing not in regiments or companies, but in platoons—even squads—heavily armed with hand bombs and revolvers, even those Shan-wei-damned repeating shotguns! Dohlaran platoons which had already been harrowed—in some cases, simply blotted out—by the deluge of shells had been a poor match for them. Half of them had still been stumbling back into their artillery-churned fighting positions—or what was left of them—when the assault came crashing in.

Those who'd made it to their positions in time had fought hard, initially at least, and the heretics had paid a heavy price to force that first wedge into the heart of the Tyzwail Line. Rahdgyrz had been in the thick of that fighting, and he'd be astonished if Hanth had suffered fewer than two or three thousand casualties of his own in just the first two hours of his attack. But those assault battalions had succeeded in their mission. In seventeen hours of the most vicious, close-quarters combat Clyftyn Rahdgyrz had ever seen, they'd fought their way completely across the line of entrenchments between St. Stefyny's Redoubt and St. Jyrohm's Redoubt, the primary anchors of the Tyzwail Line.

He'd launched a furious counterattack into their northern flank, throwing in his last five reserve infantry regiments, supported by two regiments of cavalry and six batteries of field guns. They'd made perhaps a thousand yards before the heretics' accursed portable angle-guns opened fire. Their crews had hauled them forward across the fields of Kau-yungs, the shell-torn ground, and the bodies of dead and dying heretics, and emplaced them in the Army of the Seridahn's own trenches and lizardholes. The most advanced angle-guns had been barely fifty yards behind the heretic infantry's point platoons, and they'd poured a devastating fire down upon his advancing infantry.

Those men had fought—and died—like heroes for him. They'd clawed their way forward for another hundred yards, but they'd had to advance across open ground, the heretic infantry prone behind every tiny bit of cover had poured out a tornado of accurate, aimed riflefire, and that deadly flail of shrapnel had come down on them like the hammer of Kau-yung itself.

They'd broken. For the first time ever, an attack under Clyftyn Rahdgyrz' personal command hadn't simply been stopped. It had *broken*. The survivors of those shattered regiments hadn't fallen back; they'd *fled*, abandoning the field to the enemies of God Himself.

He'd cursed them, begged them, *pled* with them, and one or two had turned back. But most had been too terrified, too broken, and even as he'd cursed them, he hadn't truly blamed them. There came a time when flesh-and-blood had simply taken more than it could endure. He knew that, but watching them flee had been more than *he* could endure. He'd drawn his saber, clapped his remaining heel to his horse, and charged the heretics single-handed.

No, not single-handed. His aides and his picked dragoon bodyguard had charged with him, although he knew at least half of them had actually been trying to catch up, seize his reins, drag him bodily back from that death ride. A third of them had died trying to do that, and each of their deaths was one more coal in the furnace of his desperate fury. But they hadn't had to drag him away from anything. A heretic bullet had felled his horse, taking him down with it, stunning him, and Colonel Mahkgrudyr had personally dragged his half-conscious body across the withers of his own horse and ridden hell-for-leather for the rear.

He'd undoubtedly save his general's life . . . and if they both lived, Rahdgyrz might someday forgive him for that. He wouldn't have cared to wager anything important on the chance of that happening, however.

Not this time, he thought grimly, bending lower over the horse's neck. *Not this time!* This *time, we turn and stop* the bastards!

It wouldn't be for long. He knew that. But Mahkgrudyr was right in at least one respect. Fahstyr Rychtyr needed all the time anyone could buy him if he was going to organize a successful defense of the Borahn Line. Whether even he could do that this time was more than Rahdgyrz could say, but he'd proven time and time again that if anyone in the entire world could do it, that man was Fahstyr Rychtyr.

And if his friend failed, it wasn't going to be because Clyftyn Rahdgyrz hadn't given him every bleeding second he could!

▼　　▼　　▼

"Stand, boys! *Stand!*" Colonel Efrahm Acairverah shouted.

He stood where the farm roads from the St. Daivyn's and Sailyr Redoubts converged, two miles east of Symyn's Farm and ten miles north of the Shan-Shandyr High Road, and the crackle of gunfire and the occasional crumping explosions of heretic portable angle-gun bombs came clearly on the wind. Those miserable, fugitive-crowded roads were the only path to the rear for almost a quarter of the Army of the Seridahn. The fork where they met *had* to be held, at least briefly, and the same engineers who'd built the Slokym Line, twenty-five miles west of the Tyzwail Line, had thrown up rudimentary breastworks, tying together a dozen bunkered firing positions that covered the crossroad. Manned by resolute troops, a company or two of riflemen could have held up fifty times their own number from behind those breastworks. But the panicked fugitives streaming west from St. Daivyn's Redoubt in a choking pall of dust were the furthest thing from "resolute troops" Efrahm Acairverah had ever seen in his life.

Gray-faced with exhaustion, many of them wounded, covered with dust and dirt, their uniforms filthy and torn, their faces blackened with powder smoke from almost two solid five-days of combat, they were ghosts of the men who'd held the Tyzwail Line before the heretics' attack.

Some of those shambling ghosts were Acairverah's own men. Not many, he thought, his eyes burning even as he shouted at them to stand, grabbed at equipment harnesses, *kicked* them when they wouldn't turn. One or two snarled at him, threatening him with rifle butts or even bayonets. One of them had actually followed through on the threat, hammering the colonel to the ground with his clubbed rifle, leaving him stunned for several seconds while the endless sea of boots trampled around him until he could get back to his own feet. But most of them simply squirmed away, flowed past him like the sea, kept stumbling westward. Most of *his* men had already died, and he wanted—wanted *desperately*—to hate these fugitives for being alive when his men weren't. But even in his fury and his despair, he couldn't. And even as they continued to stream by him, most of them still clung to their personal weapons.

They haven't given up, he thought wearily. *Not really. If they had, they'd've thrown away anything that slowed them down. But they're* beaten. *For now, for today, they're simply beaten. It's as simple as that. They're* beaten, *and until someone can convince them they aren't—*

"Stand, boys!" He heard the pleading in his own voice. "Stand and *fight* with me!"

No one even slowed. And then—

"*Turn around!*" The voice roared like thunder, like Chihiro himself come back to do battle in God's name. "*Turn around, Dohlarans!* Remember what you're made of! Remember who you are! Remember Who you fight *for* and show Shan-wei what godly men can do! *Turn around!*"

Acairverah knew that voice. Everyone in the Army of the Seridahn knew it, and the shambling shadows of that army paused. No other voice could have done that—except, perhaps, that of Sir Fahstyr Rychtyr himself. No other voice could have reached down through their exhaustion, the bitter varnish of their fear, to the core of the men they were.

But *that* voice could.

The men of the army had failed that voice once. They'd broken, fled, when that voice tried to stem the tide of disaster. Some of the very men hearing it now had failed it then, and the shame, the guilt, for having failed to follow where it led was arsenic on their tongues. They looked up, eyes huge in dirty, exhaustion-hollowed faces, as Sir Clyftyn Rahdgyrz came out of the dust, reins wrapped around the stump of his left arm to free his right hand for his saber. He tugged back on those reins, and his horse reared, foam flying from its snaffle, forehooves pawing the air.

"*Come on, boys!*" that voice they'd heard, trusted—followed—on twice a score of battlefields thundered. "*Come with me!*"

Men who hadn't even heard Efrahm Acairverah when he shouted in their faces heard *that* voice. Hands which hadn't discarded their rifles tightened on their weapons. Shoulders that had sagged and shrunken in on themselves in defeat squared themselves once more.

"*The Slash Lizard!*" someone shouted. "It's the Slash Lizard!"

"Who's with me?!" Rahdgyrz demanded. "Come on, boys! One more time! One more fight for me—for *God!* We owe Him a death, and this is a good day to give it to him! *So who's coming with me now?!*"

"We are!" One or two voices answered him, hoarse with exhaustion, cracked with thirst. "*We are!*"

The shouts spread, the flow towards the rear halted. The mob of fugitives changed somehow, solidifying, turning back into an *army* even as Acairverah watched. There was little or no unit structure to it. No one could have called it an "organized force," but neither was it a rabble.

"*We are!*" the shout went up from twice a hundred throats.

"*Then follow me!*" he shouted back, but before he could spur his horse again, a ragged sergeant grabbed his bridle.

"No, Sir!" the man said. "We'll go, but not you. We can't lose *you*, too!"

"Get your hand off my bridle, Sergeant," Rahdgyrz said almost conversationally.

"No, Sir." The sergeant shook his head stubbornly, and the general saw the tear tracks through the dust on his gaunt, filthy face. "*No, Sir.* We'll go— we'll do it for you, I *swear* we will!—but you go to the rear. *Please*, Sir! We need you. The *Army* needs you!"

"General Rahdgyrz to the rear!" more voices shouted, and men pressed in close about him, touching his legs, reaching for his bridle with the sergeant. "General Rahdgyrz to the rear!" they cried. "*Slash Lizard to the rear!*"

"Not going to happen, boys!" he shouted back, and actually managed a grin. "Not going to let you have all the fun. And none of you are going anywhere *I* don't lead you—you hear me?! You and me—we've got an appointment down that road!" He pointed his saber at the road to St. Daivyn's Redoubt, at the stream of fugitives still pouring down it only to stop as it ran into the solidifying barricade of soldiers about him. "*All of us!* Every damned *one* of us! I'm no different from you boys—from *my* boys! And if God decides this is my day to die, then so be it. Because if it is, then I'll do it with His own warriors at my back and stand *proud* beside them before Him!"

The sergeant stared up at him, the muscles of his face working, and Rahdgyrz smiled down at him.

"Let go of my bridle, Sergeant," he said gently, and, like a man moving against his own will, the sergeant did. The other voices fell silent, the other hands fell away, and he smiled at all of them, his single eye bright.

"Thank you, Sergeant. Thank *all* of you. By God, I'm *proud* to call you mine this day." Rahdgyrz' voice was soft, but then he raised it once more.

"After me, boys!" he shouted, and then, incredibly, he laughed. "After me . . . *and try to keep up!*"

He drove in his spurs, and his horse crouched on its hocks. Then it exploded forward, and the broken fugitives who'd heard his voice, the men who'd shouted for him to go to the rear, turned as one and followed him straight back into that hell of dust, smoke, and thundering weapons.

▼　▼　▼

"Sit down, Colonel," Sir Fahstyr Rychtyr said gruffly.

"I prefer to stand, Sir," Colonel Acairverah replied.

"You can *prefer* whatever you damned well want, Colonel, but what you can actually *do* is something else. Now sit the hell down before you *fall* down!"

"I—" Acairverah began, then stopped, swaying on his newly acquired crutch. He looked at Rychtyr for a long moment, eyes dark in a pale, haggard face. And then, finally, he nodded.

"I expect you're right, Sir," he acknowledged hoarsely, and settled into the chair Lieutenant Gohzail had positioned behind him.

"Thank you," Rychtyr said in a far gentler voice and leaned back in his own chair.

They sat in the farmhouse Rychtyr had commandeered for his headquarters in the village of Borahn. The mutter and rumble of artillery—most of it heretic, unfortunately—was like a distant, unending surf. But at least the "Borahn Line" was holding . . . for now. How long that would last was another matter entirely, of course.

The general glanced at Pairaik Metzlyr, standing in what had been the farm owner's parlor, gazing out the eastern windows. Dusk had fallen, although it wasn't completely dark yet, and the horizon flickered with muzzle flashes. The tempo had dropped, probably because the heretics were dragging their heavy angles forward again, but the constant skirmishes, the unending probes at his fragile positions, warned Rychtyr any diminuendo would be fleeting.

He looked down at the message on the field desk in front of him, and his jaw tightened. Acairverah had taken a very real risk in agreeing to carry that message to him. In a reasonable world, the fact that he'd lost his left leg just below the hip would have amply absolved him of any charge of cowardice for having given his parole so he might deliver it. Unfortunately, the world was increasingly *unreasonable* just now.

He ran his eyes over the message. It wasn't handwritten. Instead, it looked almost printed. It would appear the once hand-to-mouth Army of Thesmar's supply position had improved radically if Earl Hanth had taken delivery of one of the newfangled Charisian "typewriters."

Probably part of the message, Rychtyr thought. *The bastard wants me to know how good his logistics are . . . just in case I've missed how damned many shells he's been dropping on my men's heads. And how frigging many bullets and hand bombs he's got to go with them.*

Perhaps that was true, but it didn't change what the message said, and a fist of anguish closed on his heart and twisted as he read its opening paragraphs once more.

> To General Sir Fahstyr Rychtyr,
> Commanding the Army of the Seridahn;
> From Sir Hauwerd Breygart, Earl of Hanth,
> Commanding the Army of Thesmar,
>
> June 23, Year of God 898
>
> General:
>
> I deeply regret to inform you that General Clyftyn Rahdgyrz, died at 21:15 last night.
>
> From the reports of my units, he had succeeded in rallying some six or severn hundred men from several regiments which had broken under intense infantry attack and artillery fire. He led them personally into battle, and the men he'd rallied inflicted over two hundred casualties upon the Army of Thesmar before they were beaten off once more. In the fighting, General Rahdgyrz was shot through the chest. Colonel Mahkgrudyr, his senior aide, was killed fighting at his side, attempting to evacuate him from the field for treatment, but the General's wound was fatal. He died in hospital at my own advanced headquarters, under our healers' care, and one of our chaplains heard his final confession and administered last rites to him before he passed.
>
> He met his end with the same courage and the same resolute faith with which he always lived and fought, and his final request was that I pass on to you his apology for failing to hold his position. I assured him that no one could have held that position . . . or fought more bravely trying, and I now assure you that my words were no more than the simple truth. I hope that he died accepting that truth.
>
> I believe that you and he are fighting for a bad cause, but no man was ever more loyal to his commander, no man ever fought more gallantly, and no man ever died more bravely or confident in his faith than he. I envy you his friendship, and I extend my sincere condolences for your loss.

I believe him, Rychtyr thought drearily. *I really believe him.* He shook his head mentally, tiredly, amazed to realize that was true. *This isn't just polite, pro forma flattery. He means it . . . and, God, but he's right.*

The general closed his eyes in pain. He'd hoped so hard. A handful of survivors from that hopeless, valiant attack had reported that Rahdgryz had been wounded, but there'd been no confirmation of his death, and so Rychtyr had allowed himself to hope. To pray. And now. . . .

He was going to miss that great, roaring dragon of a man. That *friend.* And if anyone had ever failed another, it had not been Clyftyn Rahdgyrz. His counterattack had been an act of desperation—of atonement to God—and Rychtyr knew it. But it had also delayed the heretics' advance for two full hours . . . long enough for Rychtyr to fit four regiments from his reserve into the hole in his lines at Symyn's Farm. Far too many of his men had been trapped when the farm finally fell, but those regiments had held it for almost two more days and at least eight thousand men who would otherwise have been lost had escaped to the Borahn Line because of what they'd done.

Because of what Clyftyn Rahdgyrz had done.

"You've lost a leg, Colonel," he said softly, opening his eyes once more, looking up at the lines of pain across Acairverah's face. "You've lost a leg, and I deeply regret that. But I—I've lost my good right arm. And half my heart, with it."

"The men tried to get him to go to the rear, Sir. They truly did—and so did I. But he . . . well, he—"

Acairverah's voice broke off, his cheeks working as if he hovered on the brink of tears, and Rychtyr nodded.

"I know," he said almost gently. "Believe me, I *know*, none better. They didn't call him the Slash Lizard for nothing, Colonel. Sooner or later, this had to happen. I always knew that . . . and so did he."

Acairverah's face tightened, and Metzlyr looked up sharply. Not in disagreement with anything Rychtyr had just said, but with an expression of . . . concern, perhaps.

"My son," the Schuelerite began, "it might—"

"I only meant that when a man is so dedicated to God and Mother Church, when he commands from the front and insists on leading by example, no matter how many times he's been wounded, sooner or later that man is going to be killed, Father." Rychtyr returned the upper-priest's gaze levelly. "The men who came back from that counterattack all say he told them 'we owe God a death,' and he was right. We do. And because he believed that so strongly—because he could conceive of no higher calling, no better end—it was inevitable that eventually he'd surrender his life in God's service."

Metzlyr looked at him for several seconds, then nodded.

Not because he agrees with me, Rychtyr thought. *And not because he thinks that's actually what I meant. But he's a good man, Father Pairaik. He knows what I really meant. That's why he's worried the Inquisition may figure it out, as well.*

The general leaned back in his chair, closing his eyes and pinching the bridge of his nose as he faced the bleak reality.

His army was crumbling. Despite the twenty-five thousand reinforcements Duke Salthar had somehow found to send to him, despite the eight thousand Rahdgryz' sacrifice had saved, he was down to barely forty-eight thousand men, including his remaining militia. Many of those missing men were stragglers who'd simply been separated from their units, and at least some of them would turn up in the next few days. But that still represented the loss of over fifty-seven thousand men, seventy percent of the army he'd commanded less than three five-days ago, and he'd lost damned nearly two-thirds of his artillery to go with them. Hanth's losses had been heavy, as well. Despite his advantages in artillery—and despite the fact that, however much it galled Rychtyr to admit it, his infantry was not just better equipped but simply *better* than the best Dohlar could offer, even now—he'd paid dearly to storm those successive lines of fortifications.

But this time he hadn't stopped. He hadn't tried to flank Rychtyr out of position, hadn't sought the casualty-saving maneuvers he'd always used before. No. *This* time he'd fastened a death grip on the Army of the Seridahn and he intended to follow it wherever it went, drive it into its last desperate burrow, and then drag it out for the kill.

And he's going to do it, Rychtyr admitted bleakly. *However heavy his casualties may have been, they've been one hell of a lot lighter than mine.* His mind flinched away from the raw wound of Rahdgyrz' death. *And he's obviously been pouring in a steady stream of replacements—a hell of a lot bigger one than anyone in Gorath's been able to send* me.

Sir Fahstyr Rychtyr knew how this had to end, barring some miracle . . . and so far, God and the Archangels had vouchsafed precious few of those to Their defenders. Worse, his men knew what was coming for them, too. Their morale was collapsing, and much though that pained Rychtyr, he couldn't blame them for it. He knew the inquisitors assigned to the Army's units were increasingly concerned, even desperate, and that desperation was filling some of them with fury. But it was inevitable. Whatever else they might be, his men weren't fools. No one had told them about the spy reports or the reasons Earl Silken Hills' Harchongians had been shifted to cover the front north from Alyksberg, but they knew they were about to be totally overwhelmed by fire and death in what had always been a *secondary* theater for the heretics.

No, not for the "heretics"—for the Charisians. *You've known that for at least two years . . . and now the men have figured it out, too. This isn't about heresy, not about Charis' sudden decision to defy the will of God, and it never has been. There's a reason the boys are starting to call this "Clyntahn's War," a reason not even the Inquisition can stop the rot now. And where does that leave you, Fahstyr?*

And if the Charisians could do this, produce this sort of carnage in a *secondary* theater, what possible chance did the Harchongians stand when Charis and the Republic unleashed their *main* attack? The men could answer *that* question for themselves, as well, he thought grimly, and even men thoroughly prepared to die in God's service might reasonably turn away from a death which could accomplish nothing in the end.

We're not all Clyftyn, he thought drearily. *Not all Slash Lizards with that magnificent internal compass. The men are mortal, they have wives, children, people they love. People to live for. How can I keep feeding them into the furnace this way? But if I don't, then I fail not just the Kingdom but Mother—*

"Sir Fahstyr?"

Rychtyr lowered his hand and opened his eyes.

Acairverah had disappeared. He hadn't heard a sound, and the colonel hadn't asked his permission before withdrawing. But there was no sign of young Gohzail either, and his face tightened ever so slightly as he realized Colonel Mohrtynsyn had gestured both of them out of the room without a word. There could be only one reason for him to do that.

"Yes, Ahskar?" Rychtyr kept his tone calm, conversational, with no sign he knew what he was about to hear.

"Forgive me for asking, Sir, but . . . what about the rest of Earl Hanth's letter?"

Mohrtynsyn's voice was very quiet. Metzlyr looked up again, quickly, at the question, darting a warning glance at the man who headed Rychtyr's staff, but the colonel's eyes were steady as he looked back at the intendant.

"We have to reply one way or the other, Sir," the colonel continued, speaking to Rychtyr but never breaking eye contact with Metzlyr. "And if we accept, even only temporarily, it would give us time to reorganize. God knows we need it!"

"That's true," Rychtyr conceded. "Of course, there are a few other things to consider before we give him an answer, aren't there?"

"Yes, Sir. Of course."

Rychtyr pushed back his chair, stood, and began pacing back and forth across the narrow dining room with his hands clasped behind him.

That was the most dangerous part of Hanth's entire letter, he thought. The offer of a "temporary cease-fire." The Charisian had justified it as an opportunity for both sides to collect their wounded and bury their dead— possibly even to exchange wounded prisoners, although he must know how many fewer Charisian prisoners Rychtyr held. But however he might have *justified* it, his intent was clear enough.

"I know we could use the respite, Ahskar," he said finally, pausing beside Metzlyr to look out at that flickering eastern horizon. "God knows the men'll be hard-pressed to stand if Hanth keeps coming this way, and I'd love to have time to finish the lines around Artynsian! But you know as well as I do what he really has in mind."

Mohrtynsyn only looked at him, and Rychtyr snorted.

"Oh, trust me, Ahskar. If I could buy these boys even twenty-six hours with none of them getting killed, I'd sell my immortal soul for it. I'm sure Father Pairaik would disapprove of the transaction," he smiled briefly at the intendant, although the smile disappeared as quickly as it had come, "but I'd lay down the cash in a heartbeat, and you know it. But what he really figures is that if we ever agree to stop—to pause—even once, two-thirds of the fight will go out of our men. This—" he flicked a gesture at the message lying on his desk "—isn't really an offer of a couple of days in which to collect our wounded. *This* is the opening shot he hopes will lead to an outright surrender."

Mohrtynsyn's face clenched, but he didn't disagree, and Rychtyr turned back to the window.

Of course that was what Hanth wanted. It was what any worthwhile, sane general—especially a general who served sane *masters* like Cayleb and Sharleyan Ahrmahk—would want. Because if Rychtyr agreed to a cease-fire, however brief, however limited, it would set the entire Army of the Seridahn back on its heels. The respite would make it even harder for the men to walk back into the furnace, and who could blame them? The fact that the "heretics" had offered a cease-fire, offered a chance to spare their lives instead of simply continuing to kill them when everyone knew they could, might well confirm the Army's "Clyntahn's War" thinking. Who was the true servant of Corruption, after all? The man who spared when he might have killed . . . or the man who condemned millions of *other* men to die?

"That's exactly what he's thinking, Ahskar, and I'm not going to give it to him. Clyftyn didn't die leading that frigging forlorn hope just so I could sell out the sacrifice he and the men with him made! I won't do that. I *can't* do that."

"Very well, Sir," Mohrtynsyn said after a long, still moment. Then he smiled crookedly. "I guess I already knew what you'd say. Still, it *is* my job to point these little things out to you."

"Yes, it is." Rychtyr's smile was considerably broader—and warmer—than the colonel's had been. "And you do it w—"

The door to his improvised office opened suddenly, and he turned towards the interruption. His expression was irritated . . . but it smoothed instantly as he saw the man standing in the doorway. The brown-haired newcomer wore the purple cassock of the Order of Schueler, badged with the sword and flame of the Inquisition. The cockade in his priest's cap was the same upper-priest brown as Pairaik Metzlyr's, but his right sleeve bore the embroidered white crown of an archbishop's personal secretary.

Rychtyr had never seen him before, but he knew instantly who—or at least *what*—he had to be, and Metzlyr's reaction confirmed it a moment later.

"Father Rahndail!" his intendant said sharply. "What are you doing here? And, forgive me for pointing this out, but one usually knocks before barging in on a general officer."

"I realize that, Father," the newcomer said. "Circumstances are . . .

somewhat unusual, however." He turned to Rychtyr. "I apologize for bursting in on you, Sir Fahstyr, but I fear my errand leaves little time for normal courtesies."

"And why would that be, Father . . . ?" Rychtyr raised his eyebrows in polite inquiry as if he hadn't already realized perfectly well who the other man was.

"Evryt, Sir Fahstyr," the upper-priest said, bending his head in the slightest of nods. "Father Rahndail Evryt. I have the honor to be one of Archbishop Trumahn's personal assistants."

"I see. And could I ask—" Rychtyr began, then paused as the door opened once more, this time to readmit Lieutenant Gohzail. The lieutenant's shoulders were tight, his gray-green eyes were worried, and he was accompanied by another officer. It was a captain Rychtyr had never seen before . . . and he wore the purple tunic and red trousers of the Army of God, not the green and red of Dohlar.

"Yes, Zhulyo?"

"Forgive me, Sir, but this . . . gentleman declined to wait in the orderly room. He insisted upon joining Father Rahndail. And he appears to have brought a couple of platoons of dragoons with him. They're waiting outside."

"Indeed?" Rychtyr glanced at the Army of God officer. "And has the captain explained exactly what he's doing here?"

"No, Sir." Gohzail's tone was manifestly unhappy. "I asked him, but—"

"Excuse me, Sir Fahstyr," Evryt said. Rychtyr's eyes returned to him, and the upper-priest shrugged slightly. "I regret any confusion, and no doubt I should already have mentioned Captain Gairybahldy's presence and introduced him to you. I shouldn't have allowed the importance of my mission to distract me from that courtesy, so please, allow me to correct that oversight now and present Captain Ahlvyno Gairybahldy. When I set out for the front, Bishop Executor Wylsynn thought it best to provide me with an escort. He is, of course, aware of the way in which Duke Salthar is straining every nerve to reinforce you while simultaneously protecting the Kingdom's coasts, so it seemed best to provide that escort from the Army of God personnel who've been seconded to the Inquisition rather than requesting troops from him at such a time. Captain Gairybahldy is the commander of that escort."

"I see," Rychtyr said again. He gave the captain—who looked a shade less than completely calm and composed—a thoughtful glance, then looked back at Evryt. "And I suppose that rather brings me back to the question I was about to pose before we were . . . interrupted. So, may I ask what brings you to Borahn?"

"I've been sent to inform you and Father Pairaik that you are summoned to Gorath." Evryt's tone was level, his expression grave. "My instructions were to inform you of that as quickly as possible and then to personally escort you—both of you—back to the capital."

"I see," Rychtyr said for a third time, and glanced briefly at Metzlyr. His intendant's expression didn't look any happier than the general felt, and he returned his attention to Evryt and held out his hand. "May I see Duke Salthar's instructions, Father?"

"I'm afraid the summons wasn't issued by Duke Salthar. Or by any secular authority, Sir Fahstyr." Evryt's face hardened ever so slightly. "You've been summoned by Bishop Executor Wylsynn and Father Ahbsahlahn."

"With all due respect for the Bishop Executor and Father Ahbsahlahn, this would be a very bad time for me to abandon the Army, Father," Rychtyr said levelly. "We've just received confirmation of General Rahdgyrz' death, and I've lost close to a third of my senior regimental commanders. We're in the process of reorganizing in anticipation of the heretics' next attack, and it would be . . . counterproductive for me to leave for Gorath before that's been accomplished."

"I'm sorry to hear that, Sir Fahstyr. Unfortunately, I was granted no discretion to modify my instructions. I really must insist we depart immediately."

The iron in his tone was as unmistakable as the flint in his eyes. Rychtyr felt himself tighten internally, and the corner of his eye saw Mohrtynsyn stiffen. He also saw Gohzail take a quiet half-step backwards, which just happened to place him behind Captain Gairybahldy, while his hand dropped to the grip of the captured Charisian revolver at his side.

Gairybahldy took no apparent notice of Gohzail's movement . . . or of the way Mohrtynsyn's hand strayed towards the hilt of his dagger. But his spine stiffened and he was very careful to keep his own hand away from any weapon. The tension in that parlor could have been sawn up into pieces and used for sandbags, Rychtyr thought. Even Evryt was aware of it. It showed in the sudden tightness of his shoulders, the way his face lost all expression. It hovered in the very air, that suddenly icy, brittle tension, as Evryt realized Sir Fahstyr Rychtyr's officers might just put their loyalty to *him* above their loyalty to Mother Church.

Or to the Group of Four, at least.

"I understand your desire to discharge your instructions as speedily as possible, Father," the commanding officer of the Army of the Seridahn said calmly. "And as a loyal son of Mother Church, I am, of course, at the Bishop Executor's service at any time. I do have obligations to the Kingdom and to King Rahnyld's Army, however. I can't simply walk out the door with you right this moment. At the very least, I have to see to an orderly transfer of command. This isn't the time for there to be any confusion in the chain of command—not when fresh heretic attacks are almost certainly imminent. I'm sure you can understand that."

"I can . . . understand your reasoning, Sir Fahstyr. Nonetheless, my mission—as you've just more or less observed—is a pressing one and my instructions are nondiscretionary. How long would you require to see to that transfer?"

"General Iglaisys is my senior commander, now that we've lost General Rahdgyrz," Rychtyr replied. "At the moment, he's in St. Torrin. I presume you passed through that village on your way here?"

Evryt nodded, never taking his eyes from Rychtyr's face.

"Then you know it's only about five miles from here," the general continued. "It's too dark now to summon him by semaphore, but a courier could reach him in about an hour. Assume another hour—more probably an hour and a half—for him to hand over to his own second in command—that would be Colonel Hylz now, I believe—and then another hour to return here with the courier. So call it three and a half hours. Then it will probably take at least a couple of hours for me to bring him fully up to speed. It would take considerably longer than that if he and I hadn't already discussed our situation and our options pretty thoroughly." He shrugged. "At any rate, I'd estimate I could probably leave the Army under his command in six or seven hours. Of course, by that time it will be Langhorne's Watch, so we probably wouldn't want to leave before dawn. I could be fully packed and ready to depart by then with a clear conscience, however."

Evryt's eyes flicked past Rychtyr to Gohzail, then flitted to Mohrtynsyn's stony expression. His unhappiness was evident, but he produced something approximating a smile as he returned his gaze to Rychtyr's face.

"I'm a priest, Sir Fahstyr, not a general. I'm afraid I hadn't fully thought through the . . . complications a professional soldier would face in simply handing his command over to someone else. I'm afraid I do have to insist we depart absolutely as soon as practicable, but obviously we can't do that until you've had time to transfer command to General Iglaisys in an orderly fashion."

"I'm glad you understand, Father."

"Oh, I assure you I *understand*." Despite himself, Evryt's smile turned rather colder for a moment. Then he looked at Gairybahldy. "Captain, please inform your men we'll be staying the night here in Borahn, after all. I'm sure the General's staff will see to your quarters while we're here."

"Of course they will, Father." Rychtyr smiled at the AOG officer. "All of us understand the requirements duty imposes, Captain. Zhulyo—Lieutenant Gohzail—will see to it that you and your men are quartered together. I'm afraid all we can offer overnight will be a spot for you to pitch your own tents, but the cooks should at least be able to feed you a hot supper and I believe we'll be able to put you somewhere that lets you look after Father Rahndail's comfort and security. I trust that will be satisfactory?"

"Perfectly so, Sir," Gairybahldy replied.

"I'm glad. In that case," Rychtyr looked past him to Gohzail, "I'll leave you in Zhulyo's capable hands. He'll see you as comfortably settled as possible before he goes and oversees the packing of my own bags." He held the youthful lieutenant's eyes very steadily. "He's a very conscientious young officer. I'm sure he'll look after you to the very best of his ability."

Rebellion flickered in Gohzail's eyes for just a second, and the hand on his revolver tightened. Rychtyr's gaze never wavered, however, and after a moment, the lieutenant made himself take his hand off the weapon and his nostrils flared.

"Of course, Sir." His tone acknowledged far more than anything Rychtyr had just said. "I'll personally see to Captain Gairybahldy and his men's needs. And I'll see to it that none of our people feel any confusion or . . . concern over their presence."

"Good, Zhulyo. That's good," Rychtyr said. "And on your way out, send a courier to General Iglaisys to tell him to report to me here."

"I will, Sir," Gohzail acknowledged, then touched Gairybahldy on the shoulder. "If you'll come with me, Captain?"

"With your permission, Father?" Gairybahldy asked, looking at Evryt, and came to attention when the upper-priest nodded. "In that case, I'm at your service, Lieutenant." He saluted Rychtyr, rather more formally—and, unless Rychtyr missed his guess, much more gratefully—than an Army of God officer normally saluted someone else's officers. "Permission to withdraw, General Rychtyr?"

"Granted, Captain Gairybahldy." Rychtyr returned the salute and smiled frostily. "I look forward to your company on the trip to Gorath."

.V.
Lizard Island,
Hankey Sound,
and
Gorath Palace,
City of Gorath,
Kingdom of Dohlar.

"Sir, I think you'd better come see this."

Lieutenant Bryahn Sathyrwayt lowered his cup of hot chocolate with a frown. Sergeant Maikel knew how he hated being disturbed at breakfast. One of the very few good things about being the senior officer of the Harlysville "garrison" was the plethora of seafood taken off Lizard Island's shores and, especially, the spider crabs and shellfish harvested from Lamb Chop Shoal off the island's northwestern coast. Before he'd been assigned to the grandiloquently named Coastal Defense Force and then shuffled off to Lizard Island he'd never considered the thought of seafood for breakfast. Now it was one of the simple pleasures to which he looked forward.

"See what, Ahmbrohs?" he inquired in repressive tones, looking up from his plate. "And why can't it wait until I've at least finished breakfast?"

"Sir," Ahmbrohs Maikel was a tall, lugubrious-looking man, with a long face and thinning gray hair, who walked with a pronounced limp courtesy of the wounds he'd suffered at Alyksberg, "you can wait until you've finished breakfast if you want. No skin off my nose. Don't think Governor Alysyn'll be too happy about that later, though."

Sathyrwayt's frown deepened. Maikel took a certain pleasure in finding suitable reasons to predict doom and gloom. And he was not, regrettably, a tremendous respecter of the dignity of twenty-year-old lieutenants who'd never heard a shot fired in anger. Still, there was usually a point to his less than deeply respectful moments—what Sathyrwayt's uncle, a lay brother in the Order of Sondheim, was fond of calling a "teaching moment." All of which suggested this was a day when breakfast should be deferred.

"All right, Ahmbrohs," he sighed, took one last sip of chocolate, and pushed back from the table. "What's so damned important?" he asked, walking across the tiny dining parlor of the house assigned for his use here in Harlysville.

"Best if you see it for yourself, Sir," Maikel said, and pointed out to sea.

Harlysville lay at what was very nearly the northernmost point of Lizard Island, fronting the twenty-five-mile-wide Ghustahv Channel between

Lizard and the much larger Dragon Island, its northern neighbor. The Ghus-tahv Channel was deep, suitable for the largest galleons, and there were usually a few sails visible upon its waters. Much less shipping had passed through it since the heretics' seizure of White Rock Island, however. White Rock was nine hundred miles north of Lizard, but Charisian commerce-raiders had swarmed out from it to shut down the Trosan Channel and the Fern Narrows. What little shipping still moved across Hankey Sound came from South Harchong, not the north, and tended to hug the Sound's southern coast as tightly as possible, staying close to ports it could dash into the instant a Charisian schooner's topsails showed themselves. That meant no one was taking the shortcut through Ghustahv Channel. So what, Sath-yrwayt thought irritably, could be so damned important that he had to leave his breakfast to get cold and—

"Sweet Langhorne," he said very, very softly.

"Figure that's about the only person who could help us now, Sir," Maikel agreed with appalling cheerfulness. Sathyrwayt looked at him sharply, and the sergeant shrugged. "Already roused the platoon, Sir. Got both twelve-pounders manned, too. Don't think it'll make much difference, though."

Sathyrwayt stared at him for several seconds, then back out at the forest of sails emerging from the morning fog. There had to be at least thirty or forty galleons out there, he thought numbly. And, far worse, were the two ships heading purposefully—and absurdly swiftly—towards Harlysville's modest docks. The thick banners of smoke trailing from the single smoke-stack each of them boasted would have made their identity crystal-clear even without the silver, blue, and black banners flying from their yardarms.

Behind them, moving more slowly but trailing their own smoke, were at least two dozen much smaller vessels. They looked more like cargo light-ers than anything else, except for their spindly smokestacks and the paddle blades churning the ocean behind them. Sathyrwayt had seen pedal-powered paddle wheels on a handful of canal boats, but he'd never seen paddle wheels that spun as rapidly and steadily as *these* did.

Maikel tapped him on the shoulder and extended the spyglass Sathyr-wayt hadn't noticed hanging from his shoulder. The lieutenant took it numbly, raising it and peering through it, and his jaw tightened as he recognized the black and blue uniforms of Imperial Charisian Marines. There were what looked like at least a couple of squads—probably more—packed into each of those oncoming "cargo lighters," and his entire command consisted of a single understrength platoon of only twenty-seven men.

"I believe you're right about how much difference the twelve-pounders are going to make, Sergeant," he said, lowering the glass. "Why don't you get back to the men and suggest they stand well clear of the guns? In fact, I think it would be a good idea to shove them through the embrasures. We can always fish them back out of the harbor at low tide later."

"I think that sounds like a really good idea, Sir." There was considerably more approval in Maikel's voice than Sathyrwayt was accustomed to hearing from him. "I'll just go and take care of that right now, shall I?"

"I think that would be a very good idea." Sathyrwayt handed him back the spyglass with a thin smile. "And while you're doing that, I'll see about getting semaphore messages off to Governor Alysyn and Captain Ohygyns."

"Yes, Sir."

The sergeant touched his chest in salute and started down the narrow street towards the pathetic earthwork "battery" covering Harlysville's three fishing piers, and Sathyrwayt headed for the semaphore office.

He fully intended to send those messages, but he rather doubted they'd come as any surprise to the island's governor or the naval base's commanding officer. It seemed . . . unlikely the Imperial Charisian Navy would waste its time occupying miserable little Harlysville unless they intended to take the entire damned island. And it seemed equally unlikely the Charisians would be guilty of botched timing. If they were moving in on Harlysville, they'd probably already made their presence known off Darth Town, as well.

▾   ▾   ▾

Thunder bellowed, recoil shook HMS *Gwylym Manthyr's* fifteen thousand tons underfoot, and the waves of overpressure blew back across him like a hot, mighty fist of wind. Dense brown smoke billowed, shot through with flame, and four 10-inch and seven 8-inch shells howled from his flagship's guns.

Sir Dunkyn Yairley stood on his flag bridge—the first dedicated flag bridge ever built aboard a Safeholdian ship of war—and gazed through his double-glass. Fortunately, the wind was brisk and from the north, rolling the blinding smoke away rapidly. Despite that, the range hadn't quite cleared before those shells crashed down on the old-fashioned, stonewalled fortifications on Battery Point. He couldn't see the actual explosions as they landed like brimstone hammers, but as the smoke blew clear, he could easily see the hundred-yard section of that thick stone barrier which had just disintegrated.

The range was short, especially for *Manthyr's* guns, at barely a thousand yards, and Lizard Island's defenses hadn't received priority for the new, heavy Fultyn Rifles. It wouldn't have mattered if they had—not against *Manthyr's* armor—but the battery's 40-pounders were about as useful as stone-throwing catapults. They'd fired back defiantly as the enormous ship glided remorselessly across Darth Cove, Lizard Island's one decent harbor, into her chosen position, but they'd accomplished less than nothing and Halcom Bahrns had ignored them almost disdainfully as he closed.

In many ways, Admiral Sarmouth would have preferred to leave those fortifications alone. He took no pleasure in massacring men who couldn't fight back effectively, and that was exactly what he was doing at this moment. But if those artillery pieces couldn't harm *Manthyr*, they most certainly could harm any of his landing craft or supporting galleons. They could also kill quite a few of his Marines when the time came. He had no intention of allowing that, and so Halcom Bahrns had brought his ship to within a bare five cables of Battery Point before he'd turned and opened fire at last. Now he steamed slowly in a huge, flattened oval, maintaining a bare knot's speed through the water, while his ship's massive armament methodically pulverized the defensive positions. At that range, firing from *Manthyr*'s rocksteady platform and waiting for the smoke to clear between salvos, his gunners were capable of pinpoint accuracy, and their heavy shells drilled effortlessly into the obsolete stonework.

Sarmouth turned from the systematic destruction of the naval yard's defenses and gazed southwest at Darth Town, Lizard Island's only real town, on the far side of Darth Cove. Fortunately, neither Styvyn Alysyn, the island's governor, nor Ahlfryd Mahkgentry, Darth Town's mayor, had been stupid enough to man the even more ancient and decrepit defenses covering the civilian harbor. He'd hoped that would be the case, although it had been something of a toss-up which way Mayor Mahkgentry would decide in the end. Alysyn was a reasonable man and about as far from a fanatic as a man could get, a career bureaucrat with no hankering for glory or illusions about his island's ability to stand off an assault backed by ships like *Gwylym Manthyr* or the *City*-class ironclads. Mahkgentry was younger, a more fiery soul. He was more ardent, more impetuous . . . and more concerned about the Inquisition's reaction to anything smacking of "defeatism." In the end, though, he'd decided to abide by Alysyn's orders. Quite probably, in Sarmouth's rather cynical opinion, because those orders would offer him cover when the Inquisition came calling.

Except, of course, that the Inquisition isn't going to call on anyone ever again once this jihad of Clyntahn's is over, the baron thought grimly. *Probably expecting a bit much for people like Mahkgentry to recognize that—or admit it, anyway, even to themselves—at this point, I suppose. On the other hand, there are people in Gorath who damned well should realize it. Be interesting to see if they react to our little Lizard Island visit the way Cayleb and Sharleyan predict they will.*

He lowered the double-glass and glanced up at the sky. It was barely ten o'clock, the day's heat was only beginning to build, and it wouldn't be much longer before even Captain Ohygyns realized the only thing more resistance could accomplish would be to get more of his men killed. Major

Anthynee Frughahty, the senior officer of the troops from the Coastal Defense Force assigned to Lizard Island, had already recognized that reality. The CDF was a new organization, hastily put together by Earl Thirsk out of whatever forces came to hand, and Frughahty's contingent had been granted precious little time to shake down before it was sent out. They were scarcely what anyone could have called an effective fighting force yet, and he'd never had more than three hundred men, whereas Sarmouth was in the process of landing an entire brigade of veteran Marines. Even as the admiral watched, the steam-powered landing boats were churning back out across Darth Cove towards the transport galleons for the second wave of assault troops.

Not that it's been all that much of an "assault," Sarmouth reflected. More a matter of coming politely ashore and reminding the men to be courteous to the local civilians as long as they mind their manners. And it's remarkable how well they've done just that!

He raised the double-glass again as a fresh broadside blasted from *Gwylym Manthyr*'s guns. He didn't bother to examine the defensive battery when the smoke cleared this time. His double-glass was trained on the flagstaff above the naval yard's semaphore tower, where the green wyvern on its red field still flew defiantly.

It was only a matter of time before that banner came down and he could order Bahrns to cease fire. All that remained was to see how much time—and how many more men—Ohygyns' stubbornness was going to cost.

▾　　▾　　▾

"I won't hide the truth from you, Duke Fern." Bishop Executor Wylsynn Lainyr's voice was chill across the conference table, his expression bleak. "Mother Church finds this latest news from Lizard Island disturbing. Most disturbing."

"I hope you don't think there's anyone on His Majesty's council who doesn't find it equally disturbing, Your Eminence," Samyl Cahkrayn replied. "Lizard Island is less than four hundred miles as a wyvern flies from this very chamber. For that matter, it's less than seventy miles off Start Point and barely five hundred miles from Gorath by sea! If our reports about those Shan-wei-spawned 'steamers' of theirs are correct, that's less than two days' voyage from His Majesty's capital. And forgive me for pointing this out, but I doubt the timing of this attack—the fact that it comes when the Army of the Seridahn is already under such massive pressure—was precisely a coincidence."

"That's exactly *my* point, Your Grace," Lainyr's voice was even colder. "Governor Alysyn and Captain Ohygyns know the Army of the Seridahn's fallen back for almost a hundred and fifty miles in less than a month. Now, at the first sign of the heretic navy, they've surrendered an entire island and all of Mother Church's children living on it, to the forces of Shan-wei! *And*, in the process, provided the heretics with a naval base which—as you've just pointed out—is only five hundred miles from this very city! One cannot avoid the suspicion that news from the Army of the Seridahn's front might have . . . undermined the determination of Lizard Island's defenders."

Silence lingered for several moments in the palatial council chamber as Lainyr gazed at the Kingdom of Dohlar's first councilor with bleak eyes.

"That's a very serious charge, Your Eminence." Duke Salthar broke that silence from Fern's side of the table, and Lainyr's eyes swiveled to the Royal Dohlaran Army's commanding officer. "If I understand you correctly," the duke continued in a level, almost dispassionate tone, meeting those eyes, "you're suggesting Governor Alysyn and Captain Ohygyns surrendered out of cowardice."

The silence which followed *those* words was more intense, and considerably icier, than the last one had been. Then Lainyr cleared his throat.

" 'Cowardice' is, perhaps, a stronger word than any I might choose, Your Grace," he said. Ahbsahlahn Kharmych stirred in his chair at the bishop executor's elbow, disagreement flickering in his eyes, but Lainyr ignored him and continued steadily. "At this time, Mother Church is prepared to accept the honesty of this report." He tapped a copy of the message lying on the table before him. "But even accepting that the Governor's explanation of his thinking is completely honest, Mother Church finds it very disturbing that he thought that way in the first place. From his own words, it appears evident he never truly contemplated defending the island. He might have held out for some time had he not agreed to parley with the heretic Sarmouth within less than *six hours* of Sarmouth's arrival. Calling his decision 'cowardice' might be excessive, but I believe his entire attitude might reasonably be described as . . . defeatist. Mother Church has a right to expect at least some effort to defend her loyal children from the corruption and damnation of Shan-wei's servants, Your Grace."

"Your Eminence," Fern said before Salthar could respond, "with all due respect, I think the results of Captain Ohygyns' defense of the navy yard demonstrate that Governor Alysyn's assessment of the situation was entirely accurate. The Captain's gallant efforts produced, so far as we know, not a single heretic casualty. His artillerists, on the other hand, suffered at least eighty dead, with twice as many wounded, and all but four of his own guns had been put out of action or completely destroyed before he surrendered his command. To me, that clearly suggests Governor Alysyn, with far weaker batteries and no more than three hundred men, could have achieved nothing besides the pointless sacrifice of still more of our soldiers' lives. And that, of course, doesn't even consider the civilians of Darth Town who might have been caught in the fighting."

Lainyr's eyes narrowed ever so slightly at the first councilor's firm, almost hard tone, but Fern continued levelly.

"Lizard Island's defenses were never intended to stand off a major attack. It would have been physically impossible for Duke Salthar and Duke Thorast to defend every single mile of the Kingdom's coast, much less islands completely surrounded by sea, especially now that the heretics effectively control the entire Gulf of Dohlar. It simply couldn't be done—not out of the Kingdom's resources, at any rate. Choices had to be made, and that meant less vital objectives had to be left exposed. Just creating the Coastal Defense Force to provide at least some sort of garrisons for our smaller ports constitutes a severe drain on our available troop strength. And while I completely agree that *every* soul must be protected from the poisons of Shan-wei, Lizard Island is less than ninety miles long from north to south. Its entire civilian population is under eleven thousand. I deeply regret that any of Mother Church's children should find themselves even temporarily under heretic control, but surely the number of Lizard Islanders is minute compared to the many, many thousands who've already fled Thorast ahead of the heretic Hanth or, far worse, found themselves unable to flee, trapped behind his lines. Are you suggesting we should have attempted to reinforce someplace like Lizard Island to a level that gave it a realistic chance of resisting attack by the heretics' armored ships rather than strain every sinew to protect the far greater number of His Majesty's subjects—and Mother Church's children—on the mainland?"

Lainyr's expression was a mask for his thoughts, but Kharmych's face had darkened steadily as the first councilor spoke.

"Are you questioning Mother Church, Your Grace?" he demanded.

"I'm simply seeking clarification, Father. We have only so many men and only so many weapons to give them. Our manufactories are stretched to the limit arming them, or we might be able to put more of them into the field. We understand why Mother Church is unable to assist us with men *or* weapons at this time, and we also understand why priority's been given to equipping the Mighty Host. As the purely secular servant of His Majesty, I find those priorities . . . regrettable, but we understand what's driven them. Unfortunately, like Mother Church, we have to make decisions about where to deploy our finite—*very* finite, Father—resources. If Archbishop Trumahn or Mother Church would prefer for us to deploy them in other places, towards other ends, we need to know that."

Kharmych's face grew even darker, but Lainyr laid one hand on his arm.

"As you say, Your Grace," the bishop executor said coldly, "Mother Church's resources are strained to the breaking point at this time. I'm sure Archbishop Trumahn—and Mother Church, of course—realize this Kingdom's resources are equally strained. Under the circumstances there can be no question about the need to give you and King Rahnyld a free hand in how you employ your own soldiers and sailors. And you're quite right to point out the much greater number of Mother Church's children here on the mainland. My concern—*Mother Church's* concern—has less to do with your deployment plans, than it does with the . . . tenacity of your troops and their commanders. Especially after the recent . . . lamentable reverses your Navy and Army have suffered."

Salthar's jaw clenched, but Fern only nodded.

"We have, indeed, suffered 'reverses' in Mother Church's cause." He emphasized the last four words ever so slightly, and Kharmych's eyes flashed. "There can be no higher calling than to defend God and His Church," the first councilor went on steadily, "and this Kingdom—*and* its soldiers and sailors—remain firmly and deeply committed to it. The mainland ports, starting with Gorath, are much more heavily fortified and defended than a tiny, isolated island like Lizard Island ever could be. I regret that Duke Thorast was unable to be here to recount all the actions he's taken—*is* taking, even now—to see to that. We're currently laying up all our remaining galleons to free additional men for harbor defense, and in God's good time, when we're able to provide them with rifles, many of those men will reinforce the Army, as well. I'm confident the heretics will find it far more difficult to take a city like Gorath or Bessberg against those reinforced garrisons and batteries. But in all honesty—and I owe Mother Church nothing less than the truth—I can't guarantee a successful defense anywhere the heretics can deploy ships like the one they used against Darth Town."

The bishop executor's surprise at the frankness of that admission was obvious. Kharmych, on the other hand, looked like a man who'd swallowed a shellhorn and just felt its first sting. The silence was so intense it seemed to ring in the council room's air.

"What His Grace means, Your Eminence," Salthar said after a moment, "is that the heretics have demonstrated their ability to bombard our ports at will, just as they've demonstrated that our galleons dare not meet their ironclads at sea. So Duke Thorast has ordered that our warships' artillery be landed and incorporated into our coastal defenses."

Fern suppressed a sudden, inappropriate urge to smile at that last sentence. It hadn't been *Thorast's* idea to lay up the fleet. In fact he'd initially denied Earl Thirsk's request to do so. He'd been overruled by Fern, however, and much as it galled him to agree to *anything* Thirsk suggested, even he had been forced to admit that what had happened at White Rock Island—and now, again, at Lizard Island—had proven Thirsk was right.

"Like Duke Fern," Salthar continued, "I believe our strengthened defenses will be much more effective. The Navy is currently preparing and emplacing as many sea-bombs as possible, in addition to the new, heavy, rifled artillery. I believe the rockets which have been adapted for coastal defense may well also be effective. No one can *guarantee* that, however. Without completely neutralizing our defenses and defeating our Army garrisons, a successful *invasion* remains most unlikely; bombardments like those carried out against the Harchongians and Desnairians last year are another matter, unfortunately. Unless the sea-bombs prove even more effective than we expect, I very much fear that we'll be unable to prevent them from doing the same things to our coastal cities. If they do, the consequences will, of course, be severe."

Lainyr compressed his lips, eyes narrowed, and examined the councilors on the other side of the table for a long, tense moment. Then he nodded.

"I'm no military man. As such, I'm not remotely qualified to pass judgment on the provisions you've made to defend your Kingdom and your King's subjects. I have neither the intention nor the instructions to interfere with them in any way, and I'll pray most earnestly for their success. This is a time of grave peril when many of God's loyal children will be asked for painful sacrifices, and I deeply regret—as I'm confident the Grand Vicar himself deeply regrets—the price the people of Dohlar have already paid so gallantly in His service."

"Thank you, Your Eminence," Fern said, and the bishop executor nodded curtly to Kharmych and began to stand. But the first councilor raised a hand before Lainyr was completely out of his chair.

"A moment more, Your Eminence, if you please." The duke's tone and expression were courtesy itself, but there was a hint of granite in his brown eyes. "There's one other matter we wished to discuss."

"Indeed, Your Grace?" Lainyr's voice was neutral, and so was his face.

"Yes. Duke Salthar's received a report we find . . . somewhat troubling, and we hoped you might cast some light upon it."

"What sort of report?" the bishop executor asked even more tonelessly.

"Your Eminence, according to General Iglaisys, General Rychtyr has been relieved of command and is returning to Gorath accompanied by an Army of God escort," Salthar said. "I gave no such order, and it's my understanding that it was delivered by Father Rahndail in Mother Church's name."

The tension in the chamber ratcheted upwards abruptly and Lainyr sat back down in his chair and folded his hands on the table before him.

"General Iglaisys is correct, Your Grace," he said flatly.

"With all due respect, Your Eminence, the Army is answerable first to me, then to Duke Fern, and then to the Crown. *I* am answerable to Mother Church for the success or failure of that Army. If I feel one of my field commanders is no longer giving of his best, or if I feel he's proven ineffective, then surely it's *my* prerogative—and responsibility—to replace him."

"No, Your Grace." It wasn't Lainyr; it was Kharmych, and the intendant's eyes were fiery. "You're correct that it's your responsibility to replace in-effective or halfhearted commanders, but those commanders—like every other child of God—are directly answerable to Mother Church as God's bride. Mother Church's concerns with General Rychtyr's . . . state of mind were shared with you and Duke Fern. You chose to exercise your military judgment by leaving him in command of the Army of the Seridahn—as was your legal right. Since that time, the Army of the Seridahn has been driven back deep into the Kingdom, suffering massive casualties, and reports from our inquisitors in the field indicate that its spirit and zeal are . . . not what they might be. Indeed, those reports are one reason Bishop Executor Wylsynn expressed concern over the fighting spirit of the Lizard Island garrisons. The employment of your troops is a matter for your decision, and as you say, your responsibility—one for which you'll be accountable in the eyes of God. But if the faith, the *spiritual* strength, of those troops is being permit-ted to erode . . . *that*, Your Grace, is a matter for Mother Church and the Inquisition."

"Are you suggesting General Rychtyr is more responsible than the chaplains assigned to him for the manner in which his men's morale responds to military defeats, Father?"

A dangerous edge of challenge glinted in the depths of Salthar's tone, but Kharmych only nodded.

"Ultimately, Your Grace, the commander of an army is responsible for everything pertaining to that army, is he not? That's always been true in a secular sense—at least, as I understand it. So, yes, General Rychtyr carries a major share of the responsibility for his troops' spiritual well-being. It's pos-sible our reports are less than accurate or overstate the severity of the prob-lem." The intendant's voice made it crystal clear he didn't believe that for a moment. "If that's true, I'm sure General Rychtyr will be returning to his command quite soon."

"I hope that's the case, Father," Salthar replied. "The General is deeply respected by the entire Army, and I'm confident no man could be better qualified—from a military perspective—to command the Army of the Seri-dahn. I'm sure his removal from command would . . . sit poorly with his officers and men."

Something murderous flashed in Kharmych's eyes, but Lainyr laid a hand on his forearm again before the intendant could speak. He gazed at Salthar for a long, thoughtful moment, then stood, beckoning for Kharmych to join him.

"I understand your concerns, Your Grace," the bishop executor said coolly. "And I have no desire to . . . unsettle the Army's command at this critical time. I assure you that we'll delve to the bottom of this as swiftly as humanly possible."

"As loyal sons of Mother Church, we can ask no more, Your Eminence," Duke Fern replied for both councilors as they also stood.

"Until later, then," Lainyr said, and sketched Langhorne's scepter in blessing. Then he and Kharmych turned on their heels and swept out of the council chamber in silence.

▼ ▼ ▼

It was a far smaller council chamber, tucked away in a little used corner of the palace, and the men seated around the table had arrived very quietly, one at a time. Now Duke Fern leaned back in his chair and swept his eyes across his fellows' faces. There were only three of them: Duke Salthar; Sir Zhorj Laikhyrst, Baron of Yellowstone, who served as the Kingdom of Dohlar's foreign minister; and Hairahm Kortez, Baron Windborne, the minister of the treasury. Once again, the Duke of Thorast was conspicuous by his absence.

"I think," the first councilor said quietly, "that . . . recent events require us to reconsider our existing plans for the prosecution of the Jihad."

"Since it's coming down to a matter of survival, I think that's probably fair enough," Salthar said, and Fern nodded. The fact that Salthar was here while Thorast wasn't said quite a lot about how those "recent events" had . . . reshaped thinking in Gorath, given how supportive of the Jihad Salthar had always been, the first councilor thought.

"What sort of reconsideration did you have in mind, Samyl?" Yellowstone asked.

"There are several new bits of information we need to evaluate," Fern replied. "Our ability to continue to pay for the weapons we need is also a matter for some concern. That's one reason we've asked you to attend, Hairahm."

Windborne nodded, although from his expression, he was less than delighted to have been invited to this particular meeting.

"Before we turn to those, however," Fern continued, "Shain and I—and Aibram, of course—have rethought some of our earlier deployment plans. We've decided that the reinforcements we've assembled for the Army of the Seridahn need to be held closer to Gorath for the immediate future."

Yellowstone stiffened ever so slightly, and Windborne frowned. By straining every muscle, combing every possible man out of garrisons throughout the kingdom, they'd managed to collect and arm—after a fashion—almost sixty thousand men, exclusive of the additional Coastal Defense Force detachments Thirsk was organizing out of the seamen he'd sent ashore. Since they'd come from so many disparate sources, it was essential to give them at least some time to drill together before they were thrown into combat, and they'd been assembled outside Gorath, in close proximity to the manufactories charged with producing their rifles. Given the Army of the Seridahn's desperate situation, however, they needed to be started for the front soon. With the heretics' closure of the eastern end of the Gulf of Dohlar, they'd have to be sent up the Gorath River, to the St. Nytzhana Canal, to the Fronz River, and then northwest to Fronzport on Lake Sheryl, over a hundred miles in the Army of the Seridahn's rear, and that would take time. A *lot* of time.

"We haven't taken that decision lightly, of course," Fern continued, his expression grave. "The heretics' capture of Lizard Island, however, suggests they intend to intensify their attacks all along our coast. While the operating range of their smaller ironclads appears to be limited, the loss of Lizard Island clearly brings the capital itself into their reach, and it's obvious the operating range—and gun power—of their new, big ironclad are both much greater. Given that, we see no choice but to delay the deployment of those troops to Thorast until we're confident they don't intend an invasion in force at some vital point."

Windborne and Yellowstone glanced at one another, then nodded slowly.

"You don't suppose the heretics were so obliging as to allow Governor Alysyn's report to reach us in hopes we'd worry about exactly that, do you?" Yellowstone asked after a moment. "Or that its arrival had anything to do with Archbishop Trumahn's 'unavoidable recall' to Zion?"

"I imagine both those things are entirely possible," Fern conceded. "I can't speak to the Archbishop's schedule," he added drily, "but I'm quite sure they told us about Lizard Island—or let Alysyn tell us for them—specifically to encourage us to hold General Rychtyr's—I mean, of course, the Army of the Seridahn's—reinforcements right where they are. But whether that's the case or not, we have no choice but to honor the threat until we know more."

"And have you communicated that decision to Mother Church?" Yellowstone asked.

"Not yet. We only reached it a few hours ago, and we want your input on how best to draft a message explaining our intentions and the reason for them."

"I'm flattered." Yellowstone's tone was dry enough to turn Gorath Bay to dust.

"I knew you would be." Fern smiled briefly. Then his expression sobered. "We've made one other decision, as well. Under the circumstances, wherever those replacements end up, they'll need the best, most experienced commander we can give them—especially now that General Rychtyr is . . . temporarily unavailable."

"I can see that," Windborne said slowly. "Who do you have in mind?"

"General Ahlverez," Fern replied, and this time his tone was very flat. "Shain and I have discussed it at some length, and we can't think of a single other general as experienced against the heretics as Sir Rainos. Or—" he let his gaze meet Yellowstone and Windborne's levelly "—one with a better understanding of the Kingdom's enemies—*all* the Kingdom's enemies—and how they think."

.VI.
Tymkyn Gap,
Snake Mountains,
Cliff Peak Province,
Haidryrberg,
Glacierheart Province,
Republic of Siddarmark.

June usually isn't this nice where I come from," Captain of Swords Bryntyn Mahklyroh observed.

He slouched comfortably in the canvas sling chair, a mug of beer in one hand and a hot dog, liberally anointed with mustard and ketchup, in the other. The napkin tucked tastefully into the front of his collar protected his tunic from his chosen meal, although it threatened to fail its function as he waved the hot dog at the spectacular sunset over the Snake Mountains.

"*Please* don't tell me about all those tons and tons of snow back home in St. Cehseelya again!" Captain of Horse Gwynhai begged. "I may be a southern boy from Kyznetzov, but I have relatives all the way up in de Castro Province. I'll see your tons of snow and raise you five hundredweight of *ice*, Bryntyn!"

Mahklyroh chuckled and took a bite of the hot dog.

"All right, I'll admit it doesn't *really* snow thirty feet every winter back home. Sometimes it's only twenty-nine. And if you're going to be that way about it, I'll concede that those seventh- and eighth-cousins of yours probably get at least as much snow as we do. But it's true you know." He sat a little straighter in his chair to set the hot dog on his plate and free his non-beer hand to snag another fried potato slice. "This is really, really nice weather for June."

Now, there, Gwynhai thought, Bryntyn had a point. Even a "southern boy" could appreciate a night like this one promised to be. A few low-lying banks of cloud still glowed crimson in the west, but the sky overhead was a cobalt blue vault, a-glimmer with stars, and the moon was well above the eastern horizon. The breeze blowing out of the east was just a bit cooler than his Kyznetzov sensibilities preferred—he'd grown up spending June days wading in the shallows of Bay of Alexov, and the Snake Mountains were a lot higher than that—but the day had been a bit too warm, perhaps, despite the altitude.

And a damned good thing it was, too, he told himself rather more grimly. *I could wish we were completely dug-in, and all that sunshine and lack of rain isn't hurting a thing when it comes to getting that way. And neither is the fact that I've got Bryntyn to make sure the frigging engineers do it right!*

The truth was, he supposed, that Bryntyn Mahklyroh was as much a barbarian as any other Easterner. Certainly his taste for "good, simple food" like tonight's hot dogs and beer was a far cry from the sophisticated preferences of some of Gwynhai's more nobly born—or wealthier—Harchongese fellows. And he was a corrupting influence. He'd actually badgered the regiment's bakers into figuring out how to bake and slice hot dog "buns" for him, although he'd been unable to procure proper hot dogs to go in them. The best the cooks had been able to come up with was a mild smoked sausage, and Mahklyroh's efforts to get the "real thing" delivered through channels had probably driven at least three or four of the Southern Host's commissaries to the brink of madness. But as the 321st Infantry Regiment's commander, Gwynhai didn't really care about any of that. For that matter, the captain of horse was about as common as a Harchongian came, himself, although his family had done well for itself in the cherrybean trade before the Jihad. Perhaps that explained why he got along so well with Mahklyroh. He was fairly certain it explained the undeniably lowbrow streak of pragmatism which had gotten him chosen for his current duty.

Lord of Horse Fengli Zhywan, the Earl of Red Sun and the commanding officer, 3rd Band, of the Southern Host, had been assigned primary responsibility for the northern third of the Tymkyn Gap, with a frontage of roughly eight miles. Third Band consisted of four brigades, including the 321st's parent 5th Provisional Brigade. That gave Red Sun just over twelve thousand infantry—closer to eighteen thousand, once artillerists and other supports were added in—to cover his area of responsibility. That seemed like a lot. For that matter, it *was* a lot. But it still worked out to less than one man per yard of straight-line frontage, the way a wyvern might fly it. Since God and the Archangels hadn't seen fit to give human beings wings, the Southern Host had to cover that frontage on the ground, where hillsides, streambeds, inconveniently placed patches of woods, and Hastings only knew what else added a good thirty percent to the *actual* frontage. And Red Sun had chosen Lord of Foot Snow Mount's 5th Provisional Brigade to hold the extreme left of that line.

And Snow Mount had chosen the 321st to hold the extreme left of 5th Provisional Brigade's frontage. Which meant that if Gwynhai had been in the heretic High Mount's boots, he would have been paying particularly close attention to the 321st's positions. And that explained why he was so happy to have clear, dry weather and lots of picks and shovels.

To be fair, the Army of Tanshar had made a decent start on fortifying the Gap before everything was rearranged. But sad to say, the AOG's engineers weren't the world's greatest experts on field fortifications. It was entirely possible that the Charisian heretics could still lay claim to that title, since they were the ones who'd invented new-model weapons and tactics, but the Imperial Harchongese Army—and especially the Mighty Host of God and the Archangels—could give them a damned good run for their money these days, and the Southern Host had spent the last several five-days deepening, broadening, and strengthening the works Bishop Militant Tayrens' troops had begun.

Mahklyroh, however, was something rather out of the ordinary. He'd been a lieutenant in the Army of God, the equivalent of a mere captain of bows, when he was assigned to the Mighty Host as one of Captain General Maigwair's "advisers." Then, he'd been one more "foreigner" foisted on the Mighty Host by a batch of barbarians who obviously couldn't understand the art of war as well as *Harchongians* did. Now, he'd risen to the equivalent of an AOG major and commanded Yahngpyng Gwynhai's 1st Company, and the men of that company would have followed their round-eyed "foreign" CO straight through Shan-wei's front gate.

There weren't many Easterners still serving with the Southern Host. Or, rather, they'd been so diluted by the influx of reinforcements from the Empire that they seemed far less numerous. Mahklyroh, however, had clearly found a home, and the . . . less than exquisitely sophisticated serfs of his company adored him. The fact that he'd started as an engineering officer before being transferred to the infantry didn't hurt under the present circumstances, either.

"Yes, Bryntyn," the captain of horse acknowledged. "It is nice weather. On the other hand," his tone darkened, "if all those spy reports are accurate, there'd be something to be said for a mid-summer blizzard!"

"Since it would be highly impolitic for me to call my commanding officer a wet blanket, I'll refrain from any observations about borrowing trouble or looking on the dark side, Sir," Mahklyroh replied. Then he shrugged. "That doesn't mean you're wrong. May I ask if we've heard anything more about what High Mount's up to?"

"Nothing I haven't already shared with you." Gwynhai shook his head. "Our patrols still aren't as good as *their* patrols, unfortunately—not that I have to tell *you* that. There are obviously a lot of men over on their side of the line, and even more of their damned artillery, but we haven't been able to confirm anything concrete about his timetable. About the only thing we *have* been able to confirm is that it's going to be Shan-wei's own bitch when he finally gets around to lighting the fuse. I expect it's going to look a lot like Armageddon Reef did."

He wouldn't have allowed himself to make that particular comparison before most of his other officers, but Mahklyroh only nodded.

"You've got that part right," he agreed, his tone considerably grimmer than it had been. "And I'm grateful for every day we get to dig the boys in deeper. But, you know, there's a part of me that really wishes they'd go ahead and get down to it. We know it can't be much longer—they're burning too much summer to lie around forever—and I sometimes think the waiting's worse than the actual bleeding."

"Well, that's certainly brought supper down to earth," Gwynhai observed. "You wouldn't happen to have any other depressing thoughts you'd care to share?"

"Oh, I'm sure something will occur to me, Sir!" Mahklyroh assured him with a smile. "In fact—"

The captain of swords broke off and his head snapped around as the dark eastern horizon flared with sudden, volcanic life. The blinding trails of hundreds of artillery shells streaked across the heavens, overpowering the moon, burning away the stars. They plummeted downward and deadly flowers of flame rose from 3rd Band's frontline positions. Mahklyroh's quarters were three miles behind the front, but the ground-shaking thunder rolled over them fourteen seconds later.

▼   ▼   ▼

"How bad is it?" Zhowku Seidyng, the Earl of Silken Hills, demanded as he strode into his office.

The howling wilderness—by any civilized standard, at any rate—west of the Snake Mountains offered precious little in the way of proper housing for a Harchongese earl, but Silken Hills had become accustomed to roughing it in the Jihad's service. His steel thistle silk pavilion was a modest thing. It couldn't have cost much more than it would have taken to feed an entire village of his estate's serfs for a year or two. But it was adequate—*adequate,* if not palatial—although the section of its interior partitioned off for his office space was no more than twenty or thirty feet on a side.

"It could be far worse, My Lord," Captain of Horse Kaishau Hywanlohng, Silken Hills' chief of staff replied. "Everything we have is still very preliminary, of course." The captain of horse shrugged. "We've gotten a couple of wyvern messages from Earl Red Sun that give at least some detail, but we haven't heard anything yet from the other commanders in the Gap."

"Probably one reason the motherless demon-worshipers like to attack in the Shan-wei-damned dark, when the semaphore's useless," Silken Hills growled, and Hywanlohng nodded. He didn't doubt that was a major part of the heretics' predilection for night assaults, although he'd come to the conclusion it was *only* a part of the reason.

The chief of staff was a hard-bitten professional, who'd served in the Harchongese Army for a quarter century before the Jihad, and he'd been deeply impressed by the way the IHA's standard of training had leapt upwards under commanders like Earl Rainbow Waters . . . and Earl Silken Hills, to give him his due. He was also realist enough to recognize how huge a debt the Mighty Host owed to its AOG mentors, as well as to the manufactories pouring out the weapons with which it had been armed. By his most conservative estimate, the Mighty Host of today was at least ten or fifteen times as dangerous, on a man-for-man basis, as it had been. Yet for all its improvements, the Imperial Harchongese Army remained a far less . . . limber weapon than the Imperial *Charisian* Army. The heretics fought at night because they *trained* to fight at night. Because they embraced the darkness, moving through it with a fluid assurance Earl Silken Hills' infantry simply couldn't match. It was the same sort of small-unit capability which made heretic patrols so much more dangerous than the Mighty Host's.

"Whatever their logic, My Lord," he said out loud, "it looks like it will be sometime tomorrow morning before we get anything definitive from the bands south of Red Sun's. From what he's saying, though, it would appear High Mount's decided he needs something a little more . . . methodical than the sorts of bombardments the Dohlarans have reported."

"He does?"

Silken Hills cocked his head, one eyebrow rising, and Hywanlohng nodded. One thing about the earl, he reflected. Silken Hills was an aristocrat of the old school, with a fervor for the Jihad his chief of staff doubted the Grand Inquisitor himself could have improved upon, and he hated heresy—and here*tics*—with every fiber of his being. But it wasn't an *unthinking* hatred. He actually listened to briefings, and he'd never been too proud to learn from his adversaries, however much he might despise them for their sins. He'd spent hours discussing the Dohlaran General Rychtyr's reports with Hywanlohng and his senior subordinates, and given the nature of the anticipated assault, he'd paid special attention to Hanth's use of his angle-guns.

"Yes, My Lord. Earl Red Sun hasn't reported any of Hanth's . . . sophistication, for want of a better word. As of his last wyvern, the bombardment had been underway for over three hours, concentrated on no more than a couple of regiments' frontage. Apparently, he's really hammering those regiments, but it doesn't sound like he's spreading his fire very wide and Red Sun hasn't seen any sign of the false breaks or other deception measures Hanth has employed. I can't believe High Mount isn't aware of how successful Hanth's artillery tactics have been, so if he isn't using them, there has to be a reason. And the only one I can think of is the difference between our fortifications and the Dohlarans'."

Silken Hills nodded slowly, rubbing his chin as he gazed down at the relief map his engineers had built for him. As a place to break through the barrier of the Snakes, the Tylmhan Gap was far superior to any other choice, but that wasn't saying much. It might favor the defense less than winding lizard paths did, yet he was confident of his men's ability to bleed the heretics badly when they attacked, no matter how much artillery they might have. And the fortifications the Southern Host had built were almost certainly deeper and stronger than anything Rychtyr might have had in his confrontation with the Army of Thesmar.

"Treating it like a siege, is he?" the earl mused, still rubbing his chin.

"That's what it looks like so far, My Lord. But *only* so far," Hywanlohng cautioned. "It's much too early to decide definitively that that's what he's doing, I think. But it's clearly a possibility. And the truth is that no one's ever had to attack 'fieldworks' like the ones Captain of Horse Rungwyn's designed. I know *I* damned well wouldn't want to send in any assaults until I'd broken as many bunkers and dugouts as I could, first!"

"Well, that's one of the things Earl Rainbow Waters hoped might happen," Silken Hills pointed out. "And unlike the northern end of the front, we don't have any open flanks they can maneuver around with their frigging mounted infantry." He snorted harshly. "Damned good thing we don't, either, given how useless our *own* cavalry's likely to be!"

Another point in the earl's favor, Hywanlohng thought. He was realistic—and honest—enough to step outside the aristocracy's traditional contempt for infantry . . . and for anyone *else's* cavalry, for that matter. The same reports which had detailed Hanth's artillery tactics had described the effectiveness of his mounted infantry in terms which made it only too clear no Harchongese cavalry brigade could consider itself remotely the equal of its Charisian counterpart.

Unfortunately, the one group of people apparently unable to recognize that fact were the Mighty Host's cavalry commanders.

"I'm sure High Mount can hardly wait to break those mounted brigades loose in our rear," Silken Hills continued, "but first he's got to get through our *front*, and we can afford a lot more casualties than he can." The earl shrugged. "Add that to the way the bastards seem to be able to make shells and cannon breed like rabbits, and it probably makes a lot of sense—from his perspective—to use up as much ammunition as it takes to kick in the front gate for his infantry. If he can do that, he can damned well *create* flanks to work around, but first he's got to do the kicking."

Hywanlohng nodded. It was pure speculation at this point, but it was logical speculation that fitted everything they definitely knew.

"Shall I write up a dispatch for Earl Rainbow Waters tonight still, My Lord, or wait until we've heard from the other band commanders?"

"He's not going to be magically able to do anything about it whenever we tell him," Silken Hills observed with a grunting laugh. "All we'd do sending him bits and pieces would be to convince him we're a lot more nervous than he'd like us to be." He shook his head. "Tomorrow morning—or even afternoon—will be soon enough."

▼　▼　▼

"Your chocolate, My Lord," Corporal Slym Chalkyr murmured, gliding up behind the Duke of Eastshare and sliding the heavy mug on to the corner of his desk. "Try not t' spill *this* one on the maps."

There were drawbacks, Eastshare thought, to having long-term, trusted henchmen looking after one.

"I spilled *one* cup of chocolate on *one* map five months ago," he pointed out mildly . . . relatively speaking.

"An' spent the next three days complainin' about it," Chalkyr retorted. He seemed singularly unimpressed by the duke's scowl as he withdrew from the office as silently as he'd entered.

"For a quarter-mark and the powder to blow him to Shan-wei . . ." Eastshare muttered, and heard something very like a smothered laugh from the far side of his desk.

"You think I don't mean it?" he demanded, fixing Major Braynair with an icy brown glare.

"No, Sir. It's not that I don't think you mean it—it's that I *know* you don't," Braynair replied. "Mind, I can see where the fantasy might be tempting from time to time, but you know you'd be helpless without him."

"I put on my own boots—yes, and buttoned the fly of my trousers, now that I think about it—all by myself this morning, Lywys!"

"Of course you did, My Lord."

Eastshare glowered at his aide, but he couldn't keep it up. Partly because Braynair was entirely correct. But that was the smallest part of the reason he couldn't, he assured himself. A mere bagatelle and totally irrelevant.

"Fortunately for you, you've done an excellent job over the last several five-days," he said. "Because of that, I'm prepared to overlook your sad misjudgment of my ability to function even without Slym nagging me to within an inch of my life."

"Thank you, My Lord," Braynair said earnestly. "I appreciate it."

Eastshare snorted and returned his attention to the dispatches he'd been reading when the fresh cup of chocolate arrived. As always, whether he cared to admit it or not, Chalkyr's timing had been excellent. There was quite a mountain of those dispatches, and he and Braynair had been working their way through them for over three and a half hours . . . starting *after* supper.

He leaned back in his chair, sipping chocolate while he finished the current message, then laid it atop the "read" stack and turned the chair to face Braynair.

"Unless you're concealing some horrendous catastrophe in order to evade my ire, things are going well," he said. "In fact, they're going *so* well I'm starting to worry about when the other boot is going to fall on my toe!"

"I know, My Lord. Like Baron Green Valley always says, 'What can go wrong, *will* go wrong.'" The major shrugged. "I'm sure all kinds of things are going to prove him right before we're done, but so far—*so far*, My Lord— it really does seem to be going well."

"Um."

Eastshare climbed out of his chair, stretched hugely, and walked across to consider the enormous map. He clasped his hands behind him, rocking gently on the balls of his feet as he contemplated the arrows stretching across it. His own Army of Westmarch and Trumyn Stohnar's Army of the Sylmahn had the farthest to go to reach their objectives. At the moment, their columns were on the road, moving steadily west and—in his own case—*north*west. They'd actually begun their march well before Earl High Mount's artillery opened fire in the Tymkyn Gap, yet it would still be some time yet before they were ready to attack. But that was fine. One reason their troops had been held so far back was to prevent Zhaspahr Clyntahn's spies from getting an accurate count on their numbers or realizing where they were actually headed. Now that High Mount's guns were blazing away, even someone as canny as Earl Rainbow Waters must be looking in that direction. And since that direction happened to be seven hundred miles southwest of Eastshare's current position and the next best thing to a *thousand* miles south of his first major objective, that was just fine with him.

Have to admit, I thought Kynt and the Emperor were getting a little too clever when they came up with this one, but damned if it doesn't look like it's going to work. And anything that keeps my boys from punching straight into Rainbow Waters' front is downright brilliant *as far as I'm concerned!*

He stood a moment longer, contemplating those arrows, then sighed.

"There was a time," he said to nobody in particular as he trudged back to his desk, "when I thought things like bullets and swords were more important than reports."

"Well, My Lord, I'll grant you they're more *interesting*, anyway. I remember what the Baron had to say about that."

"What? You mean when he said there was nothing in the world quite so exhilarating as to be shot at . . . and missed?"

"That's exactly what I was thinking about," Braynair acknowledged. "He's got quite a way with words, doesn't he?"

"Probably something in the water in Old Charis." Eastshare flopped just a tad less than cheerfully back into his chair. "His Majesty turns a mean phrase on occasion, too."

"Yes, My Lord. I was particularly fond of 'Hit them where they ain't.'" It was Braynair's turn to contemplate that map. "I *like* that one . . . a lot."

.VII.
Lake City,
Tarikah Province,
Republic of Siddarmark;
and
The Temple,
City of Zion,
The Temple Lands.

T he latest dispatches from Earl Silken Hills, My Lord."

Earl Rainbow Waters looked up as his nephew deposited a thick stack of paper on his desk. It was raining hard outside his office, raindrops pounding on the roof like galloping cavalry. It was barely midafternoon, yet it was hard to see East Wing Lake through the downpour, and he heard the rumble of distant thunder, like some grim echo of the thunder rumbling in the Tymkyn Gap.

"Shall I assume you would already have informed me of anything unexpected?" he inquired, sitting back and freshening his cup of tea.

"I'd say the only unexpected thing is that none of us anticipated Earl High Mount would spend quite this much time preparing the way for his assault," Baron Wind Song replied, shaking his head.

"I feel much the same," Rainbow Waters acknowledged. "Has Silken Hills included an updated report on the state of his fortifications?"

"He has." Wind Song sorted through the stack of dispatches for a moment, until he found the one he wanted. "Here it is, Uncle. I've glanced through it, but it's very similar to his engineers' previous estimates. Apparently, Captain of Horse Rungwyn's fortifications are even more resistant than we'd expected."

Rainbow Waters held out his hand. His nephew placed the report in it, and the earl flipped through it quickly, lips pursed in a thoughtful frown. He came to the end and laid it aside to reach for his teacup and sip pensively.

"Well," he said finally, "it's gratifying to discover that the intelligence upon which our deployments is based may actually be accurate."

He had not, Wind Song noted, added the words "for once" to his statement.

"And if Eastshare and Green Valley truly intend to force the issue in the south, Silken Hills may very well be right about the reasoning behind this deliberate artillery assault. But it's been four days now, and it seems evident their artillery is proving less effective than our artillery proved when we tested it against the Captain of Horse's works." He sipped more tea. "I must admit I'm surprised—gratified, but surprised—by that. Perhaps we've overestimated the effectiveness of their artillery in general. Not that I intend to leap to any such conclusion until we've seen what happens in an open field battle."

Wind Song nodded, and the earl frowned thoughtfully for several more minutes.

"The thing which perplexes me, however, is that both Green Valley and Eastshare have abundantly demonstrated their flexibility, their ability—and willingness—to modify plans in the face of . . . operational realities. If Silken Hills' works are proving more resistant than they'd anticipated, why haven't they attempted something elsewhere? The campaigning season is short, and even shorter here in the north than in the south. I would have expected them to attempt to force the issue *here* if their original plan is bogging down *there*."

"That thought had occurred to me," Wind Song admitted. "At the same time, My Lord, it would surely be a mistake to ascribe superhuman powers to Green Valley and Eastshare. Or to the rest of their commanders, for that matter."

"Superhuman or not, they have a remarkable record of successes," Rainbow Waters pointed out. "The Siddarmarkians suffered disasters in plenty during the 'Sword of Schueler,' and the Army of God advanced almost entirely across the Republic in only two or three months. But aside from what happened to their Brigadier Taisyn on the Daivyn—and it must be painfully obvious to any but the most bigoted that he and his men understood fully from the very beginning that theirs could be only a forlorn hope—the Charisians have enjoyed a virtually unbroken chain of victories. *Decisive* victories, I might add, and they won none of them by 'playing it safe.'" He shook his head. "Their tendency to always seize the initiative, to drive home an attack and make their opponents react to *them*, has served them well. Audacity isn't *always* a virtue. It could be argued that it was the primary contributor to the handful of *naval* defeats they've suffered, after all, and no one can count on being lucky every time. But it sticks in my mind, Medyng. I still think they should have concentrated their major effort here, in the north, driving for the Holy Langhorne. It . . . bothers me that they chose otherwise, however convincing the logic behind what they actually decided to do instead. And it bothers me even more that they haven't punched with their right hand if their left hand is blocked. This reminds me of the story of the spider monkey and the tar puppet, and Green Valley, for one, is far too astute to punch both hands into the same tar."

"I understand, Uncle. And under other circumstances, I'd share your concerns to the full. Indeed, I *do* share them. But the fact remains that they're doing precisely what all of our spy reports told us they would. And as you've pointed out many times, this year's campaign is different, for both sides. We both have much larger armies in the field, there's far more artillery on both sides, and the Mighty Host and Archbishop Militant Gustyv's Army of the Center are far better dug in, equipped, and supplied than anything they've tackled yet. Not only that, but I think it's important to remember they've managed that 'virtually unbroken chain of victories' in no small part by picking their targets very carefully and by capitalizing on the opposing commanders' weaknesses."

"I believe it might be argued that that wasn't the case with Bishop Militant Bahrnabai," his uncle said dryly. "I seem to recall a somewhat audacious naval expedition halfway across the continent using *canals*. That's the sort of . . . improvisational adaptability I've come to expect out of them."

"And far better to expect the worst than simply hope for the best," Wind Song agreed. "That was rather a case of desperation as much as anything else, though. I can't *begin* to count the things that could have gone wrong, but if they hadn't mounted the operation, it's highly likely the Bishop Militant would have carried through and taken Serabor as soon as he'd been reinforced. It worked, and it was conceptually brilliant and flawlessly executed, but I'm positive it wasn't something even Charisians *wanted* to attempt.

"In the case of the Army of Shiloh and Bishop Militant Cahnyr, however, they clearly understood the minds and prejudices of their opponents. Although it's obvious they selectively fed Duke Harless the false information that helped draw him into his false position at Fort Tairys, what they provided was effective because it 'proved' what he *wanted* to be true. That sort of ploy depends upon the . . . gullibility of its victim, and with all due modesty, Duke Harless was perhaps a tenth as smart as you are, and with the exception of Ahlverez, his subordinates seem to have been no more than half as smart as *I* am." Wind Song smiled briefly. "As for Bishop Militant Cahnyr, Eastshare had defeated him inside his own mind in the Ahstynwood and on the Daivyn long before they actually attacked him at Aivahnstyn. I venture to suggest to you that I know very few people *less* defeated in their own minds than you, Uncle."

"I see all those years studying courtly speech and Shang-mi 'logic' have left their mark," Rainbow Waters said even more dryly. "I'm tempted to tell you to wash your mouth out with soap!"

He smiled at Wind Song's chuckle, but then shook his head.

"There's much in what you say," he said more seriously. "Especially given what Silken Hills has reported about the resilience of his field fortifications. And perhaps you're right. Perhaps I am allowing my . . . profound respect for Green Valley and Eastshare too much weight."

"Uncle," Wind Song said soberly, "there's no living man whose judgment I respect more than yours, but consider this, as well. No one in history has ever attempted to maneuver armies the size of those presently in the field. Certainly no one's ever tried to coordinate an offensive campaign by over seven hundred thousand men against a defending force twice that size! The most redoubtable commander in the world is bound to find that a . . . nontrivial challenge. Should it really be surprising if their footwork is a little slower than Green Valley managed with barely forty thousand men winter before last?"

"No, not surprising," Rainbow Waters agreed.

"Well, assuming the information the Grand Inquisitor's spy obtained was accurate—and everything they've done so far seems to suggest it was—their entire operational plan for the summer depends on breaking through in the south and then curling up to the north to get in behind us. And the campaign season south of Sardahn and Usher is at least a month and a half longer than it is *north* of Sardahn."

"You're saying they might well be content to sit where they are in the north?" his uncle said slowly.

"We've discussed often enough just how crucial this campaign is." Wind Song's voice was as grim as his eyes. "You and I both know how . . . difficult Mother Church has found it to sustain the Jihad this long. And despite the fact that we haven't had access to the raw reports, it's obvious the productivity of Charis' manufactories is continuing to climb. There's no doubt in my mind that they desire a decisive victory over the Mighty Host this year above all things. Yet they must be as well aware as we are of the way in which time favors *them*, not us. They'd be foolish to assume that state of affairs would apply forever, but it's unlikely to change anytime soon. So perhaps it would make sense to them to withhold that punch with their right hand even until *next year*, if they must, if they truly hope to get behind us with their left. And as slowly as their offensive in the Tymkyn Gap is proceeding, they still have ample time for someone as mobile as they've proven themselves to be to break through and get at least as far north as Jhurlahnk or even Ultyne before weather forces them to suspend operations. And if they succeed in seizing complete control of the Gulf of Dohlar and the Bay of Bess, keeping forces in Faralas, Jhurlahnk, or even Usher supplied would be relatively easy for the Charisian merchant marine."

"Now *that*, Medyng, is a very unpleasant line of speculation."

Rainbow Waters sipped at his tea, gazing at something only he could see. Then he set the cup gently down and shook his head.

"It's a very unpleasant line of speculation, and you may well be correct," he said. "Certainly it would make sense out of their southern strategy, but my instincts continue to insist they mean to attack in the north, as well. I must confess that it's largely because of my respect for their . . . audacity. Indeed, there's a part of me that finds it most difficult to believe Green Valley, in particular, could possibly resist the challenge of proving he can, indeed, force the positions we've erected against him. Still, whatever my instincts may say, logic suggests your analysis is very probably more accurate than my own at this time. Which, after all, is one of the reasons I keep you around. Unlike most of my subordinates, you remain a headstrong, intemperate, overly clever young sprout, entirely too full of your own opinions and willing to tell me—in the most disrespectful tones imaginable, if necessary—when you . . . find yourself in disagreement with me."

"Mother *did* say something to me about making sure your head would still fit into your hats when you came home again, Uncle," the baron murmured.

"No doubt she did." Rainbow Waters smiled fondly at his nephew, then straightened with an air of briskness. "No doubt she did, but now it's time for you to earn your princely salary by writing up a synopsis and an analysis of Earl Silken Hills' reports. Without inserting any intemperate observations of your own into the narrative, mind you. Do you think you could have something ready for my signature by tomorrow at dinner?"

"I may have something considerably sooner than that, Uncle. Would you like me to draft it as an endorsement of Silken Hills' analysis?"

"I think . . . yes," Rainbow Waters said slowly. "At the same time, however, be certain to enclose an addendum detailing our current analysis of Green Valley's deployments. I imagine Vicar Allayn will be astute enough to draw the proper conclusion without our belaboring the point."

There was a faint but unmistakable of warning in his tone, and Wind Song nodded. It was readily apparent from discussions with Archbishop Militant Gustyv that the Grand Inquisitor was heavily invested in the intelligence coup which had alerted them to the southern strategy. It could be . . . less than wise to imply anything which suggested the heretics could be flexible enough to depart from it at what Vicar Zhaspahr would consider to be the drop of a hat. If nothing else, it might erode the Grand Inquisitor's confidence in the Mighty Host's leadership. The consequences if he should lose faith in Rainbow Waters' judgment could well be catastrophic, and not simply for the earl and his family.

And he's certainly right about Vicar Allayn's ability to read between the lines. For that matter, Vicar Rhobair's no novice at doing the same.

"I believe I understand, Uncle," he said aloud and bowed slightly. "With your permission, I'll go gather my clerks and get started drafting it immediately."

▼   ▼   ▼

"So it would appear Zhaspahr was right."

Rhobair Duchairn refrained from adding the words "for once," but they were clearly audible anyway. Allayn Maigwair didn't reply immediately. He finished chewing the bite he'd just taken from his wyvern-breast sandwich, washed it down with a swallow of beer, and nodded.

"So far, at least," he said then. "I can't decide from Rainbow Waters' dispatches whether he's more gratified High Mount's performing according to projections or more irritated Cayleb and Stohnar seem to've been too stupid to do the smart thing and attack *him*." The captain general shrugged. "Frankly, I'm more relieved than anything else. Gustyv's most recent reports haven't exactly inspired me with boundless confidence about his part of the front. He's in pretty good shape at Talmar, but Selyk's a lot more wobbly, and he's still got less than half his cavalry up to support his front lines. We really could've used another month or so to get the rest of his troops to him."

It was Duchairn's turn to nod, and he grimaced in understanding. Gustyv Walkyr's troop movements had been seriously disrupted—and driven even farther behind schedule—by the Imperial Charisian Navy's activities in the Gulf of Dohlar. Those activities hadn't impinged *directly* upon Walkyr, but their "ripple effect" on the Church's overall logistics had forced Duchairn and Maigwair to juggle all of their transport priorities. They'd done their best to support Walkyr as fully as possible, but as more and more evidence of the extent to which the Charisians and Siddarmarkians were reinforcing their southern flank continued to roll in, they'd been forced to give even higher priority to bolstering Silken Hills. Neither of them was happy about what that meant for Walkyr's Army of the Center, and it was a vast relief to discover the Inquisition's intelligence reports had been accurate after all. Still, the treasurer couldn't rid himself of a certain lingering sense of concern.

"What do you think about the point Rainbow Waters raised about Green Valley and Eastshare?" he asked.

"I don't know," Maigwair admitted frankly. "It sounds like the most reasonable explanation, though. If they really have decided to push through the Tymkyn Gap and hook up from the south, it probably makes sense for them to delay any attacks in the north until they know whether or not that's going to work. Frankly, I have to agree with what Rainbow Waters seems to be suggesting here. *I* would've expected them to at least try some diversionary attacks farther north, too. On the other hand, there are a few indications Symkyn's moving towards the Reklair Gap. If he is, he's doing it very quietly, which could mean they hope he can take us by surprise when he attacks there. That might also explain why High Mount doesn't seem to be in a tearing hurry to hit Tymkyn Gap with any massive infantry attacks. No doubt he *is* trying to batter his way through—which looks like being a long-term challenge, given how rapidly Silken Hills' engineers make repairs every night—but he may well be waiting for Symkyn to be fully prepared to launch his own attack farther north. Or, for that matter, *Symkyn* might be waiting for High Mount's attack to break through before he launches his own."

The captain general shook his head in irritation and dipped a fried potato slice in ketchup.

"All I can say for sure," he said, waving the potato slice at Duchairn, "is that I'm just delighted they aren't hitting Gustyv's positions, and that so far, at least, they seem to be doing pretty much what all those spy reports said they were going to do. I only hope they go right on performing according to script."

.VIII.
Rock Coast Keep,
Duchy of Rock Coast;
Maryksberg,
Duchy of Black Horse;
and
Rydymak Keep,
Earldom of Cheshyr;
Kingdom of Chisholm,
Empire of Charis.

I don't know, Cousin Zhasyn. . . ."

Styvyn Rydmakyr's voice trailed off, and his gaze was troubled as it moved away from the Duke of Rock Coast's face and out the window to the Rock Coast Keep gardens. Bright sunlight spilled down over the fresh green of new leaves, and breeze sent blossoming shrubbery and spring flowerbeds dancing. It was about as peaceful a scene as could have been imagined, but Rock Coast doubted his youthful cousin even saw it.

"I know it's a big decision, Styvyn," the duke said somberly, deliberately avoiding the affectionate "Styvie" he'd accustomed the boy to hearing from him. Adolescent pride could be touchy, and this was a time to convince

Styvyn to take a man's position and make a man's choice. "And I know it's come at you more quickly—and sooner—than you expected. Well, the opportunity's surprised all of us. But if we don't take it, it's unlikely we'll see another one."

"I understand that." Styvyn's eyes moved back to Rock Coast, and the duke was struck again by how very much like his grandmother's those eyes were. At this moment, that was not an encouraging reflection. "It's just that . . . well, I've been thinking a lot about Grandmother. I've sounded her out a little, you know." Rock Coast's expression tightened a bit, but Styvyn didn't seem to notice. "She's pretty firm about her beliefs. Even more 'set in her ways' than we thought, I guess. I don't think we'll be able to convince her to support us."

"Styvyn, she's the *dowager* countess, not the countess. I truly hate to say it, but given your father's . . . invalidism, you really ought to have been confirmed as Earl Cheshyr long ago, and I told the Council that last year." The boy's eyes darkened, and Rock Coast went on quickly. "I'm not wishing your father ill, and however much I may disagree with your grandmother, I certainly respect her! I'm simply saying that whatever she feels as your father's regent, this really ought to be *your* decision. If she refuses to see reason, you can appeal directly to your people, and I'm willing to bet most of them would support you."

In fact, given how completely—and how long ago—Karyl Rydmakyr had won her husband's people's hearts, Rock Coast was confident nothing of the sort would happen. But if the old biddy realized her precious grandson had committed treason by openly declaring his allegiance to the anti-Sharleyan conspiracy, she might also realize the only way to save the little twerp's neck was to throw her own support to the conspirators and do everything she could to ensure their success.

Some things were more likely than others, and he was prepared to go to whatever length she drove him. Yet if he and Black Horse had to start right out by crushing Cheshyr, it could get . . . messy. He could live with that just fine, given what a pain in the arse Lady Karyl had been, and he could always use a little more coastline along Cheshyr Bay. On the other hand, the outright conquest of a neighbor as their very first move might undermine some of their fellow nobles' faith in their principled defiance of the Crown's tyranny.

"I don't think that would be a very good idea, Cousin," Styvyn said rather more coolly. "I'm not as confident as you are that they'd listen to me instead of her. After all, they still think of me as 'just a kid.'"

Of course they do, Rock Coast thought tartly. *You won't even be sixteen until the end of August!*

"Styvyn, there's an awful lot riding on what happens in the next few months. At the moment, practically every trained soldier in the Kingdom's been sent off to Siddarmark. That gives us our best opportunity to do this without any serious fighting. That means less people will get hurt, whether they're on our side or the Crown's. If we miss this chance, that won't be true next time around."

"I *understand* that." Styvyn's voice was sharper than it had been. "I'm only saying Grandmother isn't going to care about how good an opportunity it is, and I don't think I'll be able to change her mind in the next couple of five-days."

"One way or the other, we need Cheshyr's support." Rock Coast shook his head. "Your earldom's in a critical position—you know that; we've talked about it before. You know how concerned I am about your grandmother's safety—about your entire family's safety! I don't want anything bad to happen to her, to you, to your father, or anyone else in Cheshyr. But I'm not the only one involved in this. I don't know how well I could . . . restrain some of the others if they decided Cheshyr isn't going to join us willingly."

Something flashed in young Styvyn's eyes, and for just a moment they looked more like his grandmother's than ever. Then he drew a deep breath.

"I see your point," he said. "And I'm glad you've explained it to me so clearly. I just don't think she's going to agree to any of your proposals."

"Well, if she won't, she won't." Rock Coast made himself smile. "It's not like we have to have an answer tomorrow. I mean, nobody's going to be able to recall any of those troops from Siddarmark next five-day! So we've got some time—at least a month, I'd guess—before we absolutely have to know where Cheshyr's going to stand. Go home and think about it. You're family, and so is your grandmother—by marriage, anyway—and I really, really don't want to see my family get hurt. So go home, think about it, and use one of the messenger wyverns to let me know how things are going by, oh, Thursday of next five-day. I promise nothing's going to happen between then and now. Okay?"

"That sounds like a really good idea." The young man's relief was obvious. "Thank you, Cousin Zhasyn. Thank you a lot."

▼   ▼   ▼

"The little bastard's going to weasel," Rock Coast said grimly. "Boy doesn't have an ounce of steel in his spine!"

"Are you certain, Your Grace?" Sedryk Mahrtynsyn said. "The last time I spoke to him, he seemed fully prepared. I won't say he was *happy* about it, but he assured me of his readiness to stand with God and the Archangels!"

"He's a *teenager*, Father." Rock Coast rolled his eyes. "At his age, it's not all that hard to believe two completely contradictory things. And if it's escaped your attention, teenagers in general—and young Styvyn in particular—

tend to avoid telling their elders things they think are likely to piss those elders off." The duke shook his head. "No, now that it's starting to look like it's really going to happen, not something he can daydream about happening sometime off in the future, he's going to weasel."

Mahrtynsyn frowned and toyed with his pectoral scepter. He'd spent months working his way into Styvyn Rydmakyr's confidence, and the Order of Schueler knew a lot about . . . engendering faith in the fainthearted. He'd been careful not to terrify the boy, but there'd been no doubt in his mind that young Styvyn had become thoroughly aware of how close to the lip of hell Sharleyan and Cayleb Ahrmahk's apostasy was bringing every one of their subjects. Including, of course, one Styvyn Rydmakyr. Mahrtynsyn had been confident the boy's regenerated and strengthened faith would carry him to the decision point, despite his deep and obvious affection for his apostate grandmother.

"That could be . . . unfortunate, Your Grace," he said at last, slowly, his eyes worried.

"You mean he could go home, fling himself onto his grandmother's bosom, and confess all?" Rock Coast said derisively.

"Actually, that's very much what I'm concerned about," the under-priest replied just a bit sharply.

"Relax. I didn't time the invitation for this visit by accident, you know. First, like I said, he's a teenager. He won't *want* to go running to his grandmother to tell her he's been hobnobbing with potential traitors for the last year and a half. I think he'll probably do it in the end, if only on the theory that he'll get at least a little credit for coming clean before someone else outs him. Second, I think those talks and devotionals of yours went more than skin deep, so he's going to be worrying about pissing off God and the Archangels by betraying our confidence, too. And, finally, I've told Lahndysyl to set a new record for a slow passage. He can't be too obvious about it. The boy's been playing around in boats since he could walk and *Ahmiliya*'s a fast sailor. If Lahndysyl's too obvious about going slow, Styvyn's likely to notice." He shrugged. "It wouldn't be the end of the world from our perspective, since there'd be damn-all he could do about it aboard ship if he did notice, but I *am* fond of the boy. I'd hate for Lahndysyl to find himself forced to drop him over the side with an anchor tied to his ankles."

Mahrtynsyn winced internally at the image. Rhobair Lahndysyl was about as hard-boiled and ruthless as a man came. He was also an ardent Temple Loyalist, which was one reason the under-priest had recommended him to Rock Coast, but if he decided his employer's instructions—or the protection of his own neck—required Styvyn Rydmakyr's death, he wouldn't even blink.

"It's an eight-hundred-mile sail," the duke continued. "That's a three-day passage at the best of times. I'm confident Lahndysyl can add at least another full day or so to it without anything . . . untowards happening. So that gives us what amounts to an entire five-day before he has the chance to unburden himself."

"And, Your Grace?"

"And every word I said to the little prick about the opportunity we've got was absolutely true. I've already passed the word to the others."

Mahrtynsyn stiffened, his expression of alarmed, but Rock Coast only shrugged dismissively, and his own expression was hard.

"I know we didn't discuss my decision—not specifically, at any rate. God knows we've talked about it long enough, though! We'll never have another chance like this, and some of the others have been wavering, fluttering their hands and wondering if we won't get an even better opening. Well, we won't, and I mean to take *this* one. And to make sure no fainthearts have a different idea, I've informed them that Mahkynyn's already mustering the troops."

Mahrtynsyn's expression segued from alarm to completely blank. Fraizhyr Mahkynyn was the senior of Rock Coast's armsmen. He'd been with the duke since Rock Coast's boyhood and headed his personal guard for the last ten years, and he'd been the one in charge of quietly recruiting and drilling the additional men the duke had sworn to his service in defiance of King Sailys' Edict, the royal decree which proscribed the raising of private armies upon pain of death. If he'd ever felt a single qualm about defying that edict—or anything else the Crown might decree—Mahrtynsyn had never seen it, and if Rock Coast told him to attack Rydymak Keep tomorrow, he'd do it in a heartbeat.

In fact, judging from the duke's expression, that was almost certainly what Rock Coast *had* told him to do.

That was the under-priest's first thought. His second was that any notion he'd ever had of controlling Rock Coast no longer applied. He hadn't so much as *mentioned* this to him, far less discussed it, and by informing the others that Mahkynyn was already in motion, he'd made certain they'd follow suit. They had no choice. If he failed, their association with him was certain to come to light, so any qualms *they* might have felt had suddenly become dead letters.

"Well, in that case, Your Grace, I suppose we'd best see to getting those proclamations printed and distributed, hadn't we?" he said.

▼ ▼ ▼

"Could wish we'd had just a mite more warning, Your Grace," Dahnel Kyrbysh growled. He stood by his saddled horse in the courtyard of Black Horse Keep, the ancient pile of stone which served as the principal seat of the dukes of Black Horse at the heart of the city of Maryksberg. "Getting all

this moving—especially moving in the right direction at the right time—
on two minutes' notice isn't the easiest thing in the world!"

"A point of which I'm well aware, Dahnel," Pait Stywyrt, the Duke
of Black Horse, said sourly. "I think all this has gone to Zhasyn's head!
Somebody had to be in charge, and he seemed like the logical choice at the
time, but he's been feeling his oats here lately."

"As may be, Your Grace," Kyrbysh said with the candor of a man who'd
spent close to forty years in the service of Black Horse. "And I'll not say
you're wrong about that. But happen I'm not as unhappy about lack of warning as I'd be about worrying if the others're going to shy away and leave us
holding the lizard."

He had not said "leave *you* holding the lizard," Black Horse reflected,
and reached out to clout his armored shoulder.

"There is that," he acknowledged with something very like a grin. "None
of the others'll have any more choice about dancing to his piping than we
do, are they?"

"Not if they like their heads where they are," Kyrbysh replied bluntly.
"Speaking of which, I suppose I'd best be on the way."

"You do that," Black Horse approved. "And try not to kill anyone you
don't have to."

"Not any fonder of killing than the next man, Your Grace," the armsman replied. "Just as happy to leave Rydymak Keep to Mahkynyn, come to
that." He grimaced. "Lady Cheshyr's a stubborn old woman. She'll not open
her gates without a lot of . . . convincing."

"Probably not," Black Horse agreed, and stepped back as Kyrbysh swung
up into the saddle.

The armsman had only a short ride before him . . . today, at any rate.
The small coasting vessels Black Horse had quietly assembled were waiting to
carry him and his six hundred armsmen three hundred and fifty miles from
Maryksberg to the town of Swanyk, twelve miles inside Black Horse's
border with Cheshyr. Swanyk lay on the west side of Nezbyt Point, under
forty miles from Tylkahm, just inside Cheshyr Bay and the closest major
town of the earldom. Of course, calling either Swanyk or Tylkahm "towns"
was stretching the noun. Better to call them large fishing villages, the duke
supposed. But almost all of Cheshyr's larger villages and towns lay along the
shore of the bay. Most supported fishing fleets, and even for those that didn't,
water transportation was always easier and cheaper than moving goods
and people by land. Those towns and villages were connected by the coastal
road that ran all the way around the bay, however, and the earldom's farms
and freeholds were either threaded along that road or connected to it by
dirt tracks that stretched up into the rugged hills that separated Cheshyr
from its eastern neighbors.

The neutralization of the Bay's eastern shore in the likely event that Lady Karyl declined to join them had been assigned to Black Horse. In some ways, it would've been closer for Duke Black Bottom, but crossing the hills would have been slow going, and he had other wyverns to look to in reinforcing Swayle and Lantern Walk. So Kyrbysh would go ashore at Swanyk in two or three days and work his way north around the bay while Mahkynyn dealt with Rydymak Keep.

And welcome to it, Black Horse thought. He was scarcely a squeamish man, but the thought of what Rydymak Keep could turn into wasn't something he cared to contemplate.

▼　▼　▼

"I'm so proud of you, Wahlys," Rebkah Rahskail said.

She stood beside her son on the walls of Swaylehold, the fortified seat of the earls of Swayle on the western edge of Swayleton. The fortress had been built on a steep hill in a bend of the Lantern River three hundred years earlier and enlarged two or three times since. The river that surrounded it on three sides made it highly defensible, but it also meant its inhabitants had to deal with the inconvenience of spring floods entirely too often, and the earl-dom's capital city had spread steadily farther east, away from those floods, over the centuries.

Now the banner of the Empire of Charis had been hauled down from the staff on Swaylehold's central keep and replaced by the old flag of the Kingdom of Chisholm. It was possible the cheers of the citizens of Sway-leton had sounded a little uncertain—even a bit forced—when Earl Swayle read the proclamation setting forth the grounds upon which he and his sworn companions had bidden defiance to the tyranny of Sharleyan and Cayleb, but no voice had been raised in opposition. That wouldn't have been wise, given the large number of armsmen in the colors of Swayle who'd unexpectedly appeared here in the capital. There'd been far too many of those armsmen—under the terms of King Sailys' Edict, at least—and they'd been far too well armed for anyone to even think about arguing with them. Most of them might be armed only with swords and arbalests, although there were quite a few matchlocks and a few dozen pistols in evidence, but that was more than Swayleton's inhabitants had possessed. And there were more—and better—weapons en route to the capital.

Rebkah had known better than to try stockpiling new-model rifles—or *any* weapons, really—in her capital. If there was one person in the entire Kingdom of Charis Sharleyan Ahrmahk's minions must realize hated her with every fiber of her being, it was Rebkah Rahskail. She'd had no intention of providing those minions with the evidence to justify her arrest.

Because of that, she'd trained her armsmen up near the border with

Lantern Walk, in the backcountry where she could control access, and she'd stored her modern weapons there, as well. True, she hadn't acquired as many of them as she'd suggested she had to her fellow conspirators, but they didn't need to know that. Thinking she was better armed than she was could only help dissuade any faintheartedness on their part. She'd have had more of them if she'd had more marks, of course, and she'd tried not to feel jealous about the greater numbers of weapons flowing to Rock Coast and Black Horse when she'd been the one who'd established contact with Colonel Ainsail in the first place.

But once Elahnah Waistyn hands us the arsenal in Halbrook, we'll have lots *more guns,* she told herself fiercely. Elahnah hadn't promised to do that—not in so many words—but surely she would! They'd certainly talked around the point enough in their correspondence, and after what had happened to her own husband, how could God *not* move Elahnah to offer her full-blooded support?

"I have to admit I'm a little . . . nervous, Mother," Wahlys Rahskail said. The current Earl of Swayle was only eighteen years old, and at the moment he looked considerably younger. And frightened. "Once the Council hears about this, they're going to come straight after us with everything they've got."

"Would you rather worry about the Royal Council or about *God*?" Rebkah demanded a bit more sharply than she'd intended to. Wahlys looked at her reproachfully, and she touched his arm in apology. "I'm sorry, Wahlys. I didn't mean to snap at you. I suppose I'm a little 'nervous' myself! But what we've begun is bigger than any mortal power. Surely you understand that."

"Of course I do, Mother." Wahlys nodded sharply and his voice was much firmer than it had been. "Father Zhordyn and I have discussed that very point more times than I could count."

"I know you have." She patted his arm. "And, I don't blame you for worrying that Sharleyan's lickspittles will devote special attention to us here in Swayle." Her spine straightened proudly. "We're one of the few great families who've had the courage to stand up for Mother Church. You know what that cost your father." Wahlys' jaw tightened, and she nodded. "So of course they'll want to 'deal with us' as quickly as they can. But they'll have to fight their way clear across Holy Tree or Lantern Walk to reach us, and without the Army, they'll find that just a little bit difficult." She smiled thinly. "And when the rest of the Kingdom realizes what's happening—when the others who've been forced to hide *their* loyalty to Mother Church, *their* opposition to Sharleyan's tyranny—seize the opportunity we've offered, the 'Royal Council' will be far too busy putting out fires closer to home to worry about *us*."

▼   ▼   ▼

"Where's Grandmother?" Styvyn Rydymak demanded as he burst into Father Kahrltyn Tyrnyr's small study. "I need to talk to her—now!"

"And what might the rush be?" Father Kahrltyn asked calmly, looking up from his book and removing his reading glasses so that he could see his longtime student more clearly. He was almost seventy years old and growing increasingly frail, but he sported a thick head of white hair and a magnificent mustache, and his mind was as keen as it had ever been.

"I have to . . . tell her something," Styvyn said after a moment, downcast eyes studying something on the floor that only he could see with great intensity.

"And that might be—?" Father Kahrltyn prompted, and young Rydymak actually squirmed.

The Langhornite under-priest hid a sigh and let the reading glasses hang from the black riband around his neck as he leaned back in his chair. He'd been Styvyn's tutor almost since the lad could walk, and he loved the boy dearly. But that was rather the point, wasn't it? At almost sixteen, he shouldn't still be thinking about the heir to one of the kingdom's earldoms as a "boy."

"Since you've just gotten back from Rock Coast, should I assume this has something to do with your cousin, the Duke?" he prompted after a moment, and Styvyn flushed. Father Kahrltyn had never approved of his close association with his magnificent cousin, and he knew it.

"Well, yes," Styvyn said finally. Then he inhaled deeply and looked up to meet his tutor's eyes. "I've done something . . . really stupid, Father. Stupid enough you'll probably assign me a heavy penance once you find out about it. But right now, I've *got* to talk to Grandmother! I can't *believe* how long it took *Ahmiliya* to make the trip, and I don't think I have a lot of time."

"I see." Father Kahrltyn contemplated him for a moment longer, then shrugged. "I believe she's gone down to the armsmen's quarters to talk to Sergeant Major Ohdwiar."

"Oh." Styvyn's expression fell, and Father Kahrltyn hid a smile.

The youngster had been rather in awe of Ahzbyrn Ohdwiar ever since he'd discovered the sergeant major had served with his grandfather. He obviously didn't want to share the news that he'd been "really stupid" with his grandmother in front of someone whose respect mattered to him as much as Ohdwiar's did. But the boy inhaled again, squared his shoulders, nodded to his tutor, and marched back out the door.

He made his way through the familiar halls, still uncertain how to broach the topic with Lady Karyl. "Hi, Grandmother! Look, I don't want you to worry or anything, but I think I've committed treason. By the way, what's for lunch?"

Somehow he doubted Lady Karyl would be amused, and he'd discovered—or rediscovered—that that mattered to him. It mattered a lot, and the thought of what he was about to see in her eyes when he confessed that all her warnings about his magnificent cousin had been right made him want to throw up.

He reached the armsmen's quarters and his pace slowed, despite his determination. This section of Rydymak Keep was newer than much of the rest, built largely at the Crown's expense when his grandfather had been one of King Sailys' generals. There'd been far more men stationed in Cheshyr then, keeping an eye on Cheshyr's neighbors. Which probably should have told him his grandmother knew what she was talking about when she warned him to be wary of what those neighbors were currently up to, he thought. Given their size, they seemed almost empty, even with the thirty-odd retired soldiers Lady Karyl had provided with living space over the winter just past, and she'd put Sergeant Major Ohdwiar in what had been an officer's quarters.

He climbed the stone stairs to the sergeant major's assigned chambers, braced himself, and knocked sharply.

The door opened, and he found himself facing not Ohdwiar, but Sergeant Ohsulyvyn. That wasn't much better than facing the sergeant major himself, but he squared his shoulders.

"Good afternoon, Sergeant," he said politely but firmly. "I understand my grandmother is visiting the Sergeant Major. I'm afraid I need to speak to her."

"Of course, My Lord." Ohsulyvyn stepped back. "Come in."

Styvyn obeyed the invitation, then paused as his grandmother turned her head to look over her shoulder at him. She sat at Sergeant Major Ohdwiar's small table, with what looked like a map of the Sunset Hills spread out before her. The sergeant major stood at her right shoulder, but Styvyn had never seen the very tall, blond-haired man on her left. The stranger had a full beard, trimmed close to the jaw, and a long braid. He also had a bony face, a nose any hawk might have envied, and very, very blue eyes. Bluer even than Sergeant Mykgylykudi's.

"Styvyn!" Lady Karyl smiled. "I didn't expect you back until Monday."

"I . . . I had to come home early, Grandmother," he said. "I'm . . . I'm afraid there's something I need to tell you. Something—" He looked at the two retired soldiers and the complete stranger and his courage almost failed, but he made himself continue. "Something . . . bad," he finished in a small voice

"It can't be all *that* bad, dear," Lady Karyl said, rising from her chair to hold out her arms to him.

"Yes, it can." The words wavered and his eyes burned as his grandmother enveloped him in a tight hug. "It can. Because you were right. You were right about Cousin Zhasyn, about what he wanted, about *everything*." He raised his head, making himself meet her eyes. "I've been so *stupid*. I've—"

His voice broke completely, and he stared at her, trying to find the words.

"Perhaps I can help a bit, My Lord," the tall stranger said. Styvyn's eyes whipped to his face, and the stranger placed one hand over his heart and bowed slightly. "Permit me to introduce myself. Men call me Cennady Frenhines."

Styvyn frowned, puzzled by the outlandish name, and Lady Karyl squeezed him gently.

"Actually, Styvyn, this is *Seijin* Cennady Frenhines. He's here on behalf of Their Majesties."

"He's—?"

Styvyn swallowed hard, but Frenhines only shook his head, the expression on his bony face oddly gentle.

"My Lord, we already know everything you were about to tell us about Duke Rock Coast. In fact, we know quite a bit more than you do, because I very much doubt he was stupid enough to tell you he'd realized from the beginning that he'd have to kill your grandmother to get what he wanted." Styvyn sucked in air and his arms tightened convulsively about Lady Karyl. "I'm quite sure he didn't discuss some of his other plans with you, either. Rest assured, however, that my . . . colleagues and I know about all of them. So does Her Majesty."

"The . . . the *Empress* knows I. . . ."

Styvyn's voice trailed off in horror, and Frenhines smiled.

"Her Majesty knows you're young, that your cousin went to great lengths to flatter you into agreeing with him . . . and that in the end you'd refuse to join his treason. Everyone makes mistakes, My Lord, especially when we're young. Their Majesties know that, and the fact that you came of your own free will to inform your grandmother of their plans—and that you were willing to do it in front of witnesses—proves Her Majesty was right about your refusal to join him."

"But . . . but if you already knew what they were planning, why haven't you done anything *about* it?!"

"We're *about* to do something about it, dear," Lady Karyl replied. "We've just been waiting until all the roaches were ready to scurry out into the light. And you know what you do with a roach when that happens, don't you?"

He stared at her as he heard the cold, sharp-edged steel in her tone, a steel he'd never heard from her before.

"No, Grandmother," he said slowly.

"You step on it, Styvie," she told him in that same icy voice. "You step on it."

▼ ▼ ▼

"Think the boy beat us home, Fraizhyr?" Daivyn Mahkrum asked as he drew rein at the upper end of the street leading down to Rydymak Keep.

"Just about have to've," Fraizhyr Mahkynyn replied almost absently, steadying his spyglass to study the town below them. "Can't think of any other reason we wouldn't see *somebody* on the streets."

He lowered the spyglass. Holding the thing steady enough to see anything from the back of a horse was always a challenge, but he really hadn't needed it, anyway. There wasn't a soul to be seen. There wasn't even any smoke rising from chimneys . . . or dogs or cat-lizards on the street, for that matter.

"No, the old woman knows we're coming," he said thoughtfully as he cut a plug of chew leaf and popped it into his mouth. "She'll have that keep closed up tighter'n a landlord's heart on rent day. Be a right pain in the arse digging her out of it, too."

"Can't be too bad," Mahkrum objected. He was Mahkynyn's second in command, and the two of them had known one another since boyhood. "She can't have more'n thirty, thirty-five men in there to cover the walls, even counting those old crocks she took in over the winter, and we've got five hundred. All of 'em with rifles, come to that."

"Five hundred *outside* the frigging walls," Mahkynyn pointed out, jaw working steadily as he chewed.

"And we brought ladders!" Mahkrum shook his head. "I'll take a hundred, maybe a hundred and fifty of the lads and make all sorts of noise outside the gatehouse. Might even get her to agree to talk to me, try and 'work things out,' might say. And while I'm doing that, you take the rest of the boys, sneak around to that blind part of the wall on the south side, and throw the ladders up." He shrugged. "Might get hurt a little bit, but not enough to matter."

"You think?" Mahkynyn cocked his head, then jerked one thumb at the town's deserted streets. "You figure she's got thirty-five armsmen in there. More'n one of the Old Earl's soldiers retired to Cheshyr, you know. Could be she's got a few of them, too."

"And what's she going to arm them with? Maybe they had a decent armory in there back in the Old Earl's day, but now?" He snorted derisively and touched the butt of the prized Trapdoor Mahndrayn riding in his saddle scabbard. He had only fifty rounds for it, but every other man in their force had one of the older-style rifles, and they had plenty of ammunition for those. "You know damned well she hasn't had the marks to buy any new-model weapons! Besides, most of those 'retired soldiers' are getting as long in the tooth as *her*. Probably haven't even touched a sword in ten, twenty years. Not the kind of thing to keep a man up worrying at night."

"You're probably right," Mahkynyn acknowledged after a moment. "All right, since you're feeling all talkative, you get the front gate. Give me a couple of hours to swing around to the south."

He pointed at a stretch of hillside, just visible from their present position. It was unfortunately exposed, and once upon a time it had been a wheatfield. But that had been long ago, and there were at least some clusters of young trees that might be used for cover.

"If the boy did get home and they're watching for us, like as not they'll see us well before we get to the foot of the wall. Won't be a whole hell of a lot they can *do* about it even if they do have some arbalests or matchlocks, but the truth is we're not real likely to surprise them. So you take a half dozen of the ladders with you, too. You can hide 'em by coming in down that side street that comes in from the west." He pointed, and Mahkrum moved to look along his arm, then nodded as he found the street in question. "You can probably get to within a couple hundred yards without anyone seeing 'em from inside. Once they decide you're only a diversion and start worrying about me, your lads bring *their* ladders out and throw them up against the gatehouse. We'll come at them from two sides at once and swamp them."

"Works for me," Mahkrum said. "Put a man up there in the church steeple with a flag to tell me when you're in position?"

"Done," Mahkynyn agreed laconically.

▼　▼　▼

"There's the flag," the lookout said, and Mahkrum nodded.

It had taken longer than expected for Mahkynyn to get into position, but it wasn't like there was any rush. The old lady wasn't going anywhere, and anyone in that gatehouse had to have seen the forty men at his back. He'd decided to let them see at least that much of his force on the theory that it didn't hurt anything to give Lady Cheshyr a little extra time for worry to soften her resolve. From everything he'd ever heard, Countess Cheshyr's resolve would need more softening than most people, and the fact that no one had even *looked* in their direction, so far as he could tell, didn't seem promising.

No skin off my nose if she wants to be stubborn, he thought as he nodded to his own second and sent his horse walking steadily down the street towards the closed gatehouse. *Truth of the matter is, I'm pretty sure the Duke won't shed any tears if something pretty permanent happens to the old biddy—to the boy, too, come to that. Better if it's an accident, but I think he figures Cheshyr'd make a nice addition to the Duchy. Wouldn't be surprised if he and Black Horse plan on carving it up like a stuffed wyvern on God's Day!*

He snorted at the thought as he stopped his horse thirty yards from the closed gate and looked up at the gatehouse battlement. It was a more impressive old pile of stone from this close, and he was suddenly just as happy they weren't thirty or forty men with new-model weapons atop its walls.

"Hello, the keep!" he called.

There was silence for a moment, aside from the crackle and pop of the no less than three imperial standards flying from the keep's staffs. Then a head appeared over one of the merlons. He didn't recognize its owner—a tall, blond-haired fellow—but the man was unarmored and appeared to be armed only with a sword. He wasn't even wearing a helmet.

"Hello, yourself," he called back in a deep voice.

"Can I ask where everyone's gone?" Mahkrum inquired.

"Well, let's see," the stranger said in a thoughtful, musing tone. "Four or five hundred armsmen come riding into town in Rock Coast colors all uninvited." He shrugged. "May be silly of me, but I'd say that was probably grounds for a little concern, wouldn't you?"

"Only if it has to be," Mahkrum replied.

"Meaning what?"

"Meaning that if Lady Cheshyr—or whoever's in charge in there—is inclined to be reasonable, nobody has to get hurt."

"Why, that's remarkably generous of you, Master Mahkrum! I can't tell you how touched we all are by your deep concern over our safety."

The stranger's tone was no longer thoughtful, and its scorn cut like the flick of a whip. That was Mahkrum's first thought. Then something else registered.

"How'd you know my name?" he demanded sharply, right hand falling to the butt of the rifle at his knee.

"We know quite a lot about you . . . and why you're here," the stranger said. "In fact, we've been expecting you. So since you've been so concerned about not hurting any of us, I'll return the compliment. If you'd care to lay down your arms now and surrender without any unpleasantness, *we* won't hurt *you*, either."

"Surrender?" Mahkrum stared at the solitary lunatic in disbelief. "You're right, we've got five hundred men out here. Standing room only, you couldn't fit more'n a couple of hundred into that heap of rocks! If anyone's doing any surrendering around here, it won't be us."

"No, probably not. Or not immediately, anyway. That would take something remotely approaching brains. The survivors may change their minds about that in a bit, though. Unfortunately, you'll have to excuse me for a minute. Master Mahkynyn and his lads just came over the crest of the hill, and he's just as stupid as you and Rock Coast. Too far away for me to ask him if *he'd* like to surrender, though, so I'd better go welcome him to the party, too."

Mahkrum stiffened at the fresh evidence that the stranger knew far too much about his orders. On the other hand, there was that saying about how difficult dead men found it to tell any tales.

"You do that thing!" he shouted up at the parapet as the stranger turned away. Then he turned in the saddle and waved at the crouched men still hidden by the nearest houses, waiting to charge the wall with their scaling ladders.

▼   ▼   ▼

"Do all *seijins* have nasty senses of humor?" Zhaksyn Ohraily inquired as Cennady Frenhines stepped back from the battlements. "You know you just *guaranteed* they'll go for it, don't you?"

Despite the question, Sergeant Ohraily didn't seem particularly disapproving. At thirty-eight, he was far and away the youngest of the "gray lizards" Karyl Rydmakyr had taken in. And, unlike the others, he was an Old Charisian, not a Chisholmian. Had he been in the uniform to which he was entitled, it would have borne the crossed rifle and bayonet of a scout sniper surmounted by the stylized peep sight of a designated marksman, and he'd removed the eyepatch which had covered the left eye that had supposedly been lost in the training accident that mandated his retirement.

"Nothing nasty about it," Frenhines replied, dropping down below the level of the merlons. "I didn't say a single thing that wasn't completely true. And as for attacking, I specifically advised him *not* to. Is it my fault if he doesn't listen to advice?"

"I do believe you have a point, *Seijin* Cennady," Ohraily said, working the bolt on his M96 rifle. "We've got this. Go have fun."

Frenhines slapped him on the shoulder and went trotting down the gatehouse's internal stair towards the keep's courtyard.

▼   ▼   ▼

"All right, boys!" Fraizhyr Mahkynyn shouted. "Let's get a move on! And remember—we don't want to kill anybody we don't need to, but I'd a hell of a lot rather lose one of *them* than one of *us!*"

Someone shouted a somewhat obscene agreement, and the storming party started forward in a leisurely sort of a charge. After all, it wasn't like this was going to be difficult.

Sloppy, Mahkynyn thought, trotting along with the rest of them. *Probably nothing to worry about today, but it's not all going to be this easy. Guess I need to do a little arse-kicking when we're done. Well, won't be the first—*

He heard a sudden, strange sound—an almost *hollow* noise, muffled by the keep's walls. Then he heard another sound, a strange, warbling sound, and his face went white.

▼ ▼ ▼

"*Fire!*" Dynnys Mykgylykudi barked, and all four of the M97 mortars lined up on the keep's front courtyard coughed out round, perfect rings of powder smoke as their 32-pound bombs went rocketing upwards.

It really wasn't fair, Mykgylykudi reflected. Which was *just* fine with him; he wasn't the one planning on committing treason and probably murder at the orders of a traitor. What he *was*, was one of the Imperial Charisian Army's best mortar men. Up until his "injury," he'd been the senior instructor on the M97 at Maikelberg, and once they'd gotten everyone safely evacuated from the town, he'd ranged in on each of the surrounding hillsides with smoke rounds that left no betraying craters. He knew exactly what elevation and deflection to set.

▼ ▼ ▼

"What the—?" someone began.

Daivyn Mahkrum never found out how whoever it was had intended to complete the question. He was still trying to figure out what the concussive thumping sound on the far side of the gatehouse had been when Zhaksyn Ohraily and the other twelve men of his squad leveled their M96 rifles across the gatehouse parapet.

At such a ludicrously short range, Ohraily could have taken the shot without removing his eyepatch.

Mahkrum was dead before he hit the ground; a second and a half later the first of the mortar bombs exploded above Fraizhyr Mahkynyn's assault party.

▼ ▼ ▼

Well, that didn't go very well, did it, Master Mahkrum? Cennady Frenhines thought coldly as he loped down the stairs from the gatehouse. *Pity about that. And I'm afraid it's about to get worse.*

There was no way in the universe Sharleyan Ahrmahk would have trusted Karyl Rydmakyr's safety to anyone besides Merlin Athrawes . . . or perhaps Cennady Frenhines. Personally, he'd been quite confident the "gray lizards" were more than competent to see to her safety, but he hadn't objected at all. For someone who'd been born in the Terran Federation and raised as the citizen of a representative democracy, Merlin Athrawes had discovered he'd done a remarkable job of internalizing the far more personal bonds of loyalty that governed Safeholdian realms, and he'd never liked traitors. He liked them even less now, especially when they threatened the people he loved . . . and that was about to be very unfortunate for the treasonous armsmen outside Rydymak Keep.

He reached the keep's courtyard, staying close to the outer curtainwall as the mortars continued to cough. Twenty men were waiting for him, along with twenty-one nervous horses who obviously objected to the sounds of mortar and riflefire. Fortunately for the equine members of the group, they wouldn't have to put up with it for very much longer.

Frenhines vaulted into the empty saddle of the twenty-first horse, unbuttoned the retaining strap of his revolver's holster, and drew the katana which was very like—but not identical to—Merlin Athrawes' legendary weapon.

"All right!" he called, and young Styvyn Rydmakyr personally threw up the bar on the keep gates, then leapt aside as the mounted men thundered through the gatehouse tunnel towards the stunned and utterly disorganized armsmen who'd so fatally underestimated the task before them.

.IX.
Coast Road,
Earldom of Cheshyr;
HMS *Maikelberg*
Cheshyr Bay;
Sharylstown,
Duchy of Lantern Walk;
Sheryyn Waterfront,
Earldom of Saint Howan;
and
Maryksberg,
Duchy of Black Horse,
Kingdom of Chisholm,
Empire of Charis.

Shan-wei, but I *miss* the barracks," Rahnyld Myketchnee announced, scratching one armpit with his left hand while he held out his tea mug with the right. "Miss kitchens, too, come to that," he added sourly, glancing at the designated cooks frying bacon and eggs over the smoky morning fires.

"Some people'd bitch if they got hanged with a golden rope," Dahnel Kyrbysh replied, but his tone was a bit absent.

"Not me," Myketchnee said firmly. "Got standards, I do. Golden rope sounds about right to me."

"I'll be sure to pass that along," Kyrbysh promised, and Myketchnee chuckled.

The man had developed the soldier's traditional right to bellyache into a fine art, but he was also Kyrbysh's most reliable company commander. Now he grunted his thanks as one of the cooks poured tea into his mug. He sipped, made a face as he burned his tongue, and then ambled across to stand beside Kyrbysh.

The senior armsman glanced up, then returned his attention to the map spread out across the rock in front of him. The sky above the hill crests to their east offered just enough light for him to see it, although the predawn gloom still covered the waters of Cheshyr Bay to the west like a blanket, and he frowned as he ran an index finger down the inked line of the coast road while he tried to scratch a mental itch he couldn't quite pin down.

In some ways, the . . . expedition, for want of a better word, had gone well. He and his mounted armsmen were eighty miles inside Cheshyr now, halfway between the towns of Tylkahm and Dahryk, and they hadn't lost a man. Hadn't even lost a horseshoe! He couldn't remember a single time, even in a training exercise, when everything had gone this smoothly.

Unfortunately, one reason it had worked out that way this time was that Tylkahm had been completely deserted when they got there. So had each of the farms they'd passed en route to their present bivouac. He tended to doubt that all those people had just coincidentally decided to take a long vacation at the very moment their earldom was invaded by its neighbors.

Kind of hard to "neutralize" somebody who isn't even here, he thought grumpily. *The Duke won't be happy about it, either. Still, they have to be up ahead of us somewhere, and we're a hell of a lot faster than any batch of townsfolk moving on foot. Bound to catch up with them sooner or later.*

He'd reported the troubling lack of Cheshyrians to Duke Black Horse via messenger wyvern, but there was no way for the duke to send wyverns back to him. That meant all he could do was continue following his orders until he figured out where everyone had gone. And like he'd just told himself, he and his mounted men had to be faster than men, women, and children—and probably livestock—moving on foot. They were bound to overtake—

His thoughts paused and his eyes narrowed as he revisited that thought, pushing it around to look at it from all angles, and his frown deepened.

Damn right we're faster than they are, and we've been on the Cheshyr side of the border for two full days now. So if we're so much faster, how the hell come we haven't already caught up with them?

"They started before we did," he muttered.

"What?" Myketchnee asked. "You talking to me, or to yourself?"

"They started *before* we did," Kyrbysh repeated more loudly, turning his head to look at the other armsman.

"What're you talking about?"

"The reason we haven't caught up with them yet is that they started running before we ever started chasing them."

Myketchnee frowned, and Kyrbysh shook his head, stabbing his index finger at the dot that represented Dahryk.

"The only way all these people could've disappeared without our seeing even one of them is for them to've pulled out before the Duke ever sent us aboard the boats, Rahnyld. They must've packed up and pulled out at least two or three days—maybe even a whole five-day—before we ever got to Swanyk!"

"That's ridiculous," Myketchnee retorted, but he was frowning as he said it and he scratched one eyebrow. "Maybe a fishing boat saw us on the way in?"

"And a bunch of fishermen figured out where we were going and spread the word for everybody along our route to take to the hills in just one or two days?" He shook his head. "They knew we were coming, and they even knew what route we were going to take, before . . . we . . . ever . . . started."

He punctuated each of the last four words with another finger stab at the map, and Myketchnee's face was tight as he worked through the rest of the logic.

"But . . . that would mean. . . ."

His voice trailed off, and Kyrbysh nodded sharply.

"If they knew that much, how much *else* did they know? And who the hell is 'they,' in the first place?! *We* didn't know the Duke was going to send us out—or not when, anyway—until we got Duke Rock Coast's messenger wyvern. So how in Shan-wei's hell did somebody *else* know far enough ahead to pull all these people out of our way?"

"I don't—" Myketchnee began.

"What's *that?!*" someone demanded, and both armsmen looked up sharply.

The eastern sky had continued to lighten, and one of Myketchnee's troopers was pointing urgently out across the bay. They turned their heads, peering into the still-dim west, trying to figure out what he'd seen. Then Myketchnee drew a sharp breath.

"That's *smoke*," he said flatly.

▼　▼　▼

"I wish *I* could navigate this well," Captain Wyndayl Zohannsyn remarked to the young woman standing beside him on HMS *Maikelberg*'s bridge.

As a general rule, Zohannsyn didn't approve of women aboard ship. But there were exceptions to any rule and Ezmelda Zohannsyn hadn't raised any idiots. When a fishing boat came out of the dark to make a perfect rendezvous with his command in the middle of a moonless night, he was prepared to make one of those exceptions. Especially when the only person aboard that fishing boat happened to be wearing the blackened chain mail and breastplate of the House of Ahrmahk's personal guard.

"It wasn't really all that hard," the attractive brunette told him with a shrug. "I mean, the *hard* part was estimating how far they'd be likely to've gotten by the time we could get back here. After that, it wasn't difficult. Especially after they were kind enough to light all those fires last night."

"True." Zohannsyn nodded without lowering his double-glass, although as explanations went, that one was pretty thin in his opinion. Still, *Seijin* Merch did have a point about the line of campfires, twinkling brilliantly against the darkness of the land. With them as a reference point, putting *Maikelberg* into the proper position hadn't been especially taxing.

"Well," he lowered the double-glass at last and looked over his shoulder. "I believe we might as well get started, Master Ohldyrtyn."

"Aye, aye, Sir," Lieutenant Ohldyrtyn, *Maikelberg*'s first lieutenant, acknowledged through the conning tower view slit. "Earplugs in, Sir?"

"They are now," Zohannsyn said resignedly, tucking the protective plugs into place. He hated the damned things, but he liked his ears still working, thank you. *Seijin* Merch didn't seem particularly worried about *her* hearing, though, he noted just a bit resentfully. Well, she *was* a seijin.

The *City*-class ironclad swung slightly to starboard, paralleling the Cheshyr Bay shore at a range of three miles, and her entire larboard side disappeared behind an enormous eruption of fiery brown gunsmoke.

▼ ▼ ▼

"*Sweet Langhorne!*" someone shouted as the smoke smudge, dimly visible in the gathering light, transformed itself into a rakurai-blast of hell-spawned brilliance.

Dahnel Kyrbysh had never imagined anything like it. He'd never seen even new-model field artillery, far less the enormously greater muzzle flash of no less than *eleven* heavy naval guns firing in a single broadside. The boil of smoky brilliance was even brighter, even more blinding, coming out of the darkness, and he stared at it, mesmerized, trying to comprehend what it might be—what it might *mean*. The one thing he was certain of was that it had to be connected with however the Cheshyrians had known they were coming. But even assuming they'd known, how could anyone have arranged for one of the new ironclad steamers—and that *had* to be what it was; nothing else *smoked* that way—to be in *exactly* the right place at *exactly* the right time to—

The first salvo of 6-inch shells arrived like the end of the world and put an abrupt—and permanent—end to Dahnel Kyrbysh's questions, as well.

▼   ▼   ▼

"Are you sure this was wise, Bahnyvyl?" Mhargryt Kyvlokyn asked across the breakfast table. The Duchess of Lantern Walk was seven years younger than her husband, an attractive woman of thirty-six, with the high cheekbones, fair hair, and gray eyes of the House of Hyntyn. At the moment, those gray eyes were frankly worried, and the duke drew a deep, patient breath.

"My dear," he said, "any great venture carries a certain risk. That's a given. I assure you, however, that I considered at great length before I decided to commit our house to it."

"I don't doubt that," the duchess said a bit more tartly. "Mind you, since you've committed our entire *house* to it, I do think you might have at least warned me about it ahead of time. But my question wasn't whether or not you've considered it; it was whether or not it's *wise*."

Lantern Walk managed—somehow—not to roll his eyes.

His marriage had been arranged by his and Mhargryt's parents when she was barely ten years old. That was the way things were done here in southwestern Chisholm, whatever might be the practice in places like Cherayth, Tayt, or Eastshare. By and large, he thought it was far the wisest way to handle such things, especially among families of good blood. But Mhargryt was a distant cousin of the Earl of Saint Howan, and her father had died less than a year after the marriage was arranged. Her mother had returned to Saint Howan . . . which meant Mhargryt had been raised in a deplorably "progressive" household. She truly didn't seem to understand it was her business to bear children and raise them and *his* business to make the decisions that promoted the interests of their house.

That was why he hadn't bothered her head with any of the correspondence he'd exchanged with Rock Coast, Rebkah Rahskail, and Duke Black Horse.

"I don't really approve of Rock Coast," he said after a moment, "and, if pressed, I find Rebkah's unswerving support for Clyntahn and his associates rather tiresome. But whatever *she* may think, none of the others really believe it's possible—or even desirable—to welcome the Temple back into Chisholm, so I'm sure some accommodation will be reached with Archbishop Ulys in the end. For that matter, once Sharleyan realizes we're serious, I suspect a more . . . realistic state of affairs to be achieved in secular matters, as well. But it's possible I'm wrong about that. Not likely, I think, but . . . possible."

"Then why—?" she began, but closed her mouth as he raised one hand and waved his index finger at her.

"As I say, I think that outcome's unlikely, but if Sharleyan insists upon being unreasonable, we'll simply have to take the decision out of her hands. We have no choice, because if we don't do something now, she and Cayleb will break all the great houses. It's inevitable, given the . . . mongrelized, bastardized path on which they've set their feet. The wealthiest man in the world is a man of no blood, Mhargryt, even if they did finally make him a duke. And what were his qualifications to be elevated to that title? *Money*—money earned in *trade!*"

"I've never heard you complain about *money*, whatever its source, as long as it's in *your* purse," she replied, and he frowned.

"Don't be tiresome, dear," he said more sternly. "There's nothing wrong with money *as* money. The problem is the way Howsmyn—" he refused to use the parvenu's title "—*acquired* his. I don't blame him for amassing a fortune any way he could, but this rabid 'industrialization' he's helped loose upon the world can only destroy the existing social order. It undermines the very bedrock of society's stability, and Sharleyan is fully committed to driving through the same sort of 'progress' right here in Chisholm! If she's permitted to succeed, men of no name, no blood, will soon consider themselves the equals of the houses which have governed the Kingdom for centuries! And when that happens, our place, our wealth, and our house will be inescapably doomed to decline."

"And what about your oath of fealty?" his wife asked in a painfully neutral tone. "There are penalties set forth in that oath for its violation, I believe."

"First, that oath was initially obtained from my father at what amounted to swordpoint," Lantern Walk replied. "Mind you, I never really blamed Sailys for demanding it. In his place, I would have done the same. But the fact remains that it was given under duress, and the same was true in many ways in my own case when I swore fealty to Sharleyan. More to the point, however, she violated her responsibilities to me—and to *all* of her vassals—when she entered into that illegal marriage with Cayleb and submerged the entire Kingdom in this bastardized 'Empire' of theirs. I hardly think I can be fairly accused of treason for disregarding an oath which has already been abrogated from the other side!"

"*If* you succeed," she replied. It was obvious to Lantern Walk she was restraining her temper only with some difficulty. "If you *fail*, if the Crown wins this confrontation, I suspect *Sharleyan* will feel you can be 'fairly accused of treason'!"

"Perhaps," he conceded, reaching for his cup of chocolate. He sipped for a moment, then placed the cup back on its saucer and looked at her levelly. "Should this effort fail, then, yes, no doubt there will be penalties. This is a much more carefully planned and coordinated affair than the two attempts to . . . restrain her when she was still younger, however. Many more peers of the realm are involved, and there are limits on the penalties she might levy upon so many of the great houses without demonstrating to all of the others that our charges of tyranny are well taken. I'm sure she'll find a way to make us pay a painful price *if* we fail, but it's highly unlikely that anything the Queen's Bench might impose upon us could be any worse than what will happen to our houses anyway, within no more than a generation, if she and Cayleb are allowed to nurture the seeds of Charisian madness here in Chisholm."

Mhargryt looked at him and wondered if he even began to realize just how insufferably smug he looked and sounded at this moment.

Theirs had been a loveless marriage, and it still was, as far as she was concerned. Bahnyvyl had qualities she could appreciate—he was cultured, well read, a good dresser, a kind husband (by his own lights) in his own insufferably patronizing way, and for all his other faults, a devoted father . . . once again, in his own way. But she'd realized years ago that he was what the Bedardists called a "sociopath." He genuinely believed he was the smartest man in the Kingdom, that everyone else existed only in terms of their utility to *him*, and—worse—that nothing terrible could happen to *him*. That was the sort of thing that happened to *other* people, not to the Duke of Lantern Walk!

And she was sickly certain he'd hugely underestimated the ruthlessness of Sharleyan Ahrmahk. He hadn't been raised in Saint Howan the way she had. *His* cousin wasn't the Chancellor of the Treasury. She and Sir Dynzayl Hyntyn had grown up together. She knew and trusted Dynzayl's opinion of the Empress, just as she knew exactly how he felt about Sharleyan . . . and that he was far from the only one who felt that way. Whatever Bahnyvyl might think, this conspiracy of his wasn't going to be the walkover he believed it would.

True, he and his allies had planned it well, as far as she could tell, and the fact that virtually the entire Army was either in Siddarmark or en route to it severely limited the Crown's immediately available resources. In addition, King Sailys' Edict drastically limited the feudal levies the Crown might once have raised from nobles loyal to it in the Army's absence. That meant it was entirely possible the conspirators, who'd apparently been flouting the Edict systematically for at least a year, really did have parity, or close to it, with the forces actually available to Earl White Crag and the Imperial Council in Sharleyan's absence.

But they didn't begin to have parity with the forces Sharleyan and Cayleb could bring to bear as soon as *they* heard about this. And people like the Duke of Tayt, her own cousin, Earl Shayne, Duke Eastshare, Earl High Mount, and dozens of other greater and lesser nobles would stand by their oaths to Sharleyan to the death. Even if the conspirators won in the end, it would be only after a long and bloody civil war, and the fool sitting across from her didn't seem to have a *clue* about the "penalties" the Crown would impose if a civil war like that failed.

And he's taken me and Karyline right along with him, she thought, fury bubbling in her blood as she thought about their daughter. *He's put her life, everything she could ever hope for, on the line right along with his when she's only ten years old, and he doesn't see the slightest reason he shouldn't have!*

"Well," she said out loud, bridling her rage with an iron hand, "I certainly hope you're right about that. In the meantime—"

The breakfast room's door flew open to admit a tallish man with graying brown hair and a noticeable potbelly, and Lantern Walk's head snapped around, his eyes crackling with anger at the abrupt, unannounced intrusion.

"What's the—?" he began.

"I most humbly beg your pardon for interrupting you, Your Grace," Dygry Dyangyloh said quickly, speaking so rapidly the words were almost a gabble. "I wouldn't have intruded if the matter hadn't been so grave."

"What are you talking about?" Lantern Walk demanded, and found himself wondering if the man had been drinking, although that would have been very unlike Dyangyloh, who'd been the chamberlain of Lantern Walk for almost fifteen years. For a moment, it crossed the duke's mind to wonder if some disaster had overtaken one of his fellow conspirators, but that was ridiculous. They'd only declared their defiance of Sharleyan four days ago!

"A rider just came in from the Mayor of Stoneyside, Your Grace. A column of mounted infantry crossed the border from Tayt at Kysahndrah Falls last night. The Mayor says it's at least a full brigade, and he expected it to reach Stoneyside within no more than six hours of when he sent off his message! And from Stoneyside, they can be *here* in only two more days if they push the pace!"

"What?" Lantern Walk frowned, trying to understand what Dyangyloh meant. It sounded like he'd said. . . .

"*Mounted infantry?*" He shook his head. "That's impossible!"

"Your Grace, the Mayor's always been levelheaded. That's why we . . . ah, relied on him while we were training the men." The chamberlain shook his head, his face tight with worry. "This isn't the kind of mistake he'd make."

"But . . . but that would mean. . . ."

The Duke of Lantern Walk stared at the chamberlain, and for once, the brain of which he was so fond refused to work at all.

▼   ▼   ▼

Sir Dynzayl Hyntyn stood on the Sherytyn seawall and watched through a double-glass as the column of galleons headed towards the wharves. There were quite a few of them, and he smiled thinly as he saw the black-quartered blue and silver checkerboard of the Imperial Charisian Navy at their mastheads.

The captains transporting the last echelon of reinforcements Sir Fraizher Kahlyns had dispatched to Siddarmark had sailed under secret orders, to be opened only after they'd reached Windswept Island, between the Chisholm Sea and The Anvil. And at that point, they'd turned back around to make landfall on Wyvern Beak Head in Zebediah, where Grand Duke Zebediah—who'd once been a Marine general named Hauwyl Chermyn—had been waiting for them. The people of Zebediah had idolized Sharleyan Ahrmahk ever since she'd dealt with their previous Grand Duke and—especially—brought them their new one. The Zebediahans had been delighted to see the thousands of Charisian soldiers aboard those galleons—for that matter, a third of them had been Zebediahans themselves, by birth—and they'd been able to go ashore, along with all of their horses and draft animals, while they waited in comfort for their real mission.

They'd had it much easier than the single mounted infantry brigade which had sailed all the way back around the western coast of Chisholm, staying well out to sea, to make landfall on a remote stretch of the Eastshare coast.

That brigade had moved very quietly through the most deserted stretches of the Barony of Green Mountain and the Duchy of Halbrook Hollow. Elahnah and Sailys Waistyn might still grieve for the loss of a husband and a father, and they might still cherish doubts about where the Church of Charis was ultimately headed, but they knew where they stood. The butchery of Zhaspahr Clyntahn's Inquisition had removed any doubts they might have had about who *he* truly served, and the present Duke of Halbrook Hollow's loyalty to his cousin had proven unshakable, when the test finally came.

He'd passed the brigade across his lands to the Duchy of Tayt, where they'd been met by Sir Awstyn Tayt, Sharleyan Tayt Ahrmahk's third cousin. Duke Tayt had personally led them to Khantrayl's Hollow, hidden in the shadows of the Iron Spine Mountains, where they'd recovered from their stealthy march and prepared for their part in Empress Sharleyan's response to the conspiracy against her.

Saint Howan could easily have stayed in Cherayth. In fact, he probably should have, all things considered. His decision to come home for a visit had run the very real risk of inviting his assassination as a way to destabilize his earldom before the combined forces of Black Horse, Swayle, and Holy Tree moved in to crush it between them. But from the moment the *seijins* had told him about the conspirators' plans, he'd known where he had to be on this day.

Now the two mounted brigades aboard those galleons sailing so steadily towards him were about to deliver Sharleyan Ahrmahk's answer to the men—and women—who'd believed they could murder *her* vassals, defy *her* laws, and strip *her* subjects of the rights she and her husband had guaranteed to them.

Somehow, the Earl of Saint Howan thought, lowering the double-glass at last, he doubted they'd enjoy what she had to say.

▼   ▼   ▼

"What?" the Duke of Black Horse demanded just a bit irascibly as someone rapped sharply on the study door. It was close to midnight, he was deeply immersed in the latest wyvern messages from Rock Coast and Lady Swayle, and he was an orderly man who disliked interruptions.

"Excuse me, Your Grace," Kynton Strohganahv said, as he opened the door. "I . . . know you dislike intrusions, but . . . but I think you need to speak to this . . . person."

Black Horse's forehead furrowed in consternation. Strohganahv had been his chamberlain for well over thirty years, and he'd been the assistant to Black Horse's father's chamberlain for ten years before that. The one characteristic Pait Stywyrt associated with him most strongly was composure. Nothing ever threw Strohganahv off balance. He'd been composed even when he'd respectfully expressed his own reservations about Black Horse's current endeavors before going out and putting his instructions into effect. But today he sounded positively rattled, and his face was pale.

"And who might 'this person' be?"

"I think . . . I think I'd better let her introduce herself, Your Grace," Strohganahv said, and Black Horse's frown deepened. Then he shrugged.

"Very well, Kynton. Show whoever she is in."

The chamberlain bowed and disappeared. He reappeared a moment later, and Pait Stywyrt shot to his feet in stunned disbelief.

"Good afternoon, Your Grace," the attractive young woman in the blackened chain mail of the Charisian Imperial Guard said calmly. "Men call me Merch O Obaith, and I'm afraid I have some bad news for you."

"Wh-wh-wh . . . ?"

Dull fury—and shame—washed through Black Horse as he heard his own incoherence, but Obaith only smiled, sapphire eyes glittering in the lamplight. If the *seijin*—and with that outlandish name, that uniform, and those eyes that was what she *had* to be—was remotely concerned by the fact that he had over five hundred armed retainers right here in Maryksberg, she gave no sign of it.

"In about another five hours," she told him, "HMS *Maikelberg* is going to sail into Maryksberg Harbor. She'll be accompanied by a pair of bombardment ships and transport galleons with twenty-five hundred Charisian

Marines. Captain Zohannsyn is under orders to put those troops ashore here in Black Horse, where they'll take control of your capital, and then march into Swayle to join the two mounted brigades advancing from Saint Howan to meet them."

Black Horse swayed, his eyes wide in shock, and she cocked her head.

"Now, I realize the Army invested quite a few marks in emplacing modern artillery to protect your waterfront. I also realize that one of the very first things you did as your part in your treasonous conspiracy was to place the Army gun crews under arrest and replace them with men loyal to you. So, I suppose it's possible you'll be foolish enough to attempt to prevent Captain Zohannsyn from carrying out his orders. If you do, I'm afraid things will get very . . . messy and there probably won't be a great deal left of Maryksberg when the smoke clears."

Her calm tone never wavered, but those unearthly blue eyes—eyes exactly like the ones Black Horse had seen looking out of Merlin Athrawes' face—were hard and cold.

"I'm a simple woman at heart, Your Grace," she told him, "and I really don't like messy solutions to problems. So I thought I'd just come ahead of Captain Zohannsyn and take this opportunity to avoid one here. You see, my instructions from Her Majesty are to take you into custody for treason, and I'm sure she'll be disappointed if I'm unable to arrest you unharmed. But she's a practical woman, and I'm equally sure she'll forgive me if that turns out to be impossible. So it occurred to me that one way to prevent you from ordering the batteries to open fire and getting quite a lot of your own subjects killed would be to remove your head before you do."

Steel whispered, and Black Horse swallowed convulsively as the curved blade gleamed under his study's lamps. The katana was rocksteady in her slim hand, and she raised one eyebrow.

"Are you going to make it necessary for me to disappoint Her Majesty, Your Grace?"

.X.
Army of the Center Command Post,
Selyk,
and
Forward Lines,
Holy Langhorne Band,
Talmar,
Westmarch Province,
Republic of Siddarmark.

G o on with what you were doing." Archbishop Militant Gustyv Walkyr waved one hand as the on-duty members of his staff started coming to attention. Heads had turned and more than one eyebrow had risen as he came down the steps into the enormous bunker Earl Silken Hills had bequeathed him as his central command post. That was scarcely surprising, given the lateness of the hour.

"You've all got better things to do than stand around saluting me!" he continued, trying to defuse the tension he'd seen in one or two sets of eyes, and several staffers chuckled appreciatively as they turned back to the paperwork that never stopped in the headquarters of an army with roster strength of well over nine hundred thousand. Walkyr left them to it and crossed to the center of the bunker where Bishop Militant Ahlfryd Bairahn, the Army of the Center's chief of staff, stood by the map table at the center of the big, earthy-smelling chamber below the brightly burning oil lamps hung from the overhead.

"Have we gotten any further information from Bishop Militant Styvyn, Ahlfryd?" Walkyr asked, trying to sound concerned but confident. He was pretty sure he'd succeeded in the former. The "confident" bit came a little harder.

"No, Your Eminence, not really," Bairahn replied. Under normal circumstances, he wouldn't have been here at this hour, either, Walkyr reflected. "The Bishop Militant's been sending regular reports—until the semaphore shut down for the night, at least—but they're all very much the same as the first one. I've been compiling them for your morning brief. My impression is that he's conserving his messenger wyvern's until he's had a chance to check with all of his divisional commanders, so I don't anticipate more from him before dawn. I also queried Bishop Militant Parkair just before the semaphore closed up shop. As of thirteen o'clock, he'd observed no heretic activity on his front."

"I see."

Walkyr rubbed his mustache with the knuckle of his right hand, turning to frown down at the large map that showed the curve of the enormous eight-hundred-mile front for which the Army of the Center was responsible. Most of that front, aside from the carefully prepared defensive positions protecting the critical roads, was covered only by picket forces. Mostly, that was because the rest of the front *could* be covered only by pickets and observation posts, given the paucity of the secondary road net. It was also because only about two-thirds of his designated force had actually reached him, however. The other third was "en route" . . . and it had been that way for five-days.

Walkyr had cherished his doubts about the decision to give supporting Silken Hills maximum priority when it was made, but he'd had to agree that on the face of things, it had made sense. And it still did, based on anything he actually knew. Based on what he was beginning to *suspect*, however. . . .

"Would it happen Tohbyais is also up?"

"By the strangest coincidence, I believe he just might be, Your Eminence." Bairahn smiled. "He told me he was going for a fresh pot of cherrybean. I pointed out that that was what we had orderlies for, but you know how he is about being 'cooped up in this damned cave.'"

"Actually, I have no idea about that. He's much too tactful to express those sentiments to *me*, you know."

"We *are* talking about the same Tohbyais, aren't we, Your Eminence? You know, the one who's about as diplomatic as a baseball bat?"

"Did I just hear my name taken in vain, Your Eminence?" a tenor voice asked from behind Walkyr, and he turned his to see a tallish, very fair-haired AOG colonel.

Like Walkyr, Tohbyais Ahlzhernohn was a native of the Episcopate of St. Bahrtalam in the southern Mountains of Light. In fact, they'd grown up in the same village, and they'd both spent their boyhoods among the high peaks, where horses were relatively scarce. That made it rather ironic, in Walkyr's opinion, that Ahlzhernohn was the closest thing the Army of God had to an expert when it came to using mounted infantry on the Charisian model.

"Not by me," Walkyr said mildly. "Assuming you're the always tactful fellow I was talking about."

"Sorry, Your Eminence. You must've been thinking about someone else," Ahlzhernohn said with a grin, and Bairahn shook his head in resignation.

Despite the vast difference in their ranks, Ahlzhernohn was only two years younger than Walkyr, and they'd played on the same boyhood baseball teams before Walkyr went off to seminary and Ahlzhernohn joined the Temple Guard. No one could have been more professional when it came to the actual discharge of his duties, but Ahlzhernohn was far more comfortable than anyone else on the archbishop militant's staff when it came to exchanging jokes with him. Although, to be fair, Walkyr was far more readily approachable by *any* of his staffers than anyone else under whom Bairahn had ever served.

"Tact isn't exactly my middle name," the colonel continued now, and held up his left hand to display the three tea mugs in it. "On the other hand, I do come bearing fresh cherrybean."

"And welcome it is," Walkyr said, taking the mugs from him.

He cocked an eyebrow at Bairahn, but the bishop militant shook his head with a shudder. Walkyr chuckled and set one of the mugs aside and held the other two for Ahlgyrnahn to fill. The colonel poured the hot cherrybean, then parked the pot on a hot plate, adjusted the hot plate's wick to a slightly hotter flame, and turned back to the archbishop militant. His expression was rather more sober than it had been.

"I expect you were asking about me to see if I'd had any brilliant insight into Bishop Militant Styvyn's reports, Your Eminence?"

Walkyr nodded, and Ahlzhernohn grimaced. He took a cautious sip of the hot cherrybean, eyes thoughtful, then lowered the cup and shook his head.

"Until we can at least figure out who those people are, I'm afraid brilliant insight'll be hard to come by," he said. "The one thing I can tell you is that I don't like it one bit. There could be all kinds of harmless explanations. For example, this could just be their notion of a reconnaissance in force. Or it could even be a deliberate diversion from what they're really up to. But when we all know the heretics are launching their major offensive in the south, having a forty- or fifty-mile swath of our cavalry screen kicked in way up here. . . . Well, Your Eminence, I guess the best way to put it is that it gives one furiously to think."

"There are times, Tohbyais, when I could wish our minds didn't work so much alike," Walkyr said a bit grimly.

He sipped his own cherrybean and his tense expression eased a bit as he sighed in approval. Ahlzhernohn probably *had* seized upon the beverage-fetching mission to get out of the command post, because he'd always hated confined spaces. In fact, Walkyr knew he had a touch of what the Bédardists called claustrophobia, though he managed to conceal it pretty well from the rest of the staff. But he'd also gone to get *proper* cherrybean, made the way people who spent their winters freezing in the Mountains of Light liked it. Which explained why an effete lowlander like Bairahn had declined the elixir of the Archangels. Walkyr couldn't *quite* have floated a horseshoe on it, but he could've come close.

Now he held the mug in both hands, moving closer to the map, and his frown returned as he gazed down at it.

"It does seem odd they'd have mounted columns that strong wandering around this far from the Tymkyn Gap," he said. "And I *really* don't like it when 'odd things' start turning up in our command area."

"Henrai's queried Earl Rainbow Waters and Earl Silken Hills for any information they have that might shed any light on the heretics' intentions north of the Black Wyverns," Bairahn replied, and Walkyr nodded in approval.

Bishop Militant Henrai Shellai was the officer charged with collating every scrap of intelligence flowing to the Army of the Center. Walkyr's intendant, Archbishop Ahlbair Saintahvo, wasn't happy about that, since Shellai was neither an inquisitor nor a Schuelerite, but he was so damn good at his job that not even Saintahvo could come up with a plausible reason to replace him with someone more . . . reliable. Or pliant, perhaps. "I don't want you getting good intelligence if it conflicts with what the Inquisition's telling you" would have been just a bit too blatant even for one of Zhaspahr Clyntahn's favorites.

"So far, all we really know is that we've got lots of cavalry—Charisian mounted infantry, not Siddarmarkian dragoons—driving in our outposts along the Mahrglys-Talmar High Road," Ahlzhernohn said now, coming to stand at Walkyr's elbow with his cherrybean in his right hand. The forefinger of his left hand traced the road in question. "The fact that they've spread out to cover every lizard trail and cow path for thirty miles on either side of the road—and that the Harchongians at Marylys haven't seen a thing—makes me pretty damned nervous, Your Eminence."

He tapped the dot of the fortified Harchongese position midway between Glacierheart and Lake Langhorne, then shook his head.

"The natural tendency when something like this happens is to overestimate the numbers coming at you, and to be fair, it's usually better to overestimate than *under*estimate. Of course, that's not always the case." He glanced up at Walkyr's profile, and the archbishop militant grimaced in acknowledgment of the obvious reference to Cahnyr Kaitswyrth. "But to cover that much frontage, this has got to be at least a full Charisian mounted brigade. For that matter, it sounds like it's at least a couple of them. That's in the vicinity of sixteen thousand men. It's not enough to pose a serious threat to any of our nodal positions, but it's enough to drive our own cavalry back into our lines. That gives them a *lot* of freedom to roam around and do whatever the Shan-wei they came to do in the first place. And unless Symkyn's managed to get around Silver Moon, they almost have to be from Eastshare."

"It's not very likely Symkyn's gotten around Silver Moon, Your Eminence, but it *is* possible," Bairahn said quietly. Walkyr looked at him—not in disagreement, but clearly inviting expansion—and his chief of staff shrugged. "Baron Silver Moon has a reputation—well-deserved, as far as I can tell—as an experienced and capable commander. But he's not as . . . mobility-minded, I suppose, as some of Earl Silken Hills' other commanders. From the sound of things, Symkyn's cavalry has been quietly filtering around the flanks of Silver Moon's position for quite some time now. There's no sign of any serious movement against Marylys—not yet, at any rate—but there's been a lot of skirmishing back and forth. Mostly reconnaissance activity, probably, and our latest evaluation out of Zion—" which meant "from the Inquisition," Walkyr reflected as Bairahn shot him a sharp glance "—has been that it's an effort to distract us from the heretics' intentions farther south. They certainly haven't launched anything like a serious attack on Silver Moon's fortified positions or tried very hard to break his supply line. Whatever they're up to, though, they're managing to dominate the open space outside his lines and the chain of fortified posts he has along the High Road back to Lake Langhorne. So it's possible Symkyn might have slipped a brigade or two past him."

"It's possible," Ahlzhernohn acknowledged, "but with all respect, My Lord, you're right about how unlikely it is. Lord of Horse Silver Moon may not be as cavalry-minded as some, but he's no fool, and he spent twenty-five years in the Imperial Army before the Harchongians raised the Mighty Host. He understands flank security, and those fortified posts of his on the high roads are big enough and close enough together that getting a force this size between them without anyone seeing a thing would be . . . let's call it a *real* challenge." The colonel shook his head. "No, it's a lot more likely this is Eastshare, coming out of Glacierheart and using the farm roads northeast of Marylys." He tapped the map again. "We still don't show enough detail on this map, really, and the farm roads aren't much compared to the high road, but they're there. And the fact that every farm and village between Glacierheart and the Siddarmark border's been deserted for so long means even large forces can move long distances without being spotted just because there're no eyes left to see them. It's almost like moving through the middle of a desert."

His tone was considerably grimmer, Walkyr noticed. Tohbyais Ahlzhernohn had never been a fan of the Sword of Schueler, and the mountaineer farmboy inside him hated how much wrack and ruin had been visited upon the hard-working farm families of Siddarmark's western provinces. But he was right. And that same emptiness explained a great deal about the heretic High Mount's successful flanking march to the Kyplyngyr Forest two years earlier.

Now *there* was an unpleasant thought. . . .

"But if they're from Eastshare's Army of Westmarch, they're *seven hundred miles* from where they're supposed to be. And from their own nearest supply point, for that matter!" Bairahn pointed out.

"One thing the heretics've proved often enough is that they've got plenty of logistic flexibility," Walkyr said. "That said, *I* wouldn't want to try supplying an entire army through the sort of countryside Tohbyais is talking about. If this *is* Eastshare, I would've expected him or Symkyn—or even both of them—to hammer Silver Moon out of Marylys to free up the high road before he came so far north. On the other hand, all we've seen so far is Tohbyais' brigade or two of mounted infantry. *That* big a force could easily be hauling its supplies with it. Let's not forget what High Mount did when he cut across to get behind Harless!"

"But if it *is* Eastshare, what's he up to?"

"Now that, Ahlfryd, is the real question, isn't it?" Walkyr smiled with very little humor. "I think the one thing we can safely assume is that if we knew the answer, we wouldn't like it."

▼   ▼   ▼

"Uh, Sarge . . . I think you'd better see this."

Sergeant Owyn Lynyrd grimaced. The voice from the dugout's steep steps belonged to young Zhaik Tymahnsky, 1st Squad's youngest private. He was a city boy, from Zion itself, and a strapping, sturdy young fellow. Army life obviously wasn't what he'd expected, and he didn't much care for long marches in the rain or standing watch on a night of sleet and snow. But he didn't complain the way some of the others did, and for all his inexperience, he had a brain that worked.

Unfortunately, he also had a tendency to report every little thing to his long-suffering squad leader, no matter how trivial it might be. He'd clearly decided it was better to report things that weren't important than *not* to report something that was, and the hell of it was that Lynyrd agreed with him. Which made it just a little difficult to convince him that he needed to exercise a little discretion . . . especially while the sergeant in question was enjoying his first cup of tea after a long, long morning. Most of the platoon was finally sitting down to breakfast after an extended stand-to, starting well before dawn. No one had really expected anything exciting, but they'd all been a little concerned that it might happen anyway. And everyone knew the heretics preferred night attacks—or attacks just before dawn, anyway. Nothing had happened, but. . . .

Boy's probably still on edge like the rest of us, Lynyrd reminded himself. *Having all that heretic cavalry roaming around's enough to make anybody nervous. Shan-wei! It's making me nervous as hell!*

And, he reflected, nervous or not, at least the kid was smart enough to pester his sergeant and leave Lieutenant Ahdymsyn to enjoy *his* breakfast in peace.

Lynyrd sighed and looked regretfully down into his steaming teacup for a moment, then set it on the neatly squared earthen ledge some patient Harchongian had carved into the wall of the squad's bunker. At least he'd know where to find it when he got done inspecting whatever world-shattering discovery Tymahnsky had made *this* time. And the smell of frying bacon, coming from the fireplace carved into the wall opposite the ledge, suggested he should get the inspecting done as quickly as possible.

The thought of breakfast restored him to something approaching good humor, and he stretched luxuriously before he started for the steps. He could do that, because the bunker's roof was a good nine feet above its floor. He didn't really like to think about how much labor its excavation had required, and he was just as happy it had already been done before 3rd Regiment took over this portion of what had been the Mighty Host's frontage. Other portions of the fortifications the Army of the Center had inherited were more rudimentary, and he didn't envy the regiments assigned to those sectors. Owyn Lynyrd had developed a love-hate relationship with the shovel. Like Colonel Flymyng, 3rd Regiment's CO, Lynyrd had served with Cahnyr Kaitswyrth's ill-starred Army of Glacierheart and been fortunate enough to find himself invalided at home a few months before the heretics annihilated Kaitswyrth's command. During his time in Cliff Peak, he'd discovered the beauty of deep, heavily sandbagged holes in the ground. The deeper the better, in his opinion, especially where heretic artillery was concerned. It was just that he much preferred for someone else to do the digging.

He snorted at the thought as he climbed the steps. Not that it was really all that funny. Bishop Militant Styvyn Bryar's Holy Martyrs Division had been rebuilt from a handful of surviving cadre. For all intents and purposes, it was an entirely new division, less than eight months old, and far too many of its personnel were like young Tymahnsky—totally inexperienced and farther from home than they'd ever dreamed they might travel. They were fortunate they'd been able to take over a defensive line which had already been carefully surveyed and laid out to take advantage of every terrain feature, but they still didn't really know their positions as well as they ought to.

Captain Lynkyn, 2nd Company's commanding officer, had been running daily familiarization hikes ever since they'd occupied their sector of the front, because no map could possibly tell a man everything there was to know about the ground he was responsible for defending. In fact, Lynkyn and Lieutenant Hyrbyrt Ahdymsyn, 1st Platoon's commanding officer, had been scheduled to take both squads out today. Captain Lynkyn wanted every man in his company to know the ground intimately, well enough to find his way around in total darkness while heretic shells exploded all about him. Second

Company was still far short of that level of familiarity, and Lynyrd was in favor of spending however much perseverance, sweat, and boot leather it took to attain it.

He damned well preferred to spend them instead of blood, anyway, he thought rather more grimly. Unfortunately, they wouldn't be doing any hiking today after all.

He emerged from the dugout, circling the dogleg in the stair designed to funnel grenades into the sump at the bottom of the angle rather than allowing them to sail straight into the bunker itself. The entrance was covered by firing slits on either side of the door, and other firing slits covered the slopes leading to the bunker's position. Fighting trenches spread away from it on either side, linking it to the bunkers assigned to the company's other platoons. The outer trenches were equipped with breastworks—solid log walls two feet high and two feet deep, pierced by firing slits every six feet, and topped by a three-foot-high parapet of sandbags—and side galleries had been excavated on the forward side of each trench every ten or fifteen yards. They weren't remotely as deep or well protected as the bunkers, but a man could duck into one of them and stay out of the rain when the heretics' portable angle-gun bombs started bursting overhead in sprays of shrapnel. The long, tangled abatis covering the reverse slope running up from the main defense line to the forward trenches was guaranteed to slow any assault, and a second abatis—and a hundred-yard-deep killing ground, completely cleared of trees or brush and liberally sown with land-bombs—guarded the slope running up to the first line of defense on the far side of the crest line in front of them.

At the moment, that first trench line was more heavily manned than usual, since the cavalry which had screened the last twenty miles of the approaches to 3rd Regiment's position had been driven in. The *infantry* pickets two thousand yards in advance of the trench line were still there, of course, and Lynyrd supposed the cavalry would be sent back out again once it had been reinforced.

A second belt of land-bombs had been laid between the first and second trench lines, covered by half a dozen rifled and banded 12-pounders. Their muzzles just cleared the front lips of their gun pits, and each of them was covered by a heavily sandbagged "roof" almost five feet deep. They wouldn't help much against a direct hit from one of the heretics' heavy angle-guns, but they'd stand up to just about anything else. Twenty or thirty of the new portable angle-guns had been carefully sited behind the field guns, as well. The AOG's version was still bigger and heavier—and less portable—than the heretics', and Lynyrd doubted their gunners had acquired as much expertise, but they were one hell of a lot more than anything the Army of Glacierheart had possessed when the heretics smashed it last summer.

And, of course, there were the half-dozen rocket batteries dug in well back on the far side of the crest line behind the company's main position. Lynyrd was a little in two minds about that. He'd never actually seen them fired, but according to an artillery sergeant he'd discussed it with over a bottle of moonshine, somewhere around a fifth of all the rockets landed either long or short. Long was just fine with Sergeant Lynyrd; *short* was something he didn't want to hear about.

Private Tymahnsky had climbed back to the sandbagged observation tower at the center of the company strong point after summoning Lynyrd from the bunker. The boy actually loved sunrises, which the sergeant thought was profoundly unnatural. As far as *he* was concerned, sunrise was the perfect ending to a productive day. But since Tymahnsky actually liked being up early, and since he climbed like a damned spider-monkey, the morning overlook watch was his on a regular basis, and he'd returned to it while the rest of his squadmates settled in for their delayed breakfasts. Now the kid was beckoning urgently for Lynyrd to join him, and the sergeant sighed in resignation and started up the ladder. Given that the tower was almost fifty feet tall—it had to be high enough to see over the crest to the first trench line—and that he most definitely *didn't* climb like a spider-monkey, he'd have plenty of time to work on his properly serious "sergeant's face" while he climbed.

"What's this all about, Tymahnsky?" he growled when he topped out on the tower platform at last. "I was just about—"

"Sorry, Sarge," Tymahnsky interrupted, and Lynyrd almost blinked in surprise. The kid *never* interrupted. That was one of the things the sergeant liked about him, although he was confident Tymahnsky would get over it soon enough.

"Like I say, I'm sorry," the private went on, and Lynyrd's eyes narrowed as he heard the tension in the kid's voice and saw something very like . . . terror in his eyes. "I just—I just don't know what in Langhorne's name *that* is, Sarge!"

Tymahnsky's voice actually cracked a bit at the end, and he pointed to the east, almost directly into the early-morning sun, just barely topping the crest line. Lynyrd squinted his eyes, shading them with one hand as he peered in the indicated direction and tried to figure out what had the kid so worked up. It was a clear, cloudless morning, pleasantly warm for the month of June here in Westmarch. So what could—?

His thoughts chopped off abruptly as he saw the . . . *shape* climbing steadily into the eastern sky. It was hard to make out details, staring into the sun that way, and the thing—whatever the Shan-wei it was—had to be at least four or five miles away. It was vaguely teardrop shaped, with some sort of bulges, almost like the vanes of an arrow or an arbalest bolt, at the narrow end, and if it was as far away as he thought it was, it had to be at least a hundred feet long, probably longer.

An icy breeze blew through his bones as that thought went through his brain. Something that size couldn't just . . . float into the air! Not without demonic assistance, anyway!

The icy breeze became a whirlwind, and he swallowed hard, suddenly not at all sure he wanted breakfast after all.

"I . . . don't *know* what it is," he admitted slowly.

"Is it . . . I mean, could it be—?"

"I don't know!" Lynyrd repeated more sharply. "But what I do know is that we'd better tell the Lieutenant about it double quick!"

▼ ▼ ▼

"Think they've noticed us yet, Zhaimy?" Sergeant Kevyn Hahskyn's brown eyes glittered with malicious delight as the Wyvern-class balloon *Sahmantha* climbed steadily higher.

They'd been in ground-hover, only thirty or forty feet up, for a good ten minutes while Lieutenant Lawsyn and the ground crew triple-checked all of their equipment. Hahskyn hadn't minded the delay at all. In fact, he'd strongly approved. It had been over two months since he and his observer, Corporal Zhaimysn Ahlgood, had been allowed to take her up, and all sorts of faults could have developed in that long. For that matter, somebody could all too well have screwed something up just because he was out of practice! Better to take the time to be sure none of those things had happened. Now they were moving upwards again at last, and the sergeant grinned hugely as he tried to picture the Temple Boys' reaction when they finally saw her.

"Bet some drawers down there just got really *fragrant!*" he chortled.

"I'm glad you think it's hilarious, Kevyn," Ahlgood said tartly. "It could get a lot less humorous if they suddenly decide to send a couple of regiments out here to find out what the hell we are!"

"Nah," Hahskyn disagreed. "According to the spy reports, we could just *barely* be in range for their heavy angles. Was I them, that's what I'd send calling."

"Oh, that's *so* much better," Ahlgood said sourly, grabbing a handhold as *Sahmantha*'s nose pitched slightly.

There wasn't much breeze at ground level, but there was a little more movement a few hundred feet up. Thanks to its stabilizing fins and the carefully thought-out arrangement of its hydrogen cells, coupled with the open-ended chambers that allowed atmospheric air to fill the envelope in compensation for any hydrogen volume deficiency, the balloon was remarkably stable under most conditions. That didn't mean it couldn't bobble occasionally, though. He and Hahskyn both wore double-clipped safety harnesses, so plunging to his doom wasn't very likely—unless, of course, the entire balloon went down, which wasn't completely outside the realm of possibility. That didn't make his footing any steadier when *Sahmantha* decided to dance, however.

"Oh, relax!" Hahskyn shook his head, disdaining any handholds as he raised his double-glass and gazed westward. "Captain Poolahn didn't pick this spot at random, you know. There's no way the Temple Boys can see over that ridgeline in front of us, and I'm pretty sure Major Fhrankyl's boys would take a really dim view of letting any of Zhaspahr's artillerists get a good enough peek to actually *hit* anything this far in front of their lines."

Ahlgood grunted in acknowledgment, although it didn't really make him feel a whole lot better. Still, the section had a full battalion of mounted infantry looking after its security, backed up by an entire support platoon of M95 mortars. That didn't mean the Temple Boys couldn't push all of them back the way they'd come, but it did mean they wouldn't do it anytime soon. And with *Sahmantha* floating above them, they weren't exactly likely to creep up on them.

"They should never've let us get this close in the first place," he grumbled.

"So now you're complaining about *that*?" Hahskyn lowered his double-glass to look at him and shook his head with a grin. "I swear, Zhaimy! You are the *gloomiest* man I know."

"*Somebody* needs to keep you anchored to reality," Ahlgood shot back, unfolding the plotting table hinged to one side of the bamboo gondola. The proper topographical map was already pinned down on it, and he made sure the pencils and drafting tools in the fitted cutouts were ready for use. "You know, if they hadn't decided to use hydrogen in these things, they could've just plugged you in and filled them with hot air!"

"Oh, now that's *cold*," Hahskyn chuckled.

The balloon had continued to climb while they talked.

No one wanted to hang around generating the hydrogen to fill *Sahmantha*'s twenty-eight thousand or so cubic-foot volume anywhere close to an enemy position. Producing that much gas took a lot of zinc and hydrochloric acid, and it was best done under what might be called controlled conditions far away from any possibility of hostile interference. Besides, the massive wagon load of the generating equipment—not to mention the steadily swelling gasbag—would probably have been just a tiny bit noticeable. So the balloon had been ferried to the launch site already inflated and securely strapped down on one of the 3rd Balloon Company's 30-ton flatbed freight wagons.

Once they'd reached the deployment point, the ground crew had carefully released the tiedowns, letting *Sahmantha* float free of the wagon. Now that she'd been cleared to ascend to normal operational altitude, the steam-powered winch on the smaller 10-ton wagon had started paying out the heavy tether attached to the rigging at thirty feet per second. At that rate, it took just over two minutes to reach their optimal altitude of four thousand feet, and Ahlgood ostentatiously checked the straps of his parachute as they passed the three-thousand-foot mark. Hahskyn only shook his head and raised his double-glass again.

The terrain below was beginning to assume the appearance of one of the papier-mâché relief maps the ICA's cartographers created for senior officers, and despite his Langhorne-given responsibility to grouse, Ahlgood felt a familiar shiver of delight as he looked down from the perspective of a king wyvern at the world spread out so far beneath his feet. This was the *real* reason he'd volunteered for the Balloon Corps, although the opportunity to help break Zhaspahr Clyntahn's kneecaps had been a strong secondary motive. He felt the brisk, cold breeze sweeping through the gondola, fluttering the edges of his map, and the air was like clear wine as it filled his lungs.

"Feeling better now, are we?" Hahskyn asked as he clamped his double-glass to the bracket at the front of the gondola, but his voice was softer, almost gentle, and Ahlgood snorted.

"Guess I am," he acknowledged, pulling a pencil out of its slot.

"Good, because I believe it's time we got to work."

"Ready when you are."

"Good."

At four thousand feet, in clear visibility and with a good double-glass, an observer could pick out large objects in relatively flat terrain at up to fifty miles or even a bit farther. That was under near-perfect conditions, however. Twenty miles was a more reasonable limit, and the new Balloon Corps' doctrine really counted on less than ten. Ideally, the three wyverns of a balloon company would be deployed about fifteen miles apart, giving them plenty of overlap even in less-than-perfect visibility. For this particular mission, only *Sahmantha* had been sent forward, but the company's other sections weren't far behind, moving up close behind the mounted infantry screening the Army of Westmarch's approach march. For that matter, the 5th Balloon Wing's entire 1st Squadron would be arriving about the same time the first leg-infantry brigades did, with no less than eleven more wyverns to support *Sahmantha*.

But until they got here, *Sahmantha* was Duke Eastshare's eyes and ears, and Hahskyn focused his double-glass carefully as he swept it across the terrain below.

"Baron Green Valley was right," he said almost absently. "Nobody down there gave any thought to camouflaging their positions against somebody up *here*." He chuckled grimly. "That's going to cost them when the gun dogs get here."

The base of the mounting bracket was marked off in degrees to permit him to take accurate bearings, and he spent the first minute or so absorbing a general feel of the terrain below him. From his current altitude, he could see all the way to the once modestly prosperous town of Talmar. It wasn't very prosperous these days, and even from *Sahmantha*'s gondola it was little more than a low-lying, distant blur. The fortified zone between the balloon and Talmar was much more sharply visible in the bright morning light, and he studied it thoughtfully, then glanced at the topographical map at his own elbow to orient himself properly.

"All right," he said. "I've got a triple line of trenches starting at about five miles, running from Hill 123 to Shyndail's Farm. Call it . . . three and a half miles. First trench line follows the military crest. Communications trenches run back from there, and the second line is on the reverse slope. Distance between them is about . . . two hundred and fifty yards. Then another couple hundred yards to the third line. I'll give you hard cross bearings from the hill when you're ready to start marking up."

He was gazing through the double-glass again while Ahlgood jotted notes on a pad before he started laying details in on the map on his chart table.

"Looks like the communications trenches zigzag every twenty yards or so." He grimaced. "Be a pain trying to enfilade *that*. And we've got what look like pretty deep bunkers along the third trench line. Not the first or second, though."

"Climbing the slope on the other side of the valley?" Ahlgood asked, still writing notes.

"Yep." Hahskyn shook his head. "Looks like the same sort of setup Earl High Mount's been pounding away at down at the Tymkyn Gap."

All of the Balloon Corps' crews had been fully briefed on everything the Army of Cliff Peak had been able to tell them about the Southern Host's fortifications. Without deploying his own balloons, the earl hadn't been able to provide them with comprehensive detail, but what his scout snipers and artillery support parties *had* been able to report helped fill in the picture unrolling before the sergeant's eyes.

"Frontline trench is for riflemen to cover the abatis downslope from it," he said, "and it looks like they've got some mortars of their own dug in behind the *second* line to support them. Got some flanking sandbagged rifle pits and breastworks supporting the second line, too, but the third line's the real main line of resistance. I see at least a couple of dozen field guns dug in and sited to cover the approaches, and there's a second line of obstacles between the second and third trench lines. The first gun pit's about . . . sixty yards north of Hill 123 and just below the western edge of the valley. It gives them a good angle down the slope over their own people's heads, I'd guess.

They're spaced roughly a hundred yards apart—in fact, I'll bet they're *exactly* a hundred yards apart—between there and the woods south of Shyndail's Farm. Hard to pick out the individual bunkers from here, but looks like they've got a deep bunker—probably enough for one of the Temple Boys' big-arsed squads—every hundred and fifty yards, with a couple of smaller ones between each of the big boys. Probably not as deep as the main bunkers, but I see lots of sandbags. Willing to bet they've got good lines of fire from all of them, too."

"Better and better," Ahlgood muttered.

"Be even worse if we couldn't see what was coming," Hahskyn pointed out. "Now, looking beyond the valley, I see a couple of roads that aren't on the map, too. Looks like they've put in laterals behind their front, where they figured no one'd be able to see them." He raised his head and grinned nastily over his shoulder at Ahlgood. "Pity they were wrong about that, isn't it? Especially since I also see some canvas-covered wagons parked behind what look like dirt berms. Wanna bet those are some of those damned rocket launchers they told us about?"

"You're not making me any happier."

"Not my job." Hahskyn shrugged and returned to his double-glass. "Looking past Shyndail's Farm, the ground's all open, but it looks like they've—"

He went on detailing terrain features and deployments and Zhaimysn Ahlgood scribbled them all down, then sat at the chart table and began carefully preparing the most deadly weapon known to man: a map.

▼   ▼   ▼

"Your Eminence, I don't know *what* it is," Bishop Militant Henrai Shellai said flatly, and there was more than a little uneasiness—possibly even fear—in his eye as he made the admission.

The rough sketch Bishop Militant Styvyn had sent them lay on the map table in all its bland impossibility. That sketch had been rendered by a young sergeant in the Holy Martyrs Division's 3rd Regiment. It had also been signed by the sergeant's platoon commander, his company commander, and by Colonel Brahdryk Flymyng, 3rd Regiment's CO, all of whom attested that it was an accurate rendering. Unfortunately, no one could begin to suggest exactly what it was or how it did what it was doing.

And given the Inquisition's pronouncements of heretic demon-worship. . . .

"It's fairly obvious it has to be some sort of . . . *balloon*, Your Eminence," Ahlfryd Bairahn said. "It's the only thing it *could* be. And if this is accurate, then *this*—" he tapped the protrusion on the belly of the thing "—is some sort of cage or car. That means there's somebody in it, probably with a spyglass, looking down and seeing exactly how Colonel Flymyng's men are deployed."

"Don't be preposterous!" Archbishop Ahlbair Saintahvo said sharply. "No one could build a balloon that big, floating *that* high—assuming the altitude estimates aren't wild exaggerations!—and keep it up there that long. I've *seen* balloon ascents in Zion. None of the balloons were remotely close to the size of this thing, and they all needed hot air. They'd have to have far more fuel in this thing than they could possibly fit into it to keep it aloft this long! Besides, not one of the so-called witnesses has even *mentioned* fire or smoke! *If* the thing is really there—and I'm not so positive it is—it isn't a *balloon*, whatever it is!"

The intendant glowered at Bairahn, but Archbishop Militant Gustyv's chief of staff looked back at him levelly.

"Your Eminence," his tone was courteous but unflinching, "you're right that no one's seen any sign of a fire to heat air, so I don't pretend to be able to explain how they're keeping it up for hours on end. But when so many men tell us it's there, it's *there*. Maybe it's demons keeping it up—*I* don't know! I'm a soldier, not an inquisitor or an expert on demonology."

Saintahvo's eyes glittered angrily at that, but Bairahn went right on.

"But whether we want to call it a 'balloon' or something entirely different, what it's *doing* is only too clear. It's a reconnaisance platform. They have observers on top of the tallest observation tower imaginable, and those observers are looking down on our positions. That means the heretic commanders will know exactly where all of our men, all of our fortifications, and all our *artillery pieces* are. They don't have to send out *patrols* to get that information. All they have to do is send this *thing* up and float there, watching us and probably dropping messages to the people on the ground."

"Then do something about it!" Saintahvo snapped.

"So far, Bishop Militant Styvyn's suffered somewhere around two thousand casualties trying to 'do something about it,' Your Eminence." Gustyv Walkyr's voice was just as unflinching as Bairahn's had been . . . and considerably harder. "The St. Byrtrym Division lost an entire dragoon regiment just trying to get close enough to this thing to tell what it's *anchored* to, far less what it *is*. And, frankly, that's as alarming as the fact that they have it, whatever we call it in the end."

"What are you talking about . . . Your Eminence?" Saintahvo demanded, attaching the last two words as an obvious afterthought.

"St. Byrtrym is Phylyp Sherytyn's division," Walkyr replied, "and I know him. In fact, I recommended him for St. Byrtrym when the division was raised. He's good, Ahlbair." The archbishop militant used the intendant's first name deliberately. "He's very good, and he's also very levelheaded and very reliable. He doesn't report anything he's not certain of—or, at least, if he's not dead certain, he *tells* you that—and according to him, it's not just mounted troops out there in the woods. He ran into some of those damned 'scout snipers'—in what he thinks was at least battalion strength—and they were *waiting* for him. Probably the observers Bairahn's talking about saw him coming and passed the word. But the critical point is that we aren't talking about just mounted infantry and some kind of glorified cavalry raid. We still don't know whether these are Eastshare's or Symkyn's troops, but there are one hell of a lot of them and according to everything we were told about the heretics' plans for the summer, *they aren't supposed to be here at all*, much less present in such strength."

Saintahvo's jaw clenched. He understood Walkyr's implication only too well, but there wasn't much he could say in reply.

"I genuinely don't want to dwell on this," Walkyr said more gently. "And I don't know if this thing's demonic, but the mere fact that they *have* it is bad enough, demonic or not. I'm sure that even now we can't begin to estimate all of the advantages it's likely to give them, especially since I think we have to assume that if we've seen one of them, this far out in front of their known positions, they have to have a lot more still to show us. But all of our troop dispositions were made based on the belief that the major heretic attack would come in the *south*. I know the men of this army will fight with everything they have, but I'm still short better than a third of my total strength, and the sober truth is that we were given this sector because it was the one least threatened. For all intents and purposes, aside from the divisions Bishop Militant Tayrens brought with him, all of my units are green. They haven't been blooded, they aren't veterans, and no one can ever predict how well an inexperienced unit will actually stand up in its first combat. That's true under any circumstances. When the inexperienced unit in question sees something like *this*—" it was his turn to stab the sketch with an index finger "—floating above it, its morale will be even shakier than it would've been otherwise."

Saintahvo's eyes were shutters in a stone wall, and Walkyr shook his head.

"What I'm saying is that I think the heretics fooled us all. I think the attack in the Tymkyn Gap is a sham. I think the reason that all Earl Silken Hills has seen so far is a lot of artillery and a little skirmishing is that High Mount never really intended to attack in the south at all. Or maybe that *was* their plan, and their spies figured out somehow that *our* spies had warned us what was coming so they changed their strategy. I don't know about that. I don't know about a *lot* of things. But I do know, as sure as I'm standing here, that they're going to put in a heavy attack on the Army of the Center. I'm willing to bet that what we're actually seeing is Eastshare's Army of

Westmarch. Instead of shifting south to support High Mount, they pulled it north, and according to our best estimates, he's got damned close to two hundred thousand men with massive artillery support. If he's managed to get his guns forward—and he damned well could have, after he got around Marylys and onto the high road—our front-line positions are about to get hit by one hell of a hammer."

"And?" Saintahvo said when he paused.

"And we need to convince Zion—" the temptation to be honest and say "Zhaspahr Clyntahn" instead was almost overpowering "—that we've been drawn into a false appreciation of the heretics' intentions. I think we need to start shifting some of Earl Silken Hills' left flank units back north as quickly as possible to support my army. I've already semaphored my conclusions to Earl Rainbow Waters, and he's agreed my assessment is probably accurate. He's looking at what he may be able to shift south from his reserve, because if this is Eastshare and he's kicking off a major offensive in the center, Green Valley can't be far behind in the north. Whatever Eastshare's doing, Green Valley is damned well going to punch straight towards Lake City and the Wings. He'll go for West Wing Lake and the Holy Langhorne's canalhead like a slash lizard for a prong buck. The Earl *has* to keep him from getting there, whatever it costs or however many of his men it takes . . . and if Eastshare has these 'balloons', then it's for damn sure Green Valley has them, too."

Saintahvo looked like a cat-lizard passing fish bones. He glowered at the archbishop militant and his staff for several seconds, then shrugged angrily.

"I think you're overreacting," he said, "but I'll countersign any dispatches you send to Zion, at least in so far as their factual content is concerned. After all," he smiled thinly, "I'm a servant of the Inquisition, not a military man. As such, I'm obviously not qualified to pass an opinion on the heretics' intentions."

Walkyr's nostrils flared, but he only nodded.

"Thank you," he said. "And in the meantime, I think—"

"Excuse me, Your Eminence."

Walkyr turned in surprise as Major Ahntahn Mastyrsyn, his personal aide, interrupted him. He started to say something uncharacteristically sharp to the youthful major, but the expression on Mastyrsyn's face stopped him.

"Yes, Ahntahn?" he said instead, ignoring Saintahvo's obvious irritation at the interruption.

"Your Eminence, we've just received a semaphore message from Bishop Militant Ahrnahld. The heretics have deployed at least six more . . . whatever they are," he twitched his head in the direction of the sketch, "and opened a heavy bombardment of the Talmar lines."

.XI.
Forward Lines,
Holy Langhorne Band,
Talmar,
Westmarch Province,
Republic of Siddarmark.

The tornado of heavy angle-gun shells crunched through 2nd Company's trenches and bunkers like Shan-wei's brimstone boots. Some of those shells were far heavier than anything the Army of God had ever experienced before. They drove deep into the earth when they hit, and the craters they blew could have swallowed entire platoons. Smoke, flying dirt, dust, shell splinters, and bits and pieces of what had been the defensive abatises were everywhere, sizzling through the air at lethal velocities.

That was bad enough, but one of those heavier shells had landed directly on the roof of Captain Tymythy Lynkyn's command bunker. The bunker's depth would probably have defeated one of the 6-inch angle-guns. Unfortunately, what hit it was a shell from one of the new 8-inch guns, three times as heavy and with four times the bursting charge. Even it failed to completely penetrate the bunker, but it exploded so deep that the bunker collapsed. Only three men got out alive, and Captain Lynkyn wasn't one of them.

▾   ▾   ▾

"Captain's dead, Sir!" Sergeant Lynyrd bawled in Lieutenant Ahdymsyn's ear. He had to shout, even inside the bunker, to be heard over the howling bedlam outside it. "So's Lieutenant Sedryk! Means you're in command!"

Hyrbyrt Ahdymsyn turned from the horrific, hellish panorama of his bunker's view slit to look at his platoon sergeant in disbelief. *He* was the senior officer on the position? Impossible!

But Lynyrd twitched his head at the exhausted, bloodstained corporal standing beside him, and Ahdymsyn recognized Captain Lynkyn's senior clerk. He couldn't begin to imagine how the man had made it from the company HQ bunker through the holocaust raging across the position, but the noncom's expression told him it wasn't impossible at all.

The earth shook and trembled, quivering like a frightened animal as the torrent of shells ripped and gouged. The heretics' bombardment had begun an hour after dawn, after the men had finished the regular dawn stand-to and just had time to settle in to their breakfast chow lines. It had struck with no warning at all, with no intimation that they'd somehow managed to haul their artillery train forward and deploy it behind their screen of mounted infantry and scout snipers. It had come shrieking down out of a beautiful blue sky with mountainous white clouds, and its fury was a living, breathing monster, rampaging through the company's position and snatching men—*his* men, some of them—into its fiery maw. He couldn't believe the sheer accuracy of their fire. All the lectures he'd attended in training, everything he'd heard on the endless journey from Zion to the front, had warned him heretic artillery was more accurate, longer arranged, and more . . . flexible than Mother Church's. But *this*—!

"Any orders, Sir?" Lynyrd asked.

"There aren't any orders to give, Sergeant," Ahdymsyn retorted. "Our job's to hold this position, and that's what we're frigging well going to do! But we can't put the boys out into the trenches while *this* is coming down on them." He jabbed a finger at the smoke and dust swirling in through the view slit. "They know what to do when the artillery lifts, and I'm not about to send you or anybody else out into that kind of fire—" he smiled briefly but warmly at the corporal who'd had the guts to send *himself* out into it to tell him he'd inherited command "—to tell them anything else!"

"Can't say I disagree with *that*, Sir." Lynyrd managed his own smile. "But I'm thinking we'll need reinforcements. We're gonna be a lot shorter handed than anyone thought when the Colonel was handing out responsibilities."

"If we are, we are," Ahdymsyn said flatly. "I doubt we could even get a wyvern off to tell him we need help—or that the poor thing would live to get there through this frigging fire. On the other hand," he surprised himself with an actual chuckle, "the heretics're making enough noise I expect he'll figure it out!"

▼   ▼   ▼

"Up another hundred yards," Sergeant Hahskyn said crisply, watching the crest line on the far side of the valley vanish under a forest of explosions.

"Up a hundred," Ahlgood repeated, making certain of the correction.

"Yes," Hahskyn confirmed. "They're almost exactly on for deflection."

"Got it," Ahlgood said, scribbling the information onto the message form, then leaned over the gondola rail to hook the message capsule to the taut wire between it and the winch-wagon. He released it, it went flashing down the wire with a shrill, metallic whine, and he picked up his own, lighter double-glass to look over Hahskyn's shoulder.

The reorganized angle-gun batteries contained only half as many pieces as their field artillery counterparts, but *Sahmantha* was spotting for an entire battalion of 8-inch angles. Those guns had reduced their sector of the Temple Boy fortifications to threshed and smoking ruin, even firing from positions three miles west of their balloon, although neither of them were foolish enough to think the destruction was as complete as it looked.

Like the rest of the Balloon Corps' observers, they'd been given first-hand experience of the effects of heavy angle-gunfire. They'd trained here in the Republic, at Camp Raif Mahgail, the huge base the ICA had built on a stretch of Tanshar Bay coast in Transhar Province. Camp Mahgail was isolated enough, with sufficiently ruthless security, for them to exercise with their balloon without worrying about reports reaching the Temple, and it also housed a major artillery training ground. The balloon crews had been able to walk the fortifications Charisian engineers had produced to give the gun dogs realistic targets. As a result, they knew the AOG's defensive positions were almost certainly far more intact than they appeared to be. On the other hand, they were one hell of a lot *less* intact than they'd been when the sun rose, and the 6-inch angles currently finishing the abatises' demolition would shift to what remained of the dugouts and rifle pits when the engineers started forward to clear the footstool fields.

At the moment, the 8-inchers had a different job.

The Temple Boy planners had obviously counted on concealment to protect their rocket launchers, parking them on the far side of hills to take advantage of their high-angle trajectories. Some of them had been separated from one another by earthen berms, but Hahskyn doubted that had been to protect them from Allied artillery. It was much more likely those berms were intended to keep an accident in one launcher battery from taking out its neighbors. God knew the ICA's rocket launchers—which their spy reports said were much more reliable than anything the Temple had—could be sufficiently . . . exciting to fire, so accidental explosions were probably a very real possibility.

Whoever was in command of this part of the Temple's front was no dummy, though. He must have realized almost immediately what the Balloon Corps implied, because for the last day or two Ahlgood had spotted—and reported—frenetic efforts to give those launchers better protection. Obviously, they'd still have to come out into the open to actually fire, but like their Charisian counterparts, they'd been adapted from freight wagons. So enormous labor parties had been throwing together redoubts in which the wagons could be parked under thick, heavily sandbagged overhead protection until needed and then rolled out when it was time to fire.

Unfortunately for them, it was hard to produce overhead protection that could stop a 200-pound shell when it came howling down at fourteen hundred feet per second. It could be done—Hahskyn had seen examples of that during his artillery familiarization training, too—but not without a lot more depth than they could throw up in the time they had. A little concrete and some of the Delthak Works' new flange-beams wouldn't have hurt, either. With the materials and tools they had, there simply wasn't enough time, and he waited, watching through cold, merciless eyes, as the gun dogs of the 23rd Medium Artillery Battalion, Imperial Charisian Army, adjusted their elevation and fired.

Twenty-three seconds after that, sixteen 8-inch shells exploded in a tightly grouped pattern on the far side of the crest line which had been supposed to hide the Holy Martyrs Division's rocket launchers from its enemies.

"*Yesssssss!*" Hahskyn hissed triumphantly as at least two of those launchers disintegrated in stupendous fireballs.

Some of the rockets actually launched, shrieking up out of the devastation like damned souls with no guidance, no direction. Three of them came down again almost on top of the bunkers and trenches being pounded by the lighter angle-guns. Two of them, though, headed directly towards Talmar. They lacked the range to reach the deserted town . . . but they had enough to hit the paddocks in which Holy Martyrs' draft animals were being held.

The resulting carnage was far worse, in a way, than what was happening to those dragons' and mules' human masters, because no one could explain it to them. They shrieked in terror as devastation crashed down on them. Already spooked by the savage, unending concussions of the Charisian bombardment, they panicked and tried to stampede. Many of the paddock fences went down; some of them didn't, and scores more of the animals were trampled to death by their frantic fellows as windrows of bodies formed along the obstruction.

"Tell them they're right on!" Hahskyn said. "When they correct again, they'll want to move their point of impact about three hundred yards north. Tell them we'll notify them when the current target's neutralized."

"Maintain fire on the current elevation and deflection. Prepare to adjust north three hundred yards," Ahlgood repeated.

"Exactly."

Hahskyn heard the message go shrilling down the wire, but he never looked away from his double-glass. He did shift his focus briefly, however, and his smile was colder and thinner than ever as he studied the Temple Boys dug in artillery. He doubted their gunners were as good as the ICA's at the best of time, but that didn't matter right now, since their weapons were clearly shorter ranged. They'd attempted to counter battery the Army of Westmarch's artillery, but the few rounds they'd fired—blindly; without *Sahmantha*, they couldn't even see the Charisian gun flashes—had fallen far short of the Charisian gun pits. Hahskyn never doubted that right now they were hunkered down in the deepest protection they could find, riding out the holocaust until the inevitable Charisian attack came into their reach.

Unfortunately, their guns were well inside the range of the medium and heavy Charisian angles. The airborne Charisian spotters and observers were working their methodical way from the closest targets to those farthest away, and as soon as the 23rd Medium Artillery finished with the rocket launchers, it would be the Temple gun line's turn.

▼ ▼ ▼

"Just about time, Sir," Colonel Sailys Trahskhat said.

Brigadier Byrk Raimahn looked up from the map he'd been contemplating while he stuffed the bowl of his pipe. The brigadier couldn't have said why he was studying it, really. It was far too late to change any of his plans, much less the orders he'd already issued. It was just part of the way he was put together, this need to stand here, looking at the map, wondering what he could've done differently . . . better. He snorted at his own perversity and wondered again—briefly—how in God's name he'd ended up *here.*

When he shaved every morning, the face in his mirror wasn't so very different from the man—the boy, really, in a lot of ways—he'd seen in that same mirror before the Sword of Schueler swept over Siddar City's Charisian Quarter in a tide of blood, fire, and rapine. But that had been two and a half years—and about three lifetimes—ago, and the eyes . . . The eyes were different, and he wondered if they'd ever lose that darkness? That memory of what their owner had seen and done in those lifetimes?

He finished filling the pipe, drew a fire striker from his pocket to fire up the tobacco, and suddenly found himself chuckling with genuine humor. Someone—he suspected Sailys—had informed his grandmother that he'd taken up the vile Glacierheart custom of smoking. She'd apparently missed the fact that Charisians in plenty had smoked long before the Raimahns moved to Siddarmark to escape the heresy, which was odd, since his grandfather had smoked for several decades before he gave up the "unholy weed," as Sahmantha Raimahn was prone to call it.

She and Claitahn Raimahn had returned to their homeland after the Siddar City riots. It hadn't been easy for them—especially for Claitahn, whose principles and faith were just a little more rugged than the Mountains of Light—to admit the validity of the Church of Charis' charges against the Group of Four. But the same principles and faith which had made him a Temple Loyalist had left him no choice when Zhaspahr Clyntahn's fiery sermons actually *praised* the Sword of Schueler's barbarity. When he and his wife arrived home in Tellesberg with Sailys Trahskhat's children and sixty other Charisian and Siddarmarkian orphans in tow, he'd gone directly to Tellesberg Cathedral to tell Maikel Staynair, the man he'd blamed for so long for so much, that he'd been wrong.

Two-thirds of the fortune he'd spent a lifetime building had been lost between the Charisian investments he'd liquidated when he moved to the

Republic and the carnage the Republic had suffered afterward. But he'd pledged a full half of everything he had left to aid Charisian and Siddarmarkian refugees from the mainland. Today, he was chief administrator not just for the Church of Charis' enormous orphanages but for *all* of the Church's war-related charities, and his wife was as deeply immersed in that effort as he was.

None of which had prevented her from finding time to send the grandson she'd raised a scathing appraisal of men who smoked. She'd even included half a dozen Pasqualate tracts about the health hazards of tobacco.

Well, if kicking the smoking habit is the only thing she's going to demand when I finally get home, Byrk thought, savoring the aromatic smoke, *I imagine she'll get it. She usually* does *get what she wants, after all.*

"I suppose that if it's time, we should probably head out," he said through a wreath of smoke in a casual tone which he knew fooled neither of them.

"S'pose so, Sir," Trahskhat agreed with equally false nonchalance, and Byrk reached out to pat him on the shoulder with a broad smile.

The two of them had been through a lot in those three lifetimes since the Sword of Schueler, he thought. Sailys was still the stocky, powerfully built first baseman he'd once been, but strands of silver threaded through his brown hair now. His face carried the scars of frostbite from their first brutal winter in Glacierheart, and he walked with ever so slight a limp, courtesy of a Temple Boy bayonet at the storm of Fort Tairys. And the changes inside him were as profound as those inside Byrk Raimahn. The brigadier knew Sailys Trahskhat could never, in his wildest imagination, have pictured himself as a colonel, and especially not a colonel in the *Siddarmarkian* Army! Yet here he was. And here, for that matter, was Byrk Raimahn, who'd celebrated his twenty-third birthday just last five-day, which made him the youngest brigadier in the entire Republic of Siddarmark Army. For that matter, he was younger than any brigadier in the *Charisian* Army.

This is crazy, he thought for no more than the six-thousandth time. *I write* songs, *I don't command* brigades! *God must have an even stranger sense of humor than I ever imagined.*

Perhaps He did, but Glacierhearters didn't. They were as pragmatic, as stubborn, and as tough as their mountains, and they'd decided the over-civilized young sprout who'd commanded the riflemen escorting their beloved archbishop back to them and then fought for months to hold the Green Cove Trace was one of their own. Just as they'd decided they owed a debt to Charis when Brigadier Mahrtyn Taisyn and his Marines died to the man protecting their families from the atrocities Cahnyr Kaitswyrth's oncoming army had strewn in its wake. Their province had been more sparsely populated than most of the Republic even before the Sword of Schueler 's "Starving Winter," but they'd raised an entire fourth regiment of militia and sent it off to fight at Charis' side. Not only that, they'd specifically petitioned the Lord Protector to allow their regiment to fight under Charisian command until the end.

Greyghor Stohnar had granted their request, and the four regiments had been organized into a single brigade. But that brigade had needed a commander . . . and militia units' officers were appointed by the provincial government of the province which raised them. Which was how a Charisian boy whose first love had always been music had become the youngest brigadier in the history of the world.

It still bemused him, but perhaps it was fitting that he wasn't exactly the standard version of a brigadier, because his command was far from "standard" itself.

The RSA had retained its long-standing unit structure when it reorganized around the new-model weapons, but it had formalized the practice of consolidating the thirty-man sections of its pike companies into sixty-man platoons. They'd always tended to operate the doubled sections as single tactical units, anyway, except under very special circumstances, and many of the Army's officers had felt the rationalization was overdue even before the new weapons were added to the mix. So now there were seven platoons in each company, although Byrk had never really understood why the Siddarmarkians didn't just go ahead and call the companies "battalions," like anyone else would have. Tradition, he supposed. But by permanently combining the sections, they'd cut the number of lieutenants in each company in half. Well, almost in half. The single section of the headquarters group remained only thirty men strong but was still a lieutenant's command.

The Glacierheart Brigade had operated so long and so intimately with its Charisian allies that it was fully equipped with Charisian equipment—including the M96 rifle and Mahldyn .45 revolvers—and had adopted Charisian doctrine and tactics. But it followed the Siddarmarkian pattern as far as unit organization was concerned—which made it slightly larger than a standard, two-regiment Charisian brigade—and its men came almost equally from the ranks of the trappers and hunters who roamed the Gray Walls' majestic, snowcapped summits and the hard-as-rock miners who wrested the coal from those mountains' stubborn bones. It would have been difficult to say which group was tougher, despite many a knuckle-and-skull "empirical experiment" to find out. But that orientation—the self-reliance, woodcraft, and hunting skills of the trappers, coupled with the engineering background, teamwork, and explosive expertise of the miners—made them uniquely suited to combine the functions of the ICA's scout snipers and combat engineers.

And that explained their present assignment.

The Mighty Host's fortifications were a battlefield challenge—in degree, if not actually in kind—no one had yet faced. But the Allies had known it was coming . . . and spent a great deal of thought, time, and effort on ways to meet it. The Balloon Corps and new artillery were part of that answer, yet the ICA's gunners had realized that heavy artillery's pulverizing effect could actually hinder an attack as much as it helped. As Baron Green Valley had pointed out, artillery's function was to open a path for the infantry, not to simply churn a battlefield with ton after ton of shells. *That* was entirely too likely to create conditions in which the infantry floundered forward through muck and mire at a snail's pace while defending riflemen picked them off like roosting wyverns.

Given the current dry, sunny weather, seas of mud weren't very likely, but the army still needed a way to carry heavily fortified positions without simply relying on artillery to shatter them. So doctrine had been modified yet again. ICA tactics had always emphasized—and depended upon—the initiative of company and platoon commanders. They were told *what* to do, then figured out *how* to do it with a degree of flexibility no other army could match. Not even the RSA, which had spent the last two years absorbing what its Allies had to teach it and who came closer than anyone else, could fully equal that responsive adaptability or the mindset that made it work.

Byrk Raimahn's Glacierhearters could, however, and Duke Eastshare, who'd seen them at work in the Fort Tairys campaign, had specifically chosen them as the core and test bed for the Army of Westmarch's new assault brigades. They'd worked closely with the ICA's combat engineers, artillerists, and scout snipers, to formulate the new doctrine, and they'd suggested dozens of pragmatic improvements along the way. Three of Eastshare's other brigades had drawn the same equipment, undergone the same training, but the Glacierheart Brigade had established the training syllabus for them all. Now it was up to its officers and men to see how well all that planning, all that equipment, actually worked. Byrk's men were proud to have been chosen . . . and Byrk was only too well aware of how many of them might be about to die if it turned out the new doctrine didn't work.

"Morning, Sir," another voice said, and he looked up with a smile.

"Morning, Wahlys," he replied, and clasped forearms with Colonel Wahlys Mahkhom, who'd inherited command of the 1st Glacierheart Volunteers following Byrk's promotion.

If anyone in the world was more bemused by where he'd wound up than Sailys or himself, the brigadier reflected, it had to be Mahkhom. In retrospect, it had been inevitable, though. Always a natural leader, he'd been one of the first to begin organizing Glacierheart to resist the Sword of Schueler. He'd been instrumental in holding the Gray Walls against the onslaught from the Province of Hildermoss, and he'd exacted a savage price from the Temple Loyalists who'd slaughtered his entire family. And while he'd clearly been astonished by his promotion, he'd shouldered it with the same solid determination with which he shouldered *every* responsibility. In fact, meeting the challenge of his new rank seemed to have helped lay at least some of his demons.

He had more than enough of them left to visit carnage and ruination on the Temple Boys, though, Byrk thought, feeling the power of the older man's clasp.

"Your boys ready?" Byrk asked . . . unnecessarily, he knew.

"Might say we are," Mahkhom replied . . . equally unnecessarily.

"Then go." Byrk smiled crookedly around the stem of his pipe. "And don't get yourself shot! If they won't let me go gadding about out there with the boys, then I'm not letting you get yourself killed, either. Understand me?"

"Not rightly sure what 'gadding' is," Mahkhom replied, scratching his beard with a thoughtful air. "Sounds like somethin' you shouldn't be doin' if you're not married t' the girl, though."

"That's exactly what it is," Byrk told him with a chuckle, and punched his upper arm gently. "But I mean it, Wahlys. I'd really like to get all of you back, but we both know that isn't going to happen. Try not to be one of the ones we don't."

"If I can," Mahkhom told him much more quietly. "Happen the gun dogs and the balloon boys've made sure there'll be more of us after, this time around."

"We can always hope. Now, go. And since Archbishop Zhasyn can't be here to say it himself, I'll say it for him. May God go with all of you."

▼　▼　▼

All right," Major Sygfryd Makwyrt growled, raising his voice to be heard by his platoon commanders over the distant artillery and the thud of the mortars closer to hand. They'd been laying smoke to cover the combat engineers lifting the footstools in the Glacierheart Brigade's front; now they were laying more of it to cover the brigade itself.

"You all know what we're supposed t' do," Makwyrt continued. "Go out there, do it, and kick arse. Just make damned sure you stay in the cleared lanes till you hit the abatis, right?"

A chorus of assents came back, and he nodded sharply and pointed towards the front. They trotted off to join their platoons, and Makwyrt turned to Colonel Mahkhom.

"Wasn't much of what th' Brigadier calls a 'detailed briefing,' Sygfryd," the colonel observed as the two of them followed the lieutenants a bit more sedately.

"Heard a 'briefing' or two of yours, over the years," Makwyrt replied. "Least I used more'n three words and a grunt."

"Just didn't want t' dazzle 'em with my eloquence."

"Ha! Can't fool *me*. Learned that one from the Brigadier, didn't you?"

"Learned quite a few things from the Brigadier over the years, actually," Mahkhom said much more seriously. "Reckon all of us did. Try to bear that in mind, right?"

"Right."

They'd reached the start line, and Makwyrt gave him a firm arm clasp, waved for his command group, and his runners started forward. Mahkhom watched him go, then pulled out his pocket watch and checked the time. Another ten minutes till the barrage lifted, he thought. He and his own command group would be going in directly behind 1st Company, and he nodded to young Lieutenant Zhaikahbsyn whose 6th Platoon had been given the unenviable task of bringing up the rear . . . and watching the Colonel's arse.

"Lainyl," he greeted the lieutenant. "You boys ready?"

"Yes, Sir!" Lainyl Zhaikahbsyn replied fiercely.

"Well, just remember the idea's that the other fella's s'posed t' be the one that dies," Mahkhom said dryly.

A memory of a younger Wahlys Mahkhom in the Green Cove Trace flashed through him as he said it, but he made himself push that memory aside. Archbishop Zhasyn was right. Mahrlyn would have wanted him to live, and despite the pain that still sometimes threatened to drag him under, he meant to do what she would have wanted. And he also meant to keep as many of these young Glacierheart men alive for *their* wives and families as he could.

Maybe that could compensate—a bit—for some of the *other* things he'd done in the last couple of years.

"Yes, Sir," Zhaikahbsyn said in a slightly more subdued tone.

"Good lad!" Mahkhom clouted him on the shoulder, then twitched his head for his runners to follow him.

▼   ▼   ▼

Hyrbyrt Ahdymsyn crouched at the head of the bunker stairs, stinging eyes leaking tears as he peered into the smoke. He'd sent a runner to Colonel Flymyng during the first lull in the heretics' shelling . . . just in time to have it resume, exactly the way the Dohlaran reports Captain Lynkyn had shared with them had described. Ahdymsyn knew he'd be a long time forgiving himself for not waiting a little longer before sending Private Shandahsky off. He should've remembered those reports. He *had* remembered them; he simply hadn't had time to wait. Colonel Flymyng had to know what had happened to 2nd Company—and how badly it needed reinforcements—and he had to know as soon as possible.

I still should have waited, he thought grimly. *I knew it then, too.*

A stubborn voice that sounded a lot like Captain Lynkyn's told him he was wrong. Told him a military commander had to accept that men would die following his orders. Had to send them out *knowing* they were going to die, if the mission required it. But Hyrbyrt Ahdymsyn was still a very young man, and one who cared, and he'd discovered he didn't have whatever hardness or determination it took to accept that cold, bitter truth.

"More trouble, Sir," a voice said, and Ahdymsyn turned his head as Owyn Lynyrd reemerged from the foul-smelling ocean of smoke floating across his company's splintered position.

Ahdymsyn had sent the sergeant out fifteen minutes ago to survey what was left of that position, and he felt a vast surge of relief that he'd gotten back in one piece. But then—

"Just got a runner from Third Company," Lynyrd continued. "Captain Rychardo's dead, too. And so're Lieutenant Traivyr and Lieutenant Charlz."

"What?" Ahdymsyn stared at him in consternation. "All *three* of them?!"

"Yes, Sir," Lynyrd confirmed grimly. "They were out of their bunkers, walking the position together—*crawling* it, really, I guess—when the heretic guns opened up again. Single shell got all three of 'em. And Lieutenant Zhaksyn was already wounded. That leaves Lieutenant Pahtyrfyld as company commander." The sergeant managed a mirthless smile. "Sent a runner to let you know who's holding your right, I guess, Sir."

Langhorne, Ahdymsyn thought numbly. *Two companies* both *commanded by their most junior lieutenants? If Second and Third are this bad off, what the hell's happened to the rest of the Regiment?!*

"I see," he said out loud, and twitched his head in the direction of the fighting trenches. "How bad?" he asked.

"Pretty *damned* bad, Sir," Lynyrd replied frankly. "Wasn't able to get all the way forward, but from what I could see of the second abatis, there can't be a whole hell of a lot left of the first one. Bastards were putting shells exactly where they wanted 'em, and they ripped the shit out of the obstacles and the trenches. Second line's close enough to in one piece we can probably man it; first line has to be just about completely gone, and they're dropping portable angle shells all along the hillcrest. Got a mess of shrapnel and explosive mixed in with the smoke, too. We'd probably lose a third of the boys we've got left just getting to the first line. Only good news is that we got just about everybody out of there before the really heavy shelling started."

Ahdymsyn nodded. Earl Rainbow Waters' new tactics specifically called for pulling back from the exposed trench line during the artillery bombardment and then reoccupying it once the shelling lifted, and despite the pounding 2nd Company had endured, he knew its casualties would have been far worse if the men had been out in the open during the hurricane bombardment.

The question was whether or not he applied the *rest* of the new tactics. Did he move back forward to man the forward trench lines, or did he concede those and concentrate on the final line, here by the bunkers.

He listened to the heretic shells, continuing to fall not on 2nd Company's position, but *behind* it, laying down a wall of fire and steel to prevent the division reserve from coming to his support, and his mouth was a grim, hard line.

Owyn's right, he told himself coldly, *the* first *line almost has to be gone. Oh, I could probably get the boys into it—and back out, any of them that survived— without losing as many to the portable angles as he's suggesting. That's what the communication trenches are for, and they can't* all *have been taken out! But we were only supposed to hold it until the reserve came up, and that's not going to happen with those damned shells ripping hell out of the lateral roads behind us. Besides, I don't have enough men left to man it even if it's still there!So that only leaves the lines on* this *side of the valley, and I don't have enough men left to man both of them, either.*

The forward line had less overhead protection even before the heretics kicked the crap out of us, but it also has the better field of fire up to the eastern crest. Visibility sucks with all this smoke, but the heretics have to ease up on the shelling, even with their portable angles, if they're sending in their own infantry. So we might still *have a chance to catch them silhouetted when they come over the crest.*

All of that was true, but deep inside, he knew the real reason he wasn't going to man that forward line.

If I put them that far forward and the bastards start shelling us again, I'll lose half the boys I've got left before they make it back to their bunkers.

He couldn't do that. He just . . . couldn't.

"Turn them out, Owyn," he said. "We don't have enough men for the original defense plan, and Colonel Flymyng and Bishop Militant Styvyn won't get any reinforcements to us through *that*." He jabbed one thumb over his shoulder at the curtain of death thundering between his men and the rest of the Holy Langhorne Band. "We'll make our stand here on the bunker line. And be sure we've got plenty of hand-bombs forward. In all this smoke, they'll probably have as much range as our rifles do."

▼   ▼   ▼

"*Hsssst!* Right here, Sir—an' watch your feet!" Corporal Tymyns hissed.

Lieutenant Greyghor Ohygyns, CO, 2nd Platoon, 1st Company, the 1st Glacierheart Volunteers, froze. Zackery Tymyns, the assistant squad leader of Sergeant Braisyn Mahktavysh's 1st Squad, was well into his forties—the next best thing to a septuagenarian from Ohygyns' perspective. He was also shrewd, solid, steady, and unflappable, however, and he'd have been an officer himself if he hadn't been the next best thing to functionally illiterate.

If Tymyns wanted him to be careful with his feet, then he'd damned well be careful with his feet!

"Good, Sir!" Tymyns emerged from the smoke with a gap-toothed grin. "Got our markers, Sir, an' Braisyn said t' tell you the engineers did us proud. Got a clear path marked clear through the first belt. Only they's a passel of footstools kinda stacked t' the sides, so it's best you stay t' the middle of the path."

"I appreciate that, Zackery," Ohygyns said. "No telling where I would have put my feet as I went strolling along whistling and drinking a beer."

"'S why I'm here, Sir, t' keep you out of trouble," Tymyns replied with an even broader grin, and Ohygyns shook his head. Then he looked over his shoulder at Klymynt Ohtuhl, his platoon sergeant.

"Pass the word back, Klymynt," he said much more seriously. "Single file from here, and we stay right in the middle of the tapes!"

"Got it," Ohtuhl acknowledged with typical Glacierheart informality, and Ohygyns started forward once more, following closely on Tymyns' heels.

The "crump, crump, crump" of bursting smoke rounds rolled steadily back from the west, getting louder as they came closer. There were no shrapnel or explosive rounds in the smoke falling on this side of the crest line—or their damned well weren't *supposed* to be—and the combat engineers had cleared several lanes through the belt of footstools.

He passed a couple of motionless bodies in Charisian uniforms, and his mouth tightened. Those engineers had paid a price to accomplish their task, yet he knew that price had been infinitesimal compared to what it would have been without the massive artillery support they'd received, and the smoke had probably been even more valuable than the high explosive and the shrapnel. The engineers had trained to find and lift the footstools in total darkness—for that matter, the Glacierheart Volunteers had trained to do it, as well—but that was always tricky, and too often costly. That was why the infantry support squads' mortar crews had hauled such vast numbers of smoke bombs forward with them. With the rifles covering the footstool fields blinded, the engineers had been able to go about their dangerous work in daylight.

Of course, there's always the second belt on the other side of the hill, he reminded himself, but the engineers were supposed to be working on that at that very moment.

He reached the crest and found Sergeant Mahktavysh waiting with the rest of 1st Squad spread out to either side, heads up and weapons ready.

"Good to see you, Braisyn," he said.

"And you, Sir. See Zackery got you here in one piece."

"So far, at least. What's the situation down below?"

"Don't rightly know yet, Sir. Still waiting for—"

"Cahnyr!" one of the riflemen barked suddenly, and the sergeant broke off.

"Staynair!" came back, and the private who'd challenged relaxed—slightly at least—as he was answered with the proper counter.

"Come on in," he called, and a figure materialized out of the smoke.

The engineer sergeant was very careful about how he approached Mahktavysh's ready riflemen, despite the invitation. Then he saw Ohygyns and trotted briskly over to him and saluted.

"Got a lane clear to the obstacle belt for you, Lieutenant," he said.

"Good!" Ohygyns nodded, and turned as Platoon Sergeant Ohtuhl arrived along with Sergeant Tymythy Ohlyry's 2nd Squad.

"Fourth and Fifth're right behind us, Sir," Ohtuhl said, indulging in what was an orgy of formality for him.

"Then I reckon it's time we follow the sergeant here—" Ohygyns indicated the engineer "—and get down to it."

▼　▼　▼

Lieutenant Ahdymsyn and his remaining men manned their positions while portable angle-gun shells continued to thud about them. The protective bays in the front walls of their trenches, coupled with what remained of the overhead sandbags, provided reasonable cover against the small shells' sprays of shrapnel. It would be another matter if one of the explosive rounds landed directly in one of the trenches, but that was unlikely, despite the weight of fire still coming at them.

At least they weren't being scourged by the devastating fire of the heretics' heavy angles any longer. Ahdymsyn was grateful for that, but it was a very mixed blessing. The only reason the heavy guns would have stopped pounding them had to be because the heretic infantry was moving in for the kill.

I wish to hell we had a frigging breeze! Something to move the damned smoke along.

The smokescreen was like the worst fog he'd ever seen—ever imagined—and at least half the portable angle-gun shells falling on his position were solely to replenish the smoke any time it even looked like thinning. And that meant—

▼　▼　▼

As nearly as Lieutenant Ohygyns could tell—which wasn't nearly as well as he would have *preferred* to tell, thanks to the lifesaving smoke which had gotten them this far—2nd Platoon was where it was supposed to be . . . give or take a few dozen yards. The large-scale maps prepared by the Balloon Corps' cartography section had helped enormously in the initial approach, but once

2nd Platoon entered the cratered wilderness of the main bombardment zone, they'd become a lot less useful. There didn't seem to be any recognizable landmarks or topographic features anymore, and he'd been forced to hope the engineers had managed to maintain *their* bearings as they cleared the footstools.

He'd been surprised to find the Temple Boys' second trench unmanned when they reached it. It had been hammered almost as badly as the first one, and it was more than half-collapsed in many places, but he'd been impressed, when he slithered down into the trench, revolver in hand, by how well it had held up, all things considered. It would still have offered a daunting fighting position, and some of the craters behind and in front of it were deep enough to have offered very effective improvised defensive points to support it.

His Glacierhearters had found some bodies and even a couple of wounded who might survive if 1st Company's healers got to them in time, but it was obvious the Temple Boys had pulled back from this trench, as well as the first, almost the instant the bombardment began. Well, that was only sensible. Ohygyns didn't even want to think about how *he* would have reacted with every heavy angle in the world dropping shells on top of *him*. But they hadn't moved back into it when the heavy shellfire lifted, either.

First Platoon had filtered out of the narrow lane the engineers had cleared, climbed cautiously across the shattered but still formidable abates . . . and found no one waiting for them. They'd been able to spread out along the abandoned trench, gathering their full strength without having to fight their way into it, and that had been a priceless boom. Now Ahbnair Mahkneel's 4th Platoon had come up to join them, Zheppsyn Mahkwaiyr's 5th Platoon was on Mahkneel's heels, and the trench was almost as defensible from the west as it had been from the east. Whatever else happened, letting the better part of two hundred Glacierhearters establish a secure foothold in their lines was a *serious* mistake on the Temple Boys' part, because they'd play hell pushing the company back out of it again.

Not going to happen, he thought coldly, listening to the background rumble of artillery and the quieter crumping sounds of smoke rounds landing less than three hundred yards in front of them. *Any pushing that gets done around here'll be going the* other *way!*

Major Makwyrt was coming up with the 5th, but he wasn't here yet. Besides, he wasn't the sort to reach for the reins even if he had been. This was Ohygyn's responsibility, and he checked his watch again. Timing wasn't really all that critical, given the nature of the assault plan and what must have already happened to the poor damned Temple Boys in front of them. The fact that it wasn't critical didn't mean that it wasn't *important*, however. Second and 3rd Companies were moving up to assault the sectors to either side of 1st Company's, and they were supposed to go in as close to together as they could. On the other hand, they were already six minutes past the designated time. Not surprisingly, given all the uncertainties involved in their approach. But he was here now, and *somebody* had to open the ball . . .

He closed the watch case with a snap, drew his revolver, made sure the speedloaders in the case on his left hip were secure, and nodded to Platoon Sergeant Ohtuhl.

"Go," he said simply, and Ohtuhl pulled the rocket's priming ring.

A standard flare pistol would almost certainly have gotten the job done, but Brigadier Raimahn wasn't a great believer in "*almost* certainly." He'd wanted something he was positive would be visible above the smoke and dust raised by the Charisian artillery and support squads, and the signal rocket soared upwards and burst at an altitude of several hundred feet.

▼   ▼   ▼

"Flare!" Sergeant Hahskyn snapped.

He swung his bracket-mounted double-glass quickly to take a bearing on it.

"It's one of ours," he said as the bearing confirmed it was in *Sahmantha*'s sector. "Orange, and right about in the middle of Golf Three!"

"Orange at Golf Three," Ahlgood confirmed, and Hahskyn nodded sharply.

The observer drew a deep breath. He believed the people who told him what he was about to do was actually safe—he really did! Any hydrogen that leaked would have risen well above the gondola. There wasn't *really* any chance of igniting the huge floating bomb above them. Really there wasn't.

He fought down the temptation to close his eyes and reached for the flare pistol.

A moment later, three orange flares arced away from *Sahmantha* and burst one-by-one, in a steady sequence . . . well over a hundred yards clear of the balloon. The artillery—and especially the mortars—responsible for suppressive fire on 1st Company's frontage took note, and the last of the explosive rounds whistled off, to be replaced solely by smoke.

▼   ▼   ▼

"*Heads up!*" someone screamed out of the smoke. "*Heads u—!*"

The words disappeared, but the scream continued, a wordless shriek of pain as the heretic hand-bomb exploded. Hyrbyrt Ahdymsyn shoved his whistle into his mouth and blew it shrilly.

"Stand to!" he bellowed. "*Stand to!*"

▼   ▼   ▼

Second Platoon swept forward with practiced lethality.

Each squad had broken down into three four-man teams, moving forward in the separate, coordinated, mutually supporting rushes which were the hallmark of Charisian small unit tactics. The first two teams in each squad consisted of three men with bayoneted pump shotguns and a dedicated grenadier, armed with a revolver and plenty of Mark 3 grenades, with the much more powerful Lywysite bursting charge. Each of his teammates carried a rucksack of additional grenades as well as his own ammunition. The third team in each squad had only two shotguns. The third man carried five satchel charges, each packed with just under twelve pounds of Lywysite . . . and the fourth carried an M97 flamethrower.

The M97—christened "Kau-yung's fire striker" by the troops—consisted of two steel tanks, one containing fifteen gallons of fire vine oil and one filled with compressed air, connected to a steel wand forty-two inches long by a flexible hose. With a full fuel tank, it weighed just over a hundred and twenty pounds, which wasn't an inconsiderable burden. To the men of the Glacierheart Brigade, however, it was worth every pound.

▼   ▼   ▼

Lieutenant Ahdymsyn clutched his St. Kylmahn rifle as he fought to sort out the savage, smoky confusion. More shouts and screams cut through the bedlam, and he heard the flatter, duller sound of Church hand-bombs, clearly distinct from the sharp, ear shattering blast of the new heretic hand-bombs. He also heard rifle shots coming from his men . . . and an impossibly rapid "boom-boom-boom" in reply. Not even a heretic bolt action rifle could be fired that quickly, but *something* out there in the smoke was—

The heretics were no longer dropping as many smoke shells onto 2nd Company's positions now that their own infantry was in contact, and the thinning smoke cleared for just a moment. In that window, Ahdymsyn could see for almost fifty yards, and his eyes widened as a belly-crawling heretic reached the sandbagged breastwork to his left and came up on one knee to shove the muzzle of a rifle that didn't look quite right through the firing slit. He squeezed the trigger, and Ahdymsyn's eyes widened in shock as he pulled the entire forestock of his rifle back, slid it forward once more, and fired again. And again!

The lieutenant's belly was a frozen knot as the sheer speed of the heretic's fire registered. But then another heretic rolled up beside the first one. His arm moved sharply, and both of them ducked back down to avoid the blast of one of their powerful hand-bombs as it blew back out the firing slit.

Even as the explosion roared, two more heretics, with the same bizarre-looking rifles, vaulted up and over the breastwork. They dropped into the trench behind it, and the earthen walls deadened the staccato booming of their weapons.

The heretic who'd thrown the grenade pushed up off his belly, and

Ahdymsyn squeezed his trigger. The grenadier flew sideways, his head a bloody ruin, and Lynyrd Owyn fired at the dead grenadier's squadmate. He hit the rifleman in the thigh, and the heretic rolled sideways and disappeared into one of the bombardment's shell craters.

Ahdymsyn opened the breech on his St. Kylmahn, stuffed another round into the chamber, capped the lock, and brought the rifle back up as another quartet of heretics came out of the smoke, directly in front of him and less than twenty yards away. His and Lynyrd's shots had marked their position for the heretics, and they were charging straight at him. He got the shot off and another heretic went down. Beside him, he was distantly aware of Sergeant Owyn raising his rifle while he began reloading his own with frantic haste, but somehow he knew there wouldn't be time.

There wasn't. The heretic behind the one he'd just wounded was carrying some sort of rod in his gloved hands. A bizarre, misshapen backpack swelled his silhouette grotesquely, and Ahdymsyn just had time to see the rod swinging in his direction.

The M97 flamethrower had a maximum range of fifty yards, twice the distance to Lieutenant Ahdymsyn firing slit, and the lieutenant's world dissolved in shrieking agony as the river of fire roared through the opening to envelop him.

.XII.
The Temple,
City of Zion,
The Temple Lands.

The quiet ticking of the corner clock was clear and sharp in the stillness of Rhobair Duchairn's office. The Church of God Awaiting's treasurer sat at his desk, expression grim as he worked through the latest reports from his logistics management staff. A ripple of chiming notes broke the stillness, and he frowned, then touched the God light on his desk, and the office door slid open to reveal one of his assistants.

"I apologize for interrupting you, Your Grace," the under-priest said, and while his tone was sincere it included none of the trepidation one of Zhaspahr Clyntahn's aides might have exhibited.

"I know you wouldn't have without a good reason, Father." Duchairn's response explained *why* that trepidation was so thoroughly absent.

"Vicar Allayn's here to see you. I told him you were studying the latest dispatches, and he indicated that those dispatches were part of what he wanted to discuss with you."

"I see. In that case, by all means, show the Vicar in, please."

"At once, Your Grace." The under-priest bowed and vanished. Less than a minute later, he was back, escorting Allayn Maigwair.

"The Captain General, Your Grace," he murmured, and disappeared once more. The door slid shut behind him, and Duchairn rose to clasp forearms.

"Don't tell me you've got even more bad news," he said by way of greeting.

"Actually, I do," the captain general growled, and Duchairn's eyebrows knitted. "I got a fresh dispatch from Rainbow Waters an hour ago." He shook his head, and his expression was grim. "It's gone from bad to worse. The center of the Talmar Line's gone, and Symkyn's finally moving from Aivahnstyn . . . and not south. He's driven what looks like an entire corps between Mahrlys and Lake Langhorne, and Eastshare's left a corps of his own on the high road about two hundred miles north of Mahrlys. Silver Moon's dug in to hold until relieved, but with Eastshare north of him and Symkyn pushing up from the west, I don't think there's much chance anyone's *going* to relieve him. Before the heretics pulverized a third of Brydgmyn's band at Talmar, I'd have expected Silver Moon to be able to hold for two months, at least, and probably for as much as four or five. Now?" He shook his head. "If the Charisians are serious, they can blast his entire position to bits in a couple of five-days. Even if they don't, there's no way he can fall back to rejoin Silken Hills *or* Gustyv. That's another twenty thousand men gone."

Duchairn stared at him in shock for several seconds, then shook his head like a man trying to shake off a punch to the jaw.

"I don't understand," he said. "This is your area, not mine, but I read the memos you and Rainbow Waters exchanged. I *know* how tough those positions are! How in God's name are the Charisians *doing* this? The troop movements, the advances across country, I can understand, but those defensive positions were . . . they were *formidable*, Allayn!"

"Yes, they were, and yes, they *are*," Maigwair replied. "And a big part of the Charisians' success so far's due to sheer surprise. It's pretty damned obvious they must've spent a lot of time thinking about exactly how to break through fortifications like the ones the Host's been building, too. But the bottom-line answer to your question is their frigging *balloons*."

"The balloons?" Duchairn repeated.

He'd been too deeply immersed in the frantic realignment of their logistic priorities in light of Eastshare's sudden appearance before Talmar to follow the dispatches about the newest Charisian innovation, as well. They'd clearly upset Maigwair deeply, but for the life of him, the treasurer still couldn't see what a novelty like a balloon had to do with military operations. He'd taken two of his nephews to a balloon ascent right here in Zion two years ago as a special treat and a way to forget, however briefly, the terrible reality of the Jihad. He had to admit it had been fascinating, but still. . . .

"Of course the balloons!" Maigwair snapped, much more sharply than he was in the habit of speaking to Duchairn these days.

"But . . . I don't understand," the treasurer said. "I want to, and I'm *trying* to, but how can a balloon be a *weapon*? I can see where one might be frightening to some Harchongese peasant. And I suppose one of them could give a general a peek at the other side's positions. But they can't stay up very long. The one I took the boys to see year before last could only stay up about twenty minutes, and it never got higher than a couple of hundred feet. I talked to one of the aeronauts afterward and he said the limitation's in the fuel. It's heavy, and a balloon can't carry enough fuel to heat enough air to stay up much longer than that. Theoretically one *could* stay up longer, but he said that the hot air doesn't generate enough 'lift' to support very much fuel."

"That may be true, but it also doesn't matter a good goddamn. They aren't *using* hot air."

"What?" Duchairn asked blankly. "They have to! The aeronaut I spoke to explained that a balloon is basically a chimney with a top that catches the hot smoke from the fire and rides it. There are a couple of passages in *Jwo-jeng* and *Sondheim* that talk about it, too. But all of them stress that it's the *heat* that makes the trapped air so much lighter."

"I know. I checked the same passages. But these aren't using hot air. I don't have the least damned clue what they *are* using, but there's no smoke from them, and no sign of flames. For that matter, there's no . . . flue, for want of a better word. There's just this . . . this great big *bag*, probably steel thistle silk. God knows the Charisians seem to be able to produce *miles* of the stuff! They're cigar-shaped, too, not round, and according to Rainbow Waters, they're ascending to as much as several *thousand* feet. And they're *staying* there, Rhobair. I can't begin to tell you how big an advantage that gives someone like Green Valley or Eastshare! If they park a couple of observers up *there*—" Maigwair waved a hand at the ceiling in a sort of distracted corkscrew motion "—they can see everything—*everything*—and drop reports to their own people on the ground!"

"Several thousand feet?" Duchairn repeated very carefully, and Maigwair jerked a sharp nod.

"At least. And I don't have any idea how damned far someone can see from that far up. Assuming anyone they can see looking down can see them by looking *up*, though, it's got to be at least fifty or sixty miles. That's an *awful* long way—more than two days' march, for infantry—and knowing where the other side is and what they're doing at any given moment is a tremendous advantage. It's like a fistfight when one fellow has a bag over his head!"

"Sweet Langhorne." Duchairn signed himself with Langhorne's scepter. "And none of Zhaspahr's spy reports warned you this was coming?!"

"Not one damned word about it," Maigwair confirmed grimly.

"How serious is it, really?"

"I don't know . . . yet," Maigwair said with bleak honesty. "From what's happened so far, I can already tell you it's going to be bad, though. Really bad. Bishop Militant Ahrnahld got precious few of his people out from Talmar—Holy Martyrs Division and Rakurai Division are basically just gone, and St. Byrtrym's down to less than half strength—so we don't have a lot in the way of firsthand reports. From the little we do have, the Charisians' artillery was even more effective than it's ever been before. For one thing, no one ever worried about hiding things on the ground from someone floating around in the air. That means their damned balloons could see *everything*, including angle-guns and rocket launchers hidden on reverse slopes, and tell their gunners where to find them. There's no reason they can't spot for their own artillery during an actual bombardment, either. That's an enormous tactical advantage, and it probably explains how they were able to punch out Talmar so quickly.

"On the other hand, no matter how well their aeronauts can see our troops and fortifications, their troops on the *ground* won't be able to see any farther than our boys can when they actually attack us. Without knowing how good the balloons' ability to communicate with troops who aren't directly below them might be, I can't estimate how much of a tactical effect they'll have at that point. But even if they don't have any effect at all—at that point—they'll still let their commanders pick the best spots to attack. And there's no way anyone on our side's going to deploy troops unobserved, no matter what the terrain's like, in daylight. That means effectively zero chance of hitting them by surprise. That's bad enough, but judgng from what happened at Talmar, they can finally take *full* advantage of their heavy angle-guns' range. If they can see forty or fifty miles, then they can damned well spot for artillery at four or five miles—or *ten* miles, for all I know!—no matter what kind of terrain obstacle's in the way."

"How many of these balloons has Rainbow Waters reported so far?"

"He can't say for certain," Maigwair said, and snorted with something like true humor when Duchairn looked at him incredulously. "You know how meticulously he differentiates between what he can and can't confirm, Rhobair! And apparently all their balloons are identical. So he can tell us how many he's seen at any given moment or on one sector of the front, but not how many the bastards have in total. He does have reports of at least five simultaneously in the air across sixty or seventy miles of his front, though."

Duchairn nodded his head sickly as understanding flowed through him at last. No wonder Maigwair was so worried. The sophistication of the Charisians' artillery had always been one of their deadliest advantages. He doubted he could fully appreciate the consequences of the new balloons, even after the other vicar's explanation, but the mere thought of the artillery capabilities Maigwair had just sketched out was enough to freeze his blood.

"I hope you don't have any other surprises up the sleeve of your cassock," he said after a moment.

"Actually, I do," Maigwair said flatly. "That's the real reason I came to see you. If you were still wondering if the heretics meant to throw their main weight south, you can stop. Rainbow Waters' forward commander at Ayaltyn's come under heavy artillery fire . . . and he's got at least two or three more frigging Shan-wei-damned balloons floating in *his* sky, too. And Rainbow Waters just got a dispatch from his pickets on the Hildermoss. It would appear the Charisians have the locks at Darailys back in service."

"What do you mean?" Duchairn asked sharply.

"I mean there are at least five of their ironclads steaming upriver with 'dozens'—that's the local commander's number—of steam-powered tugs towing barges behind them. Whether they're stuffed with troops or 'just' supplies, that's really bad news for Rainbow Waters' left flank. Especially with Green Valley finally starting to move *south* of Cat-Lizard Lake."

"My God," Duchairn said, his face pale, and Maigwair shrugged.

"It's not like we haven't seen this coming, Rhobair. Oh, we didn't have a clue about the damned *balloons*, but we always knew they'd hit us and eventually hit us hard. The way they tricked us into focusing on the south makes it a lot worse, but Rainbow Waters still has a *very* strong position on a relatively narrow front north of the Great Tarikah Forest. He's got good east-west roads *and* the canal behind him if he's forced to give ground, too. I know Zhaspahr plans on putting Rychtyr's head on a stick, but the man's tactics against Hanth were brilliant, and Rainbow Waters is at least that good and has a hell of a lot more to work with. The front may be *breaking*, but it doesn't have to collapse unless we give him and Gustyv another of Zhaspahr's 'no retreat' orders."

He met the treasurer's eyes, and the ticking of the clock was deafening.

"That's the real reason I'm here," he said quietly. "You and I had better have a brief discussion before our meeting with Zhaspahr. And Zahmsyn, of course," he added as an afterthought. "He's going to be in full bore frothing mode over Talmar, *especially* after he hears about the frigging 'demonic' balloons. The news about Green Valley and the ironclads on the Hildermoss'll only make that worse, and we need to be sure we're both on the same page if we're going to keep him from doing something else outstandingly stupid."

Maigwair's eyes were worried and his tone was grim, but he sounded far from defeated, Duchairn noted. Given that lack of defeat, and assuming it was genuine, then the two of them might not be on the same page after all.

"You know he has to have eyes in my staff and that those eyes will tell him you and I are conferring before the meeting," he pointed out.

"He doesn't need any reports that we're *actually* discussing this before the meeting, and you know it. By now he automatically assumes you and I are conniving behind his back any time some less than cheerful bit of news arrives, whatever his spies tell him! If they don't report we're doing it, it's only because we've done better than usual at sneaking around and hiding it."

Now *there*, Duchairn thought, he had a point.

"You're probably right," he sighed, and pointed at the comfortable chair which was Maigwair's usual choice. "So, since he's going to assume we're plotting anyway, I suppose we might as well get to it. Exactly what's on that 'same page' in your thinking?"

"Well, the first thing—"

▼　　▼　　▼

"I thought you'd assured us Walkyr was the man for this command, Allayn," Zhaspahr Clyntahn said sourly.

"I told you he was at least as good as any other commander we might have assigned and that Earl Rainbow Waters specifically requested him," Maigwair corrected in a cool tone. "Having said that, however, yes. I *did* think he was the best man for the command, and nothing that's happened has changed my opinion."

"Then you may be even more incompetent than I *thought!*" Clyntahn snarled. "The man's fighting from fortified positions against enemies coming at him in the open and he's *still* telling us he'll have to retreat!"

"That sort of thing happens when the other side can float around up in the sky and see every damned thing you do on the ground," Maigwair riposted. "And as if that weren't bad enough, a third of his troops—and more like *two*-thirds of his artillery—hadn't arrived when the enemy attacked. Under the circumstances, frankly, I'm amazed he hasn't *already* retreated! That *is* covered in the strategy Earl Rainbow Waters put together—and explained to all of us in his dispatches—when we pulled Silken Hills off the Talmar Front and sent him south."

"Those arrangements were part of Rainbow Waters' *interim* plans!" the Grand Inquisitor shot back. "I didn't see anything in there about running the hell away now that Walkyr's had time to settle into those positions!"

"He hasn't *had* a whole lot of time to settle in," Maigwair pointed out. "For that matter, half his band commanders have had only a few months to learn how to command and handle their troops. Even the best musician's music depends on how well tuned his instrument is, you know."

"What a wonderful analogy!" Clyntahn sneered. "How long did you spend thinking it up before you just tossed it off?"

Maigwair only gazed at him levelly, disdaining any response and Clyntahn's already angry expression grew even tighter.

"Zhaspahr, Earl Rainbow Waters' dispatches all emphasize how hard Archbishop Militant Gustyv and his men are fighting for every inch of ground," Duchairn said. "They simply don't have enough experienced men and enough artillery to hold their current positions—especially with these new balloons that nobody warned him might be coming—" he was very careful about the emphasis he didn't put on the last six words, but Clyntahn's eyes glittered with rage as he continued calmly "—looking down on him. That's why he's requested Rainbow Waters' permission to begin an orderly withdrawal to the positions at Salyk."

"And what the hell makes you think he'll stand and fight *there?*"

"He's fighting hard right this minute, Zhaspahr," Duchairn said more sharply, "and so far his troops' fighting spirit seems to be holding. Frankly, I'm deeply impressed by that, especially given the way the heretics' new heavy angles are pounding them. But they've punched a five-mile hole right through the center of his line at Talmar. They're pushing troops through it this very minute, and those troops are flanking his main positions. It's like driving a splitting wedge into a log. Their advance is driving his men on either side of the hole farther and farther apart. At the moment, Brydgmyn's still holding a line ahead of them with Holy Langhorne Band's remnants and four divisions from the Army's reserve—it's shaky as hell, but it's there—and it's preventing the heretics from hooking around into the rear of the divisions on either side of the break. But that line's being forced to give ground. It's retreating slowly, for now, but it's under enormous pressure and the pressure's getting worse. Eventually, it's gong to break. And in the meantime, the heretic guns are going right on chewing the hell out of the troops on either side of their salient. Walkyr needs to get those men out of their trenches and dugouts before they turn into deathtraps, and Brydgmyn needs to get his people out of artillery range—and out of sight of those damned balloons—while he reorganizes."

"They'll only follow him up and hit him again," Clyntahn pointed out nastily, once again choosing not to directly address the matter of the balloons none of the Inquisition's agents had seen coming.

"Of course they will," Maigwair agreed. "And they'll pay in blood for every mile . . . *if* we let him retreat in good order while his men are still prepared to fight an effective delaying action. If Walkyr just sits there, 'standing his ground,' the way Kaitswyrth did at Aivahnstyn, we'll lose every soldier he has. His center's already collapsed; Holy Langhorne Band is hanging on by its fingernails And—" he added bitterly "—only because its present line seems to be out of range of the heavy angles . . . for now. That's going to change, though, and if we don't let him plan for an orderly retreat now, before he comes under the same sort of fire that smashed Talmar, we'll be lucky if *any* of his units get out. Brydgmyn's not proposing to run the hell away, Zhaspahr, and neither is Walkyr! They only want authorization to fall back on their terms, at *their* pace. There are ninety thousand men in the Talmar Line—or there *were*. Brydgmyn's already lost something like ten thousand of them. If he's ordered to hold his ground at any cost, that lets the heretics dictate everything that happens. At that point, Walkyr'll be lucky to get twenty thousand back . . . and that twenty thousand will be as brutalized and demoralized as the survivors of the Army of Glacierheart."

Fresh fury flashed in Clyntahn's eyes at the reference to Cahnyr Kaitswyrth, but he didn't fire back instantly. It was remotely possible that was because even he could recognize the simple truth of Maigwair's statement, Duchairn reflected. Not *likely*, perhaps, but possible.

"If Walkyr's so damned understrength and he's got so few of his frigging guns, what the fuck have the two of *you* been doing?" the Grand Inquisitor demanded instead. "What about all those thousands of artillery pieces both of you were promising us over the winter?!"

"Quite a few of them are at the front shooting at the heretics right this minute!" Duchairn said much more sharply than he normally addressed Clyntahn when the Grand Inquisitor was clearly working himself into a full-fledged fury. "More of them are strung out along the Holy Langhorne, though. And the reason they are is that we moved Silken Hills south—based primarily on intelligence your 'Sword Rakurai' provided—and then the heretic navy completely closed the Gulf of Dohlar. According to the last report I've received—it's the better part of a five-day old, thanks to the fact that it had to be relayed around several breaks in the semaphore chain—there are over four thousand field guns, two hundred heavy angle-guns, and more than ninety thousand rifles in South Harchong waiting to be shipped to the front . . . except that the heretic navy's in the way!"

Clyntahn glared at him, and Duchairn braced internally for yet another diatribe against Dohlar and the Earl of Thirsk, but he also continued speaking.

"There were other factors involved, of course. But it just wasn't possible to get all of the Archbishop Militant's men and artillery to the front while meeting Silken Hills' needs as he redeployed. And that was made *enormously* more complicated by the loss of South Harchong's production and our own inability to ship men and matériel from the Malansath Bight to the Bay of Bess and then up the Dairnyth-Alyksberg Canal. Allayn and I—and every man on our combined staffs—have had to juggle priorities just get enough *food* to the front! I don't have the complete numbers in front of me, but there are at least—*at least*, Zhaspahr—eighteen hundred artillery pieces and almost as many rocket launchers stuck along the Holy Langhorne, still trying to get forward. And all of those weapons were already supposed to be in Walkyr's hands!"

Clyntahn's glare could have ignited a condemned heretic's pyre, but then he drew a deep breath and shoved himself farther back into his chair.

"If Walkyr can fall *back*, why can't Rainbow Waters move troops *up* from his own reserve to support him where he is, instead?" His eyes were still fiery, but his tone actually approached one of reason.

"The north-south road net—such as it is—behind the Mighty Host's front isn't good." Maigwair's own tone was less confrontational as if in recognition of Clyntahn's version of what passed for self-restraint. "Rainbow Waters spent a lot of time over the winter and spring improving it as much as he could, but there are limits to what engineers can do in a high northern winter. We've had a little experience of our own with that right here in Zion, you know!"

His grimace was actually close to a smile, but it faded quickly.

"He could move troops and supplies south, but it's unlikely he could move enough of them rapidly enough to make much difference. It would actually be better to leave the roads behind the Army of the Center clear for it to fall back in an orderly fashion in case Walkyr has to retreat from Salyk than to clog them with troops and wagon trains that can't get there in time to make a difference anyway.

"But that's only part of Rainbow Waters' problem. He's coming under increasingly heavy pressure *north* of the Tarikah Forest, too.

"After Green Valley's performance last winter, I don't think anyone wants to suggest he's less competent than Eastshare, and it looks like he pushed mounted infantry cross country to cut the roads west of Ayaltyn. They were on the road before anyone realized what he was up to—I imagine those damned balloons helped him choose the best routes for his advance—and that means he's effectively surrounded Lord of Foot Morning Star's brigade. That's another five thousand men gone, and the heretic thrust coming up the North Hildermoss will be past Mardahs within the five-day. It may be headed for Cat-Lizard Lake to reinforce Green Valley, but I don't think so. I think it's headed for Sanjhys, and with six or seven ironclads to lead the advance and shoot a way through any opposition, they'll damned well get there. Rainbow Waters has planted sea-bombs and obstructed the river as thoroughly as he can, but sea-bombs are less reliable than land-bombs and there are no locks between them and Sanjhys.

"That means the troop strength coming upriver will get at least as far as Sanjhys before it's forced to come ashore. With Green Valley already past Ayaltyn and the river ironclads no more than a few days from Sanjhys, it looks like Rainbow Waters is going to need all of his reserve on his northern flank really soon. According to his last dispatch, he's already detached one band from his reserve—that's three Harchongese brigades, or about ten thousand men—to support Gustyv. They're moving as quickly as they can, but, frankly, it's unlikely they'll reach him in time to change the situation south of Salyk. Besides, he's worried about how quiet his own front's been *south* of Ayaltyn. We've confirmed that it's Eastshare's Army of Westmarch at Talmar, and we've identified at least one corps from their Army of the Daivyn at Marylys. But there's still no sign of Stohnar or the rest of Symkyn's army. For that matter, the only heretics we've actually seen on the ground in the Tymkyn Gap so far appear to be light infantry."

" 'Light infantry'?" Clyntahn pounced on Maigwair's final sentence. "What do you mean 'light infantry'?"

"I mean we haven't seen any of their mounted infantry, we haven't seen any of the Siddarmarkians that were transferred to High Mount's command, and aside from a few battalion-level attacks to take out advanced observation posts and screening positions, he hasn't launched a single assault." Maigwair shrugged. "I'm not prepared to say he won't, but, to be honest, I think we've been played by the heretics' spymasters, Zhaspahr."

"Meaning what?" Clyntahn's eyes were slitted, his expression hard.

"Meaning that, coupled with how hard Eastshare's hit Talmar and the fact that Silken Hills hasn't seen a single one of their new balloons anywhere near the Tymkyn Gap, I've come to the conclusion they deliberately fed us false information to pull Silken Hills south, knowing we'd have to replace him with our own troops in the center."

Maigwair shrugged, his own expression almost as bitter as Clyntahn's.

"They know our new divisions can't have many veterans after last year and that they haven't had as long to train as Rainbow Waters' Harchongians," he continued. "So if they did deliberately draw us into deploying our troops to hold the central part of the front, it was because that's where they *really* plan to break it. I can't prove that yet, but it sure as hell *looks* like what's happening. If the strength estimates from Rainbow Waters' forward commanders are anywhere near accurate, Green Valley's got somewhere around a hundred thousand men, and this army coming up the Hildermoss is probably another eighty or ninety thousand men strong. That's a heavy enough attack it may very well be designed to break through on its own, but it could also be intended to pin Rainbow Waters' left while they punch through the Army of the Center and swing up behind him from the south.

"According to your inquisitors' best estimates—and understand that my people's estimates are very close to yours—the heretics have a combined strength of seven or eight hundred thousand men deployed in western Siddarmark, not counting artillery or transport battalions. If Green Valley has—or is about to have—somewhere around two hundred thousand of them, and if Eastshare has about the same number, that still leaves at least another three hundred thousand they haven't committed yet. At the moment, I'm pretty damned nervous about where those three hundred thousand men are and what *they're* planning to do."

Clyntahn's face had turned to stone while Maigwair was speaking. It was obvious he didn't care for the notion that Charis and Siddarmark might have deceived him so thoroughly.

"I have to agree with Allayn and Rainbow Waters, Zhaspahr," Duchairn said quietly. "I don't know whether the heretics managed to fool us or whether they simply realized what we were doing—we've had ample proof of how good their spies are—and decided to take advantage of it." Clyntahn looked at him, and the treasurer shrugged. "As Allayn's just pointed out, whether we want to admit it or not, the Harchongians are likely to be tougher than our new divisions. If their spies told them we'd started moving Harchongese troops south—and replacing them with the Army of God in the center—they may have decided to switch their own plans and hit us there rather than carry through with their original intentions in the south. In a lot of ways, it doesn't really matter which it was. What *matters* is that it appears to be what they're actually *doing*."

He waited, hoping the combination of logic and the sop to Clyntahn's pride might carry the day. Personally, he was convinced Maigwair was right; the Charisians and Siddarmarkians had played them from the beginning. But if Clyntahn wanted to believe they'd changed strategies in response to his brilliant intelligence coup, that was fine with Duchairn . . . as long as he was willing to listen to the voice of sanity afterward.

"If that's their plan, then surely it's more important than ever for Walkyr to hold his positions as far east—and south—as possible to protect Rainbow Waters' right flank," Clyntahn replied after several seconds.

"If he *can*, then, yes," Maigwair agreed. "But if he *can't*, it becomes even more important to authorize him to retreat, because Rainbow Waters will need every man if the heretics manage to turn this into a mobile battle. That would've been true under any circumstances, given their advantages in mounted infantry. If their balloons are mobile enough to keep up with their mounted infantry, it's going to be even worse, though. That's why we can't afford to lose the ninety thousand men spread out between Talmar and Salyk. We just can't."

Maigwair leaned back in his chair, bracing his forearms on the armrests, and his expression was very serious as he met Clyntahn's eyes.

"This is almost certainly the decisive campaign, Zhaspahr," he said quietly. "If we lose it, then from a military perspective, we also lose the Jihad. I'm not going to tell you God and the Archangels can't still show us a road to victory, because if They choose to do that, then of course They can. But if the heretics succeed in destroying or crippling the Mighty Host and the Army of the Center, any road They show us will have to rely on something besides our military capabilities. My men—*our* men—and Rainbow Waters' Harchongians are fighting hard. I believe they'll continue to fight just as hard for every scrap of ground. But if we lose *them*, we lose the Jihad. That's why our commanders at the front *have* to have the flexibility to make strategic withdrawals if that's what it takes to avoid their troops' destruction."

Clyntahn's eyes met his across the conference table, and it was very, very quiet in the luxuriously furnished chamber.

JULY

YEAR OF GOD 898

✦

.I.

Baron Green Valley's HQ Wagon,
70 Miles South of Vekhair,
The Tairyn River Line,
and
23rd Division Headquarters,
50 miles South of Lake City,
Tarikah Province,
Republic of Siddarmark.

"Come on in, Ahrtymys," Baron Green Valley invited as General Ohanlyn climbed the steps into his command trailer.

The dragon-drawn vehicle was fifty feet long and nine feet wide, which provided room for a small sleeping compartment at one end, a slightly larger working office, and a very large map compartment with working space for staffers and clerks. It provided a weather-proof mobile headquarters that was far more efficient than anything Green Valley had possessed before, and it was also one more sign of the Imperial Charisian Army's steadily growing sophistication.

Now he led the way across the map compartment where his staff was laying out the latest information into the greater privacy of his office with Captain Slokym at their heels.

"Have a seat," the baron invited, waving at a chair as he unbuckled his pistol belt and hung it on the rack in one corner. "See about finding us something to eat, Bryahn," he continued to Slokym. "I'm pretty sure the General and I will be having a working supper."

"Yes, My Lord." Slokym saluted, then withdrew, closing the door behind him, while Ohanlyn accepted Green Valley's invitation and seated himself. The baron stepped past him and settled gratefully into the custom-made swivel chair behind his desk and opened the bottom desk drawer. He extracted a bottle of Chisholmian whiskey and two glasses and poured generously.

"The good stuff," he said, shoving one towards his subordinate, and Ohanlyn chuckled. Then his eyebrows rose after he'd sipped.

"It *is* good," he said.

"*Seijin* Merlin sent it to me." Green Valley took a sip of his own. "The man's unnaturally good at just about everything, even picking whiskeys."

"And thank God for him," Ohanlyn said sincerely.

Green Valley nodded soberly and the truth was that Ahrtymys Ohanlyn knew far more about Merlin Athrawes' contributions to Charis than most people outside the inner circle would ever suspect. At forty-two, he was a little older than Green Valley, and he'd been a protégé and junior colleague of Doctor Rahzhyr Mahklyn at the Royal Collegewhen *Seijin* Merlin appeared in Tellesberg. As such, he knew the source of the new "arabic numerals," and he knew Merlin had been instrumental—although even he didn't realize quite *how* instrumental—in many of Mahklyn's subsequent brilliant theoretical breakthroughs.

He'd also helped refine quite a few of those breakthroughs, including the invention of the slide rule. He'd gone on to assist Ahlfryd Hyndryk and Ahldahs Rahzwail in the creation of the ICA artillery's indirect fire techniques and personally proposed the special-purpose slide rules, matched to the ballistic performance of each mark and model of gun. And if there were times Green Valley thought Ohanlyn really should have been assigned to Eastshare or High Mount, given the fact that he probably understood the new artillery even better than Ohanlyn did, he wasn't even tempted to give him up.

"So," he said now, putting down the whiskey glass and tipping back in his chair as he found his pipe and began filling it, "how bad is it?"

"I wouldn't say it was *bad*, My Lord," Ohanlyn said thoughtfully, leaning back with his own whiskey glass. "It's just . . . less *good* than it was."

That was certainly one way to put it, Green Valley reflected. His Army of Tarikah had pushed Rainbow Waters' St. Bahzlyr Band back for over a hundred miles since launching its offensive. In fact, if he counted Ayaltyn, he'd driven Lord of Horse Yellow Sky's band west for well over a hundred and *seventy* miles. Rainbow Waters had never intended to hold Ayaltyn, however. Lord of Foot Morning Star's brigade of Yellow Sky's 23rd Division had been supposed to fall back slowly, both to delay Green Valley while the Mighty Host's main positions prepared for attack and—hopefully—to encourage Green Valley to demonstrate any new tricks the Allies might have come up with before the true grapple. Unfortunately for Rainbow Waters' hopes, the Army of Tarikah's engineers had thrown no less than four pontoon bridges across the Hildermoss River south of Ayaltyn in a single, moonless night. Two full brigades of mounted infantry had crossed them just before dawn, advanced twenty miles, then swung north to cut the Ayaltyn-Lake City High Road west of the city. Between them, they'd outnumbered Morning Star's single brigade almost four to one, and they'd been accompanied by both their organic mortar squads and four batteries each of the new 4-inch breech-loading field guns. They'd closed the mouth of the sack, leaving no way for the lord of foot to escape, and Ohanlyn's gun dogs had pulverized Morning Star's supporting artillery before the infantry assaulted.

There'd never been any doubt about what was going to happen then, but the Harchongians' stubborn refusal to surrender had been an ominous indicator of the Mighty Host's morale. Green Valley's infantry had been forced to clear Morning Star's fortifications with flamethrowers and satchel charges literally bunker-by-bunker, and he'd lost almost six hundred men in the process. That was only about thirteen percent of the Harchongese casualties, but he'd suffered them against a completely isolated position, stripped of all long-range artillery support, while his own artillery and assault columns had enjoyed the advantage of aerial spotting. He hadn't really wanted to think about what was likely to happen once he came up against the main Harchongese positions.

He'd done that now, and while it hadn't been quite as painful as he'd feared it would after the Ayaltyn experience, it had been quite painful enough.

"It's mostly just that Rainbow Waters is a fast learner, My Lord," Ohanlyn continued. "Worse, it looks like he's encouraged a lot of his senior officers to be fast learners, too. They've figured out a lot of the implications of the Balloon Corps, and they're putting what they've deduced to good effect."

Green Valley nodded gravely. He already knew pretty much everything Ohanlyn was about to tell him, but he couldn't have explained how he'd come by that knowledge. So it was a good thing that Ohanlyn, one of the smartest people he'd ever met, was about to hand him a plausible source for the knowledge he already possessed.

"I don't know where they got it, although if I had to guess, Rainbow Waters or Zhyngbau probably requisitioned it from the Wing Lakes' fishing fleet," the artillerist continued, "but they've come up with an awful lot of netting. They're using it to help hide their angle-guns. It looks like they're moving the guns only under cover of darkness, whenever they can, and stringing the netting across their new positions. Then they cover it with cut branches, grass, anything to make it blend into the background." He shrugged. "Nobody ever had balloons before, so no one ever needed that kind of over-head concealment. I could wish it had taken these people a little longer to come up with it, though."

"You and me both," Green Valley agreed sourly.

"They're hiding their field guns better, too," Ohanlyn continued after a thoughtful sip of whiskey. "They were already putting them under over-head cover to protect them from our angles, but they were more concerned with stacking the sandbags high than with trying to *hide* them. Now they're piling more cut greenery across them, wherever that works. Where it doesn't, it looks like they're stretching tarps and then covering them with dirt. Or just stacking the dirt without the tarps, when they have time." He shrugged. "That gives them both the concealment and better cover, and they're pretty careful about fairing the contours. They're not giving my boys in the baskets a lot of sharp angles and vertical shadows. My observers're still spotting a lot of them, but there's a big difference between 'a lot' and 'all.'"

Green Valley nodded again. Ohanlyn was certainly right about the speed with which the Harchongians learned. The first few times they'd tried to hide their dug-in field guns under canvas, they'd simply draped the tarps across them. That hadn't helped as much as they'd obviously hoped it would, so they'd begun using larger tarpaulins and stretching them farther, over irregularly rounded forms, before they applied the dirt to blend them into the background.

"Frankly, I'm less worried about the field guns than the frigging rocket launchers," Ohanlyn said much more grimly. "That was really ugly Monday. We shouldn't have let it happen."

"Every so often the other side gets something right, Ahrtymys," Green Valley said. "And in Rainbow Waters' case, that's going to happen a lot more often than we like. You and your gun dogs—and your balloons—are saving a lot of lives, and I know you wish you could save *all* of them, but you can't."

Ohanlyn stared down into his whiskey for several seconds. Green Valley knew exactly what he was seeing, and it wasn't a glass of whiskey. It was the torn and mangled bodies of a pair of infantry battalions which had been caught on their approach march by a Harchongese rocket bombardment. Between them, they lost almost seven hundred men, better than thirty percent of their roster strength, and lucky it hadn't been worse.

"How did it happen?" the baron asked quietly. "I've read Colonel Tymyns' report, but I'm still not clear on the details."

"The Harchongians are hiding those damned mobile rocket launchers of theirs under tarps and netting, too," Ohanlyn replied. "It's a lot easier to hide converted freight wagons than it is to hide angle-guns, and they're keeping them covered up until they need them. I'm pretty sure they're stretching the tarps high enough off the ground for the launcher crews to get under them and aim the damned things before they ever remove their camouflage. Then they whip the tarpaulins off, fire the rockets, and run for their own trenches." He shrugged. "What's worst about it is that my boys in the balloons can see *exactly* what they're doing but there isn't enough time to get word to our artillery to take the launchers under fire before they get the rockets away. We're demolishing every launcher they show us, but we're getting too many of them after the fact, and, frankly, I don't see a good way to stop this particular tactic."

"I don't either," Green Valley said after a moment, and the hell of it was that he didn't. "I guess the best we can do is try to make it harder for them to spot us on the approach. More smoke shells, maybe. And I've already put out the word that I want as many approach marches as possible made under cover of darkness. I know nights aren't very long, this time of year, but if the bastards on the other side're managing to move artillery and dig it back in between dusk and dawn, we should at least be able to move our troops up to their jumpoff points while they're doing it."

"Yes, My Lord."

"Are they applying this . . . overhead awareness of theirs to other aspects of their positions?"

"They're trying to, but it's a lot harder to hide a trench line." Ohanlyn smiled thinly. "They may be able to conceal individual strong points, but we know where they are well enough to strip away any camouflage with our initial bombardment."

"Good." Green Valley nodded in satisfaction, then let his chair come upright and pulled a folder out of the upper drawer of his desk.

"All right, two things. One is that two Victory ships started offloading in Rainshair yesterday, and the river barges are headed this way now. The first of the new shells should arrive sometime five-day after next." Ohanlyn's eyes widened and Green Valley smiled as the artillerist sat suddenly straighter. "Doctor Lywys and Duke Delthak have done us proud. They've got them into genuine *volume* production, and they held the initial deliveries to make sure you and I didn't get the chance to give away the secret by using a handful here and a handful over there just because we had 'em. There's twenty thousand *tons* of them coming up the New Northland Canal—probably enough for that fire plan you've been working on for so long."

"*Outstanding*, My Lord!" Ohanlyn's eyes were positively glowing now, and his smile would have done any kraken proud. "I've been looking forward to that for what seems like forever!"

"I know you have, but we can't take the pressure off them in the meantime," Green Valley cautioned, "so here's what I've got in mind for Thursday." He pulled a thick sheaf of typescript from the folder and passed it across. "Let's take a look at the objectives and kick around the best use of your medium angles. It occurred to me that—"

▼ ▼ ▼

"I'll be damned. You guys're still here?"

Corporal Jwaohyn Baozhi looked up as Sergeant Huzhyn rolled into 5th Section's fighting position overlooking the Tairyn River.

"Glad to see you, too, Sarge!" he said as Huzhyn slid to the bottom of the crater, and it was true. Third Platoon's senior noncom was probably the most experienced—and competent—sergeant in the entire 4th Company, and he knew how to lead, not drive. That was something a lot of Harchongese noncoms still had a little trouble with, but Huzhyn had taught the platoon's corporals—including one Jwaohyn Baozhi—to do the same thing.

"Thought I'd come check up on you," the sergeant replied as five more men scrambled down after him. "You get those rockets?"

"Yep. Right there." The corporal pointed to the corner of the position.

"Good. And I suppose you know what to do with them?"

"Trust me, we've got it straight, Sarge."

"Good," Huzhyn said again, and looked around the noisome hole approvingly. "Smells like a latrine in here, but it's a damned good position," he observed, and it was.

The heretic artillery had produced a *lot* of large craters over the past five-day or so, and Baozhi and his section had spent an entire night covering one of them over with logs and a five-foot-deep pile of sandbags. They'd left a ten-inch gap at the bottom, all the way around, giving them a three-hundred-sixty-degree field of fire, and then shoveled dirt over the sandbags to hide their angularity. Its height on the bank gave clear lines of fire all the way down to the river's edge—and, for that matter, let them drop hand-bombs right onto the heretics' heads when they got close—and whenever the heretic smoke shells let up, they could see a good thousand yards back on the eastern bank. That was why the artillery had provided them with the half-dozen signal rockets to send up the next time the heretics got ready to cross . . . assuming the range was clear enough for Baozhi's section to see them assembling, at least. Whether there'd still be any artillery to respond to those rockets was an open question, but if there was. . . .

"Figured you boys were probably getting a little low out here at the sharp end," the sergeant continued. A smile creased his dirty face, and he slipped the heavy rucksack off his back. He heaved it across to Baozhi, who staggered as he caught it; the thing had to weigh at least sixty or seventy pounds. "Two of 'em are rifle ammunition," he said, jerking a thumb at the equally heavy rucks the other men with him were shedding with obvious relief. "This one and those two—" he indicated the two biggest and strongest carriers "—are hand-bombs."

"We can use them," Baozhi said grimly while heretic bullets slapped into the face of the fighting position like slow, erratic hail. "Tried us again about an hour ago. I figure we'll see them again sometime around sunset. Maybe sooner. We lost Dyzhyng last time."

He jerked his head at the body lying in the corner of the position, its face covered by a scrap of blanket, and Huzhyn grimaced.

"Sorry to hear that. Seems like it's always the good ones, doesn't it?"

"Yeah." Baozhi shook his head. "Damned freak thing, too. Bullet came in through the firing slit, hit something, and ricocheted. Hit him in the back of the neck, right below the helmet." The corporal shook his head again. "Doubt he even realized he was dead before he reported in to Langhorne."

"Best way to go." Huzhyn looked around, listening to the tempo of incoming fire, and pursed his lips. "How are you boys fixed for water and rations?"

"We're good for food, but if you could get a water party up, we're down to about a half canteen each. Kind of . . . irritating with the river so close and all."

"See what I can do," Huzhyn promised, "but it'll probably be after dark. Lot of bullets flying around right now."

"Whenever you can," Baozhi agreed, not commenting on the fact that Huzhyn had just come through that "lot of bullets" and was about to go back out into it.

"Later, then," the platoon sergeant said, jerking his head to gather up his ammo carriers, then climbed back up and out and headed for the rear once more.

Baozhi watched them go, then crossed to the firing slit again and stood at Private Gangzhi's shoulder to peer out it. He supposed it didn't really matter—it seemed unlikely that even one of the heretic snipers could actually *see* him—but he was always careful to stay to one side of the slit. The heretics who could see it tended to put their rounds right down the middle.

The ground between their position and the river had been torn and churned into a blasted, cratered wasteland, dotted with the splintered remains of trees, by heretic artillery—and by their own, he reflected. Not that he expected a lot more friendly support. The heretics' artillery was more accurate than the Mighty Host's at the best of times; at the *worst* of times, their gunners seemed capable of putting a shell into a specific five-gallon bucket, and they were really, really good at counter battery. Baozhi's ten-man section was down to only seven, now that they'd lost Fynghai Dyzhyng, but he knew his men were still better off than the IHA's artillerists, especially now that the heretics had their damned balloons.

Baozhi had listened carefully when Captain of Spears Zhwyailyn explained that the balloons weren't really demonic. He believed the company XO had been telling him the truth . . . at least as much of it as Zhwyailyn knew, anyway. He would have found the explanation more convincing, however, if the captain of spears had been able to explain exactly how the monstrous things managed to stay up there if they *weren't* demonically empowered. He would have liked explanations for quite a few of the heretics' innovations, to be honest, but the balloons were front and center of his concerns at the moment. Without them, the heretics would still be east of St. Tailar instead of pushing their way across the Tairyn River.

Baozhi was happy enough to be shut of St. Tailar. He was as devout as the next man, but the endless expanse of unmarked mass graves, stretching literally for miles around the ruins of the concentration camp the Inquisition had built on the town's site, had been enough to give him nightmares, especially when the artillery began ripping those graves open. The bones and the bodies—high northern winters tended to slow decay, and the stench of bodies and body parts, making up for that delay under the hot July sun—had been like a curse from the un-restful dead. He couldn't truly believe all those people, especially the children who'd been exhumed by the terrible thunder of the shells, had been heretics. Surely not *all* of them—not the *kids!* That was the sort of thought it was unwise to voice where the Inquisition might hear, but he was pretty sure he wasn't the only one who'd thought it.

Yet however glad he might have been to leave St. Tailar behind, he was a lot less happy about how far the heretics' Army of Tarikah had driven the St. Bahzlyr Band since it launched its offensive. The heretics' new super-heavy angle-guns seemed to be slower-moving than the rest of their artillery, but the lighter angles—and their own version of Mother Church's rocket launchers—seemed to keep right up with their mounted infantry.

They hadn't had it all their own way, at first, because Lord of Horse Yellow Sky, St. Bahzlyr's commander, had ordered his artillerists to survey every suitable artillery position between Ayaltyn and his main forward defense line. His plans had envisioned counterattacking to relieve Ayaltyn if it was attacked, and he'd wanted to know where to put his guns when he did. The speed with which Green Valley had enveloped Baron Morning Star's brigade had prevented that, but his gunners' surveys had helped them predict the firing positions the heretic artillery was most likely to choose coming west. Once it became obvious no counterattack could save Morning Star—that, instead, the heretics would be calling on the band's main positions very soon—his batteries had pre-registered their guns on as many of those points as lay within their range. They couldn't actually see most of them when the heretics opened fire on the main defensive line, but they'd counter batteried with blind fire, using the previously recorded elevations and deflections. They'd scored in at least one case, too, silencing a pair of heretic batteries within a half hour of their opening fire. But their triumph had been short-lived. The heretic angles, guided by two of their balloons, had started eliminating St. Bahzlyr's guns with steady, dreadful precision.

And that was what had happened again and again over the last several five-days. Each time the heretics bounded forward, the out-ranged and out-gunned Harchongese angle-guns had a fleeting opportunity to inflict casualties before they were hunted down by the heretics' aerial spies and subjected to a deadly cascade of counter battery fire. By now, the Mighty Host's angle-gun crews had started limbering their guns after firing only a dozen shells and attempting to withdraw before the heretics' counterfire came down upon them.

Sometimes, it even worked.

Baozhi suspected the new camouflage schemes were working better for the field guns and the rocket launchers, so 4th Company might actually get some effective fire support next time the heretics tried to cross the ford in front of it. For a while, at least. Until the combination of balloons and angle-guns crushed the Harchongese batteries again. The rocket launchers could be devastating when they actually got their rockets off, but the smaller, portable infantry angles were really the most effective. They were far smaller, which probably made them harder to spot from the air, and they could set up much closer to the front, in any convenient shell hole or behind any handy hill, and their size made them smaller, harder to hit targets. Plus, they were far more mobile than any of the Mighty Host's other artillery and the tactic of moving as soon as they fired worked better for them. One of his buddies, the gun captain on an infantry angle, called it "shoot and scoot," and it seemed to work . . . after a fashion, at least.

But none of that changed the fundamental fact that the Mighty Host was being driven steadily westward. It didn't take a genius to realize where that had to end if they couldn't find a way to stop Green Valley's advance.

At least they seemed to have a stopper in his path at the moment. The Tairyn River was narrow, little more than a hundred and fifty yards across, but it was also deeper over most of its length, and had a faster current, than the Tarikah River between East Wing Lake and the North Hildermoss. It was the most substantial terrain obstacle yet in the heretics' path, and the St. Bahzlyr Band and its sister St. Zhyahng Band were solidly dug-in on its western bank. Langhorne knew the heretic engineers seemed able to produce pontoon bridges in the blink of an eye, but they'd have a hard time getting one across the Tairyn unobserved, and every ford was covered by positions just like 4th Company's.

As long as they held the fifty or sixty miles between East Wing Lake and the tangled, impassable obstacle of the Great Tarikah Forest, Green Valley wasn't getting past them, however much artillery he had.

▼   ▼   ▼

"I'm looking for Captain Bahrtalam," the combat engineer lieutenant said. "Anyone know where I can find him?"

"Up at the CP, Sir," a private in one of the rifle pits said, and pointed back into the drifting mist. "Straight up the bank. Big tree, still about ten, twelve feet of it left. Turn left there and it's about fifty yards."

"Thanks," the lieutenant said, and started climbing the bank.

It wasn't all that steep, but the pounding both sides' artillery and mortars had delivered made for treacherous footing in the misty dark. The lieutenant didn't mind, though. Misty dark was ever so much better than bright, clear daylight with bullets whistling around his ears.

He found the tree the private had described. Once upon a time, it had been a lot taller, judging by the three-foot-diameter trunk that remained. He turned north, feeling his way carefully through the remnants of the dead tree's companions until he saw the faint gleam of a shaded light ahead of him.

"Halt!" someone barked, and he froze. "Who goes there?"

"Mahrsyhyl," he called back, "Ninety-Seventh Combat Engineers. I'm looking for Captain Bahrtalam."

"You've found him," a different voice, this one with a pronounced accent, replied. "Come on in."

Lieutenant Mahrsyhyl advanced cautiously, keeping his hands well out from his sides. The gleam of light he'd seen would have been completely invisible from the far side of the river, even without the fog, he realized. Bahrtalam's command post was in a natural hollow, with a solid earthen slope between it and the river. The lieutenant slithered down into it and tried not to notice the shotgun-armed sentry watching him alertly.

"Captain Bahrtalam?" he asked as a tallish, broad-shouldered man loomed against the light.

"Bahrtalam," the captain confirmed in an accent that never came from Chisholm or Old Charis. He must have been one of the very first Zebediahans to enlist, Mahrsyhyl thought. "What can I do for you, Lieutenant?"

"I understand you've got a problem the Ninety-Seventh might be able to help out with," Mahrsyhyl replied. "Captain Kwazenyfsky sent me to find out what it was."

"He did, did he?" Bahrtalam smiled. "Can't say I'm sorry to hear *that!* Step into my office, Lieutenant."

▼   ▼   ▼

"You sure this is the right place, Sarge?" Corporal Waryn Meekyn asked dubiously. "Not saying you're *lost*," he continued. "Heck, it's been—what? At least three, four days since the last time *that* happened! Just kinda hard picking up landmarks in this crap."

"And just as hard for some Temple Boy sniper on the other side of the river to deprive me of your invaluable services," Platoon Sergeant Hauwerd Paitryk retorted. "Sort of makes me wish we'd waited for daylight."

"Aw, don't be that way, Sarge!" Meekyn chuckled. "You know you'd miss me in the morning."

"Like a hangover, Meekyn. Like a hangover."

The men of Meekyn's squad shook their heads, grinning in the darkness. He and the platoon sergeant went back a long way, and Paitryk had already dropped off 3rd Platoon's other three squads. It was obvious he was saving 2nd Squad for something special.

"Hold it!" someone called, and Paitryk's raised hand stopped the squad dead. "Looking for someone?" the voice continued.

"Looking for First Platoon," Paitryk confirmed. "Sergeant Paitryk, Ninety-Seventh Combat Engineers."

"Good!"

The satisfaction in the one-word response was obvious, and Paitryk beckoned for the men pulling the equipment carts to take five. The obeyed with alacrity. The carts had outsized wheels and were fitted so that as many as four men could tow each of them, but they were still a bitch to get through this sort of terrain. Not that they didn't beat hell out of trying to *backpack* their gear!

Paitryk left them to it while he and Meekyn moved forward again. A corporal emerged from the dark and nodded for them to follow him, and another fifty yards brought them to a foxhole scratched in the muddy riverbank. There were a couple of feet of muddy water in its bottom, but Paitryk doubted anyone much cared about that when the bullets were flying. A fair-haired lieutenant—probably two-thirds of Paitryk's age, if that—sat on the edge of the foxhole, his feet a couple of feet clear of the water, waiting for them.

"Lieutenant Mahkdahnyld?"

"That's me. What do you need, Sergeant?"

"I understand there's a couple of bunkers on the other side of the river that've been giving your boys some problems."

"You might say that." The lieutenant sounded considerably grimmer than a moment ago. "Lost a quarter of my platoon this afternoon. The bastards waited till we were halfway across, then opened up. There's one position in particular—don't think it's actually a bunker, more like something they threw up after the gun dogs blew the crap out of their original entrenchments. It's high enough the bastards in it can toss grenades straight down to the ford. Wouldn't be surprised if it's been spotting for their artillery, too. It's the only position we've seen that's high enough to see back onto our side, and judging by how quick their mortars hit us, *somebody* sure as hell saw us before we hit the river last time. I don't think the balloon boys can pick it out from all the churned-up shit. For that matter, our support squad spent a couple of hours trying to take it out. No luck. I think they hit it a couple of times, but it must have a shitpot of dirt piled on top of it."

"But you can spot it for us when we've got a little light?"

"Sure." The lieutenant shrugged. "We've been pecking away at it—at all three of them—with riflefire, but it doesn't seem to do a lot of good. One of my boys almost got a rifle grenade through the firing slit, but it's the better part of two hundred yards and we don't have an unlimited supply of them to waste."

Paitryk nodded. The ICA's Lywysite-filled rifle grenades were lethal when they hit, but two hundred yards was right on the edge of their maximum range, even with the new smokeless ammo, and a rifle grenade didn't have the punch to take out a bunker unless someone managed to pop it past one of its firing slits. It wasn't an *impossible* shot, but hitting any sort of pinpoint target with an RGL at that range depended a hell of a lot more on luck than it did on skill.

"Well, Sir," he said, laying one hand on Meekyn's shoulder, "I believe my friend here may be able to help you out. Don't let that low forehead and those monkey lizard arms fool you. He's actually almost as bright as most hamsters."

"I see." The lieutenant surprised himself with a chuckle. Then he cocked his head. "And just how is Corporal Monkey Lizard going to help me out?"

"I'm glad you asked that, Sir."

▼ ▼ ▼

"Roll out." Corporal Baozhi prodded Private Yangkau with his toe, then stepped back as the private snapped awake. "Dawn in about twenty minutes," he continued, twitching his head at the opening to the rear of their position. "Last chance to take a dump before we settle in for the day."

"Gee, thanks," Yangkau said, coming to his feet with a long, stretching yawn.

"Well, I don't want to say anything about stinks," Baozhi told him, "but there's a reason Pasquale has us dig latrines, and it's bad enough when we have to take a leak inside here. Besides, I've always found the sound of bullets a little distracting when I'm communing with nature."

"Got a point," the private said, and climbed out of the improvised bunker.

Baozhi watched him go, then peered out into the dimness. It was too dark still to see the bodies which had bobbed uneasily in the ford yesterday, and he wondered if the heretics had recovered their dead overnight. He hadn't taken any pleasure out of killing them, but a man did what he had to do, and he was sure their friends would be back to try to return the compliment.

Hell of a way for people to spend their time, he thought, shaking his head. *Hell of a way.*

▼ ▼ ▼

The eastern sky glowed its salmon and rose way towards sunrise, and stomachs tightened on both sides of the river. The St. Bahzlyr Band had held the Army of Tarikah's advance for four solid days, and Baron Green Valley's men—especially the men of the 21st Brigade—were tired of that. The 21st was one of the Army of Tarikah's assault formations, especially trained in and equipped for the new assault trooper tactics, and they took their failure yesterday—and the painful loss of friends—as a personal failure. They were confident they could have carried through and taken their objectives anyway, but their casualties would have been brutal, and their lives—and training—were too valuable to waste when it could be avoided. Sometimes it *couldn't* be, but the Imperial Charisian Army regarded the lives of its soldiers as its most precious resource. Which was why the 97th Combat Engineer Battalion had been sent up to lend them a helping hand.

▼　▼　▼

"Are you sure about this, Corporal?" Lieutenant Mahkdahnyld asked.

"Yes, Sir," Corporal Meekyn replied. "If we can see it, we'll take it out for you."

Mahkdahnyld looked at the corporal's contraptions a bit dubiously. He'd heard about them, but he'd never actually seen one of them used. His inclination had been to call for plenty of smoke from his support squad—there was a lot less breeze today, so the smoke ought to be more effective—and put his men across under its cover. He was confident he could get them across the ford more or less intact this time—as long as no one called the mortars in on them—but then they'd face the tangled remnants of the abatis the Harchongians had built along the western shore. They'd have to clear those under fire, smoke or no smoke, and that damned bunker at the right end of the Harchongese line would be rolling the damned grenades down on them the whole time. So if Meekyn and his team really could take out the bunkers, especially the one on the right . . .

"'Bout enough light, I think, Sir," Meekyn observed. "Point them out to us?"

Mahkdahnyld peered through his double-glass, scanning the western side of the river as the last of the mist began to lift. After a moment, he lowered the double-glass and pointed.

"All right, the one on the left is at about twenty degrees," he said. "See what's left of that clump of talon branch? It's about fifteen yards this side of that. Got it?"

Meekyn gazed across the river. The range wasn't great enough to need a double-glass once someone had pointed the target out, and he nodded.

"Got it," he said.

"Okay, the next one's about thirty, forty yards to the right of that. If you follow the trench line, you should be able to pick it up."

"Beside that communication trench running up the slope?"

"Right. Okay, now the third one—the one that's been such a bitch—is harder to see, but if you look another sixty yards or so to the right and up near the crest line. . . ."

▼　▼　▼

"Any sign of the heretics yet, Corp?"

"Not yet," Baozhi replied.

He stood peering out the firing slit, wishing he had a spyglass . . . and that the sun wasn't so much in his eyes. He was a little surprised the heretics hadn't tried to take advantage of that, time their crossing for when he couldn't make out details because of the sun glare. But they probably didn't realize how bad it was from up here, so—

His thoughts paused, and his brow furrowed. What the hell was that?

▼　▼　▼

"All right, Lieutenant," Corporal Meekyn said. "Ready whenever you are."

"Fine." Lieutenant Mahkdahnyld looked first to his left, then to his right. His platoon crouched or lay prone behind downed trees or in muddy shell holes. Farther behind them, hopefully still invisible from the far side of the river, all three of 2nd Company's other platoons waited to follow them across.

Assuming they *got* across this time, of course.

He looked back at the weapons Meekyn's squad had positioned. They certainly looked outlandish enough. Each consisted of a tripod—like a shortened surveyor's tripod, only much, much heavier—with a long piece of six-inch pipe on it. The "pipe" was fitted with a laddered peep sight, adjustable for range, and mounted in a sturdy pivot with outsized wing nuts to lock it in elevation and deflection once it was properly aligned. A length of quick match trailed from the rear of each pipe to meet a single, heavier fuse that ran back to the wooden box at the corporal's knee where Meekyn crouched beside him.

The noncom's squad had set up six of them, two targeted on each of the dug-in positions Mahkdahnyld had pointed out. Now the lieutenant nodded.

"Anytime, Corporal."

"In that case. . . . *Fire in the hole!*"

Meekyn yanked the ring on the wooden box. The friction fuse ignited the lengths of quick match and the glaring eyes of combustion flashed along them.

▼　▼　▼

Despite the sunlight in his eyes, Corporal Baozhi saw the bright flare of the fuses clearly against the riverbank's shadowed dimness. He didn't realize what he was seeing, though. Then the fuses reached their destinations, and Jwaohyn Baozhi realized—briefly—what those tripods were.

The rockets designed by Major Sykahrelli streaked out of the launch tubes in a belch of flame that was awesome to behold. That back blast was the problem Sykahrelli had been unable to overcome in his quest for a shoulder-launched weapon. But it was no problem fired from a remote platform, so he'd designed a somewhat heavier version of his original model.

The six rockets roared across the Taigyn River like fiery comets, and Baozhi dropped to the floor of his improvised bunker.

"Down! *Down!*" he shouted, and the men of his squad were veterans. They didn't ask why; they simply flung themselves down.

Three seconds later, the rockets reached their targets. One of them, aimed at the bunker on the southern end of the line, wandered off course and missed its mark by at least thirty yards. The other five flew straight and level, accelerating the entire way, drawing fiery lines across the river. Then they impacted, and each of them carried a twelve-pound charge of Lywysite. That was the equivalent of *thirty* pounds of black powder, twelve percent more than the charge in an 8-inch high explosive shell, and the walls of the bunkers—and of Baozhi's improvised position—were far, far thinner than their roofs.

All three strongpoints disintegrated in a rolling peal of thunder, and Mahkdahnyld raised his flare pistol. The crimson flare was pale in the brightening light, but it was visible to the support squads waiting for the signal. The mortars began coughing a moment later and smoke rounds thumped down on the farther bank, between the river's edge and the surviving trench lines. Heavy angle-gun shells rumbled across the sky, as well, impacting on confirmed—and suspected—artillery and mortar positions farther back from the western bank, and Mahkdahnyld smacked the engineering corporal on the shoulder.

"Outstanding!" he said with a huge grin, reaching for his whistle as the far side of the river disappeared beyond the rolling banks of smoke. "Drop by once we pull back from the line, Corporal! I know forty or fifty people who're going to buy you *lots* of beer!"

▼ ▼ ▼

"I hate those accursed things, Sir!" Lord of Foot Shyaing Pauzhyn snarled as another salvo of heretic shells—the big ones this time, from the super-heavy angle-guns no one had seen coming—rumbled overhead and crunched down on the 23rd Division's rear area. He wasn't talking about the shells, however, and Lord of Horse Myngzho Hyntai knew it. He was talking about the *other* thing no one had seen coming—the Shan-wei-damned balloon floating serenely in the cloudless sky and directing those shells with such fiendish accuracy.

"Unfortunately," Hyntai said, "there seems to be little we can do about them—yet, at least. I understand the gunners are trying to construct carriages which will let us elevate Fultyn Rifles high enough to engage them."

He put as much optimism into his tone as he could. That wasn't a great deal, although the look Pauzhyn gave him suggested he'd still sounded rather more optimistic than the lord of foot, who commanded his 95th Brigade felt the statement deserved.

Well, it was hard to blame young Shyaing, Hyntai admitted. Although, he supposed that at thirty-seven, Pauzhyn might have resented the adjective "young." From Hyntai's seventy-two-year-old perspective, however, it was certainly apt, even if Pauzhyn was much less young than he'd been a month or two ago.

Another salvo of heavy shells growled their way across the heavens. The sound they made was like nothing anyone had ever heard before. At least it was less terrifying than the shrieking, howling, tumult of a mass rocket launch, but the thunder as those massive projectiles struck got into a man's bone and blood. Each of them was its own private volcano, erupting in fire and death, and only the deepest bunker could hope to resist a direct hit.

The good news was that for all their fury, all the carnage they could wreak, accomplishing the sort of pinpoint accuracy to produce direct hits upon demand was beyond even the heretics' artillerists. So far, at least. Hyntai didn't like adding that qualifier, and he'd been careful not to say anything of the sort in front of his subordinates, but the heretics had a most unpleasant habit of sprinting ahead just whenever it seemed Mother Church's defenders might be closing the gap between their relative capabilities. The balloons which taunted the Mighty Host from their inviolable height were an excellent case in point.

"I know you're anxious to get back to your command, Shyaing," the lord of horse continued, "so I won't keep you long." He showed his teeth in a brief, humorless smile. "I was always taught that bad news is best delivered briefly."

"Bad news, Sir?" Pauzhyn sounded wary but scarcely surprised. There'd been very little *good* news since the heretics' offensive began.

"I fear we've been ordered to retreat," the division commander said much more heavily.

"Retreat?" Pauzhyn repeated sharply.

"Yes." Hyntai tapped the map on the boulder between them. "To here."

Pauzhyn peered down at the map and his mouth tightened. In the five-day and a half since the heretics had forced the line of the Tairyn, 95th Brigade had been pushed back another twenty-five miles. It was actually rather remarkable they hadn't been pushed even farther, he thought, given the paucity of prepared positions in their immediate rear. Hastily dug trenches and lines of lizardholes tended to come apart quickly when the heretic artillery got to work.

On the other hand, there was something to be said for hastily constructed fieldworks, too. The heretics' new assault tactics turned bunkers into death-traps once they'd broken into the trench line. Sometimes they paid a stiff price to do that, but once they had—once they were in among the bunkers, close enough to find targets for those accursed, rapid-fire shotguns, throw their damnable satchel charges, or use their horrific flamethrowers—very few defenders got out alive.

His brigade had been reduced from a beginning strength of forty-six hundred to barely two thousand, despite the influx of almost a thousand replacements, and the 23rd's total casualties mirrored his own. Then there was what had happened to Baron Morning Star's brigade. But the men were still stubbornly full of fight, he thought.

"Sir, I realize there are prepared positions waiting for us there," he said after a moment, "but the new line will increase our total frontage by almost a quarter. And our backs will be directly against the Sairmeet-Lake City High Road. If they push us back any farther, reach the high road. . . ."

His voice trailed off, and Hyntai nodded in unhappy agreement.

"You're right, of course. On the other hand, we're actually being pulled back behind the line to rest and refit. Three other bands—St. Tyshu, St. Ahgnista, and St. Jyrohm—are already holding the fortifications. We're going into reserve, at least for the moment."

Relief showed in Pauzhyn's eyes, but the worry remained to keep it company.

"I know the Host's front line will be very close to the high road," Hyntai said soberly, "but we have no choice. Sanjhys fell three days ago, and the heretics' balloons are already directing artillery on the approaches to Vekhair. This is for your private information, not to be shared with any of your officers, but Earl Rainbow Waters has ordered Vekhair's evacuation." Pauzhyn stiffened, but Hyntai continued steadily. "It's to be carried out very quietly, by night, with the transport flotilla lifting the men out and ferrying them to Lake City."

"And their heavy weapons, Sir?"

"And their heavy weapons will have to be abandoned," Hyntai acknowledged gravely. "The flotilla has barely sufficient lift for the men; artillery and rocket launchers will have to be left behind . . . along with a rearguard to prevent the heretics from breaking through once they realize what's happening. The Earl has no choice but to save what he can, though. The heretic general on their right flank—General Klymynt—is already pushing mounted infantry around to cut the road along the north shore of the lake. With those damnable balloons spying on him, Lord of Horse Mountain Flower would be trapped against the lake before he made fifty miles if he attempted to break out overland. If he had more depth—or perhaps I should say more *width*—he might be able to evade the heretics despite the balloons, although, to be honest, I doubt there'd be much chance even then. He has too many infantry and too few dragoons to win a footrace against them.

The good news is that the locks between Sanjhys and Vekhair have been destroyed, so at least Klymynt can't simply continue across the lakes with his ironclads!"

Pauzhyn nodded with the air of a man trying hard to find something positive in what he'd just heard, and Hyntai laid a hand on his shoulder.

"I know it's far harder to gird yourself for battle when all you see before you is an endless retreat, Shyaing, but you and your officers and men have made me proud—very proud. And unlike last year, or the year before, the heretics are being forced to fight for every foot, even with *those* spying for them." He jerked his head at the balloon. "All we can do is continue the fight, and it's already July. The campaigning season won't last beyond September— early October at the latest—this far north. If we can hold them to this slow an advance, then we should be able to stand along the line of the Ferey River this winter."

"And *next* summer, Sir?" Pauzhyn asked very, very softly.

"And next summer will be in God's hands," Hyntai replied even more softly.

.II.
Gorath Bay Approaches
and
Hankey Sound,
Kingdom of Dohlar.

O h, *shit*," Seaman Ahlfraydoh Kwantryl, late of His Dohlaran Majes-ty's Ship *Triumphant*, whispered as the image swam clear through the spyglass.

"*What* was that?" someone asked rather pointedly from behind him.

It was Kwantryl's misfortune to be assigned to Lieutenant Bruhstair's six-gun section in Battery Number One. He hadn't much liked Bruhstair when they'd served together aboard *Triumphant*, and he'd decided he liked him even less now that the ship had been laid up and they'd been trans-ferred ashore. It wasn't that Bruhstair was incompetent. In fact, he had a real knack for the new model artillery, and for someone who'd turned twenty— less than half Kwantryl's age—barely five months earlier, he was damned good at his job. He was, however, a prude in every sense of the word. He'd been remarkably unsympathetic when a seaman—whose last name happened to be Kwantryl—over-imbibed (and overstayed his leave) in an establishment run by ladies of negotiable virtue. On top of that, he disliked even the mildest profanity, and God help anyone who took God or the Archangels in vain in his hearing.

And of *course* the little snot had to have the sharpest damned ears in the entire Royal Dohlaran Navy.

"Sorry about that, Sir," Kwantryl said with what might have been a tiny edge of prevarication. "I think you'd better have a look, though," he added more seriously, stepping back from the spyglass on the observation tower's railing.

Bruhstair gave him a sharp look, then bent to the spyglass himself.

Under other circumstances, Kwantryl might have been amused by the way the lieutenant's shoulders tightened so suddenly. At the moment, however, all he felt was agreement with Bruhstair's response.

"Just this once, Kwantryl," the lieutenant said finally as he straightened up from the spyglass, "I think your vocabulary may have been . . . appropriate."

He snapped his fingers at the other seaman sharing the lookout duty at the moment. Seaman Ahlverez looked up quickly, and Bruhstair pointed at the observation tower ladder.

"Get down there and tell Lieutenant Tohryz we've—that *Kwantryl* has—just spotted several columns of smoke headed this way. Tell him I estimate there must be at least a half-dozen heretic steamers out there but the ships themselves are still below the horizon, so I don't know how many are ironclads."

Ahlverez paled visibly, but he also nodded and darted down the ladder so rapidly Kwantryl was afraid the idiot would hang a toe and plunge to the bottom with a broken neck.

"And now, Kwantryl," Bruhstair said with a razor-thin smile, "I suppose you and I should see if we can't get a better count. Even at their speed we should have time for that before we go to quarters."

▼   ▼   ▼

"*Riverbend* reports Cape Toe in sight, Sir," CPO Matthysahn announced, still bent behind the swivel-mounted double-glass focused on the signal flags above the leading ironclad, three cables ahead of *Gwylym Manthyr*. He peered through the double-glass for a few more seconds, then straightened. "Bearing four points off the starboard bow, she says, Sir. Range twelve miles."

"Thank you, Ahbukyra," Halcom Bahrns replied. He did a little mental math, then turned to the midshipman of the watch. "My respects to Admiral Sarmouth, Master Ohraily, and *Riverbend*'s sighted Cape Toe, four points off the starboard bow. Range from the flagship is approximately thirteen miles."

"Your respects to the Admiral, Sir, and *Riverbend*'s sighted Cape Toe, four points off the starboard bow and the range from *Manthyr* is thirteen miles," young Ernystoh Ohraily repeated back. Bahrns nodded, and Ohraily touched his chest in salute and headed for the bridge ladder while *Gwylym Manthyr* and the reinforced 2nd Ironclad Squadron, now up to a total of six units, continued plowing towards Gorath Bay at a steady ten knots.

▼　▼　▼

"Thank you, Master Ohraily," Baron Sarmouth said gravely. "Please present my compliments to Captain Bahrns and inform him that, with his permission, I'll join him on the navigation bridge directly."

"Your compliments to Captain Bahrns, My Lord, and, with his permission, you'll join him on the navigation bridge directly," Ohraily repeated.

Sarmouth nodded, and the youngster saluted and withdrew from the admiral's dining cabin. Sylvyst Raigly closed the door behind him, then turned to cock one eyebrow at the admiral.

"Yes, I'll want my good tunic, Sylvyst," Sarmouth sighed, with a resigned headshake. "Have to look my best when we're all being shot at, I suppose. But there's damned well time to finish breakfast, first. I'll call you when I'm ready."

"Of course, My Lord," Raigly murmured, and Sarmouth felt his lips twitch as the valet bowed himself out of the dining cabin. The extra few minutes would give Raigly more time to assemble his personal arsenal before they went on deck, although the probability of a desperate boarding action aboard *Gwylym Manthyr* struck Sarmouth as rather unlikely.

He snorted at the thought, then scooped up the last bite of poached egg and washed it down with the last of his cherrybean. Then he pushed his chair back and turned towards his day cabin, marveling once again at the spaciousness of his quarters. Admittedly, *Manthyr* was ten times *Destiny*'s size, and all the *King Haarahlds* had been designed to serve as flagships, but he'd still been astonished by the amount of space set aside for the flag officer's use. He had a day cabin, an office, a chart room, a dining cabin, *and* a sleeping cabin. And, as if that weren't enough, he also had a sea cabin—half the size of his day cabin and equipped with a comfortable bed—and a second, larger chart room right off the flag bridge.

It was more space than he'd ever needed—or could conceive of ever needing—and it seemed . . . wrong somehow for his quarters to remain inviolate when the ship cleared for action. His possessions were supposed to be sent below, the dividing partitions were supposed to go with them, and the heavy guns which shared his quarters were supposed to be loaded and run out, ready to fire. But there were no cannon in *these* quarters and no reason to strip them before battle. Although his most prized possessions had been sent below yesterday evening in preparation for today, there'd be no hustle and bustle for him this morning. He supposed he'd get used to it eventually, but he hadn't yet. In fact, he'd been surprised to discover he actually missed it, as if he'd lost some unspoken connection with the rest of his flagship's crew.

He smiled a bit crookedly as he admitted that to himself, but his amusement faded quickly as he crossed the day cabin and stepped into the chart room. The lamp hung from the deckhead had been lit, but more and better light actually came in through the three scuttles in the outboard bulkhead. Trumyn Lywshai, his flag secretary and clerk, had opened all three of them and latched them back, letting the fresh sea air sweep through the compartment. Probably to help clear the lingering tobacco smell, Sarmouth reflected as he drew his cigar case from his breast pocket. He selected a cigar, returned the case to his pocket, and stood frowning down at the chart spread across the table as he clipped the cigar's end. That chart had been liberally marked with penciled notations, and his frown deepened as he studied them.

Gorath Bay offered several advantages as a harbor, including approach channels deep enough for the largest ships. Unfortunately, it also offered quite a few advantages when it came to *defending* those passages.

The peninsula Dohlarans had named The Boot curved up from the south, enclosing a bay that ran over two hundred and thirty miles from north to south. For all its size and the depth of its channels, the bay was more than a little constricted, however, and its half-dozen-plus islands provided numerous sites for defensive batteries. Cape Toe at the tip of The Boot was a case in point, covering the Lace Passage, between Hankey Sound and the Zhulyet Channel . . . which just happened to be the approach which had been forced upon Sarmouth's squadron. Sandbottom Pass, northwest of Lace Passage, would have stayed well clear of the Cape Toe batteries, but its deep water channel was much narrower . . . and the Royal Dohlaran Navy had scuttled no less than thirty galleons to obstruct it. If he wanted to enter Gorath Bay, he had to fight his way past Cape Toe first. It wasn't going to get a whole lot better even after he ran the Lace Passage gauntlet, either, because Thirsk clearly believed in a defense in depth.

The next minor difficulty would come when he had to force one of the passages through the barrier of shoals and islands stretching well over two hundred miles from Broken Keel Shoal in the west to Senya Point in the east. One would have thought two hundred miles offered ample opportunity, but one would have been wrong. There were only three possible routes he could take, and he frowned as he ran his finger across the chart, remembering one of Cayleb Ahrmahk's favorite observations, acquired from an ancient Old Terran military theorist via Merlin Athrawes. In war, everything was very simple, but achieving even simple things was immensely difficult.

He'd never seen a better example of that than the one on the chart before him, and he wasn't looking forward to what this operation might cost.

The damage Hainz Zhaztro's flagship had suffered in Saram Bay had been made good by HMS *Urvyn Mahndrayn*, the first steam-powered repair ship in Safeholdian history. It had taken over a month, and Zhastro had transferred his flag to the newly arrived HMS *Tanjyr* until he could get *Eraystor* back. Sarmouth had a copy of *Mahndrayn*'s report on *Eraystor*'s damages, and it had given him rather more respect for the current generation of Temple Boy artillery. He doubted even the rifled 10-inchers which had pummeled *Eraystor* so brutally represented a threat to his flagship, but the Dohlarans had managed to mount several dozen *12-inch* rifles to protect their capital. He didn't like to think about the labor involved in working a 12-inch muzzle-loader, and it had a very low rate of fire, thanks to its barrel length and the need to swab out between rounds. But if one of them hit, it was going to hit with authority.

And that doesn't even count the rockets and the sea-bombs, he thought grimly, puffing his cigar alight while he glowered at the chart. *I know why we have to do this and how it's going to end, assuming everything works the way it's supposed. I even know it'll be worth whatever it costs . . . if everything does work. But I also know it's damned well not going to be the painless romp some of the boys are predicting.*

He drew on the cigar, brooding down at the chart, then blew out a long streamer of smoke, straightened his spine, and headed back to collect his good tunic before he joined Bahrns on the bridge.

▼　▼　▼

"I make it at least twelve smoke clouds now, Sir," Kwantryl reported, never looking up from the spyglass. "I can see two of their ironclads, too. One of the single-chimney ships is leading, but that big bastard's right behind it. Can't get a good look at number two yet—too much smoke from the one in front. And until they get closer, I can't tell how many of those other clouds're ironclads, either."

"Two of them would be more than enough for me." Lieutenant Bruhstair's tone was light, but his expression was grim as he jotted down Kwantryl's latest count. "Range?"

" 'Bout ten miles to the single-chimney, Sir," Kwantryl replied. "Looks like there's two, maybe three cables between them, and they're coming on pretty damned fast. Figure they'll be right up to us in 'bout another hour."

Bruhstair nodded without even commenting on Kwantryl's language, added that information to his note, then tore the page out of his notebook and handed it to one of the ship's boys who'd been sent up the tower to serve as runners.

"Lieutenant Tohryz, quick as you can!"

"Aye, aye, Sir!"

The youngster scurried down the ladder like a spider-monkey, and Kwantryl raised his head to watch him go, then glanced at Bruhstair. But the lieutenant wasn't looking in his direction. He'd stepped to the edge of the observation tower, looking down on the section of guns along the battery wall that were his responsibility.

"Make sure we've got plenty of dressings!" he called down to one of the gun captains. "And get those water tubs refilled—especially the ones for drinking water! Don't want any of you layabouts collapsing from thirst just to get out of a little honest work!"

Someone in the section shouted back. Kwantryl couldn't make out the words, but from the tone, they were probably a bit saltier than Bruhstair normally tolerated. This time, the lieutenant only laughed, and Kwantryl nodded in approval. He could forgive any young twerp quite a lot when he was as devoted to his men as Dyaygo Bruhstair.

It was just sort of hard to remember that *between* times like this.

He snorted with amusement at the thought, and the lieutenant gave him a sharp glance.

"Something humorous about the situation, Kwantryl?"

"No, Sir. Not really. Just an old joke. Funny how a man's mind goes on these little walks every so often."

"Well, I recommend you walk it right back to that spyglass," Bruhstair said a bit more tartly. "That *is* why we're up here, you know."

"Yes, Sir!" Kwantryl replied and bent back over the spyglass. It was probably just as well the lieutenant couldn't see his huge grin from behind him. Explaining what was really so funny would land him in a shitpot of trouble as soon as the battle was over.

▼   ▼   ▼

"Range is down to ten miles, Sir," CPO Mathysyn reported. "The range-finder has the southern battery in sight."

"Thank you, Ahbukyra."

Halcom Bahrns glanced at his admiral, and Sarmouth nodded that he'd heard the report. Ten miles would have been in range for *Gwylym Manthyr*'s 10-inch guns, assuming they'd had the elevation for it. Which they didn't. At six degrees, their maximum reach was "only" twelve thousand yards, just under *seven* miles.

We'll just have to keep going until we are *in range,* he thought. *At least it won't be that much longer, and* Riverbend *should be into* her *effective range in another twelve minutes. I just wish to hell there was some way to tell* Whytmyn *everything I know about the defenses.*

Unfortunately, there wasn't. Thirsk had made several adjustments in the last couple of days, only after the squadron had sailed for the attack. There'd been no time for a "*seijin*" to legitimately learn about those adjustments *and* get word to Sarmouth. He'd done everything he could to adjust his own plans in the tradition Cayleb had established in the Armageddon Reef Campaign by "playing a hunch," but there were limits.

He'd seriously considered asking Owl and Nahrmahn to deploy some of the SNARCs' small incendiary devices. In fact, he'd discussed the possibility with all the inner circle's senior members, only to discover their opinions were as divided as his own. Sharleyan, Merlin, Pine Hollow, and Maikel Staynair had all favored their use as the best way to save lives . . . on both sides. But Cayleb, Rock Point, Nimue, Nahrmahn, and Nynian had all opposed it because of the potential political consequences. In the end, after hours of debate, Cayleb and Sharleyan had declared that the decision was his, as the commander on the spot and the man whose officers and men would bear the action's brunt.

A part of him wished they'd gone ahead and made the call rather than leaving it up to him, but he told himself that was his inner coward talking. And so he'd made the decision. In fact, he'd made it three times, flipping back and forth with a degree of indecisiveness that was most unlike him.

Explosions in carefully selected strategic locations—like battery magazines—could have gone a long way towards easing his task. But this attack was as much a calculated political maneuver as a purely military operation or even the pursuit of long-delayed justice, and that political maneuver depended on a fine and delicate balance of factors in the city of Gorath itself. However helpful in a military sense, those magazine explosions might raise eyebrows—the *wrong* eyebrows—especially if they were *mysterious* explosions without some readily identifiable cause. It was probable that those inclined to assign demonic powers to the "heretics" would do just that—and that those inclined *not* to assign them demonic powers wouldn't—whatever happened. But he couldn't be positive of that, and as Nynian and Nahrmahn had forcefully pointed out, events in Gorath would depend at least in large part on the perceptions of two or three key individuals whose reactions they simply couldn't predict.

And so, in the end, he'd decided against it. He only hoped it wasn't a decision he'd regret.

And even if I'm not going around blowing things up with joyous abandon, and even if I can't tell my people everything, we've already told them about one hell of a lot. It's just going to have to be good enough. And young Makadoo may be able to buy me a little bigger "information bubble." Speaking of which. . . .

He glanced up at the lookout pod. *Gwylym Manthyr*'s navigation bridge was thirty-five feet above the water, which gave it a visual horizon of just under eight miles in clear weather. His flag bridge was ten feet higher, which gave it another mile or so of visibility. The rangefinder on its raised pedestal atop the forward superstructure was twenty feet higher still, and its powerful range-finding angle-glasses could see over ten miles, about two-thirds of the lookout pod's visual range. That was good, but he could do better.

"Is Master Chief Mykgylykudi ready?" he asked.

"Yes, My Lord." Halcom Bahrns straightened from the voice pipe into which he'd been speaking and smiled. "I figured you'd be asking that right about now, and he says he's ready to start paying out cable anytime we want. He also says, and I quote, 'Master Makadoo's been squirming like his breeches are full of bees for the last quarter hour.'"

Despite his inner tension, Sarmouth chuckled. Young Zoshua Makadoo was *Gwylym Manthyr's* fifth—and youngest—lieutenant. He was also a slightly built, quick-moving fellow, like many of the Charisian Empire's new aeronauts.

"Well, we can't have Zoshua driving the Bosun crazy," the admiral said. "Best tell him to get started."

▼　▼　▼

"What the fuck?!"

The startled obscenity escaped before Ahlfraydoh Kwantryl could stop it and Lieutenant Bruhstair looked at him sharply. But the seaman only straightened and gestured at the spyglass.

"Sir, you'd better have a look yourself."

The urgency in Kwantryl's tone erased any temptation to rebuke him for his language, and the lieutenant put his eye to the spyglass. For a few moments he couldn't understand what had startled Kwantryl so, but then he inhaled sharply as he saw the large white . . . shape rising above the biggest heretic ironclad. It was already considerably higher than the big ship's mast, and it went on climbing higher, rapidly and smoothly, as he watched. It was shaped something like a flattened cigar, he thought, but it had some sort of stubby vanes, or wings, or something, and it was clearly harnessed to the ship somehow.

"What *is* that thing, Sir?" Kwantryl asked, and the tough, veteran seaman was obviously shaken. Not surprisingly, Bruhstair thought, feeling a cold shiver as he remembered all the fiery sermons damning the heretics for trafficking with demons. But. . . .

"I think it's a balloon," he said slowly, forcing himself to take his eye from the spyglass and stand up straight . . . and rather surprised by how much better he felt when the *shape* faded into an unthreatening blur with distance.

"'Balloon,' Sir?"

"Yes. I've never seen one myself," Bruhstair replied more confidently, "but one of my uncles saw a demonstration in Gorath and told me about it when I was a kid. If you heat the air inside a balloon, it floats up into the air."

"Floats into the air?" Kwantryl looked decidedly uneasy. "Can't say I like the sound of *that*, Sir!"

"There's nothing demonic about it," Bruhstair said quickly. "The Bishop Executor himself pronounced that when Uncle Sailys was in Gorath. It's only fire and air, and both of those are permitted."

"If you say so, Sir." Kwantryl didn't seem very convinced, Bruhstair noted.

"It's not demonic," the lieutenant repeated reassuringly. "But it *is* going to let them see a lot farther. Don't know how much good it'll do them, though. And whatever somebody perched up there can see, he'll still need some way to get word of it back down to the ship. Might be just a bit of a problem getting that done in time to do any good."

▼　▼　▼

"End of the cable, Sir," Petty Officer Hahlys announced.

"Thank you, Bryntyn," Lieutenant Makadoo acknowledged.

The lieutenant lay prone in the nose of the streamlined gondola. Unlike the balloons of the ICA's Balloon Corps, the Navy's kite balloons had a lifting shape, with stubby airfoil wings that generated a *lot* of lift when their motherships towed them at fifteen knots or so. Or when they were towed at a mere five or ten knots into a *twenty-five* knot wind, like today's. That meant they needed less hydrogen to loft a given weight—although, to be fair, that lift wasn't available when their motherships *weren't* steaming into the wind—and they could probably have squeezed a third passenger into the gondola, as long as whoever it was was no bigger than him or Hahlys. The quarters would have been tight, though.

At the moment, Makadoo's elbows were braced on the padded rest in front of him while he peered through his powerful double-glass. The front of the gondola was glassed in to protect the crew from the wind generated by the balloon's forward motion, but Makadoo had the center section of window latched back. Duke Delthak could say whatever he wanted, but Zoshua Makadoo was firmly convinced the visibility was better with the window out of the way.

Besides, he and Hahlys *liked* the wind.

"Check the drop cylinder," he said, never looking away from the view ahead.

"Aye, Sir," Hahlys replied.

The young petty officer stuffed the test message into the small bronze cylinder and made sure the lid was properly screwed down. Then he snap-hooked its traveler onto the messenger line deployed on one side of the balloon's braided steel thistle silk tether. He let go and it disappeared, flashing down the messenger line to the deck far below.

Looking down, Hahlys could see one of the other signalmen pounce on the canister, unhook it, and hand the note inside it to Ahndru Mykgylykudi, *Gwylym Manthyr*'s bosun. Mykgylykudi glanced at it, then nodded to the party of seamen gathered around the steam-powered "donkey" engine beside the winch that controlled the balloon's tether.

The second messenger line was spaced well over a foot on the *other* side of the tether. It was also doubled and ran over a sheave at the top of the gondola's open rear. Now that line hummed sharply as it sped through the sheave until the canister hooked to it thumped against the rest at the base of the sheave, and Hahlys nodded approvingly.

The messenger canisters were a faster means of communication than a signal lamp would have been. They were also *safer*. *Mhargryt*—they'd named it for Makadoo's mother, since the lieutenant said she'd always had an explosive temper—was basically a great big bomb, just waiting to explode. That was why there was no iron or steel anywhere in the gondola's construction, and why there were no iron nails in its crew's boots.

The powered messenger line was the fastest way to get a message up to *Mhargryt*, but the free-falling line was much faster when it came to getting a message back to the ship. And since *Mhargryt*'s primary duty was to be *Gwylym Manthyr*'s eye in the sky—and to spot the fall of the big ship's shots from above the clouds of gun and funnel smoke likely to blind her gunners—speed of communication was a very good thing to have.

"Both lines are working fine, Sir," he reported to Makadoo.

"Good."

Makadoo sounded just a little distant, and Hahlys smiled. From their present altitude of eighteen hundred feet, the lieutenant could see for almost sixty miles. That meant he could see all the way across Cape Toe. In fact, he could probably just make out the low-lying blur of Sandy Island on the far side of the Outer Ground, the stretch of water between The Boot and the barrier islands separating it from the Middle Ground, closer to Gorath. At the moment, he was focused closer to home, slowly and methodically sweeping the waters of the Lace Passage for any sign of the Royal Dohlaran Navy. Hahlys would be astounded if any of the Earl of Thirsk's surviving galleons or screw-galleys were crazy enough to engage the squadron, but Admiral Sarmouth's instructions before they'd launched had been clear. He wanted to know the instant they spotted anything bigger than a rowboat.

Several minutes went by as Makadoo switched his attention from the channel to Cape Toe itself. He studied the fortifications equally carefully, then lowered the double-glass and rolled onto his side, looking back towards Hahlys.

"Message," he said, and the petty officer pulled out his pad and pencil. "Ready, Sir."

"Message begins. 'No vessels currently underway within visual range. Several small craft moored north of Cape Toe at Battery Number Two's jetty. Have also spotted several large canvas-covered freight wagons behind Battery Number One's parapet in what appear to be well dug-in positions.'"

He paused, rubbing the tip of his nose thoughtfully while he considered what he'd just said. Then he shrugged.

"Read it back," he said, and nodded when Hahlys did. "It never ceases to amaze me that *anyone*, including you, can read your handwriting, Bryntyn. But once again, you've gotten it right. So let's get the word back to the ship."

▼　▼　▼

"Coming down on six miles' range, Sir," Commander Pharsaygyn murmured, and Sir Hainz Zhaztro nodded without ever lowering his double-glass.

He understood the unspoken part of his chief of staff's announcement. Lywys Pharsaygyn thought it was about time his admiral retired to the interior of HMS *Eraystor*'s conning tower and put its armor between him and the Dohlaran defenders. On the other hand, the possibility of a Dohlaran gunner's hitting a target—even one *Eraystor*'s size—at better than ten thousand yards was remote, to say the least, and the field of view from the conning tower, even using one of the angle-glasses, wasn't anything Zhaztro would have called adequate.

"Tell Alyk I'll be along shortly," he said, then lowered the double-glass to smile crookedly at Pharsaygyn. "And if you're going to tell me he wasn't your accomplice in coming out to drag my arse into the conning tower, please don't."

"That obvious, were we?" Pharsaygyn returned his smile unrepentantly.

"Let's just say subtlety isn't your strong suit," Zhaztro said. "Besides, if it's six miles for us, it's only four and a half for *Riverbend*, which means—"

▼　▼　▼

"Range eight thousand, Sir," Lieutenant Gyffry Kyplyngyr said, looking up from the voice pipe which connected HMS *Riverbend*'s gunnery officer to her conning tower. "Lieutenant Metzlyr requests permission to open fire."

Unlike Admiral Zhastro, Captain Tobys Whytmyn had already retired into that conning tower. It wasn't because he was any more concerned about Dohlaran artillery at this range than his admiral, but there was going to be plenty of concussion, blast, and smoke from *Charisian* artillery all too soon.

Under the circumstances, he preferred having the conning tower's armor between himself and the muzzle blast of eleven 6-inch guns.

Call me a wuss, but I'd really like to keep my eardrums intact a little longer, he reflected.

"Very well," he acknowledged, peering through the starbard angle-glass at their target. "Bring us another two points to larboard, Helm."

"Two points larboard, aye, Sir."

Petty Officer Riely Dahvynport turned the wheel easily, despite the fact that *Riverbend*'s rudder was far more massive—and much, much heavier—than any of galleons' or galley's rudder had ever been. The gleaming hydraulic rams deep in *Riverbend*'s bowels answered to his touch, and the ironclad's course curved to the west. She continued to approach Cape Toe, but her new heading would open her broadside, allowing every one of her starboard guns to bear on the batteries.

Whytmyn let his ship settle onto her new course, then looked over his shoulder at *Riverbend*'s second lieutenant.

"Very well, Gyffry. Tell Tairohn he can open fire whenever he's ready."

"Aye, Sir!" Lieutenant Kyplyngyr acknowledged with a huge grin and disappeared down the ladder like a lizard into its hole.

▼ ▼ ▼

Well, that *can't be a good sign,* Ahlfraydoh Kwantryl thought, standing in the embrasure beside his assigned 10-inch Fultyn Rifle.

Lieutenant Bruhstair's section was fully manned now and Lieutenant Rychardo Mahkmyn, Battery Number One's commanding officer, had taken over his and Bruhstair's post on the observation tower. As far as Kwantryl was concerned, he was more than welcome to it, too. The tower had been heavily sandbagged, but there was an enormous difference between sandbags, however thickly piled, and the solid earth of the battery's thick, protective berm.

That was particularly pertinent at the moment, since the lead ironclad had just turned far enough to present its broadside to Cape Toe. Somehow, Kwantryl doubted they would have done that if they didn't figure they were—

▼ ▼ ▼

"*Fire!*" Tairohn Metzlyr barked into his voice pipe at the base of HMS *Riverbend*'s rangefinder.

Not only did the rangefinder give him an accurate distance to his target, but his present perch was also high enough—and the lenses in the rangefinder's angle-glasses were strong enough—to give him an excellent view of it.

Nothing happened for another five seconds. And then—

▼   ▼   ▼

"*Langhorne's balls!*" someone gasped.

Fortunately, whoever it had been was somewhere behind Lieutenant Bruhstair, impossible to identify. Not that even a stickler like Bruhstair would have wasted time and energy castigating the malefactor under the circumstances.

The heretic ironclad disappeared behind a stupendous gush of fiery smoke.

HMS *Triumphant* had been entirely too close to a Charisian galleon when it exploded in the Kaudzhu Narrows. The stunning concussion of that moment, the flaming wreckage flying across his own ship, setting fire to *Triumphant's* main topsail, was something Ahlfraydoh Kwantryl had no desire to repeat. Yet the volcanic eruption that blotted out his view of the ironclad was at least as bad. It was also eight thousand yards away, but that had its own drawbacks. Like the fact that at that range it took several seconds for the heretics' shells to reach their targets, which gave a man all too much time to think about what was headed his way.

Kwantryl stepped back from the mouth of the gun embrasure. He was no more obvious about it than he could help, and he had ample time to put some of that nice, solid berm between him and the incoming fire.

Ten seconds after they'd been fired, eleven 6-inch shells came shrieking down on Battery Number One. They weren't as tightly grouped as Lieutenant Metzlyr would have preferred. Five of them actually overshot the battery entirely, but that wasn't a complete loss, because one of them scored a direct hit on one of the wagons Lieutenant Makadoo had reported to Admiral Sarmouth.

The heavy freight wagon disappeared in a savage explosion as the 12-foot-long coast defense rockets in its launching frame exploded. A huge mushroom of smoke, flame, and dirt rose over two hundred feet into the air and half a dozen fire-tailed comets screamed out of it at crazy angles. But the defenders had built high earthen cofferdams between those wagons, putting each of them into its own mini-redoubt, and those cofferdams channeled the blast upwards rather than out to the sides, where it might have taken other wagons with it.

Five of the other six shells slammed into the battery's berm, drilling into it as *Eraystor's* shells had drilled into Battery St. Charlz in the attack on Saram Bay, and Ahlfraydoh Kwantryl's jaw tightened as their powerful explosions sent shockwaves rippling through his flesh.

The eleventh and final shell sizzled just above the top of the parapet and crashed into the base of the observation tower. The heavy sandbags smothered much of the explosion, but shell fragments sliced upwards through the tower platform's floor like white-hot axes, killing three of its seven occupants . . . including Lieutenant Mahkmyn.

And then, eleven seconds after their shells, the thunder of HMS *Riverbend*'s guns rolled over the battery.

▼　▼　▼

"Eleven thousand yards in four minutes, My Lord," Ahrlee Zhones announced. He had to speak fairly loudly as he stood at Baron Sarmouth's elbow because both of them had already inserted their protective earplugs.

"Thank you, Ahrlee," Sarmouth acknowledged.

He and his youthful flag lieutenant stood on the flag bridge's starboard wing as Halcom Bahrns followed *Riverbend* and *Eraystor*. *Gwylym Manthyr* wouldn't be approaching Cape Toe quite as closely as her smaller consorts, partly because she drew more water and partly because no one could be certain the Dohlarans hadn't planted any of their sea-bombs to protect those waters.

Actually, Sarmouth knew exactly where Earl Thirsk had put his mine-fields. As a result, he knew all of the armored ships could have come within as little as four thousand yards of the battery. There was no way he could have explained how he'd come to possess that knowledge, however, and he had a reputation as a canny, methodical officer to maintain.

Besides, even if there weren't any sea-bombs, there were those rocket wagons he hadn't been supposed to be able to know about. If worrying about mines he knew weren't there kept his ships outside the range of rocket launchers he knew *were* there, that was fine with him. He'd been delighted when the first wagon exploded under *Riverbend*'s fire, and three more of them had been destroyed since.

Which only leaves twelve *of the damned things*, he thought grimly, looking down on the vortex of smoke and flame through an overhead SNARC.

▼　▼　▼

"Sweet Bédard," Zoshua Makadoo murmured as *Gwylym Manthyr* opened fire at last.

Unlike anyone else in the squadron—aside, if he'd only known, from its commander—he and Bryntyn Hahlys had an unobstructed view of the incredible vista, and his double-glass was glued to his eyes. He'd never imagined anything like the huge billows of brown Charisian gunsmoke, the equally huge jets of dirty gray-white spurting from the battery's earthen ramparts as the Dohlarans' banded rifles returned fire, the black smoke pouring from the squadron's funnels, and the white smoke of burning barracks rising From Battery Number One's interior. Even at the kite balloon's altitude, it quivered and bounced in the shockwaves as the flagship's main battery spat out an even more enormous mountain of smoke.

Four 10-inch shells howled through six miles of empty space, and seven 8-inch shells came with them.

Twelve seconds later, they struck.

▼ ▼ ▼

Kwantryl coughed harshly, despite the water-soaked bandanna across his nose and mouth, and stared into the blinding smoke through red-rimmed, tear-streaming eyes. He and the rest of Lieutenant Bruhstair's gun crews—his *surviving* gun crews, at any rate—had only the vaguest notion of their target's position. The gunsmoke was bad enough; the wood smoke pouring from the blazing barracks, mess hall, sickbay, and what had once been the battery commander's office was worse.

"*Clear!*" the gun captain shouted, half-screaming to be heard, and Kwantryl and the other crew members jumped clear of the slides. The captain peered along the barrel while the heat of firing rose from it as if from a stove, looking for the funnels protruding from the impenetrable fog bank of gunsmoke. They were all he could really hope to see, and even then only fleetingly.

"*Firing!*" he shouted and jerked the lanyard.

The 10-inch rifle thundered like Chihiro's trump of doom. It recoiled fiercely, and the gun crew swarmed over it, shoving the water-soaked swab down the barrel to quench the last shot's embers. The barrel was so long it took two men to manage the swab, and the men with the next powder charge waited impatiently.

"*Handsomely*, boys!" Lieutenant Bruhstair shouted. "*Handsomely!*"

The lieutenant paced steadily, unhurriedly, up and down the line of his guns. There were only four of them now. One had been buried in its embrasure by an exploding heretic shell, but another had burst four feet in front of the trunnions. Half of that crew had been killed or wounded, and the survivors were distributed among the remaining guns, replacing other men who'd been cut down.

At that, they were lucky only one gun had burst. The cast-iron guns which had been issued to Lieutenant Bruhstair's section were far more likely to fail than the newer steel rifles. It hadn't made his gunners feel one bit more confident when he'd gone to the 15-pound bombardment charge rather than the standard 12-pound charge. Not that anyone had been tempted to argue. Given what the heretics' shells were doing to Battery Number One it struck most of his men as unlikely they'd live long enough to be killed by a bursting cannon.

"*Load!*" the gun captain bellowed, and the man with the bagged charge reached for the gun's overheated muzzle and—

▼   ▼   ▼

Two tons of steel slammed into Battery Number One as *Gwylym Manthyr's* first broadside landed. The 10-inch shells' effect on the protective berm was devastating, but one of the 8-inch shells drilled straight into the face of the battery's number two magazine with freakish accuracy.

The explosion was like the end of the world.

▼   ▼   ▼

Ahlfraydoh Kwantryl dragged himself to his knees, shaking his head like a punchdrunk fighter. He didn't remember the explosion that had picked him up and tossed him aside like a child's doll. He didn't remember landing, either, and he looked down with a sort of detached bemusement as he realized his left arm was broken in at least three places.

Better off than the rest of the lads, though, a corner of his brain told him.

The entire section was gone. The breeches of two of its guns still protruded from the churned earth which had once been a protective berm. The others were simply gone, dismounted and buried, and two-thirds of the gunners who'd served them had gone with them. A gaping, crescent-shaped bite had been ripped out of the battery's parapet, and two more rocket wagons exploded even as he came to his feet. At least he *thought* it was two of them, but his ears didn't seem to be working very well, and it could easily have been more than that.

He turned in a slow circle, clutching his broken arm, watching as men who'd been wounded or simply stunned began struggling upright, and his jaw tightened as he saw Dyaygo Bruhstair.

The young man's—the *boy's*—left leg ended at mid-thigh, and blood poured from the ragged stump. More blood pulsed from a deep wound in his left shoulder, but he'd fought his way into a sitting position somehow, clutching at the stump of his leg, and his face was paper-white, his eyes glazed with shock.

Kwantryl staggered to his side and went back to his knees. It was harder than hell with only one working arm, but he managed to pull his belt free and looped it around the truncated leg. Another member of the section knelt beside him, helping to tighten the crude tourniquet, but Kwantryl couldn't have said who it was. It didn't really matter. They'd just gotten the tourniquet tightened when another 6-inch shell exploded and a white-hot splinter decapitated whoever it had been.

He moved behind Bruhstair, gripped his collar in his good hand, and heaved, dragging the lieutenant towards the nearest supposedly shellproof dugout. After what had just happened to the section, he had his doubts about that "shellproof" guarantee. The engineers who'd made the promise had never seen heretic shells. But it would be better than nothing.

Another salvo tore into the shattered and broken battery. Steel splinters shrieked overhead and screams answered as they drove into men who'd just discovered they were all too mortal.

"Leave me!" Bruhstair's voice was barely audible through the bedlam, but he reached up, pawing feebly at the hand locked onto his collar. "*Leave me!*" The words were half-slurred, but their intensity came through. "Get under cover!"

"No, Sir," Kwantryl panted, staggering like a drunken man as he hauled the lieutenant towards the dugout.

"Damn you, Ahlfraydoh! Just *once* do what I say!"

"Not happening," Kwantryl gasped. "'Sides, we're almost—"

The 10-inch shell landed less than five feet behind them.

▼　　▼　　▼

"Repairs completed, Sir. Or as close as we're getting without *Mahndrayn*, anyway."

Lieutenant Anthynee Tahlyvyr's face and uniform were both filthy. In that respect, he was no different from most of the rest of HMS *Eraystor*'s crew. In his case, however, a liberal coating of oil and coal dust had been added to the grimy gunpowder residue, and Captain Cahnyrs shook his head with a smile as he regarded his senior engineer.

"How bad is it?"

"We're not getting that breech block on Number Seven six-inch back anytime soon, Sir," Tahlyvyr said sourly. "Same thing for the larboard engine room blower, and there's still a hole in Compartment Sixty-Two we can't reach to plug. Must be pretty good-sized, too, judging by how much water's coming in, but the pumps're holding it. Until I can get the funnel uptakes patched, I can't give you enough draft for full steam pressure, but she's still good for thirteen, maybe even fourteen knots."

"Outstanding!" Cahnyrs said sincerely, and patted him on the shoulder. "Not go scrub some of that crap off your hands and grab something to eat. We'll be finding more work for you soon, I'm sure."

"What I'm here for, Sir," Tahlyvyr replied with a weary, off-center smile. "And food sounds really good right about now."

"Well, make it quick," Cahnyrs warned. "You've got about forty minutes."

"Aye, aye, Sir."

The engineer touched his chest in salute and climbed down the exterior bridge ladder to *Eraystor*'s narrow side deck. Cahnyrs watched him go, then turned to the admiral at his side.

"I wonder if he understands just how good he really is, Sir Hainz?"

"I don't know if *he* does, but I sure as hell do," Zhastro said. "I assume your after-action report will bring him to my attention in suitably glowing terms?" Cahnyrs nodded, and Zhaztro snorted. "Well, see that it does! That young man deserves a medal or two. Not the only member of your ship's company that's true of, either, Captain. For that matter, *you* haven't been too shabby today."

"Day's still young, Sir. Plenty of time for me to screw up."

"And if I thought that was likely to happen, I might actually worry about it," Zhaztro replied dryly.

Cahnyrs chuckled, and Zhaztro gave him a smile. Then he moved out to the end of the bridge wing and lifted his double-glass to observe *Eraystor*'s next challenge and his smile faded.

The shattered ruins of the Cape Toe fortifications lay five hours and the better part of forty miles astern as she steamed steadily up the Zhulyet Channel towards its narrowest point, between Sandy Island to the east and the far smaller Wreckers' Island on the western side of the channel. Even at its narrowest, that channel was twenty-six miles wide. Unfortunately, Slaygahl Shoal lay right in the middle of it, running almost thirty-five miles from north to south. Slaygahl was just awash at low tide, and even at high tide there were barely four feet of water across it. The shipping channel was far deeper—at least six fathoms everywhere—but it was also barely five miles wide on the western side of the shoal, and about ten miles wide on the eastern side. And, even more unfortunately, Sir Lywys Gardynyr wasn't the sort of commander to miss the possibilities that offered. According to the *seijins*, he'd laid a dense field of sea-bombs on either side of the shoal.

Right where anyone trying to find a way through them would come under the heavy fire of at least a dozen 12-inch Fultyn Rifles.

This is going to be . . . unpleasant, *Hainz*, Zhaztro told himself. *You thought Battery St. Charlz was bad, but this is going to be worse.*

He and Baron Sarmouth had discussed their unpalatable options exhaustively and come up with the best approach they could. Which wasn't remotely the same thing as saying they'd found a *good* one.

In many ways, they would have preferred to use Needle's Eye Channel, between Meyer Island and Green Tree Island. It was broader, but it was also shallower, and there were even more guns on Green Tree than on Sandy and Wreckers'. That ruled out the Needle, and at least they'd managed, courtesy of Admiral Seamount, to come up with one wrinkle Zhaztro was pretty sure hadn't occurred even to someone as canny as the Earl of Thirsk.

He trained his double-glass astern and smiled again—thinly, but with genuine satisfaction—as he watched the converted steam powered landing barges churn steadily along off *Eraystor*'s quarter. They'd been towed all the way from Lizard Island by the larger steamers, because they weren't the best seaboats in the world, and their relatively low speed now that they were no longer on tow was the reason it had taken five hours to reach the squadron's current position, but he wasn't about to complain.

He swung his double-glass back towards Wreckers' Island and felt himself tighten internally. The entire island was barely eight miles long, and it reminded him ever more strongly—and unpleasantly—of Battery St. Charlz as it drew steadily closer. According to the *seijins*, the batteries along its eastern shoreline not only mounted heavier guns but were even better protected than St. Charlz' had been, and no one had ever accused Dohlaran gunners of faintheartedness. On the other hand, this time he'd have *Gwylym Manthyr* in support.

He knew Sarmouth would actually have preferred to take the lead with his far more powerful, better armored flagship. In fact, he'd initially planned to do just that, but Zhaztro had convinced him it was out of the question. *Manthyr* was less maneuverable, she drew more water, and she was far less expendable. There was also the minor consideration that it would be . . . less than desirable to blow up the expedition's commanding officer on a drifting sea-bomb. Sarmouth had seemed less than overwhelmed by *that* part of the argument, but he hadn't been able to ignore the rest of it, and his expression had been almost petulant when he finally accepted Zhaztro's alternate suggestion.

Now Zhaztro snorted in amused memory and lowered the double-glass.

"Signal *Manthyr* that we're prepared to proceed," he said.

▾　　▾　　▾

"Admiral Zhastro is ready to proceed, Sir," Ahrlee Zhones reported, holding up the message slip in his hand.

"Good," Sir Dunkyn Yairley said in a tone which was considerably more confident than *he* was. He didn't like what the SNARCs were showing him one bit, but there wasn't much he could do about it at the moment. No one aboard *Manthyr* was in any position to see the threat that worried him most, and he couldn't exactly order Halcom Bahrns to open fire on something no one—or at least no one without access to the SANRCs—even knew was there. Especially not if that fire produced the spectacular result it almost certainly would. That might well validate his bizzare orders, but it certainly wouldn't *explain* them, and there was only so much that he could wave away as blind chance and luck.

"Remined Lieutenant Makadoo that I want to know the instant he sees anything—*anything* at all—out of the ordinary," he directed. "Especially if he sees any sign of warships or floating rocket launchers."

"Yes, My Lord. At once."

Zhones sounded a little perplexed, and Sarmouth didn't really blame the youngster. He'd already prodded Makadoo with that message—or a variant on it—several times, and he wondered if Zhones thought the fight the Cape Toe batteries had put up had shaken his nerve. Unfortunately, he couldn't explain his motives to his flag lieutenant . . . any more than he could come right out and explain them to Makadoo.

He thought again about ordering *Manthyr* to take the lead, but all Zhaztro's arguments against that decision still stood.

Yes, they do. And you don't know that it's going to be anywhere near as bad as you're afraid it could, Dunkyn, he told himself. *For that matter, even if you told Hainz all about it, he'd only point out that we still have to force the channel and clear the damned sea-bombs and tell you it didn't change a thing, and he'd be right. It doesn't change anything . . . except which men—and how many of them—may be about to get killed, perhaps.*

"Very well," he said. "Hoist the signal to proceed."

▼   ▼   ▼

"We're moving in, Sir," PO Hahlys said, and Zoshua Makadoo finished chewing and swallowed hastily.

"Got it," he said, and shoved the rest of the sandwich into his pocket and crawled forward. Hahlys squirmed past him as they exchanged positions and the lieutenant settled back into place with his double-glass. After better than six hours aloft, he and Hahlys had been ravenously hungry when Bosun Mykgylykudi sent their lunch up on the powered messenger line. Hahlys had eaten first, while Makadoo maintained a lookout, then the petty officer had relieved him.

And I almost got done eating, the lieutenant thought with a chuckle as he raised the double-glass.

It was a bit strained, that chuckle. Zoshua Makadoo was about as irrepressible as a young man came, but his wyvern's eye view had shown him far too much carnage this day. He'd seen *everything,* and it was almost worse that it had been so far away, so tiny. He'd heard the thunder of the squadron's guns and watched shells bursting all over the Dohlaran fortifications, but it had been like watching toys fighting toys . . . until he raised his double-glass and saw the dying "toys" writhing in broken agony whenever the smoke parted. He'd seen Dohlaran shells hitting *Eraystor, Riverbend,* and *Gairmyn,* as well, and he wondered how many men he knew aboard those ships had been killed or wounded.

No one ever promised it would be easy, he reminded himself, focusing the double-glass on *Eraystor* as she steamed steadily towards the enemy once again.

"Message from Admiral Sarmouth, Sir," Hahlys said. Makadoo looked over his shoulder at the petty officer, who held up the slip of paper he'd just taken from the message cylinder.

"Read it."

"Yes, Sir. 'Remember to report anything—' that word's underlined twice, Sir '—out of the ordinary. Especially—' three underlines on that one, Sir '—any warships or floating rocket launchers.' That's it, Sir."

Makadoo grunted in acknowledgment and frowned as he turned back to the vista below, swinging his double-glass across to Wreckers' Island. Admiral Sarmouth had personally briefed them before they launched, and his instructions had been very clear. It was unlike him to repeat himself—and, especially, to repeat himself this *often*—and Makadoo couldn't help wondering if the admiral knew something the rest of them didn't. If he did, the lieutenant couldn't imagine what it might be. He'd already examined Wreckers' Island as meticulously as he could from this distance, and reported everything he'd seen.

It was obvious this target was going to be a tougher slabnut than Cape Toe had been. Only the very muzzles of the battery's long, lethal Fultyn Rifles were visible, peeking out of much smaller—and harder to hit—embrasures than the Cape Toe batteries had shown. The parapet itself looked half again as thick, as well. He'd already passed that information along, and he was just as glad they hadn't waited another few five-days, since it was clear the Dohlarans had still been piling up fresh dirt to add even more breadth and depth to the parapet. In fact, they must have been doing that right up to the very last minute, he thought, as he studied the half-dozen barges moored behind the island. They were obviously very shallow draft, given how little depth of water there was on Broken Keel Shoal, between the island and the mainland. In fact, given the state of the tide, they had to be hard aground at the moment, which probably explained why they hadn't run away. Two of them—quite a bit smaller than the others—were empty, although there were still a few heaps of dirt scattered around their open-topped holds. Clearly whoever had been swinging the shovels hadn't been all that worried about getting *all* of it. But the other four were mounded high with still more dirt destined for the parapet. In fact, the dirt was heaped so high he was surprised they'd been able to float the damned things across the shoal at all.

Left it just a little late, though, he thought with a thin smile. *Don't know how much the extra dirt would've helped, but we'll never find out now, will we?*

▼   ▼   ▼

"Looks like they're finally getting down to it, Sir," Lieutenant Commander Zhordyn Kortez said grimly.

"Surprised it's taken them this long," Captain Ezeekyl Mahntayl replied. Mahntayl was forty-six, ten years older than his executive officer, and he'd lost a leg and an eye in the Kaudzhu Narrows. He was also one of the Royal Dohlaran Navy's two or three most expert gunners, which explained his present command.

"I guess Captain Dynnysyn's boys hammered them pretty hard," Kortez observed.

"Probably. Not hard enough, though," Mahntayl growled. "Should've done a lot better!"

"Yes, Sir."

Some people would have taken Mahntayl's words as a criticism of Cape Toe's CO, but Kortez knew better. Mahntayl and Cayleb Dynnysyn had been friends for years. The anger in Mahntayl's voice had a lot more to do with that friendship and the reports they'd received about Cape Toe's casualties than with the fact that the heretics hadn't lost a single ship . . . so far, at least.

"I know the lads are ready," the captain went on now. "But there's still time for another walk-through. Well, for somebody who still has both feet, anyway." He actually managed a smile. "See to that for me, if you would."

"Of course, Sir." Kortez saluted and headed for the deeply dug-in and heavily sandbagged command post's entrance. Unlike Cape Toe, the garrison of Wreckers' Island could depend on the enemy coming in close enough to be seen from sea level. There *was* an observation tower in the center of the island, but it was unmanned at the moment. If the heretics wanted to waste a few shells demolishing *it* instead of shooting at his artillery, Mahntayl would be delighted.

And the guns aren't all I have for you, either, you bastards, he thought harshly, peering through the tripod-mounted spyglass. *You just keep right on coming. I don't think you're going to enjoy your reception very much.*

▼   ▼   ▼

"Open fire!"

The first broadside thundered from *Eraystor's* larboard broadside in a fresh volcanic cloud bank of brown smoke, and Sir Hainz Zhaztro found himself— again—wishing he was still on the bridge wing.

But I don't wish it very hard *at the moment*, he told himself, peering through a view slit as the Wreckers' Island battery disappeared behind a swirling cloud of its own gunsmoke.

Shells screamed overhead or hurled up huge columns of white, mud-stained water, and he felt his belly muscles tighten as the size of those fountains confirmed the weight of the artillery his men were about to face.

▼   ▼   ▼

"What the hell?" Ezeekyl Mahntayl muttered.

The heretics' shells came shrieking in like vengeful demons, slamming

610 / DAVID WEBER

into his battery's earthem defenses, blasting craters deep into them. But some of those shells didn't explode. *Some* of them gushed dense billows of smoke, instead. Which had to be the most unnecessary thing he'd ever seen in his life! His guns were already making *plenty* of smoke. Even with the brisk northeasterly blowing lengthwise down the Zhulyet Channel, it was thick enough to severely restrict his gunners' visibility, and that could only get worse, despite the 12-inch rifles' slow rate of fire. For that matter, the heretics were producing more than enough gunsmoke of their own to obscure their ironclads! Surely they'd be better served hammering Wreckers' Island with explosives than churning up still more *smoke!*

Unless there was something *else* they didn't want him to see.

▼　▼　▼

"All right, Wahltayr," Commander Tahlyvyr Sympsyn said as smoke enveloped Wreckers' Island . . . and hopefully blinded its gunners. "Let's get this circus moving."

"Aye, aye, Sir!" Lieutenant Wahltayr Rahbyns replied, and glanced at the grizzled petty officer at the converted landing barge's helm. "You heard the Commander, PO. Take us in."

"Aye, Sir," PO Styv Khantrayl acknowledged and eased the wheel expertly.

"A bit more speed, I think," Rahbyns added, looking ahead through his double-glass, and the seaman acting as engineer opened the throttle a bit wider.

The paddle wheel thumped and vibrated, churning the water as *Bombsweeper One*—the only name the converted barge had ever been given— gathered speed.

"Stream the kites!" Rahbyns ordered in a louder voice, and four more seamen bent over the winches mounted on either side of *Bombsweeper One*'s blunt bows. It took two sets of hands on each winch to control the speed with which the heavy wire cable paid out, and Rahbyns watched critically.

He'd been a less than happy man when he first heard about the Temple Boys "sea-bombs." A floating explosive charge, just waiting for a ship to sail over it? A charge that didn't care how heavily armored the ship in question might be? A charge that hid invisibly in the water until the fatal moment? The very thought had been enough to send an icy chill through any sailor.

But he should have known Admiral Seamount would find a solution, and so he had. It wasn't perfect, and it was one hell of a long way from anything a man might call "safe," but he doubted the Dohlarans would like it very much.

The cables finished paying out, and *Bombsweeper One* labored more heavily as the tethered objects someone from Old Terra would have called paravanes spread outward on either bow. The cables angled sharply back, and the depth-maintaining vanes had been carefully set to keep the sea-kites in precisely the right position relative to their mothership.

If *Bombsweeper One* happened to run directly into one of the sea-bombs, the consequences would be . . . unfortunate. But no matter how dense the field of sea-bombs might be, the odds were heavily against a direct bows-on collision. A sea-bomb attack was actually more likely to succeed if its target sailed *past* it, close enough for the wake to suck it into contact with the hull.

But the sea-kites' cables would intercept the mooring cables of any sea-bombs caught in their path and guide the explosives not inward, towards the bombsweeper, but *outwards*, towards the kite. That meant the only real danger spot was directly ahead of her and no wider than her own beam . . . in theory, at least. Hopefully, the mooring cable would actually break and the sea-bomb would float to the surface, where the M96-armed riflemen standing along the rails on either side would be waiting for it, rather than be drawn directly into the kite. Their magazines were loaded with a special incendiary bullet designed to punch through the sea-bomb's casing and detonate its gunpowder filler.

There were drawbacks to the system, of course. The bombsweepers had to steam straight ahead on painstakingly plotted courses if they wanted to have any idea where the swept channel was when they finished. That would make them unpleasantly easy targets. And clearing a sufficiently broad channel required the combined efforts of several bombsweepers, steaming in a carefully maintained formation so that their deployed kites overlapped without fouling one another. At the moment, Rahbyns' sweeper was the head of a blunt triangle three sweepers—and just over three hundred yards—across. The other two were what Admiral Seamount had christened his "wingmen," steaming far enough back that their inboard kites were at least fifty yards inside *Rahbyns'* kites but a minimum of seventy-five yards astern of them. The overlap guaranteed—in theory, at least—that no sea-bombs would be missed.

Lieutenant Mahkzwail Charlz steamed parallel with Rahbyns at a distance of just under five hundred yards in *Bombsweeper Five*, leading a second triangle of bombsweepers. Theoretically, the entire formation would sweep a six hundred-yard wide channel through the middle of the Dohlaran sea-bombs in a single pass, although the plan called for them to turn around, find their navigation marks, and sweep a second channel that overlapped the first, clearing a path approximately a thousand yards wide.

It all sounded good, and the training exercises had gone well, but no one had been shooting at them during the exercises, and none of the "sea-bombs" they'd swept had actually contained gunpowder.

That was why there nine more bombsweepers in reserve, waiting to replace any casualties.

▼   ▼   ▼

"What the hell are they're doing?" Lieutenant Commander Kortez demanded, and Captain Mahntayl looked up from the spyglass with a scowl.

"I presume you're talking about the little bastards?" Mahntayl had to raise his voice to be heard over the thunder of artillery and the roar of bursting shells, despite the command post's thick walls, and Kortez nodded.

The captain hadn't heard his second-in-command return to the bunker, which probably shouldn't have surprised him, given the ungodly bedlam of the artillery duel. Now Kortez stood beside him, glaring out through the same view slit. The blinding walls of smoke, reinforced by the heretic's damned smoke shells, made visibility spotty as hell, but the wind had shifted ever so slightly. The smoke remained as dense as ever, possibly even denser, between his gunners and the ironclads, but the range to the small steampots churning towards the sea-bombs was actually clearing.

"Well, the only thing *I* can think of," he said sourly, "is that they know about the sea-bombs and they think they've found a way to clear them."

"That's ridiculous," Kortez muttered, but he sounded like someone who *wanted* Mahntayl to be wrong, not someone who thought he was.

"If you can think of another reason for those pissant little boats to run around in the middle of a Shan-wei-damned artillery duel, I'm all ears," Mahntayl replied.

He and Kortez looked at each other for a moment. Then the lieutenant commander shrugged.

"No, Sir, I can't. The question is whether or not they can really do it, and I wouldn't think—"

He broke off as one of the bombsweepers' kites brought a sea-bomb to the surface. The tide was ebbing steadily towards dead low-water, and it was obvious the Charisians had planned their attack for a time when the sea-bombs would be closest to the surface and most visible. Now the sea-kite's cable did precisely what it was supposed to do, guiding the captured sea-bomb towards the kite. Rifles cracked from the sweeper's deck, raising quick little spits of white around the sea-bomb. Nothing else happened for four or five seconds. Then it exploded ferociously—but harmlessly.

Less than a minute later one of the other bombsweepers detonated another sea-bomb. Then two more exploded in quick succession, and Mahntayl swore.

"Pull the guns off the frigging ironclads!" he snapped. "Let's see how one of those little pricks likes a twelve-inch shell up his arse!"

▼ ▼ ▼

"Be damned, Sir! It's actually *working!*" Lieutenant Rahbyns shouted jubilantly, and Commander Sympsyn nodded.

He hoped like hell that they didn't lose a kite, but each of his bomb-sweepers had two additional kites, ready to stream the instant an exploding sea-bomb destroyed one of the ones they'd already deployed. In the meantime, though, Rahbyns was right; it was working almost exactly as Admiral Seamount had predicted.

"Signal to the Flagship," he said, turning towards the signalman standing by the stubby mast which had been rigged solely as a way to pass signals. "Hoist Number Nineteen."

"Aye, aye, Sir!" the youthful signalman replied with a smile. According to the signal book vocabulary, Number 19 meant "I have mail on board."

▼ ▼ ▼

"Signal from Commander Sympsyn, relayed from Gairmyn," Zhones said jubilantly. "Number Nineteen, My Lord!"

"Good, Ahrlee! Excellent!" Sarmouth said, as if he hadn't already known exactly how Sympsyn's efforts were proceeding.

And it truly was good tidings. But there were bad ones to go with it, including the fact that the new 12-inch Fultyn Rifles were, indeed, capable of punching through a *City*-class ironclad's armor. So far, two had penetrated *Eraystor* and one had penetrated *Riverbend*. The good news—such as it was—was that the Dohlaran armor piercing shells were thicker walled and contained far less powder than their Charisian counterparts and their fuses were less reliable. A Dohlaran 12-inch shell was actually only a little more destructive than a Charisian *6-inch* shell.

Not that enough six-inch shells won't rip the guts right out of any ship, the admiral thought grimly.

Eraystor had twenty casualties already, nine of them fatal, and *Riverbend* had three dead and seven wounded. Zhaztro's flagship had lost two guns on her engaged side, as well, and the damage control parties had had a difficult time extinguishing the fire one of the hits had started in her paint stores.

Gwylym Manthyr's much heavier guns had taken Wreckers' Island under fire as well, but Mahntayl's guns were even more deeply dug-in than the Cape Toe batteries had been. It was going to take time to neutralize them, and—

▼ ▼ ▼

The first 12-inch shell hit the water almost five hundred yards from its intended target. The next three were at least equally wide of the mark.

Number five hit *Bombsweeper Three* almost directly amidships.

The converted barge was too lightly built to activate the shell's unsophisticated fuse, so *Bombsweeper Three* wasn't simply blown out of the water. But the shell that slammed completely in one side and out the other side of the bombsweeper also punched straight through its boiler.

The explosion of steam killed two of the bombsweeper's crew outright. Three more were savagely scalded—one of them fatally—and only the fact that the boiler was on an open deck, with no overhead to trap any of the explosion's fury, prevented it from blowing the converted barge apart.

The reprieve, unfortunately, was brief.

Without power, the bombsweeper slowed quickly, and as it lost speed, its kites began angling back inward rather than spreading broadly. Half of *Bombsweeper Three*'s assigned riflemen were dead or dying, but the survivors fired desperately at the sea-bomb trapped by the starboard kite as it glided steadily closer. It took almost thirty shots to score a hit, and the sea-bomb was barely forty yards clear when it detonated.

The explosion shook *Bombsweeper Three* like a spider-rat in a cat-lizard's jaws. Another dozen seams started, sending fresh streams of water spurting into the slowly settling vessel.

And then the sea-bomb which *hadn't* been caught on a kite's cable slammed directly into *Bombsweeper Three*'s hull and the sweeper—and every man aboard it—disintegrated in a white column of death.

▼　▼　▼

"*Yes!*" Ezeekyl Mahntayl shouted. The heretics' guns had hurt his battery badly and he knew the damage was only beginning, but he wheeled to Kortez. "Put the eight-inchers onto them, too, and tell the lads to pour it on! Sink those frigging pissants!"

▼　▼　▼

"Shan-wei take them!" Sir Hainz Zhaztro snarled.

He'd had ample proof the Dohlarans had finally found a gun *Eraystor*'s armor couldn't simply shrug off. He didn't know how many of his flagship's crew had been killed already, but he knew there were more than he'd ever find it easy to live with. And he knew there'd be more of them if he continued the engagement. But he also knew her armor offered better protection than anything the bombsweepers had. For that matter, it had defeated everything *lighter* than a 12-inch shell to come her way. She could be hurt badly, possibly even killed, but she was immeasurably more survivable than any of the bombsweepers, and unless the sweepers could clear a path through the sea-bombs, the entire attack on Gorath would ultimately fail.

"Take us closer," he told Alyk Cahnyrs grimly. "Make the bastards concentrate on *us*, instead."

▼　▼　▼

"That's odd," Lieutenant Makadoo muttered.

"What's odd, Sir?" Bryntyn Hahlys demanded.

The petty officer couldn't think of anything "odd' enough to distract *him* from what had just happened to *Bombsweeper Three*—especially since shell splashes had begun rising like loathsome, poisonous fungus around two more of the sweepers. The three leading ironclads were moving to interpose between the remaining sweepers and the Dohlaran gunners, and their new course angled perilously close to the sea-bomb field boundaries on the charts the *seijins'* spies had provided. It also took them entirely too close to the battery's guns for Hahlys' piece of mind, and the fury of the artillery duel had redoubled.

"Well, *I* sure as Shan-wei wouldn't be running out into the open with shells falling all around my ears," Makadoo replied.

"Excuse me, Sir? Running *out?*" Hahlys shook his head. "That doesn't make any sense!"

"What I thought, too," Makadoo agreed, staring through his doubleglass. "But looks like there's at least a hundred of them."

"Where do they think they're going to go?" Hahlys wondered out loud. Wreckers' Island was over eight miles from the mainland coast. That struck him as one hell of a swim!

"Looks like they're climbing onto those construction barges." Makadoo sounded as if he couldn't quite believe his own words as he watched the fleeing Dohlarans and *Gwylym Manthyr's* 10-inch and 8-inch shells began walking back and forth across the battery's parade ground. "They must be out of their minds! If I was going to panic and run, I'd look for the deepest hole I could find, not head for—"

He broke off and stiffened, leaning forward as if that would somehow help him see better.

"Oh . . . my . . . *God!*" he whispered and whipped around, showing Hahlys a bloodless face.

"Signal—quick!" he snapped, and the startled petty officer jerked the pad out of his pocket.

"'Urgent,'" Makadoo barked, beginning to dictate even before Hahlys had his pencil ready. "'Six barges behind Wreckers' Island loaded with rockets!' Get that the hell down to the ship!"

"Yes, Sir!"

While Hahlys grabbed the signal cylinder and stuffed the sheet of paper into it, Makadoo turned back around, watching sickly through his double-glass as the Dohlaran seamen swarmed across the barges. Even now, the lieutenant felt a surge of respect for the courage it took for those men to charge out into the open in the midst of such a furious bombardment, but that respect was swamped by a much stronger sense of dread as they stripped away the earth-colored tarpaulins which had covered the squat, vertical cylinders of the defensive rockets.

▼   ▼   ▼

"Message from Lieutenant Makadoo, Admiral!"

Sarmouth turned quickly to the midshipman. He already knew what Makadoo's message said, and a part of him wanted to scream curses at the lieutenant for not mentioning those "construction barges" sooner.

"What?" he demanded harshly, impatiently, resenting the lost time while Zhones told him something he already knew.

" 'Urgent,' " Zhones read. " 'Six barges behind Wreckers' Island loaded with rockets!' " The young man looked up from the note and his eyes were dark. "*What* barges, My Lord?" he demanded.

"Immediate signal to Admiral Zhastro!" Sarmouth snapped. "Execute General Order Six!"

"Yes, Sir!" Zhones jerked his head at a pale-faced signalman, and Sarmouth whipped around to the ladder which connected the flag bridge level of the conning tower to the navigating bridge level. He pressed the inside edges of his boots to the outside of the ladder frame and slid down it like a midshipman down a shroud without ever touching a single tread.

"My Lord?" Halcom Bahrns sounded surprised at his sudden, unceremonious arrival, and Sarmouth didn't blame him.

"Rocket barges, Halcom!" he said quickly. "Makadoo's spotted half a dozen of them behind Wreckers' Island. We have to get Zhaztro and the *Cities* out of there!"

Bahrns' eyes flared, but he jerked a nod of almost instant understanding, and Sarmouth swung towards one of the vision slits and stared out of it. No one could possibly have seen the Dohlaran battery through the enormous clouds of smoke, but he didn't need to. The overhead SNARC saw it just fine, and his jaw clenched as the swarming Dohlaran seamen stripped away the canvas which had been deliberately painted and then rigged over a supporting framework to resemble rounded piles of dirt.

Thirsk's too damned smart, the baron thought grimly. *And he—or, rather, Ahlverez—has gone too far out of his way to establish his own information conduits. That's how the two of them found out about the frigging Balloon Corps so damned fast! And then Thirsk had to go and move the goddamn barges after we'd sailed! I wonder if he was still strengthening the earthworks just to give him cover to hide the rocket barges. Or did he just realize he could hide them from a balloon that way?*

There was no way to answer those questions, but there was still time to avoid the wost consequences of Thirsk's forethought. The Dohlarans would need several minutes—probably as much as a quarter of an hour—to clear away the launchers and bring them to bear, and those barges were firmly aground now, unable to move or alter their point of aim. That meant they'd have to wait until Zhaztro moved into their coverage zone. He'd have to come close enough for them to reach *and* sail into the immobile barges' fixed field of fire, so if he only reversed course quickly enough. . . .

"Shift your fire, Halcom," he said, turning back from the view slit. "Forget about the battery for now. Put everything you can on the channel between it and the mainland." He bared his teeth. "No frigging barge full of rockets will like a hit from a ten-inch shell!"

▼　▼　▼

"Any response from *Eraystor*?" Captain Gahryth Shumayt demanded.

He stood on HMS *Gairmyn's* open bridge wing, heedless of the heavy Dohlaran fire. He'd suffered from claustrophobia all his life, but that wasn't why he'd eschewed the protection of his ironclad's conning tower. He simply couldn't *see* anything from inside it, so he'd insisted his first lieutenant stay there, where he'd be able to take over if anything untowards happened to Shumayt himself, while he got on with the business of seeing where the hell his ship was going.

Now he glared at the signalman who'd joined him on the bridge wing, and that hapless—and obviously nervous—young man shook his head.

"No, Sir." The petty officer looked up at the colorful bunting flying from *Gairmyn's* yardarm, then ducked instinctively as another Dohlaran shell screamed overhead before it smashed into the water well beyond the ironclad. The fountain rose high as her crosstrees, pattering back across her decks like salty rain, and he climbed cautiously back to his feet and looked sheepishly at his captain, who'd never even flinched. "Nothing so far."

"Shit," Shumayt growled.

"It must be the smoke, Sir," the PO said, and Shumayt swore again.

Of course it was. The *Cities'* masts were shorter than those of any galleon, and the billowing gunsmoke—and funnel smoke—could only make their signals even more difficult to see. But surely one of the other ships *had* to see the signal and relay it to Zhaztro! They couldn't *all* be invisible to *Eraystor*!

▼　▼　▼

Damn it! Sarmouth snarled mentally as he realized Shumayt's signalman was exactly right. Zhaztro *couldn't* see the signal, and the cushion of time which would have let him withdraw was spinning away with terrifying speed.

The baron ripped open the heavily armored conning tower door and stormed out onto the navigating bridge. Someone shouted his name, but he ignored it, racing to the outer edge of the bridge and raising his double-glass as if he were trying to see *Eraystor* through the blinding smoke. But that was the farthest thing from his mind at the moment.

"Nahrmahn!" The thunder of *Manthyr's* artillery drowned his voice. No one could have heard him from more than three or four feet away, but Nahrmahn Baytz and Owl had far better hearing than any flesh-and-blood human being.

"We're already deploying them!" Nahrmahn's voice came sharply over the com plug in his ear, and Sarmouth felt a huge surge of relief. Of course the portly little prince had been monitoring the situation! But Narhmahn wasn't done speaking.

"The remotes are on their way, but it's going to take time, Dunkyn. At least another ten minutes. The remotes are stealthy as hell, but they aren't very fast!"

"I should've just gone ahead and blown the damned things up as soon as we came in range! *Damn* it! We're throwing enough frigging shells their way to explain just about *anything's* blowing up over there now!"

"But you didn't know this was going to happen," Nahrmahn pointed out. "If Sir Hainz could just see the signal, you'd've gotten him out of the field of fire in plenty of time."

"And if I were God, we wouldn't need to worry about goddamned Clyntahn!" Sarmouth snarled. "But I'm not and he can't! And *don't* remind me about the 'political consequences'! None of them mean squat until after the frigging battle, and unless we *win* the damned thing, no one'll be able to do a single thin—"

▼　▼　▼

"Signal from Admiral Sarmouth, Sir!" Lywys Pharsaygyn's voice was sharp as he threaded his way across the crowded conning tower with the message slip in hand. "Relayed from *Gairmyn*. 'Urgent. Number Eighty. Numeral Six.'"

"*What?*" Zhaztro stared at his chief of staff in disbelief.

Number 80 was "Execute previous orders," and Number Six was the order to break off the attack and withdraw immediately. He'd thought Sarmouth was taking caution to the extreme by arranging that sort of order in advance, and he wondered what in Shan-wei's name had triggered it now, of all possible times! *Eraystor* and *Riverbend* were barely six thousand yards from Wreckers' Island. They'd taken several more hits to get there, and *Riverbend* was on fire aft, but Captain Whytmyn had just signaled that his damage control parties were on top of it. They were finally in close enough for the deadly rapidity of their 6-inch guns—coupled with the more deliberate, longer ranged fire from *Gwylym Manthyr*—to beat down the battery's fire. They could simply pour in far more shells than the slow-firing muzzleloaders could send back, and barring some sort of catastrophic hit in a magazine or something equally severe, they were *winning*. So why—?

Doesn't matter, Hainz, he told himself harshly. *Dunkyn's not the kind to jump at shadows, and even if he was, he's your commanding officer.*

"I don't know what it's about, Alyk," he said, turning to his flag captain, "but turn her around and signal the bombsweepers to follow us back out to—"

▼   ▼   ▼

"*Fire!*" Lieutenant Fhrancysko Dyahz barked.

He'd lost thirty men clearing away the concealing canvas. And, he admitted, he'd thought the idea of "camouflaging" the barges when they were already hidden behind the island was ridiculous. But then he'd seen the balloon floating above the heretic flagship and realized Admiral Thirsk must have already known the heretics had it.

Now he yanked the friction primer that ignited the fuse and turned to follow the last of his men back into the protection of the battery's shell-proof dugouts. He was twenty feet from the entrance when one of *Gwylym Manthyr*'s 8-inch shells exploded seventy yards away from him and a steel splinter four inches long hit him in the back like a hyper-velocity buzz saw.

He was dead by the time he hit the ground.

Ten seconds after that, the rockets began to fire.

▼   ▼   ▼

Each of Lieutenant Dyahz' four barges contained a hundred and twenty of the squat, ugly rockets Dynnys Zhwaigair had designed for harbor defense. They didn't all fire simultaneously. Instead they launched in a carefully arranged sequence, roaring heavenward in a fountain of flame on a far slower, far steeper trajectory than the ICN's high velocity guns could produce. His number two barge had fired only forty-three rockets before one of *Gwylym Manthyr*'s 10-inch shells exploded eleven feet from it. The explosion ripped the side of the hull to pieces, set off the sympathetic detonation of nineteen more rockets, and blasted the broken and burning barge up onto its side. The sudden upheaval scattered its remaining fifty-eight rockets in a flat, broad arc that came nowhere near any Charisian.

Of the three hundred and sixty rockets aboard the remaining three barges, forty-nine malfunctioned in one fashion or another. Three of them actually snaked around and slammed into the rear face of the battery's parapet, killing sixteen more of Captain Mahntayl's men. But the other three hundred and eleven screamed heavenward in an endless avalanche of fire and smoke, then came shrieking back down.

They weren't very accurate weapons—not individually—but there were over three hundred of them. They couldn't *all* miss . . . and they didn't.

▼   ▼   ▼

Gahryth Shumayt watched sickly from the open bridge wing as at least five and possibly six of those rockets came crashing down on HMS *Eraystor*. He couldn't tell how many of them actually hit her and how many were "only" near misses—not through the smoke and the enormous columns of spray rising from the tortured sea as hundreds of other rockets plunged into it and exploded. He saw at least two fireballs, though, and the forward half of the ironclad's funnel simply disappeared in a rolling wave of destruction.

He could see *Riverbend* more clearly, and he swore vilely as Tobys Whytmyn's ship staggered around, turning directly south-southeast, away from Wreckers' Island. The flames which had been almost extinguished aft belched up in a fresh, towering inferno, and propellant charges for her 6-inch guns began exploding as they cooked off in the flames. She was clearly sinking, settling swiftly by the stern, and Shumayt found himself praying the inrushing water would quench the flames before they reached her magazine. She was fighting towards deeper water, trying to get clear, clawing her way towards the reserve bombsweepers who might be able to pick up her survivors when she finally sank.

It was all she could do, and as the billowing clouds of smoke belched from the wounded, dying ship, he wondered if Whytmyn was still alive on that flame-enshrouded bridge, still trying to get at least some of his people out alive.

He didn't wonder about *Eraystor*.

The last rockets slammed into the water and exploded a good thousand yards from *Gairmyn*, and *Eraystor* thrust through the smoke and spray. She was still making at least ten knots, but her entire forward superstructure—everything forward of her crumpled funnel—was a solid mass of flame. Her navigation bridge was simply *gone*, ripped away, leaving only a few twisted support girders to show where it once had been, and her conning tower had become a chimney, the flue of hell's own furnace. Flames roaring ferociously up that chimney leapt masthead-high, and the ship was clearly out of control with no living hand upon her helm.

She staggered around, still turning in response to Captain Cahnyrs' final helm order, and as Shumayt watched, she steamed directly into the field of sea-bombs.

She got three hundred yards before she hit the first one. Within three minutes' time she struck two more.

The fourth exploded directly under her forward magazine, and HMS *Eraystor* disintegrated in a massive ball of flame.

.III.
East Point Battery
and
Royal Palace,
City of Gorath,
Kingdom of Dohlar.

The Earl of Thirsk stood alone at the observation tower's front rail, watching the eastern horizon turn lavender and rose. Captain Stywyrt Baiket, who'd become his executive officer ashore when his longtime flagship was laid up to release her manpower for shore defense, stood several feet behind him, watching him a bit anxiously, and half a dozen aides and runners stood behind Baiket. For all that, Thirsk had been alone—alone with his thoughts, his worries . . . his responsibilities—as the black, moonless sky had slowly, slowly turned to gray. And now, as dawn crept timidly closer and he stared out across the Five Fathom Deep from the East Point Battery, his weary eyes strained to pierce the waning dark.

There were eighteen 12-inch Fultyn Rifles in that battery, which ought to make short work of any attacker . . . if, of course, the attacker in question chose to face them, and it was far from certain he would. Indeed, the choice of invasion routes for the Kingdom of Dohlar's capital came down to a guessing game—the deadliest Thirsk had ever played—with thousands of lives on the line.

There were three avenues to choose between, now that the Charisians had forced the Zhulyet Channel and reduced Wreckers' Island to churned, smoking wreckage.

East Gate Channel, the passage between East Point and Fishnet Island, was twelve and a half miles wide. That water gap could be closed—barely—by rifled artillery, as long as the batteries on both sides remained in action, although striking power and accuracy would be less than stellar against a target sailing straight down the center of the passage. They could hit it, but accuracy would be poor and the ability to penetrate Charisian armor plate would be . . . questionable, at best. That was why he'd laid the densest sea-bomb field of all squarely across East Gate's center. An attacker could choose to pass close to one of the batteries—East Point or Fishnet—and endure the worst its guns could do, or he could sail down the center of the channel, where those guns would be far less effective, and accept the sea-bomb threat. The sea-bomb fuses remained much less reliable than he could have wished, and about thirty percent of them leaked badly enough to become useless within a five-day or two, but his men had laid hundreds of the things. If anyone was foolish enough to sail *into* that field, he would never sail out of it again.

The Middle Gate, between Fishnet Island and Alahnah Island, to its immediate west, was less than half that wide, which made it far easier to defend with artillery. But Tairayl's Gate, the gap between Alahnah and Chelsee Point on the mainland, was over twenty miles across. No Dohlaran gun could hope to engage a target sailing down the middle of that broad expanse.

Fortunately, the water was shallower in Tairayl's Gate than in East Gate Channel. The Middle Gate was actually the deepest of the three channels, and tidal scour combined with the current of the Gorath River to keep it that way. All three of them were deep enough for even the largest galleons, at least at high tide, but the deepwater channel through Tairayl's Gate was more tortuous than most. In fact, it curved and twisted so sharply it was seldom used by galleons, since a wind that was fair for one leg of the passage was almost always dead foul for the next one. Threading a way through it could be a tricky piece of piloting even for a galley—or a steamer—no matter how well it was marked . . . and just now, it wasn't marked at all. If any navy could navigate that passage even after someone had removed every buoy and extinguished every lighthouse, it was undoubtedly the *Charisian* Navy, but their armored steamers were far too valuable to risk casually. That was especially true after what had happened to them off Wreckers' Island, he thought grimly, and he'd done what he could to make the choice even less attractive by placing sea-bombs at the trickiest points along the channel.

The Middle Gate had been harder to cover with sea-bombs because of the set of tide and current. The mooring cables kept breaking, and the Dohlaran merchant marine had discovered the hard way that a drifting sea-bomb had no friends. He'd persevered with the effort, but he couldn't pretend he was satisfied with the result. On the other hand, its maximum width was under ten thousand yards. That was why the batteries on Alahnah and Fishnet accounted for well over a third of his total heavy rifles—including all six of the 15-inch rifles the Temple Lands foundries had managed to deliver—despite the islands' small size. He had only twenty-five rounds for each of the 15-inchers, and the guns were actually shorter ranged than the 12-inch pieces, but they hit with devastating power and they were backed by twenty-four more 12-inchers and thirty 8-inch weapons. He rather doubted anyone who'd already experienced what the heavy Fultyns could do would choose to run that gauntlet at such a short range unless he had to.

All of that was true, but it was also true that it had never occurred to him when he'd planned the capital's defenses that the Charisians might be able to sweep the sea-bombs out of their way. His reports from the previous day's fighting were less complete than he might wish, but almost all of them agreed that they'd demonstrated an ability to do just that, even under heavy fire, and that made all of his planning suspect. From the reports he'd received, he doubted their bombsweepers made Tairayl's Gate any more attractive, since the technique they'd developed apparently required them to steam in straight lines. Tairayl's Gate didn't lend itself to those sorts of courses.

The East Gate, unfortunately, did.

That was why he was standing atop this observation tower awaiting the dawn. If he'd been in Baron Sarmouth's shoes, and if those fragmentary reports were accurate, his decision would have been simple. Assuming his converted barges truly could clear the sea-bombs, the East Gate's simpler piloting, coupled with how much farther from the defensive batteries he could stay, made it his obvious choice. It was always possible he'd choose another route simply because it was *less* obvious. His tactics in the Trosan Channel and off Shipworm Shoal indicated how well he understood the advantages of surprise. But the Imperial Charisian Navy was equally well aware of the risk in being *too* clever, and East Gate's attractions were simply too compelling to be ignored.

If the sea-bombs could be cleared.

That was why he'd committed the last fifteen screw-galleys of the Royal Dohlaran Navy last night.

He hadn't planned on using them at all, even though he'd drilled them in night attacks ever since the Battle of Shipworm Shoal. That battle had made it obvious daylight attacks were suicidal even against ironclad *galleons*, far less the ICN's steam-powered monsters, but he'd hoped the darkness might allow them to finally employ their spar torpedoes . . . until yesterday, at least. He hadn't truly allowed for how fast and maneuverable—and incredibly hard to kill—the steamers were. True, his men had sent two to the bottom and severely damaged a third. Numerically, that was almost half the attacking force. But given the difference between the smaller steamers and the one the Charisians had named for *Gwyllym Manthyr*, it represented barely a quarter—if that—of Sarmouth's firepower. Against that sort of armored target, *only* the spar torpedoes could hope to have any effect, but he'd quickly realized that the chance of a screw-galley getting a torpedo into attack range of something that fast and heavily armed, even in the dark, had been so slim as to be nonexistent.

But the bombsweepers were much smaller, unarmored, un*armed*, and— if the reports were accurate—*slower* than the screw-galleys. They'd be easy meat for the screw-galleys' massive forward batteries, most of which now mounted 8-inch rifles, and they represented the Charisians' only path through the sea-bombs. So if the screw-galleys could get through to them, destroy or cripple enough of them to prevent the survivors from clearing the East Gate. . . .

There'd never been much chance of accomplishing anything more than a temporary delay, even if the attack succeeded, but the Navy's honor—and the increasingly evident agents inquisitor patrolling Gorath's streets—had demanded they try. And so he'd sent them out, knowing the Charisians had to be on the lookout for exactly that sort of attack, and their officers and men had never flinched. The black-painted screw-galleys, stripped of masts and sails to make them even harder to see, had slipped silently out of the harbor in the very last of the fading sunset, with scarcely a ripple to mark their passing, and Thirsk had planted himself atop this very tower to await their return.

He was still waiting.

You know what happened, he told himself grimly. *They'd've been back by now if they were coming. The only real question is how many more hundred men you just sent to their deaths, Lywys.*

His jaw tightened, but he refused to lie to himself. Those hadn't been lightning flashes last night. They'd been too distant for him to hear anything over the steady, rhythmic wash of waves against the East Point beaches, but he'd known they were the savage flashes of artillery and the glare of Charisian star shells. The firing hadn't gone on very long, and if any of his screw-galleys had survived it, there'd been plenty of time for them to return by now.

I am so tired of sending young men out to die for those bastards in Zion, he thought bitterly. *But at least I—*

A rim of blinding sunlight heaved itself over the eastern horizon, and Lywys Gardynyr's jaw clenched painfully as the rich golden light raced out across the sixty-mile-wide stretch of water called Five Fathom Deep.

▼ ▼ ▼

Had Thirsk only realized it, he was less alone than he thought he was. Sir Dunkyn Yairley might be standing beside Halcom Bahrns on Bahrns' navigation bridge, but that didn't prevent him from looking out over Five Fathom Deep with the Dohlaran earl through the eyes of the tiny remote on Thirsk's shoulder, and his expression was grimly satisfied at the view they shared.

HMS *Gwylym Manthyr* steamed straight for the center of East Gate Channel, gliding across the smooth, sun-gilded water under the vigilant white eye of her kite balloon while a banner of coal smoke trailed astern. A double trio of bombsweepers swept the waters ahead of her; HMS *Bayport*, HMS *Cherayth*, and HMS *Tanjyr* followed her; and four more bombsweepers flanked the slow-moving column of armored warships. The badly damaged

Gairmyn, half her guns out of action, her casemate blackened by fire, her funnel bleeding smoke from dozens of splinter holes, listing four degrees to starboard, and riding well over a foot deeper than her design waterline, brought up the rear with the ammunition colliers . . . and the three crippled Dohlaran screw-galleys which had survived long enough to surrender.

Those screw-galleys had been Sarmouth's greatest anxiety after the savagery of the Zhulyet Channel. They'd been slower, less maneuverable, and far more vulnerable than *Manthyr* or his remaining *Cities*, but if they'd been able to creep in close enough in the darkness. . . .

Fortunately, the ICN had evolved a doctrine to deal with them, and it had worked well. The combination of star shells and rockets had stripped away the darkness, and *Manthyr's* 4-inch breechloaders had been absolutely lethal, far deadlier than the *Cities'* slower firing 6-inch guns. Only three of the screw-galleys had gotten in close enough to engage with their own guns; none had managed a torpedo attack; and all their efforts had managed to sink only one bombsweeper.

He'd felt more like a murderer than an admiral, in many ways. Not one of the screw-galleys had tried to run. Every one of them had been sunk or crippled trying to *close* with their enemies with an unswerving gallantry which deserved far better than it had achieved. Their courage had won his ungrudging respect, but that hadn't prevented him from crushing the attack, and if he'd regretted their deaths, at least it had been gratifying to find something working as planned.

He'd be a long time forgiving himself for what had happened to *Eraystor* and *Riverbend*, even though he still knew intellectually that Zhaztro had been right about which ships could be risked. The consequences if Mahntayl's rockets had hit *Manthyr* instead of the *Cities* would almost certainly have been far worse, even just in terms of absolute casualties. No one could argue with that, but. . . .

But if you're not cheating, you're not trying hard enough, he thought. *You forgot that one, Dunkyn, and now Hainz and all those other men are gone.* His eyes hardened. *Avoiding any appearance of "demonic intervention" had damned well better be worth it in the end.*

That remained to be seen, but there was one thing he could do this morning, "demonic intervention" or not, and he really didn't care if it compromised that political objective. He was through seeing his men die if it could be avoided.

Better get out from under, My Lord, he thought in Thirsk's direction. *You're not supposed to be part of the body count today, but if it happens, it happens.*

"I believe it's about time, Halcom," he said.

"Of course, My Lord," Bahrns said after the slightest of hesitations, and Sarmouth hid a bittersweet smile. His flag captain had seemed a bit . . .

bemused when he issued his instructions this morning. But whatever he might have thought, he hadn't argued, and now he bent over the bridge pelorus and took a careful bearing on the observation tower upon which the Earl of Thirsk stood. Then he swung the pelorus and took a cross bearing on the flagstaff of Fishnet Island's East Battery.

"All stop," he said, still gazing across the pelorus.

"All stop, aye, Sir," the telegraphsman acknowledged. He rocked the engine room repeaters' big brass handles, moving the pointer in the engine room. "All stop," he confirmed, and the pulse of *Gwylym Manthyr's* engines stilled, as if some great sea creature's heart had suddenly stopped beating.

"Prepare to anchor," Bahrns said.

"Prepare to anchor, aye, Sir," Lieutenant Bestyr acknowledged.

"Very good," the captain murmured, still bent over the pelorus, as *Manthyr's* momentum carried her silently onward, like some fourteen-thousand-ton ghost. He stayed that way for several more minutes, then raised his head as *Manthyr* reached exactly the correct bearing from East Point.

"Let go the stern anchor!" he said crisply, and *Gwylym Manthyr's* stern anchor plunged into the water with a massive roar of anchor chain. Bahrns straightened and crossed to the forward edge of the bridge, then stood patiently, fingers of his right hand drumming against his thigh while *Manthyr's* momentum sailed out the anchor chain and her speed bled away. Then—

"Let go the bow anchor!" he said, and *Manthyr's* starboard bow anchor plunged. "Power on the after capstan," he continued. "Veer cable forward."

Gwylym Manthyr edged slowly backwards for two or three minutes as the after capstan sucked in anchor chain and the forward capstan paid it out. Bahrns watched critically, balancing her between the two anchors with finicky precision until, at last, she came to rest, the current of the outgoing tide raising a tiny ripple around her stem, exactly equidistant from the batteries on Fishnet and East Point.

"Secure the capstans," he said then, and waited while the order was carried out. Then he turned to Sarmouth once more.

"Prepared to engage, My Lord," he said simply.

▼   ▼   ▼

The Earl of Thirsk stared in disbelief.

The Charisian ironclad's captain had handled his enormous command with impressive skill, almost as if she'd been one of the ICN's nimble schooners. That had been his first thought. He'd been a bit puzzled by how slowly she'd moved, but it had been obvious she meant to split the difference between East Point and Fishnet. That had suggested a lot more trust in the bombsweepers' ability to protect her than he'd expected out of someone as experienced as Sarmouth.

He has to know I'd have laid as many sea-bombs as I could to cover the East Gate, and somehow I doubt those sweepers of his can guarantee to clear all of them out of his path! He can't be going to deliberately *take that ship straight into them!*

The very thought had been insane, yet that had been exactly what was happening, and he'd felt himself tightening internally, waiting for the first explosion. But then his eyes had gone wide. She was anchoring—*anchoring!*—just over eleven thousand yards from East Point . . . and exactly the same distance from Fishnet. What struck him first was the fact that Sarmouth was anchoring at all, surrendering the mobility which would have made his flagship a far more difficult target. Then he realized *Manthyr's* position allowed her gunners to engage with both broadsides at once, from an absolutely stable and unmoving platform, while simultaneously placing her at the very limit of his own range. Just reaching her would require his gunners to use dangerously heavy charges—the kind that led to burst guns and dead and mangled gunners—and even so, their shells would have precious little penetrating power when they got there.

And then the rest of it struck him.

She hadn't just anchored, hadn't just positioned herself perfectly to engage both batteries simultaneously. No, she'd also anchored when the bombsweepers in front of her had been a mere two hundred yards, less than half a cable, outside his sea-bombs. And Sarmouth hadn't anchored because anyone had suddenly spotted the sea-bombs or because his sweepers had abruptly brought one to the surface. There'd been no haste, no urgency, to the maneuver. No, he'd anchored with slow, deliberate precision, exactly where he'd intended to anchor from the very beginning. And that meant—

He knows *where they are.* The thought ran through Thirsk's brain. *He* knows *exactly where they are. Shan-wei! Either he's the luckiest flag officer in the entire world, or else he knows where they are even better than I do!*

An icy shiver went through him. It was entirely possible Charisian spies had watched those sea-bombs being laid. He'd had ample proof of how effortlessly at least *one* Charisian "spy" could penetrate Gorath undetected. But they could scarcely have found a spot to take detailed bearings on the vessels laying the sea-bombs without someone *seeing* them. And without those bearings, they couldn't possibly have provided Sarmouth with information accurate enough for him to accomplish what he'd just done. Even *with* that kind of information, Thirsk doubted any Dohlaran captain could have duplicated that maneuver.

He wanted to think it had been only a spectacularly lucky guess on Sarmouth's part, but then two of the ironclad's escorting bombsweepers crossed in front of her on opposite courses, dropping buoys over the side, and Thirsk's jaw clenched as he realized they were deploying floater nets. Floater nets designed to catch any drifting sea-bomb well short of *Gwylym Manthyr.*

Obviously Sarmouth *did* know where they were, and he was taking no chances on one of them breaking loose.

▼   ▼   ▼

"Handsomely done, Halcom," Sarmouth congratulated his flag captain.

"Thank you, My Lord." Bahrns smiled crookedly, his eyes on the bomb-sweepers deploying the protective nets. "I hope it won't offend you if I admit I was a little nervous about the whole thing."

"Offend?" Sarmouth chuckled. "No, Halcom. Sanity never offends me. I suppose I *was* guilty of what His Majesty likes to call a 'calculated risk'—when he's the one taking it, at least—but we did have the sweepers out front, you know."

"Yes, My Lord, I do."

Sarmouth heard the hint of repressiveness in his captain's tone and chuckled again. But then his expression hardened.

"Well, here we are, the men've had breakfast, and we've got the entire day to work with." He smiled grimly and began fitting the plugs into his ears. "Under the circumstances, I believe we should be about it."

▼   ▼   ▼

"You should leave now, My Lord," a voice said quietly.

Thirsk turned his head. Stywyrt Baiket stood at his right shoulder, spyglass raised to his eye, and his voice was so low no one could have heard him from more than a very few feet away.

"I don't think so," Thirsk replied, turning his own eyes back to the massive, anchored ironclad.

The pair of heavy guns fore and aft were rotating to starboard with mechanical smoothness, obviously powered by the same steam that drove the ship's propellers. Sarmouth had decided which of his two targets deserved their attention first, the earl thought, watching the muzzles turn in his direction.

"Then you're wrong, My Lord."

Baiket's voice was even lower, but it had acquired a steely edge, and Thirsk looked at him again. The captain lowered his spyglass to meet his eyes levelly.

"I know what you're thinking," he said. "I know *why* you're thinking it. But this is my job now, not yours, and there's not a man in the entire Navy who doesn't know how badly we'll need you going forward. We can't risk losing you, My Lord. Not when you have so much still to do after the battle."

His tone said more than his words, and Thirsk's heart sank as he realized what the other man was truly saying . . . and that he was right.

"You're not 'abandoning your post,' My Lord," Baiket said almost gently. "You're making sure you'll be available for a job only *you* can do."

"You're right . . . Shan-wei take it," Thirsk muttered and clasped Baiket's shoulder with his good hand. "You're right. But watch yourself, Stywyrt. I don't have that many friends left—see to it I don't lose another one!"

"Dying's not on my to-do list, My Lord," Baiket assured him with a smile. "I've got too much to look forward to! This next little bit's going to be a mite on the . . . unpleasant side, maybe, but later—!"

His smile grew broader and much, much colder as their gazes held for a handful of seconds. Then he twitched his head at the observation tower stair.

"Best you were going now, My Lord. In fact, I'll go with you as far as the command post. Somehow," he raised his spyglass for one last glance at the long, slender guns elevating in his direction, "I think it's going to get a little *noisy* around here."

▼   ▼   ▼

The smoke was thicker than a Fairstock fog, Bishop Executor Wylsynn Lainyr thought grimly.

There was virtually no wind to disperse it, and it had settled like a curse, growing thicker and thicker while the fires burned. He hadn't had this much difficulty picking his way through a city's streets, even after dark, since his last visit home in Hayzor. His carriage's powerful lamps penetrated no more than a few yards—barely far enough for the coachman to see the heads of his horses—and the pedestrians they passed had wet cloths tied over their mouths and noses.

Of course, there weren't many of those pedestrians.

The streets and avenues of Gorath were deserted, turned into ghostly, smoke-shrouded places abandoned to fear and the night. It wasn't really *dark*, though. The roaring flames consuming the Royal Dohlaran Navy's massive dockyards and warehouses turned the smoke into a glowing cocoon. The short coach trip from Gorath Cathedral to King Rahnyld's palace had been like a voyage through clouded amber, but it was an amber tinted with the red of the flames, not warm and golden, and it pulsed like the beating of some enormous heart as those flames roared and danced all along the south-eastern end of the city.

There were more flames farther north, where the foundries which had produced the kingdom's heavy artillery had been reduced to rubble, and the entire city had shivered like a terrified animal when a heretic shell landed directly atop the Navy Arsenal and touched off its main magazine in a stupendous, roaring explosion that had rolled on and on for what had seemed an hour.

Yet for all of that, the city itself had suffered remarkably little damage.

The heretics had blasted their way in through East Gate Channel, demolished the East Point batteries, and swept away the sea-bombs Earl Thirsk and Duke Fern had promised would be so effective. Then they'd advanced on the city itself.

The smaller ironclads had smashed the batteries protecting the waterfront and the Navy Yard, then turned their attention to Gorath's famous golden walls. They'd obviously come to deliver a message to the city which had delivered their sailors to the Inquisition not once, but twice, and they'd reduced the entire seaward face of its walls to broken and blasted wreckage with shell after methodical shell, fired with the metronome steadiness of a formal salute. And while they were doing that, the enormous ironclad—the ironclad named for the accursed heretic Mother Church had given to the Punishment in Zion itself—had trained its guns on rather different targets. It had anchored again—*anchored*—in full view of any citizen of Gorath who'd cared to look, and begun the careful, systematic, *unhurried* destruction of the shipyards, manufactories, foundries, and warehouses which supported the Royal Dohlaran Navy and Army.

The implications of its obvious and utter contempt for anything Gorath's defenders could do had been terrifying, but the reach and accuracy of its fire had been even more frightening. Lainyr was no military man. He'd had no idea how the heretics could drop their shells so accurately, with a precision the finest surgeon might have envied, on targets that couldn't even be *seen* from Queen Zhakleen Harbor, but he didn't doubt Captain Gairybahldy's explanation was correct. It was the balloon. It was the accursed, no doubt demonic, *balloon*. It hung above the ironclad, watching the fall of its shells, sending down corrections, and the thunderbolts of destruction had marched across their targets with devastating effect.

And the bastards were careful not *to hit the residential areas*, Lainyr thought grimly.

For all the pervasiveness of the smoke, only a handful of shells had landed anywhere near the city's houses or apartment buildings, and they'd obviously missed their intended targets. The Navy Yard, the manufactories and warehouses, the city's walls had been demolished by hit after hit, yet it had been painfully obvious the heretics were carefully avoiding civilian casualties.

And the people of Gorath knew it. They knew the navy which had every reason to hate their kingdom, whose monarchs had declared the basis for those reasons time and again, whose dead sailors had been dropped into Gorath Bay like so much refuse, denied even burial in consecrated ground, and whose living sailors had been delivered to the hideous provisions of the Punishment, were deliberately *not* killing them. Destroying their city's manufactories, smashing its walls and its fortifications, yes; killing the civilians of that city, no.

The word that the heretics—the savage, bloodthirsty heretics the Inquisition had assured them sacrificed babies to Shan-wei and routinely burned Temple Loyalist churches to the ground, generally with their congregations locked up inside them—were trying not to kill them or their families and children had spread rapidly among the capital's inhabitants. Ahbsahlahn Kharmych's agents inquisitor had already confirmed that, and Lainyr didn't want to think about the speculation that restraint was bound to spawn, especially after all the casualties Dohlar had suffered in the service of Mother Church. King Rahnyld's subjects' confidence in the Jihad—and in its justification, little though Lainyr liked admitting that—had been crumbling for months. Langhorne only knew what would happen to it now, but the bishop executor didn't expect it to be good.

"Five more minutes, Your Eminence."

Lainyr turned his head as Captain Gairybahldy leaned from the saddle and spoke through the open carriage window. Like everyone they'd passed, the captain had tied a wet bandanna across his face. It made him look like a highwayman, Lainyr thought. Or like some other sinister criminal, at any rate. That was an image Mother Church's protectors didn't need to be projecting just now, and a petty, petulant part of him thought about snapping an order to take it off—and for *all* of Gairybahldy's men to do the same.

But there's no point, he thought wearily. *And how likely is that, really, to add to the . . . demoralization this city's already suffered?*

"Thank you, Captain," he said, courteously, instead, and leaned back in his seat opposite Kharmych and closed his eyes in silent prayer.

▼　▼　▼

Closed windows and doors might keep the worst of the city's smoke at bay, but the stink of it penetrated even to the heart of the royal palace. Lainyr would have preferred to think it had come in on his own clothing, but the faintest haze was visible in the longer palace corridors, hanging in nebulous halos around the lamps which lit them.

He followed their guide down the crimson runner and the council chamber doors opened wide at their approach.

"The Bishop Executor and Father Kharmych, My Lords," the liveried footman announced, and stood aside as the clerics passed through the doors, followed by Captain Gairybahldy. The men seated at the table—the Duke of Fern, the Duke of Salthar, and Baron Yellowstone—rose as they entered.

"Your Eminence, Father," Fern greeted them.

"Your Grace," Lainyr replied, but he also paused just inside the doors.

"Is something wrong, Your Eminence?" Fern inquired.

"I was about to ask *you* that," Lainyr replied. "May I ask where Duke

Thorast is? And it was my impression His Majesty intended to be present for the discussion of the capital's defense."

"Duke Thorast has been unavoidably detained, I'm afraid," Fern replied, gesturing with one hand towards the comfortable chairs waiting for Lainyr and Kharmych. "And His Majesty is currently with the healers."

"With the healers?" Lainyr repeated sharply, resuming his progress towards the table. "Was he injured during the attack?!"

"No, Your Eminence. I assure you, if he had been you would already have heard. No, he's simply experiencing some difficulty with his breathing because of the smoke. The healers don't think it's anything serious, but his personal physician wants to keep an eye on him until they're positive of that."

"I see." Lainyr extended his ring for Fern to kiss, then settled into his chair, Gairybahldy at his back like an armsman, as the Dohlaran councilors sat back down. "And do we know how long Duke Thorast will be delayed?"

"For quite some time, I'm afraid, Your Eminence," another voice said, and Lainyr's head whipped around.

He hadn't heard the well-oiled hinges when the doors opened again behind him. Nor had he heard the boots crossing the thick, expensive carpet. But he recognized that voice, and his eyes flared as he saw the Earl of Thirsk.

The Admiral wasn't alone, and the color drained from the bishop executor's face as he saw Sir Rainos Ahlverez at Thirsk's left shoulder . . . and Bishop Staiphan Maik at his right. There was a pistol in Ahlverez' hand, aimed directly at Captain Gairybahldy's head, and the general shook his head very slightly when the Guardsman whipped around and his hand started towards his own pistol.

Gairybahldy froze, standing very still indeed under the blank, cold eye of that pistol muzzle, but Ahbsahlahn Kharmych shot to his feet.

"*What's the meaning of this?!*" the intendant thundered. "What do you think you're *doing?!*"

"I should think that would be clear even to you, Father," Thirsk replied coolly. "For your information, however, units of the Army and Navy are currently arresting every agent inquisitor in Gorath." He shrugged slightly at Kharmych's stunned expression. "We may miss a few, and I'm afraid there may be a little breakage. The officers and sergeants assigned to that duty are mostly survivors of the Army of Shiloh or veterans from the Army of the Seridahn. I'm afraid they're unlikely to show a great deal of patience if any of your agents offer resistance. For some reason, they aren't very fond of inquisitors."

Kharmych stared at him, frozen, as he and Bishop Staiphan walked around the end of the table to the Duke of Fern's chair. The bishop's face was stone, his eyes harder than flint as they met Lainyr's horrified gaze, and the bishop executor's frozen heart plummeted as he read the message in that unyielding countenance. Ahlverez stayed where he was as another half-dozen men in Army uniform filtered into the room, bayoneted rifles carried at a position of port arms, and Duke Fern rose once again, to stand beside Thirsk and Staiphan Maik.

"At this moment," the earl continued, "Sir Rainos' senior aide, Captain Lattymyr, is at the Cathedral with two platoons of Army of Shiloh veterans. It's a pity Archbishop Trumahn's business in Zion has continued to prevent his return, but I'm confident Father Rahndail will be able to direct the Captain to General Rychtyr's chambers so that the General can accompany Sir Lynkyn back to the Palace. In the meantime," he smiled thinly and settled into the chair Fern had just vacated, while Bishop Staiphan moved to stand at one shoulder and the first councilor—the *former* first councilor, Lainyr realized numbly—moved to stand at the other, "I think we should by all means begin that discussion about how to defend this city.

"And against whom."

.IV.
Royal Palace,
City of Cherayth,
and
Braigyr Head,
Duchy of Rock Coast,
Kingdom of Chisholm,
Empire of Charis;
and
Symyn's Farm,
Duchy of Thorast,
Kingdom of Dohlar.

Rebkah Rohsail sat in the comfortably furnished chamber, staring out the window at the palace gardens, hands folded in her lap, and tried to understand how it could all have gone so wrong.

It's as if they knew exactly what we planned the entire time, she thought. *They* were *waiting for us. And that* bitch *Elahnah—!*

White-hot rage fisted her hands in her lap as that familiar thought went through her once again. She knew now why Elahnah Waistyn hadn't promised her support. She'd been back over their correspondence a thousand times in her mind, and her teeth ground together as she went through it yet again. She'd read what she'd wanted to see into Elahnah's letters—she knew

that now—but she also knew Elahnah had realized *exactly* what she was reading into them. That without ever quite committing perjury, the Dowager
Duchess of Halbrook Hollow had encouraged her plans without actually
committing to support them in any way. That would have been bad enough,
a great enough sin against God, but the traitorous bitch hadn't stopped there.
She must have been passing Rebkah's letters directly to White Crag and
Stoneheart, as well!

She wanted, desperately, to believe Elahnah's treachery was what had
given the entire conspiracy away, but deep inside she knew it couldn't have
been. The Crown's response had been too devastating, too complete, and
far too well planned to have been based solely on the vague hints and sug-
gestions Rebkah had penned to her. No, they'd been betrayed from *within*—
they had to have been . . . unless. . . .

She inhaled deeply. No, it couldn't have been the false *seijins*. No matter
what they might claim, *she* knew who they truly served, and God would
never have permitted Shan-wei's minions to cast down His champions this
way!

But it didn't really matter what had begun the chain of disasters leading
to this palace chamber and its genteel confinement. What mattered was the
chain itself, and the totality of the trap which had closed upon her and her
allies.

Virtually all of them were in custody now. The speed and decisiveness
with which Sir Ahlber Zhustyn's agents had pounced was almost as breath-
taking as the obviously preplanned military movements which had crushed
their motley collection of armsmen in less than two five-days. Every one
of the senior guildsmen who'd corresponded with her or with Zhonathyn
Clyntahn had been arrested in the space of less than twenty-six hours. Brekyn
Ainsail, the man she'd trusted to divert weapons to the cause, had not only
been arrested, but he'd personally led Zhustyn's agents to the weapons caches
he'd set up for her. Father Zhordyn was in custody, as well, and so were more
than two dozen clerics who'd secretly pledged their loyalty to the Temple
and promised to bring their congregations with them.

It was disaster, total and complete. A handful of the conspirators had so
far eluded arrest, although she couldn't imagine how. The most prominent
was Rock Coast himself, and she found herself torn between the hope that
at least one of them would escape the Crown's net and a vengeful desire for
the man who'd obviously botched the entire plan to share his fellows' fate.

In the meantime, though—

Someone knocked on her chamber door, and the maid assigned to her—
not her own maid from Swayleton—opened it. Voices murmured, and then
a captain in the uniform of the House of Ahrmahk bowed to her.

"Excuse me, Milady, but your presence is required," he said courteously.

She gazed at him for a moment, considering a spiteful refusal to accompany him. To make him drag her through the halls, spitting her defiance the entire way. But then she squared her shoulders defiantly, ran her hands over her braided hair, and stood.

"Of course, Captain," she said in a voice of ice.

▼   ▼   ▼

The council chamber was rather more crowded than usual, with half a dozen Imperial Charisian Guardsmen standing respectfully, silently, but very watchfully against the wall. Rebkah glanced around and her mouth tightened as she realized Duke Lantern Walk, Duke Black Horse, Duke Holy Tree, and Duke Black Bottom were already present. And, unlike her, all of them were in chains.

They stood before the council table, facing Sylvyst Mhardyr, the Baron of Stoneheart, across it. Sir Ahlber Zhustyn sat at the Lord Justice's right elbow, and Stoneheart's brown eyes were as hard as his barony's name.

"What's the meaning of this?!" Lantern Walk raised his manacled hand. "I'm a peer of the realm—a *duke!* How *dare* you treat me like a common felon?!"

"Actually," Stoneheart said coldly, "it's easy. You *are* common felons."

Lantern Walk's face turned beet-red, but Holy Tree was obviously terrified, hovering on the brink of collapse, and Rebkah felt a deep, searing contempt for her prospective son-in-law. The least he could do was be a *man* now that they'd been found out! Still, he hadn't completely collapsed yet, which was more than she could say for some.

"There's been a terrible misunderstanding!" Black Horse said. "I realize this looks bad—looks *terrible*—My Lord! But, surely, when you've reviewed all of the evidence, you'll realize I was coerced. This was . . . this was all Rock Coast's idea! His and Lady Swayle's! *I* wanted nothing to do with it, but they told me all my neighbors were already committed to their treason! That if I didn't join them, they'd attack me, *force* me to support them! The first I heard of it was barely a month ago, and by then their plans were already in motion! It was too late for me to tell anyone or do anything except—"

"Save your breath, Your Grace." Stoneheart's cold contempt shut Black Horse's mouth with a snap. "The Crown knows you were one of the two original instigators of this entire plot. It was at least as much of your making as of Duke Rock Coast's *or* Lady Swayle's. And unlike Lady Swayle, neither you nor Rock Coast were inspired by the depth of your faith, whatever you have told *her.* We have documentary evidence of your involvement at every step, Your Grace, and this time, you—*all* of you—will face the penalties laid down for treason."

Rebkah felt her face pale, Holy Tree swayed, and Black Horse stared at Stoneheart as if he couldn't believe his ears. Black Bottom only shrugged—the thought of any mortal penalties clearly meant little to a man of his age in his health—but Lantern Walk ony laughed scornfully.

"Don't be a fool," he sneered. "And don't think *we're* fools, either! You're talking to four of the Kingdom's six ranking dukes! We failed, and of course there'll be consequences. But not even Sharleyan—not even *Cayleb of Charis*—is stupid enough to think they could execute all of us without bringing the entire rest of the nobility down around their ears!"

"I beg to differ, Your Grace. I very much doubt the other peers will be particularly fond of self-serving traitors who attempted to provoke outright civil war. You might want to consider that the first and fourth ranking dukes of this Kingdom live in Tayt and Eastshare. Neither of *them* will raise a hand in your defense. Nor, I venture to suggest, will anyone else, when the full scale of your treason is revealed."

"Full scale?" Lantern Walk jeered. "You actually think you can convince the House of Lords of all these ridiculous charges? Where's your *proof*? And don't tell me about 'eyewitness testimony' from our 'fellow conspirators'! Everyone knows what can be coerced or tortured out of someone accused of this sort of crime!"

"Unfortunately for you, Your Grace, we don't need eyewitness testimony." Stoneheart smiled thinly. "We'll be presenting quite a lot of it, but we don't *need* it, because we have your correspondence—*all* of it. We have complete copies of your secret files, and we can demonstrate every step of your communications chains. We know which days Father Sedryk carried letters to Lady Swayle, what day one of Rock Coast's messenger wyverns arrived in your wyvern cot. We have the names of your couriers, copies of the written promises you made to Master Clyntahn and the other guilds, and every bit of Lady Swayle's correspondence with Colonel Ainsail. We have the serial numbers of the stolen weapons that were diverted to your purposes, and we know when and where you recruited your armsmen in violation of King Sailys' Edict. Trust me, Your Grace—we have more than enough evidence to prove our case against you five times over."

Even Lantern Walk had paled at that devastating catalog, but he shook himself and glared at Stoneheart.

"Prove it and be damned!" he snapped. "You may be able to threaten the others into tearful confessions to escape the noose, but Sharleyan knows the entire Kingdom will go up in flame if she executes this many peers!"

"Indeed?" Stoneheart cocked his head, then opened the folder on the table before him and extracted several sheets of paper.

"This is a letter from Her Majesty to her Council. In case you're interested, the date is February ninth. Allow me to share a short passage from it.

" 'My Lords, it has come to Our attention through the service of Our loyal servants and, particularly, through the offices of Our especial servant, *Seijin* Merlin, and his companions that certain nobles of Our Realm of Chisholm have once more set their hands to the commission of foulest treason. We append in a separate letter the names of twenty-seven peers, major and minor, who have signified to one another their willingness to raise armed insurrection against Our Crown and Our subjects.' "

An invisible fist punched Rebkah in the belly. If that letter truly had been written in February, and if it really had been accompanied by that list of names, then Sharleyan had known—known for *months*—exactly what the conspirators were doing . . . and who they were.

" 'These traitors,' " Stoneheart continued, " 'have expressed to one another their readiness to murder those loyal to Our throne, be they noble or common, and to overthrow the rights and prerogatives Our Crown has most solemnly vouchsafed to Our loyal House of Commons. They have chosen to do this at a time when Our Empire is locked in life or death struggle with the very embodiment of evil, a struggle in which thousands of Our subjects have already died and in which thousands more will die before the victory is won. It was Our hope, when last treason reared its head, that a few salutary executions might teach Our great nobles the lesson of Our unwillingness to tolerate such blatantly criminal acts. Clearly, they have not done so, and it is Our firm purpose to finally and forever break the cycle of rebellion and treason among Our nobility. More, it is Our intention that this time, not only they but *all* Our subjects, will learn that the law applies to all. That those proven and adjudged guilty will pay the full penalty set forth by law, regardless of state or birth. Their lives and their lands are forfeit by their own actions, and We will have the head of every individual who has personally set his or her hand to this enterprise. Those of noble birth will be first attainted of their treason, and their titles will escheat to the Crown to be held in trust by Us until they be bestowed upon those worthy of such honor. There will be no exceptions, no exemptions, because of high birth. It is Our hope that *this* time others will learn from example so that We need never again root out rebellion, treason, and betrayal among those who have sworn their most solemn fealty "of heart, will, body, and sword" upon their immortal souls and the *Holy Writ*.' "

He laid the letter back on the table in a ringing, stunned silence. Then he leaned back and looked into the shocked eyes of a slack-jawed Lantern Walk.

"Is there any part of Her Majesty's letter you failed to understand, Your Grace?"

▼　▼　▼

Zhasyn Seafarer, who dared not use his own name or even whisper the words "Rock Coast," crouched over the small fire, stirring a battered, blackened pot of pork and dried beans. It was a far cry from the palatial life of the Duke of Rock Coast, and his jaw tightened as he thought about the disaster which had engulfed all he'd ever held dear.

He looked up to watch Sedryk Mahrtynsyn tend to their horses, if one could call such miserable beasts horses. Rock Coast would have sent them straight to the knackers if they'd been found in *his* stables, but he supposed it was better than walking . . . and certainly no one would ever suspect that the rider of such a wretched excuse for a mount might be a duke of the realm.

Mahrtynsyn no longer wore his cassock, his priest's cap, or his ring of office. Instead, he was as roughly dressed as Rock Coast himself, and they were free and alive—so far, at least—only because the priest had planned for all eventualities. The sorry horses and the farmer's clothing had been tucked away in a barn on the outskirts of Rock Coast Keep long before the galleons loaded with Charisian Marines sailed into Rock Coast Sound behind HMS *Carmyn*.

The priest finished with the horses, settled onto a rock on the far side of the fire, and started getting out their battered Army-style mess kits.

"I should've stayed," Rock Coast growled, glaring down into the pot. "I should've taken personal command of the water batteries and damned well shown them how a Duke of Rock Coast dies!"

Mahrtynsyn managed not to roll his eyes, but it was difficult. The duke had been carrying on about what he *should* have done almost from the moment the sound of the ironclad's guns had faded in the distance behind them. He'd evinced no desire to die gloriously when *Carmyn*'s captain called his bluff and opened fire on the waterfront batteries, however. Still, he was a duke, and a *Chisholmian* duke, at that. That made him a very valuable piece—a duke of the realm driven from heretic Chisholm for his steadfast faith in Mother Church and his noble defiance of the apostate rulers who'd led so many millions of their subjects into the very shadow of Shan-wei's wings. The Inquisition could do quite a lot with a hero like that . . . assuming Mahrtynsyn could get him to safety. And since he had to get *himself* to safety, anyway. . . .

"Your Grace," he soothed, "I understand your feelings, but, truly, it took more courage to come away with me than it would have taken to stay. Perhaps you could have . . . negotiated your surrender. After all, you *are* a duke, not some nobody Sharleyan and Cayleb could simply sweep under the carpet. But once we reach Desnair and find a way to get you to Zion, the Grand Inquisitor himself will greet you as a true son of Mother Church. Believe me, you'll find the respect your birth and your sacrifices in God's cause deserve, and the time will come when Mother Church's victorious armies will restore all you've lost and more."

"Well," Rock Coast half-mumbled, "I suppose. . . ."

His voice trailed off, and Mahrtynsyn finished unpacking the mess kits with a sigh of relief.

▼　　▼　　▼

Night wind hissed in the tall seagrass and waves roared softly, rhythmically, across the rocky strand. Braigyr Head, on the border between Rock Coast and the Earldom of MaGuire, loomed above the beach like a sentinel, shielding the bonfire burning above the high tide line from inland eyes. Or Sedryk Mahrtynsyn certainly hoped it did, anyway.

"You're sure they're out there?" Rock Coast demanded.

"They've been here every Monday, Tuesday, and Friday night for the last three five-days, and they'll be here for the *next* two if they miss our fire tonight, Your Grace," Mahrtynsyn told him . . . for no more than the thirtieth time. "It's not that terrible a hardship for them, and they won't raise any suspicion. The fishing off Braigyr Head is actually quite good."

"As long as someone hasn't slipped them enough marks to betray us," the duke growled fretfully.

"That isn't going to happen," Mahrtynsyn said rather more flatly than he normally spoke to the duke. Rock Coast looked at him in the fire-spangled darkness, and the priest shrugged. "These are faithful sons of Mother Church, Your Grace, tried and tested in the fire. Believe me, they would never betray me—I mean, us."

The duke looked skeptical and started to say something else when Mahrtynsyn laid one hand on his forearm and pointed out to sea with the other.

"And here they are, Your Grace!" he announced, and felt Rock Coast's taut muscles relax under his grip as the dinghy came through the surf and grated on the rocky beach.

One of the small boat's two-man crew climbed nimbly over the side and waded the rest of the way ashore. He carried a bull's-eye lantern, and light glowed as he opened the slide and trained it on the two men waiting for him.

"That you, Father?" he asked in a rough MaGuire accent.

"It is, my son," Mahrtynsyn assured him, turning his head to let the fisherman see his face clearly even as he signed Langhorne's Scepter in blessing. "Langhorne and Schueler bless you for your faithfulness!"

"Thank you, Father." The fisherman ducked his head, but he also peered suspiciously at Rock Coast. "And this would be . . . ?" he said dubiously.

Rock Coast started to reply to the insolent familiarity with a sharp set-down, but Mahrtynsyn squeezed his forearm again.

"He's a friend, my son, another son of Mother Church. I vouch for him."

"That's good enough for me, Father," the fisherman declared, and closed the lantern slide. "Best be getting into the boat, then."

The four of them filled the dinghy pretty much to capacity. Rock Coast clearly didn't think much of the battered, paint-peeling little boat, but at least he came from a coastal duchy, and he'd spent enough time in small craft to manage not to encumber the oarsmen.

The boat waiting for them was larger than the dinghy. That wasn't saying a great deal, however, for it was little more than thirty feet long, and the smell of fish was overpowering. Rock Coast gagged quietly on it as he climbed aboard, but he made no complaints. Mahrtynsyn's grip on his forearm had warned him that the fishing boat's crew didn't know who he was, and the duke approved of keeping them in ignorance. He had rather less faith in the goodness of men's hearts than Mahrtynsyn appeared to cherish. If they realized they had the fugitive Duke of Rock Coast in their hands, they might just decide they could retire as rich men after selling him to the Crown.

"What's next?" he asked Mahrtynsyn quietly as the boat came onto the wind and headed farther out to sea.

"Now we make rendezvous at dawn with something a bit larger and more comfortable than this, Your Grace," the priest replied equally quietly, standing with him in the bow. "I'm afraid it still won't be the sort of passenger galleon you're accustomed to, but it will be fast and well armed."

"Really?" Rock Coast raised an eyebrow, and Mahrtynsyn chuckled.

"Technically, Your Grace, what we're meeting is a privateer out of Desnair."

"A privateer?" the duke repeated sharply and frowned when the priest nodded. "Given what the Navy's been doing to privateers, what makes you so confident this one will have survived to be waiting for us?"

"Because, as I said, it's only *technically* a privateer. In fact, it's been chartered by Mother Church and paid—paid very handsomely, as a matter of fact—*not* to take prizes. Its only job for the past month has been to wait for me—for *us*, now—at this rendezvous on the proper nights."

"And how did it know to be waiting here *this* month?" Rock Coast sounded skeptical, and Mahrtynsyn shrugged.

"Your Grace, I didn't know precisely when you and the others would make your attempt, but I knew roughly what the window of opportunity had to be. So last month, a different 'privateer' was waiting. The month before that, it was yet another 'privateer' . . . and *next* month, it would have been still a fourth."

Rock Coast looked at him narrowly, and Mahrtynsyn hid a smile as he watched the duke reevaluating just how high in Mother Church's hierarchy his "chaplain" actually stood. Or how high in the confidence of the adjutant of Mother Church's Holy Inquisition, at least.

"Trust me, Your Grace," the priest soothed. "The ship will be there, and once we're aboard, her crew will see that both of us arrive safely in Desnair."

▼　　▼　　▼

"Sail on the larboard bow!"

Duke Rock Coast sat up from where he'd actually managed to fall asleep against the side of the fishing boat's wretched little deckhouse. The fishermen had offered to let him go below, but he'd declined. The stench was bad enough on deck; he didn't even want to think about what it must be like *below* decks.

Now he rubbed his eyes, peering in the indicated direction, and poked Mahrtynsyn in the ribs. The priest snorted awake and jerked upright, then stretched hugely.

"Yes, Your Grace?" he half yawned, and Rock Coast pointed.

"Unless I'm mistaken, that's your 'privateer,' Father."

Mahrtynsyn shielded his eyes with his hand, then nodded sharply as the two-masted schooner tacked in their direction. Desnair's black horse on a yellow field flew from its foremast head, and he was pleased to note that it was even larger than he'd expected. Ideally, no one would even see them on the voyage to Desnair, but the big, obviously well-armed schooner looked more than capable of taking care of itself if it had to.

"About twenty minutes, I'd say," Rock Coast said, estimating times and distances with an experienced eye, and grimaced. "I'm sure these fellows truly are the loyal sons of Mother Church you called them, Father, but I hope you won't take it wrongly if I say I'll be happy to be shut of their boat."

"To be honest, Your Grace, I can't fault you," Mahrtynsyn admitted with a smile. "They're fine fellows, but it is a bit . . . fragrant, isn't it?"

"Nothing burning our clothes as soon as we get out of them won't cure," Rock Coast said dryly.

▼　　▼　　▼

As it happened, Rock Coast's time estimate had been almost perfect, and the big schooner rounded up into the wind as she hove-to with a smooth professionalism that drew a nod of approval from him. It was nine thousand miles to Desnair. Having a crew skilled enough to get them there struck him as a very good idea.

The fishing boat ran up into the schooner's lee and took in its single baggy sail.

"Hello there!" Mahrtynsyn called through his cupped hands, standing at the fishing boat's rail. "We're glad to see—"

His voice broke off as nine blunt carronades snouted out of the schooner's gunports. At the same instant, the Desnairian colors plummeted from the masthead and another flag—this one a terrifyingly familiar black-quartered silver-and-blue checkerboard—shot upwards in their place. A dozen riflemen in the uniform of the Imperial Charisian Navy appeared at the quarter deck rail, and a wiry young man in a lieutenant's uniform raised a speaking trumpet.

"I think you might consider surrendering, Your Grace!" he called.

Rock Coast stared at him in horrified recognition, and the lieutenant shrugged. He was barely thirty yards away, and the movement was easy to see.

"I'm afraid *your* schooner ran afoul of the Navy some five-days ago, Father Sedryk," he said. "Her secret orders made interesting reading, and once the Duke's little rebellion failed, it wasn't difficult to guess who would be traveling with you. Earl White Crag and Baron Stoneheart decided it would be rude to leave the two of you stranded, and I just happened to have delivered Baron Sarmouth and Earl Sharpfield's latest dispatches to Port Royal, so they sent me to provide you with transportation. Unfortunately, I can't take you to Desnair right now." The Duke of Darcos smiled coldly. "I'm afraid we have an errand in Cherayth, first."

▼   ▼   ▼

"Excuse me, Sir."

The Earl of Hanth looked up from the ribeye steak, fork paused in mid-air, and his expression was not happy. Too many of his meals got interrupted for one reason or another, and he'd missed lunch completely. He'd been looking forward to supper ever since, and his steak was done exactly the way he liked it, with a cool red center, and smothered in sautéed mushrooms. He was . . . less than eager for some last-minute detail to interfere with it while it—and the baked potato steaming gently beside it—got cold.

"Yes?" he said just a bit repressively, and Major Karmaikel grimaced.

"I regret interrupting you, My Lord, but there's someone here to see you, and I'm pretty certain you wouldn't want me to keep him waiting."

"Who the hell could be so frigging important I can't even finish *this* first?" Hanth demanded waving the bite of steak on his fork irately. "Couldn't you have . . . I don't know, *delayed* whoever it is for fifteen whole minutes?"

"Yes, My Lord. And if I had, you'd have taken my head off."

"I find that rather difficult to believe," Hanth sighed. "But you don't usually do things that are *totally* insane." He contemplated the morsel of steak mournfully, then drew a deep breath. "At least give me long enough to chew and swallow *one* bite," he said, and popped the steak into his mouth.

"Of course, My Lord," Karmaikel murmured with a hint of a smile.

The tall, broad-shouldered major withdrew, and Hanth chewed slowly—it was just as delicious as he'd expected, of course—then swallowed. He'd just lifted his beer stein to take a sip when the door opened again.

"I apologize for interrupting your supper, My Lord," the brown-haired, bearded man in the uniform of a Royal Dohlaran Army colonel said. "My name is Mohrtynsyn, Ahskar Mohrtynsyn. I have the honor to be General Sir Lynyrd Iglaisys' chief of staff, and he's sent me to request a cease-fire while my King's ministers—and Earl Thirsk—negotiate with Admiral Sarmouth in Gorath."

.V.
Earl Rainbow Waters' Pavilion
Cherayk,
220 Miles North of Selyk;
and
Lake City,
Tarikah Province,
Republic of Siddarmark.

Your Eminences."

Earl Rainbow Waters stood in welcome as Gustyv Walkyr and Ahlbair Saintahvo followed Captain of Horse Wind Song into the compartment at the heart of his headquarters pavilion. Walkyr gave him a weary but genuine smile and the earl returned it; Saintahvo held out his ring hand imperiously.

Rainbow Waters bent to kiss the ring with scrupulous courtesy, but his face was expressionless as he straightened, with no hint of the smile he'd bestowed upon the archbishop militant. Nor did Walkyr extend *his* ring to demand the same obeisance, and Saintahvo's mouth tightened.

"I thank you for meeting me," the earl continued after a moment.

"You've traveled rather farther than we have, My Lord," Walkyr pointed out. "And from all reports, you're being pressed as heavily north of the forest as we are here."

"Unfortunately, yes," Rainbow Waters conceded. "But our front is in no immediate danger of an outright rupture, Earl Crystal Lake and my other band commanders understand both their orders and my intentions, and I'm in touch with them by semaphore and messenger wyvern. Still, it's true that events there are the reason I felt it was essential we meet personally to discuss the situation."

"The 'situation' *here* is about as bad as it could be," Walkyr said bluntly. He nodded to Major Mastyrsyn, who raised his eyebrows in a polite request to the earl. Rainbow Waters waved at the lacquered table at the center of the sizable compartment, and Mastyrsyn unrolled the map he'd carried under his arm.

"As you can see, My Lord," Walkyr said, indicating the newest positions marked on that map, "Eastshare's pushed us all the way back to Selyk in the center. Unfortunately, he's also gotten around us with a spearhead and cut the road behind Bishop Militant Lainyl at Mercyr. We attempted a relieving attack, but it failed." Archbishop Saintahvo stood behind the archbishop militant and scowled at his back as Walkyr shook his head, his eyes shadowed. "My boys tried hard, My Lord—they truly did—but with those damned balloons and the heretics' mounted infantry. . . ."

"Your Eminence, I fully appreciate the tenacity with which your men have fought," Rainbow Waters said quietly, oblivious to Saintahvo's expression. "None of us anticipated the weight of attack that would fall upon you—especially not now that Symkyn's brought so much of his army up past Marylys to join Eastshare's assault. By our best estimate, you're now faced with almost three hundred thousand men."

"Which is barely half the strength—indeed, *less* than half the strength—of the Army of the Center," Saintahvo pointed out unpleasantly. Walkyr flushed, but Rainbow Waters simply looked at the intendant.

"That's true, Your Eminence," he said after a moment. "But Eastshare and Symkyn are far more mobile than our own forces and, as such, have the advantage of the initiative. And in addition to their mobility and artillery's superior range and rate of fire, they now have the advantage of those balloons no one warned us might be coming."

It was Saintahvo's turn to flush at the reminder of the Inquisition's failure to uncover yet another devastating Charisian surprise.

"The enemy," the earl continued calmly, "always possesses the ability to choose his time and place to attack. Archbishop Militant Gustyv has over six hundred miles of front to defend, and unlike him, the heretics can see *precisely* where their enemy's forces are deployed and in what strength. He cannot—*no one* could—prevent the heretics from massing a decisive local superiority at their chosen point of attack under those circumstances."

Saintahvo glared at him for a moment, but then he nodded choppily. Obviously, he wasn't prepared—yet, at least—to challenge Rainbow Waters' authority. Walkyr wondered how much longer that would last if—when—the situation continued to worsen.

"In addition to the situation at Mercyr," the archbishop militant continued into the silence, "Eastshare's pushed a column west of Blufftyn. In fact, the head of that column's no more than a hundred and fifty miles south-east of Cheryk at this moment, My Lord. I'm afraid you've come rather closer to the front than might be wise against an opponent who's so much more mobile than we are."

"I am accompanied by three entire brigades of cavalry and Baron Wind Song and I brought our finest horses," Rainbow Waters replied with a faint smile. "I believe we can safely outdistance any pursuit if we must, although I thank you for your concern."

"Well, we can't afford to lose *you* whatever else happens," Walkyr said gruffly. "And at least Bishop Militant Ahntohnyo managed to get his entire command out of Blufftyn and rejoin my main force. In fact, he's currently dug in on the high road between here and Eastshare's column. I judge that the tree cover on his line of retreat helped a great deal by obstructing the balloons' visibility."

"I'm most relieved the Bishop Militant was able to extract his band," Rainbow Waters said. "Unfortunately, I've just received semaphore dispatches which indicate that the Siddarmarkian Stohnar has finally appeared. At least one entire corps of the Army of the Sylmahn is driving along the Five Forks–Sairmeet High Road. A second spearhead has swung south from Five Forks and then turned northwest. Apparently, the intention was to trap Bishop Militant Ahntohnyo between the Army of the Sylmahn and the Army of Westmarch. He's escaped that trap, but his retreat means the road from Blufftyn to Sairmeet is now open to the heretics as well."

Walkyr's face tightened. Earl Golden Tree's position blocking the high road at Sairmeet, at the heart of the Great Tarikah Forest, was the true key to the terrain feature which shielded the Mighty Host's southern flank. It was a strongly fortified position, powerfully held by forty thousand men, with no less than three additional defensible river lines in its rear. If Golden Tree was forced to fall back, the heavy tree growth would offer his flanks formidable protection, and those river lines would offer him places to stand. But once he *started* falling back . . .

"Your Eminence," Rainbow Waters faced Walkyr squarely, "we cannot afford for Eastshare to separate your left from my right . . . and at the moment, that seems to be precisely what the heretics are accomplishing." Walkyr nodded. Saintahvo gave him a stony glance, then looked back at Rainbow Waters, and the earl shrugged. "I believe Eastshare and Symkyn hope to . . . peel you away from the western flank of the forest and simultaneously break through between Selyk and Glydahr to prevent you from retreating into Sardahn. Whether or not they intend to pin the entire Army of the Center—or as much of it as they can—into one enormous pocket is more than I'm prepared to say at this time. That would certainly be an extremely valuable prize for them, if they could accomplish it. However, I feel confident their *primary* objective is to drive you towards St. Vyrdyn, away from the forest and from the Ferey River."

Walkyr gazed down at the map and his jaw clenched. Eastshare's most northern spearhead was within ten miles of the Sair-Selyk Canal, already across the original boundary between the Army of the Center's area of responsibility and the Mighty Host's. Ahntohnyo Mahkgyl's twenty thousand men from Blufftyn had retreated across that boundary in their effort to delay the heretics, but under Mother Church's contingency planning, if the Army of the Center was forced to retreat, it was supposed to fall back *west*, on Glydahr, not to the north, in line with its orders to cover the gap between the Black Wyverns and the Tairohn Hills. But Rainbow Waters was right; Eastshare and Symkyn were obviously attempting to drive him northwest, towards Four Point and St. Vyrdyn . . . both of which also lay in the Mighty Host's area of responsibility and were too far west to play any significant role in the fighting in Tarikah.

"What do you need me to do, My Lord?" he asked, looking up from the map.

"I need you to form a new line. Almost a quarter million of your troops have yet to reach the front. I intend to ask Vicar Allayn and Vicar Rhobair to debark them at Transyl. From there they can move down the high road from the Holy Langhorne Canal, hopefully as far as Glydahr. If, however, the heretics attack Glydahr in strength before they can arrive, I desire your garrison there to retreat up the high roads towards Four Point. I do *not* wish you to attempt to defend Glydahr under those circumstances. Instead, I wish you to withdraw all but perhaps one band from the Glydahr front, reinforce your center, fall back to form an east-west line between St. Vyrdyn and the Forest, and hold it as long as possible. In the meantime, I am pushing forces of my own southwest along the Ferey and my engineers are preparing defensive positions west of the river. Hopefully, I'll be able to offer you additional support forward of the river. I can't guarantee that, however, and whether I can reinforce you or not, you *must* slow the heretics and buy my engineers time."

It was very quiet in the tent.

"I realize this is a distinct departure from our previous plans, and from any discussions with Vicar Allayn." The earl's voice sounded almost shockingly loud against that quiet as he looked at the two archbishops . . . and carefully failed to mention Zhaspahr Clyntahn. "In the end, however, no plan survives unmodified in the face of the enemy. I fully recognize the danger that pulling your forces north, away from Glydahr, presents to Sardahn. I hope the diversion of your reinforcements will offset that, but, frankly, the critical consideration at this time is the defense of the Mighty Host's communications. If the heretics succeed in driving Earl Golden Tree out of Sair-meet and clear the road for Stohnar to advance directly through the forest while Green Valley and Klymynt continue their advance on Lake City, my position east of West Wing Lake will become untenable. In that case, the Ferey River becomes our final stop line for their advance on the Holy Lang-horne. And, Your Eminence," the earl looked the archbishop militant squarely in the eye, "if they succeed in cutting the Holy Langhorne, at least half of the Mighty Host will have no option but to attempt to retreat across the Barony of Charlz . . . with winter coming on. I estimate that as many as three in ten of my men may survive under those circumstances."

"I'm sure that's true, My Lord," Saintavho said after a moment, "and we must obviously give great weight to your views. At the same time, however, the Archbishop Militant's instructions from Vicar Allayn are very clear. And I'm sure you realize how . . . unhappy Vicar Zhaspahr would be if the Inquisition's camps at Glydar should fall into heretic hands. Or if Bishop Militant Tayrens should find himself forced to execute all of the camps' inmates to prevent the heretics from freeing them before they can be sifted." He held the earl's eye coldly. "There are many responsibilities in play at this moment, My Lord. It might be wise for you to discuss these matters with Bishop Merkyl before rushing to decisions based purely on military consid-erations of what the heretics may or may not do at some future time. May I ask if it would be possible for him to join our discussion here?"

Rainbow Waters' expression hadn't so much as flickered at Sainthavo's reference to Bishop Merkyl Sahndhaim, the Mighty Host's intendant. Now he shook his head with what appeared to be genuine regret.

"I fear Bishop Merkyl's age and gout made it impractical for him to ac-company me on a journey which must be made in such haste, Your Emi-nence. We did, however, discuss these points at some length before I departed from Lake City, and he expressed his agreement with my intentions. Indeed," he held out a hand to his nephew, who opened his briefcase and handed him a document several pages thick, "the Bishop was good enough to send along his own appreciation of the situation."

The earl extended the document to Sainthavo, whose expression could have soured all the milk within a hundred miles as he took it.

"In the meantime, Your Eminence," Rainbow Waters continued, "I think—"

He broke off, eyebrow rising, as a member of his staff appeared in the compartment entrance.

"Yes, Giyangzhi?" he said.

"I'm afraid an urgent dispatch has just arrived, My Lord."

There was something odd about the officer's voice and his expression was taut as he extended a single sheet of paper. Rainbow Waters accepted it and his eyes ran over the tersely worded dispatch. They seemed to widen for a moment, then he handed the message to his nephew and looked at the two archbishops.

"Your Eminences, I fear the situation on the northern front has just been . . . simplified," he said.

▼   ▼   ▼

Kynt Clareyk, Baron Green Valley, rode briskly down the broad, deserted avenue through a windblown drift of cinders and ash, surrounded by an entire watchful company of mounted infantry. An inferno roared all along the lakefront, a solid wall of fire that stretched for miles as it consumed warehouses packed with sufficient supplies for a million men for at least three months in a roiling torrent of flame and dense, choking black smoke.

He felt a profound sense of satisfaction as he looked around at the prize his army had taken, but he wished the Earl of Crystal Lake had been just a bit less decisive. Greedy of him, he knew, but he'd hoped the earl would find it difficult to cope with the sheer scope and surprise of Ahrtymys Ohanlyn's new bombardment plan. Unfortunatey, Rainbow Waters had chosen what amounted to his deputy commander because he trusted that deputy's capabilities, and the earl was an excellent judge of men. Mahzwang Lynku might be seventy-nine years old, and he might be increasingly frail physically, but age had done nothing to dull his quick intelligence and, despite his frailty, he had more energy than many officers who were two-thirds his age.

He'd needed both those qualities—badly—over the last few days. It was simply the Allies' misfortune that he had them.

The arrival of twenty thousand tons of shells filled with Sahndrah Lywys' Composition D had provided Ohanlyn's gunners with an entirely new level of lethality. The new filler was both much safer to handle and twice as powerful, on a pound-for-pound basis, as black powder. It was also much denser, so twice the weight could be poured into the same shell cavity. That made a shell filled with it four times as destructive as one filled with black powder . . . and that meant the new 8- and 10-inch shells, in particular, had just become utterly devastating.

While the new shells were being distributed to his batteries, Ohanlyn had used the Balloon Corps to map the deployments of the three Harchongese bands holding the twisty sixty-seven miles of the Tairyn River line between the Great Tarikah Forest and East Wing Lake. There'd been close to ninety thousand men in those bands, and Lord of Foot Crystal Lake had put sixty thousand of them into the actual trenches while he held the other thirty thousand in reserve behind them, beyond even Charisian artillery's effective range and ready to counter attack any fresh breakthrough. That hadn't counted the battered bands refitting their divisions in Lake City it-self, of course.

Unfortunately for the Mighty Host, Green Valley hadn't had to attack the entire front. Instead, he'd chosen a ten mile segment of it for which the St. Ahgnista Band was responsible, five miles south of the lake, and Ohan-lyn had deployed almost five hundred medium and heavy angle-guns and a hundred and twenty rocket batteries against it. That was a heavier density of artillery than in the vast majority of attacks in Old Terra's World War One, and unlike the armies who'd faced one another on the Western Front in 1916 or 1917, the Mighty Host, with no balloons of its own, had been totally unable to keep track of Charisian movements beyond two or three miles—if that—of their own front lines. They hadn't had a clue that Ohan-lyn's batteries were in motion as he assembled his sledgehammer . . . until that hammer came down.

The artillery general had spent two full five-days on his preparations while Green Valley held his infantry south of the lake in place, resting his assault brigades and continuing to pound away at the shrinking Vekhair pocket with his right. It was remarkable how ineffective Hainryk Klymynt's artillery had been at Vekhair, but his showy bombardments—with old-style shells—had kept even someone as sharp as Crystal Lake looking in *that* di-rection while Ohanlyn and Green Valley's brigade commanders made their preparations. Ohanlyn had pre-registered all of his heavy batteries, but he'd done it one battery—indeed, one *gun* in each battery—at a time, and he'd been careful not to use any of the new ammunition while he was about it.

And then, at 11:20 in the morning, when the majority of the Tairyn River Line's men were sitting down to lunch, Ohanlyn had unleashed a savage, howling hurricane of a bombardment. The Mighty Host had expe-rienced heavier bombardments than anyone else in the entire history of Safehold . . . but not even they had yet experienced anything like *this*. The sheer, stupendous weight of shells was beyond belief, and the rocket bom-bardment had laid a solid carpet of high explosives across the defenders' front lines. Not only that, but each launcher had been provided with three reloads, and all four of them were launched within the space of barely an hour while the aerial observers directed the heavy guns' fire with deadly accuracy.

And then the bombardment ceased.

It didn't slow, didn't taper off. It simply *stopped*. Every single gun ceased fire in the same minute . . . and when they did, the assault brigades stormed forward with their shotguns, their flamethrowers, and their satchel charges. Ohanlyn "gun dogs" had reopened fire, switching their attention to known Harchongese artillery positions that might have interfered with the attack, smothering them in a blanket of shells—using the older, black powder-filled projectiles—which silenced them completely.

The defenders had been too stunned, too mentally devastated by the suddenness of the holocaust—and by how rapidly the attack had followed on that holocaust's heels—to offer anything like effective resistance. Green Valley's lead assault companies had flowed through the wrecked Harchongese positions like the sea, bypassing the handful of points at which defenders were still capable of fighting back, leaving the follow-up echelons to deal with the holdouts. They'd cut completely through the two-mile-deep fortified zone in barely two hours, and in those two hours the St. Ahgnista Band had simply ceased to exist as an organized formation. Almost a quarter of the St. Jyrohm Band, on St. Ahgnista's left, was wiped out along with it, and what remained of St. Jyrohm's forward deployed regiments were pinned between the Charisians who were suddenly in their rear and the lake. Green Valley didn't bother to storm that portion of the front. There'd been no need; the troops trapped in those fortifications couldn't withdraw, and he had no intention of losing any lives assaulting them.

Earl Crystal Lake, with only an incomplete appreciation of the scale of the disaster, did what any determined, intelligent commander would have done: he threw in a heavy counterattack from his reserve. But that counterattack ran into a devastating curtain of artillery, brought down upon it by the Balloon Corps' now highly experienced observers. It recoiled and fell back hastily—the only thing it could possibly have done under the circumstances—and by nightfall, the Army of Tarikah's spearhead had advanced fifteen miles beyond its start point and started digging foxholes of its own while the mortars dug in behind it.

Green Valley had watched through the SNARCs as reports of the disaster flowed into Crystal Lake's headquarters, and he'd been deeply impressed by the Harchongese commander. Despite the proof of the Army of Tarikah's crushing power—despite the loss of over thirty-five thousand men in the space of a few hours—the redoubtable earl had refused to panic. Nor had he allowed himself to be paralyzed by the sheer scale of the catastrophe. He'd reached his decision by midnight, barely fifteen hours after the bombardment began, and the orders had gone out by courier to the brigades continuing to cling to the southern stub of the Tairyn River Line.

Those brigades, aside from sacrificial rearguards, had been in motion westward by dawn. Nor had Crystal Lake stopped there. With Green Valley's advanced infantry less than fifteen miles from Lake City's outer defense perimeter, and with no way to estimate how quickly the Charisian guns could bring their devastating new power to bear against that perimeter, he'd had the moral courage to order the evacuation of Tarikah Province's capital city, as well.

Green Valley didn't even want to think about how Zhaspahr Clyntahn was likely to react to that, but Crystal Lake hadn't hesitated. He'd ordered the systematic destruction of as much of his own fortifications as possible, and any artillery that couldn't be on the road within twelve hours was blown up in place. The thunderous explosions had rolled around the city for hours as the guns—and the mountains of supplies Rainbow Waters had collected at Lake City—were blown up or put to the torch. Meanwhile, the capital's garrison had been ordered back to the Gleesyn-Chyzwail Line south of East Wing Lake and what remained of the Tairyn River Line's defenders were ordered to form a defensive front between the Tarikah Forest and the Gleesyn-Chyzwail Line, covering the Gleesyn-Sairmeet High Road to protect the Sairmeet garrison's lines of communication.

Crystal Lake had made his decisions and implemented them so swiftly not even Charisian mounted infantry could have interfered with his movements. Or not, at least, without operating beyond the support of their own artillery, and even with the Army of the Hildermoss added to his command, Green Valley remained too hugely outnumbered by the Northern Mighty Host to take that sort of liberties with Harchongians.

It was difficult even for the SNARCs to provide definitive numbers on Earl Rainbow Waters' casualties to date, but Owl's best estimate was that, combined with the Tairyn River Line disaster, the Mighty Host had suffered close to a hundred and seventy-five thousand dead, wounded, and prisoners. That was a staggering number, greater than the entire combined initial strength of the Army of Tarikah and the Army of the Hildermoss . . . and represented less than fourteen percent of the Northern Mighty Host's starting strength. Green Valley and Klymynt between them, on the other hand, had suffered around fourteen thousand combat casualties—only about a third of them fatal, thank God—which was only eight percent of the Harchongians' losses. With "nonoperational" casualties from accidental injuries and illness included, his and Klymynt's total casualties rose to just under seventeen thousand, which was ten percent of their initial strength. That might not sound too dreadful, aside from the agonizing human cost hidden behind those bland numbers, especially given the new troops arriving from Chisholm to reinforce them. But their losses were overwhelmingly concentrated in his specially trained and equipped assault brigades. Some of the battalions in those brigades were down to little more than forty percent of their assigned strength, and rebuilding them with replacements straight from Chisholm, without time for those replacements to integrate into their new formations, could only compromise their combat effectiveness.

And that's exactly what Rainbow Waters intended to do to us, Green Valley thought grimly. *He meant to hurt us worse than this—and expected to do it faster than this—because he didn't have a clue the Balloon Corps was coming or just what that would mean for artillery and operational movements. But he's no more likely to panic than Crystal Lake did, and there's the next damned best thing to six hundred thousand fresh Harchongese infantry en route to the front. They'll take a while to get here, but within the next three five-days—by the end of August, at the latest—he'll have received enough fresh brigades to replace every man he's lost. In the same time-frame, Hainryk and I are looking at maybe another forty thousand. We're costing him one hell of a lot of casualties, but in absolute numbers, including current field strengths and reinforcements in the pipe, the loss ratio is actually slightly in his favor.*

Of course, there came a point at which comparative loss ratios became meaningless. A point at which those in command realized their own losses were simply unsustainable, whatever the other side's might be. And however tough-minded Rainbow Waters, Crystal Lake, and the Mighty Host's other field commanders might be, they weren't really the psychological target of the current offensive. No, *that* target lay elsewhere . . . in a city named Zion.

He shook that thought aside as his escort drew up before the modest two-story palace beside Tarikah Cathedral. He looked around again, noticing the firefighting parties his brigade commanders had organized to prevent sparks and drifting embers from spreading the warehouses' blaze to the city's civilian housing, and swung down from the saddle. He handed the reins to one of his escorting troopers and ascended the palace's front steps, with Bryahn Slokym and half a squad of infantry at his heels.

A very nervous looking upper-priest opened the huge, carved door as the baron reached it. The cleric was brown-haired and brown-eyed, with long, stork-like arms and legs, and he bobbed an awkward bow.

"General Green Valley?" He sounded tentative, his tone anxious, and Green Valley nodded.

"I am . . . Father Avry."

The Chihirite stiffened in surprise as Green Valley addressed him by name, but he clearly had other things to worry about, and he drew a deep breath.

"The Archbishop is waiting in his office," he said. "If that would be convenient, of course, My Lord," he added quickly.

"That would be entirely convenient, Father. Please, take me to him." The priest nodded, and Green Valley looked at the bodyguards standing behind Slokym. "I think you lads can stay here," he said.

The squad leader looked rebellious, and Green Valley frowned.

"Let me rephrase that," he said pleasantly, "you lads not only *can* stay here, you *will* stay here. Would it happen that I need to be any clearer than that?"

The corporal looked appealingly at Captain Slokym, but the captain only shook his head.

"No, My Lord," the corporal said finally, looking back at Green Valley. "That's . . . clear enough."

"Good," Green Valley replied, then relented a bit. "Don't worry, Corporal. I'm armed, Captain Slokym is armed, and the last thing anyone in this palace wants is to harm me in any way. Isn't that correct, Father Avry?"

He cocked an eyebrow at the priest, who nodded quickly.

"There, you see?" Green Valley said cheerfully. "And now, Father, if you'd lead the way?"

The man who came to his feet as Green Valley entered the large, book-lined office had thinning silver hair, a receding hairline, and intelligent—and worried—gray-blue eyes behind the lenses of wire-rimmed spectacles perched on a beaky nose. He wore the white cassock of an archbishop, badged with the green of Pasquale, and he looked far more composed than Father Avry had.

He also, Green Valley thought with a surge of sympathy whose warmth surprised even him just a bit, looked absolutely and totally exhausted. The baron compared the man before him to the imagery Owl had captured of him two years before, and there was at least *ten* years' difference between them.

"Baron Green Valley," the archbishop said.

"Archbishop Arthyn," the baron replied, and bowed rather more deeply than simple courtesy required. Arthyn Zagyrsk's eyebrows rose, despite his formidable self-control, and Green Valley straightened. "I've been looking forward to this meeting for some time, Your Eminence."

"Indeed?" Zagyrsk smiled bleakly. "I don't suppose I should be surprised. Lake City is—*was*—the last provincial capital in Mother Church's hands. And I imagine I'm the last of her archbishops in Siddarmark. The end of an epoch, one might say."

"One might," Green Valley agreed. "And I won't pretend I don't feel a certain . . . satisfaction in knowing Zhaspahr Clyntahn's invasion and the butchery it perpetrated on the Republic is about to be brought to a crushing end." His brown eyes were far bleaker than the archbishop's smile had been. "There isn't enough justice in the world to compensate for the suffering, anguish, and death that man has inflicted, Your Eminence."

"No. No, I don't suppose there is." Zagyrsk shook his head, then squared his shoulders. "And I'm sure 'justice' figures into your instructions about any of Mother Church's prelates who fall into your custody, My Lord. I'm prepared to submit to whatever your Emperor and Empress—and the Lord Protector, of course—have decreed. I would beg for mercy, or at least leniency, for those like Father Avry who had no choice but to obey me as their ecclesiastic superior."

Father Avry's face tightened as if he wanted to reject Zagyrsk's words, but Green Valley shook his head before the Chihirite could speak.

"I don't think you quite understand, Your Eminence. Yes, I feel an enormous satisfaction at having liberated Lake City from Zhaspahr Clyntahn and his butchers. And I do have instructions concerning you. But those instructions are to inform you that Emperor Cayleb, Empress Sharleyan, and Lord Protector Greyghor are fully aware of how long and how hard you, Father Avry, and Father Ignaz fought to mitigate the excesses of the Inquisition. They know you insisted on proper food and medical care for the concentration camp prisoners assigned to forced labor in Tarikah. They know you opposed the Inquisitor General. They know Father Ignaz smuggled over eight hundred children out of Camp St. Tailahr in clear defiance of his direct orders from his own superiors. And they know how hard—and how successfully—you fought to keep the Inquisition away from the citizens of Tarikah Province. You couldn't prevent what happened elsewhere, Your Eminence, and you couldn't stop what the Sword of Schueler did to the people of your archbishopric. But you did every single thing you could to protect them—Reformist, as well as Temple Loyalist—from the very beginning. So, yes, I do have instructions concerning you. And those instructions are to leave you here, in your archbishopric, doing what you've done so well for so long. Whether or not it will be possible for you to remain permanently, once this jihad ends, is another question, but the *Writ* says the sheep will know the good shepherd, and so do Their Majesties and the Lord Protector."

.VI.
The Temple,
City of Zion,
The Temple Lands.

I suppose you're still going to insist Walkyr was the best man for his command, Allayn?" Zhaspahr Clyntahn asked unpleasantly.

The heavyset Grand Inquisitor leaned forward, forearms planted on the conference table as he thrust his face belligerently in Allayn Maigwair's direction. Rhobair Duchairn sat on the opposite side of the table, beside Maigwair, and the pile of reports and memos in front of him was almost as tall as the one in front of the captain general. Zahmsyn Trynair sat at the head of the table, because it was nominally his responsibility to chair their meetings this five-day, but the table in front of him was almost completely bare and it was painfully obvious he would have preferred to be just about anywhere else.

He wasn't about to attempt to exert any actual control over Clyntahn, at any rate. He simply sat there, and Maigwair gave him a disgusted look before he turned his attention to Clyntahn.

"Given the fact that Gustyv's managed to hold his army together despite getting the shit hammered out of it by two entire heretic armies, yes, I'm going to do exactly that," he said, meeting the other vicar's belligerent gaze levelly. "He's managing to *retreat*, Zhaspahr, when a lot of armies would have broken and run, and Rhobair here—" the captain general twitched his head in Duchairn's direction "—has actually managed to get Ahubrai Zheppsyn's band—that's another thirty thousand men and close to two hundred guns—forward to join Klemynt Gahsbahr at Glydahr. That brings the Glydahr garrison back up to almost forty thousand, despite the troops he pulled out in response to Rainbow Waters' request, and Zheppsyn and Gahsbar are continuing to extend and improve the entrenchments Silken Hills left when he moved south." Maigwair emphasized the last four words ever so slightly. "And in the meantime, Gustyv is building a solid line between St. Vyrdyn and the headwaters of the Sair."

"A 'solid line' over *three hundred* miles north of his original positions!" Clyntahn pointed out nastily. "Chihiro preserve us from more military triumphs like that! And then there's the little matter of what happened at Mercyr, isn't there?"

"I won't pretend that doesn't hurt," Maigwair conceded. "If we'd had more dragoons forward it might not have happened, but without a bigger mounted force of his own, Brygham couldn't prevent Eastshare from getting his mounted infantry around behind him. And after that, there was no way he could have gotten the bulk of his troops out, whatever he'd done. As it is, he's still putting up one hell of a fight and locking down that part of the high road. Would I rather have his band out of the trap and available to Walkyr? Damned right I would. But he and his men have nothing to be ashamed of. For that matter, they're still accomplishing the objective they were assigned in the first place!"

Clyntahn made a disgusted sound, but he didn't pursue it, Duchairn noted. That probably had something to do with the fact that Lainyl Brygham was the son of one of his longtime allies on the Council of Vicars. He also happened to be a capable commander who'd shown plenty of bulldog tenacity, however, as he was demonstrating yet again even now, and appointing him to command one of Walkyr's bands had been one of Maigwair's more inspired personnel decisions.

The captain general was undoubtedly right about how Brygham had ended up trapped at Mercyr, and the fact that Maigwair had tried so hard for so long to build a mounted force which might match—or at least offset— the Imperial Charisian Army's mobility probably didn't make the captain general feel one bit better. But, by the same token, mounted infantry was scarcely at its best amid the dense trees of the Great Tarikah Forest, and Brygham had refused to panic. Instead, he'd settled in with just over forty percent of his original infantry—and *all* his artillery—to hold his blocking position and deny the high road to the oncoming Siddarmarkian Army of the Sylmahn for as long as humanly possible. The remainder of his infantry had been ordered north to join Ahntohnyo Mahkgyl's band at Blufftyn, banking on the forest to slow and hamper any pursuit. Unfortunately, only about a thousand of them had made it before Mahkgyl was forced to retreat; the rest had been cut off when Stohnar's and Eastshare's spearheads met at Blufftyn.

With that position in their hands, the Siddarmarkian general was theoretically able to join the advance of Eastshare's right flank, but his logistics remained badly constrained by the limited capacity of the farm roads and dirt tracks between Blufftyn and the Waymeet-Five Forks High Road. He simply couldn't get enough food, ammunition, and—especially—artillery forward. So as long as Brygham held Mercyr and Earl Golden Tree's forces continued to block the high road at Sairmeet, the Great Tarikah Forest retained its value as the roadblock covering the Northern Mighty Host's right against Stohnar's army.

Of course, all of that paled into insignificance compared to what had happened *north* of the forest, the treasurer reflected gloomily. He was less worried by the loss of Lake City—he'd recognized that Rainbow Waters would never be able to hold the provincial capital the same day he'd realized how badly they'd been fooled about the Charisians' southern strategy—than by the way in which Green Valley had blasted his way through the last defensive line before the city. He didn't have as much information on that as Maigwair did, but the information he did have was terrifying to the man in charge of providing Mother Church's weapons. It was clear the Charisians and Siddarmarkians had brought more than just their infernal balloons to this year's campaign, and not even Brother Lynkyn could begin to suggest how they'd made their shells so much more destructive virtually overnight!

"I can't say *any* of our peerless military commanders fill me with a superabundance of confidence," the Grand Inquisitor observed bitterly. He'd begun to criticize even Rainbow Waters, especially after the earl had strongly defended Earl Crystal Lake's decision to retreat from Lake City . . . and since he'd received Ahlbair Saintahvo's report about the earl's meeting with Gustyv Walkyr. "And what's this business about *Silken Hills* planning to retreat, too?"

"It's a *contingency* plan, Zhaspahr." Maigwair shook his head. "It's obvious now that the heretics have no intention of attacking the Tymkyn Gap . . . if they ever actually did. At the moment, his forces at Tallas are holding firm, though. The problem is that High Mount seems to be throwing most of his weight against the Reklair Gap and it's pretty clear at least a third of Symkyn's army's turned *south* to join him instead of continuing farther north, with Eastshare. When you combine that with how hard the heretics worked to convince us they meant to attack the Tymkyn Gap, that strongly suggests that what they really want is for Symkyn and High Mount to punch through at *Reklair*—and Tallas, if they can, no doubt—to capture Wedthar. That's the biggest South March town we still hold, which would make it valuable enough under any circumstances, but it gets one hell of a lot *more* valuable given what's happening in Dohlar."

Clyntahn's sour expression turned thunderous at the mention of Dohlar. He continued to hold Earl Thirsk personally responsible for the Dohlaran Navy's reverses, and the fact that the earl remained that navy's commander stuck in his craw like a sliver of bone. The fact that no one could have fought more effectively—or with more imagination—against the Imperial Charisian Navy's armored fleet meant nothing to him. He continued to rail against Thirsk's "defeatism" and "unreliability," and he'd predicted nothing but disaster when word reached Zion that Charis had begun its long-awaited assault on the city of Gorath.

"I know you don't want to hear about Dohlar, Zhaspahr," Maigwair continued, facing the issue squarely, "and I know we're all worried about what's happening in Gorath right now. But even if the Dohlarans beat off this attack, the heretic navy will keep the Gulf effectively shut down indefinitely. We simply don't have any way to keep them from doing that, and that's what makes Wedthar so important. It's a critical road junction, and with the Gulf . . . unavailable, it's the linchpin for Silken Hills' supply line. If the heretics punch through to it, we can write off all of his artillery, at an absolute minimum, because he won't be able to get it out." He shrugged. "I'm actually relieved that he's drawing up movement plans already. It doesn't mean he's planning *to* retreat, Zhaspahr; it means he's planning *how* he'll retreat—and fight the most effective delaying action possible while he does it—if he's *forced* to retreat. That's a pretty important distinction."

"All *I* see is that every Shan-wei-damned army we have is moving *west*, not east!" Clyntahn snarled. "It's bad enough when a gutless bastard like Thirsk bends over and invites the frigging heretics to bugger him, but now every commander we've got is too damned busy thinking about 'contingency plans' and 'fighting withdrawals' to give any goddamned thought to actually *defeating* the heretics! If it's all the same to you, Allayn, I'd like to see just one of them—just *one!*—with the guts to actually stand his ground and *fight* like someone worthy of the trust God's placed in him!"

Desperation must really *be getting to him, given how he's starting to criticize the Harchongians, not just our own people,* Duchairn thought, watching the Grand Inquisitor's angry expression.

It was easy enough to understand the reasons for Clyntahn's anxiety. Charis and Siddarmark hadn't achieved an outright breakthrough anywhere . . . yet. Lake City came close, but Crystal Lake's prompt withdrawal had prevented a complete rupture of Rainbow Water's front north of the Tarikah Forest. Yet they were pushing the Church's forces back everywhere, and the junction between Eastshare's Army of Westmarch and Stohnar's Army of the Sylmahn was enough to frighten anyone. It was also what made Brygham's continued stand at Mercyr so important. But sooner or later, Mercyr was *going* to fall, however valiantly Brygham and his men fought. Even Clyntahn had to realize only a direct miracle could prevent that now. And once Eastshare and Stohnar's quartermasters were able to use the high road through the Great Tarikah Forest, they'd be ready for their next lunge forward.

The question was the direction in which they'd do the lunging.

If they struck due west and threw their full weight against Walkyr's retreating army and successfully stormed Glydahr, they'd almost certainly drive the Princedom of Sardahn out of the Jihad. It would also cut the primary supply line for any of the archbishop militant's forces which survived Glydahr's fall and let them threaten the Holy Langhorne Canal west of the Tairohn Hills, which would cut *Earl Rainbow Waters'* line of supply—or retreat—as well.

But they might also choose the option Rainbow Waters obviously believed was their best choice and continue *north*west instead of west, across the line of the Ferey River, and strike for Mhartynsberg in the Barony of Charlz in order to cut the Holy Langhorne *there*. Or, for that matter, they could continue due north, along the western face of the Tarikah Forest, and attempt to envelop Rainbow Waters' West Wing Lake positions from the south while Green Valley's frontal attacks held the earl in place.

So far, Mother Church's generals had continued their stubborn fighting retreat, giving ground slowly or, like Brygham at Mercyr, digging in and continuing to resist ferociously even when surrounded. In the process, they were inflicting heavy casualties on their enemies, especially the Charisian Army. But Charis and the Republic were clearly prepared to pay the price. There was no sign Green Valley's offensive in the north was weakening, their artillery's newly revealed capabilities were a terrifying portent of what might be about to come, and if they truly were about to launch a fresh, major offensive against Silken Hills in the *south*, it seemed likely that—

The treasurer's gloomy train of thought came to a sudden halt as the council chamber door slid unexpectedly open.

"Forgive me for interrupting, Your Graces," Wyllym Rayno said quickly, addressing all four of the vicars, although his attention was obviously focused on Clyntahn. "I'm afraid we've just received some . . . disturbing news."

"What sort of 'disturbing news' would that be?" Clyntahn demanded. "Schueler knows we've already heard enough of it without your bursting in to deliver still more, Wyllym!"

"I realize that, Your Grace. Unfortunately, I saw no option but to bring this to you immediately." The Archbishop of Chiang-wu drew a deep breath and braced himself visibly. "Your Grace, it appears Duke Fern has resigned and King Rahnyld has named Earl Thirsk to replace him as First Councilor."

"*What?!*" Clyntahn shot upright in his chair, his face darkening. "*Thirsk?!*"

"I'm afraid so, Your Grace." To his credit, Rayno met his superior's suddenly fiery eyes without flinching. "We have only fragmentary information at this point, but according to first reports, he's placed Bishop Executor Wylsynn and Father Ahbsahlahn under arrest. Many of our agents inquisitor in Gorath have also been seized, apparently by Dohlaran Army troops under Sir Rainos Ahlverez' command. And—" the archbishop's eyes wavered finally "—Thirsk has negotiated a cease-fire with the heretic Sarmouth."

"*I knew it!*" Clyntahn slammed both fists on the conference table. "I frigging well *knew* it! I've been telling the rest of you for *months* that that gutless bastard would turn his coat the first moment he could! But this—*this!*" He pounded his fists up and down, his face purple with rage. "The whole damned *kingdom's* turned against Mother Church—betrayed God Himself! Shan-wei must be cackling in hell, and you three are the ones who kept me from hauling Thirsk back here and dealing with him before he could sell his entire kingdom to her! What do you think's going to happen now that he's gotten *away* with it? You think some of the other weak-kneed gutless wonders out there won't be thinking about doing exactly the same thing? Of course they will!"

Duchairn glanced at Maigwair from the corner of one eye, but neither of them spoke, and Clyntahn's lip curled in contemptuous fury. Then he turned back to Rayno, jabbing the air with an emphatic forefinger.

"I want every Dohlaran in the Temple Lands taken into custody—immediately!" he snarled. "Every *one* of them, Wyllym—do you understand me?! I want them arrested, and I want them sifted, and any of them—*any of them*—with any connection to Thirsk or the other traitors to Mother Church will face the Question and the Punishment! I don't give a spider-rat's arse who they are, what they are, or who they're related to. I want every one of them in custody within twenty-six hours!"

"I've already directed our agents inquisitor to bring in the most prominent of them, Your Grace," Rayno replied. "There are a great many Dohlarans in the Temple Lands, however. Many of our foundry and manufactory supervisors are Dohlaran, in fact, and so is quite a bit of our labor force. I'm not certain we have enough manpower to arrest all of—"

"Don't frigging tell me we don't have enough *manpower!*" Clyntahn barked. "*Find* it! Transfer whoever you have to transfer, but *get it done,* Wyllym!"

"Of course, Your Grace!" Rayno bowed deeply. "I'll see to it immediately."

"See that you damned well do. Now go get started!"

"At once, Your Grace!"

Rayno bowed again, deeper even than before, and vanished, and Clyntahn settled back into his chair. Fury continued to radiate from him, and the council chamber's very air seemed to quiver with it.

"I told you this would happen." The words came out remarkably quietly, but they were wrapped around a core of white-hot rage. "I *told* you, but would you listen? No, of course you wouldn't!"

"We don't know for certain yet what's happening," Duchairn said very cautiously. Clyntahn's furious glare focused on him, and the treasurer shrugged. "I'm only saying that Wyllym himself said his reports were fragmentary, Zhaspahr."

"Of course we know!" Clyntahn snapped. "This is what the miserable prick's been planning from the beginning—from the first time he didn't want to surrender his precious heretics to the Punishment!"

Duchairn started to reply, then stopped himself, and a deadly silence fell as the implications of a complete Dohlaran collapse went through all of their minds.

In many ways, it really changed nothing, Duchairn thought. Charisian control of the Gulf of Dohlar had already severed both South Harchong and Dohlar from the Temple Lands and the northern front, where the decisive grapple was underway. A Dohlaran withdrawal from the Jihad would free Earl Hanth's Army of Thesmar to reinforce High Mount, making Silken Hills' withdrawal even more urgent, but it would take time, and probably a lot of it, for Hanth to redeploy. Not that it really mattered how long it took—not in the end.

Mother Church had been reduced to the resources of the Temple Lands, whatever minor contribution the Border States could make, and North Harchong. And what that really meant was that her field armies had been reduced solely to the Temple Lands for their support.

The Mighty Host might still be in the field, and additional troops might still be on the march from the Empire, but Charisian control of the Harchong Narrows had already cut off every North Harchong foundry, mine, and farm west of the Chiang-wu Mountains from the day they'd retaken Claw Island. Now, with the entire Gulf closed, the only remaining Harchongese water transport to the Temple Lands was down the St. Cahnyr River out of the Langhorne Mountains or along the Hayzor-Westborne

Canal out of the extreme eastern edge of Maddox Province. Those routes served less than five percent of the total Empire; everything else might as well be on the moon for all the good it did the Jihad.

And the Border States won't be able to supply anything remotely close to our requirements, Duchairn thought. *For that matter, how many of them will even try to? Because Zhaspahr has a point, damn him . . . especially if Charis and Siddarmark are smart enough to offer Thirsk generous terms. With Charisian and Siddarmarkian armies marching steadily deeper into their own territories, the Border State rulers will be looking at the example of Dohlar—and Chisholm, and Emerald, and Corisande, and Tarot, and every other realm that's made its peace with Charis or simply dropped out of the Jihad, like Desnair.*

It's over.

The thought went through his mind softly, quietly, with something almost like a sense of . . . relief. No, not relief. That was the wrong word. But he couldn't think of the *right* word for the strange empty, singing silence deep within him.

It doesn't matter what Brygham or Walkyr or Rainbow Waters can do in the field, he thought. *Not anymore. There's simply no physical way we can haul enough food, enough ammunition, or enough men forward to support them. They could fight like Chihiro himself come back to earth, and it wouldn't change one damned thing in the end.*

He saw the same awareness, the same recognition, in Allayn Maigwair's eyes, and he started to open his mouth. He wasn't certain what he was going to say, how he'd find the words, and someone else spoke before he found them.

"I think it might be time to . . . seek direct contact with Cayleb and Sharleyan and Stohnar."

The hesitant voice was Zahmsyn Trynair's, and Duchairn's eyes widened in astonishment as the Chancellor looked nervously at Clyntahn.

The Grand Inquisitor seemed not to have heard him for a handful of seconds. Then he turned his head, looking back at Trynair.

"What did you say?" he asked, and Duchairn's astonishment grew.

The question had come out calmly, almost courteously, as if Trynair's suggestion had been perfectly reasonable, and now Clyntahn cocked his head. His expression was almost as calm as his tone, and he made a little encouraging motion with his right hand.

"I said . . . I said it might be time to seek contact with Cayleb and Sharleyan and Stohnar," Trynair said, and leaned forward slightly. "I know none of us want to even contemplate that, but if . . . if the situation's as . . . as *serious* as it seems to have become, then it seems unlikely we can expect a . . . successful resolution on the battlefield. So perhaps it's time we sought a diplomatic approach."

"A diplomatic approach," Clyntahn repeated. He leaned back in his own chair, folding his hands across his midsection, and raised his eyebrows. "What sort of 'diplomatic approach' did you have in mind, Zahmsyn?"

"Well," Trynair said a bit hesitantly, "I think we probably have to begin by forming a . . . a realistic view of what Mother Church's prospects are if we continue the war. I mean, we need to have an accurate understanding of our capabilities—and how they compare to the heretics'—before we can assess what we can realistically ask for."

"Ask for at the negotiating table, I presume you mean?"

"Yes." Trynair nodded, his expression more animated at the evidence of Clyntahn's willingness to hear him out. "It's always important to decide ahead of time what points are and aren't negotiable, Zhaspahr. And it's just as important to evaluate the strengths and weaknesses of both sides' positions before sitting down at the table. Each of them is going to assess what it demands—or what it's willing to concede—based on what it expects continuing the war would cost it."

"And I imagine it's equally important to decide what's the minimum you're prepared to accept from the other side. Especially when you're negotiating on God's behalf," Clyntahn observed in that same calm, reasonable voice, and something in his eyes sent a thousand tiny, icy feet scuttling up and down Duchairn's spine.

"Oh, absolutely!" Trynair nodded again, firmly, and Duchairn could almost physically feel the Chancellor's eagerness. It was like watching someone awaken from a trance, rousing as he realized his diplomatic competence and experience had suddenly become relevant once more.

"You always have to understand what you can and can't bargain away," he went on. "And it's always important to remember that you're not going to get everything you ask for. In this case, I think we're all in agreement that Mother Church can't bargain away her religious authority. That has to be guaranteed at an absolute minimum. But we might be willing to offer some accommodations to the Reformists' less outrageous demands."

"I don't think it would be acceptable for Mother Church to surrender any significant doctrinal points, Zahmsyn," Clyntahn said thoughtfully.

"Oh, no! Not *permanently*," Trynair agreed. "I'm not suggesting we should do anything of the sort! But we might need to convince them we'd be willing to, if only to get them started talking to us. If we tell them we're prepared to negotiate and both sides agree to a cease-fire in place while we do, I'm sure we could spin the talks out at least to the end of summer. Trust me, my people and I are old hands at that sort of thing!" He smiled. "If we get them talking in the first place, I'm confident we can *keep* them talking until the first snow shuts down the fighting. That would give us all winter to improve our military position, and if we did *that*, we'd be able to hold out for much better terms next year. The longer they give us to recover, the more expensive it becomes for them to defeat us militarily. And the more expensive that becomes, the more . . . amenable to reason they'll be."

"And you genuinely think you could negotiate an acceptable balance of authority between Mother Church and someone like Cayleb Ahrmahk or Greyghor Stohnar? Forgive me if I seem just a trifle skeptical about that, after all this time and all this bloodshed."

"I don't know," Trynair said frankly. "I only know it's our best chance— our *only* chance, really—given how bad things look. I may not be able to get them to agree to our minimal terms, but there's at least the *possibility* that I can. On the other hand, if we continue the Jihad and lose—and that's exactly what seems to be happening, Zhaspahr—they'll be in a position to dictate any terms they want, and I think we can all imagine what *those* terms would be like."

"I imagine we can," Clyntahn agreed. He sat for several more moments, his lips pursed in thought, then gave a small nod and stretched out an arm. He passed one hand over the glowing God light on the table before him, and the council chamber door slid open once more as one of the purple-cassocked agents inquisitor in the antechamber answered the soft chime.

"Yes, Your Grace?" he said, signing himself with Langhorne's scepter and bowing to the Grand Inquisitor.

"Arrest him," Clyntahn replied conversationally, and pointed at Trynair.

Zahmsyn Trynair slammed back in his chair, staring at Clyntahn in disbelief, but the agent inquisitor only nodded, as if the order to arrest Mother Church's Chancellor was nothing out of the ordinary. The sound of his heels was loud in the brutal, echoing silence as he crossed to Trynair's end of the table.

"If you'll accompany me, please, Your Grace."

The words were courteous, but the tone was icy and Trynair shook his head, still staring at Clyntahn.

"Zhaspahr, *please*," he whispered. "You can't! I mean—"

"I know *exactly* what you mean, Zahmsyn," Clyntahn said, and the veneer of thoughtful, interested curiosity had vanished. "You mean you're willing to sit down across a table from that bastard Cayleb and that harlot Sharleyan and bargain away God's own authority to save your worthless arse." His voice was as implacable as his frozen eyes. "I should've realized long ago that you'd betray Him and His Archangels anytime you saw an advantage to it. But just as God knows His own, His Inquisition knows how to deal with *Shan-wei's* own."

"But I'm *not!*" Trynair rose from his chair, holding out an imploring hand. "You *know* I'm not! I'm trying to save Mother Church from losing *everything* if the heretics defeat our last armies!"

"Don't be any stupider than you have to be," Clyntahn sneered. "Mother Church is God's Bride. She *can't* lose—not in the end—so long as one faithful, loyal son stands to fight for her! But I don't suppose a traitor to God could be expected to understand that, could he?"

"I—"

Trynair broke off, his face paper-white, terror beginning to flare in his eyes as panic leached away the anesthetic of shock. He stared at Clyntahn, and then his eyes darted desperately to Duchairn and Maigwair.

"Don't expect them to save you," Clyntahn said flatly, jerking the Chancellor's eyes back to him, and contempt edged his voice. "Unlike you, they're dutiful sons of Mother Church. They understand their responsibilities . . . just as they understand the consequences of failing to *meet* those responsibilities."

Duchairn's jaw clenched so tightly he expected his teeth to shatter, but he managed to hold his tongue. It wasn't easy when he saw the horror in Trynair's eyes, but he couldn't miss the message in *Clyntahn's.* The Grand Inquisitor was perfectly prepared to make a clean sweep, to have *all* of them arrested to free his own hand for the Jihad. If he did, the consequences would be disastrous for Mother Church, but none of them would be there to see it when he took the entire Church down in ruin with him.

He's mad, Duchairn thought. *He's finally gone completely mad. He knows— intellectually, he knows as well as I do—the Jihad's lost. As Allayn and Zahmsyn do. But he'll never admit it. Or maybe he just doesn't care. He's ready to ride the Jihad all the way to Mother Church's total destruction if God isn't willing to validate him by producing the miracle it would take to prevent that. And he'll kill anyone who disagrees with him.*

The awareness, Clyntahn's challenge, lay between them, stark and ugly, and Rhobair Duchairn made himself sit back in his chair. He forced himself to meet Clyntahn's cold serpent's eyes without flinching . . . but he said nothing.

Clyntahn's nostrils flared and his lip curled. Then he looked back at the agent inquisitor.

"Take him," he said, and the agent inquisitor laid a hand on Trynair's arm.

Trynair stared down at it for a single heartbeat. But then his eyes closed and his shoulders slumped. He stood a moment longer, until the agent inquisitor tugged. When his eyes opened again, they were empty—empty of fear, of hope, of anything at all—and he followed the agent inquisitor from the chamber, walking like a man lost in nightmare.

Clyntahn watched him go, then rose from his own chair and stood facing Duchairn and Maigwair across the table.

"Nothing can excuse the treason of a vicar—especially of Mother Church's own Chancellor—when she's fighting for her very life against the forces of hell unleashed upon the world." Every word was carved out of ice, and his eyes were colder still. "Understand me well, both of you. Anyone who betrays the Jihad, regardless of position or power, betrays *God*, and that will never be tolerated, never pass unpunished. *Never.* The Inquisition's rod will find him out, and it will *break* him."

He held them with those frozen eyes, daring them to speak, then inhaled deeply.

"Perhaps it's as well this has happened," he said then. "It's time all of God's children were made aware that *anyone* who fails God must pay the price. And so they will. The Holy Inquisition will teach them that when Zahmsyn faces the Punishment tomorrow."

He gave them one final, icy look, then stalked from the chamber in silence.

AUGUST
YEAR OF GOD 898

The Halberd Rest Tavern,
City of Zion,
The Temple Lands.

I'll be honest," Captain Ahksynov Laihu said somberly as the waitress set the fresh tankard on the table and disappeared with the latest empty one, "I never thought I'd see anything like today. Never."

He buried his nose in the tankard, swallowing a deep draft of the honeyed mead he favored, then set it down with a thump. The background noise was more muted than one ever heard in The Halberd Rest. The raucous shouts of greeting, the cheerful ribaldry directed at the long-suffering waitresses—who normaly gave back as good as they got—and the clink and rattle of cutlery were all subdued, as if a cloud of silence hung suspended in the tobacco smoke among the rafters.

"Don't know why not, Sir," Sergeant Phylyp Preskyt said from the other side of the square table. Laihu looked at him, and Preskyt shrugged. "Not exactly the first vicar to face the Punishment," he pointed out.

Trust Preskyt to put it into perspective, Ahrloh Mahkbyth thought, nursing his own glass of whiskey.

He sat between the captain and the sergeant at the small table tucked into an alcove in the back of the tavern's dining room. It was a very inconveniently placed alcove, right beside the swinging doors from the kitchen. The traffic was heavy as waiters and waitresses shuttled back and forth past it with trays of food, and the noise as orders were shouted to the cooks through the huge, square window beside the doors made it difficult for people sitting in it to hear one another without raising their voices. On the other hand, it was almost impossible to see into it from most of the dining room floor, and if the people around the table found it difficult to hear one another, it was even more difficult for anyone else to hear them.

I really shouldn't be doing this, Mahkbyth told himself now, looking back and forth between the two Temple Guardsmen. *What I should be doing is sitting at home, keeping my head down and making damned sure I don't draw any attention to myself!*

Unfortunately, that had turned out to be rather more difficult than usual.

He'd gone to witness Zahmsyn Trynair's Punishment for a confused tangle of reasons he couldn't completely sort out. Part of it, and he was honest enough to admit it to himself, was that he'd *wanted* to see Trynair's death. If any man had ever deserved to suffer the Punishment, it had to be one of the four who'd launched the madness of the Jihad and condemned so many millions of others to the same fate. He didn't really want to see and hear anyone screaming as the white-hot irons were applied, or as the roaring pyre consumed his tortured body, but if it had to happen to anyone, he couldn't think of a better candidate. Well, no, that wasn't quite true. He could *definitely* think of a better candidate, but the odds against anyone condemning Zhaspahr Clyntahn to that fate were . . . slim.

He'd also gone because he'd been quietly underlining his piety ever since Zhorzhet Styvynsyn and Marzho Alysyn died in the Inquisition's custody. It turned his stomach, but he knew the value of protective coloration. And he'd gone to touch base with two or three old comrades from his own days in the Guard. Maintaining those contacts was part of his public persona, and their willingness to share barracks scuttlebutt with an old retired sergeant often provided Helm Cleaver with useful tidbits of information. Besides, many of them had been his friends for decades—like Laihu and Preskyt—and he missed them.

He hadn't expected them to invite him to The Halberd Rest for sausages and beer, though. Food was the last thing he would've thought of after the hideous spectacle they'd just witnessed. But he'd forgotten the pragmatism of serving guardsmen, just as he'd forgotten the way in which familiar food and drink could comfort a man when he needed it worst.

Laihu was quite a few years younger than Mahkbyth, with the dark hair and eyes of his Harchongese ancestry. He was also an intelligent, insightful fellow who'd learned the realities behind the Temple's façade only too well over the course of a thirty-year career, and once upon a time, long, long ago, Mahkbyth had been the senior sergeant in *Lieutenant* Laihu's platoon for almost five years. He'd come to know the other man well during those years, and it amazed him sometimes that Laihu could have served that long a career, well over half of it right here in Zion, without succumbing to the cynicism that was so much a part of Temple duty. It amazed him even more that Laihu was still on active duty in Zion, given the doubts he knew the captain had cherished for many years about the fashion in which the vicarate's morality reflected—or didn't—the Archangels' true intentions.

Of course, you always knew he was a smart fellow, Ahrloh. Certainly smart enough to keep his mouth shut about the sorts of things that get a man killed!

He did, indeed, know that. In fact, he'd considered attempting to recruit Laihu for Helm Cleaver more than once. But the captain was also a man of stubborn integrity who took his oaths seriously. There'd never been much chance he'd violate those oaths, even for an old friend.

Not before the Jihad, anyway, Mahkbyth reflected. *Might be a little different these days. But it might not, too.*

"You've got a point, Phylyp," Laihu said now, his expression that of a man who'd just tasted something spoiled. "Never sat right what happened to Vicar Hauwerd. *Never.* And I'll tell you what." He looked Mahkbyth straight in the eye. "Vicar Hauwerd and his brother? No way they were guilty of all the *crap* they were accused of! I never knew Vicar Samyl well, but I served under Hauwerd when he was with the Guard. So did you, Ahrloh! *You* think the two of them would've conspired against Mother Church?"

"*I* think you may have had a little too much mead, Ahksynov," Mahkbyth replied. "That's not exactly the sort of question a dutiful son of Mother Church ought to be asking another dutiful son of Mother Church at a time like this."

"If you can't ask another *dutiful* son of Mother Church, who can you ask?" Laihu shot back.

"Pretty sure that's not exactly what Ahrloh meant, Sir," Preskyt said. The sergeant was a solid, square shouldered fellow with a stolid, intensely loyal personality. He'd been Mahkbyth's senior corporal when they'd both served in Laihu's platoon, and he'd been with Laihu ever since. Now he shook his head. "Business of a good sergeant is to keep officers from doing the stupid stuff," he pointed out. "And I hate to say it, but asking the wrong question where the wrong set of ears can hear comes under the head of *really* stupid stuff right now."

Despite himself, Mahkbyth chuckled. Then he looked back at Laihu.

"That's exactly what I meant," he said. "Mind you, Phylyp's much more eloquent than I am, but he's grasped the nub of my thought."

Laihu snorted into his mead, and Mahkbyth shook his head with a smile. But then the smile faded, and he shrugged.

"Having said that, no. I don't think for a second the Wylsynns were guilty of everything they were accused of. I'm not prepared to say they weren't guilty of *anything* they were accused of, but I'll guarantee you they were never in this world involved in Shan-wei worship or an effort to destroy Mother Church."

"Exactly," Laihu said, although he was careful to keep his voice even lower than it had been, low enough that Mahkbyth had to strain to pick it out of the background sound even though they were less than three feet apart. "Exactly." The captain shook his head. "Too many personal scores are getting paid off, Ahrloh. I always knew there'd be things I wouldn't much like doing, but believe me—you're a hell of a lot better off as a civilian." He looked moodily down into his mead. "Some mornings, it's awfully hard to get up and report for duty."

"I'm not surprised." Mahkbyth reached out and patted him on the shoulder lightly. "There were days like that for me even before the Jihad, and I don't see how it could've gotten anything but worse since the Jihad started. But it's like the *Writ* says. There are going to be dark days as well as happy ones. What matters is how well we bear up on the dark ones."

"I know." Laihu threw back another swallow of the mead, then put down the empty tankard and gazed down into it. "And you're right," he said with the air of a man who'd come to an important decision. "I *have* had too much mead tonight. So, with your permission, Sergeant Mahkbyth, I believe I'll invite Sergeant Preskyt to escort me back to barracks and pour me safely into bed." He grimaced. "I'm pretty sure Shan-wei's going to be using the inside of my skull for an anvil when I wake up in the morning."

"Oh, probably won't be *that* bad, Sir," Preskyt said encouragingly as Laihu stood almost steadily. "I've seen you *lots* drunker than this," the sergeant continued with a wink at Mahkbyth. "A little tomato juice, some raw egg, some tabasco sauce, and you'll be right as rain by, oh, thirteen o'clock!"

"Your sympathy is always such a comfort to me, Sergeant." Laihu patted Preskyt on the shoulder, then nodded to Mahkbyth.

"And on that note, I'll bid you good night, Ahrloh. Was good seeing you. We'll have to do this again."

"Hopefully on a happier occasion," Mahkbyth agreed, and watched the two of them weave their way across the crowded dining room and out into the late summer twilight.

He finished his own beer, tossed a handful of coins onto the table, nodded to the waitress, and followed them out the door. He turned and started along the street, ignoring the trams rattling by behind their draft dragons. Nights were short in Zion this late in summer, and he enjoyed walking. Besides, it was only a few blocks, and—

"Good evening, Chief Sergeant," a voice said behind him, and he stopped. He hesitated for just a moment, then turned to face the officer standing behind him. The officer in the uniform of the Temple Guard but with the flame and sword of the Inquisition on his shoulder flash.

"Evening, Captain," he replied, then corrected himself. "Major, I mean. Sorry, I'd heard about the promotion, just forgot it."

"Not surprising when you've been out of the Guard so long, Chief Sergeant," the other man said with an easy smile. "What's it been? Fifteen years now? Sixteen?"

"More like twenty-five, Sir. Since about three months after Dahnyld died."

"That long?" The major shook his head. "It doesn't seem like it could have been. I heard about your wife's death, though. I'm sorry you lost her . . .

and I wish the Guard had figured out who was responsible for that. And for your boy."

"So do I," Mahkbyth said levelly.

They stood silently for a moment, then the major shrugged.

"Could I ask where you're headed?"

"Home." It was Mahkbyth's turn to shrug. "I've got a cat-lizard who's probably wondering where the Shan-wei I am right now." He smiled crookedly. "You know how cat-lizards are."

"Always refused to be owned by one of them, myself," the major replied with an answering smile. "But I'd sort of hoped you were headed by your shop. A friend of mine tells me you've got the best selection of whiskeys in Zion."

"I don't know if it's *the* best, but it's certainly one *of* the best, if I do say so myself. We're closed right now, but if you'd like to come by tomorrow, I'll be happy to prove that."

"I've got the duty all next five-day," the major said. "And your shop's sort of on the way home, isn't it?"

Mahkbyth frowned. Something about this conversation was making his antennae tingle, but there was no point lying. Especially to an officer assigned to the Inquisition who obviously already knew the answer to his own question.

"About a half-block out of the way, Sir," he said.

"Well, I don't want to sound like I'm *wheedling*, but I really would appreciate it if you could open up just long enough to sell me a couple of bottles. I've got some serious entertaining to do, and I'm afraid the liquor cabinet's bare just now. And at least one of the friends I have coming over has some . . . sophisticated tastes. I've already tried three other shops here in Zion without finding his preferred blend."

Mahkbyth managed not to frown. He *really* didn't want to open his shop, and especially not on such short notice for an officer who'd been seconded to the Inquisition. By the same token, pissing off someone with the sort of connections the major had could be dangerous. More to the point, people might start wondering why he'd been stupid enough to *risk* pissing him off.

"I'm sorry to hear that, Sir," he said after only the briefest of hesitations. "Of course, if you've been to that many other shops, it's likely I don't have it in stock either." He grimaced. "I'm sorry to say quite a few labels have been in short supply since the Jihad began."

"Oh, trust me!" The major rolled his eyes. "I'm only too well aware of that, Chief Sergeant!"

"What are you looking for, exactly, Sir?" Mahkbyth asked pleasantly. If it was as rare as the major was implying, he could always deny he had it in stock, either. For that matter, he thought with a smile, he might even be telling the truth! "I'm assuming it's one I've at least heard of!"

"Oh, I'm pretty sure you have," the major said, looking him straight in the eye. "I'm looking for Seijin Kohdy's Premium Blend, Chief Sergeant. Do you think you could find me a bottle?"

.II.
Tellesberg Palace,
City of Tellesberg,
and
The Delthak Works,
Earldom of Hanth High Rock,
Kingdom of Old Charis,
Empire of Charis,
and
Charisian Embassy,
Siddar City,
Republic of Siddarmark.

I have to say, I never really thought I'd see something like this," Sharleyan Ahrmahk said.

She and Maikel Staynair sat in a sunny council chamber with Trahvys Ohlsyn, the Earl of Pine Hollow and the Kingdom of Old Charis' first councilor, and Bynzhamyn Raice, Baron Wave Thunder, the Empire of Charis' senior spymaster. Or, rather, the Empire of Charis' senior *breathing* spymaster.

"I rather doubt Trynair saw it coming, either," the electronic personality who was the empire's true spymaster said dryly over their com earplugs. "There's a certain poetic justice to it, though, I suppose."

"I don't think there's enough poetry in my soul to appreciate it properly, Nahrmahn," Ehdwyrd Howsmyn, the Duke of Delthak, put in from his office at the Delthak Works and looked at the red-haired upper-priest sitting across his desk from him.

"Mine either," Paityr Wylsynn agreed, his eyes dark. "I'm ashamed to say there's a vengeful part of me that feels nothing but satisfaction after what happened to Father and Uncle Hauwerd and all their friends. But that's an ugly part I try not to listen to very often, and the rest of me. . . ."

His voice trailed off, and he shook his head, looking down into the tumbler of Glynfych in his hand.

"I didn't mean to sound flippant, Paityr," Nahrmahn said. "But I'm afraid my vengeful side's better developed than yours is. And it may be petty of me, but I tend to carry a fairly personal grudge against people whose allies have me murdered."

"That would tend to give someone an interesting perspective," Cayleb Ahrmahk observed from the dining room attached to his quarters in the Charisian Embassy. He and Merlin Athrawes and Nynian Rychtyr had just finished breakfast, and he grimaced. "On the other hand, Paityr has a point. That's an ugly, ugly way to die."

"I don't want to appear insensitive, but dead is dead, and none of the four of them could have gotten that way soon enough to satisfy me," Nynian said grimly. "As for being surprised, I'd always figured Trynair was the one most likely to be the first to get thrown off the ice floe to check for krakens." She shrugged. "His problem was that he was always the smartest one in the room, even when he wasn't. I don't know for sure what he really did to piss Clyntahn off, but he should've borne in mind that his area of expertise hasn't been in much demand since the jihad started. In fact, I'd be willing to bet that at least half the reason he went to the Punishment was to help Clyntahn make a point to Maigwair and Duchairn. *They* have skills he still needs, so why not use someone he *doesn't* need as what the Inquisition likes to call 'a teaching moment'?"

Her eyes were very dark, her expression cold, and Merlin regarded her thoughtfully as he nodded.

"I wouldn't be at all surprised if you're right about that, love," he said. "I know you're right about the way Clyntahn's mind works, anyway. And you definitely know all the players involved better than any of the rest of us do. But that does leave an interesting question. What inspired him to arrange a 'teaching moment' at this particular time?"

"I can't answer that, but I'd bet my ruby eardrops it has a little something to do with what Kynt, Eastshare, and the others are doing to the Temple's armies." Nynian took a sip of chocolate. "Clyntahn's got to be getting desperate, and he's the sort who works out his fears by killing other people. If I had to guess, Trynair was probably stupid enough to suggest negotiating with us. Either that or one of the two Clyntahn figures he still needs said something he needed to discourage by killing someone else."

"You don't think Clyntahn would support negotiations even if they were nothing but a ploy to win time, Nynian?" Nahrmahn asked.

"I doubt he'd even consider it," Maikel Staynair responded before Nynian could. He shook his head, his expression grim. "After all this bloodshed, he has to know he, personally, won't survive defeat, no matter what else happens. As Cayleb would say, that's *so* not going to happen. And even if he didn't realize we'd demand that as a matter of justice, he knows perfectly well that in our shoes, *he'd* demand it out of vengeance. He's not going to do any-thing that could open the door to that result."

"I think you're exactly right, Maikel," Nynian agreed. "And I'd add that he'd see a willingness to negotiate, whether it was genuine or not, as a fatal sign of weakness. He'd believe that as soon as word got out, any remaining support for the jihad would evaporate. After all, if the Temple's willing to negotiate, then clearly this hasn't really been a life-or-death grapple between God and Shan-wei from the beginning. God doesn't negotiate with the Mother of Lies. If the Group of Four—well, Group of Three, now—*is* will-ing to negotiate, then they're effectively declaring that we've been right all along. This has been a war against mortal men *claiming* to speak for God, and now that they're losing, they're trying to salvage whatever they can of their own positions and power."

"That's pretty much what I've been thinking, too," Wave Thunder put in. "Especially the bit about its validating our position that we've been fight-ing against men who have perverted God's will. Clyntahn's about as arro-gant as they come, but he's smart enough to recognize that."

"Don't overlook the possibility that his own beliefs could be involved in this," Ohlyvya Baytz said. Her image sat on the terrace of Eraystor Palace—or, rather, of its electronic doppelgänger in the VR computer in Nimue's Cave—beside her husband. He cocked an eyebrow at her, and she shrugged.

"We've never been able to really decide how much of him is corrupt cynicism and how much is genuine zealotry," she reminded him. "For that matter, I very much doubt *he* could separate them. But we've always known he's been driven at least partly by a genuine commitment to his own twisted vision of what God's like, and I think it's entirely possible—probable, really—that he's retreating into—what was it you called it the other day, Merlin? A 'bunker mentality,' wasn't it?"

"It was indeed." Merlin tipped back in his chair and folded his arms, his expression thoughtful. "And I think you've got a point. Clyntahn's not the sort who could ever really believe in the possibility that he'd fail. It's just not in his makeup. But now the proof that he *has* failed is there for everyone to see, even him. So it's actually pretty likely he'd insist that God and the Arch-angels will come swooping in to the rescue, no matter what happens. But for that to happen, he and the others have to prove they're worthy of divine in-tervention, and that means fighting to the last drop of everyone else's blood."

"That's what I was afraid you were all going to say," Nahrmahn sighed. "Because the way I've been reading this, it's not a good sign from our per-spective. If he's able to send Trynair to the Punishment, then he's obviously in total control, and that means he really is going to fight 'to the last drop of everyone else's blood' rather than let even a scrap of rationality to creep into the Temple's position."

"I hate to say this," Pine Hollow said slowly, "but is that really a bad thing from our perspective?"

The others all looked at him, and he waved one hand, his expression troubled.

"From the perspective of ending this damned war without killing any more people than we have to, it's a *terrible* thing," he said. "I know that. But the truth is that from our perspective, the inner circle's perspective, this war isn't really about *reforming* the Church. It's about *overthrowing* the Church, about breaking the *Writ* and the Proscriptions, and hopefully doing it before any millennial visitors drop in on us. If Clyntahn's willing to continue the fight until we drag him out of his last lizardhole by the scruff of his neck, we'll be in a far better position to impose terms that break the Church's moral authority once and for all. He's already done a pretty damned good job of *undermining* that authority; now he may be giving us a chance to complete its destruction."

"Something to that," Cayleb said after a moment, and sighed. "In fact, I should probably admit I've been thinking pretty much the same thing. It's just that I'm so *sick* of all the blood, all the dying."

"We all are, sweetheart," his wife said gently. "But that doesn't make Trahvys wrong."

"No, it doesn't," Nynian agreed. "On the other hand, Zion's turning into a snake pit right now. There's no way to predict how Trynair's Punishment will affect that, but I doubt it's done anything to tamp down the tension. Between what's happening at the front, Trynair's execution, Helm Cleaver, and those broadsheets of Owl's, there's an awful lot of pressure building in the city. Right this minute, it *looks* like the Inquisition's in total control, but the truth is, there's no such thing as 'total control.' I'd say there's a possibility—probably remote, at the moment, but still there—of a genuine insurrection if Clyntahn and his inquisitors push it too far. And if that happens, all bets are off."

.III.
Earl Rainbow Waters' Headquarters,
City of Chyzwail,
West Wing Lake,
Tarikah Province,
Republic of Siddarmark.

Y ou sent for me, Uncle?"
Taychau Daiyang looked up from the endless stream of reports
and rubbed his eyes as Baron Wind Song entered his office. That office had
once belonged to the Mayor of Chyzwail, but the mayor didn't need it anymore . . . and Earl Rainbow Waters did.

"Yes, I did," he said, and pointed at the chair beside his desk. "Sit."

Wind Song obeyed, and if his expression was calm, his eyes were worried. The silver streaks in his uncle's dark hair had grown far broader, and
although he remained immaculately groomed, his eyes were red rimmed
from too little sleep and too much reading, too much poring over maps
and orders of battle. He'd always been a physically robust man, but his
hands had developed a tremor. It was still a tiny thing, one only the eyes of
someone who knew him very well might have noticed, but Wind Song *did*
know him.

"I've been reading our dispatches from home," Rainbow Waters said
after a moment. "And from Zion." Their eyes met, and the earl shrugged
ever so slightly. "It seems matters are coming to a head—here at the front, I
mean, of course."

"Of course," his nephew agreed.

"I'm not certain everyone back in Zion and Shang-mi fully understands
the gravity of our position here," Rainbow Waters continued after a moment.
"Oh, they clearly understand that Green Valley and Klymynt are pressing us
hard here in Tarikah, but I've just received a report that Eastshare's mounted
infantry have occupied Bauskum. Charisian mounted patrols have been spotted by our Ferey River pickets as well, and there are reports his scout snipers
are reconnoitering around Rainyr's Hollow."

Wind Song's face tightened. Rainyr's Hollow was a small farming
town—a ghost town, now, like every other village and town in this part of
Tarikah—barely a hundred miles by road from the Sairmeet-Gleesyn High
Road. For that matter, it was little more than a hundred and fifty air-miles
from Chyzwail. Once upon a time, a hundred and fifty miles would have

offered a comfortable degree of security, but Charisian mounted infantry, balloons, mobile field artillery, and infantry angle-guns had changed that.

"We can't say which way his main body will advance, but from all reports, Bishop Militant Lainyl will be forced to surrender at Mercyr any day now. Coupled with Eastshare's activity, that strongly suggests it will be Golden Tree's turn at Sairmeet next. He's already under heavy pressure from Stohnar from the east. If Eastshare swings in behind him as he did to Brygham at Mercyr, the consequences would be . . . unfortunate."

That's certainly one way to describe the collapse of our most critical blocking position, Wind Song thought.

"The Baron has requested permission to begin planning for a withdrawal," Rainbow Waters said. "I've granted it with, of course, the understanding that he must hold his ground as long as he reasonably can."

"Of course." Wind Song nodded. "May I ask if Bishop Merkyl has countersigned that permission?"

"I haven't yet had the opportunity to discuss it with the Bishop," Rainbow Waters said. "I'm confident that, when I do, he'll find himself in agreement."

Wind Song nodded again, although he wouldn't have cared to wager on the Mighty Host's intendant's agreeing to anything of the sort. Merkyl Sahndhaim had grown steadily more querulous as the situation worsened. It couldn't be very much longer before he began countermanding Rainbow Waters' decisions rather than simply criticizing them, at which point. . . .

"As I say," Rainbow Waters went on after a moment, "I've also been reading the correspondence from Zion and Shang-mi. The letters from the capital, in particular, cause me some small concern. It's essential that we continue moving troops forward. While I remain fully confident of the Mighty Host's fighting spirit, the possibility that we may be forced to retreat to the far side of the Tairohn Hills, or even as far as the Kingdom of Hoth, must be faced. Should that happen, we'll need every man we can get to bolster our new front."

He paused, regarding his nephew for several seconds, until Wind Song nodded. In fact, of course, if they were forced back that far, there weren't enough reinforcements in all of Harchong to save the Jihad. Far too much of the Mighty Host's irreplaceable artillery would have to be abandoned in the face of the obscenely mobile Charisians, and losses in small arms were already far beyond anything the Church could quickly replace.

"I'm not confident His Majesty's ministers have a proper sense of urgency in this matter," Rainbow Waters resumed once Wind Song had nodded. "Accordingly, I've composed a detailed report, laying out our current status and my best projections and earnestly urging them to expedite

troop movements to the very best of their ability. Given the vital importance of the entire matter, I've also decided that rather than relying upon
the semaphore, it's necessary to send an officer of sufficient stature—and
one sufficiently familiar with my thinking to answer any questions—to deliver my messages in person."

Wind Song stiffened in his chair. It was over six thousand miles for a
wyvern from Chyzwail to Shang-mi. The battle for West Wing Lake would
be decided five-days before any messenger could reach the capital.

"I'm sure I can find the proper messenger, Uncle," the baron said, holding Rainbow Waters' eyes levelly.

"In my view, there's really only one choice," Rainbow Waters replied.
"Of all of my staff officers and aides, you're the one most fully privy to my
thinking."

"Which is precisely the reason I can be least readily spared." Wind Song's
gaze never wavered.

"I must insist upon making my own determinations in this matter," his
uncle said sternly. "I'm quite prepared to make it a direct order."

"I would most respectfully urge you not to do that, My Lord. It would
grieve me to defy your wishes."

"It would not be my *wish*, Baron Wind Song. It would be my direct
order as your superior."

"In which case I would most regretfully be forced to resign my commission. After which, of course, your orders would no longer be applicable
to me."

"Some might consider your resignation an act of cowardice in the face
of the enemy!"

"It would be difficult to construe it that way, My Lord," Wind Song
said serenely, "when I then volunteered to serve in the ranks."

Rainbow Waters glared at him for several tense seconds. Then his
shoulders slumped.

"Please, Medyng," he said, and his voice had frayed around the edges.
"I promised your mother I would bring her son home to her."

"And I promised to bring her *brother* home, My Lord," Wind Song said
softly. "I've never in my life done anything as important as what you and
the Mighty Host are doing right here, right now. And I've never felt so privileged as I have to serve as your aide while you do it. There are no words to
express my pride in you, Uncle, so I won't embarrass both of us by trying.
But I will be here at your side, whether as an officer or a common trooper,
to the end, whatever that end may be."

Their eyes held, and then, slowly, Rainbow Waters smiled. It was a sad
smile, but genuine, and he shook his head.

"Your grandmother always said I was the most stubborn of her children," he said then. "Personally, I always believed she was wrong, since your mother was always far stubborner than I. It would appear she's passed that trait on to you, as well."

"I believe she's said something to that effect to me herself, Uncle."

"An excellent judge of character, your mother." Rainbow Waters nodded, then drew a deep breath and picked up one of the heaped folders on his blotter.

"Very well, Captain of Horse Wind Song, I'll send my dispatches by semaphore . . . for whatever they're worth. In the meantime, please review this estimate of the portability of the heretics' balloons and give me your thoughts on it."

.IV.
Merlin Athrawes' Chamber,
Siddarmarkian Embassy,
and
Cayleb Ahrmahk's Study,
Charisian Embassy,
Siddar City,
Republic of Siddarmark.

M erlin? *Merlin!*"

Sapphire eyes popped open. A PICA had no real need for sleep in the biological sense of the word, but Cayleb Ahrmahk had been right when he'd insisted, years ago, that Merlin get at least six hours of "down-time" every night.

It wasn't quite like biological sleep, although he and Owl had worked out a subprogram which actually gave him the equivalent of REM sleep. And there were times when he simply ignored Cayleb's orders and capitalized on the ability of a PICA to remain alert, active, and deadly for days on end.

In this case, however. . . .

"This had better be *really* important, Nahrmahn," he subvocalized over his built-in com link, glaring at the image Owl projected into his vision and very careful not to disturb the head resting peacefully on his shoulder or the body nestled close against him.

"I never realized Nynian snored," Nahrmahn replied with a twinkle. "That's actually sort of reassuring. I mean, she's so formidable in so many ways."

"You may already be dead," Merlin told him, "but I don't think you'd like what a good, strong power spike would do to you."

"Point taken." Nahrmahn chuckled, but then his smile faded. "And I'm sorry to disturb you, but there's something we need to discuss. And it's a good thing Nynian's here, because we definitely need her input on this one."

▼ ▼ ▼

"So this fellow just walked into Mahkbyth's shop?" Cayleb Ahrmahk said skeptically, gazing at Merlin and a silken-robed Nynian across the chocolate cup in his hands. "Why does that make me feel all suspicious?"

"Because paranoia is a survival tool," Sharleyan said tartly from her own bedchamber. Dawn was just gilding the sky over Tellesberg, and she sat before her mirror, brushing her hair.

"All of our sources—everything we've gotten from the SNARCs, and everything Helm Cleaver and the Sisters have reported—underline how tense the situation in Zion's gotten," Nynian pointed out. "I don't find it difficult to believe it's going from tense to critical very quickly, Sharley. Especially not in the wake of what happened to Trynair!"

"I just don't like the way this 'opportunity' has dropped onto us out of the clear blue sky," Cayleb said. "It's got 'trap' written all over it."

"I don't think so," Merlin said thoughtfully, leaning back in an overstuffed armchair. "For it to be a trap, the Inquisition would have to know who Ahrloh is—or *what* he is, at least—and we know from what happened to Zhorzhet and Marzho exactly what they'd do in that case. Do you really think Rayno or Clyntahn would mount some sort of elaborate ploy at this point instead of producing a real, live terrorist for the Punishment?"

"And there's always the question of just who they could plan on trapping," Nynian added. "They've obviously figured out our communications loop lets us turn messages around at least as quickly as their own semaphore, so I don't doubt they expect Ahrloh to be able to pass the message on to us quickly, assuming he really is one of our people. But I doubt they could expect anyone from outside Zion to just . . . appear in Ahrloh's shop tomorrow. So the only people they could logically try to 'trap' would have to be already in Zion, or at least very close to the city. And if whoever they're after is *that* close, the Inquisition's typical thinking would be to grab Ahrloh and torture his superior's location out of him. Rayno might be more subtle under some circumstances, but not under the current ones." She shook her head. "No, at this point, Clyntahn would want *fast* results. He'd settle for whatever he could get quickly, and he definitely wouldn't take a chance on a fish like Ahrloh wiggling out of the net."

"What I find most interesting," Maikel Staynair said slowly, "is the use of the Seijin Kohdy code phrase. That suggests at least some knowledge of Helm Cleaver and the Sisters."

"Which could simply mean they managed to torture at least some information out of Zhorzhet and Marzho before they died," Cayleb said harshly, his eyes grim.

"True." Staynair nodded in his archbishop's palace's bedchamber, sitting up in bed while he scratched the belly fur of the purring cat-lizard luxuriating across his lap. "And I suppose they're really simply attempting to bait Ahrloh into confirming his own membership in Helm Cleaver by responding to the code phrase. But I have to agree with Nynian. It doesn't have that sort of feel to me."

"And whether it's a trap or not, it has to be explored," Wave Thunder said. "The possibility of making a contact at that level simply can't be ignored."

"Well, that leaves us in a bit of a quandary," Nahrmahn pointed out. "Owl and I picked up on this as soon as Ahrloh put the message into the system, but if we want to explore this—in time for it to do any good, at least—we can't wait for that message to reach us. Besides, most of Nynian's conduits are down now. Nobody's passing any semaphore messages or couriers across the front lines at the moment. In fact, the only conduit that's still up is the messenger wyvern route through Dohlar and the South March, and they're running out of wyverns. We won't be able to get them replacements anytime soon, either."

"Then there's really only one way to do it," Merlin said calmly.

"You'd be in awfully close proximity to the Temple if something goes wrong!" Duke Delthak said sharply. "Ahrloh's shop's well inside the safety margin you set for any active use of Federation technology. If this *is* a trap, you couldn't get the recon skimmer in close enough to pull you out of it."

"I don't see that as a deal breaker," Nimue said from the late-afternoon Manchyr. "Maybe the skimmer couldn't pull us out, but having a pair of *seijins* cut their way out of the city on foot against everything the Guard could throw at them couldn't exactly help Clyntahn's position!"

"Perhaps not," Nynian said, "but I'm afraid there is no 'us' in this for you, Nimue."

"I beg your pardon?" Nimue's tone was on the sharp side, Nynian only shook her head with a thin smile.

Either it's possible for a PICA to get out of Zion even if something under the Temple wakes up, or it's not. If it is, we don't need two PICAs. If it *isn't*, we can't afford to lose both the PICAs we have. That means only one of you is going. Since Ahrloh's met *Seijin* Zoshua, Merlin's the logical choice instead of you. And if Merlin's going, so am I."

There was a moment of profound silence over the com link, and Nynian turned her head to meet Merlin Athrawes' cybernetic eyes. Their gazes locked, and he saw the unyielding steel behind *her* eyes.

"I'm not sure that's necessary," he said, after a moment.

"*I* am."

Her voice was flat, as unyielding as her expression, and he sat back in his chair. He doubted she could have fully analyzed her own reasoning, but that didn't really matter. Everything within him wanted to argue, to tell her no, to *refuse* to take her . . . and he couldn't. She'd given too much, risked too much, *lost* too much getting to this point for him to even try to protect her against her will.

"Then that's good enough for me," he said simply instead. "Owl, we'll need the recon skimmer."

.V.
Ahrloh Mahkbyth's Fine Wines and Spirits,
Mylycynt Court,
City of Zion,
The Temple Lands.

If I'd known you were going to come in person, I'd never have forwarded the message," Ahrloh Mahkbyth said grimly.

"And if I'd had to wait for your message to reach me, I wouldn't have gotten here in time for you to worry about it," Nynian told him, looking up from the bottle of wine whose label she'd been examining. "This is a very good year, Ahrloh. How many more bottles of it do you have?"

"I'd have to check the ledger," he said repressively. "And don't try to distract me."

"I'm not trying to distract you from anything. I'd just like to take a dozen or so bottles with me when we leave." She slid the bottle gently back into the rack with the reverence the vintage deserved and smiled at him. "Helping you get established really was one of my better investments . . . in a lot of ways."

He glared at her for a moment, then turned to her much taller companion.

"Can't *you* make her show a little sense, *Seijin* Zoshua?" he demanded.

"I doubt anyone's *made* her do anything since she was six years old," Zoshua Murphai replied philosophically. "And I'm fairly sure her nanny had to negotiate bath times with her for at least three years before she *turned* six."

"I don't understand why everyone thinks I'm so *stubborn*." Nynian shook her head as she crossed to a display of paper-thin, hand-blown Harchongese brandy snifters. She picked one up and held it to the light, admiring the exquisite workmanship. "If people would just recognize the impeccable logic of my position in the first place, we could save a lot of time that otherwise gets wasted arguing."

"That's all well and good," Mahkbyth said. "But it's entirely possible they managed to break Zhorzhet or Marzho before they died, and you know it. That could explain exactly how he got that recognition phrase. And if it is, if this truly is some sort of trap, you're the one person in all the world we can least afford to deliver to them, Ahnzhelyk!"

"And we won't," she told him calmly, setting the snifter back on the display stand, and turned to face him with a serene smile. "I can't guarantee it isn't a trap, but if it is, they aren't going to take us by surprise the way they must have surprised Zhorzhet and Marzho." She stepped closer to him and laid one hand on his forearm. "And if they can't surprise us, they won't be *capturing* anyone will they?"

He looked at her grimly for a moment, but then, finally, he shook his head.

"That's not really all that much better an outcome from Helm Cleaver's perspective, you know," he pointed out.

"Maybe not, but it's a *far* better one from *my* perspective." She squeezed his forearm gently. "And it wouldn't really be all that disastrous from Helm Cleaver's point of view, either. Inconvenient, perhaps, but Axman is safely back home in the Republic, in contact with Cayleb and Sharleyan and all of *Seijin* Zoshua's . . . associates. They're fully capable of coordinating Helm Cleaver's operations if anything unfortunate were to happen to me."

Mahkbyth nodded a shade unwillingly. He didn't know that "Axman" was Sandaria Ghatfryd, but he'd received several messages from Axman over the years in which he'd commanded Helm Cleaver.

"Besides, I have to be sure your new friend's telling us the truth, don't I?" Nynian continued.

"And how, pray tell, do you intend to do that?" he inquired just a bit caustically. "I'm willing to concede that you're better than most at picking out lies, Ahnzhelyk, but he wouldn't have been chosen to contact us if he wasn't better *at* lying than most." The ex-sergeant shrugged. "That would be true whether he's an honest messenger or an Inquisition provocateur."

"Oh, I'm fairly confident I'll be able to sort the chaff from the grain," she told him, touching the pectoral scepter she wore around her neck.

It was larger than most, and more spectacular, almost like something designed for a high-ranked churchman's formal wear. It was certainly more ostentatious than anything he'd ever seen her wear before, and for all its superb workmanship, it was rather too massive for someone as slender as she. It was also far more eye-catching, although that was actually a point in its favor. Publicly displayed evidence of piety was a sound investment in Zion just now.

"And, in the meantime, it's nice to see Zion again," she continued, turning to gaze out the shop windows at the peaceful, lamplit square. "I hadn't

realized I was actually feeling a little homesick until the *seijin* delivered me."
She shook her head. "Odd, really. I wouldn't have expected to feel that way."

"We're all creatures of habit, one way or another," Murphai pointed out,
coming to stand beside her. "And I'm sure you had a lot of good memories
to go with the bad."

"Of course. It's just that recently the bad seem to've outnumbered the
good so badly."

"Times change. That's why we're here, after all."

"True enough." She nodded, still gazing out the windows, then turned
her head to look up at him. "True enough. You do have a way of helping
me keep things in perspective, don't you, Zoshua?"

"One tries," he told her with a lurking smile, and bowed ever so slightly.

She chuckled warmly, and one of Mahkbyth's eyebrows rose as he gazed
speculatively at their backs.

"And some of us do it much better than—"

The sudden jingle of the bell over the door interrupted her, and she
turned as a customer entered the store.

It was very late—thirty minutes or so after Mahkbyth's normal closing
time, in fact, although his hours had always been flexible—and he'd sent
Zhak Myllyr home almost an hour ago. Fortunately, he'd been doing that
for the last couple of five-days, since Myllyr's wife was in the final month of
her third pregnancy and she'd been having a difficult time of it. That had
provided a perfect pretext for ridding himself of the Inquisition's spy in his
shop.

Unless, of course, another and far more dangerous spy had just entered
it by the front door.

"Major," he said, and the newcomer stopped just inside the shop vestibule, blue eyes a shade or two lighter than Nimue Alban's narrowing as he
saw Nynian and Murphai.

He was a tall man, only two or three inches shorter than Murphai, with
longish brown hair worn in the rather old-fashioned style of braid favored
in his native Trellheim, and he wore the uniform of the Temple Guard.

"Ahrloh," he replied after a moment. "I hadn't realized you'd have other
customers. This late, I mean."

"I'm not surprised," Murphai said easily before Mahkbyth could respond.
"On the other hand, Major, *we've* been after hours customers of Ahrloh's for
quite some time."

"I see." The major looked back and forth between the tall, fair-haired
seijin and Mahkbyth. "Of course, I'm sure you can understand why a man in
my position might feel a little . . . uneasy, under the circumstances."

"I'd be astonished if you didn't," Nynian said, standing a couple of strides behind Murphai as she spoke for the first time. "I'm sure you'd be equally astonished if *we* didn't feel the same way, Major."

"I suppose I would be," he acknowledged, frowning slightly as he looked at her. "That *would* be the natural response, wouldn't it . . . Madam Phonda?"

"Of course it would," she said calmly. If she was particularly perturbed by his recognition, she didn't show it.

"I was under the impression I'd be meeting only with Ahrloh," the major said. "In fact, he's the only one I'm *authorized* to meet with tonight."

"Then I'm afraid you're in something of an awkward situation," Nynian told him. His shoulders tightened ever so slightly, and she smiled. "You're the one who initiated contact. And I'm afraid that the fact that you've recognized me provides you with information you didn't have—information that might start the Inquisition looking in directions I'd really rather it didn't if you were to pass it along to someone like, oh, Wyllym Rayno or Allayn Wynchystair. That being the case, I'm afraid we have to insist you lay your own cards on the table."

"There's a limit to how many cards I'm authorized to show," he replied slowly. "And I was only authorized to show even them to *Ahrloh*."

"Understandably," Murphai said, eyes narrowing slightly at the confirmation that the major wasn't acting solely on his own. "I'm afraid Madam Phonda has a point, though."

"And I'm afraid I can't go beyond that point without discussing it with . . . my superior first," the major said firmly. "I'm sure he'll authorize me to tell you a great deal more than he already has, but until he does, I'm not in a position to do that."

"Then we're at an impasse, because I really can't allow you to leave until Madam Phonda is satisfied with your bona fides."

"You can't *allow* me to leave," the major repeated, eyeing the taller but obviously unarmed *seijin*. "Forgive me for asking this, but what are the odds you could *stop* me from leaving?"

"Better than average," Murphai replied with a slow smile.

"I think not." The major's hand started for the butt of the pistol holstered at his side. "With all due—"

He broke off as Murphai's hand darted out with impossible speed, almost too quickly to be seen. That hand swept in past his own and plucked the pistol effortlessly from his holster.

Alarm flared in his eyes, and he reached for the hilt of his sword, instead. But he never touched it. Murphai's other hand snapped out and closed on his forearm like a hand-shaped version of one of the hydraulic presses in Lynkyn Fultyn's foundry. It wasn't a brutal grip, or a punishing one. It was simply totally inescapable and unbreakable, and Murphai's hand didn't so much as quiver even when the major threw his full, solidly muscled weight against it.

He wasted a full ten seconds trying to wrench free, then stopped. It was obviously useless, but that wasn't the reason he'd stopped, and a strange, eager, deeply *relieved* light seemed to glow in his blue eyes.

"You truly are a *seijin*, aren't you?" he said very softly.

"People keep saying that," Murphai replied, with an odd little smile.

The major looked back and forth between him and Nynian, then inhaled deeply.

"The *Writ* says *seijins* are God's chosen champions—His and Mother Church's," he said. "If that's true, then I know you'll understand why I *can't* tell you more than I was authorized to."

"Of course I do." Murphai released his grip on the major's arm, although he kept the pistol, and stepped back half a stride. That happened to place him directly between the Guard officer and Nynian. "But at the same time, I know you'll understand our position. And while I can respect your loyalty, I think I could probably make a pretty fair guess at who your 'superior' is. If I'm right, he needs all the help he can get . . . and you're the one who first made contact with *us*. So if you and he truly want our help in doing anything about this insanity, you really need to talk to us, Major Phandys."

.VI.
Nimue's Cave,
Mountains of Light,
The Temple Lands.

You're joking."

Nahrmahn seemed oddly put out, Merlin reflected.

"No, we aren't. You've seen the imagery yourself. For that matter, I know damned well you were listening in while he had the conversation."

"Well . . . yes," the deceased little prince admitted.

"Then what seems to be the problem?" Merlin asked suspiciously, and Nynian snorted.

Merlin looked across at her. The two of them sat in comfortable chairs in Nimue's Cave with glasses of forty-five-year Glynfych—a parting gift from Ahrloh Mahkbyth—in front of them, and now she shook her head at him.

"His professional pride's offended," she explained, and smiled affectionately at Nahrmahn's avatar. "That's it, isn't it, Nahrmahn? You never saw this coming, and that offends you."

"I probably wouldn't choose the verb 'offend,'" he replied. "I *do* feel a trifle . . . irritated, however."

"Oh, for the love of—!" Merlin shook his head, torn between amusement and irritation of his own. "Look, if it makes you feel any better, *Nynian* never saw this coming, either!"

"Do you really want to tick off *both* of us?" Nynian inquired with a commendably straight face only slightly undermined by the twinkle in her eye.

"No, I want both of you giving us your best analysis," Merlin said.

"Second the motion," Cayleb threw in from Siddar City.

"As do I," Maikel Staynair added. "And unlike Nahrmahn, I was unable to watch the conversation as it happened. Perhaps you could go over the high points for those of us not already familiar with them? Because I have to agree with Nahrmahn that the whole business seems flatly impossible!"

"Yes," Paityr Wylsynn said, and his voice was far softer than the archbishop's, almost husky. "Please. I was otherwise occupied at the time, myself. If I'd had any idea what Duchairn had to say, I would've made time to watch it! But I didn't, and I can't believe. . . . I mean, I *want* to believe, but. . . ."

"Believe me, I understand that, Paityr," Nynian said gently. "He was your uncle, but he was my friend—my very *dear* friend. And now I know he died the way he did at least in part to protect me. And whatever qualms you may feel about being directly descended from Androcles Schueler, the 'Stone of Schueler' proves Phandys was telling us nothing but the truth. I don't think he told us everything—for that matter, he *told* us he wasn't telling us everything. But what he did tell us was the truth, and that means we can thank your Uncle Hauwerd for all of it."

"And Rhobair Duchairn," Nimue Chwaeriau said soberly from Manchyr Palace. She stood behind Irys as the princess and the Earl of Coris sat on a palace balcony, looking out over Manchyr Bay as the sun settled towards the horizon behind them. "I have to say I didn't see *that* one coming, either."

"I'm . . . less surprised than I might have been," Sharleyan said slowly from Tellesberg. "If I'd ever suspected anything like this was possible, I'd have picked Duchairn as the one most likely to be behind it. It's been obvious from his actions in Zion, especially his efforts to properly care for the poor and the destitute, that he's had something like a genuine regeneration of his faith. In fact, I'd wondered how he'd avoided openly breaking with Clyntahn long since—how a man who obviously hated everything Clyntahn stood for with every fiber of his being could have continued to make one accommodation after another with him. I put it down to cowardice, in the end, and God knows he had ample proof that any rational human being should be terrified of Zhaspahr Clyntahn. But this . . . this puts a very different face on those 'accommodations' of his."

"It does, indeed," Merlin agreed, then turned slightly in his chair to face Paityr Wylsynn's projected image squarely.

"The short version of it, Paityr, is that your uncle was a . . . more pro-active fellow than your father in many ways. He absolutely supported your father's candidacy for the Grand Inquisitorship, and he agreed a hundred percent with the need to collect the evidence your father would need to clean up the abuses and the corruption of the vicarate. But he also knew what really happened to Saint Evyrahard, and he was determined to keep that from happening to your father if he could. Unfortunately, according to Major Phandys, he also knew your father wouldn't have approved of his efforts, so like a lot of younger brothers, he just . . . neglected to mention them to him.

"After Clyntahn won the election—or, rather, after Rayno cooked the vote to *give* him the election—your uncle continued quietly pursuing his efforts. I don't know exactly what he hoped he might achieve by them, but remember that there was no Army of God, no Mighty Host, when he set out. The only real armed force in Zion—or anywhere else in the Temple Lands, if you come down to it—was the Temple Guard. I suspect he hoped he might eventually recruit a large enough cadre from its junior officers to actually let him convince your father a military coup against Clyntahn and the Inquisition could succeed."

"I think that's exactly what he hoped," Nynian murmured, her eyes soft with affectionate memory. "Of course, Samyl never would've agreed to anything of the sort. You know what he was like, Paityr!"

"Yes." Paityr had to stop and clear his throat. "Yes," he said then, more strongly. "I do. But I also know how . . . convincing Uncle Hauwerd could be. I'm not prepared to say he couldn't have brought Father around to it in the end."

"Well, if anyone in the world *could* have, it would've been Hauwerd," Nynian conceded, then she chuckled. "And if he *couldn't* convince Samyl, I wouldn't have been one bit surprised to see him stage the coup on his own and then offer your father a fait accompli!"

"Whatever he might have done under other circumstances," Merlin continued, "when he and your father realized Clyntahn intended to purge them and all their friends, he must have been bitterly tempted to try a coup then. But he wasn't ready, and he refused to ask the officers and men who'd given him their allegiance to throw away their lives in a vain effort to save *his* and his friends'. I think, from some of the things Phandys said—and, even more, from the way he said them—that he had a hard time keeping them from trying, anyway."

He shook his head, his eyes distant, then refocused on Paityr.

"Phandys had a hard time getting out the truth about how he died. He confirmed the rumor that your uncle killed your father himself rather than permit him to be taken for the Question and the Punishment." Anguish twisted Paityr's face, but it was anguish for the decision his uncle had been forced to make, not condemnation, and he nodded. "And Phandys also confirmed that he was the one who actually killed your uncle. In fact, he was also the one who denounced your father and your uncle to Zhaphar Kahrnaikys. He was actually the one who inserted the passage request that sent Kahrnaikys after your uncle into the logbook to begin with." Paityr stared at him, his face white. "It was the best way your uncle could think of to divert any possible suspicion from Phandys . . . and Phandys was your uncle's guarantee that he'd never be put to the Question. Could never be made to tell anyone about the names on that list. Or about anyone else he suspected of . . . anti-Inquisition activities."

Merlin's eyes flitted ever so briefly to Nynian, then returned to Paityr.

"And Phandys did it," he said very softly. "That's a tough, hard man, Paityr, and he broke down twice telling us about it, but he by God *did* it. And he didn't do it to protect himself. He did it as the last service he could ever perform for a man he *profoundly* respected. I know a little something about the kind of human being it takes to engender that kind of loyalty, Paityr. I wish to God I'd had the chance to know your uncle."

"He was . . . special," Paityr agreed.

"And a good judge of character," Nynian said. "When he realized what was going to happen, that there was no escape, he passed the names of the guardsmen he'd recruited to Rhobair Duchairn, of all people. To the *one* member of the Group of Four who'd experienced a genuine spiritual rebirth. My God, what that must've been like for Duchairn! He had in his hands the names of dozens of 'traitors.' All he had to do was hand them to Clyntahn and Rayno, and he would've proved his loyalty to them at a time when anything they saw as *disloyalty* was a death sentence. And if he *didn't* hand them over, especially if he actually tried to take up Hauwerd's task, he *guaranteed* himself the Punishment if a single thing went wrong. Can you imagine what a man who could accept the charge Hauwerd passed to him must have felt when he was compelled to play the part of Clyntahn's *accomplice*?!" She shook her head slowly, her beautiful eyes huge and dark. "It must have been a living hell for him, a thousand times—a million times—worse than anything Thirsk had to endure."

"I'm sure it was," Baron Rock Point said after a moment from his flagship in Tellesberg Bay, but his voice was considerably harder and colder than Nynian's had been. "I'm sure it was, and I have to respect the courage he's shown since Hauwerd handed him the list. And I don't have any doubt that Maikel would tell me that any soul can be redeemed and that good works are part of how that redemption works, sometimes. But let's not forget the role he played in creating this entire jihad."

"I'm not suggesting we do anything of the sort," Nynian said. "But I've seen an awful lot of what the human heart's capable of, for good or ill, Domynyk. In this case, I'd have to come down on your brother's side. This is a man who's been working his passage for years now, from the very belly of the beast. I'm prepared to cut him some slack."

"And I'm inclined to agree with you," Cayleb said soberly.

"But how did Phandys make the connection to Mahkbyth?" Irys asked.

"It would appear that whatever Paityr's father may have thought, his Uncle Hauwerd cherished a few suspicions about Ahnzhelyk Phonda," Merlin said. "It would also appear—" he smiled almost mischievously at Nynian "—that he and Ahnzhelyk were . . . rather closer friends than most people realized."

"That was then, and this is now," Nynian said, and Merlin chuckled. But then he looked back at Paityr again.

"We'll never know exactly what he suspected about 'Ahnzhelyk,' but he'd obviously figured out she was involved with her own activities, as well as the role she'd taken in your father's circle of Reformists. I wouldn't be surprised if part of it was just the recognition of a kindred soul. Whatever else happened, however, he clearly overheard a conversation he wasn't supposed to overhear."

"I wouldn't put it that way," Nynian said thoughtfully. "It's more likely that I was too impressed with my own cleverness. I'm willing to bet I knew perfectly well he was listening to the conversation when I spoke with one of the members of Helm Cleaver right there in my mansion. A lot of them passed through, you know. In fact, Sandaria wasn't the only member who worked for Ahnzhelyk." She smiled. "All those remarkably handsome, muscular young footmen who kept themselves handy to protect my ladies belonged to Helm Cleaver, you know."

"No." Merlin chuckled and shook his head. "Actually, that never even occurred to me, Nynian!"

"Well, I wouldn't want to suggest I could be *devious* or anything. . . ." She smiled. "But from the way Phandys described it, I'd be willing to bet that Hauwerd caught something I thought would go right past him, since he didn't know about Helm Cleaver's existence. At any rate, that's where the 'Seijin Kohdy's Premium Blend' came from."

"And as far as Phandys' decision to approach Ahrloh, Irys," Merlin said, "that was a combination of an inspired guess on Hauwerd's part and desperation on Duchairn and Phandys' part. Hauwerd was the one who convinced Zhustyn Kyndyrmyn to write up an accurate report of what happened to Ahrloh's son and his wife. I wouldn't be surprised if he'd been tempted to approach Chief Sergeant Mahkbyth himself when he was recruiting his list of potential traitors, but he didn't. Probably because he figured that a man who'd already lost his only child and was caring for an invalid wife had enough responsibilities—and had suffered enough—without dragging him into a possible coup against the Inquisition, as well. But he knew about Ahrloh and his family, and because he'd passed that report on to Nynian, he knew *she* knew about them. Phandys knew Ahrloh, too—they'd served together—and your uncle knew 'Ahnzhelyk' had been instrumental in setting Ahrloh up as a shopkeeper in Zion. So when he saw the sort of clientele she was subtly steering in his direction, he concluded there was an excellent chance he'd been recruited for whatever organization *she* was involved with. That was one of several things he discussed with Phandys when he realized Clyntahn was closing in on him and his friends . . . just before he ordered Phandys to denounce him."

"And why did the Major approach him *now*?" Irys asked, her expression intent.

"Because of what happened to Zahmsyn Trynair," Merlin said. "I don't think they've acted out of fear for their own lives. If they'd been going to do that, they'd have done something a long time ago. I think what we're seeing is a combination of factors. Trynair's death—and Clyntahn's threats to Duchairn and Maigwair—have convinced both of them that he's prepared to pull the entire Church down with him rather than face the personal consequences of defeat. At the same time, Zion's become a pressure cooker. When you combine the news from the battle front with the casualty totals, the number of families who've lost someone they loved, the number of people the Inquisition's 'disappeared' in the capital, Helm Cleaver's actions and the way they've provided detailed lists of their victims' crimes, and the way the broadsheets we've been putting up all over the capital for years now flatly contradict Clyntahn's version of events, the reservoir of reverence and piety that always supported the Inquisition has pretty much evaporated. There are a lot of people in Zion who no longer believe a single thing Zhaspahr Clyntahn says, Irys. A *lot* of them. And there's a much smaller but still significant number of people who find themselves actively *opposing* him, passively at least. That's been a factor in the success of several of Helm Cleaver's operations. People who might have been able to give information to Rayno's agents inquisitor frequently don't.

"What it boils down to is that Clyntahn's maintaining his power through a reign of terror, and every report that comes in from Tarikah or Cliff Peak or the South March—every word about the front that goes up in one of our broadsheets—is one more piece of evidence that the Temple is about to lose the Jihad. Clyntahn and his core supporters are unwilling to admit that, but they're probably the only people in Zion—maybe even in the entire Temple Lands—who don't understand that the war's lost. And it's a funny thing, Irys. People have a strong aversion to seeing their sons and husbands die in a war that's already lost, especially when they realize they were systematically lied to about the reasons that war was begun in the first place. That's true even when they haven't come to the sneaking suspicion that God Himself is on the *other* side.

"So right now, Clyntahn's control is stretched thin—maybe even thinner than he realizes—in Zion at the very moment when he's about to commit the Church and every Temple Loyalist to an apocalypse that will kill millions of more people. If Duchairn's ever going to act, it has to be now, and he doesn't think he can succeed, even now, solely out of his own resources. So he sent the Major out to see if he could find the help he needs."

"So Phandys was on a fishing expedition when he approached Master Mahkbyth," Earl Coris murmured. "He didn't *know* anything for certain, and all he had was what might or might not have been a code phrase Vicar Hauwerd overheard used in a conversation more than a decade ago. Is that about it?"

"Just about," Nahrmahn agreed. "And that's one reason my 'professional pride' is offended. This isn't the sort of carefully calculated, exquisitely coordinated, brilliantly polished strategy upon which *I* pride myself, and it's still about to do one hell of a lot of damage to Zhaspahr Clyntahn."

"That remains to be seen," Maikel Staynair said rather more somberly. "There are a million things that could go wrong. And even if there weren't, we haven't actually decided we're going to give Duchairn the help he's looking for."

"What?" Irys twitched upright in her chair. "Of course we are!" She looked around the images projected onto her contact lenses, then turned to Coris . . . and saw the expression on his face. "Aren't we?" she asked almost plaintively.

"Irys, if we help Duchairn—and, I'm pretty sure, Maigwair, even though Phandys refused to name anyone besides Duchairn—we may sabotage our own ultimate objective," Sharleyan said quietly. "If Duchairn, with or without Maigwair, topples Clyntahn and manages to retain control afterwards—which is scarcely a given, I realize—he'll offer us everything the Church of Charis has been demanding from the start. He's already pledged to do that through Phandys, and while he may have lied to Phandys, Phandys definitely didn't lie to Merlin or Nynian."

Irys looked at Sharleyan's image, her expression perplexed, and Coris sighed.

"Irys, we want to *overthrow* the Church of God Awaiting. Duchairn wants to *reform* it. He wants to stamp out its abuses, rein in the Inquisition, root out the corruption and the corrupters, and make as much honest, forthright restitution and recompense as he can for all the atrocities Clyntahn's version of the Church has committed. If he offers to do those things, *we can't reject the offer*. We can't explain to our own people, much less to Greyghor Stohnar or all the other people trapped in this war, that we need to destroy the entire religion in which all of them believe. We just can't do it, for the same reasons we haven't been able to openly explain it to anyone already. So if we help Duchairn *save* the Church rather than continuing the war in hopes Clyntahn will ultimately destroy it, we may throw away our best chance to accomplish Nimue Alban's true mission."

"But all those *people*, Phylyp," Irys half whispered. "All those people who might not have to die!"

"And that's the heart of the problem, Irys," Sharleyan said compassionately. "How far are we prepared to go to accomplish the objective we can't tell anyone else about? And how many good and courageous people—like Major Phandys—are we willing to abandon to death while we do it? Because the one thing I can tell you for certain from having watched his conversation with Merlin and Nynian is that whether we support them or not, he and Duchairn are *going* to try."

A long moment of silence hovered over the com link, and then Merlin smiled crookedly.

"You said this wasn't one of your brilliant strategies, Nahrmahn," he said, "and you're right. What it *is* is more up Maikel's alley than yours."

"I beg your pardon?" The archbishop arched his eyebrows.

"It's what you've talked about again and again, Maikel—the finger of God moving in the hearts of men. Think about how much how many people have sacrificed to bring us to this moment, to this decision point. Think about Samyl and Hauwerd, think about Zhorzhet and Marzho, about Duchairn and Phandys, and about the Sisters and Helm Cleaver. Think about *all* of that, and the chance Duchairn and Phandys took just contacting us in the first place. And then think about all the lives—our soldiers' lives, not just those on the other side—we could save. That we *might* save. Do you *really* think we have a choice?"

He shook his head, and Nimue Chwaeriau's holographic eyes met his across the link. Met his and agreed with them.

"God wouldn't have given us this opportunity if He didn't want us to take it," Merlin said softly. "Maybe I'm wrong about that, but you know what? If I am, I don't care. Not now. We've killed enough people. *I've* killed enough people. We're not going to kill any more than we have to, whichever side they're on, and we'll just have to trust God to give us another opportunity somewhere down the road to accomplish Nimue's mission. Because if He doesn't want us to do this, then He's been Zhaspahr Clyntahn's God all along, and I know damned well He hasn't."

.VII.
Great Tarikah Forest,
and
Chyzwail,
West Wing Lake,
Tarikah Province,
Republic of Siddarmark.

Zhwozhyou Puyang, Earl Golden Tree, rubbed his eyes wearily. It didn't help a lot. He was sixty-one years old, and those eyes no longer took candlelight in stride. Unfortunately, he was out of lamp oil, courtesy of the heavy heretic angle shell which had landed directly atop his headquarters bunker. He hadn't been in it at the time, but most of his staff had, and all of his lamp oil—and the lamps to burn it and the fragments of all of his personal possessions—had been left strewn in the crater where the bunker once had been.

Along with the bloody bits and pieces of the staff who'd served him for over two years.

Golden Tree didn't know what in Kau-yung's name the heretics filled their goddamned shells with now, but some of them, at least, struck like Langhorne's own Rakurai. The sheer size of the craters they left was enough to turn a man's bowels to water. Actually seeing one of them explode—and surviving the experience—could destroy the resolve of even the most faith-filled.

He was proud of his men. It wouldn't have done to admit that, of course, since most of them were the scum of the earth—peasants, at best, and conscripted serfs, the most of them. But they'd stood tall and fought hard for God even after the heretics managed to cut their only line of retreat behind them.

Golden Tree still didn't know how the heretics had done that, either. In fact, there were Shan-wei's own lot of things he didn't know . . . including how God expected him to get his command out of this trap. All he knew for certain was that eight days ago the heretic Stohnar had somehow gotten one—at *least* one—of his outsized infantry brigades deep enough into the Great Tarikah Forest to overwhelm his pickets on the South Tairyn River. Now the heretics controlled his only avenue of supply . . . or escape. And even if they hadn't held the river, only God and the Archangels knew if the Mighty Host still held the other end of the high road, where it exited the forest. Earl Rainbow Waters' last dispatch had indicated that Gleesyn was still holding and that the line he'd stitched together to cover the high road beyond the forest remained intact. But that dispatch was eight days old.

Golden Tree lowered his hand from his aching eyes and picked up the common pottery mug on the corner of his improvised replacement desk. He grimaced as he sipped and reminded himself—again—not to ask the cooks what they were using for "tea" these days. He was quite sure he wouldn't have liked the answer to that question any more than he'd liked the answers he'd already gotten to a whole host of questions.

He sipped more "tea" and scowled down at the report he'd been reading. Or trying to read, at any rate. Captain of Foot Hiyang's handwriting was atrocious. Then again, four years ago Zynghau Hiyang had been a small shopkeeper in the imperial capital. He'd never expected to be a soldier, much less an officer, and *far* less an officer battling heresy, apostasy, and demon-worship. He had his rough edges, did Captain of Foot Hiyang, and no one would ever accuse him of brilliance. But when his regimental commander had been killed, he'd taken over the regiment and fought it with more gallantry and determination than Golden Tree had seen out of any of his other commanders, and that was a very high bar, given how magnificently his entire command had fought.

Yet there was nothing left of Hiyang's regiment. Not anymore. That was how the captain of foot had come to be available when Golden Tree's staff died under the shell he'd somehow avoided. And now, glaring down at Hiyang's latest casualty report, Golden Tree faced the truth.

He'd entered the Sairmeet position with two almost full strength bands of infantry, over forty thousand men—closer to fifty, when his artillery and engineers were added in. They'd settled into a well laid out set of defensive works under the loom of the massive northern spine trees of the unconsecrated forest and been grateful for the evergreens' deep, cool green shade. It had been like living at the bottom of one of the ornamental koi ponds back home.

Now those trees were broken stumps. Now the branches which had shielded them from the sun—and from the heretic balloons—were gone, or stripped bare and ugly by heretic shells. Now the well laid out entrenchments were churned and broken, their perimeter littered with decaying bodies, too many of them Harchongese and too few of them Charisian or Siddarmarkian. And now the ammunition and supply dumps which hadn't been destroyed outright by the heretic artillery were empty.

As of sunset tonight, by Hiyang's best estimate, he had twenty-three thousand effectives left, and the captain of foot estimated the artillerists had barely a dozen rounds per piece. His riflemen were down to their last forty rounds per man, and hand-bombs were in even shorter supply. He had rations for two more five-days . . . if he fed the men one meal a day. His healers were out of Fleming moss, reduced to boiling whatever rags they could find for bandages—when they could find fuel and the heretics' harassing infantry angle shells let them—and they'd exhausted all their painkillers . . . and the alcohol and Pasquale's Cleanser to keep their surgical instruments clean of corruption.

He'd hung on desperately, hoping for the supply column Earl Rainbow Waters had promised to fight through to Sairmeet . . . if he could. The Mighty Host's commander was a man of his word, and Golden Tree had known that if mortal men could get those supplies through, then the Mighty Host would do it.

But it hadn't.

Face it, Zhwozhyou, he told himself. *Your men are done. It's not that they won't fight any longer; it's that they* can't. *Not without food and medical supplies. Not without shells and hand-bombs. Langhorne! Not without* bullets! *And if the heretics have pushed the Host back from Gleesyn, there's no point in your getting more of these men killed holding Sairmeet. They may be peasants, they may be serfs, but even serfs' lives have to count for* something.

He shivered at the thought of what Zhaspahr Clyntahn's Inquisition might demand of his and his officers' families, but he knew what he had to do.

▼   ▼   ▼

Earl Rainbow Waters rose as his nephew ushered Gustyv Walkyr and Ahlbair Saintahvo into his office. He kissed Saintahvo's proffered ring, then waved an invitation at the chairs awaiting his guests. They settled into them, and the ugly rumble of artillery formed a backdrop of distant thunder. The Charisian gunners couldn't possibly see their targets in the darkness, even from their accursed balloons, but they didn't seem to care, and their profligate expenditure of ammunition in what amounted only to harassing fire was its own message. It said *their* supply lines were capable of delivering everything they needed, and that *their* manufactories—and the treasuries behind them—were capable of *producing* everything they needed.

Neither of which was true of Mother Church any longer.

"I thank you for coming," the earl said quietly as Wind Song poured wine into the waiting porcelain cups and then silently withdrew, leaving his uncle with his guests. "I realize both of you are sufficiently busy without my dragging you away from your headquarters in the middle of the night."

"It's not like we had that far to come, My Lord," Walkyr observed with what might a trace of genuine humor, and Rainbow Waters' lips twitched.

The Army of the Center had fought hard since his meeting with Walkyr and Saintahvo at Cheryk. Its inexperience and lack of artillery had shown, but its survivors had *gained* experience far more rapidly than they'd undoubtedly desired, and they'd inflicted severe casualties on the heretics when a brigade from the Army of Westmarch moved too precipitously against St. Vyrdyn and been caught in column by AOG rocket launchers.

The Charisians had probably lost in excess of two or three thousand men in that single disaster, and the Army of the Center's gunners had been jubilant. But then the Charisian angle-guns had been brought up once more and the balloons the advancing column had outrun had caught up with the front. The Army of Westmarch had resumed its methodical advance, and Army of the Center had been driven back once again.

By now, Walkyr's army had been driven clear back to Rainbow Waters' Ferey River Line. It had lost contact with St. Vyrdyn—which the heretics had entered yesterday, if Rainbow Waters' latest intelligence was correct—but its right flank continued to cling to the edge of the Tairohn Hills sixty or seventy miles north of the city. The garrison at Glydahr continued to hold out, but the heretics had punched two mounted brigades between St. Vyrdyn and Glydahr and taken Four Point, cutting the high road between Gyldar and the Holy Langhorne Canal. It was only a matter of time before the isolated Sardahnan capital fell . . . a point the Army of the Daivyn's heavy artillery was making clear as it steadily and mercilessly obliterated the city's outworks. It would be interesting to see how long the intendants and inquisitors in Glydahr could . . . inspire Archbishop Militant Klymynt Gahsbahr's men to resist.

In the meantime, the portion of Walkyr's army still under his direct command—perhaps a hundred and sixty thousand men, all told—had become the Mighty Host's reserve behind the southern end of the Ferey River line, and the archbishop militant had moved his own headquarters to Chyzwail to facilitate conferences just like this one.

No, Rainbow Waters reminded himself. *Conferences, yes. But like* this *one? I think not.*

"May I ask why you needed to see us, My Lord?" Saintahvo asked, leaning forward and ignoring the wine glass at his elbow. "I assume it's to share still more *bad* news," he added caustically.

The archbishop inquisitor had become steadily more querulous—although Rainbow Waters would have denied he *could* have become more querulous after their first meeting—as the situation worsened. He'd made it amply clear that he knew the true reason for all their reverses could be found in the fecklessness of their commanders. He'd become increasingly strident, and he no longer hesitated to show his displeasure with Rainbow Waters as clearly as with Walkyr. The earl had been unable to decide whether that was simply because *Saintahvo* was such a natural pain in the arse or if it reflected the tone of the private dispatches the archbishop inquisitor received regularly from Zion.

700 / DAVID WEBER

"In fact, I'm afraid it is, Your Eminence," the Mighty Host's commander said now, his tone calm and his expression curiously serene for a man about to impart news of still more disaster to Zhaspahr Clyntahn's personal representative. "I received a messenger wyvern from Earl Golden Tree this evening. At dawn tomorrow, Sairmeet will surrender to the heretics."

"*What?!*" Saintahvo jerked upright in his chair, his face twisting with rage.

"Regrettable," Rainbow Waters said, "but scarcely unexpected, Your Eminence." He shook his head. "Sairmeet's been completely isolated for almost two five-days, but Earl Golden Tree has continued to get occasional messenger wyverns out. I've shared his dispatches with you and Archbishop Militant Gustyv, and it's been evident for some time that unless we reopened the high road, Sairmeet's loss was inevitable. According to the Earl's final dispatch, he has less than forty rounds of ammunition per rifle and enough food to feed his men for less than a five-day. The heretics haven't even assaulted his position in over six days. They're simply dropping shell after shell upon it and killing somewhere between three and six hundred of his men every day without ever exposing their own infantry to his fire." The earl shrugged. "Under those circumstances, a surrender which might save the lives of his remaining men is the only logical recourse."

"*Logical?!* What does *logic* have to do with a war for the entire world's soul?" Saintahvo demanded. "This Jihad isn't about *logic*, My Lord! It's about defeating Shan-wei and her minions and saving the soul of every loyal child of Mother Church, living or yet unborn. Beside *that*, what does simple life or death matter?!"

"With all due respect, Your Eminence, I think that might be just a little difficult to explain to the sons and daughters of the men in Sairmeet. I don't question the importance of protecting Mother Church and defending God's will even at the cost of our own lives. But it would seem to me that when dying for God can accomplish nothing *except* to die for God, one might be excused for not wishing to create any more orphans and widows than one must."

Saintahvo flushed puce at the Harchongian's cool, unruffled tone, but the earl seemed not to notice.

"Were it possible to relieve and resupply Earl Golden Tree," he continued, "then it would, indeed, be his duty to continue to hold his position until our columns reached him. Unfortunately, that isn't going to happen."

"And why not?" Saintahvo demanded. "Why *haven't* you relieved him?"

"Because to this point, the Mighty Host has suffered in excess of thirty-two thousand casualties attempting to do just that, Your Eminence." Rainbow Waters leaned back in his chair. "That means our losses in the effort to *relieve* him now exceed the total strength still under his command by fifty percent. The math is irrefutable. I cannot afford to continue losing men at that rate attempting to reinforce failure. And even if it made some sort of military sense to continue the attempt—which, I repeat, it does *not*—it would no longer be possible."

"Why not?" Saintahvo snarled.

"Because the Army of Tarikah took Gleesyn this afternoon," Rainbow Waters said flatly. "They are now across the Ferey at Gleesyn and at two points south of Gleesyn in at least brigade strength, covered by their heavy angle-guns from the eastern bank of the river. The bridges at Gleesyn were demolished before the position was overrun, but heretic engineers have already thrown at least—*at least*, Your Eminence—five pontoon bridges across the stream. I feel confident there are additional bridges we haven't seen yet. If they do not exist now, they will by morning."

Silence gripped the office for several seconds, enhanced somehow by the distant, vicious mutter of the Charisian artillery.

"I estimate the heretics have suffered something in excess of eighty thousand casualties, Your Eminence," the earl resumed quietly. "But the Mighty Host has suffered in excess of *four hundred* thousand, which doesn't count the casualties your own Army of the Center has suffered, nor the casualties Earl Silken Hills and the Southern Host have taken now that Symkyn and High Mount have broken through at Reklair and Tallas. When all are combined, the total is probably very close to twice that number.

"Our men—and *your* men—have fought with the utmost courage and tenacity, and I assure you that the heretics' casualties have been far heavier than any they've suffered in any of their campaigns since Bishop Militant Bahrnabai was stopped in the Sylmahn Gap. Indeed, I believe they may be heavier than *all* the casualties they've suffered in *all* of their campaigns since then. That's certainly true for the Charisians, at any rate. And our forces are still intact, still a viable fighting force, despite the heretics' advantages in artillery and mobility—even despite their balloons. But the loss ratio is tilting more and more sharply in their favor, not ours, and our lines are strained to the breaking point, as what just happened at Gleesyn demonstrates. And, perhaps even more to the point, they're driving spearheads *past* our lines. They're about to turn this from a battle of fortified positions into a war of maneuver, of movement, where their mobility and their balloons will be even more decisive than they've been to this point."

"So what do you propose to do?" Saintahvo grated.

"There's only one thing I *can* do, Your Eminence." Rainbow Waters met the archbishop inquisitor's furious gaze levelly. "If I don't order the immediate retreat of every man north of Gleesyn, the heretics will drive northwest, cut them off, and do to them *exactly* what they've just done to Sairmeet. But once I evacuate that end of the Ferey River Line, there are no other suitable defensive positions short of Mhartynsberg. Indeed, given the heretic force at Four Point's threat to the Holy Langhorne at Transyl, it may prove necessary to withdraw all the way to that city. At the very least, I believe it would be necessary to dispatch Archbishop Militant Gustyv and his entire remaining force to hold that position."

"That's over *seven hundred miles* from here!" Saintahvo blurted. "And if you retreat past Mhartynsberg, you surrender the entire Barony of Charlz and Sardahn to heretics and demon-worshipers!"

"And if I *do not* retreat, Your Eminence, then my army—and yours—will be destroyed. At which point there will be no organized force to defend anyone *else* against heretics and demon-worshipers."

"And have you discussed this with Bishop Merkyl?" Saintahvo demanded.

"I have. And it's only fair to admit that he felt much as you appear to feel, initially at least. In the end, however, I believe he recognized the unfortunate but inescapable logic of my analysis."

"And why isn't he here to tell me that himself?"

"The gout which has plagued him for so long has become much worse, Your Eminence. I believe his natural . . . unhappiness with recent events has aggravated the condition. At any rate, he is currently with the healers, although I believe he'll be available to confer with you by tomorrow or the next day."

"Tomorrow or the next day?" Saintahvo repeated in an ugly tone. "Well, My Lord, whatever Bishop Merkyl may feel or not feel—assuming his medical condition hasn't . . . compromised his state of mind—I categorically reject your 'logic'! We're *God's* warriors. We owe him our lives—and our deaths, if it comes to that—and He expects us to fight on in His cause, trusting that in the day of battle, He will be our fortress and our refuge. You will *not* retreat, My Lord!"

"Your Eminence, I might point out that for all your high ecclesiastic rank, you aren't *my* intendant; Bishop Merkyl is. As such, I question whether or not you have the authority to countermand my intentions if he approves them."

"Whatever *you* may think about my authority, My Lord, *I* disagree." Saintahvo quivered visibly with the force of his rage. "And while I might officially be 'only' Archbishop Militant Gustyv's intendant, I'm also the Grand Inquisitor's *personal* representative. Are you prepared to tell *him* I lack the 'authority' to countermand your cowardly intention to run away from the enemies of God?"

His tone was scathing, his eyes contemptuous, but the earl only shrugged.

"I anticipated that you might . . . disagree with my analysis, Your Eminence," he said in that same calm, almost conversational tone, "so I took the precaution of informing Vicar Allayn of my intentions."

"You did?" Saintahvo asked in a rather different tone, obviously taken aback by Rainbow Waters reasonable sounding response.

"I did, indeed," Rainbow Waters replied. "And I received his reply by semaphore shortly before sunset. Somewhat to my surprise, there was a second response, addressed to Archbishop Militant Gustyv in the Captain General's personal cipher. Vicar Allayn was sufficiently alarmed by the . . . sweeping nature of my intentions that he wished to make his own and his colleagues' view of them as clear as possible to the Archbishop Militant."

He extracted a single sheet of paper from a folder on his desk and handed it to Walkyr. The archbishop militant didn't seem especially eager to take it, but he did. Then he unfolded it and read it slowly. His face was expressionless as he reached the bottom, then reread it carefully and even more slowly. He looked up and folded the message very neatly and precisely. Saintahvo held out an imperious hand for it, but Walkyr seemed not to notice as he gazed across the desk at Rainbow Waters, who looked back at him with one raised eyebrow.

"May I ask if you find yourself in concurrence with the Captain General's instructions, Your Eminence?"

"Yes," Walkyr replied. There was something odd about his voice, a combination of trepidation and something else, something almost like . . . relief. "Yes, I do, My Lord."

"Very good," the earl said. Saintahvo looked back and forth between them, hand still extended for Vicar Allayn's message, and Rainbow Waters picked up the small handbell on the corner of his desk and rang it once.

The sweet, musical sound seemed utterly incongruous against the backdrop of heretic artillery, but it was surprisingly clear and sharp. It hung on the ear for a moment, then the office door opened and Baron Wind Song reentered, accompanied by a half-squad of infantry in the uniform of the Emperor's Spears, the Harchongese military police.

"Yes, My Lord?" the baron inquired, and the earl waved a graceful hand at Saintahvo.

"Arrest him," he said.

Yes, Your Eminence?" the under-priest said, entering Wyllym Rayno's office in response to the archbishop's signal.

"Have we heard anything from Father Allayn this morning?"

"Why, no, Your Eminence." The under-priest shook his head. "Were you expecting a report or a message from him?"

"I was *expecting* to see him here in my office twenty minutes ago." Rayno looked less than amused. The archbishop had always started his days early; given the current situation, he'd taken to beginning them well before dawn, and all of his senior subordinates had learned to do the same. "Send someone to find out what's delayed him. And why he didn't *tell* me he was going to be delayed!"

"At once, Your Eminence."

The under-priest bowed and disappeared, and Rayno climbed out of his chair and stomped his way to his corner office's window. Unlike the space made available to vicars, his office boasted none of the mystically changing scenes of woodland, forest, or mountain. He did have an excellent view across the Plaza of Martyrs to the harbor, however, and he stood with his hands clasped behind him, glowering at the scenery.

Allayn Wynchystair had better have a damned good reason for his tardiness—and an even better one for his failure to warn Rayno he'd be late! More than enough was going wrong without one of his most senior deputies suddenly deciding he had better things to do than bring him up-to-date on the Fist of Kau-Yung's latest atrocities.

The archbishop growled a curse.

The scene before him looked perfectly ordinary. A huge, blazing arm of the sun had only just heaved itself above the eastern horizon, white wave crests chased themselves across Lake Pei, and the bright banners of Mother Church snapped gaily on the sharp breeze whipping in from the lake. Sails moved across the lake, the first few pedestrians of morning moved along the streets, and all of it was reassuringly normal, even tranquil.

And it was all a lie.

He sighed, his expression far more anxious than he'd allowed the under-priest to see, as he faced the truth.

Zion was a powder keg, and for the first time in his career, he couldn't predict what was about to happen in its streets. The panic he couldn't see from his window hung over the city of God like a foul miasma. Like a pestilence. The news from the front lines was devastating, and despite Rayno's opposition, Zhaspahr Clyntahn had decreed that the Inquisition would suppress word of Earl Golden Tree's surrender, just as it had attempted to suppress news of Bishop Militant Lainyl's. And, just as it had failed in Lainyl Brygham's case, it had failed in Golden Tree's. Those accursed broadsheets—those impossible, *demonic* broadsheets—had shouted the news from every wall, every doorway. And whatever Clyntahn might tell himself, whatever he might insist upon in his increasingly savage—and rambling—conferences, the people of Zion believed those broadsheets more than they believed Mother Church herself.

Of course they did, and with good reason. That was why Rayno had argued in favor of telling the truth from the outset. Censor news if they must, but tell the truth in the official news they *did* release, lest the people reading those broadsheets decide it was God's enemies who told the truth and His champions who lied. The Inquisition had never had to worry about that before those broadsheets, though, and Clyntahn seemed unable to admit that the techniques which had always worked before would work no longer.

Then there was the upsurge in the "Fist of God's" attacks on senior clergy, especially among the episcopate. That was bad enough, but over the last five-day, eighteen regular agents inquisitor had been ambushed as they went about their duties. Seventeen of them were dead, the eighteenth was in a coma, and no one—not one single soul—had seen a Shan-wei-damned thing. *No one.* When the Inquisition couldn't turn up a single witness to the brutal slaying of one of its own—when *everyone* insisted they didn't have a clue what had happened—they were entering uncharted seas. Nothing like that had *ever* happened before. And the one thing he was certain of was that those murders hadn't been committed by the Fist of God. The attacks had been too . . . sloppy. Too impassioned. They were the handiwork of outrage, not of a calculated strategy. Besides, the Fist of God had always disdained casual attacks on randomly chosen street agents inquisitor. No. Those attacks were the work of ordinary Zionites, the result of the rage boiling just beneath that tranquil surface outside his window.

It doesn't mean the city's entire population's caught up in it, Wyllym, he told himself. *How many people does it take to kill eighteen men, especially when they're caught alone or with only a single companion to help them? It could be no more than a handful of malcontents! So Zhaspahr's right. The attacks don't prove the . . . disaffection is general.*

No, it didn't conclusively prove anything of the sort. But Wyllym Rayno had been an agent inquisitor—and a prosecutor inquisitor—in his day. He couldn't have begun to count the number of cases he'd made on far flimsier evidence than the seventeen bodies in the Inquisition's morgue.

And now Wynchystair couldn't even be bothered to keep his appointment! Well, he was going to get an earful when he *did* arrive, and—

"Excuse me, Your Eminence."

Rayno turned from the window. The under-priest was back, and his face was pale, his expression visibly shaken.

"What?" the archbishop demanded, fighting a sudden sinking sensation.

"Father Allayn—" The under-priest swallowed. "Father Allayn is dead, Your Eminence. He and Father Zhaksyn, Father Paiair, and Father Kwynlyn . . . they're *all* dead."

"*All* of them?!" Rayno stared at the aide.

"All of them," the under-priest confirmed. "I just heard from Father Allayn's secretary. He says . . . he says Father Allayn had summoned the others to an early meeting—over breakfast, I think—to hear their reports before his meeting with you. Someone threw a hand-bomb through the breakfast parlor window."

"*Schueler,*" Rayno whispered. He stared at the under-priest for several seconds, then shook himself. "Tell Bishop Markys I want to see him *immediately!*" he snapped.

▼   ▼   ▼

"*That* doesn't sound good," Father Elaiys Makrakton observed, his expression uneasy. The under-priest glanced at his assistant, Brother Riely Stahrns, then looked at the Temple Guard sergeant in command of the squad assigned to support them.

"Don't ask *me*, Father," the sergeant said edgily, head cocked as he listened to the shouts coming around the corner ahead of them.

"Well, I guess there's only one way to find out," Makrakton said, his tone considerably heartier than he actually felt.

"If you say so, Father."

The sergeant sounded as doubtful as Makrakton truly felt, but he jerked his head at his men.

"You heard the Father. Look sharp!"

Heads nodded, and Makrakton tried to pretend he hadn't noticed the bayonets being fixed on the Guardsmen's rifles. Then he drew a deep breath and nodded to Stahrns.

The daily briefing had all sounded so . . . routine this morning. It wasn't a duty anyone wanted, of course, but *someone* had to go tear down the blasphemous broadsheets that went up every night, and today it was their turn. Makrakton had done his share of avoiding it any way he could. There was something about just *touching* the things, about coming into contact with something so obviously unclean. And even if they were torn down, they only reappeared the next morning. Never in exactly the same place, but there were parts of town—stretches like Zheppsyn Avenue—where they *always* appeared. They might be on a different building—on St. Nysbet's today and on the Zheppsyn Avenue Library tomorrow—but they were always here. Anyone willing to believe their lies, could always find a fresh load of them on Zheppsyn.

He led the way around the corner, turning into the avenue, and his jaw tightened as he saw the crowd standing around the message board outside St. Nysbet's. That was where the parish priest posted the day's scripture every morning, but that wasn't what they were reading today, and he felt beads of sweat under his priest's cap as he realized how big the crowd was. There had to be fifty or sixty men standing around the message board, voices raised in an indistinct but angry surf of sound, and even as he watched, more trotted down the street, heading for the crowd.

Well, they couldn't have *that*, now could they?

"Follow me," he growled out of the corner of his mouth and went striding towards the growing knot of men.

"Here, now!" he shouted. "What's all this, then?! You people know better than to believe the sorts of lies in those things!" He jabbed an accusatory finger at the broadsheets he could now see tacked to the message board. "Move along! Go about your business before I have to start taking names and—"

"*No more lies!*"

Makrakton's head jerked up as the shout rang out. He didn't know exactly where it had come from. It didn't seem to have come from the men around the message board, but he couldn't be certain. What he *was* certain of was that the entire crowd had turned to face him.

"I said—" he began again.

"*No more lies and no more murders!*" the same voice shouted. "The broadsheets are right, lads! *Show Clyntahn what we* really *think of him!*"

Makrakton couldn't believe his ears. Sheer shock held him motionless for a moment, and that was one moment too long.

The crowd surged suddenly, but not to disperse. No, it surged towards Makrakton and his escort.

"What do you think you're—?" He heard Brother Riely begin, but then the lay brother's voice chopped off as a hurled cobblestone struck him squarely in the face.

Stahrns went down with a strangled scream, clutching at his ruined face, and the sergeant was suddenly shouting orders. The squad's rifles came down, leveled, and a sheet of smoky fire lashed out across Zheppsyn Avenue. There were screams from the other side of that smoke, but the single, rushed volley didn't stop the oncoming Zionites. They came out of the smoke, at least a quarter of them with cobblestones or other improvised weapons in their hands, and hurled themselves straight at the Guardsmen.

"*Kill the bastards!*" someone bellowed.

"No more murders!" someone else shouted, and then—

"*Death to the Grand Fornicator!*"

The enraged mob rolled over the Guard squad. Two or three of them went down on the Guardsmen's bayonets, but the squad was too shaken, too taken aback. It wasn't a disciplined force; it was simply a group of confused, disbelieving men with rifles in their hands, and they never had a chance.

Makrakton had a momentary glimpse of a stolen rifle butt coming at his face, swung like a baseball bat by a burly civilian in a bricklayer's apron. It was only a blur, then it smashed into his jaw and he went down, three-quarters stunned.

The boots were waiting.

▼   ▼   ▼

Zheppsyn Avenue was not unique.

The broadsheets had, indeed, gone up again the night before, the way they always did. But *these* broadsheets were different. For months—years—they'd appeared, morning after morning, and all they'd ever done was to report news. At first, they'd been dismissed by every loyal son or daughter of Mother Church as the lies they obviously were. But over time, five-day-by-five-day, month-by-month, the citizens of Zion and the Temple Lands—of Harchong, and Desnair, and Dohlar—had realized they *weren't* lies. They were truth, and yet that was *all* they'd been. They'd never called for action, never urged anyone to rebel. In fact, they'd gone out of their way to avoid anything of the sort.

But these broadsheets weren't like that. *These* broadsheets were written in fire and quenched in rage. They recounted the hideous casualty totals from the front. They enumerated the millions of Siddarmarkians who'd died in the Inquisition's holding camps, listing the grim total camp-by-camp. They gave the totals for the numbers of Zionites who'd simply disappeared in every borough of the city . . . and broadsheets in each borough gave the names of the agents inquisitor responsible for that borough's disappearances. The broadsheets nearest the Temple listed all of the vicars and bishops and priests Zhaspahr Clyntahn had purged. The broadsheets nearest the Plaza of Martyrs gave the numbers for how many people had been tortured and burned to death as the Punishment decreed. The broadsheets on individual church doors gave the names of Inquisition informants, parish-by-parish.

And this time, they didn't simply give information.

Children of God!

The day has come to retake God's Church from the evil men who make a mockery of God's law and His love for His children! Zhaspahr Clyntahn is no servant of God. He is evil and corruption, and he is *death*! Death for any who oppose him—who oppose *him*, not God! Death for your sons and fathers and brothers fighting not for God, but for Clyntahn the Corrupt! Death for children and infants in arms in the camps of Siddarmark! Death for *your* children, for *anyone* who dares to question the monster he's made of the Inquisition! And death for Mother Church herself if no one stops him before he transforms her forever into an image of his own cruelty and vile ambition!

　　Strike! Strike now! *Strike hard!* Take back your Church in the name of God and the Archangels!

　　Death to the Inquisition! *Death to Zhaspahr Clyntahn!*

And *this* time members of Helm Cleaver—and the hidden audio remotes of an electronic being named Owl—were scattered about the city in strategic locations to be the voices of rage . . . and the sparks of holocaust.

▼　　▼　　▼

No one had seen it coming.

Perhaps they should have, but they'd been the forces of Mother Church for so long, spoken with the full authority of the *Holy Writ*, of the *Book of Schueler* and the Proscriptions. They'd spoken for *God*, and who would dare to argue with Him?

They'd never been able to eradicate the accursed broadsheets, but they'd become accustomed to them. They'd hated them, feared them, understood the way in which the truth they proclaimed gnawed away at the Inquisition's narrative, but that was all they'd done. It had never occurred to them that one day that might change. Nor had they realized the way in which those broadsheets' proven veracity, the fact that they'd never—*not once*—been caught in a lie, would validate them on the day they did change.

A third of Zhaspahr Clyntahn's agents inquisitor disappeared in the first two hours. Most of them suffered the same fate as Elaiys Makrakton and Riely Stahrns. Some were less fortunate and spent far longer dying. And some—either out of simple prudence or because some deep-seated part of them had always known those broadsheets spoke the truth—simply stripped away the purple badges of the Order of Schueler, discarded their cassocks, and vanished into the streets of the city.

▼   ▼   ▼

"What should we do, Father?"

Father Zytan Kwill stood on the mounting block before the gate of the Hospice of the Holy Bédard, the largest homeless shelter in the city of Zion, and stared at the vast crowd filling the square before him.

"What should we do, Father?!"

The question went up again, and Kwill drew a deep breath. He would never see ninety again, and the frailty of age had wrapped itself about him, but in that moment, with every eye—every heart—in that enormous crowd focused upon him, he was a giant. A giant who knew at last exactly what to say.

"My children—*God's* children—you *know* what to do! The *Writ* itself tells you! Remember the words of the Archangel Chihiro!

"'In the day of wickedness, be not wanting. In the day of corruption, be not afraid. In the day of evil, stay not your hand. When Darkness comes before you, pretending to be Light, when those who should be your shepherds become slash lizards devouring the sheep, when darkest night consumes the sun, cling to God with all your might and all your strength, and know that He will send you the true shepherd, the good shepherd! Find that shepherd. Seek him out, for you will know him by his works. Trust him who leads you to Light. Follow him, fight for him, bear him up and do not let him fail, for the good shepherd loves the flock. The good shepherd nurtures the flock. And the good shepherd dies for the flock. Be you also good shepherds. Face those who would do evil in God's name, and cut them from you forever!'"

There was silence for a moment—a moment in which he could hear the distant roar of the furious city. In which he could hear distance-faint screams, occasional shots, and over all of it the sigh of God's own wind filled with the bright, clean sunlight of summer.

"You know who the false shepherd is, my children," Zytan Kwill said then. "You know him by his works, by his darkness, by his destruction. *And you also know the good shepherd!* The good shepherd who's been here for you—for *all* of you—and who you know will lay down his life for you if God wills it! Go! Find him! *Fight* for him! Be you also good shepherds and do what God has called you to do this day!"

Another moment of stillness, and then—

"*Death to the Inquisition!*"

▼   ▼   ▼

The column of dragoons trotted down the avenue. The horses seemed uneasy—probably from the smell of smoke—and their riders were grim faced. But they rode in disciplined silence, accompanied only by the sound of shod hooves on cobbles, the jingle and rattle of tack and weapons.

"Thank God," Father Zhordyn Rahlstyn murmured fervently.

He and Brother Anthynee Ohrohrk crouched inside the deserted shop-front, peering through its windows into the street. They'd been fortunate Ohrohrk had remembered the shop had been closed ever since its owners had been taken into custody. They'd managed to get inside before anyone spotted them in the street, and they'd hidden there, wondering what to do next.

Given what they'd seen happen to half a dozen of their fellow agents inquisitor—and, for that matter, to the squad of Temple Guardsmen who'd been assigned to support *them* that morning—wandering around the streets struck them as a very bad idea. They were fortunate their Guardsmen had lasted long enough, drawn enough of the mob's attention, for them to run, but they couldn't count on that sort of good fortune lasting forever.

"I can't believe this, Father," Brother Anthynee said, hands still trembling as they watched the mounted column coming towards them. "I can't *believe* it! How could they all *turn* on us like this?!"

"When Shan-wei's loose in the world, *anything* can happen, Anthynee," Rahlstyn replied almost absently. "And those eternally damned and accursed broadsheets—*that's* what set them off! But don't think they've turned *all* of Zion against us. Against God, I mean." He shook his head. "God and the Archangels don't desert their own! That's why They've sent us this cavalry, and in the fullness of time, They'll take back control of God's city for His rightful servants."

"Of course They will, Father." Ohrohrk sounded less than totally convinced, but he nodded sharply when Rahlstyn looked at him.

"Then let's go out and greet our rescuers," the upper-priest said.

The two Schuelerites opened the shop's front door and stepped out into the street as the front rank of the column drew even with it. The officer at its head touched his horse with a heel, and the big roan swung around, trotting over to where Rahlstyn stood.

The upper-priest's heart rose as he recognized the rider's insignia. It was that of a full bishop militant, a division commander, and there must have been two thousand men in the column behind him.

"Praise Langhorne and Schueler you've come, My Lord!" Rahlstyn cried. "May I ask your name?"

"Kradahck," the bishop militant said. "Dynnys Kradahck. And yours, Father?"

"Zhordyn Rahlstyn, My Lord. And this is Brother Anthynee Ohrohrk." Rahlstyn's spirits rose still higher as he recognized the bishop militant's name. He wasn't "just" a division commander. Bishop Militant Dynnys Kradahck

commanded the Holy Martyrs Training Camp, the main Army of God training facility twenty-two miles from the City of Zion. To have reached the
city so soon he must have been summoned by semaphore—or perhaps messenger wyvern—almost the moment the outbreaks began. The proof that
the Grand Inquisitor and Captain General had reacted so promptly and
strongly was a tremendous relief.

"I never thought I'd be so relieved to see the Army here in Zion," he
said frankly, "but some sort of madness seems to have seized the city! Thank
God you've arrived! Are more troops on the way?"

Kradahck looked down at him thoughtfully, and Rahlstyn suddenly
found himself wondering if his anxiety—and his sudden relief—had betrayed
him into what might be misconstrued as impertinence. He was an upper-
priest of the Inquisition, of course, and Kradahck was only a bishop *militant*,
which was just a military rank, really. He wasn't certain, but he rather thought
Kradahck had been a mere under-priest a few years earlier. For that matter,
he might be one of the Army of God officers who'd been directly consecrated from the laity in answer to the desperate need for senior officers.

"Yes, Father," the bishop militant said after a moment. "There are quite
a few additional troops en route. Infantry, for the most part, so they'll be
some few hours behind the mounted men."

"May I ask what your orders are?" Rydach asked in a deliberately more
courteous tone, and Kradahck nodded.

"I'm on my way to relieve the Temple Annex and restore order."

"May Brother Anthynee and I accompany you?"

"Oh, I think that can be arranged, Father," Kradahck replied, and looked
over his shoulder at the youthful, brown-haired major who'd just cantered
up to join him, accompanied by a quartet of noncoms. "Father Zhordyn, this
is Major Sahndyrsyn, my aide." Rahlstyn nodded to the major, and Kradahck
waved a hand at him and Ohrohrk. "Hainryk, these are Father Zhordyn
and Brother Anthynee. Arrest them."

Rahlstyn was still staring in goggle-eyed disbelief when four very tough-
looking dragoons grabbed the agents inquisitor.

They weren't particularly gentle.

▼　▼　▼

"What in Shan-wei's name is happening?!" Zhaspahr Clyntahn demanded
furiously. "Wyllym! What's the meaning of this?!"

"Your Grace, it's . . . it's—"

Rayno broke off, unable for once to find the words to answer the Grand
Inquisitor.

"Don't just *gobble*, damn it!" Clyntahn snapped. "Why hasn't this rabble
already been dispersed!"

He stabbed an angry finger at the sea of rioters crowding into the Plaza of Martyrs. Most wore civilian clothing, but here and there Rayno saw men in AOG uniform. The vast majority of them seemed to be armed only with improvised bludgeons, or paving stones, or even nothing at all, but there were dozens—possibly even scores—of rifles in that enormous crowd, and the rumbling snarl coming from it was enough to freeze a man's blood.

"Your Grace," the archbishop said finally, taking his courage in both hands, "they haven't been dispersed because the Army is *supporting* them."

"*What?!*" Clyntahn wheeled around, and Rayno shook his head.

"Your Grace, this has to've been carefully planned, and the treason was spread more broadly than anyone could have imagined! Officers of the Temple Guard—our own officers!—opened the Guard arsenals and distributed weapons to the mob. Others actually led rioters into municipal and Church buildings! Many of the Guard remained loyal, I believe, but they had no more idea this was coming than we did. Most of them were seized before they could even begin to react, and every agent inquisitor we had in the street when this . . . this *madness* began had to run for his life. I'm afraid a great many of them couldn't run fast enough, and the situation's only continued to spiral farther and farther out of control. Vicar Rhobair's occupied the Treasury and seized control of the semaphore office and the dock master's offices, and it looks like Major Phandys is actually *leading* the mutineers who followed his orders to seize the buildings. As soon as I realized what was happening, I sent agents inquisitor to arrest Vicar Allayn, but none of them have returned, and Army troops—apparently under his personal command—have surrounded St. Thyrmyn. The prison is on fire—they're using infantry angle-guns to drop shells into its courtyard!—and none of our brethren inside the facility have been able to escape."

"How the *fuck* did you let this happen?!" Clyntahn snarled.

"Your Grace, even the Fist of Kau-Yung is involved in this!" Rayno snapped back. "Three quarters of my senior people—Wynchystair, Gahdarhd, Ohraily, Zhyngkwai, at least a dozen more—were assassinated almost simultaneously this morning. Nobody even saw whoever threw the grenade that killed Gahdarhd and his senior assistant!"

Clyntahn stared at him speechlessly, and Rayno made himself draw a deep breath.

"Your Grace, if it had been only Duchairn and Maigwair, or if it had been *only* the Fist of Kau-Yung—or even if it had been *all* of them, perhaps— we might have been able to retain control. I can't say for certain; *no one* could! But I *can* tell you for certain that it was *this*—" it was his turn to jab his finger out the window "—this . . . this *mob*—that guaranteed we *couldn't* control it." He shook his head again. "The entire city caught fire, probably in the space of less than one hour. It certainly didn't take more than two! How were my people supposed to deal with something that sudden, on that kind of scale? We simply couldn't do it, Your Grace!"

"My God," Clyntahn whispered

He looked back out at the Plaza of Martyrs and his face tightened as a straw-stuffed effigy in an orange cassock was dragged across the plaza to one of the charred posts to which so many heretics had been chained. The effigy was lashed to the post, and a torch flared.

And over it all, he heard the shouts.

"Death to the Inquisition! *Death to the Grand Fornicator!*"

And, more terrifying—and far more infuriating—even than that, a single name, chanted over and over and over again.

"Du-*chairn!* Du-*chairn!* Du-*chairn!*"

The shouts rose above the vast, indistinguishable crowd surf of the mob, and he swallowed hard.

"Your Grace, we have to go," Rayno said urgently.

"Go?" Clyntahn turned back to the archbishop. "You mean *run?* Run away like a dog with my tail between my legs?!"

"Your Grace, we've lost. For today, at least, we've lost. I have reports of additional Army troops moving into the city from the Holy Martyrs Training Camp. I don't doubt more are coming from farther away. Apparently there's been some fighting in the ranks, some resistance by men who understand where their true loyalty lies, but their resistance has been crushed. Most of the men marching into the city seem to be prepared to follow their officers' orders even against the Inquisition, and at least a quarter, probably more, of the Temple Guardsmen we'd counted upon to support our agents inquisitor have gone over to the traitors. And between the cordon around St. Thyrmyn and what happened to our people who were caught in the streets, I doubt there are more than twenty percent of our agents inquisitor in any position to help us. Without more men, we can't hold the Temple. We just can't. So it's time to get you out of Zion to someplace where you can rally the Faithful to *deal* with this."

"Someplace like where?" Clyntahn demanded.

"This madness can't have infected the entire Temple Lands," Rayno replied. "There are too many Faithful out there, and they couldn't possibly have coordinated something like this all across the Temple Lands without our picking up *some* indication of what was coming. They obviously believe that if they can take Zion, if they can control the Temple itself—and if they can take *you*—the rest of the Temple Lands will fall into line. That means this is the focal point of their entire rebellion. So if we can get you away, outside the area of their control, I'm sure we can rally forces from the other episcopates. And, in a worst case, if we can get you to Harchong—where we know we can count on the people's loyalty and faith—God will surely show us the path to reclaim Zion in His good time."

Clyntahn stared at him for a handful of heartbeats. Then he nodded sharply.

"You're right, Wyllym," he said crisply. "Let's go."

▼　▼　▼

No one knew why the tunnel had been dug in the first place. It was obviously as ancient, or almost as ancient, as the Temple itself, because it was illuminated by the same mystic panels that lit the Temple. Its walls were lined with brick, however, not with the smooth, solid stone the Archangels had used. According to the oldest rumors, it had been built after the Archangels' servitors had withdrawn to the Dawn Star and it had departed in glory.

Wyllym Rayno didn't know about that, but he did know it was one of the Inquisition's most tightly held secrets. It was over seventeen miles long, from the Temple's cellars all the way across Templesborough and Langhornesborough to the countryside beyond, and its exit was hidden under a vineyard the Order of Schueler had very quietly owned for well over three centuries.

The tunnel was amply large enough for the thirty picked agents inquisitor escorting him and the Grand Inquisitor to safety. Every one of those bodyguards was an experienced veteran of either the Temple Guard or the Army of God—men who'd distinguished themselves in rooting out heresy and proven their loyalty time and again. Of course, simple loyalty and zeal weren't enough to gain a man admission to the Grand Inquisitor's own guard. They also had to have thoroughly demonstrated their competence, and there wasn't a man of that guard who wouldn't have qualified easily for an officer's commission in the AOG.

Another seventy men waited at the vineyard, sent ahead to secure the exit and arrange horses. Rayno wished they had horses in the tunnel itself, but although it was wide enough, its roof was far too low, which was . . . unfortunate. The Grand Inquisitor was a poor rider, but he was even more poorly accustomed to seventeen-mile hikes, and the entire party had to pause for rest far more often than Rayno preferred. Every time they did, he worried that someone they'd believed was loyal might have betrayed the tunnel's existence to the traitors. That they were being pursued even as they stood guard, waiting for Clyntahn's breathing to settle back into a normal range.

But, eventually, they reached the far end and went hurrying up the steps. They emerged into another cellar, quiet and cool, shadowed by enormous wooden vats, and Rayno heaved a vast sigh of relief. But then he frowned. He'd expected to find at least one of the men he'd sent ahead waiting to guide them to the others. On the other hand, it wasn't as if the bodyguards surrounding him and Clyntahn weren't fully capable of finding their own way up the stairs. Besides—

They reached the head of the stairs, emerged into the early afternoon sunlight, and froze.

At least they knew why there hadn't been anyone waiting for them at the tunnel exit, a tiny corner of Wyllym Rayno's mind thought numbly.

All seventy of the men he'd sent ahead lay scattered about. Or he thought they were all there, anyway. It was hard to be certain, given all the blood and body parts, and he felt his gorge rise. Everywhere he looked, there was more blood, more carnage.

There's not even one *intact body*, he thought, staring at corpses which had lost heads, or arms, or legs, or some hideous combination of all three. And standing there, amid the butchery, were two people.

Only two.

His heart froze and his breathing stopped as he realized who—or at least *what*—those people were. The Inquisition's entire intelligence apparatus reported directly to him. He'd seen more than one sketch of a so-called *seijin*, and especially of the two most infamous false *seijins* of them all: Merlin Athrawes and Nimue Chwaeriau. But neither of these were Athrawes or Chwaeriau. He didn't know who the shorter, female *seijin* was, but he'd seen at least one sketch of her taller companion.

Dialydd Mab, the *seijin* who'd made the destruction of the Inquisition and all its works his personal crusade.

"Don't just stand there!" Clyntahn bellowed. "*Take them!*"

If their escort had been given time to think about it, they might not have obeyed that thunderous order. They might have paused, looked upon the bodies of their fellows, reflected that they might fare no better, and considered an alternative reponse. But they weren't given that time, and the reflexes of their training took over.

They charged the two *seijins*, half of them shouting war cries, and the *seijins* came to meet them.

The *seijins* didn't charge. Neither did they shout. They simply walked into the agents inquisitor, and if the fact that they were outnumbered fifteen-to-one concerned them, they showed no sign of it.

Then the charging agents inquisitor were upon them, and the carnage began.

Rayno's eyes bulged in stunned disbelief. He'd read report after report about the *seijins*—especially about Athrawes—and their incomparable lethality, and he'd rejected them as the obvious exaggerations they were.

But they hadn't been exaggerations after all.

The *seijins*' swords moved so swiftly they weren't even blurs, and they struck with deadly accuracy. They truly were capable—even the woman, despite her smaller, more delicate frame—of decapitating a man with a one-hand blow. That was one of the things Rayno had refused to believe, but he could disbelieve no longer as heads and limbs and blood *exploded* away from those deadly swords.

It was over in a bare handful of seconds, before Rayno could have poured himself a cup of tea. And the only reason it had taken even *that* long, he realized, was because the killers had had to wait for the falling bodies to get out of the way.

They walked out the other side of thirty fresh corpses, and Rayno swallowed sickly as he realized they'd never even broken stride.

"Archbishop Wyllym and Vicar Zhaspahr, I believe." Mab's deep voice was colder than a Zion winter, and his smile was even colder as blood ran down his sword blade and pearled from its chisel-like tip. "We've been waiting for you."

"Please," Rayno heard someone whimper, and realized it was him. "Please, I don't—I mean—"

"What's this?" Mab arched one eyebrow. "You're not prepared to die for your faith after all, Your Eminence? I'm shocked."

"I . . ." The archbishop shook his head and held out his hands pleadingly. "I don't want to—"

He rose on his toes, his mouth opening in a perfect circle of agony, as the dagger drove into his back. He went to his knees, reaching back with both hands, trying in vain to reach the wound, and looked back over his shoulder with a fresh gasp of pain as Zhaspahr Clyntahn wrenched the dagger from his flesh.

"*Traitor!*" the Grand Inquisitor hissed. "You can at least *die* like a servant of God, you miserable, fucking excuse for an inquisitor!"

Rayno's mouth worked, then he collapsed forward, quivered once, and lay still.

"That's one sort of retirement package, I suppose," Mab said thoughtfully, gazing down at the body. Then he raised his arctic eyes to Clyntahn. "And about the kind of loyalty I'd have expected out of you, Your Grace."

"Go to hell," Clyntahn said almost conversationally, and pressed the bloody dagger to the side of his own throat. "You're not taking *me* anywhere! Unlike that miserable bastard, I'm not—"

His eyes were on Mab, not that it mattered very much. Even if he'd been watching her, he couldn't have reacted before Gwyliwir Hwylio moved.

He cried out, in shock as much as in pain, as a small, impossibly strong hand locked on his wrist. It twisted, and his cry of shock became a squeal of anguish as his wrist snapped and the dagger fell from his hand. He struck at her with the other hand, beating at her in clumsy panic, but her forearm batted his punch effortlessly aside, and he cried out again as three of his fingers shattered as easily as his wrist. Then he was on his knees, staring up at her in horrified disbelief, terrified by the raw demonic strength of her, and she smiled.

She *smiled*.

"I'm sure Merlin would have preferred to be here in person," Mab said as his companion held the Grand Inquisitor effortlessly, "but not even a *seijin* can be in two places at once. Don't worry, though. You'll get your opportunity to meet him."

Clyntahn's mouth worked, and Mab nodded to the woman. She lifted the taller, far heavier vicar to his feet as if he'd been a sack of feathers.

"I'm sure you'll be brokenhearted to hear that Vicar Rhobair and Vicar Allayn have pledged us their word to try you within Mother Church and sentence you to whatever punishment Church law decrees for your offenses. Unless I'm very much mistaken, that would mean the Punishment . . . as a minimum."

Clyntahn swallowed hard, and Mab shook his head.

"Don't worry, Your Grace. There's been a small change of plan. You don't have to worry about Mother Church at all, because you'll be facing a rather different venue. There's an Imperial Charisian Navy ship waiting off the mouth of the Zion River. By this time tomorrow, you'll be aboard her. And you'll stay there, until she reaches Siddar City."

Clyntahn's normally florid face was pasty with combined shock, pain . . . and fear, and Mab's smile was a razor of ice.

"I hope you enjoy the voyage, Your Grace."

FEBRUARY
YEAR OF GOD 899

"I'm sorry it took this long to get you back to our city, Your Majesty,"
Greyghor Stohnar said, accepting a fresh wine glass from one of the efficient Charisian servants.

"Well, I've been a little busy," Sharleyan Ahrmahk replied with a smile,
and looked across the informal sitting room at her husband, who—exhibiting
the restrained dignity appropriate to one of the two most powerful monarchs in the world—was busy crawling around on the carpet while he tickled their daughter. Crown Princess Alahnah, who would be five in another
two months, was equally busy squealing, and her mother shook her head
with a smile. Then she looked back at the lord protector, and her smile faded.

"I could wish it was a joyous occasion, My Lord, rather than simply a . . .
satisfying one."

"I think all of us feel that way," Stohnar acknowledged. "Not your
daughter, of course." It was his turn to shake his head, his lined face—several
years older than it had been when Zhaspahr Clyntahn unleashed the Sword
of Schueler—wreathed in a smile of his own. "Mine are all grown, but I
remember that age. And I know how much Cayleb missed both of you. I
don't know whether to envy the two of you for the partnership you have or
to pity you for how long and how often it takes you apart."

"Well, one thing about being married to a sailor, My Lord, is that you
learn to deal with those lengthy separations. And—" she brushed the slight
swell of her belly "—he's always so happy to see me after them, you know."

Stohnar's lips twitched.

"I'd . . . ah, heard the Crown Princess is about to acquire a sibling," he
said.

"And at least one more cousin."

"Really?" Stohnar cocked his head.

"Yes. Duchess Darcos is married to a sailor, too, you know."

"Princess Irys is expecting another child? I hadn't heard!"

"It hasn't been announced. The last time, saluting guns started going
off all over Manchyr Harbor fifteen minutes after the healers confirmed her
pregnancy. Flattering, but she'd prefer a little more . . . private time with
Hektor before going public with this one. In fact, she's decided to make the

announcement right after Zhan and Mahrya's wedding. I think she hopes it will get lost in the festivities." Sharleyan shook her head. "I believe that's what they call a triumph of optimism. And I happen to know Mahrya is secretly hoping the news of Irys' pregnancy will divert some of the public attention from *her*."

"You do have an interesting family, Your Majesty."

"As Merlin would say, 'one tries,' My Lord." Sharleyan chuckled. "And that's especially true of Cayleb. He can be *very* trying upon occasion."

"I'm sure he can. But having him here in Siddar City made a tremendous difference, you know. And we couldn't have had him without the way you two work together. I don't think there's ever been another marriage—another pair of monarchs—like the two of you."

"Most of the secret's simply *trusting* one another, My Lord, but another part—a huge part, really—is having councilors you can trust. Ministers whose judgment is sound and who you know are both capable and loyal. And, frankly," she dimpled suddenly, "having Maikel Staynair on your side helps enormously!"

"And so did Merlin Athrawes' council—and sword—I'm sure."

"No, having Merlin at our side didn't hurt a bit," Sharleyan agreed softly. "But, to be honest, the thing that really made it work was Cayleb." She looked back at her husband, who was upright now, with Alahnah on his shoulders. She had both hands on top of his head while her heels drummed on his chest, and Sharleyan's smile softened. "He was the one who had the courage to propose a joint crown when we'd never even met. And would you like to know the truly remarkable thing about my husband, My Lord?"

"Yes, Your Majesty. I would."

"The most remarkable thing about Cayleb Ahrmahk," she said, "is that he doesn't think he's remarkable at all. He's never flinched, never even considered turning aside, even when Charis faced the entire world alone . . . and he thinks anyone would have done the same things he's done in his place."

"Then I'd say you're well matched, Your Majesty," Stohnar said. She looked at him and she shrugged. "You didn't do very much flinching either, from what I've seen. Like that business in Chisholm."

Sharleyan's smile faded, and he felt a stab of remorse for having reminded her of where she'd been only three five-days ago, before *Gwyllym Manthyr* had borne her and her husband from Cherayth to Siddar City for tomorrow's grim duty.

The last of the convicted traitors had faced the headsman a month ago, and Sharleyan and Cayleb had been present for every execution. Some might believe they'd been there because Sharleyan wanted to see those traitors pay for their treason, but those people were fools. Sharleyan Tayt Ahrmahk hadn't wanted to see *anyone* die, but her presence had been the final facet of the lesson she'd taught her nobles: she would never flinch from the harsh responsibilities of her crown . . . and she would never hide behind her ministers.

That lesson had gone home this time. All Stohnar's sources agreed on that.

"Forgive me," he said after a moment. "I didn't mean to—"

"You didn't take my brain anywhere it wouldn't have gone anyway, My Lord." She shook her head quickly and smiled once more. "And Cayleb and I really have accomplished a *bit* more than just keeping the imperial heads-men busy!"

"That's one way to describe redrawing the map of the entire world," Stohnar said dryly.

"Oh, I wouldn't say we've gone quite *that* far, My Lord." Sharleyan's lips twitched. "Most of the borders are still where they were, after all."

"Oh? Would that include Tarot, Emerald, Zebediah, and Corisande?"

"Their borders are still exactly what they were. They've simply been integrated into something even larger. Actually," her expression turned thoughtful, "you're probably in a better position than most to understand that. The Republic's provinces have always enjoyed a lot of local autonomy, yet they're part of a single whole. We're a lot alike that way."

"You may have a point," he agreed. "And if Grand Vicar Rhobair has his way, I suspect the Temple Lands will be a lot more like us, too."

"We'll have to see how that works out." Sharleyan's expression was doubtful, but then she shrugged. "If anyone can make it work, it's probably him, but he's taken on an awfully ambitious task."

"I hadn't realized what a gift for understatement you have, Your Majesty," Stohnar said dryly.

Grand Vicar Rhobair was clearly determined to restore order—and decency—to the Church of God Awaiting. And, as Sharleyan had suggested, he had his work cut out for him.

Between Zhaspahr Clyntahn's purges and the Fist of God, the vicarate had been reduced by more than a third since the Armageddon Reef campaign, and well over a quarter of the survivors had retired to private life, mostly to avoid lengthy imprisonments, over the past few months. Forty-two of their fellows hadn't been given that option. Much of the evidence against what had come to be known as "the Forty-Two" had been assembled over decades of patient effort by the murdered Wylsynn brothers and their allies, and Grand Vicar Rhobair had pressed their prosecutions relentlessly. Thirty-four had already been sentenced—eighteen of them to death—and the remaining eight trials were in their closing stages. Acquittal was . . . unlikely, and Stohnar suspected the Grand Vicar had been motivated almost as much by his debt to the Wylsynns as by the need to see justice done.

Yet justice must be done—not only done, but *seen* to be done—if anyone was ever to trust the Temple again. The man Zion called the Good Shepherd understood that the Church of God Awaiting must be cleansed, restored and—especially—*reformed* as transparently as possible. That was one reason he'd refused to fill the vacancies in the vicarate by appointment. That had been the grand vicar's prerogative under church law that went back over five centuries, but these vacancies would be filled by election by their fellow vicars.

Not that he wasn't prepared to use his prerogatives ruthlessly where he deemed necessary.

The Temple Lands were in the process of a major political reorganization. Stohnar suspected the Grand Vicar would have preferred to shift from direct ecclesiastic rule to some form of secular government. That clearly wasn't going to happen, but he *had* managed to end the practice which had developed over the last two hundred years of appointing vicars to govern the episcopates. Instead, they'd become what they'd been originally: archbishoprics, governed by prelates appointed by the Grand Vicar with the advice and *consent* of the vicarate. He'd also abolished the Knights of the Temple Lands and eliminated the special privileges and exemptions of the Temple Lands' clerical administrators. And, for good measure, he'd decreed that henceforth Mother Church's archbishops would follow the Charisian model and spend a minimum of eight months out of every year in their archbishoprics, *not* Zion.

He'd overhauled the system of ecclesiastic courts just as completely as the vicarate and the episcopate. They'd been removed from the Order of Schueler's jurisdiction and restored to the Order of Langhorne. The office of Grand Inquisitor had been abolished and a new Adjutant, Archbishop Ignaz Aimaiyr, had been appointed to oversee the Inquisition's complete reform. Aimaiyr was about as popular a choice as anyone could have been . . . which, admittedly, wasn't saying a great deal at the moment.

The Grand Vicar had come under enormous pressure to push even farther and simply abolish the Punishment, or, at least, to renounce its use as the Church of Charis had, but he'd refused. Horrible as the Punishment was, it was too deeply established within the *Holy Writ* to abolish it without fundamentally rewriting the *Writ*, and that was farther than a man like Rhobair Duchairn was prepared to go. Yet he'd taken steps to prevent the way in which it had been abused and perverted.

To insure there would be no more Zhaspahr Clyntahns, he'd replaced the office of Grand Inquisitor with a new three-vicar Court of Inquisition with its members drawn from the Orders of Langhorne, Bédard, and Pasquale; the Order of Schueler was specifically denied a seat. The Grand Vicar would formulate policy for the Inquisition; the adjutant would administer it; and the Court would determine who had—or hadn't—violated fundamental doctrine. Never again would a single vicar possess the authority to condemn even a single child of God, far less entire realms, for heresy. Moreover, any conviction for heresy by the Court of Inquisition could be appealed to the vicarate as a whole, and the Punishment of Schueler could be inflicted only after the sentence had been confirmed by a majority vote of the entire vicarate and the Grand Vicar.

The Punishment would remain . . . but whether it would ever again be *applied* was another matter entirely, given the restrictions with which Grand Vicar Rhobair had hedged it about.

There were some—including Greyghor Stohnar—who had mixed feelings about that. The Lord Protector could think of at least two dozen Inquisitors who'd thoroughly earned their own Punishment. But if they'd escaped *the* Punishment, they hadn't escaped punishment. The Grand Vicar had promised justice as the critical component of the minimum peace terms the Allies would accept, and he was keeping that promise. Over three hundred ex-Inquisitors, most of them from the concentration camps, had been stripped of their priestly office so that they might be arraigned before secular *Siddarmarkian* courts for crimes which ran the gamut from theft and extortion to rape, torture, and murder.

There were those, Stohnar knew, who felt the Grand Vicar was casting too wide a net. Who pointed out—quietly—that some of the accused had acted not as Zhaspahr Clyntahn's tools but from the genuine belief that God Himself had called them to extirpate heresy by any means necessary.

Maybe they truly thought they were serving God, the lord protector thought now. *And maybe in some grand scheme of things that makes a difference. But it doesn't make one to* me, *by God.*

Twenty-six million people had lived in the third of the Republic which had been occupied by the Army of God. Seven million of them had been murdered in Zhaspahr Clyntahn's concentration camps. Another four and a half million had died during the Sword of Schueler's violence or perished more slowly from starvation or exposure trying to escape it. And *another* four and a half million had fled from the Republic, or been forcibly resettled to the Temple Lands by the Church's military. Eleven and a half million dead and four and a half million refugees represented twelve percent of the Republic's pre-Jihad population, and that didn't count the military casualties suffered by the Siddarmarkian Army, both during the Sword of Schueler and after it.

The refugees, especially, were going to be a thorny issue. The hatred between the Temple Loyalists who'd supported the Sword of Schueler and the Church's invasion and those who'd remained loyal to the Republic was arsenic-bitter and as deep as the Western Ocean. Stohnar didn't know if it could ever be healed . . . and even if it could, it would be the work of generations.

Ultimately, we'll have to find some *way to address the refugees' status. Figure out if they can ever come home—or, for that matter, what happens to property they abandoned when they refugeed out. But I'll be damned if I* see *any answers. Hell, at least a quarter of them are probably guilty of murder! So do we insist on trying to investigate them all somehow? Figure out who's guilty and hang the bastards? Or do we admit we can't do that at this point? Just let them all come home with some sort of blanket amnesty, if that's what they want? And how the hell do I keep the Sword's survivors from massacring them all if they do?*

A solution—or, at least, a resolution—would have to be found . . . eventually. That was why he and the Grand Vicar had appointed Arthyn Zagyrsk, the Archbishop of Tarikah, Zhasyn Cahnyr, and Dahnyld Fardhym to a commission which was very quietly attempting to address the issue. Stohnar didn't expect them to succeed, but if anyone could find an answer, it would probably be those three.

And the truth is that dealing with that *one is probably the* easy *part!*

Despite all Grand Vicar Rhobair's efforts, a chasm yawned between the Temple and Siddarmark, one Stohnar doubted could ever be fully bridged. Too many in Siddarmark had lost too much—and too many—to the atrocities the Temple had permitted to happen. Perhaps a quarter of Siddarmark's remaining population self-identified as Temple Loyalists. Another twenty percent had formally embraced the Church of Charis. But that left over half who weren't prepared to become members of the Church of Charis but were equally determined never to submit to the doctrinal authority of the Temple again.

I can't say I'm looking forward to seeing how all that settles out. At least Duchairn's been smart enough to officially proclaim that neither the Church of Charis nor the "Church of Siddarmark" is—or ever was—heretical.

The Church of Charis continued to deny the authority of the Grand Vicar, *whoever* that Grand Vicar might be, which constituted a significant violation of church law. But Grand Vicar Rhobair had declared that there was a difference between church law and church *doctrine*, and that so long as any church adhered to the teachings and requirements of the *Holy Writ*, it could never be *heretical*. He held out hopes—officially, at least—that reconciliation and reunification might someday be possible.

Might get the first of those, Stohnar thought. *No way in hell is he going to get reunification—not with Charis. But maybe reconciliation and peaceful coexistence will be good enough. Surely to God we've all learned that oceans of blood aren't the way to resolve doctrinal dis—*

"Excuse me, Your Majesties."

A deep voice pulled Stohnar up out of his thoughts.

"Yes, Merlin?" Emperor Cayleb said, turning to face the *seijin* who'd just entered the sitting room.

"Merlin!" the crown princess squealed, holding out her arms to her godfather, and the tall, armored *seijin* laughed.

"Sorry, sweetheart," he told her, touching the tip of her nose with an index finger. "I've got the duty tonight."

"Oh." Alahnah frowned, but she was the daughter of monarchs. She'd already started learning about duty. "Breakfast?"

"Probably not." Merlin's sapphire eyes met Cayleb's. "There's something the grown-ups have to do tomorrow morning. I think it'll probably keep us busy at least until lunchtime, but I'll see you then."

"Promise?"

"Yes, promise. Satisfied, Your Imperial Highness?"

"Yes," she said, lifting her nose in a credible imitation of one of her father's sniffs. Merlin chuckled, but then he looked back at Cayleb and Sharleyan.

"Earl Thirsk and his daughters have arrived," he told them. "I showed them to the dining room. Irys and Hektor are keeping them company, and I told them you'd be joining them shortly."

"Was Archbishop Staiphan able to come?" Sharleyan asked, reaching up to lift Alahnah down from her perch.

"Not yet, Your Majesty. Earl Thirsk tells me the Archbishop's been delayed but still hopes to be able to join you this evening. The Earl's best estimate is that he'll be another hour or so. And he says the Archbishop specifically ordered him to tell you not to wait supper. Something about warming pans, chafing dishes, and desecrating the second-best kitchen in Siddar City."

"That sounds like him." Cayleb chuckled, then looked at his daughter. "Now, let me see. Would you rather eat the supper with a bunch of boring grown-ups or eat upstairs in the nursery with Zhosifyn and Zhudyth?"

"Upstairs!" Alahnah said promptly, and Cayleb shook his head mournfully.

"Abandoned again," he sighed.

"I'll take her, Your Majesty," Glahdys Parkyr said, and Sharleyan kissed the top of her head before she passed her across to the nanny.

"I wonder how many dynastic alliances come out of suppers in nurseries?" Stohnar mused as Alahnah was carried away, waving a grand farewell to the adults, and it was Sharleyan's turn to chuckle.

"I don't know if it's going to turn into a 'dynastic alliance,' My Lord, but I can't see how well she and Earl Thirsk's granddaughters get along *hurting* anyway!"

That was one way to put it, Stohnar reflected. Lywys Gardynyr had been confirmed not simply as First Councilor of Dohlar but as regent to King Rahnyld V, following Rahnyld *IV*'s abdication. It would be a four-year regency, and given Thirsk's age, he'd probably retire as soon as he'd seen his new king take up his crown in his own right. It looked as if the youngster would be a marked improvement on his father, who—to be fair—had never *wanted* to be king, and if Thirsk planned on retiring, Sir Rainos Ahlverez, the newly created Earl of Dragon Island and the Duke of Salthar's successor on the Royal Council, would maintain a certain continuity. For that matter, Staiphan Maik, the new Archbishop of Dohlar, was also a member of the Regency Council, and unless he wound up elevated to the vicarate—a distinct possibility, at least in a few years—he'd be yet another steadying influence on the youngster.

In the meantime, the Kingdom of Dohlar had established remarkably cordial relations with the Empire of Charis. The fact that Cayleb and Sharleyan's *seijin* allies had saved Thirsk's family from almost certain death despite what had happened to Gwylym Manthyr and his men hadn't been lost on the kingdom at large. Nor had the care Baron Sarmouth had taken to avoid civilian casualties in the attack on Gorath . . . or Caitahno Raisahndo's return, unharmed, along with every Dohlaran sailor, soldier, and officer who'd surrendered to the Charisians. A lot of Dohlarans and Charisians had killed one another over the last eight years, but compared to the carnage in Siddarmark, they'd fought a remarkably clean war. It had ended in mutual respect, and according to Henrai Maidyn, at least a dozen Charisians, including Duke Delthak, were already pursuing Dohlaran investment opportunities.

In fact, Dohlar seemed poised to come out of the jihad in remarkably good shape. There were moments when Stohnar found himself resenting that, but Charis was making even more investments in Siddarmark. And however well Dohlar might be doing, Desnair and Harchong were a rather different story.

The Desnairians still had their gold mines. That was about it, and Desnairian fury had been unbridled, albeit impotent, when the Allies announced that the Republic and Empire of Charis jointly guaranteed the independence of the Grand Duchy of Silkiah in perpetuity. And Stohnar took a certain pleasure out of contemplating the reaction in Desnair the City when Emperor Mahrys learned about Charisian plans to deepen and broaden the Salthar Canal to permit actual oceanic shipping to cross the grand duchy without ever touching a Desnairian seaport. Delferahk probably wouldn't be hugely pleased by the notion, either.

As for the Harchongians, *South* Harchong appeared to be relatively comfortable with Grand Vicar Rhobair's reforms. For that matter, the South Harchongians were in the process of extending cautious feelers towards Charis and the acquisition of the new manufacturing techniques, as well. They weren't pleased with the outcome of the war, and South Harchong had shown no desire to embrace the Church of Charis or the Church of Siddarmark, but they were . . . pragmatic. And they were eager to finalize a peace settlement with the Allies in order to reclaim their captured military personnel.

It was a very different story in North Harchong. The North Harchongians were clearly digging in to resist the changes sweeping towards them. Their aristocrats continued to reject the existence of the schismatic churches for a lot of reasons, including their "pernicious social doctrines." And while their political establishment, including the professional bureaucracy, had professed its loyalty to the Temple, they were clearly unhappy with Grand Vicar Rhobair's "liberalism." In fact, the Church in North Harchong was dragging its feet about surrendering the Inquisition's power, and Stohnar wouldn't be surprised to see a Church of *Harchong* emerge. *That* could produce all sorts of interesting—and unfortunate—consequences. And while the South Harchongians wanted their soldiers returned home, North Harchong wanted nothing of the sort. Its aristocrats had been infuriated by Captain General Maigwair's insistence on arming and training thousands upon thousands of serfs. The last thing they wanted, especially in light of Grand Vicar Rhobair's reforms, was the Mighty Host back, and there was no doubt in Stohnar's mind that Earl Rainbow Waters and most of his senior officers would be assassinated within five-days if they ever dared to go home.

"I suppose we should head on down to the dining room," Cayleb said, pulling the lord protector back up out of his thoughts. "Wouldn't want to keep our guests waiting. And—" he smiled, and his smile was suddenly cold "—I imagine they're going to enjoy supper rather more than *your* guest, Merlin."

"One tries, Your Majesty," Merlin said. "One tries."

▾   ▾   ▾

Zhaspahr Clyntahn looked around the chamber in which he'd been confined for the last three months.

It wasn't a very large chamber, and its furnishings were austere, to say the least. Despite which, he felt a familiar flicker of contempt at the heretics' flabby softness. He'd come to terms with his fate. He didn't look forward to death, and especially not to execution like a common felon, but the cowards who'd condemned him lacked the courage—the strength of their own convictions—to send him to the Punishment. He took a certain pleasure out of that, out of reflecting upon the thousands upon thousands of heretics *he'd* sent to the Punishment as God demanded. In a way, it was almost as if he'd had his vengeance upon his captors before he ever fell into their grasp.

As for the traitors who'd deserted Mother Church in her hour of need, who'd betrayed *him* by their gutless incompetence, they'd learn the error of their ways in the end. The cowards who'd run at the heels of those bastards Duchairn and Maigwair like frightened dogs would know the full cost of their sin when they beheld him sitting in glory at Schueler's right hand, waiting as the Archangel passed judgment upon them. And there'd be a special corner of hell, a pit deeper than the universe, for Rhobair Duchairn who'd betrayed God Himself and surrendered Mother Church to the perversion, the apostasy, the depravity of the "Church of Charis" and the so-called *Reformists!*

He looked at the remnants of his meal. His *last* meal, this side of Heaven. It was a far cry from the repasts he'd enjoyed in Zion, and the wine had been barely passable. Of course, that had been true of all the meals they'd allowed him, and he'd lost a lot of weight, although he could scarcely say he'd wasted away.

He pushed away the tray and stood, crossing to the window that looked out across the vast square in front of Protector's Palace. It was too dark to see it now, but he'd seen the gallows waiting for him. They'd made sure of that.

He glanced at the copy of the *Holy Writ* on the shelf beside the window, but he wasn't like Duchairn. He didn't need to paw through printed words to know he'd been God's true champion! Shan-wei had proved stronger this time, gotten her claws and fangs into too many men's hearts, but in the fullness of time, God would avenge him. God knew His own, and Zhaspahr Clyntahn treasured the damnation, the devastation and ruin God, Schueler, and Chihiro would decant upon His enemies—His and Zhaspahr Clyntahn's—in the fullness of time.

He turned his back on the window and the *Writ* and stalked across to the narrow bed with the plain cotton sheets. He sat on it, irritated with himself when he realized that even now, even knowing Schueler and God waited to greet him as their own, there was the tiniest tremor in his fingers. Well, God's champion or not, he was only mortal. The weakness of the flesh must overpower the strength of even the most brightly burning soul at times. And he'd shown his steel during that farce of a trial. For over a month they'd paraded their "witnesses," adduced their "evidence," whined to the judges about the death and the destruction—as if *that* could matter to a man defending God Himself!

He'd ignored them. Hadn't deigned to cross-examine any witness, to challenge any evidence. It had been obvious the entire "trial" was only for show. The verdict had been passed before he'd ever been dragged off of that accursed Charisian ship in Siddar City. Everything else had been window dressing. But perhaps not. Perhaps they were such moral cowards that they'd really needed the entire circus, the entire pretense of justice, to steel their spines for what they'd intended to do all along.

It didn't matter. Nothing *they* did could matter. All that mattered was

that the Archangels would be waiting to reward him as his services deserved
and—

A quiet sound interrupted his thoughts. The chamber door opened, and
his stomach tightened as he looked up. He hated that reaction, but even God's
own champion could be excused for feeling an edge of physical fear when
he found himself face-to-face with Shan-wei's foul servants.

The tall, broad-shouldered Guardsman stepped through the door, and
Clyntahn's jaw clenched as a woman, a head shorter than he but clad in the
same blackened chain mail and breastplate, followed him. Her red hair showed
coppery highlights in the lamplight, and her eyes were the same dark sapphire as her companion's.

Clyntahn glared at them, refusing to give them the satisfaction of speaking. They didn't glare at him, however; they only looked at him with cold,
disdainful contempt, and he discovered that contempt cut far deeper than
any rage.

"Well?" he snapped finally. "Come to gloat, I suppose!"

"'Gloat' isn't the word I'd choose, Your Grace," Athrawes told him in a
cold, thoughtful tone. "I prefer to think of it as . . . enlightening you."

"*Enlightening!*" Clyntahn spat on the chamber floor. "There's a special
place laid up for you in hell, Athrawes! A pit of fire will consume your flesh
for all eternity, and I'll be standing on its brink *pissing* on you!"

"He still doesn't get it, does he?" the false *seijin* said, glancing at his companion.

"No, he doesn't." She shook her head. "He doesn't even realize that we
requested the duty tonight so we'd have this opportunity to . . . explain to
him."

"You have *nothing* to explain to me, woman!" Clyntahn snarled.

"Oh, now, there you're wrong," she said, and the last Grand Inquisitor
of Mother Church felt his eyes narrow as her voice began to *change* somehow. "We have quite a lot to explain to you, Your Grace. And we've waited
a very long time for the opportunity."

Clyntahn paled, and he felt himself shrinking back as her voice shifted,
deepened, until it was no longer a woman's voice at all. It had become a deep
bass, identical to Athrawes', and Athrawes smiled coldly as his eyes darted
back and forth between them.

"The thing you need to understand, Your Grace, is that you're won't be
sitting at Schueler's right hand, passing judgment on anyone. If there truly
is a hell, you'll see it better than most, and I suppose it's possible you *will* get
to spend time with Schueler, Langhorne, and Chihiro . . . because that's
where every one of them will be."

"*Blasphemy!*" Clyntahn snapped. He grasped his pectoral scepter and shook himself. "Blasphemy! And nothing but what I should expect from heretics!"

"You have no idea what you're really facing at this moment, Your Grace," Athrawes said softly. He reached one hand to the solid wooden table at the center of the chamber. He didn't even look at it, only reached down and grasped it by one corner. And then, one-handed, he lifted its legs six inches off the floor . . . and held it there. His arm didn't even quiver, and Clyntahn swallowed hard.

"You talk about 'demons' and 'archangels,'" Athrawes told him. "But Langhorne and Schueler weren't *archangels*. They were men—*mortal* men who lied to an entire world. Mass murderers. Pei Shan-wei was no archangel, either—only a woman who spent her entire life helping others. Only a woman who made it possible for humans to live and prosper on this world. Only a woman who was murdered by Langhorne and Chihiro and Schueler because she was so much *better* than they were."

Clyntahn's eyes were huge, darting back and forth between his face and that motionless table, suspended in midair. But then that same voice came from the woman, and his eyes whipped to her face.

"Only a woman," she said, "who was my *friend*."

"*Demons!*" Clyntahn whispered hoarsely, raising his scepter between them. "Demons! Creatures of hell!"

"Hell, Your Grace?" She laughed, and the silvery sound was cold and cruel. "You don't know the meaning of the word . . . yet. But I think tomorrow, after the trap springs, you'll find out."

"Stay back!" he snapped.

"We have no intention of harming you in any way, Your Grace," she told him. "None. As Merlin said, we've come to enlighten you. You've talked a lot about your special relationship with Schueler and the archangels, so we thought you might like to meet them—before your hanging, I mean."

"What do you mean?" the question was betrayed out of him, and he closed his mouth with a snap as soon as he realized what she'd said.

"She means your *Holy Writ* is a lie," Athrawes said. "She means every word about the Creation of Safehold is alive. That every page of the *Commentaries* was written by someone who'd been lied to by Langhorne, and Bédard, and Chihiro. She means she and I are older than your *Writ*. She means we died before the first human being ever set foot on this world. And she means that tomorrow morning when they hang you, there won't be any archangels waiting for you."

"Lies!" he shouted desperately. "*Lies!*"

"Oh, there've been *lots* of lies on this planet," the woman told him, "but not from us."

Clyntahn leapt off the bed, pressing his back against the wall, trying to sink into the solid stone as both false *seijins'* eyes began to glow a hellish blue.

"*Stay away from me!*" he screamed.

"Of course, Your Grace," Athrawes said.

He set the table down as if it were a feather and the woman withdrew a shiny object from her belt pouch. She set it on a corner of the table and smiled at Clyntahn while those demonic eyes glowed past her lashes.

"Allow us to introduce you to your 'archangels,' Your Grace," she said. "This is what we call 'file footage.' We put together an hour or so of it. I think you'll find it interesting. Especially the bit where Langhorne is explaining himself to Pei Shan-wei."

She pressed the shiny object, and breath caught in Clyntahn's throat as the image of a breezy room appeared before him, no more than two feet tall, but perfectly detailed. He'd seen images like it in the Temple, in the Inquisition's secret records, and he heard someone whimpering with his voice as he recognized many of the faces in that room. He recognized the Archangel Langhorne, the Archangel Bédard, the Archangel Chihiro . . . the fallen Archangel Kau-yung . . . and Shan-wei the Accursed herself.

"—and we implore you, once again," the slender, silver-haired mother of hell said, and he shuddered as that dreadful voice fell upon his ears for the first time, "to consider how vital it is that as the human culture on this planet grows and matures, it *remembers* the Gbaba. That it understands *why* we came here, why we renounced advanced technology."

"Stop it," Clyntahn whispered. "*Stop it!*"

"We've heard all these arguments before, Dr. Pei," the Archangel Langhorne said, and it was the Archangel's voice. He knew it was, because unlike Shan-wei's, he'd heard it before. "We understand the point you're raising. But I'm afraid that nothing you've said is likely to change our established policy."

"Administrator," Shan-wei said, "your 'established policy' overlooks the fact that mankind has always been a toolmaker and a problem solver. Eventually those qualities are going to surface here on Safehold. When they do, without an institutional memory of what happened to the Federation, our descendants aren't going to know about the dangers waiting for them out there."

"That particular concern is based on a faulty understanding of the societal matrix we're creating here, Dr. Pei," the Archangel Bédard said. "I assure you, with the safeguards we've put in place, the inhabitants of Safehold will be safely insulated against the sort of technological advancement which might attract the Gbaba's intention. Unless, of course, there's some outside stimulus to violate the parameters of our matrix."

"I don't doubt that you can—that you have already—created an anti-technology mindset on an individual and a societal level," Shan-wei replied levelly. "I simply believe that whatever you can accomplish right now, whatever curbs and safeguards you can impose at this moment, five hundred years from now, or a thousand, there's going to come a moment when those safeguards fail."

"They won't," the Archangel Bédard said flatly. "I realize psychology isn't your field, Doctor. And I also realize one of your doctorates is in history. Because it is, you're quite rightly aware of the frenetic pace at which technology has advanced in the modern era. Certainly, on the basis of humanity's history on Old Earth, especially during the last five or six centuries, it would appear the 'innovation bug' is hardwired into the human psyche. It isn't, however. There are examples from our own history of lengthy, very static periods. In particular, I draw your attention to the thousands of years of the Egyptian empire, during which significant innovation basically didn't happen. What we've done here, on Safehold, is to re-create that same basic mindset, and we've also installed certain . . . institutional and physical checks to maintain that mindset."

"No, *nooooooo*," Clyntahn moaned. Five or six centuries, *thousands of years?!* It was lies, *it was all lies!* It had to be!

But the voices went right on speaking, and he couldn't look away.

"The degree to which the Egyptians—and the rest of the Mediterranean cultures—were anti-innovation has been considerably overstated," Shan-wei told the Archangel Bédard. "Moreover, Egypt was only a tiny segment of the world population of its day, and other parts—"

▼   ▼   ▼

His torment lasted more than the hour the hellish woman had promised. It lasted a century—an age! They made him watch it all, made him absorb the blasphemy, the lies, the deception. And, far worse than that, they made him realize something more dreadful, more hideous than any torment the Punishment had ever inflicted upon the most hardened heretic.

They made him realize it was the *truth*.

"Lies," he whispered, staring up at them from where he'd slid down the wall to hunker on the floor. "*Lies*." Yet even as he said it, he knew.

"Go on telling yourself that, Your Grace," Athrawes said as the woman slid the object back into her belt pouch. "Be our guest. Tell yourself that again and again, every step of the way between this cell and the gallows. Tell yourself that when the rope goes around your neck. Tell yourself that while you stand there, waiting. Because when that trap door opens, when you fall through it, you won't be able to tell yourself that any longer. And how do you think the real God, the true God, the God men and women like Maikel Staynair worship, will greet you when you hit the *end* of that rope?"

Clyntahn stared at him, his mouth working wordlessly, and the *seijin*—the *seijin*, he knew now, who was a young woman a thousand years dead—smiled at him while his companion—the *same* dead woman!—unlocked the chamber door once more.

"Tell yourself that, Your Grace," Merlin Athrawes said as he turned to follow Nimue Chwaeriau through that door. "Take it with you straight to hell, because Schueler and Langhorne are waiting for you there."

▼　▼　▼

Greyghor Stohnar sat on the reviewing stand beside Cayleb of Charis. Empress Sharleyan sat on the Emperor's right, with Aivah Pahrsahn to *her* right, and young Prince Nahrmahn Garyet and King Gorjah of Tarot sat with them. The Duke of Darcos and his wife sat on the rows below theirs, and so did Earl Thirsk, Archbishop Staiphan, Archbishop Zhasyn Cahnyr, Archbishop Klairmant Gairlyng, Archbishop Ulys Lynkyn. . . .

It was a very long list, scores of names. And for every name on it, there was another name that wasn't there. Gwylym Manthyr, Mahrtyn Taisyn, Dabnyr Dynnys, Clyftyn Sumyrs, Samyl and Hauwerd Wylsynn, even Erayk Dynnys. As he sat there in the crisp, cold morning sunlight, bundled in his warm coat, wearing his gloves, his breath rising in a golden, sun-touched mist, he thought about all those missing names. The men—and the women—who couldn't be here to see this morning, to know that justice had finally been done in their names.

Justice. Such a cold, useless word. It's important—I know it's important—but . . . what does it really achieve? Does it bring them back? Does it undo anything the bastard did?

He remembered the cold contempt in Clyntahn's eyes as the verdict was finally read. Remembered the arrogance, the way he'd stared at all of them secure in the knowledge—even *now*, after everything—that the final victory would be his. That he truly had served God. He'd wanted to vomit that day, but today would be an end. And as he thought that, he realized what justice achieved.

It's not about him, *really. Oh, there's vengeance in it, and I won't pretend there isn't. But what it's about—what it means—is that we're better than he is. That there are some acts, some atrocities, we won't tolerate. That we will punish them to make our rejection of evil clear but we won't resort to the butchery, the flaying knives, the castration, the white hot irons, or the stake that he used on so many people. We will remove him from the face of this world, but with a decent respect for justice and without—*without*—becoming him when we do. That's what this morning is about.*

A trumpet sounded. The background murmur of conversation died, and the only sound was the snapping of the banners atop Protector's Palace and the faint, distant cry of a wyvern. Then the door opened, and the escort, an enlisted soldier chosen from every army that had fought against the Group of Four—and from the Royal Dohlaran Army, the Army of God, and the Mighty Host of God and the Archangels, as well—came through it, surrounding the prisoner in the plain black cassock.

Stohnar watched them come, and his eyes widened slowly as Zhaspahr Clyntahn drew closer. The arrogance was gone, the shoulders slumped, the hair was wild and uncombed, and he walked like an old, old man, eyes darting in every direction. They fastened on the tall, blue-eyed *seijin* standing behind Cayleb and Sharleyan, and the smaller *seijin* standing behind the Duke of Darcos and his wife, and even from his seat, Stohnar could see the terror in their depths.

They reached the foot of the gallows stairs, and Clyntahn stopped. The escort paused, and he raised one foot, as if to set it on the lowest stair tread. But he didn't. He only stood there, staring now up at the noose swaying in the breeze, and not at the *seijins* standing post in the stands.

Seconds trickled away, and—finally—the sergeant in Charisian uniform touched him on the shoulder. The Charisian pushed gently, giving the prisoner the option of dignity, but Clyntahn whirled. He stared up at the stands again, his face white, his hands trembling.

"*Please!*" he cried hoarsely. "Oh, *please!* It was—I thought—I *can't*—!"

He went to his knees, holding out his hands imploringly.

"I thought I was *right!* I thought . . . I thought the *Writ* was *true!*"

Stohnar stiffened. The man was mad. Here at the very end, finally face-to-face with death, with retribution for his millions of victims, he was mad.

"*Please!*" he half-sobbed. "*Don't!* It's not my fault! They *lied!*"

The sergeant who'd tried to leave him the gift of dignity drew back. Then he glanced at his companions, and four of them reached down, pulled the prisoner to his feet, and bore him towards the gallows. He fought madly, twisting and kicking, but it was useless. They dragged him across the platform, held him while the executioner put the noose about his neck. He tried to cry out again, but one of the guards clamped a gloved hand across his mouth while a young brigadier in the uniform of the Glacierheart militia unfolded a sheet of paper.

"'Zhaspahr Clyntahn,'" he read, "'you have been tried and adjudged guilty of murder, of torture, and of crimes too barbaric and too numerous to enumerate. You are cast out by the Church, stripped of your offices, deprived of your place among God's children by your own actions. And so you are condemned to be hanged by the neck until dead, and for your body to be burned into ashes and the ashes scattered upon the wind so that they do not pollute sacred ground. This sentence to be carried out on this day at this hour.' "

He paused and folded the paper, then nodded to the sergeant whose hand was clamped across Clyntahn's mouth.

"Do you have anything you wish to say?" Byrk Raimahn asked as that hand was removed, remembering the Starving Winter in Glacierheart, remembering all the Glacierhearters who would never come home.

"I . . . I—" The voice wavered around the edges. It cracked and died, and the mouth worked wordlessly.

▼   ▼   ▼

"I wish the Commodore and Shan-wei were here to see this," Nimue Chwaeriau's voice said quietly in Merlin Athrawes' ear, and he knew every other member of the inner circle heard her in that same moment, even if none of the others could reply.

"And Gwylym," he replied over his own built-in com, sapphire eyes hard as he watched the trembling Grand Inquisitor with the noose about his neck. "Everyone else the bastard had murdered."

"I know. But we've come a long way from where you started, Merlin. A long way."

"Maybe. But we've got an even longer way to go, and there's that 'Archangels' return' to worry about. The way Duchairn's salvaging the Church, finding some way to deal with that should keep us . . . occupied."

"Of course it will," Nahrmahn Baytz' voice said. "But since you're so fond of Churchill quotes, what about this one? 'This is not the end. It is not even the beginning of the end. But it is, perhaps, the end of the beginning.' "

▼   ▼   ▼

Byrk Raimahn waited another ten, slow seconds. Then he stepped back.

"Very well," he said coldly, and nodded to the executioner.

The trap opened, the rope snapped tight, and the body jerked once as the neck broke cleanly. There was a sound from the watching crowd. Not of jubilation, not of *celebration*. Only a vast, wordless sigh.

▼   ▼   ▼

"I don't know how it looks from your perspective, Merlin," Nahrmahn said quietly, "but from mine? It's been one *hell* of a beginning, my friend."

Merlin gazed at the body, watching it sway slowly, and put his hands on Nynian's shoulders. She covered the hand on her right shoulder with her own and turned her head to look up at him. He looked away from the body, meeting her eyes, and smiled slowly.

"It has that, Nahrmahn, it has that. And if we've got a long way to go," he squeezed Nynian's shoulders gently, "at least we've got good company for the trip."

Author's Note

Some of you may have noticed that there is no character list in this book. Some of you may have felt a certain relief that there's no character list in this book.

A combination of factors came together to cause its omission this time around. Part of it was the simple length of the manuscript and the thought of what adding another forty thousand or so words to it would have done in terms of my readers' skeletal muscular injuries. Part of it was that I was delayed getting the book in and that, in fact, Tor has done a remarkable job to get it through production in time for delivery.

And part of it was that I intend—eventually—to post a comprehensive list of all the characters in all the Safehold novels on my website at davidweber.net. I will also be posting the master electronic map of Safehold. It requires some work before it's ready for prime time, however, and the same is true of the character list. So if you come looking for either of them in the immediate future, you probably won't find them. Give me another month or so, and you should be able to.

Thanks for coming along for the ride this far. I promise Merlin still has lots more story to tell.

Glossary

Abbey of Saint Evehlain—the sister abbey of the Monastery of Saint Zherneau.

Abbey of the Snows—an abbey of the Sisters of Chihiro of the Quill located in the Mountains of Light above Langhorne's Tears. Although it is a working abbey of Chihiro, all of the nuns of the abbey are also Sisters of Saint Kohdy and the abbey serves as protection and cover for Saint Kohdy's tomb. The Abbey of the Snows is built on the foundation of a pre-Armageddon Reef structure, which is reputed to have been a resort house for Eric Langhorne before his death.

Angle-glass—Charisian term for a periscope.

Angora lizard—a Safeholdian "lizard" with a particularly luxuriant, cashmere-like coat. They are raised and sheared as sheep and form a significant part of the fine-textiles industry.

Anshinritsumei—"the little fire" from the *Holy Writ*; the lesser touch of God's spirit and the maximum enlightenment of which mortals are capable.

Ape lizard—ape lizards are much larger and more powerful versions of monkey lizards. Unlike monkey lizards, they are mostly ground dwellers, although they are capable of climbing trees suitable to bear their weight. The great mountain ape lizard weighs as much as nine hundred or a thousand pounds, whereas the plains ape lizard weighs no more than a hundred to a hundred and fifty pounds. Ape lizards live in families of up to twenty or thirty adults, and whereas monkey lizards will typically flee when confronted with a threat, ape lizards are much more likely to respond by attacking the threat. It is not unheard of for two or three ape lizard "families" to combine forces against particularly dangerous predators, and even a great dragon will generally avoid such a threat.

Archangels, The—central figures of the Church of God Awaiting. The Archangels were senior members of the command crew of Operation Ark who assumed the status of divine messengers, guides, and guardians in order to control and shape the future of human civilization on Safehold.

ASP—Artillery Support Party, the term used to describe teams of ICA officers and noncoms specially trained to call for and coordinate artillery support. ASPs may be attached at any level, from the division down to the company or even platoon, and are equipped with heliographs, signal flags, runners, and/or messenger wyverns.

Bahnyta—the name *Seijin* Kohdy assigned to his *hikousen*.

Band—the AoG and Harchongese equivalent of an army corps. The word "corps" itself can't be used because of the Inquisition's opposition to the adoption of that "heresy-tainted" term.

Blink lizard—a small, bioluminescent winged lizard. Although it's about three times the size of a firefly, it fills much the same niche on Safehold.

Blue leaf—a woody, densely growing native Safeholdian tree or shrub very similar to mountain laurel. It bears white or yellow flowers in season and takes its name from the waxy blue cast of its leaves.

Bombsweeper—the Imperial Charisian Navy's name for a minesweeper.

Borer—a form of Safeholdian shellfish which attaches itself to the hulls of ships or the timbers of wharves by boring into them. There are several types of borer: the most destructive of which continually eat their way deeper into any wooden structure, whereas some less destructive varieties eat only enough of the structure to anchor themselves and actually form a protective outer layer which gradually builds up a coral-like surface. Borers and rot are the two most serious threats (aside, of course, from fire) to wooden hulls.

Briar berries—any of several varieties of native Safeholdian berries which grow on thorny bushes.

Cat-lizard—furry lizard about the size of a terrestrial cat. They are kept as pets and are very affectionate.

Catamount—a smaller version of the Safeholdian slash lizard. The catamount is very fast and smarter than its larger cousin, which means it tends to avoid humans. It is, however, a lethal and dangerous hunter in its own right.

Chamberfruit—a native Safeholdian plant similar to a terrestrial calabash gourd. The chamberfruit is grown both as a food source and as a naturally produced container. There are several varieties of chamberfruit, and one common use for it is in the construction of foamstone pipes for smoking.

Cherrybean tea—a "tea" made from the beans (seeds) of the cherrybean tree, especially favored in Emerald and Tarot and a highly esteemed luxury in North Harchong and the Temple Lands, although its expense limits it to a very wealthy group of consumers.

Cherrybean tree—the Safeholdian name for coffee trees. There is only one variety on Safehold, a version of robusta genetically engineered to survive in a wider range of climates. The cherrybean tree is still limited to a fairly narrow belt of equatorial and near equatorial Safehold because of the planet's lower average temperatures.

Chewleaf—a mildly narcotic leaf from a native Safeholdian plant. It is used much as terrestrial chewing tobacco over much of the planet's surface.

Choke tree—a low-growing species of tree native to Safehold. It comes in many varieties and is found in most of the planet's climate zones. It is dense-growing, tough, and difficult to eradicate, but it requires quite a lot of sunlight to flourish, which means it is seldom found in mature old-growth forests.

Church of Charis—the schismatic church which split from the Church of God Awaiting following the Group of Four's effort to destroy the Kingdom of Charis.

Church of God Awaiting—the church and religion created by the command staff of Operation Ark to control the colonists and their descendants and prevent the reemergence of advanced technology.

Cliff bear—a Safeholdian mammal which somewhat resembles a terrestrial grizzly bear crossed with a raccoon. It has the facial "mask" markings of a raccoon and round, marsupial ears. Unlike terrestrial bears, however, cliff bears are almost exclusively carnivorous.

Cliff lizard—a six-limbed, oviparous mammal native to Safehold. Male cliff lizards average between one hundred and fifty and two hundred and fifty pounds in weight and fill much the same niche as bighorn mountain sheep.

Commentaries, The—the authorized interpretations and doctrinal expansions upon the *Holy Writ*. They represent the officially approved and Church-sanctioned interpretation of the original Scripture.

Composition D—The Charisian name for TNT.

Cotton silk—a plant native to Safehold which shares many of the properties of silk and cotton. It is very lightweight and strong, but the raw fiber comes from a plant pod which is even more filled with seeds than Old Earth cotton. Because of the amount of hand labor required to harvest and process the pods and to remove the seeds from it, cotton silk is very expensive.

Council of Vicars—the Church of God Awaiting's equivalent of the College of Cardinals.

Course lizard—one of several species of very fast, carnivorous lizards bred and trained to run down prey. Course lizard breeds range in size from the Tiegelkamp course lizard, somewhat smaller than a terrestrial greyhound, to the Gray Wall course lizard, with a body length of over five feet and a maximumn weight of close to two hundred and fifty pounds.

Crusher serpent—a huge Safeholdian predator roughly analogous to a boa constrictor. Crusher serpents are warm blooded, which better suits them to Safehold's colder climate, and can reach lengths of up to sixty feet. They are ambush hunters which prefer flight to fight in threat situations, and they can sometimes be faced down even by relatively small prey animals. Nonetheless, they are fearsome foes if cornered and have been known to take down even adolescent slash lizards.

Dagger thorn—a native Charisian shrub, growing to a height of perhaps three feet at maturity, which possesses knife-edged thorns from three to seven inches long, depending upon the variety.

Dandelion—the Safeholdian dandelion grows to approximately twice the size of the Terrestrial plant for which it is named but is otherwise extremely similar in appearance and its seeds disperse in very much the same fashion.

De Castro marble—a densely swirled, rosy marble from the de Castro Mountains of North Harchong which is prized by sculptors, especially for religious and Church art.

Decrees of Schueler—the codified internal directives, regulations, and procedure manual of the Office of the Inquisition.

Deep-mouth wyvern—the Safeholdian equivalent of a pelican.

Doomwhale—the most dangerous predator of Safehold, although, fortunately, it seldom bothers with anything as small as humans. Doomwhales have been known to run to as much as one hundred feet in length, and they are pure carnivores. Each doomwhale requires a huge range, and encounters with them are rare, for which human beings are just as glad, thank you. Doomwhales will eat *anything* . . . including the largest krakens. They have been known, on *extremely* rare occasions, to attack merchant ships and war galleys.

Double-glass or **Double-spyglass**—Charisian term for binoculars.

Dragon—the largest native Safeholdian land life-form. Dragons come in two varieties: the common dragon (generally subdivided into jungle dragons and hill dragons) and the carnivorous great dragon. *See* Great dragon.

Eye-cheese—Safeholdian name for Swiss cheese.

Fallen, The—the Archangels, angels, and mortals who followed Shan-wei in her rebellion against God and the rightful authority of the Archangel Langhorne. The term applies to *all* of Shan-wei's adherents, but is most often used in reference to the angels and Archangels who followed her willingly rather than the mortals who were duped into obeying her.

False silver—Safeholdian name for antimony.

Fire striker—Charisian term for a cigarette lighter.

Fire vine—a large, hardy, fast-growing Safeholdian vine. Its runners can exceed two inches in diameter, and the plant is extremely rich in natural oils. It is considered a major hazard to human habitations, especially in areas which experience arid, dry summers, because of its very high natural flammability and because its oil is poisonous to humans and terrestrial species of animals. The crushed vine and its seed pods, however, are an important source of lubricating oils, and it is commercially cultivated in some areas for that reason.

Fire willow—a Safeholdian evergeen tree native to East Haven's temperate and subarctic regions. Fire willow seldom grows much above five meters in height and has long, streamer-like leaves. It prefers relatively damp growing conditions and produces dense clusters of berries ranging in color from a bright orange to scarlet.

Fire wing—Safeholdian term for a cavalry maneuver very similar to the Terran caracole, in which mounted troops deliver pistol fire against infantry at close quarters. It is also designed to be used against enemy cavalry under favorable conditions.

Fist of Kau-Yung—the unofficial name assigned to Helm Cleaver and its operatives by agents inquisitor attempting to combat the organization.

Five-day—a Safeholdian "week," consisting of only five days, Monday through Friday.

Flange-beam—Safeholdian term used for what a Terran engineer would call an "I-beam."

Fleming moss—an absorbent moss native to Safehold which was genetically engineered by Shan-wei's terraforming crews to possess natural antibiotic properties. It is a staple of Safeholdian medical practice.

Foamstone—the Safeholdian equivalent of meerschaum. This light-colored, soft stone takes its name from the same source as meerschaum, since it is occasionally found floating in the Gulf of Tanshar. Its primary use is in the construction of incense burners for the Church of God Awaiting and in the manufacture of tobacco pipes and cigar holders.

Forktail—one of several species of native Safeholdian fish which fill an ecological niche similar to that of the Old Earth herring.

Fox-lizard—a warm-blooded, six-limbed Safeholdian omnivore, covered with fur, which ranges from a dull russet color to a very dark gray. Most species of fox-lizard are capable of climbing trees. They range in length from forty to forty-eight inches, have bushy tails approximately twenty-five inches long, and weigh between twenty and thirty pounds.

Gbaba—a star-traveling, xenophobic species whose reaction to encounters with any possibly competing species is to exterminate it. The Gbaba completely destroyed the Terran Federation and, so far as is known, all human beings in the galaxy aside from the population of Safehold.

Glynfych Distillery—a Chisholmian distillery famous throughout Safehold for the quality of its whiskeys.

Golden berry—a tree growing to about ten feet in height which thrives in most Safeholdian climates. A tea brewed from its leaves is a sovereign specific for motion sickness and nausea.

Grass lizard—a Safeholdian herbivore, somewhat larger than a Terrestrial German Shepherd, which is regarded as a serious pest by farmers. There are several subspecies, which are found almost everywhere outside the arctic regions.

Grasshopper—a Safeholdian insect analogue which grows to a length of as much as nine inches and is carnivorous. Fortunately, they do not occur in the same numbers as terrestrial grasshoppers.

Gray-horned wyvern—a nocturnal flying predator of Safehold. It is roughly analogous to a terrestrial owl.

Gray mists—the Safeholdian term for Alzheimer's disease.

Great dragon—the largest and most dangerous land carnivore of Safehold. The great dragon isn't actually related to hill dragons or jungle dragons at all, despite some superficial physical resemblances. In fact, it's more of a scaled-up slash lizard, with elongated jaws and sharp, serrated teeth. It has six limbs and, unlike the slash lizard, is covered in thick, well-insulated hide rather than fur.

Group of Four—the four vicars who dominate and effectively control the Council of Vicars of the Church of God Awaiting.

Gun dogs—ICA infantry and cavalry nickname for their own army's artillerists.

Hairatha Dragons—the Hairatha professional baseball team. The traditional rivals of the Tellesberg Krakens for the Kingdom Championship.

Hake—a Safeholdian fish. Like most "fish" native to Safehold, it has a very long, sinuous body but the head does resemble a terrestrial hake or cod, with a hooked jaw.

Hammer-islander—Safeholdian term for a sou'wester; a waterproof foul-weather hat made of oilskin or tarred canvas. It takes its name from Hammer Island, which experiences some of the harshest weather on Safehold.

Hand of Kau-Yung—the name applied by agents of the Inquisition to the anti-Group of Four organization established in Zion by Aivah Pahrsahn/ Ahnzhelyk Phonda.

Helm Cleaver—the name of *Seijin* Kohdy's "magic sword," and also the name assigned by Nynian Rychtair to the covert action organization created in parallel with the Sisters of Saint Kohdy.

High-angle gun—a relatively short, stubby artillery piece with a carriage specially designed to allow higher angles of fire in order to lob gunpowder-filled shells in high, arcing trajectories. The name is generally shortened to "angle-gun" by the gun crews themselves.

High Hallows—a very tough, winter-hardy breed of horses.

Highland lilly—a native Safeholdian perenial flowering plant. It grows to a height of 3 to 4 feet and bears a pure white, seven-lobed flower 8 to 9 inches across. Its flower is the symbol of martyrdom for the Church of God Awaiting.

Highland lily—a tulip-like native Safeholdian flower, found primarily in the foothills of the Langhorne Mountains and the Mountains of Light. Its snow-white petals are tipped in dark crimson, and it is considered sacred to martyrs and those who have fought valiantly for Mother Church.

Hikousen—the term used to describe the air cars provided to the *seijins* who fought for the Church in the War Against the Fallen.

Hill dragon—a roughly elephant-sized draft animal commonly used on Safehold. Despite their size, hill dragons are capable of rapid, sustained movement. They are herbivores.

Holy Writ—the seminal holy book of the Church of God Awaiting.

Hornet—a stinging, carniverous Safeholdian insect analogue. It is over two inches long and nests in ground burrows. Its venom is highly toxic to Safe-holdian life-forms, but most terrestrial life-forms are not seriously affected by it (about ten percent of all humans have a potentially lethal allergic shock reaction to it, however). Hornets are highly aggressive and territorial and instinctively attack their victims' eyes first.

Ice wyvern—a flightless aquatic wyvern rather similar to a terrestrial pen-guin. Species of ice wyvern are native to both the northern and southern polar regions of Safehold.

Inner circle—Charisian allies of Merlin Athrawes who know the truth about the Church of God Awaiting and the Terran Federation.

Insights, The—the recorded pronouncements and observations of the Church of God Awaiting's Grand Vicars and canonized saints. They rep-resent deeply significant spiritual and inspirational teachings, but as the work of fallible mortals do not have the same standing as the *Holy Writ* itself.

Intendant—the cleric assigned to a bishopric or archbishopric as the direct representative of the Office of Inquisition. The intendant is specifically charged with ensuring that the Proscriptions of Jwo-jeng are not violated.

Journal of Saint Zherneau—the journal left by Jeremy Knowles telling the truth about the destruction of the Alexandria Enclave and about Pei Shan-wei.

Jungle dragon—a somewhat generic term applied to lowland dragons larger than hill dragons. The gray jungle dragon is the largest herbivore on Safehold.

Kau-yung's striker—(also simply "striker") the ICA's combat engineers' nickname for a flamethrower.

Kau-yungs—the name assigned by men of the Army of God to antiperson-nel mines, and especially to claymore-style directional mines, in commem-oration of the "pocket nuke" Commander Pei Kau-yung used against Eric Langhorne's adherents following the destruction of the Alexandria Enclave. Later applied to all land mines.

Keitai—the term used to describe the personal coms provided to the *seijins* who fought for the Church in the War Against the Fallen.

Kercheef—a traditional headdress worn in the Kingdom of Tarot which consists of a specially designed bandana tied across the hair.

Knights of the Temple Lands—the corporate title of the prelates who govern the Temple Lands. Technically, the Knights of the Temple Lands are *secular* rulers who simply happen to also hold high Church office. Under the letter of the Church's law, what they may do as the Knights of the Temple Lands is completely separate from any official action of the Church. This legal fiction has been of considerable value to the Church on more than one occasion.

Kraken (1)—generic term for an entire family of maritime predators. Krakens are rather like sharks crossed with octopi. They have powerful, fish-like bodies; strong jaws with inward-inclined, fang-like teeth; and a cluster of tentacles just behind the head which can be used to hold prey while they devour it. The smallest, coastal krakens can be as short as three or four feet; deepwater krakens up to fifty feet in length have been reliably reported, and there are legends of those still larger.

Kraken (2)—one of three pre-Merlin heavy-caliber naval artillery pieces. The great kraken weighed approximately 3.4 tons and fired a forty-two-pound round shot. The royal kraken weighed four tons. It also fired a forty-two-pound shot but was specially designed as a long-range weapon with less windage and higher bore pressures. The standard kraken was a 2.75-ton, medium-range weapon which fired a thirty-five-pound round shot approximately 6.2 inches in diameter.

Kraken oil—originally, oil extracted from kraken and used as fuel, primarily for lamps, in coastal and seafaring realms. Most lamp oil currently comes from sea dragons (*see* below), rather than actually being extracted from kraken, and, in fact, the sea dragon oil actually burns much more brightly and with much less odor. Nonetheless, oils are still ranked in terms of "kraken oil" quality steps.

Kyousei hi—"great fire" or "magnificent fire," from the *Holy Writ*. The term used to describe the brilliant nimbus of light the Operation Ark command crew generated around their air cars and skimmers to "prove" their divinity to the original Safeholdians.

Land-bomb—Temple Loyalist armed forces' term for a land mine.

Langhorne's Tears—a quartet of alpine lakes in the Mountains of Light. Langhorne's Tears were reportedly known as Langhorne's Joy before the destruction of Armageddon Reef.

Langhorne's Watch—the 31-minute period which falls immediately after midnight. It was inserted by the original "Archangels" to compensate for the extra length of Safehold's 26.5-hour day. It is supposed to be used for contemplation and giving thanks.

Levelers—a reformist/revolutionary Mainland movement dedicated to overturning all social and economic differences in society.

Lizardhole—Temple Loyalist armed forces' term for "foxhole."

Marsh wyvern—one of several strains of Safeholdian wyverns found in saltwater and freshwater marsh habitats.

Mask lizard—Safeholdian equivalent of a chameleon. Mask lizards are carnivores, about two feet long, which use their camouflage ability to lure small prey into range before they pounce.

Master Traynyr—a character out of the Safeholdian entertainment tradition. Master Traynyr is a stock character in Safeholdian puppet theater, by turns a bumbling conspirator whose plans always miscarry and the puppeteer who controls all of the marionette "actors" in the play.

Messenger wyvern—any one of several strains of genetically modified Safeholdian wyverns adapted by Pei Shan-wei's terraforming teams to serve the colonists as homing pigeon equivalents. Some messenger wyverns are adapted for short-range, high-speed delivery of messages, whereas others are adapted for extremely long range (but slower) message deliveries.

Mirror twins—Safeholdian term for Siamese twins.

Moarte subită—the favored martial art of the Terran Federation Marines, developed on the colony world of Walachia.

Monastery of Saint Zherneau—the mother monastery and headquarters of the Brethren of Saint Zherneau, a relatively small and poor order in the Archbishopric of Charis.

Monkey lizard—a generic term for several species of arboreal, saurian-looking marsupials. Monkey lizards come in many different shapes and sizes, although none are much larger than an Old Earth chimpanzee and most are considerably smaller. They have two very human-looking hands, although each hand has only three fingers and an opposable thumb, and the "hand feet" of their other forelimbs have a limited grasping ability but no opposable thumb. Monkey lizards tend to be excitable, *very* energetic, and talented mimics of human behaviors.

Mountain ananas—a native Safeholdian fruit tree. Its spherical fruit averages about four inches in diameter with the firmness of an apple and a taste rather like a sweet grapefruit. It is very popular on the Safeholdian mainland.

Mountain spike-thorn—a particular subspecies of spike-thorn, found primarily in tropical mountains. The most common blossom color is a deep, rich red, but the white mountain spike-thorn is especially prized for its trumpet-shaped blossom, which has a deep, almost cobalt-blue throat, fading to pure white as it approaches the outer edge of the blossom, which is, in turn, fringed in a deep golden yellow.

Narwhale—a species of Safeholdian sea life named for the Old Earth species of the same name. Safeholdian narwhales are about forty feet in length and equipped with twin horn-like tusks up to eight feet long. They live in large pods or schools and are not at all shy or retiring. The adults of narwhale pods have been known to fight off packs of kraken.

Nearoak—a rough-barked Safeholdian tree similar to an Old Earth oak tree. It is found in tropic and near tropic zones. Although it does resemble an Old Earth oak, it is an evergreen and seeds using "pine cones."

Nearpalm—a tropical Safeholdian tree which resembles a terrestrial royal palm except that a mature specimen stands well over sixty feet tall. It produces a tart, plum-like fruit about five inches in diameter.

Nearpalm fruit—the plum-like fruit produced by the nearpalm. It is used in cooking and eaten raw, but its greatest commercial value is as the basis for nearpalm wine.

Nearpoplar—a native Safeholdian tree, very fast-growing and straight-grained, which is native to the planet's temperate zones. It reaches a height of approximately ninety feet.

Neartuna—one of several native Safeholdian fish species, ranging in length from approximately three feet to just over five.

NEAT—Neural Education and Training machine. The standard means of education in the Terran Federation.

Nest doll—a Harchongian folk art doll, similar to the Russian Matryoshka dolls in which successively smaller dolls are nested inside hollow wooden dolls.

New model—a generic term increasingly applied to the innovations in technology (especially war-fighting technology) introduced by Charis and its allies. *See* new model kraken.

New model kraken—the standardized artillery piece of the Imperial Charisian Navy. It weighs approximately 2.5 tons and fires a thirty-pound round shot with a diameter of approximately 5.9 inches. Although it weighs slightly less than the old kraken (*see* above) and its round shot is twelve percent lighter, it is actually longer ranged and fires at a higher velocity because of reductions in windage, improvements in gunpowder, and slightly increased barrel length.

Northern spine tree—a Safeholdian evergreen tree, native to arctic and subarctic regions. Spine tree branches grow in a sharply pointed, snow-shedding shape but bear the sharp, stiff spines from which the tree takes its name.

Nynian Rychtair—the Safeholdian equivalent of Helen of Troy, a woman of legendary beauty, born in Siddarmark, who eventually married the Emperor of Harchong.

Offal lizard—a carrion-eating scavenger which fills the niche of an undersized hyena crossed with a jackal. Offal lizards will take small living prey, but they are generally cowardly and are regarded with scorn and contempt by most Safeholdians.

Oil tree—a Safeholdian plant species which grows to an average height of approximately thirty feet. The oil tree produces large, hairy pods which contain many small seeds very rich in natural plant oils. Dr. Pei Shan-wei's terraforming teams genetically modified the plant to increase its oil productivity and to make it safely consumable by human beings. It is cultivated primarily as a food product, but it is also an important source of lubricants. In inland realms, it is also a major source of lamp oil.

Operation Ark—a last-ditch, desperate effort mounted by the Terran Federation to establish a hidden colony beyond the knowledge and reach of the xenophobic Gbaba. It created the human settlement on Safehold.

Pasquale's Basket—a voluntary collection of contributions for the support of the sick, homeless, and indigent. The difference between the amount contributed voluntarily and that required for the Basket's purpose is supposed to be contributed from Mother Church's coffers as a first charge upon tithes received.

Pasquale's Cleanser—the Safeholdian term for Carbolic acid.

Pasquale's Grace—euthanasia. Pasqualate healers are permitted by their vows to end the lives of the terminally ill, but only under tightly defined and stringently limited conditions.

Persimmon fig—a native Safeholdian fruit which is extremely tart and relatively thick-skinned.

Prong lizard—a roughly elk-sized lizard with a single horn which branches into four sharp points in the last third or so of its length. Prong lizards are herbivores and not particularly ferocious.

Proscriptions of Jwo-jeng—the definition of allowable technology under the doctrine of the Church of God Awaiting. Essentially, the Proscriptions limit allowable technology to that which is powered by wind, water, or muscle. The Proscriptions are subject to interpretation by the Order of Schueler, which generally errs on the side of conservatism, but it is not unheard of for corrupt intendants to rule for or against an innovation under the Proscriptions in return for financial compensation.

Rabies—a native Safeholdian disease which produces symptoms very similar to those associated with the terrestrial disease of the same name. It does not affect imported terrestrial fauna, however, and the terrestrial disease was not brought to Safehold with the colonists.

Rakurai (1)—literally, "lightning bolt." The *Holy Writ*'s term for the kinetic weapons used to destroy the Alexandria Enclave.

Rakurai (2)—the organization of solo suicide terrorists trained and deployed by Wyllym Rayno and Zhaspahr Clyntahn. Security for the Rakurai is so tight that not even Clyntahn knows the names and identities of individual Rakurai or the targets against which Rayno has dispatched them.

Rakurai bug—a Safeholdian insect analogue similar to a Terrestrial firefly but about three times as large.

Reformist—one associated with the Reformist movement. The majority of Reformists outside the Charisian Empire still regard themselves as Temple Loyalists.

Reformist movement—the movement within the Church of God Awaiting to reform the abuses and corruption which have become increasingly evident (and serious) over the last hundred to one hundred and fifty years. Largely underground and unfocused until the emergence of the Church of Charis, the movement is attracting increasing support throughout Safehold.

Rising—the term used to describe the rebellion against Lord Protector Greyghor and the Constitution of the Republic of Siddarmark by the Temple Loyalists.

Round Theatre—the largest and most famous theater in the city of Tellesberg. Supported by the Crown but independent of it, and renowned not only for the quality of its productions but for its willingness to present works which satirize Charisian society, industry, the aristocracy, and even the Church.

Saint Evehlain—the patron saint of the Abbey of Saint Evehlain in Tellesberg; wife of Saint Zherneau.

Saint Kohdy—a *seijin* who fought for the Church of God Awaiting in the War Against the Fallen. He was killed shortly before the end of that war and later stripped of his sainthood and expunged from the record of the Church's *seijins*.

Saint Zherneau—the patron saint of the Monastery of Saint Zherneau in Tellesberg; husband of Saint Evehlain.

Salmon—a Safeholdian fish species named because its reproductive habits are virtually identical to those of a terrestrial salmon. It is, however, almost more like an eel than a fish, being very long in proportion to its body's width.

Sand maggot—a loathsome carnivore, looking much like a six-legged slug, which haunts Safeholdian beaches just above the surf line. Sand maggots do not normally take living prey, although they have no objection to devouring the occasional small creature which strays into their reach. Their natural coloration blends well with their sandy habitat, and they normally conceal themselves by digging their bodies into the sand until they are completely covered, or only a small portion of their backs show.

Sandrah's Doorknocker — (also simply "doorknocker") ICA engineers' slang term for the Composite Demolition Charge, Mark 1; the Safeholdian equivalent of the Bangalore Torpedo.

Scabbark—a very resinous deciduous tree native to Safehold. Scabbark takes its name from the blisters of sap which ooze from any puncture in its otherwise very smooth, gray-brown bark and solidify into hard, reddish "scabs." Scabbark wood is similar in coloration and grain to Terran Brazilwood, and the tree's sap is used to produce similar red fabric dyes.

Sea cow—a walrus-like Safeholdian sea mammal which grows to a body length of approximately ten feet when fully mature.

Sea dragon—the Safeholdian equivalent of a terrestrial whale. There are several species of sea dragon, the largest of which grow to a body length of approximately fifty feet. Like the whale, sea dragons are mammalian. They are insulated against deep oceanic temperatures by thick layers of blubber and are krill-eaters. They reproduce much more rapidly than whales, however, and are the principal food source for doomwhales and large, deepwater krakens. Most species of sea dragon produce the equivalent of sperm oil and spermaceti. A large sea dragon will yield as much as four hundred gallons of oil.

Sea-bomb—Temple Loyalist armed forces' term for a naval mine.

Sea-kite—the Imperial Charisian Navy's name for a minesweeping paravane.

Seijin—sage, holy man, mystic. Legendary warriors and teachers, generally believed to have been touched by the *anshinritsumei*. Many educated Safeholdians consider *seijins* to be mythological, fictitious characters.

Shan-wei's candle (1)—the deliberately challenging name assigned to strike-anywhere matches by Charisians. Later shortened to "Shan-weis."

Shan-wei's candle (2)—a Temple Loyalist name given to the illuminating parachute flares developed by Charis.

Shan-wei's footstools—also simply "footstools." Charisian name for nondirectional antipersonnel mines which are normally buried or laid on the surface and (usually) detonated by a percussion cap pressure switch. See Kau-yungs.

Shan-wei's fountains—also simply "fountains." Charisian name for "bounding mines." When detonated, a launching charge propels the mine to approximately waist height before it detonates, spraying shrapnel balls in a three-hundred-and-sixty-degree pattern. *See* Kau-yungs.

Shan-wei's sweepers—also simply "sweepers," Charisian name for a Safeholdian version of a claymore mine. The mine's backplate is approximately eighteen inches by thirty inches and covered with five hundred and seventy-six .50-caliber shrapnel balls which it fires in a cone-shaped blast zone when detonated. *See* Kau-yungs.

Shan-wei's War—the *Holy Writ*'s term for the struggle between the supporters of Eric Langhorne and those of Pei Shan-wei over the future of humanity on Safehold. It is presented in terms very similar to those of the war between Lucifer and the angels loyal to God, with Shan-wei in the role of Lucifer. *See also* War Against the Fallen.

Shellhorn—venomous Safeholdian insect analogue with a hard, folding carapace. When folded inside its shell, it is virtually indistinguishable from a ripe slabnut.

Sisters of Saint Kohdy—an order of nuns created to honor and commemorate Saint Kohdy. The last of the "angels" used kinetic weapons to obliterate their abbey and the tomb of Saint Kohdy shortly after the last of the original Adams and Eves died.

Sky comb—a tall, slender native Safeholdian tree. It is deciduous, grows to a height of approximately eighty-five to ninety feet, and has very small, dense branches covered with holly tree-like leaves. Its branches seldom exceed eight feet in length.

Slabnut—a flat-sided, thick-hulled nut. Slabnut trees are deciduous, with large, four-lobed leaves, and grow to about thirty feet. Black slabnuts are genetically engineered to be edible by humans; red slabnuts are mildly poisonous. The black slabnut is very high in protein.

Slash lizard—a six-limbed, saurian-looking, furry oviparous mammal. One of the three top land predators of Safehold. Its mouth contains twin rows of fangs capable of punching through chain mail and its feet have four long toes, each tipped with claws up to five or six inches long.

Sleep root—a Safeholdian tree from whose roots an entire family of opiates and painkillers are produced. The term "sleep root" is often used generically for any of those pharmaceutical products.

Slime toad—an amphibious Safeholdian carrion eater with a body length of approximately seven inches. It takes its name from the thick mucus which covers its skin. Its bite is poisonous but seldom results in death.

Snapdragon—the Safeholdian snapdragon isn't actually related to any of the other dragon species of the planet. It is actually a Safeholdian analogue to the terrestrial giant sea turtle. Although it is warm-blooded, its body form is very similar to that of a terrestrial leatherback sea turtle, but it is half again the leatherback's size, with fully mature male snapdragons running to body lengths of over nine feet. No living Safeholdian knows why the snapdragon was given its name.

SNARC—Self-Navigating Autonomous Reconnaissance and Communications platform.

Spider-crab—a native species of sea life, considerably larger than any terrestrial crab. The spider-crab is not a crustacean, but more of a segmented, tough-hided, many-legged seagoing slug. Despite that, its legs are considered a great delicacy and are actually very tasty.

Spider-rat—a native species of vermin which fills roughly the ecological niche of a terrestrial rat. Like all Safeholdian mammals, it is six-limbed, but it looks like a cross between a hairy gila monster and an insect, with long, multi-jointed legs which actually arch higher than its spine. It is nasty-tempered but basically cowardly. Fully adult male specimens of the larger varieties run to about two feet in body length, with another two feet of tail, for a total length of four feet, but the more common varieties average only between two or three feet of combined body and tail length.

Spike-thorn—a flowering shrub, various subspecies of which are found in most Safeholdian climate zones. Its blossoms come in many colors and hues, and the tropical versions tend to be taller-growing and to bear more delicate blossoms.

Spine fever—a generic term for paralytic diseases, like polio, which affect the nervous system and cause paralysis.

"Stand at Kharmych"—a Siddarmarkian military march composed to commemorate the 37th Infantry Regiment's epic stand against an invading Desnairian army in the Battle of Kharmych.

Steel thistle—a native Safeholdian plant which looks very much like branching bamboo. The plant bears seed pods filled with small, spiny seeds embedded in fine, straight fibers. The seeds are extremely difficult to remove by hand, but the fiber can be woven into a fabric which is even stronger than cotton silk. It can also be twisted into extremely strong, stretch-resistant rope. Moreover, the plant grows almost as rapidly as actual bamboo, and the yield of raw fiber per acre is seventy percent higher than for terrestrial cotton.

Stone wool—Safeholdian term for chrysotile (white asbestos).

Sugar apple—a tropical Safeholdian fruit tree. The sugar apple has a bright purple skin much like a terrestrial tangerine's, but its fruit has much the same consistency of a terrestrial apple. It has a higher natural sugar content than an apple, however; hence the name.

Surgoi kasai—"dreadful" or "great fire." The true spirit of God. The touch of His divine fire, which only an angel or Archangel can endure.

Swamp hopper—moderate-sized (around fifty to sixty-five pounds) Safeholdian amphibian. It is carnivorous, subsisting primarily on fish and other small game and looks rather like a six-legged Komodo dragon but has a fan-like crest which it extends and expands in response to a threat or in defense of territory. It is also equipped with air sacs on either side of its throat which swell and expand under those circumstances. It is ill-tempered, territorial, and aggressive.

Swivel wolf—a light, primarily antipersonnel artillery piece mounted on a swivel for easy traverse. *See* Wolf.

Sword Rakurai—specially trained agents of the Inquisition sent into the enemy's rear areas. They operate completely solo, as do the Inquisition's regular Rakurai; they are not suicide attackers or simple terrorists. Instead, they are trained as spies and infiltrators, expected to do any damage they can but with the primary mission of information collection.

Sword of Schueler—the savage uprising, mutiny, and rebellion fomented by the Inquisition to topple Lord Protector Greyghor Stohnar and destroy the Republic of Siddarmark.

Talon branch—an evergreen tree native to Safehold. It has fine, spiny needles and its branches are covered with half-inch thorns. It reaches a height of almost seventy feet, and at full maturity has no branches for the first twenty to twenty-five feet above the ground.

Teak tree—a native Safeholdian tree whose wood contains concentrations of silica and other minerals. Although it grows to a greater height than the Old Earth teak wood tree and bears a needle-like foliage, its timber is very similar in grain and coloration to the terrestrial tree and, like Old Earth teak, it is extremely resistant to weather, rot, and insects.

Tellesberg Krakens—the Tellesberg professional baseball club.

Temple, The—the complex built by "the Archangels" using Terran Federation technology to serve as the headquarters of the Church of God Awaiting. It contains many "mystic" capabilities which demonstrate the miraculous power of the Archangels to anyone who sees them.

Temple Boy—Charisian/Siddarmarkian slang for someone serving in the Army of God. It is not a term of endearment.

Temple Loyalist—one who renounces the schism created by the Church of Charis' defiance of the Grand Vicar and Council of Vicars of the Church of God Awaiting. Some Temple Loyalists are also Reformists (*see* above), but all are united in condemning the schism between Charis and the Temple.

Testimonies, The—by far the most numerous of the Church of God Awaiting's sacred writings, these consist of the firsthand observations of the first few generations of humans on Safehold. They do not have the same status as the Christian gospels, because they do not reveal the central teachings and inspiration of God. Instead, collectively, they form an important substantiation of the *Writ*'s "historical accuracy" and conclusively attest to the fact that the events they describe did, in fact, transpire.

Titan oak—a very slow-growing, long-lived deciduous Safeholdian hardwood which grows to heights of as much as one hundred meters.

"The Pikes of Kolstyr"—a Siddarmarkian military march composed to commemorate a Desnairian atrocity in one of the early wars between the Republic of Siddarmark and the Desnairian Empire. When played on the battlefield, it announces that the Republic of Siddarmark Army intends to offer no quarter.

Tomb of Saint Kohdy—the original Tomb of Saint Kohdy was destroyed by the same kinetic weapons which destroyed the Abbey of Saint Kohdy. Before that destruction, however, the Sisters of Saint Kohdy had secretly moved the saint's body to a new, hidden tomb in the Mountains of Light, where it remains to this day.

Trap lizard—a medium-sized (for Safehold) predator. Trap lizards run to an adult body length of approximately four feet. They have outsized jaws and are ambush hunters who normally dig themselves into dens near game trails and then pounce on prong bucks and other herbivores using those trails.

Waffle bark—a deciduous, nut-bearing native Safeholdian tree with an extremely rough, shaggy bark.

War Against the Fallen—the portion of Shan-wei's War falling between the destruction of the Alexandria Enclave and the final reconsolidation of the Church's authority.

Wing warrior—the traditional title of a blooded warrior of one of the Raven Lords clans. It is normally shortened to "wing" when used as a title or an honorific.

Wire vine—a kudzu-like vine native to Safehold. Wire vine isn't as fast-growing as kudzu, but it's equally tenacious, and unlike kudzu, several of its varieties have long, sharp thorns. Unlike many native Safeholdian plant species, it does quite well intermingled with terrestrial imports. It is often used as a sort of combination hedgerow and barbed-wire fence by Safehold farmers.

Wolf (1)—a Safeholdian predator which lives and hunts in packs and has many of the same social characteristics as the terrestrial species of the same name. It is warm-blooded but oviparous and larger than an Old Earth wolf, with adult males averaging between two hundred and two hundred and twenty-five pounds.

Wolf (2)—a generic term for shipboard artillery pieces with a bore of less than two inches and a shot weighing one pound or less. They are primarily antipersonnel weapons but can also be effective against boats and small craft.

Wyvern—the Safeholdian ecological analogue of terrestrial birds. There are as many varieties of wyverns as there are birds, including (but not limited to) the homing or messenger wyvern, hunting wyverns suitable for the equivalent of hawking for small prey, the crag wyvern (a flying predator with a wingspan of ten feet), various species of sea wyverns, and the king wyvern (a very large flying predator with a wingspan of up to twenty-five feet). All wyverns have two pairs of wings, and one pair of powerful, clawed legs. The king wyvern has been known to take children as prey when desperate or when the opportunity presents, but they are quite intelligent. They know that humans are a prey best left alone and generally avoid inhabited areas.

Wyvernry—a nesting place or breeding hatchery for domesticated wyverns.

Zhyahngdu Academy—perhaps the most renowned school for sculptors in all of Safehold, located at the port city of Zhyahngdu in the Tiegelkamp Province of North Harchong. It dates back to the days of the War Against the Fallen and has trained and produced the Church of God Awaiting's finest sculptors for almost nine hundred Safeholdian years.

The Archangels:

Archangel	Sphere of Authority	Symbol
Langhorne	law and life	scepter
Bédard	wisdom and knowledge	lamp
Pasquale	healing and medicine	caduceus
Sóndheim	agronomy and farming	grain sheaf
Truscott	animal husbandry	horse
Schueler	justice	sword
Jwo-jeng	acceptable technology	flame
Chihiro (1)	history	quill pen
Chihiro (2)	guardian	sword
Andropov	good fortune	dice
Hastings	geography	draftman's compass

Fallen Archangel	Sphere of Authority
Shan-wei	mother of evil/evil ambition
Kau-yung	destruction
Proctor	temptation/forbidden knowledge
Sullivan	gluttony
Ascher	lies
Grimaldi	pestilence
Stavraki	avarice

The Church of God Awaiting's Hierarchy:

Ecclesiastic rank	Distinguishing color	Clerical ring/set
Grand Vicar	dark blue	sapphire with rubies
Vicar	orange	sapphire
Archbishop	white and orange	ruby
Bishop executor	white	ruby
Bishop	white	ruby
Auxiliary bishop	green and white	ruby
Upper-priest	green	plain gold (no stone)
Priest	brown	none
Under-priest	brown	none
Sexton	brown	none

Clergy who do not belong to a specific order wear cassocks entirely in the color of their rank. Auxiliary bishops' cassocks are green with narrow trim bands of white. Archbishops' cassocks are white, but trimmed in orange. Clergy who belong to one of the ecclesiastical orders (see below) wear habits (usually of patterns specific to each order) in the order's colors but with the symbol of their order on the right breast, badged in the color of their priestly rank. In formal vestments, the pattern is reversed; that is, their vestments are in the colors of their priestly ranks and the order's symbol is the color of their order. All members of the clergy habitually wear either cassocks or the habits of their orders. The headgear is a three-cornered "priest's cap" almost identical to the eighteenth century's tricornes. The cap is black for anyone under the rank of vicar. Under-priests' and priests' bear brown cockades. Auxiliary bishops bear green cockades. Bishops' and bishop executors' bear white cockades. Archbishops' bear white cockades with a broad, dove-tailed orange ribbon at the back. Vicars' priests' caps are of orange with no cockade or ribbon, and the Grand Vicar's cap is white with an orange cockade.

All clergy of the Church of God Awaiting are affiliated with one or more of the great ecclesiastic orders, but not all are *members* of those orders. Or it might, perhaps, be more accurate to say that not all are *full* members of their orders. Every ordained priest is automatically affiliated with the order of the bishop who ordained him and (in theory, at least) owes primary obedience to that order. Only members of the clergy who have taken an order's vows are considered full members or brethren/sisters of that order, however. (Note: there are no female priests in the Church of God Awaiting, but women may attain high ecclesiastic rank in one of the orders.) Only full brethren or sisters of an order may attain to rank within that order, and only members of one of the great orders are eligible for elevation to the vicarate.

The great orders of the Church of God Awaiting, in order of precedence and power, are:

The Order of Schueler, which is primarily concerned with the enforcement of Church doctrine and theology. The Grand Inquisitor, who is automatically a member of the Council of Vicars, is always the head of the Order of Schueler. Schuelerite ascendency within the Church has been steadily increasing for over two hundred years, and the order is clearly the dominant power in the Church hierarchy today. The order's color is purple, and its symbol is a sword.

The Order of Langhorne is technically senior to the Order of Schueler, but has lost its primacy in every practical sense. The Order of Langhorne provides the Church's jurists, and since Church law supersedes secular law throughout Safehold that means all jurists and lawgivers (lawyers) are either members of the order or must be vetted and approved by the order. At one time, that gave the Langhornites unquestioned primacy, but the Schuelerites have relegated the order of Langhorne to a primarily administrative role, and the head of the order lost his mandatory seat on the Council of Vicars several generations back (in the Year of God 810). Needless to say, there's a certain tension between the Schuelerites and the Langhornites. The Order of Langhorne's color is black, and its symbol is a scepter.

The Order of Bédard has undergone the most change of any of the original great orders of the Church. Originally, the Inquisition came out of the Bédardists, but that function was effectively resigned to the Schuelerites by the Bédardists themselves when Saint Greyghor's reforms converted the order into the primary teaching order of the church. Today, the Bédardists are philosophers and educators, both at the university level and among the peasantry, although they also retain their function as Safehold's mental health experts and councilors. The order is also involved in caring for the poor and indigent. Ironically, perhaps, given the role of the "Archangel Bédard" in the creation of the Church of God Awaiting, a large percentage of Reformist clergy springs from this order. Like the Schuelerites, the head of the Order of Bédard always holds a seat on the Council of Vicars. The order's color is white, and its symbol is an oil lamp.

The Order of Chihiro is unique in that it has two separate functions and is divided into two separate orders. The Order of the Quill is responsible for training and overseeing the Church's scribes, historians, and bureaucrats. It is responsible for the archives of the Church and all of its official documents. The Order of the Sword is a militant order which often cooperates closely with the Schuelerites and the Inquisition. It is the source of the officer corps for the Temple Guard and also for most officers of the Temple Lands' nominally secular army and navy. Its head is always a member of the Council of Vicars, as Captain General of the Church of God Awaiting, and generally fulfills the role of Secretary of War. The order's color is blue, and its symbol is a quill pen. The Order of the Sword shows the quill pen, but crossed with a sheathed sword.

The Order of Pasquale is another powerful and influential order of the Church. Like the Order of Bédard, the Pasqualates are a teaching order, but their area of specialization is healing and medicine. They turn out very well-trained surgeons, but they are blinkered against pursuing any germ theory of medicine because of their religious teachings. All licensed healers on Safehold must be examined and approved by the Order of Pasquale, and the order is deeply involved in public hygiene policies and (less deeply) in caring for the poor and indigent. The majority of Safeholdian hospitals are associated, to at least some degree, with the Order of Pasquale. The head of the Order of Pasquale is normally, but not always, a member of the Council of Vicars. The order's color is green, and its symbol is a caduceus.

The Order of Sóndheim and the Order of Truscott are generally considered "brother orders" and are similar to the Order of Pasquale, but deal with agronomy and animal husbandry respectively. Both are teaching orders and they are jointly and deeply involved in Safehold's agriculture and food production. The teachings of the Archangel Sóndheim and Archangel Truscott incorporated into the *Holy Writ* were key elements in the ongoing terraforming of Safehold following the general abandonment of advanced technology. Both of these orders lost their mandatory seats on the Council of Vicars over two hundred years ago, however. The Order of Sóndheim's color is brown and its symbol is a sheaf of grain; the Order of Truscott's color is brown trimmed in *green*, and its symbol is a horse.

The Order of Hastings is the most junior (and least powerful) of the current great orders. The order is a teaching order, like the Orders of Sondheim and Truscott, and produces the vast majority of Safehold's cartographers, and surveyors. Hastingites also provide most of Safehold's officially sanctioned astronomers, although they are firmly within what might be considered the Ptolemaic theory of the universe. The order's "color" is actually a checkered pattern of green, brown, and blue, representing vegetation, earth, and water. Its symbol is a compass.

The Order of Jwo-jeng, once one of the four greatest orders of the Church, was absorbed into the Order of Schueler in Year of God 650, at the same time the Grand Inquisitorship was vested in the Schuelerites. Since that time, the Order of Jwo-jeng has had no independent existence.

The Order of Andropov occupies a sort of middle ground or gray area between the great orders of the Church and the minor orders. According to the *Holy Writ*, Andropov was one of the leading Archangels during the war against Shan-wei and the Fallen, but he was always more lighthearted (one hesitates to say frivolous) than his companions. His order has definite epicurean tendencies, which have traditionally been accepted by the Church because its raffles, casinos, horse and/or lizard races, etc., raise a great deal of money for charitable causes. Virtually every bookie on Safehold is either a member of Andropov's order or at least regards the Archangel as his patron. Needless to say, the Order of Andropov is not guaranteed a seat on the Council of Vicars. The order's color is red, and its symbol is a pair of dice.

▼   ▼   ▼

In addition to the above ecclesiastical orders, there are a great many minor orders: mendicant orders, nursing orders (usually but not always associated with the Order of Pasquale), charitable orders (usually but not always associated with the Order of Bédard or the Order of Pasquale), ascetic orders, etc. All of the great orders maintain numerous monasteries and convents, as do many of the lesser orders. Members of minor orders may not become vicars unless they are also members of one of the great orders.